RATS
OF
MURK
BOUND TO THE FAE
7-9
EVA CHASE

Rats of Murk: Bound to the Fae - Books 7-9

3 in the Bound to the Fae Box Sets series

All rights reserved. This book or any portion thereof may not be reproduced or used in any manner without the express written permission of the author, except for the use of brief quotations in a book review.

This is a work of fiction. Any resemblance to actual persons, living or dead, or actual events is purely coincidental.

First Digital Edition, 2022

Copyright © 2021, 2022 Eva Chase

Cover design: Malice & Mayhem Book Covers

Case design: Story Wrappers

Front character art: Pradesta

Back character art: Salome Totladze

Ebook ISBN: 978-1-990338-93-9

Hardcover ISBN: 978-1-990338-94-6

LIES OF MURK

BOUND TO THE FAE #7

CHAPTER ONE

Sylas

When I first glance toward the platform by the Heart's pulsing light and notice that Talia is no longer perched on its edge, I don't think much of it. No doubt she's rejoined the dancing or stepped aside to chat with her dressmaker friend from our pack. Astrid will be watching over her, as will Corwin's coterie.

I amble through the crowd of revelers, still in a celebratory mood myself. Just a couple of hours ago, I finally claimed the extraordinary human woman who's won my heart as my official mate—alongside my two cadre-chosen who've earned her affections as well, and with the approval of her Unseelie soul-twined mate. The peace between Corwin's winter realm and ours of summer feels more solid than it's ever been.

I'm far from the only one wanting to celebrate both those things. It seems as if the whole of the fae world is laughing and whirling on the field around me and in the surrounding forest, moving with the rollicking music. Their eager toasts lace the air with the scent of duskapple wine. And why shouldn't they be as happy as I am?

Whitt draws up beside me, tipping a wine glass of his own to his mouth. My spymaster taps my arm with his elbow and cranes his neck to peer through the crowd. "Where's our mighty mate gotten to?"

"I'm not entirely sure." I scan the revelers myself, my deadened eye adding the occasional after-image, both fleeting and vague, to the scene before me. Talia should be easy to pick out with the vivid pink and purple dye in her hair, a hue few even true-blooded fae could match, but I'm not seeing her.

She could have gone off into the forest, but a twang of uneasiness breaks through the joy inside me. At the same moment, Corwin appears at my side. The winter arch-lord rarely shows much emotion, so the obvious distress on his bronze-brown face puts all my senses on the alert in an instant.

"Have you seen Talia?" he asks in a low, urgent tone, his gaze flicking over the fae around us. "I wasn't focused on our bond, so I'm not sure exactly where she was, but all of a sudden my impression of her vanished completely."

Whitt stiffens. "She's *gone*?"

Before an even deeper horror can grip me, Corwin shakes his head. "She must be alive and clearly not in any conscious distress. The bond is still *there*. I just can't sense her on the other end. It's similar to when she's sleeping and not dreaming, although often I can pick up a bit of her emotional state even then. And she wouldn't have fallen into sleep in a snap like that."

"She was sitting on the platform just a few minutes ago," I say, moving to weave through the crowd. Perhaps we'll find some sign of what became of her there. "Did you notice nothing at all before she disappeared? There was no pain or panic?"

Corwin and Whitt follow me. The raven shifter's mouth twists. "I caught a brief jolt of what felt like confusion and fear, but it was so abrupt I didn't have time to reach out or study it all that carefully. I caught it and immediately focused on her presence, and she'd already gone blank."

"That doesn't bode well." Cold apprehension winds through my body.

At the platform, we find no signs of any kind of scuffle or of where Talia might have gone from here. As we examine the area, August catches up with us. He looked so jovial the last time I saw him just minutes ago, but his frown now shows he's noticed our change in mood.

"What's wrong?" he asks, his substantial muscles flexing across his broad shoulders. "Did something happen to Talia?"

"That's what we're trying to determine," Whitt says in a tense voice so unlike his usual carefree tone that I know he's on the verge of panic himself.

"We need to find Astrid," I say. "She's always kept a close eye on Talia." As we should have been too. I just hadn't imagined anything could happen to her during this gathering with so many of us who care about her so close by. Guilt congeals in my gut alongside my worries.

Corwin makes a gesture, and within moments, his coterie woman Zelpha is at his side. She takes in our expressions and knits her brow. "Is there a problem?"

"Talia's missing," Corwin says. "She was here by the platform just a little while ago. Did you see where she went from there?"

The brawny woman's eyes widen. "I was glancing over at her now and then, and she seemed fine. But I haven't seen her in… maybe ten minutes? A little scuffle broke out between two men near me who must have had too much wine, and I was busy making sure they didn't come to fatal blows. I'll start searching the woods for her—and check with the rest of the coterie if I cross paths with them."

"We could make an announcement," August says, but he sounds doubtful. We both know that if we make it clear to all the fae celebrating around us that something's happened to the human woman they've begun to revere, the festivities will turn chaotic in an instant.

"Let's see what we can piece together on our own before we cause a mass panic," I say. "Having all of the fae here upset might make it harder to determine what happened rather than easier."

My eyes catch on Astrid's gray hair and wiry form near the opposite end of the platform. I hurry over to the newest of my cadre-chosen, and she heads toward me when she notices me coming. "Is

Talia with you?" she asks with obvious hope. "I lost track of her for a moment."

Blast it. I can't give her any relief. "So have we, and from her soul-twined mate's impressions, we have reason to believe she's been incapacitated. Did you see her leaving the platform?"

Astrid's expression darkens with worry. "No. As soon as you went over to the refreshment table, I was keeping her in my line of sight. But then one of the dancers stumbled into me and knocked the feet right out from under me, and a few of us fell in a jumble..." She grimaces, rubbing her elbow where I can already tell a bruise is forming. "By the time I managed to get up, she'd moved. I haven't seen her since."

My apprehension is expanding by the second. I can't shake the growing suspicion that it's unnaturally convenient that our colleagues who would have been watching over Talia were all suddenly diverted shortly after we left her side.

"Make inquiries," I tell her. "Discreetly, but we want to know which way she went and whether anyone was with her."

Astrid nods with a jerk of her head. She heads back into the crowd, stopping to murmur to fae here and there.

Corwin appears to spot something farther away in the crowd. He beckons for us to follow him toward one of his other coterie members, an older man whose name I believe is Verik, who I assume Zelpha brought in on the search. He's standing near Donovan and one of my colleague's cadre-chosen.

Donovan's forehead is furrowed. "You're looking for Talia?" the younger arch-lord says. "Jagan saw her heading into the woods a few minutes ago."

His cadre man nods and motions to the woods to the south. "She was walking with Kyo, one of our pack-kin. I'm sure Kyo wouldn't have meant or done her any harm. She's always spoken highly of Talia and her generosity in healing our curse."

"Then perhaps something befell both of them." I set off in the direction he indicated, knowing the other men will follow me.

As my chief warrior, August pushes a little ahead. At the edge of the forest, he scents the air and then drops into wolf form to lope between the trees. When I follow suit, I catch a slight hint of Talia's sap-sweet smell in the air. It urges me onward.

Whitt's wolf bounds through the woods a few feet to my left. A rustle of feathers tells me Corwin and perhaps his coterie man have taken flight in their raven forms. If Talia's been taken beyond these woods, they'll spot her faster than we Seelie can. But if it's only been a matter of minutes, we may find her just as quickly here on the ground.

Her scent thickens just enough to lead us toward Donovan's pack village. We leave the last of the reveling fae behind, and August stops with a bark of alarm several paces ahead of me. He straightens up into his usual shape and immediately kneels by a crumpled figure.

My pulse stutters with a jolt of alarm. I dash the last short distance to him, but it isn't Talia's smell that fills my nose, though I still catch traces of her essence around. The woman slumped at the base of the tree is old and fae.

As I shift out of my wolf, both Whitt and Donovan come up beside me. August is murmuring with his hand over the woman's forehead. After a moment, her eyelids flutter. She stares up at him and then jerks into a sitting position. "What am I doing here? What happened?"

Donovan crouches down next to August, his tone urgent but full of compassion. "That's what we're hoping to find out, Kyo. One of my cadre-chosen saw you walking this way with Lady Talia. What were the two of you talking about?"

"Lady Talia?" The woman's puzzled expression makes my heart sink. "I—I don't think I've seen her since the ceremony. I went back to my house to fetch a shawl—the night brings a chill to these old bones more often than not—and…" She frowns. "That's the last thing I remember: walking up to my house. Lady Talia certainly wasn't there." Her gaze darts around us, concern flashing across her wrinkled face. "Is she all right?"

I don't sense any hint of pretence in her. She honestly doesn't know.

Restraining a growl, I let loose my wolf once more. I'll be more likely to pick up Talia's trail with my canine nose given full rein.

I prowl through the forest with all my senses on the alert. There are whiffs of her scent here and there in this spot and along the trail she must have walked to reach here—but nothing in any other direction. She didn't touch anything, with her feet or any other part of her, after she arrived in this part of the forest. Which means she was most likely carried off.

By *whom*?

Other than the scents of my companions and the old fae woman, I don't pick up any indication of another presence that passed through. My deadened eye refuses to offer me any glimpses beyond the ordinary, no matter how I urge it to. Clenching my fangs, I dip my nose even lower, drag the air even deeper into my lungs. There *has* to be something. She couldn't utterly disappear.

Whitt and August pad between the trees nearby. Donovan continues talking with his pack-kin in quiet tones, but I can tell he isn't getting anything more useful from her. With a hoarse caw, Corwin's raven alights on a branch near us and cocks his head. He doesn't appear to have any news either.

Then, some distance from the spot where we found Kyo, the faintest hint of something bitter touches my nostrils. I freeze, weaving my head until the smell catches just a little more in my nose. No sniff around that area brings more of it to my awareness, but my fangs are already clenched. I've tasted enough to know what it is.

I spring up onto my feet, every muscle braced. Whitt and August hustle over, shedding their wolves as they come. Corwin drops down to join us, shifting in an instant.

My voice comes out just shy of a snarl. "There was a rat here. It covered its tracks well, but not perfectly. We must find it and whatever other Murk vermin slunk here with it as quickly as possible. Return to the celebration and send off every fae who's able-bodied and still has enough of their wits about them to seek out the mangy rodents."

Whitt's eyes flashed the moment I said "rat." He springs off into the forest, racing toward the field around the Heart with August swiftly overtaking him. As I move to join them, Donovan catches my arm. I'm so furious I nearly snap his nose off.

"Sylas," he says hastily, with a hint of apology, "what would the rats want with Talia?"

That is the question, isn't it?

My thoughts trip over all the minor intrusions of the Murk into our lives over the past few months. Vandalism and a murder at Aerik's castle. The destruction of several homes in the Unseelie's summer fae settlement and a woman who warned of more to come. A plume of toxic, iron-laced smoke, guarded by a man who lunged at Talia when she tried to put it out.

The story I heard from Aerik just a few days ago of how he stumbled on Talia's town in the first place… hunting down a rat.

Have the Murk been sneaking through our lives even more than that without us realizing it? Have they had some interest in Talia all along? I still don't fully understand, but clearly I should have acted on what I did know sooner, more thoroughly.

I should have never given the slightest opportunity for one of those vermin to get anywhere near my mate.

"I don't know," I reply, the rage mixing with my guilt into a searing ache within my chest. "To disrupt our celebration? To send us into a panic? Whatever their reason, it can't be good—for us or her."

Then I hurtle after my cadre, hoping my error won't cost me the woman I love. Because if the rats wrench her beyond the boundaries of the Mists into their haunts in the human world before we find her, we may never find her at all.

CHAPTER TWO

Talia

As I emerge from sleep, the first thing I register is the smell. Or smells, really, because there are an awful lot of them colliding and clashing, most of which I'd never expect to find in my nose when I wake up.

Sylas's castle smells of warmed wood, and Corwin's carries a faint mineral scent. Both of those mingle together in my bedroom in our new joint castle. Now, I'm assaulted by a mix of bitter metal, acrid smoke, and a thick mildewy odor that has me recoiling before I'm even fully conscious.

My muscles tense, and a twinge runs through my scalp down the back of my head. And inside my head…

Inside my head there's a horrible blank.

The emptiness echoes from behind my forehead down to my gut. I have no sense of Corwin at all, not even the dulled impression of a barrier between us like when he's fully raised his walls against our connection. There've been times he's shut me out before, but this is the first time I've ever felt completely detached from him since the moment our soul-twined bond sprang into existence like a lightning bolt down the center of my being.

My pulse stutters, and my eyes pop open. I shove myself upward, my thoughts spinning. My mind is still blurred with the unnatural sleep I'm shaking off. Staring at the scene around me, I have trouble processing what I'm seeing.

I'm lying on a thin blanket on a tiled floor in a corner of an immense room, larger than even the ballrooms in the fae castles. It's split in three, with the tiled floor I'm sprawled on stretching the full length to the distant wall, falling away into some sort of chasm several feet from me, and then rising into another span of tiles on the other side. At either end of the chasm, an opening to a dark tunnel looms. Pipes, wiring, and metal beams crisscross the dim ceiling high above me.

Scattered across the tiled sections stand little shacks made of a hodgepodge of metal sheets, wooden boards, plastic siding, and all sorts of debris from car tires to tattered scarves. Figures are moving between those buildings, ducking in and out of them, and climbing up and down makeshift ladders along the length of the chasm. Some of them appear to be working, hauling sacks or crates of supplies or fixing materials together into objects I can't identify. Others are simply sprawled in small groups chatting with each other.

Assorted sounds, from rustling to clanking, emanate from all around me. I suspect the smoky smell is drifting from a large, battered steel contraption partway along my side of the room, which whirs and growls with sputterings of sparks. Most of the light streams from flickering panels fixed at seemingly random intervals along the ceiling.

None of the figures are all that close to me. A few of those nearby have glanced my way and then averted their gazes. My voice stays locked in my throat. I'm not sure whether I should call out to them or avoid them.

Where the hell *am* I? What happened to me? I remember—we had the ceremony for me to take Sylas, Whitt, and August officially as my mates. There was music and food and dancing—an old woman from Donovan's pack wanted to give me a gift—a fae man appeared out of nowhere and knocked me out with some kind of magic.

My hand jerks to my waist, instinctively reaching for my knife for protection, but of course I wasn't wearing my usual belt with this lovely dress for the ceremony. In the same instant, the man from my memory steps into my view, so easily he's probably been watching me from just behind me the entire time. My entire body goes rigid, bracing to defend myself.

I still have the bronze bracelet Sylas gave me, smooth against my wrist. If I have to, I might be able to transform it into some kind of blade in time to fend him off… or at least make attacking me a little harder.

The man peers down at me with an air of mild disdain. In the wavering light, I can't tell what color his heavy-lidded eyes are, only that they're dark. Straight, straw-blond hair falls across his pale forehead. It points in a jagged line toward a long nose with a slight bump partway along its length as if it's been broken before.

There's nothing directly threatening in his casual stance, but the human-style collared shirt he's wearing is fitted enough to show the muscular definition in his well-built shoulders and chest. He isn't quite as brawny as Sylas or August, but there's no mistaking the strength he could wield if he chooses to. That he's *already* chosen to wield, against me.

If the magic he used wasn't enough confirmation, the ears with lightly pointed tips that poke from between the mussed strands of his hair confirm my original assumption. Despite his clothing and our surroundings, he's definitely some kind of fae.

"Looking for this?" he asks in the low, faintly hoarse voice that greeted me in the forest before he knocked me out. My gaze falls to his hand. He's dangling a circlet of gold and silver—

My crown. The crown my mates gave me at the end of the ceremony—to celebrate our union, the peace between the summer and winter realms, and everything I've done to help the fae on both sides of the border. I *wasn't* looking for it, hadn't even realized it was missing, but now that I see it in his grasp, my fingers itch to snatch it back.

But I have more important considerations first.

"Who are you?" I say, jerking my attention back to the fae man's face. "Where are we? Why did you bring me here?"

The man flicks the crown in a slow rotation around his fingers. He ignores all but my last question. "My king felt it was time you met him. I'll bring you to him now."

His *king*? I don't understand any of this. I open my mouth to press for more answers—but a twitching motion by the man's leg catches my eyes, and my voice dies.

A long, slender shape, sinuous and covered with a thin sheen of pale beige fur, grazes his calf and then tucks back behind him. I gape for a second before comprehension dawns on me. Even then, my gaze darts toward the other, more distant figures throughout the room to double check.

Between the distance, the erratic light, and my initial daze, that one detail didn't fully sink into my mind when I scanned the space before. Now that I'm looking for it, my gut twists at how obvious it is. A woman climbing out of the chasm there has a similar but dark shape slanting along her leg to twine around her ankle. A man on the other side has a gray one looped around the leg of the table he's poised at.

Not ropes or cables or any separate tool. With each glimpse, my understanding solidifies.

They all have tails. Long, tapered, lightly furred tails. I've never seen fae with tails before, but if this is their home, why shouldn't this kind flaunt them like the wolf shifters can let out their fangs and claws, like the ravens can unfurl their wings? A fresh wave of panic washes over me.

I've been taken by the Murk. The rat-shifting fae despised by both the Seelie and the Unseelie; the fae best known for playing vicious pranks and taking malicious satisfaction out of hurting both humans and other fae.

I cringe back against the wall instinctively. When I focus on the man in front of me again, there's something hard in his face that wasn't there before. He motions to me with his empty hand. "Let's go. There's no point in delaying it."

My hands press against the cool tiles. "I don't want to go anywhere except home."

"Well, too bad for you that's not in the cards. You can walk, or I can carry you. Either way, we're going *now*."

His voice stays low, but I can tell from the edge that creeps into it that he means it. He's more than half a foot taller than me, and he's got fae strength and magic on his side. There's no way I'm beating him in a struggle, bronze bangle or not. I weigh my options for a few seconds and decide I'd rather go on my own two feet than have him lay one hand on me, if I'm going to end up going either way.

I push myself upright. The silky fabric of the dress my friend Harper made me for the ceremony swishes around me. It's marked with dirt and grease stains now, but I still feel a little elegant in it.

I'm Lady Talia, mate to four of the most powerful fae alive, and I will meet my fate with dignity—and as much defiance as I can manage.

The fae man ushers me to a set of narrow stairs built against the side of the chasm by the nearest tunnel. I walk slowly, catching my balance on my initially wobbly legs. The ache of my recent wound—dealt by one of this man's Murk kin—wakes up in my thigh, and I'd limp anyway because of my warped foot, but I keep my pace as steady as possible.

It isn't much of a drop, no more than five or six feet down. As I pick my way down the steps, I take in the metal bars and slats that run along the concrete floor of the chasm. Recognition clicks in my mind, taking the setting immediately from alien to familiar.

"This is a subway station," I say, the revelation slipping out of me before I can catch it.

"Not anymore," my kidnapper says. "The humans abandoned it, and we reclaimed it."

I guess I should be glad that my situation can't be made even worse by a speeding subway train rumbling down those tracks. It's hard to feel very optimistic as I limp along beside the fae man into the dank, shadowy tunnel.

Small, furry bodies scuttle past us in the darkness, and I can't tell whether they're Murk in rat form or regular rats. Maybe a mix of both. More haphazard structures jut from the walls here and there, little more than vague shapes to my eyes. My escort strides along with an impatient air, navigating the darkness without hesitation.

The mildew smell gets thicker as we walk deeper into the tunnel. Twice, a small light flares in the distance against the thicker blackness. As my eyes adjust, I notice a dull orange glow seeping across the tracks up ahead. It brightens as we near it. A quiver ripples through the air, prickling over my skin with an unsettling erraticness. I can't help rubbing my bare arms.

As we come up on the glowing area, the dissonant hum of energy intensifies. The wall falls away to reveal a deep alcove about the size of the grand meeting room in the Bastion of the Heart back in the summer realm. Tailed fae stand in a line leading up to a large dais at the far end, which holds a tall throne.

The throne appears to have been constructed out of the rubble of the destroyed section of wall, packed together with clay. The woman at the front of the line is speaking to the man sitting in that high seat. A glowing mass behind him is what's emitting the orange light, which catches off his pale, spiky hair. Three other figures lounge on the dais around him with a vaguely menacing air.

At the sight of my kidnapper, the man waves the woman and the rest of the line away. "Return in an hour," he barks in a tone that manages to sound both terse and flippant.

As the other fae scatter, my escort leads me toward the throne.

Closer, I can see that any color in this man's hair is only reflected from the quaking light behind him, which twitches in time with the erratic energy now trickling right through my flesh. The narrow spikes along his scalp are pure white. But that can't be a reflection of his age, because the face they frame is smooth and sharp-edged without a hint of wrinkles. His yellow eyes track our every step. A white-furred tail swings casually over the arm of the throne.

Like my kidnapper, this man is dressed in human clothes: tight dark jeans and a satiny shirt with a blue-and-maroon pattern, the collar gaping open to show off the wiry muscles and dappling of scars on his lean chest. He's barefoot, his narrow toes tipped with claws like the ones that slashed open my thigh. They gleam on his fingertips too. When we stop in front of him, one more feature captures my attention.

His ears. At first I mistook them for more tufts of his spiky hair. They're pointed as sharply as Whitt's, and Whitt is nearly true-blooded.

From what the other fae have told me about how much the Murk have mingled with humans to bear their children, I didn't think any of the rat shifters had that much fae blood left in them. But then, there are obviously a lot of things the Seelie and Unseelie don't know about their greatest enemies.

The Murk who must be the king my kidnapper mentioned and the… guards? poised around him on the dais watch us silently. My kidnapper dips into a rough bow and nudges me half a step ahead of him. "I brought her to you as soon as she woke up."

"Thank you, Madoc," the king says in the same tone as before, careless and yet brusque. I hold myself stiffly still as he looks me over from head to toes and back again. "Well, they have draped you in a lot of pretty wrapping, haven't they? I hear that you've even won over not just the man your soul was bound to but three others besides—and to the point of them declaring you their mate. You've outdone my expectations. Excellent work."

I blink at him, my stomach balling tighter. "I don't understand. What are you talking about? Why did you have me brought here?"

He shrugs, a cool glint lighting in his yellow eyes. "Everything important about you came from me. You've served the purpose you were intended for. And now you'll serve me by being here while those idiotic fae of the seasons scramble around in desperation." He grins, revealing a row of crooked teeth.

His words repeat in my head. *Everything important about you came from me.* A thicker chill coils around me. "I've never even met you."

He cackles with apparent glee and stretches out in his throne, tossing one leg over the arm next to his swaying tail. "Oh, little girl, you met me before you met almost anyone. You didn't really think you gained the power to cure curses and win an arch-lord's soul all by yourself, did you?"

My lips part, but no sound comes out. I close my mouth, swallow, and finally stammer, "But how—how could *you*—?"

"I stole you when you weren't even a day old," the king says, his gaze wandering away from me as if the story barely matters to him. "Swapped you out for one of our own infants cloaked in an illusion. Your dimwitted parents never noticed. Then when I'd worked my magic, I swapped you back. You already held the kernel for the rest to sprout. I planted it in your grandmother, urged it on in your mother—these things take time to fully bloom, you know. We've been playing a long game here."

A rush of nausea flips my stomach. Nuldar the sage said something about that, didn't he? That my grandmother had met a fae who planted the seed… We assumed he meant that my grandfather had fae blood in him, that it'd caused my powers somehow. But it wasn't that—it was this spiteful villain working some kind of magic on my family?

Even as the pieces click together, every cell in my body balks at accepting what he says as truth. I grope for some kind of argument. "But—we went to a pool that shows the past—I asked about when I was born, and when I first met the fae—it showed—"

"Only darkness, right?" The king's gaze focuses on me again, his lips curving into a nasty smirk. "Oh, I know the tricks the fae of the seasons have up their sleeves, and I matched them with my own. I stole you in total darkness, and in total darkness you remained until you were returned home. Nothing for them to unravel with their visions and magic ponds."

Nuldar's creaking voice comes back to me. *She started in darkness. Then she came into the light.*

No. This can't be possible. A tremor courses through me, leaving me shaking despite my best efforts to hold myself steady. "But *why*…"

"I'd have thought that'd be obvious. You have a lot of experience with the viciousness of those fae, don't you? Keeping you half-starved in a cage? Mangling your body? Attacking you at every turn? And you their supposed savior." He shakes his head in mock disbelief. "They've spent millennia trying to crush us Murk, shunning us, savaging us, killing us as often as they can. It was time they got not just a taste but a whole banquet of their own medicine. And you delivered it for me."

One of the fae beside the throne speaks up, his voice cruel in its amusement. "We'll see them all on their knees soon, Orion!"

Orion. Some distant part of my mind files that away as the king's name. The rest is still reeling, but he doesn't wait for me to reply.

"It's all worked out perfectly," he says. "I laid the curse while I placed the seed of the temporary cure in your family line all those decades ago. Drive the wolves wild, freeze the ravens feather by feather—what could be more fitting?"

My jaw goes slack. It shouldn't surprise me after everything he's already said, but still—the enormity— "*You* placed the curse on both of the realms?" The curse that's been afflicting the Seelie and Unseelie for… for decades, like he said.

The curse that's been steadily growing more horrible until I showed up with just the right components to cure it. How else could he have managed that if he wasn't responsible for the curse itself? But I still don't understand *how*.

Orion's lips pull into a mocking sneer. "They never suspected, did they? So sure of themselves and so dismissive of us. Now they've seen our power, and before much longer they'll know who orchestrated their downfall." He chuckles to himself. "The worse the curse got, the more frantic they all got. And then you appeared as if out of nowhere, a beacon of hope. With a little encouragement, we had them all seeing you as their blessed savior, the one figure standing between them and despair. And now I've yanked you away from them."

He has. Away from *all* of them, more completely than I'd ever imagined was possible.

My voice comes out thin. "My—my soul-twined bond. I can't feel—"

Orion snorts. "Oh, we couldn't have you drawing your supposed beloved here, could we? Since my magic created the spark for that connection, I can shield it well enough. He won't reach you while you're within my home."

He isn't saying the bond is gone completely. Maybe there are some limits to what his powers can accomplish.

But that doesn't help me while I'm stuck here.

I swallow thickly. "And what happens next?"

"Oh, I'll let them stew in their misery and panic for a little while, and then we'll sweep in and claim all the Mists for ourselves. I'm sure you'll continue to be a useful tool throughout that mission. And you'll get to watch all those who mistreated you laid low."

Orion speaks as if I should be happy. I wrap my arms around myself, finally getting enough control to stop shaking, but nausea is still clamped around my gut. My thoughts whirl, shying away from accepting anything he's said as the truth.

I thought—I thought the Heart *had* blessed me, to push back the curse, to bring the realms together.

The Murk are known for mischief, for playing tricks on people. Maybe he's just trying to make me believe all this so he can manipulate me somehow, or simply for his own amusement. I don't have to accept his story at face value.

None of it really makes sense, after all. The Murk are supposed to be the weakest of all the fae by a huge margin, living so far from the Heart, constantly breaking its laws. How could they have managed to orchestrate a curse so massive it affects every one of those he calls the "fae of the seasons," controlling their behavior, even killing them?

"I don't believe you," I say, raising my chin. "You couldn't do even half of that when you can barely draw on the Heart's power at all."

Orion laughs again, but for the first time true hostility darkens his expression even as his eyes gleam brighter. "Oh, I don't have any need for the Heart of the Mists, little girl. I made my own." He swings his arm toward the stuttering mass of orange light that fills the space at the back of the platform.

I stare at it and then at him again. "You *what*?"

His lips peel back over his uneven teeth. “I made my own Heart. A Heart for the Murk, to fuel our powers by our own rules. With every bit of confusion and agony we provoke, it grows stronger, fiercer. Just in the past few hours I can feel it beating even more furiously. And that’s all thanks to you.”

CHAPTER THREE

Madoc

The woman hasn't touched the plate of food one of Orion's servants brought her. The scraps scavenged from the homes and eateries above us probably don't compare to the elaborate feasts she enjoyed in the castles of the Mists, so maybe she thinks she's too good to bother with the stuff.

Orion follows my gaze and pops a grape into his mouth. "If she wants to starve herself, she can give it her best shot. I doubt she'll keep it up for very long."

Having watched Talia from afar many times over the past several months, I'm not so sure about that. The memory comes to me of seeing her poised within one of those floating carriages, her knife at her own throat, holding herself hostage to ensure she wasn't taken captive. She meant it. I could taste her resolve even at a distance.

But I keep my mouth shut on the matter. There's no point in arguing with the king unless you're sure it's something worth pissing him off over.

Something about the way she's sitting hunched in the corner of the throne room, the skirt of her fancy but tarnished dress tucked around her slim legs, niggles at me. Her usually vibrant hair droops around her face. She hasn't let any tears fall, but there's a burning in her gaze that suggests a deep anguish.

Which is to be expected. *I* expected it. It shouldn't bother me.

It might be just that the pose reminds me a little too much of the one glimpse I was able to get of her in that summer fae Aerik's cage. As if *we've* caged her, even though there's nothing holding her in that spot.

"She doesn't seem particularly enthusiastic about the plan," I say, keeping my tone carefully mild—and quiet, even though there's little chance her human ears could pick up our conversation from over there near the tracks.

"It's shock," Orion says. "Humans have such fragile constitutions, don't they? She'll get over it, and then she'll realize that I've given her a great gift. She's been instrumental in bringing down all those haughty bastards in the Mists. From what you and my other spies reported, most of them have been horrible to her. It'll just take a little time for the deeper understanding to sink in."

"Of course." I roll the tension out of my shoulders and consider the other fae lounging in our king's company. One of the men meets my gaze with narrowed eyes. The woman who's most frequently been warming Orion's bed these days shoots me a lascivious grin I'm sure is intended as a taunt rather than an invitation.

Even if she were inviting me, I know better than to lay my hands on anything my king has claimed as his own.

Most of Orion's closest colleagues are several decades if not centuries older than me. They established themselves at his side when I was still a young man proving my worth. Some of them had a hand in the tests of my loyalty and determination. I'm never quite sure whether they're happy I passed those tests or annoyed to have one more fae sharing access to the king's ear. Who knows what they say to him during the long stretches when I'm away overseeing his plans in the Mists?

But if they've snarked about me, it hasn't seemed to affect Orion's opinion. I've shown how far I'm willing to go for him. Every time he's called for support, I've stepped up first. He knows he can count on me.

And the others don't like each other any more than they like me or I like them. Whatever sort of court our Murk king has, it's a cutthroat one. But it needs to be if we're going to carve our way through those we hate even more to bring our people to the home they deserve.

My gaze slides back to Talia. She's pushed her hair back from her face and is tentatively scanning the room, her eyes warily alert.

"Should I assign guards to monitor her movements?" I ask. "Or will we be limiting the parts of the Refuge she has access to?"

Orion shrugs, his tail flicking in the air. "All the entrances are well-sealed. Not even a fae could get past them easily without knowing the right tricks, let alone a human. I see no need to waste our energy keeping that close an eye on her. We'll give her plenty of rope and see what she does with it."

The hint of a smirk that touches his lips makes the hairs on the back of my neck rise, but I tamp down my apprehension. Talia will learn quickly enough not to cross any of the fae here, especially Orion. She *has* to learn that. This is her life now, and she'd better get used to it.

We're giving her more freedom than those bastards in the Mists did, despite all the rhetoric they've spewed at her that I can tell she's bought into. The horror on her face when she noticed my tail…

I shake that memory off too. "Would you have me return to the Mists and observe how the fae of the seasons are reacting to losing her?"

Orion shakes his head. "Oh, no, Madoc. I have a much more important task for you." He tips his head toward the woman. "I may not be concerned about her escaping, but it will be much more fun digging in the knife if we can decimate those puffed-up pricks with their savior on our side. And she's been so close with their leaders, I'm sure she knows plenty of things we'd want to know too."

My trepidation returns. I smooth it out of my tone. "What would you have me do, then?"

"I have to spell it out?" My king rolls his eyes. "You've watched her more than anyone else here. You know her well enough. Cozy up to her, win her over, and coax whatever information you can about the workings of the arch-lords' courts out of her. If you can lure her into your bed as well, so much the better."

A twinge shoots through my abdomen down to my groin. "You want me to seduce her."

"Wouldn't that be the perfect cherry on the sundae?" Orion says, idly tossing another grape. "Transfer her loyalty from those she calls her mates to you. I can't imagine it'd be that hard, considering how many of the idiots she gave herself over to. And it shouldn't be any great trial for you. She's easy enough on the eyes."

None of the other men she's welcomed into her heart and her bedroom have been reviled rat shifters, though. Her distrust of the ravens was only overcome by the soul-twined bond Orion manufactured. I don't have any benefit of that—not that I'd want her poking around in my head.

But he isn't wrong that she's pretty enough. I've studied that face from afar enough times to know it becomes outright stunning when lit up with a full smile. She just isn't likely to aim any of those smiles at me.

"I'm the one who took her," I point out. "She has enough animosity against the Murk in general—no doubt right now she hates me even more than the rest."

Orion waves off my subtle objection. "Then consider it a challenge to grow your skills. She feels alone and frightened. She'll be eager for an excuse to cling on to someone. Make yourself that someone."

He turns away to speak to Grigor at his other side about something to do with the scavenging runs. It's a clear dismissal. A prickle runs down my spine with the sense that he expects me to show I'm up to the task immediately. If I hesitate, he'll question why.

It would be awfully satisfying to know we've conquered the fae of the seasons by turning the woman they've celebrated so much against them, wouldn't it?

I step off the dais and amble over to Talia, leaving a few feet of distance when I stop. Her gaze darts up over me, and her whole body tenses, her jaw clenching. She automatically assumes I'm here to hurt her somehow, when I brought her all this way without a single injury other than a few stains on her elaborate dress.

She bought into the other fae's accusations about the Murk so easily. I'll happily start by tearing down as many of those lies as I can. What can I offer her that'll upend her misconceptions about us?

I crouch down so I'm level with her. I need to at least get her talking with me first. This won't be something I can rush, no matter how easy Orion thinks it'll be.

"Not hungry?" I ask with a motion toward her plate.

Talia glances down at the food and then at me. "I don't trust that I'll feel better rather than worse after I eat whatever you've given me."

She's sharp enough to have learned at least that much about faerie food. I let out a light chuckle. "There's nothing enchanted there. This is all pure mortal food. We don't often indulge in faerie delicacies down here."

"And why should I believe you?"

"Why would we want to get you drunk or high?" I ask. "If Orion wanted you not in your right mind, he could arrange that much more quickly with his magic. He doesn't, though. You're one of us now. You've helped us more than most of the fae around me. He might not show it all that well, but he appreciates your contribution. I certainly do."

Talia's shoulders stiffen even more. "I didn't make that 'contribution' on purpose."

"And that isn't your fault. There's no way you could have known. You didn't betray anyone, if that's what's bothering you."

She slowly unfolds her pose, settling her legs on the ground and drawing her back up straighter. I can't suppress the flicker of admiration both at the admittedly appealing curves hugged by the fabric of her dress and the studied defensiveness in her stance.

Before, she was mindlessly shielding herself. Now she's prepared for some kind of battle.

A battle with me. I haven't made any progress yet.

"I don't want to be here," she says. "I want to go home. But obviously you're not going to let me do that. You can't expect me to be happy about it."

"That's fair." I will my voice to soften, to shed any irritation I might feel at her devotion to the fae of the seasons, as if *they're* the victims in the grand scheme of things. "Orion's said that you can roam anywhere you'd like in the King's Refuge here. You might not be happy, but I could help you find a spot where you'd be more comfortable. We could even construct you a house of your own."

She studies me for a long moment, still wary but taking in my words. "I don't think there's anywhere here I'll be comfortable."

"You haven't seen much of the place yet, or given it much of a chance." I hold up my hands. "I realize you're probably not ready to hear this yet, so I'll just lay it out there and you can make of it what you will. The stories you've heard about the Murk are just that—stories. Told by those who've always wanted to keep us beneath them, who need excuses to justify how they've pushed us aside. We have craftspeople. We have artists. We bleed and love and sometimes even cry more than any of the fae currently living in the Mists can bring themselves to do. No one here intends to harm you. I'll be patient with you, but whenever you're ready, there's so much I can show you."

Talia's expression has shuttered. She's definitely not ready now. "No, thank you," she says firmly. "I just want you to leave me alone."

"I can do that too. But I'll be easy to find if you need any help later on."

I back away, returning to the edge of the dais. She might not be won over, but at least I planted a few seeds of my own—doubt about the overblown tales the bastards of the seasons have filled her head with, curiosity about everything the Murk truly are.

It's a start. Orion took several decades growing his seeds that've come into fruition in her. He can allow me a week or two.

And I've scored one minor victory already. I don't watch her overtly, but from the corner of my eye, I see her reach toward her plate and bring a grape to her lips.

CHAPTER FOUR

Talia

Down in the subway tunnel, it's impossible to tell what time of day it is—or whether it's even day at all. The only light comes from the flickering panels and the erratically pulsing glow of what Orion called the Murk's Heart.

So I'm not sure how many hours I've been hunched in the corner at the far end of the huge alcove from Orion's throne and his Heart, gathering myself. My breaths ebb and stutter, sometimes so shallow I start to feel dizzy. My heart skips beats, racing now and then sluggish and then skittering again, as uneven as the dissonant energy that's washing over me.

I want to get away from that unnatural thing, but where would I go? Would the Murk even let me wander around, like my kidnapper—Madoc—suggested, or are they just looking for an excuse to punish me even more?

Except they don't really seem to think they're punishing me in the first place. Their king talked as if I'd been part of some grand mission. The way he sneered when he talked about the fae of the seasons, maybe it's hard for him to imagine why anyone would want to go back to them.

No one has paid much attention to me since he stopped talking to me, other than the woman who brought me a plate of food with barely a glance my way. I forced myself to eat as much as I could stomach, knowing I have to keep my energy up, and nothing horrible has happened to me. Someone else snatched up the plate with my leftovers before I'd quite decided whether I could swallow more.

That was what feels like ages ago. My stomach is still knotted with tension, but one of those knots now aches of hunger. My throat has gone scratchy with thirst.

I don't see any obvious place to get a drink here, though, and I have to admit I'm scared to ask. Madoc left the throne room a little while ago. The only person still in this immense hollow that I've spoken to is the king himself, and the thought of going up to Orion again, of pleading for anything from him, makes my skin crawl.

Plenty of others are approaching him. A steady trickle of fae slink in and out of the throne room, all of them with the long, twitching tails that mark them as rats. Some bring small trinkets that he motions for them to add to a pile at the back of the dais. Some crouch low and make requests I can't hear from where I'm sitting. Others appear to be reporting to him about whatever activities they've been carrying out.

I should probably creep closer so I can overhear what they're saying, so I have a better idea what the Murk are up to and what I might do about it. But then I'd risk drawing Orion's attention again —and I'd be absorbing even more of that unsettling, erratic energy.

My gaze moves behind the king to the orange glow of the Murk's Heart. A tremor runs through my body, and my pulse starts thumping hard all over again. Can it be true that Orion managed to conjure a force that rivals the Heart of the Mists?

But then, how else could he have cast such a huge curse on all the summer and winter fae? From what my mates told me, it started out with only a mild effect: an hour of wolfish savagery, ravens falling ill but not dying. But as their distress grew, their pain fueled that awful thing and allowed Orion in turn to strengthen the curse so it got worse and worse… A horrible vicious cycle.

A cycle I'm a part of. *I* was one of the Murk's tricks, getting the Seelie's and Unseelie's hopes invested in me and then yanking me away from them. All the panic they must be feeling over my disappearance is only making the Murk more powerful.

I had no idea about any of this, but that fact doesn't lighten the guilt clamped around my lungs.

I only ever wanted to help the other fae, and instead I've set them up for even greater misery than they were facing before. And who knows what else, if Orion sees through his awful plans.

Gradually, through my horror and hunger, resolve gathers deep in my gut. I've been used as some sort of weapon against the place I've taken as my home, against the men I love more than anything, but there has to be a way I can undo some of the damage. I should find out everything I can about this place and what happens here, about Orion's sadistic plans and what else the Murk are up to. And then I have to find a way out of here so I can warn the fae back home.

I'm just stirring, stretching my limbs before I attempt to stand up and slip out into the tunnel, when Madoc strides back into the throne room. A couple of other Murk carrying large platters of food come in behind him. The spread they've brought looks like more of a meal than the collection of scraps I was given earlier. The creamy, buttery scent that reaches my nose makes my stomach gurgle. I tuck my arm around my belly as if I can hold in the sound.

Maybe Orion heard it from across the room—rat ears must be keen too—because he flicks his hand toward me. "Bring her. I'd dine with my human accomplice."

Madoc steps toward me and motions for me to follow. I straighten up tentatively, studying him.

He tried to reassure me when he spoke to me earlier, but I'm not sure why. He was pretty cold to me when I first woke up in this place. And he's the one who dragged me here to begin with.

If I've learned anything about the Murk, it's that you can't trust any of them, no matter how they appear.

I did want to find out more about what's happening here, though, and who better to hear it from than the king and one of his right-hand men? As much as my instincts might be urging me to cringe away and huddle in a ball until the world rights itself, I know that's not going to get me anywhere.

I've faced all kinds of horrors before. Maybe none of them were quite as gut-wrenching as this one, but that doesn't mean I can't find my way through this too.

Keeping a careful distance from Madoc, I limp up to the dais. Orion eases off his throne to lean against its base with his legs sprawled out. His tail coils next to him. One of the servants sets the largest platter, which holds several plates, by his side. The other brings around plates to the fae who've lingered on the dais around him, who I'm guessing are among his inner circle.

Do Murk have cadres or coteries? Do they even have lords? I have no idea what the hierarchy here is other than Orion clearly rules over them all.

"Sit," he tells me briskly when I reach the dais. I sink onto the low platform with its scarred wooden slats where I can reach the platter without getting too close to him or any of the other fae. Madoc sits across from me. He waits until Orion grabs a handful of the fettucine that's giving off the creamy scent before reaching for what looks like a spring roll on one of the other plates.

Orion slops the pasta down on one of the empty plates the servants brought, licks the sauce off his hand without any hint of concern, and then picks up a fork to dig into the noodles. I watch Madoc take a bite of his spring roll and decide those must be decently safe. As delicious as the fettucine smells, I don't want to eat anything Orion's fingers have been in.

"Well," Orion says, peering at me, "you've been tucked away taking everything in for quite a while. What do you make of my kingdom?"

I take a bite of the spring roll to give me a chance to think while I'm chewing. A mix of pork and vegetable juices with a tang of spice washes over my tongue, and it's all I can do not to stuff the rest in my mouth all at once. It's not August-level cooking, but after the day I've had, it might as well be.

I clear my throat, and Madoc sets a bottle of water near me in offering. I guess it's not too hard to figure out that I'd be thirsty at this point. Orion takes a swig from a bottle of wine with a company label on it, obviously human made.

One thing I'll say for the Murk: they don't seem to be as disdainful of anything human as the other fae are. Maybe it's possible to end this war before it goes any further. I've managed to talk down fae who hated me and what I stood for before, managed to help negotiate a peace treaty between summer and winter when both wanted to strike out at the other.

If Orion's even a little more willing to take my thoughts into account than the fae of the seasons, I might have a chance at swaying him. I just need to know what he wants.

"You obviously have a lot of subjects working to carry out your plans," I say, measuring my words and keeping a close eye on his reactions. "It's amazing that you were able to create a Heart of your own. I can see why they'd follow you."

Orion grins, but there's a bit of a cruel edge to it. "You have some brains, then. Good. I doubt the fae of the seasons gave you much chance to use them."

My mates and at least a few of the others did, but I bite back a protest. I need to get on his good side if he's going to listen to me. "As a human among the fae, I've needed to use every skill I do have to survive."

He hums to himself and gulps down another forkful of pasta. "I suppose I didn't equip you as well as I could have. The cure and the mate bond—more unusualness than that and it might have become too suspicious. It does seem to have been enough to keep you alive."

"Yes," I say, hiding my surprise as well as I can. The cure and the mate bond aren't the only things unusual about me.

Does he not know about the fact that I can use true-name magic to some small extent? It doesn't sound like it. Could that talent have been an unintended and unknown side effect from the magic he worked on me?

If that's the case… I catch myself before my hand reaches for the bronze bracelet Sylas gave me. I have a secret weapon—in more than just the cuff I could transform into a blade. I can manipulate air and light a little bit too.

And I have Whitt's true name. I can't reach out to Corwin—the hollow of the muted bond digs into my chest—but I might be able to talk to another of my mates. Tell him where I am, as much as I can determine that. Warn him.

I can't let that hope show on my face while Orion is watching me. I reach for what looks like a flaky yellow pastry that turns out to be filled with spiced ground beef and take a couple of bites before speaking again. "What are you going to do next, now that you've taken me back? You said you want to win the Mists for yourself?"

Orion nods with a careless wave of his hand. "Leave the scheming to us, little girl. It's our specialty, after all. If you want to stick it to the fae who treated you like dung, you're welcome to come along for the ride."

"What are you going to do to the summer and winter fae?" I venture. He can't mean to *kill* every one of them, can he?

"They'll meet the fate they deserve." The king peers at me more intently. "You're concerned about the ones you made your mates, aren't you? Don't bother yourself about them. You never mattered to them for more than what you could do for their people. You'll find much better companionship here, and none of *my* people will shun their own for associating with a human."

That last point might be true, but my throat closes up with a swell of emotion. I grasp the water bottle and take a swig from it just to have something to do with my hands.

I know my mates care about me far more than Orion believes. The ache of missing them brings a burn to the back of my eyes that I don't want the Murk king to see.

When I feel like I've gotten a better grip on myself, I let myself speak again. "I'm glad to hear that. But why do you want the Mists anyway? It seems like you've made yourself really at home here, and you have access to everything the human world offers." I motion to the food.

Orion snorts. "The Mists belong to the fae—they should belong to *all* the fae. They're where we truly belong. Oh, we'd still make our visits to this world when we wanted to, but we've been driven to the shadowy corners of our true home for too long. It's time those tables were turned and we claimed what should have been ours all along."

He throws back more wine and sets the bottle down with a thump. "Less about that subject while we're eating. It's giving me indigestion thinking about the bastards who've rooted us out."

"You seem to have accomplished a lot already," I say meekly, feeling awkward and like I'm going to swallow my tongue at the sort-of praise I'm offering this man. I'm not going to say I approve of his campaign against the fae of the seasons. I just want him to get the sense that I'm trying to understand. But it sounds like I've gotten as far as I can with him right now.

I finish my bottle of water and several more tidbits off the platters. The pangs of thirst and hunger fade away.

Orion lifts his chin toward me. "Don't feel you need to keep to this room. You're with us now—almost one of us. Don't disturb any of my people at work, but they shouldn't hassle you either."

"Okay," I say, wondering how true that actually is. A pinching low in my belly alerts me to a more pressing concern than exploration. "Um, are there some kind of bathrooms down here?"

Orion throws back his head with a laugh and motions to Madoc. "We aren't *animals.* Show her to the facilities."

Madoc gets up without a word. I follow him out of the throne room. As we walk along the dark subway tunnel to the next station over, I find myself trying not to stare at the bobbing of his tail with his steps. The question itches at me too much to keep it in, though.

"Why does everyone have their tails out all the time down here?" I ask. I haven't seen any of the Murk really *using* their tails, other than occasionally nudging items closer or holding them steady. "I know you don't have to." The Murk who attacked me by the burning patch that let off that awful iron smoke didn't have a tail, and I don't think Madoc did when I ran into him in the woods by the Heart.

"Orion likes us to embrace our full nature," Madoc says. "Too many of us have spent our whole lives hiding what we are so that we can get by without a backlash. He's trying to change that."

I sympathize with that reasoning more than I want to. I suppose, no matter how villainous many of the Murk have been, there are probably at least a few who don't have much interest in playing pranks or hurting anyone, who don't deserve the treatment they'd get as soon as anyone discovers what they are. I shouldn't assume they're all the same any more than it was fair for the summer and winter fae to assume the worst of each other.

I don't agree with Orion's intentions or the way he's used me, but his people have raised him up as a king and supported his campaign for a reason.

That thought sticks with me as I duck through the doorway at one end of the station platform that Madoc points me to. Inside, I find a row of urinals on one side and stalls on the other.

My nose wrinkles at the faint smell of urine, but it's not as bad as I'd have expected if these aren't working at all. The toilet I use flushes. The fae must have managed to reconnect them to the sewer system, or else the people who abandoned this stretch of subway forgot to disconnect them in the first place.

I gaze at my reflection in the dingy mirror for a few seconds. My hair is rumpled, my face even paler than usual. I look almost as frail as I did right after Sylas rescued me from Aerik's cage.

How much of the pain I've been through did Orion plan, and how much was simply chance?

Madoc is waiting for me on the platform when I emerge. This station looks a lot like the one where I woke up, with structures that I guess are houses scattered all along the platforms and fae moving around them and across the tracks.

He answered my last question. I might as well try him with another. "How many stations do you have in the—what did you call this place?"

"The King's Refuge," Madoc says, and glances toward the next tunnel entrance. "There are five stations all connected and a maintenance area as well. It's the biggest Murk colony I'm aware of."

From the number of houses and fae that I've seen, it's probably bigger than any of the fae villages in the Mists.

"Would you like to see more of it?" Madoc asks in a cautious tone. "I could show you around."

Does he really want to act as my tour guide? I scrutinize him, and he gazes steadily back at me. Maybe he doesn't have any real animosity toward me, only the fae I've associated with. As if that's much better.

Either way, when I do my exploring, I don't want company for it.

At my hesitation, he goes on, offering a small, slanted smile. "I know this can't be easy for you, finding out so much about your life that you had no idea of, losing the home and the people you'd gotten used to. Of course you'll need time to adjust. And if you want to talk about any of it—I may not be fond of the fae you left behind, but I can still listen."

I don't know how to believe his apparent kindness. I swipe my hand across my mouth, and the niggling inside me deepens. "The Murk have been paying attention to what's happened to me in the Mists, haven't they? Orion would have wanted to know how his plan was progressing."

Madoc nods. "We have many people keeping an eye on the realms there. I've visited often myself."

Without the other fae realizing it. With the magic of the Murk's Heart, they must have developed spells for better concealing their scent and other signs of their presence.

I wet my lips. "But it wasn't only watching. There were Murk who destroyed part of the Unseelie village in the summer realm. And one who started a fire with iron in the smoke. What was all that about?"

Madoc pauses before he answers. His eyes, which I can now tell are gray, momentarily turn even darker. "Sometimes we just meant to keep them on their toes. But Orion wanted to be sure the fae on both sides of their border cared about you as much as we could encourage them to. The ravens were all but worshipping you with just a little nudge here and there, remarks we let them overhear, but the wolves had taken your blood for granted. With the iron-laced fire, we arranged a bit of a spectacle where you could show what a hero you were to them too."

The whole problem with the smoke had been a setup—specifically that only a human could stop. And the Murk who'd sprang at me…

My hand drops to my thigh where the lingering wound still aches a little. Unlike the fae of the seasons, the Murk can end their own lives. They're too separate from the Heart of the Mist's power for it to stop them the way it has other desperate fae like Corwin's mother.

"The man who attacked me," I say slowly, "I didn't do anything to him at all. He had a spell on him to make it look like I'd killed him, but really he did it to himself."

The corner of Madoc's mouth twitches. I can't tell if it was heading toward a greater smile or a frown. "You catch on quickly. Orion is bringing us out of the darkness we've dwelled in for so long. Many of us are happy to give our lives for that cause."

My arms come up to wrap around my chest. I look out over the fae moving through the subway station again, my heart sinking.

An enemy that committed to destroying my home will be awfully hard to defeat. But will I really be able to convince Orion that there's another way before it comes to full-out war?

CHAPTER FIVE

Talia

The second time I wake up in the Murk colony they call the King's Refuge, I'm alone in the little house of corrugated steel Madoc arranged for me, which is about the size of a large tent. He assured me that I could have something larger prepared if I wanted it, but all I wanted was somewhere to sleep without so many rat shifter eyes on me.

I'm far enough away from the Murk's Heart that it isn't rattling my nerves anymore, but I catch a faint, erratic quiver of my skin as I rub my eyes. Is there anywhere in this network of tunnels where I'd be able to escape it completely?

Maybe not, but I need to attempt a bigger escape. Which means I have to get a better idea of what and who I'm dealing with out there.

I tug at my new clothes—a long-sleeved tee and sweatpants Madoc had one of the other fae bring me so I could change out of my dress—and glance at the silky bundle I've left carefully folded in the corner. I'm glad for the change because I don't want the other Murk paying particular attention to me when I'm wandering around, and the dress definitely stands out here. But other than my bracelet, it's the only thing I have that connects me to the home I left behind.

I will get back there. And I can get started on making that happen now.

Cautiously, I clamber out of the hovel. The same unpleasant mix of smells reaches my nose, and there's a faint metallic tapping sound carrying from farther down the subway station. The rat shifters must be at work there.

My head still feels muggy. I didn't exactly sleep *well* in the nest of blankets Madoc left for me, with everything I've discovered in the past day buzzing around in my mind.

I go over to the bathroom and splash some water onto my face at the sinks, which thankfully work, although I'm not sure I'd want to attempt drinking the water their faucets spew out. Madoc pointed out the cases of bottled water that stand in one corner of every station and that the Murk must replenish regularly. If they don't trust the tap water, I certainly don't.

My stomach grumbles. I make my way along the platform to where a long table is set up. A couple of Murk are laying out an odd variety of food across it: bagels and a huge tub of cream cheese, a large tray of fried meat patties that appear to have cooled, various boxes of cereal with no bowls or milk to use with them, all sorts of fruit from bananas to mangos that look a bit bruised but otherwise all right, and more.

I pick up a muffin and a pear, biting into one and then the other tentatively. Fae brush past me to take their own meals from the table. Other than a few evaluating glances, which give me the sense that they know who I am, they ignore me. I guess that's better than overt hostility. Madoc at least didn't lie that his people wouldn't hurt me.

As one of the rat shifters who laid out the spread steps away, wiping her hands together, I venture a question. "Where did you get all the food from?"

She studies me with sharp eyes and gives me a tight smile. "We take whatever we can find and make off with what doesn't put us at too much risk. It should all be fine for you."

So they steal it from the humans above. Although from the looks of some of the items, they might have already been discarded before the Murk took them. The rat shifters can't have much choice, living the way they do. Where would they grow or hunt for their own food like the fae of the seasons do?

"Thank you," I say, because even though I don't trust any of the fae around me, she was at least patient enough to answer.

"Take anything you want," she adds, with a tip of her head toward the table. "We bring more throughout the day. You're Orion's—no one will fight you over it."

Do the Murk sometimes fight each other over the best scavenged morsels? But what really sends a shiver through me is her casual reference to Orion, as if I *belong* to him.

In his subjects' eyes, I probably do.

I thank her again and wander on along the subway platform, scanning the activity on both sides of the tracks and down in their chasm. A lot of the Murk don't appear to be doing much of anything other than lounging around and talking. But maybe the ones here are those who don't currently have any work to do. I spot others vanishing into the tunnels and emerging from them. One man heaves a large box onto the platform just a few feet from me.

"What's in there?" I ask, feeling a little more confident that he's not going to snap at me for daring to talk to him.

He scrambles onto the platform next to his cargo, his tail swishing to help him balance. "Lead bars," he says. "Bringing them to the crafting workshop."

Because presumably it's easier for the Murk to work with materials they've already gathered rather than summoning them out of the earth, just like I need a bronze object in my hands before I can shape it. I motion to the box. "What are you going to craft with them?"

A sly smile flashes across his face. "Whatever our king asks of us to further our plans."

I'm not sure I like the sound of that, but he's carting the supplies away before I can pry any further.

I continue exploring, picking my way carefully through the dark subway tunnels, where only occasional magically-charged lanterns provide a faint illumination, and making my way through two more stations. The last tunnel leads to a larger sort-of cavern filled with unfamiliar machines and other tools. This must be the maintenance area Madoc mentioned.

No fae are in that space now. I move along the walls, checking all the equipment over in case I spot something that might be useful, and notice a square opening on the back wall, a few feet over my head. A cover of interlaced steel bars is fixed over it.

I can't reach it right away, but I manage to shove one of larger machines up to the wall beneath it and climb up on top to reach the opening. The square space is just large enough that I'm sure I could fit inside it.

A faint, cool draft washes over me when I bring my face close. It's got to be an air vent of some sort. I think I catch a hint of car exhaust. Does it lead all the way outside?

It doesn't appear to be an entrance the Murk use. I can't see any way to open or close the cover. The steel panel is held in place by several heavy bolts, dappled with rust that's starting to meld them into the cover itself.

I look down at my bracelet, hope flickering up in my chest. Maybe it isn't a blade I'll need most to defend myself—maybe it's a wrench. I could shape the metal into one if I concentrated, couldn't I? It shouldn't be all that much harder than making a knife.

I'll remember this spot for later. I don't want to use up any of my meager magical energy on that right now. I might need all the strength I can summon to reach out to Whitt.

My mates need to know that I'm all right and that the Murk are trying to destroy them.

I slide down off the machine and crouch next to it, leaning against its solid metal side. No footsteps or rustlings of a rat's passing reach my ears for several minutes. Can I trust that I'm actually alone?

Orion didn't seem all that concerned that I might leave. Maybe he's convinced that's impossible anyway. I didn't notice any Murk following me as I explored.

I bite my lip, waiting a little longer just to be sure. Then I cup my hands around my mouth to muffle as much of the sound as possible, close my eyes, and picture Whitt's handsome face: his sun-kissed brown hair, his sparking ocean-blue eyes, his typical crooked grin.

Homesickness wrenches at me so hard it brings a flood of tears to the back of my eyes. My breath turns ragged.

I'll get back to him—him and my other three mates and the home we've made. I *have* to.

"*Wye-con-ell*," I murmur under my breath, putting all the concentration I can into reaching out to him across the vast distance between our worlds. "*Wye-con-ell.* I need to talk to you. Hear me. Let me hear your answers."

My voice gets more urgent with each word. A fizzing sort of static rushes through my mind.

Then, all at once, a hint of my mate's warm sandy scent grazes my nose. I have a vague impression of him, somewhere out there—far more ephemeral than when I tried out using his true name after he first gave it to me, but definitely something apart from the dark, dank room I'm hidden away in.

Talia? Whitt's voice says in my mind, as if carried on the wind across miles, so faint I can barely make it out. *Talia, where are you?*

I squeeze my eyes tighter shut and train all my attention on my sense of him far away in the fae world. An ache spreads over my scalp with the effort. *The Murk took me. I'm in the human world. Some kind of—*

A more jabbing pain splits through my focus. I press my hand to my forehead as if I can force the discomfort back. How much of a message do I have the strength to convey to him before I lose this connection completely?

Whitt's voice fades in and out as the magic between us wavers. *Have they hurt you? Where… you? We've been… we can.*

I struggle to decide on the most important information I need to pass on to him. I don't think I know enough for my mates to figure out where this Murk colony is and come for me, not yet. And… I'm not sure I'd want them to anyway. Will they be able to overpower Orion and his people on their own ground, with their Heart so close and the Heart of the Mists so far away? They have no idea—they won't be prepared.

It's bad enough being torn away from them. I won't lead them to their doom.

My hands clench in my lap. I put every shred of energy I have into the few words I can send him. *I'm all right. Working to find a way back to you. Watch out for the Murk. They mean to invade the Mists.*

The ache digs deeper. A sweat breaks out on my back, and I gasp in a breath. I can't tell whether all of that reached Whitt. His voice and my impressions of him are fragmenting even more. *We'll… soon… if they… in there… love you.*

I love you too, I think back at him with a pang through my heart, but in the same moment, the tenuous connection snaps.

I rock backward, banging my shoulders on the machine I'm sitting against. The headache has expanded all through my skull. When I turn my head, pinpricks of pain stab at the backs of my eyeballs.

I'm obviously not going to be holding extended conversations with Whitt any time soon. But at least he knows I'm alive and reasonably okay. Hopefully he heard enough of my warning to tell everyone to be even more on guard against the Murk.

Gripping a bar that protrudes from the machine, I haul myself to my feet. My head spins, the pain turning blaring for several seconds before it retreats just a little. I take shallow breaths in and out.

Am I even going to be able to make it back to the nearest station?

Holding my head as still as I can, I take careful steps toward the tracks, setting my hands against the machines for balance. I manage to find a slow but steady pace that doesn't provoke the throbbing in my skull too badly.

When I reach the tracks, I focus on the gravel path between the rails. One step, then another, with a rasp of my boots over the gritty stones. After all my wandering, my ankle is starting to hurt too, a duller throb echoing up my leg.

It feels like years later that the starker glow of the station touches the edges of my vision. I take my next steps faster and immediately regret it.

Agony whirls up behind my temples. I sway to the side, the toe of my boot catching on one of the rails. I tumble forward toward the sharp gravel—

—and firm hands grasp me just as my knees brush the ground with a faint sting.

"Steady there," Madoc says, easing me into a sitting position. As I wince and press my palms to my temples, he cocks his head at me. "What's happened to you?"

"I—" I can hardly find my words amid the pain. "My head hurts."

He peers closely into my eyes, so near that his scent washes over me, cool and faintly electric like the atmosphere just before a thunderstorm. Is he actually worried about me?

"Maybe the sudden, jarring change in environment is affecting you," he says, lowering his voice even more as if he's guessed hearing any sound at all sets off fresh sparks of pain. "Let me do what I can, and then I'll get you back to your house and bring one of our healers to you."

He touches his knuckles to my forehead and murmurs a few words. A welcome chill floods through my skull, dulling the pain. It's still *there*, but the throbbing has become more distant. My thoughts seem to fade in volume at the same time.

"Better?" Madoc asks, and I manage to nod. "Wait right here. I'll get you a cart so you don't need to walk."

In my dulled state, a mumbled plea slips out of me. "I want to go home."

Madoc obviously knows I don't mean the hovel I slept in. He brings his hand to my cheek with unexpected gentleness. "You'll find a good home here among us. We'll *make* it a good one for you. I promise."

He strides off, leaving me puzzling over the raw emotion that crept into those words, as if he meant them more than I'd ever have expected.

CHAPTER SIX

Corwin

"You and your companions can make use of these rooms for as long as you need them," I say to the man I've just ushered into one of the larger guest apartments in the palace of Heart's Cadence. My gaze slides past him to the cursed woman—his mate—hunched on the bed, and my stomach clenches with the knowledge that they will only need the space here until she passes.

At the moment, I'm starkly aware of the horror of losing one's mate. At least I can take some small measure of hope from the fact that based on the message Talia managed to convey to Whitt, she's nowhere near death. That still doesn't get us any closer to retrieving her from the wretched Murk that wrenched her away from me.

And with her gone, anyone the curse touches among my people have no hope at all.

A punch of tangled anger and grief hits me in the chest. I set my jaw and steady myself as well as I can. My guests are watching me.

"Let me know if there's anything we can do to make you more

comfortable," I say. "My staff will be ready to see to your requests or summon me if necessary."

"Thank you, arch-lord," the man says with a dip of his head and a tight smile, and I feel I can finally step away from them.

It's unlikely they'll be the last to require my hospitality. Since Talia's disappearance three days ago, they're already the second travelers to arrive seeking her cure. My colleagues and I explained the situation in as calm a way as we could and sent the larger entourage of folk-flock who'd joined the curse victims back home. Terisse has taken the other victim and her family into her palace.

Being helpless to do anything to hold back the curse on my own only multiplies my anguish. And I can imagine how torn up Talia would be to think of the people who may die in her absence. The Murk have dealt us a harder blow than they may even realize.

Or maybe this is exactly why they've stolen my mate—to strike out at us in ways not just personal but with consequences for our entire realm and the summer realm besides. It's by far the most immense gambit they've ever pulled off.

How were they able to sneak past so many sentries to reach Talia? To bewitch the Seelie woman before that and force her to draw Talia away from the celebration to the forest where she was more vulnerable? It's beyond anything we've ever seen or heard of the Murk before, and that leaves uneasiness twisted all through my gut.

I've only made it partway down the hall from the guest quarters when one of my staff hurries over to me. My heart sinks with the thought that yet another curse victim has arrived, but what he actually says doesn't make me feel much better.

"Arch-Lord Laoni is waiting in the terrace room, my lord," he says. "She wishes to speak to you."

I grit my teeth and set off to see what my most hostile colleague wants now.

It doesn't surprise me to discover that Laoni hasn't even bothered to sit down. She's standing between the scattered chairs, gazing out the tall windows that look over the terrace and the sweeping landscape beyond. As if to remind me that she doesn't jump to my bidding, she stays there for a moment after I've entered the room before deigning to turn to face me.

"Corwin," she says, studying my face. "You look frazzled."

Her tone gives the observation an implied criticism, as if I should be totally at peace even with my soul-twined mate in the hands of our greatest enemies. I bite back the cutting remark that leaps onto my tongue, pulling together the appearance of professionalism. "I'd imagine that's not surprising, considering the circumstances. It hasn't affected my duties."

Her eyes narrow, and I suppose she's thinking about my mother —about how completely *she* fell apart when she lost her own soul-twined mate with my father's death. The other arch-lords have always questioned my fitness for the position based on their fears about my familial "instability." Even after Talia cured Laoni and kept her curse secret as Laoni wished, she's still out to pick at me every way she can.

"What progress have you made toward finding your mate?" she demands, as if the only reason we haven't retrieved Talia yet is some failing on my part.

"I have sentries and soldiers, including three of my coterie members, scouring every inch of the realm for any trace of Murk presence," I say tightly. "Arch-Lord Sylas is doing the same on the summer side."

"And yet they've turned up nothing."

No doubt she's only concerned because of what fate *she'll* meet if we don't rescue Talia within the next few weeks, before the curse returns to her. I fold my arms over my chest. "If you wish to see faster proceedings, you're welcome to add more of your own flock to the search."

Laoni's chin comes up. "I've sent several on that quest already. I can't leave my domain completely undefended if the filthy rats decide to strike out in some other way."

"Well, I'm doing everything I can," I say, my patience fraying too much for me to keep the irritation out of my voice. "It is *my* soul-twined mate they have, and I won't rest until she's back by my side. If you have a suggestion that might actually help, by all means, share it. Otherwise, as far as I can tell you're only here to harass me."

Laoni's expression twitches, and her gaze hardens. A flash of shame rushes through me. I've worked so hard on keeping a controlled front, especially with my colleagues. My fears for Talia *are* unraveling me.

"I'll leave you to your work, then," Laoni says stiffly, and marches off to the terrace to fly to her own domain.

After she's soared off, I remain in the room for several minutes, gripping the back of one of the armchairs. My pulse thuds in a heavy rhythm. With every beat, the emptiness where my connection to Talia should be reverberates through me, digging the pain of her absence deeper.

I can't let my distress shatter me completely. I'll have no chance of fighting for Talia then, and I'll fail my flock and all the other people I rule over as well. But how can I center myself when such a huge piece of my soul is missing?

My gaze rises to the ceiling. There *is* someone in this palace who has an idea of what I'm experiencing. I don't know if she'll be at all coherent, but maybe talking to her will help me sort through the turmoil inside me at least a little.

I move through the halls swiftly, not wanting to be interrupted while I'm so unsettled. As I climb up the staircase that leads to my mother's quarters, I consider casting the usual calming spell to soothe her nerves before I enter. But perhaps she deserves the respect of being faced in her genuine state, with all the anguish she's dealing with that I rarely see these days.

I wish there was a better way to keep her from harming herself without locking her up. But the memories of the horrific scenes that resulted from her past attempts at ending her life, always in vain but not without gore and bloodshed, make the thought of offering her the freedom she deserves impossible.

"Mother, it's me," I call through the locked door. "I'm coming in."

When I open it, I find her crouched near the stairs that lead up to her bedroom. She takes a leap forward as if to spring for the open entrance, but I close the door and quickly lock it.

Mother's shoulders slump. She darts over to the table she's upended yet again and then hunches there, swaying slightly.

"Hello, Mother," I say quietly, my heart wrenching all over again. I can't imagine being reduced to the near-feral state she's in, but I can understand the agony she's gone through better than I ever could before.

I walk across the room and sit on the floor against the built-in shelves, across from her current refuge. She mutters under her breath and then adds in a voice that's almost a whimper, "Let me out. Let me end it."

I swallow hard. "You know you can't, no matter where you go or what you do. The Heart won't let you destroy the life it's given you."

Her chest heaves with a strangled sob. She drops her head into her hands.

"You feel like that life has already been destroyed, don't you?" I murmur. "Part of your soul ripped away from you. I—I may have to face the same thing."

Mother twitches, and then lifts her gaze to take me in. "Your mate…"

"You might remember Talia? She's come to see you before. She… The Murk have taken her. They've interrupted our soul-twined bond somehow. I can't sense her at all."

Another surge of emotion rolls over me with the admission, even though it isn't new. I bring my hand to my mouth as if I'm in danger of sobbing myself.

Coming here might have been misguided. Am I only making myself feel worse?

But before I can decide to leave, Mother eases forward. Haltingly, she crosses the room until she's squatting right in front of me. Her head cocks as if she's trying to make out who I am.

Then she reaches and, for the first time since her grief overwhelmed everything else, takes my hand.

"My son," she says in a small, thin voice.

I squeeze her fingers, a bittersweet ache forming in my chest at the gesture. "I'll—I'll make it through. I have to. But I just wanted to see you. You're the only one I know who's been through it and won't judge me for my pain."

She stares at me for a long moment. Something clears in her eyes, just briefly. "If I could have shielded you from the horror of it," she says, and lapses back into silence.

"I know you couldn't have, any more than I could have protected you. I still can't really help you, as much as I'd like to. But… you're not alone."

Mother sways back and forth as if to some imaginary song and then swipes her forearm past her reddened eyes. "I am, but I'm not. I —" She focuses in on me again, gripping my hand. "It's the deepest pain for the deepest bond. But for all the pain, I wouldn't have given it up. We are lucky to have ever been so blessed—to have gotten what time we had—" She inhales raggedly and drops her head again, a tremor running through her. "If I could only follow that bond to its end…"

"I know," I say, my own voice raw, but something inside me has steadied.

Disturbed as she is, there's truth in what she said. I'm lucky to have been twined so closely with a woman like Talia for as even as short a time as I was. I need to focus on that and not the loss of it—on what I'll *still* have, when we defeat the Murk, not on anticipating an even greater loss.

"Thank you," I say. "For hearing me. For your words. Is there anything I can bring you—"

The wildness is already returning to her eyes. She flings her arm toward the door. "To go out—to find a blade or a cliff—"

My throat constricts. "It won't work. But maybe, if we can finally end this curse, you'll find at least as much peace as you just gave me."

CHAPTER SEVEN

Talia

The last thing I actually *want* to do is spend more time in Orion's unpredictable presence with the glow of that horrific Heart pulsing over us. But when my searing headache has finally faded enough that I can think coherently, I know I have to try.

I'm obviously not going to be able to construct any kind of complex plan with Whitt or rally the fae in the Mists when I can barely get across two sentences over the distance without incapacitating myself. My only real hope of helping stop the war Orion is intent on waging is to change his mind. If that task seems impossible, well, I've just got to take it one step at a time.

I limp through the station toward his throne room. It looks as if the Murk are just rousing for the day—if it is day. The lights that had been dimmer when I first emerged are glimmering brighter now.

When I reach the immense alcove, the Murk king is standing beside his regal seat, stretching his arms with a small yawn. A servant hustles over to bring him a steaming mug. I catch a whiff of coffee as she passes me.

His usual companions aren't with him right now—the dais around him is empty. I guess they must go back to their own houses to sleep.

Where does Orion spend his nights? I glance around, but nothing in the throne room looks like the kinds of houses the rest of the Murk have. Does he just lie there on the platform basking in his Heart's erratic light?

A shiver travels down my spine at the thought, but at the same moment the Murk king takes notice of me. He gives me a grin as jagged as his spiky white hair and motions me over. "Decided to join me for another breakfast, have you?"

With the first breakfast being just yesterday, was it? I think I only lost the better part of a day to that headache. Does that mean I've been gone from the Mists for nearly three full days now? I'm not sure how long they kept me unconscious after Madoc grabbed me in the forest.

I could have been missing for over a week for all I know.

All the Unseelie fae who'll have been struck by the curse since then—all the efforts my mates must be going to trying to find me—

I can't do anything about that until I find a way out of here.

Pushing the uncomfortable thoughts aside, I make my unsteady way over to the dais and sit on the edge. Orion appears to have forgotten about me as quickly as he noticed me. He paces along the dais, giving orders in a low mutter to the various underlings who are now gathering in the throne room.

Just as he's sent the last of them off, a couple more servants stride in carrying platters of food like yesterday. The king drops into the same spot at the base of his throne to consider their offerings.

"Do you want coffee?" he asks, and it takes me a second to realize he's talking to me, since he didn't even look up.

I wouldn't mind being perked up with caffeine, but the bitter scent trailing from his mug makes my tongue recoil. I'm not sure I'd be able to get down the kind of stuff he's drinking. "No, thank you."

"Well, eat. We won't be starving you here." He snatches up a chicken wing and pulls a strip of meat off it with his teeth. His gaze lingers on my boots, and I suspect he's thinking of the other mistreatment I suffered at the hands of the Seelie. A pang runs through the arch of my foot at the memory of Aerik's cadre man snapping the bones.

"I wondered if you've had any news from the Mists," I venture, taking a small roll dusted with dried coconut. "About how they're doing with me gone?"

He makes an amused sound and peers into my eyes for the first time. The predatory gleam in his yellow ones makes the hair on the back of my neck stand on end. "You're worried about the pricks you left behind."

I tuck my feet closer to me. "They weren't all awful to me. Some might have hurt me, but others did a lot to help me heal. I don't think you should see them all as horrible."

"I have many more centuries of experience with the other fae kinds than you do," he says in a tone that makes me wonder just how old he is despite his smooth face. "But yes, I have people monitoring the Mists. Everything is proceeding well."

He doesn't elaborate on that, although I've heard enough from him before to assume that "well" by his standards is "badly" by mine. His gaze slides away from me, and he raises his hand in greeting. Madoc has just appeared at the entrance to the throne room.

"I've already eaten," the other fae man says when Orion gestures to his spread, but he sits down on the dais across from me anyway and considers me. "Feeling better now, Talia?"

I nod, my hand instinctively moving to my forehead. "It's completely gone."

"You shouldn't strain yourself," Orion declares. I assume Madoc told him about the state he found me in. "If I feel I need you to pitch in, I won't hesitate to tell you. Otherwise you're at your leisure."

Does he suspect that I was doing something he wouldn't like? I fumble for words. "I—I think it was just the stress of… everything."

He hums to himself. I can't read him at all.

I've got to put out some kind of feelers. "If the fae of the Mists are upset with me gone—you could use that without even needing to attack them, couldn't you? Negotiate with them. There's lots of unclaimed land in both realms. I'm sure there's room for all the Murk to live there as well."

Orion snorts. "And make ourselves subject to their arch-lords and rules, for however little time until they find some loophole to kick us out again? Didn't you learn anything about them in your time there?"

I'm not going to get very far if I'm too argumentative. I can already tell he doesn't like having *his* authority challenged either. "You might be right about that," I say. "But—wouldn't it be better for your own people to try to find some kind of compromise instead of battling to take over all of the Mists? If there's fighting, some of the Murk will die too."

"My people are willing to make the necessary sacrifices to bring us to a better place for the rest of eternity." Orion takes a big gulp of his coffee and blows out a puff of steam. "The Seelie and Unseelie will never meet us as equals. As far as they're concerned, we're dirt under their boots."

"But you have me now. That gives you leverage. You could even ask for a chunk of the Mist lands to be given completely to the Murk. They'd have to live with displacing a bunch of lords, but oh well. You *should* have a place there. You're fae too."

I must manage to sound reasonably convincing, because Orion pauses for a second as if he's thinking my statement over. But then he shakes his head. "I can't risk avoiding a smaller slaughter in the beginning only to lead us to a much larger one later on. To be sure of getting what we deserve, we have to take it by force—all of it. The fae of the seasons have owned the entirety of the Mists for millennia; it's our turn now. Besides, they deserve some bloodshed of their own after stomping us down for so long."

"The ones who first cast you out won't even be alive anymore, will they?" I have to point out.

"I'm sure a few of those pricks have held in there. And their heirs haven't been any kinder."

I bite back the urge to point out that the Murk haven't done anything to warrant kindness from the other fae recently. Does he really expect the summer and winter realms to extend an olive branch when his people are causing all the havoc they can both there and here in the human world?

I'm not sure what else I can say, so I take a handful of raspberries and pop them into my mouth to cover my uncertainty. At least I know more than I did before about what's driving Orion, what matters to him. There has to be *some* way I can present a compromise that'll appeal to him. Even if it only gets him face to face with the fae of the Mists to talk—so that they can get the upper hand and end this war before it really starts.

A couple more of the men from Orion's inner circle amble into the throne room. Orion grabs a drumstick to take with him and walks over to consult with them by the far end of the dais. I swallow the berries, their juice turning sour in the back of my mouth.

"You're worrying too much," Madoc says. "You'll give yourself another headache." He gets up and beckons me. "Come. I'll show you part of the Refuge you won't have seen yet. Maybe it'll even reassure you about the future."

I can't imagine what in this place could accomplish that, but I get up anyway. Orion seems to trust Madoc quite a bit. Maybe Madoc will listen to me more than his king has and be able to translate my arguments into a version Orion will accept.

He leads me in the opposite direction from the way I went exploring yesterday, through one station and another. The other fae are getting to work throughout the Refuge, more supplies coming and going, more sounds of construction echoing off the ceilings. My skin prickles with apprehension.

Just how long do I have before Orion decides to launch the next phase of his attack? What is he waiting to see in the Mists before he decides to go ahead?

Even if he's planning on waiting months, I have to get out of here before then. The Unseelie's curse will be gripping more and more of them, taking their lives without me there to banish it. And how bad will the summer curse be if I haven't returned by the next full moon? Orion may have ramped up the strength of the curses even more now that he's taken me away from them.

I can't express any of those worries to my companion. Madoc

clearly doesn't see anything wrong with his king's approach. I don't know where to begin with him.

Thankfully, he starts up the conversation first. "The way we run things here is pretty different from what you got used to in the courts of the Mists, isn't it?"

A cool draft tickles over my skin in the dark tunnel. I rub my arms as I consider my answer. "I guess. The way everyone supports Orion, it isn't that different from how things work between a lord or lady and their pack or flock."

"We're all united, though," Madoc says. "Every Murk is happy to follow Orion's guidance. The fae of the Mists are constantly arguing between themselves, from what I've seen. Even the arch-lords. The ones you weren't tied to picked on you plenty of times, didn't they?"

I can't deny that. Maybe I shouldn't want to if I'm trying to get into his good graces. "They did. There are definitely plenty of them who were… less than kind." Not that I could call any of the Murk I've met exactly "kind" so far either.

Madoc nods. "It must have been hard, being thrust into a situation like that and needing to find your footing with them while showing powers none of them understood. As much as it benefitted us, I'm sorry you had to deal with them on our behalf, unknowingly."

I blink, peering at him through the shadows. Is he really sorry? His tone has stayed soft, with that hoarse note it always seems to have as if he's never quite cleared his throat enough.

It's hard to believe his sympathy isn't just more Murk trickery.

"What are you showing me?" I ask, wanting to change the subject.

A mysterious smile plays with his lips. "You'll see. It's a spot I set up for myself for when I need to think beyond what's right in front of me." He glances sideways at me. "When we do go to the Mists, we won't treat every fae the same, of course. If there's anyone who particularly deserves to be crushed, or any you think we should go easier on, we could take your suggestions into account with whatever guidance you can offer."

My chest constricts. I don't want them crushing anyone at all, not even the vicious fae like Aerik and Tristan who barely see me as worthy of having a life. But that definitely isn't what he wants to hear.

"I'll think about it," I say instead.

He seems to accept my answer. I study what I can see of his profile in the darkness. "It doesn't bother you at all, the thought of all that violence? It's not really the Murk way to get into direct combat, is it?"

Madoc lets out a dry chuckle. "That much might be true. But some fighting will be worth it to claw our way back to the position and the home owed to us. And I'm sure we'll find ways of bringing our own approach to the battles that lie ahead."

He touches my arm, just a brief graze of his fingers over the skin above my elbow that makes the muscle there jump, guiding me with him into a narrow passage I hadn't noticed in the tunnel wall. It's a stairwell, the steep concrete steps leading up to a narrow landing and then another. After the first couple of flights, a faint ache wakes up in my warped foot. I wonder how far under the ground we are here.

At the third landing, Madoc pushes open a door with a creak of its hinges and moves to usher me into the room on the other side. My legs balk automatically. It's just starting to sink in how far we are from the other Murk now… not that I could expect any of them to leap to my aid if Madoc wanted to hurt me in front of them. But being in an enclosed space with him sets my nerves jangling.

Madoc watches me, maybe guessing at the reasons for my hesitation. "If you don't want to see it after all, we could leave," he says without a trace of judgment.

His lack of urgency and my desire to earn his trust win out over my worries. In his eyes, I belong to his king, don't I? He wouldn't want to damage his ruler's belongings.

I shake my head and limp past him into the room.

It's a small space, windowless like every other part of the Refuge I've seen, with a few cushions along one side and a box that holds an assortment of human snacks—chip bags and prepackaged brownies and that sort of thing—by the other. Papers tacked to the walls show a speckling of penciled dots, some with lines sketched between them.

But what draws my gaze is the telescope set up at the far end of the room, pointed at the spot where the wall meets the ceiling.

"I know it looks ridiculous," Madoc says, going to it, "but it's enchanted. Not easy to get a good look at the stars when slinking through the human world. When our Heart grew strong enough that I had enough power, I tied this telescope magically to one in a science lab up above. Its view of the universe is projected to this lens."

He runs his fingers over the device, and in that moment I can tell I'm seeing genuine appreciation. Whatever else he cares about, that telescope matters to him.

"Why do you want to see the universe?" I ask.

Madoc shrugs, dropping his hand with an abruptly sheepish air. "I've always found the stars fascinating. All that energy and light, so far out of reach. And there's something both wonderful and awful about the thought of how much more there is beyond the worlds we can visit here." He makes an awkward gesture as if he thinks he's said too much and tips his head toward the drawings on the walls. "There's also an art to it, a sort of soothsaying you can perform looking at the constellations. I've been developing my skill at that."

I take a closer look at the patterns of dots and lines. "And what have you found out from them?"

"As I imagine you've realized, any kind of fortune-telling magic is never very exact." He considers the drawings as I do. "But I believe they show a better, less confined future for the Murk. What I do outside this room is to make sure as many of us reach that future as can. Hope shouldn't be as distant as the stars."

Something in those words resonates straight through my chest and brings a lump to my throat. "You know," I say, quietly but with total honesty, "I hope you get that better future, all of you." I just don't want it to happen through the deaths of everyone I care about back in the Mists.

Madoc's gaze jerks to me. In that instant, he looks startled. But then his expression relaxes with another smile, and he motions me over to the telescope. "Here, get a glimpse of the universe and see if it doesn't put everything in some perspective."

He pushes one of the cushions over so I can kneel at it by the telescope's eyepiece. I bring my face to it tentatively.

As I peer through the device, closing my other eye, my whole vision fills with a dark sky dotted with blazing stars, closer than I've ever seen them when gazing up at the sky on my own.

I thought it was morning, but it's actually night outside, at least in whatever part of the human world we're near. I guess it isn't surprising that the Murk have their schedules upside down, sleeping through the day instead.

And now, after hearing the way Madoc talked, I can't help wondering if there's more to him than I've realized as well. I can't believe he's only looking to "sow spite," no matter what the old rhyme says.

But if his goal is still to see the fae of the summer and winter realms fall, does that really make a difference? I'm not any closer to stopping that destruction.

He's right about one thing. Staring up into the heavens makes me feel very, very small.

CHAPTER EIGHT

Talia

The disturbance starts with a few shouts that echo into the station from the nearest tunnel. There's a strange quality to them, both exhilarated and vicious, that makes my head snap around where I was sitting near the scavenged food table eating a hasty dinner.

Several of the fae around me leave off their conversations or work to glance in the same direction. When more voices join the chorus, they slip off the platform onto the tracks and head for the tunnel.

The commotion is coming from the direction of Orion's throne room. Uneasiness coils around my stomach as I follow the fae. I'm not sure I *want* to find out what's going on, but I know I need to. I can't afford to stay ignorant of anything that's going on with my captors, no matter how horrible.

Maybe especially the horrible things.

In the tunnel, the orange glow of the Murk's Heart wavers even more than usual over the many figures streaming into the throne room. I manage to slip inside among them and find a crate by the wall that I can scramble onto for a view over their heads. Keeping my balance with a hand against the cool concrete beside me, I peer over the crowd.

Orion is standing in front of his throne, his head cocked to one side with an expression I can only call cruel amusement. The lash of his tail from side to side suggests he's not actually all that *happy*, though. A few of his close hangers-on have gathered around him, looking a little more alert than usual.

I don't see Madoc among them. Stupidly, his absence sends a flash of worry through me, as if I should be concerned about whether something's happened to him.

He's the one who stole me from my home and my mates. But… he's also the only one of the Murk who's shown much concern for my well-being. I can't help suspecting I'd be even worse off here without him.

The swarm of fae have left a small open space in front of the dais. Just a couple of Murk stand there, one with scars dappling every plane of his hardened face and another with her hair cut into a broad, bristly mohawk. A slim fae man with floppy black hair and umber skin crouches on the floor between them. I can't see his face, but his posture is taut with terror.

"We found him crying in one of the store rooms," the bristly woman says, her voice harsh as sandpaper. "*Sniveling* like an infant, when he was supposed to be bringing materials to the forges."

Forges? I haven't come across those yet. Is that what those lead bricks were for too?

I don't know what they're making, but the first place my mind goes is *weapons*. My muscles tense. I strain my ears to hear better over the murmuring of the crowd.

Orion steps right to the edge of the dais, looming over the three of them. His tail sweeps back and forth like the snap of a whip. "You swore to stand strong in my service, Bren. I have no need for whimperers and cowards."

"I'm not a coward," the floppy-haired man says in a determined youthful voice that makes me think he might not even be an adult yet by fae standards. "I—I only took a moment. Evie—she and I—we were going to be mates, but she hasn't come back from her last scouting trip, and it's been weeks, and I— It seems like she isn't coming back. I won't let it affect my work for you again!"

Orion's lips curl with skepticism. "If it's happened once, it can happen again. We suffer all kinds of losses under the heels of the fae of the seasons. That's why we have to stay focused on overturning them. How can I count on you if you behave so feebly when we're not even in the thick of a battle?"

I wince inwardly. The poor boy—he's lost his intended mate, probably to some violent end, and he isn't allowed to show his grief without being berated for it?

"I'll conquer it and come out stronger," the young man insists. "I swear it. I want to destroy every one of those bastards from the Mists."

Orion hums to himself. "You've aspired to stand right beside me, Bren. I don't think a few words are enough to convince me I should still consider you for that honor." Even from across the room, I can see the feral gleam in his yellow eyes. "Action means so much more than words. Let's see that strength in action now. I need to know just how dedicated you are to this war."

Bren's shoulders twitch, but he shoves himself to his feet. "Of course. Whatever you want, my king."

Orion's gaze skims over the gathered figures and lands on someone in the crowd. He raises his hand with a beckoning gesture. "Colby, you've been begging for more recognition lately. This is your chance to prove yourself too. Let's see which of you is actually prepared to do whatever it takes for your people."

An icy shiver runs down my back. What's he talking about?

The crowd parts to allow another young man to squeeze through to the clear area in front of the dais, this one a little shorter and stouter than Bren. I can't tell how much of that stoutness is muscle and how much fat. Bren eyes him, his hands balling into fists at his sides, and Colby juts out his jaw in defiance.

The two older fae who brought Bren in front of Orion pull back to the edge of the crowd. I catch the woman's satisfied grin.

The other Murk gathered in the throne room start to whoop and cheer as if egging the two men on. Orion folds his arms over his chest and glowers down at Bren and Colby. "You know how it works. Only one of you can stay. You decide which that is. Or if you aren't willing to face the challenge, you can turn tail and scamper off now."

Bren shakes his head, though his wide eyes look panicked. Colby draws himself up taller. They start to circle each other, staring each other down. Another shiver crawls across my spine to shudder through my gut.

All at once, Colby lunges at Bren. He knocks him to the ground, punching him in the face and clawing at his neck. Bren flails at him with fists and knees, managing to roll away with blood streaking from a row of scratches across his throat. He smacks his tail into Colby's ankles and flings himself at the other man's legs when he wobbles.

As they roll around, clawing at and grappling with each other, the cheers of the crowd rise. Orion watches with a pleased smirk stretching across his face.

My stomach lurches queasily. My own hands clench with the urge to slap that look right off his smug face.

The two young men wrestle with each other with increasing fervor. Bren gets in a slash with his claws that rips through Colby's shirt and spills blood down the side of his torso. Colby batters Bren's nose hard enough for it to spurt more blood across them both. Torn hair flies up; grunts and groans echo off the high ceiling. They're both panting raggedly between each blow. I stand rigid on the edge of the crate, my heart thudding.

Colby scrapes his claws across Bren's cheeks and forehead deeply enough that the other man shrieks and I flinch. But then Bren whips his arms around Colby's knee and wrenches with a wild heave and a slap of his tail against the ground. The cracking of breaking bone carries through the raucous encouragement of their audience.

Colby topples onto his back with a cry. In an instant, Bren is on him. With his face twisted into an expression that looks more beastly than human, he digs his fingers into Colby's hair, claws splitting the scalp, and slams his opponent's head against the hard floor. And again. And again. Blood starts to splatter the pale concrete. Colby goes limp, but Bren snarls and rams his head down even harder.

He's going to kill him, smash his skull right in two. It's over—can't they see that? Isn't this enough?

A noise of protest breaks from my throat, but it's swallowed by the eager clamoring of the audience. Before I've even though about what I'm doing, I jump off the crate and throw myself into the crowd toward the fighters. If I can just get there in time, if I can make them stop—

An errant elbow clocks me in the temple. I reel to the side and push myself forward again—and firm arms catch me from behind.

Madoc's hoarse voice reaches me, his breath warm against my ear. "You can't do anything about it. Charging in there will only make things worse—for you and them."

I squirm against his hold, but he pulls me right against his solid chest, his arms wrapping tighter around me. A sputter of denial escapes me. "I have to— If I just—"

"It's already over." He nods toward the dais. Over the heads of the crowd, I can just see Bren's floppy hair, damp with blood, where he's straightened up. "What's one more dead Murk anyway?"

Madoc asks the question flippantly, but I sense a hint of bitterness in his tone. Does he really think I see things that way?

"I've never wanted *anyone* to die like that," I say. "Colby didn't have to. They could have ended the fight when he passed out. They could have found some other way to decide that wasn't fighting!"

Madoc's grip loosens just a little. He eases around enough to study my face. "It really matters that much to you?"

I glare at him. "Yes. I wouldn't want to see even *actual* rats forced to tear each other to bits. I might not agree with everything the Murk have done, but I can still think you deserve better than that." I fling my hand toward the dais.

Madoc doesn't seem to know how to respond to that declaration. And then my attention is drawn back to the platform—to Orion, who's bringing his hands together in a slow, emphatic clap of approval. He applauds Bren's performance with so much enthusiasm I feel sick all over again. Then he motions the young man up beside him.

Blood is streaking down Bren's face, and not all of it is his own. But he smiles fiercely at his king, who claps him on the back.

"You've shown what you're made of," Orion declares. "Someone fetch Nami to patch up my new knight. And get rid of the trash on the floor, will you?" He lifts his chin disdainfully toward the spot where Colby's battered corpse is lying.

A cold wave of certainty washes over me. I swallow hard, my stance loosening enough that Madoc lets go of me completely.

There's going to be no reasoning with Orion. He clearly doesn't operate on reason in the first place. He *enjoys* violence and pain, like the worst stories told about the Murk.

It's because of fae like him that the others hate the Murk so much. He even enjoys turning his bloodlust on his own people, fae who are desperate to serve him and please him—the fae he claims to care so much about bringing to a better world.

I can't think of a single thing I could say to him that I'd have any hope of getting through.

My shoulders square of their own accord. Why should I even bother *trying* to get through to him?

I've spent so much of the past several months wrapping my head around different points of view and working toward compromises with people who hate me… and I'm done. This is my limit. I'll play along to Orion's tune as much as I have to in order to survive and get back to the people who care about me, but I won't waste one more particle of energy on considering his warped point of view.

I deserve more than that.

I'll find out whatever I can about the Murk's Heart and Orion's plans while working toward my escape, and then I've got to get the hell out of this place to warn all the people he means to slaughter.

CHAPTER NINE

Whitt

I know I've spent too long staring at ink on parchment when the words begin to blur together on the page in front of me. I lean away from my desk and tip my head against the back of my chair, closing my eyes.

Scrawled handwriting continues to taunt me on the insides of my eyelids. I let out a sound of frustration that's half growl, half groan.

There's nothing in all the historical records I've accumulated that suggests the Murk should have had the ability to accomplish anything close to the kidnapping of our mate. We had guards all around the celebration area. That woman from Donovan's pack should have scented trouble the second the man who charmed her stepped anywhere near her, well before he had a chance to addle her mind. Whoever he was and whoever might have been working with him, he should have left so much more of a trail.

But somehow the Murk have learned to disguise all sign of their presence so well that our wolfish noses can completely miss it. Not only that, but they've been able to dull the soul-twined bond between Talia and Corwin so thoroughly he's sensed nothing at all from her these past few days. I don't know whether they've stifled her talent with true names or she's simply so distant it's a struggle for her to reach me, but she barely managed to convey any message to me at all either.

The worst part is, there were warning signs before this. The blasted buildings in the Unseelie's summer settlement. The iron-laced smoke it appeared the Murk created at the edge of the arch-lords' domains. We *knew* they were showing more skill and strength than we'd believed could be possible.

But we still never considered they might be able to pull off a crime this immense.

We shouldn't have left Talia's side for even a second that night. We should have ensured one of us or a trusted guard was within hand's reach of her any time she left our shared castle. Maybe even within the castle—can the Murk eschew the Heart's vow when entering the border territory?

I have no idea. The weight of all the things I don't know presses in on my skull.

I rub my forehead as if I can alleviate the pressure that way. I'm the strategist and spymaster. It's my blasted *job* to have all the information we need and the understanding to make use of it. And yet I missed whatever clues might have allowed us to be better prepared, and in all my searching, I've come up with nothing that's been able to bring Talia back to us.

The mite is counting on me, and I couldn't even promise her we'd get her back soon.

There's a soft rap on my door. I open my eyes and straighten up in my chair, catching my lord's scent. "Come in."

Sylas steps inside, his expression as grim as it's looked since we first discovered Talia's disappearance. I'd swear his deadened eye gleams an even starker and more deathly white than it did before. He looks around my study, at the books and scrolls scattered across the shelves where I haven't bothered to reorganize them properly, at more of the same heaped on my desk, and at my own expression. His mouth twists with a trace of sympathy.

"Still nothing?" he asks.

I shake my head, knowing it's the same for him. If he or any of our people scouring the realms for Talia had picked up any hint of her location, he'd have led with that news.

Sylas sighs and then draws his head up into a more authoritative stance. I've never seen as much anguish in him as he's let show over the past few days, but he's still an arch-lord, and he knows he has to act like one regardless of his personal concerns. He fixes his gaze on me. "Has she managed to reach out to you again?"

I offer another shake of my head and an apologetic gesture. "I got the impression it was very difficult for her even the first time, and what she was able to pass on to me was fragmented. It might be better that she's not attempting it again if she isn't sure she can inform us yet of anything that would actually bring us to her, so she can conserve her strength."

Or she may have been caught and prevented from trying again, or be otherwise incapacitated. I don't want to voice those possibilities.

At least we know she's alive. Corwin may not be able to make use of their bond, but it hasn't broken for him either. I saw how the loss of Isleen, even after her many betrayals, hit Sylas. The pain of a shattered soul-twined bond is impossible to ignore.

"Yes," Sylas says. He doesn't remind me to tell him as soon as she does make any sort of contact, because he trusts that I will regardless. He walks restlessly to the other end of the room and then back before meeting my gaze again. "I'm concerned about Corwin."

My mind snaps to sharper alertness. I haven't seen much of our Unseelie counterpart since our initial discussions about Talia's capture—he's been busy organizing his own people's efforts. "In what way?" I ask.

"When I've spoken to him recently, I've had the sense that he's withdrawing. He's brushed off all my offers of help and kept our conversations unusually brief even by his typical standards. Her loss is a blow to all of us, but to him, with the bond gone silent… I think it may be taking a much graver toll than he wants to let show."

I frown. "Can't you get him to open up a little about it? You have your own experience along those lines."

Sylas makes a hopeless gesture. "I'm also his equal in standing, and I suspect he feels even more that he needs to keep up a professional front with a fellow arch-lord. I thought… You're adept at reading people, and you have some idea of what that deep a bond is like. Perhaps you'd be able to get through to him or at least make sure he isn't faltering too badly. It might be good for you to step away from the books as well."

I can't argue with him there. I glance down at my desk and rub my aching eyes. "I'm not sure how fond of me Lord Bird is, but I can certainly give it a shot."

Sylas manages a brusque chuckle. "I expect he'll be more fond if you refrain from calling him 'Lord Bird' to his face."

"You asked for my help. Don't question my methods," I retort in an attempt at light-hearted teasing that I can tell doesn't quite hit the mark. Exhaling raggedly, I stand up and shake the tension out of my limbs. "I'm sorry. I'll see what I can do. Is he off in that diamond fortress of his?"

"I heard from the last guard change that he entered the border castle not too long ago," Sylas says. "I'd start there."

I nod and head out.

Stepping into our shared castle from the summer side and gazing around the grand entrance hall makes my throat constrict. We built this place specifically to give Talia a home where she could fulfill all her responsibilities and spend time with all her mates without needing to constantly travel back and forth between the realms. It feels *wrong* for the place to be standing without her in it or anywhere nearby.

We'll get her back, I think at the walls, as if they need the reassurance as much as I do. *The Murk will not win in the end.*

I walk through the rooms on the first floor to where the wooden construction blends into the diamond of the winter side. Down one of the halls, Corwin's scent reaches my nose. I follow it up the stairs and toward the castle's private chambers, but it doesn't lead me to his own bedroom. I find myself standing outside Talia's, right in the center of the castle.

After a moment's hesitation, I knock on the door. "Corwin?"

There's a faint rustling that suggests he's getting off the bed. He opens the door a moment later, dressed as impeccably as usual in his Unseelie arch-lord finery but with a slightly sheepish expression on his face that softens any snarky thoughts I might have had.

Our interloping raven cares a lot about formalities and appearances, but he isn't made of ice underneath. I've seen outright fire in him when it comes to defending Talia.

"I was about to head out and rally another search party," he says, with a flick of his gaze back toward the room. "I— The covers still smell of her. It helps bolster my spirits."

I hold up my hands. "I won't judge." I pause and then decide it's safe to add, "I understand why you'd want to seek out any semblance of a connection to her that you can."

Corwin opens his mouth, closes it again, and ducks his head just for a second. "Well, I should go on to speak to my flock. Unless there's news?"

"No. I only thought I'd see how you're coping. I could join in the search—perhaps the cold air will sharpen my senses."

But the raven shifter is already shaking his head. "That's all right. This is my realm, and it's my duty to ensure the security of all its people. I'm sure you have plenty to attend to on the summer side."

He's trying to brush me off like Sylas mentioned. Only I'm much less polite than my lord is. I grasp his arm before he can literally brush past me. "Just a moment."

Corwin levels his dark gaze at me. "What?" he says with a hint of irritation, but the gleam shimmering in those eyes speaks of a whole heap of other emotion he's holding in, most of it painful.

I grope for the right words to get across what I think I need to say. "When I first noticed how lovely Talia is, I thought I couldn't have her. There were… circumstances in my past that made me feel ill-equipped to be a good mate to anyone. So I pushed her away through no fault of her own, because I didn't want her to discover those failings."

Corwin's forehead furrows. "Why are you telling me this?"

"Because I was wrong. Because it was better to have the subjects that were gnawing at me aired out than to hide them away. I wish I'd trusted her sooner. There's a strength in standing with someone over standing alone, as I'd imagine you've discovered too."

He inclines his head, still looking uncertain. "But I can't stand with her now. That's why I have to do everything in my power to find her."

"Of course. But that principle doesn't only apply to her." I tap my chest. "We're in this together. You know that Sylas, August, and I will fight just as hard to bring her back. Your pain isn't the same as ours because your bond is different, but we're not going to judge you for that either. So I hope you won't push *us* away to try to stop us from noticing it. We'll be stronger searching for her if we collaborate, just as we have been in so much else."

Corwin's shoulders come down just a little, releasing a subtle tension I might not have noticed if I hadn't been watching for it. He glances away with an audible swallow and then meets my eyes again. "You're right. I shouldn't turn away help that's offered, and I should recognize that you're all just as entwined in her loss as I am, even if it's in different ways. I haven't meant—"

I wave off his apology before he can do more than begin it. "It wasn't my intention to chide you, only to knock a little more sense into that already sensible bird brain of yours." I smile to offset the hint of mockery in my words. "Before you go rushing off on another search, perhaps we should try putting our brains together? None of the past searches have turned up anything, have they?"

Corwin grimaces. "No. But we can't stop trying."

"Of course not. My point is just that it's becoming increasingly clear that however the Murk stole Talia away, they have enough magical power to both cover their tracks and mute her bond with you."

He nods slowly. "I suppose that's true. But how could those vermin—"

I cut him off with a gesture. "We can't know how, so there's no point in worrying about it. Let's just focus on what is. The rat shifters have a substantial amount of magical power, far more than we'd ever have guessed. Perhaps enough to rival our own kind."

"Now there's a horrifying thought," Corwin mutters, sardonically enough that I like him more.

"Indeed. So…" I cock my head. "If *you* were going to use magic to erase all sign of your presence and passage through various types of terrain, what sort of spells would you turn to?"

I consider the same question as Corwin falls into silent pondering. I hadn't let myself really accept the idea of the Murk being on the same level as us before. But if they were—if they could pull off the same kinds of careful yet potent spellwork…

"They might rely on the wind, to some extent," Corwin suggests. "Strong gusts to disperse their scent."

I snap my fingers. "Yes. And perhaps they've made use of some sort of carriages of their own that don't need to touch the ground."

"They would need to include visual illusions as well, so that they're not seen. Especially when they're on the winter side where the terrain is generally more open."

I'm not used to dealing with ice and snow. "What sorts of illusion would work best for that?"

Corwin rubs his jaw. "If *I* were attempting an effect like that, I might make use of light and reflections. Replicate the glare of sunlight on frozen surfaces so it seems completely natural."

A smile springs to my lips. "*That* sort of magic would leave some traces behind, at least in the short term. What do you say we conduct a quick search just the two of us, tracking any traces of warped light on and around your plateau here?"

Corwin doesn't look fully convinced, but a little more energy has come into his tone. "What did you have in mind?"

I motion toward the winter-side doorway. "We make a circuit of the plateau and then drop to the lands below if necessary. Cast periodic seeking spells for that specific type of magic. I'll prowl the treed areas in wolf form, and you scan the open areas as a raven.

We'll see if either of us come upon anything questionable—and signal the other as soon as we do."

Corwin draws in a slow breath. "That sounds reasonable," he says, which from him I know is significant praise. "Shall we see to it immediately?"

I grin. "No time like the present."

It does feel good to be out in the real world *doing* something other than digging through records, even when the real world I'm currently in has bitingly cold air and rather a lot of that quite natural, glaring reflected sunlight Corwin mentioned. My spirits stir eagerly as I intone a spell I send off to the north, through the rest of Corwin's domain. He adds his voice to mine to strengthen the seeking spell. Then we leap forward into our animal forms.

The ice prickles under my wolfish paws, but my fur fends off the worst of the chill. I stalk through the sparse forest, my nerves on edge to catch any quiver of alert from the spell we cast. When I emerge, Corwin circles overhead with a low caw that seems to voice his own lack of results.

Gradually, we make our way through the other arch-lords' domains, thankfully avoiding the rulers of those domains so far. I've nearly reached the edge of a strip of forest to the southeast when a tingling races over my skin.

I let out a forceful bark and spring forward. The tingling intensifies as I narrow in on the spot. Right at the edge of the woods, where the needled branches would hide the view from above but anyone lurking here could keep an eye on both the nearest palace and the flock village by it, a faint magical glimmer remains embedded in the snow.

I dart out from under the tree cover to show Corwin the spot and wheel back, shifting upright as I do. Corwin lands beside me mere seconds later.

He notes the same glimmer I did. "It's relatively recent," he says with an edge in his voice, kneeling by it. "I'd guess it was conjured in the past day."

"But no scent of the rats," I point out. "No prints or other marks of their presence. It's possible it wasn't them. Would there be any reason for your own people to be casting those illusions here?"

"I doubt it." Corwin stands and frowns down at the trace of magic. Then he looks at me. "They're slipping past even all the guards and sentries we've called to the task—they're still spying on us. Are they just enjoying seeing our distress over Talia's loss? Or…"

My gut clenches, the momentary lifting of my spirits fading. I fill in the question he couldn't quite voice. "Or are they planning something even worse?"

CHAPTER TEN

Talia

I wait until the Murk around me have settled into their homes to sleep, during what I guess must be daytime in the world outside the Refuge. I hear a few still roaming past my little hovel, probably patrolling. When I poke my head out, the overhead lights have dimmed enough that I have to squint to make out any shape more than a few feet away.

Orion always appears to be up when the rest of his people are. I assume he has to sleep sometime. I gaze into the dark stillness for a while longer before gathering the boldness to slip over the edge of the platform and creep along the tracks.

The tunnel swallows me in an even deeper black, but only for a few breaths. As I feel my way along across the gravel between the rails, the glow of the Murk's Heart comes into view up ahead, seeping out over the tunnel walls with its sporadic flickering. I fix my gaze on it to guide me, even though the sight of it makes my pulse skitter.

When I reach the entrance to the throne room, I peer inside carefully. The dais stands empty, no figures lounging on its well-worn surface or in the king's chair. There's no sign right now of the king himself. The entire room is empty other than the jittering glow and the erratic jolt of the Heart's energy over my skin.

Setting my feet as silently as I can, I limp across the rough cement floor to the glowing orange mass. With so little other light, its erratic energy niggles at me even more than usual, sending a crawling sensation through my body in waves. I shudder, hugging myself, and force my feet to carry me all the way onto the low platform.

I skirt the throne and walk right up to the Murk's Heart. Bracing myself against the spurts of energy that waft over me, I scan the ground beneath it and the wall around and behind it for any clues to its full nature.

Is it drawing on any kind of fuel here? Has Orion used some kind of magical artifact to help power it? Is there anything at all I could disrupt to damage the Murk's source of magic—to weaken them enough that I could reach Corwin again, that the fae of the seasons could challenge the rat shifters on their own turf and win?

Or even just to prevent the war Orion's planning. I'd settle for that, regardless of what happens to me.

But I can't see anything except the immense patch of condensed energy, which stands a few feet taller than me and equally wide. Not as big as the Heart of the Mists, but still formidable. Still potent enough that the roots of my hair are starting to prickle the longer I'm standing so close.

I wave my hand into the midst of the glow, and a searing pain stabs through my fingers. I yank them away so quickly I almost stumble backward. My skin doesn't look damaged as far as I can tell in the orange light, but it takes several seconds before the sharp ache starts to fade.

Okay, that definitely didn't get me anywhere.

I shuffle to one side and the other to see if I can make out any other clues from a different angle, but nothing that looks at all useful presents itself. Sucking a frustrated breath through my teeth, I wander around the rest of the dais, prodding the surface with my toes, testing the assortment of concrete chunks that make up the throne, checking the walls on either side for supplies or other items that might be important to Orion.

I find a few newspapers from the past few weeks tucked away on one ledge, but they don't give me any clue about my location. Either Orion has his people raiding newsstands with international subscriptions, or they leap through the portals to visit cities all over the world. The paper that's in English is from Sydney, Australia. There's another written in what I think is Spanish, and two others in letters I can't even read to guess what countries they're from.

Can Orion read all these languages, or did he want them for some other purpose?

I'd like to take them with me in case they'll prove useful, but when they're the only thing left around here other than a few scraps of food waste, it'll be too obvious they're missing. I worry my lip under my teeth and then set the newspapers back in their nook.

I slink back toward the entrance staying close to the wall, searching for other alcoves. There's one narrow opening I hadn't noticed before because of the angle of its entrance, which falls away into a passage of total darkness. I can't tell how deep it is, and there's nothing in view in the area the Heart's glow touches.

When I lean close, a rasp that sounds like an exhaled breath reaches my ears. I stiffen and cautiously retreat.

I think someone's sleeping down there. Orion or someone else?

Whoever it is, I doubt they'll be all that friendly to someone sneaking into what's essentially their bedroom.

Disheartened, I limp the rest of the way to the tunnel. I should probably get some sleep. Tomorrow I'll slip away to the maintenance room again and see if I can loosen up the bolts on that vent cover. If I can't find anything here in the Refuge that'll help me stop the war, then the best thing I can do is get the hell out of here to let the other fae know exactly what they're up against.

I've only just stepped over the nearer rail when the rattle of gravel farther down the tunnel freezes me in place. My heart thumping, I glance over my shoulder. It takes a few moments for enough light to catch on the approaching figure for me to recognize him, and even then, I don't totally relax.

Madoc comes to a stop a few feet from me and raises his eyebrows. "What were you doing in there at this hour?" he asks, his voice quiet.

"I thought of something I wanted to ask Orion," I say, spitting out the first excuse that pops into my head. "I figured he might still be up." I shrug as if to say, *oh well.*

Madoc gives me a penetrating look that sends a quiver of apprehension through me, but he doesn't question my story. "I'd imagine he'll hear your question tomorrow. Do you need help finding your way back to your house?"

"I made it here; I'm sure I can find my way back."

He motions for me to walk alongside him. "I was heading this way anyway. Had a desire I couldn't shake for a middle of the night snack. Not that it's actually night in many places above us."

"A noon snack?" I can't help suggesting.

The corners of his lips twitch upward. "Something like that. You're obviously feeling a bit restless yourself if you're seeking out answers when everyone else is sleeping. Maybe you could do with a snack too."

My first instinct is to refuse, to avoid his company—but I second-guess that impulse before the words work their way up my throat. Orion's not worth trying to convince, but Madoc… Madoc didn't seem exactly *happy* about what happened earlier with the two young Murk men, even if he saw their skirmish as unpreventable.

He's close to Orion. He must know more about his king's strategies and magic than just about anyone else here. I might as well take whatever opportunity presents itself to see what I can get out of him. At least he can talk, unlike their Heart.

"Thank you," I say. "That would be nice. Is there much food around at this time?"

He chuckles lightly. "I keep my own stash."

I remember the box of human snacks I noticed in his telescope room. Unsurprisingly, that's where he leads me—past the station with my house and through another into a farther tunnel, then up the stairs. On the way up, he murmurs a string of syllables I immediately recognize as the true name for light—*sole-un-straw*—

and a gleaming white sphere appears at the top of the stairs to guide our way.

In the small room, I settle onto one of the pillows. Madoc paws through his box of snacks, his tail curling around his feet, and asks, "Do you prefer sweet or salty?"

It's been so long since I've had human-made junk food that I'm not sure how to answer. When it comes to August's cooking, the answer would definitely be "Sweet," so that's what I say.

Madoc tosses me a crinkly package that holds what looks like a chunk of chocolate cake in the shape of a half moon. I manage to tear the plastic open and take a bite.

The pastry is weirdly fluffy and yet sticky in my mouth, the white icing adding an extra punch of sugar. A memory wavers up—Mom didn't like us having junk food much, but I think I had one of these at a friend's house way back when…

Madoc has taken a cake of his own. He watches me as he eats his in quick but neat bites. "Not to your liking?" he asks in a tone I can't totally read.

"It's fine," I say. "I just—it's making me think of a long time ago, when my life was normal." It's hard to say whether the nostalgic sensation is good or bad. Maybe a bittersweet mix of both.

"Your life was never normal," Madoc says. "You were meant for this from before you were born. You just didn't know it until recently."

I grimace at him. "It's pretty much the same thing." I pause. "Am I the only human Orion used that way?"

Madoc eyes me again, and I suspect he's deciding how much it's safe to say to me. "You're obviously the only one he's sent into the Mists to win over the fae of the seasons," he says. "Which is for your good too, even if you didn't get asked permission first."

"Because I'm going to be in such a great position after he finishes his plans and conquers the entire fae world?" I say, reining in the sarcasm that wants to seep into my voice.

"You will be," Madoc says, ignoring whatever he picked up from my tone. "You'll have more freedom than you ever did under those fae, whatever favors the few who catered to you might have promised, and you'll be respected as an instrumental part in seeing through our plans. But you'll still get to be a part of a magic most humans never get close to."

Does he really believe all that? I tip my head to one side, studying him in turn. "I saw today just how well Orion treats his own people who're only trying to help with his plans. If that's the kind of respect I can expect, I'm not sure I'm better off with it."

Madoc's gaze flickers. "Anyone who wants to join the fight right at Orion's side has to be tested to make sure they won't crumble under the real pressure. You've already accomplished everything he'll ask of you."

I'm not so sure about that. "So why do you stand with him?" I ask, partly out of real curiosity and partly in the hopes of unraveling a little more of his king's plans. "Are you expecting some kind of great reward once the fae world is his? Assuming you even survive the battle, of course."

"We'll survive," Madoc says darkly. "The Seelie and Unseelie are hardly prepared for what they're going to face when we're ready to launch our full attack. And I don't care about any reward."

My eyebrows arch. "Nothing at all?"

He gazes evenly back at me. "Nothing other than seeing all the other Murk like me throw off the bullies who've been treating us like dirt for so long. Every fae in this place and all the other colonies deserves to regularly breathe air that isn't filtered through miles of subways system, to stay out in the sun rather than having to cringe in the shadows. They deserve to *live*—the centuries upon centuries most of the other fae get but we rarely see."

Passion rings through his voice. I think he really means everything he's just said. I can't quite wrap my head around those words in combination with his support for Orion, though.

My defiance tumbles out before I can catch it. "You want to save your people. As far as I can tell, Orion is more interested in hurting fae—and not just the fae of the seasons. I saw how excited he was watching the fight. He's insane."

Madoc's expression shutters. His voice comes out stiff. "If he is, then it's the kind of insanity that allowed him to do what no Murk before ever has—to create our Heart, to bring us all together ready to take what's ours. We'd have no chance at all without him." He stands up abruptly. "I think you'd better be getting to bed now."

The last of the packaged cake turns chalky in my mouth. I get up and follow him down the stairs, still puzzling over how a man who could profess such honorable goals so genuinely could also accept so much sadistic cruelty from the king he serves.

Was I wrong, and Madoc didn't really mean the rest after all? He could be just as bad as Orion underneath, only better at hiding it.

I can't count on either of them shifting their views, that's for sure.

CHAPTER ELEVEN

Talia

I meander around the outer portion of the maintenance room for several minutes, acting as if I'm just exploring, listening hard for any sign that I'm not alone. I didn't pass any fae during the last part of my walk here. I can't hear anything but the thumping of my pulse.

Of course, the rat shifters have been able to hide their presence from all the other fae in the past, so I can't assume my senses will be enough to notice them.

Madoc seems to turn up pretty often when I'm around. Is that just coincidence, or has he been following me? I try a little experiment, letting my warped foot snag on a pipe and toppling onto the ground. I suck in my breath and swear, gripping my knee as if it's badly hurt, though I only banged it a little.

No one leaps from the shadows to come to my aid. The room around me remains silent. After a few more minutes, I feel confident enough to stand up and weave through the machines to the one beneath the air vent.

I'm going to have to risk this move eventually. I'll never be totally sure that I'm alone. If they catch me at this, well, can they really blame me for wanting to get out?

I focus on the thought of sucking fresh air into my lungs, hearing Corwin's voice through our bond, seeing the blue sky again. But once I'm settled into a secure position on the knobby top of the machine with the vent at shoulder height, I have to let the uneasy images of what Orion and his followers might do to me for my disobedience rise up.

It's fear and defiance that fuel my ability to manipulate bronze.

Unfortunately, I'm not exactly an expert on tools. I can't remember if I've ever held a wrench before—I watched Dad use one doing minor repairs around the house now and then, but my impressions of how exactly it's shaped are vague.

I study the bolts, picturing how I'll need the tool to grip their heads, and hold that image in my mind as I grip the bracelet Sylas gave me. "*Fee-doom-ace-own*," I murmur as quietly but forcefully as I can, willing the metal to shift to match the imagined tool.

The bracelet releases my wrist and straightens into the approximate shape, a long handle with a rounded head. The opening that's meant to wrap around the bolts proves to be too small the first time—I can't get it around them at all. When I encourage it wider, it slips right over them. Gritting my teeth, I repeat the true name once more, nudging it just a tiny bit smaller again and ignoring the splinter of a headache that's just starting to pierce my forehead.

This time, the tool catches on the bolt head and holds there. But that wasn't even the hardest part.

I wrap both sets of fingers around the handle and yank—then yank harder. It takes so much effort the muscles in my arms burn before I feel the bolt budge just a bit. I catch my breath and haul on it again.

It takes a long time before I've loosened that first bolt enough that I could remove it from the vent cover. I've stopped every few minutes to rest and listen for any approaching figures, but those breaks haven't reduced the strain by much. When I finally feel the bolt totally give, my shoulders and biceps are throbbing. I'm not sure I could have kept it up much longer anyway.

I tug the bolt out just to confirm that I can and then slip it back into the hole so that it's not obvious I've loosened it. Then, with the ache of the workout radiating through my body, I contemplate the other seven bolts holding the vent in place.

I don't think I can tackle more than one a day. So, I'm spending one more week here at the very least, and that's assuming I'm able to come and work on them every day uninterrupted. I swallow thickly.

How long is left until the next full moon? How many more Unseelie will freeze to death in the curse's grasp before then?

What if Orion launches the next part of his war before I can get out of here?

There's nothing I can do about that. I'll just keep coming back when I can and giving it my best shot.

I push back the nagging reminder in the back of my head that I don't even know if this air vent will give me a clear passage to the outside world. It's the only chance I have.

My skull prickles with a renewed headache when I transform the wrench back into a bracelet—one that hopefully looks almost identical to the one I was wearing before—but it fades quickly as I limp along the tracks. Which is good, because I've only just emerged into the nearest station when one of the Murk comes hustling over to me.

Not just any of them. It's Bren, his eye socket still mottled purple and brown with bruising, scabs mottling his cheeks from Colby's scratches. When he opens his mouth, I realize he must have lost a tooth in the fight. There's an obvious gap.

And the king he fought so hard for hasn't let the Refuge's healer fix any of that. Maybe Orion wanted to leave the superficial wounds as a testament to the kind of devotion he expects.

"Orion wants you to attend to him," Bren says, a little breathlessly. "You should hurry—it took me a while to find you."

There's a hint of irritation and a question in that statement, but I pretend I don't hear the latter part. "Of course," I say, the battered face in front of me also a stark reminder of just how careful I have to be around the Murk's king. "Is he in the throne room like usual?"

Bren bobs his head and trails behind me as I hobble on through the station and into the tunnel behind. I'd point out to him that I can't walk any faster and he's welcome to carry me if he's so impatient, but I'm a little worried he'd take me up on that suggestion, and I don't actually want his hands on me.

I guess I can't blame him for wanting to be sure he's completely fulfilled his orders. He's even more aware of his king's temperament than I am.

"I saw your fight with Colby," I venture, keeping my tone mild. "Are you all right?"

"I'm proud that I proved I can stand with my king," the young fae man says brusquely.

Something about the boyish smoothness of his face and the determination in his tone reminds me of Jamie. I'm not sure Bren is any older than my little brother in fae terms. My hand drifts to my bracelet, thinking of the spell August cast on it to connect me to my brother. Does the fact that it hasn't alerted me mean Jamie's still safer than I am right now, or has Orion's magic disrupted that spell like my bond with Corwin?

I glance down at my hands, and my heart stutters. My fingertips are stained dark with dirt and grease from clambering over the machines and working away at the old bolt. Bren doesn't appear to have noticed, but I doubt Orion's sharp eyes will miss that detail.

"I, um—I have to use the bathroom," I say quickly. "I'll go see Orion right after. But you can wait if you want to make sure."

Bren frowns, but he walks with me to the nearest bathroom and only sighs once while he stands by the doorway. I use the toilet just so he can hear the flush and then scrub my hands as quickly as I can at the sink.

When I'm done, the tips are ruddy, but I've managed to wash off most traces of my work. Any lingering smudges I can attribute to feeling my way along the walls in the shadowy tunnels.

When we finally reach the throne room, Orion doesn't look particularly concerned about the delay. He glances over with a nonchalant wave and goes back to talking with two fae women who keep bobbing their heads beseechingly as they speak to him. But after I've sat down a short distance from the throne and Bren has vanished, the Murk king cocks his head at me. "It took you some time getting here."

I shrug as if I assume it isn't any big deal. "I was wandering around the Refuge, getting to know this place—since it's my new home, for now at least. It's pretty big."

"It is. I've put a lot of work into making this colony a city in itself." Orion smiles and waves off the women. Sitting down in his throne, he beckons me closer so I'm practically sitting at his feet. His tail flicks in the air just inches from my arm.

I don't enjoy having to gaze up at him like some kind of pet, but I suspect he wouldn't take it well if I insist on standing and putting myself on his level.

"How long will we be staying in the Refuge?" I ask, wondering if I can get more information out of him if I come at it from a different angle. "It's impressive, but I can't pretend I wouldn't like to be back in the open air in the Mists. That's the goal, right?"

"It is." Orion folds his hands in his lap and stretches out his legs. "But there's no rushing a revolution. We'll know when the time is best to strike."

It sounds like even *he* doesn't know when he plans to attack. Hopefully that means it won't be incredibly soon.

I want to know as soon as he makes any decisions about that. I weigh my words and then say, "Is there any way I could help? There are a lot of fae in the Mists who've treated me badly. I feel like I should be there, standing up to them."

Orion's expression doesn't appear to change, but a shiver runs over my skin as if his attention has become more penetrating. "Starting to come around, are you?" he says casually.

I motion to the room around me. "It's easy to see that the Murk are more than I was led to believe, and obviously you have some legitimate issues with the other fae. You've got just as much a right to the Mists as they do. I spent too long in their world locked away, not able to contribute much… I don't want it to be that way again."

"You know I can't let you leave the Refuge until there's no chance that raven you're bound to could sense anything through you that would damage our efforts." Orion considers me as if evaluating whether leaving this place was my intended goal.

It's easy to nod as if it doesn't matter to me, because I never expected he'd let me wander around in the human world right now anyway. "I understand. I'm thinking more about the preparations down here, and being ready to step up once you set off for the Mists."

"Hmm." He taps his lips. "Interesting when that's nearly the reason I called you here. I'd like to rub some salt into the wound—only figuratively, for now. I'm sending a letter into the Mists to remind the fae there how much they've lost. I'd like to add a little of your blood to it so they can be sure we do actually have you. Will you volunteer it?"

Is it really voluntary when his authority and brutality are hanging over me? I don't feel like I have much more choice than the two men who fought to the death yesterday must have.

You don't need to do that, I want to say. *They already know I'm with the Murk.* But then I'd have to reveal how I communicated with Whitt.

And besides, Orion would probably want to taunt them with my blood regardless of whether they already know.

"Of course," I say, with more confidence than I feel. "You've offered me so much here; it's the least I can do in return. Should I do it now?"

He gets up and motions for me to follow him. There's a sheet of paper sitting in one of the little alcoves that I found empty last night. I was hoping that I'd be able to read some of the message he's sending, but it's in the same odd lettering as many of Whitt's books, which wakes up my headache when I look at it for more than a few seconds.

Is there any way I can pass on a message of my own with this act? What message should I even pass on?

Orion doesn't give me much time to think about it. He produces a small pocket knife and reaches for my hand. I let him take it and prick my forefinger.

He keeps his fingers around my wrist as he brings my hand to the paper. I press down, leaving a slight smear, pushing just a little harder one, two, three, four times. I'm not sure it'll say much to my men, but I want them to know I'm thinking of the four mates I left behind, that I'm still enough in my right mind to do so. That I'm figuring out a way back to them.

Orion intones a few syllables to close my finger. He studies the bloody mark at the bottom of the page for long enough that my skin starts to creep. But when he turns back to me, he's smiling.

"Very good. I clearly made you well. If you want to be useful, I'm sure I can find a few more jobs for you. Let's get you started right now."

CHAPTER TWELVE

August

The forest along the border in Donovan's domain is the stillest I've found it in the past few days since the Murk stole Talia from this spot. Everyone else has finally gone off to search farther afield. I've joined those efforts, but I keep getting drawn back here.

The last place we know for sure she was. The place that's offered so few clues. But what if there's something we're missing?

I have to keep looking. Have to keep going over every inch of ground with my wolfish nose to the dirt, dragging in every trace of scent. Have to scour every twig for scraps of hair or fabric. Just one little thing could lead us to our missing mate.

I'm not sure how many hours I've been at it when I sit back on my haunches and gaze around me with now-bleary eyes. I haven't turned up any evidence at all.

Another wolf trots over to me through the trees. I recognize Astrid by her pale fur and wiry limbs. Unable to suppress the tiny flicker of hope that maybe she's come with good news, I straighten into man form as she shifts too.

Her expression offers the opposite of hope. "The party we sent through the portal to Talia's brother's town just returned. Jamie is fine, but there's no sign that Talia's been there any time recently."

I nod in acknowledgment, my stomach sinking. I'm glad the Murk haven't threatened her brother as well, but if they had, it'd at least have given us one more avenue to locating them. And we have so little.

I shouldn't wish that a teenaged boy was kidnapped to make my own job easier, I chide myself. I shouldn't have failed in the first place.

Rubbing my hand over my face, I consider what to say. "Our pack-kin had a long trip. Tell them to rest and eat and whatever else they need to do for a couple of hours. Then I want them to take up the patrol west of Copperweld. And we should send another contingent to the fringes to check the other portals."

Astrid dips her head. Technically we're equals in authority now that she's part of Sylas's cadre, and she has several centuries of experience on me, but she defers to my orders when it comes to the defense of our pack. That's supposed to be my strength. And yet—

"If I may, August?" she says, in a patient voice.

Her hesitation sends a prickle of shame through me. She shouldn't need my permission to speak her mind to me. "Say whatever you need to. I'll hear it."

She motions to the forest around us. "*None* of us were prepared for the Murk to pull off anything like this. It isn't your fault that you weren't either. I have every intention of finding Lady Talia and tearing apart every Murk that tries to stand between us and her, but tearing *yourself* up isn't going to help her."

My embarrassment grows with a rush of heat over my face. "It was my duty more than anyone else's to make sure she was safe. On the very night when I swore to be there for her in every possible way, I let her out of my sight—I let those mangy rats—"

"No," Astrid says, more firmly now. "You didn't 'let' them do anything. They had a very clever scheme that slipped past all of us. All that matters now is unraveling that scheme so we can get her back."

"Of course," I say. "I appreciate your honesty." I know she's right. But my gut stays knotted as she lopes off to pass on my instructions to our warriors.

It isn't just the fact that I didn't catch onto the Murk's plan ahead of time that's gnawing at me. From the very first moment I started falling for my mate, I was haunted by the thought of how easily my affection could end up hurting her. I allowed myself to set those worries aside… but maybe I was wrong to. By taking Talia as our partner, we drew even more attention to her than she'd have had otherwise.

I don't know what I'd have done differently, but I can't shake the sense that I've let both her and myself down.

There's no point in continuing this search over well-trodden ground, though. I can admit that to myself—I'm not going to find anything new. Inhaling the warm, piney air, I let loose my wolf and trot across the terrain, debating where to turn my focus next.

I've spent a lot of recent days telling squads of our pack-kin and other volunteers to go one place or another. Whitt said that he and Corwin came across signs that the Murk are monitoring our efforts regardless. While so many of our people are searching farther abroad, maybe I should give our own lands a closer inspection.

I pause at the castle for a goblet of water and a bite to eat to refresh my senses, and then I slink off into the woods that cover our side of the hill around the Heart. Our domain stretches all the way down and a few miles farther, most of that area forested. It'd give the rats plenty of shelter if they wanted to spy on us in our distress.

The thought makes me draw my lips back from my fangs. I allow myself a moment to dream of ripping into those vermin.

I make a steady sweep of my patrol, back and forth from one end of our domain to the other, lower down the hill with each pass. No hint of ratty scent reaches my nose. No odd glimmers of light catch my eyes. Maybe they use different strategies in the shadows, though. I pause once or twice to cast out a spell to detect magically conjured shadows or other sorts of deflective illusions.

My efforts turn up nothing, but on my next pass through the

woods, a different unexpected smell tickles into my nose. It's wolf, and vaguely familiar, but not any I recognize as our pack-kin.

Of course, there's a cacophony of wolfish scents all around. It could be from any of the other Seelie coming and going to report on the search. But this one caught my notice because it's particularly thick in this spot, as if the person stayed here for some time.

I don't see anything around to explain why they'd have lingered here. And something about the vague familiarity sends a wave of uneasiness through my chest.

Frowning inwardly, I sniff around and pick up the trail a little farther down the hill. As I follow it, a twinge of recognition wavers up from my memory.

Jax. The dark-haired woman from Lord Tristan's cadre—the one who once threatened Talia. It's her scent; I'm sure of it.

Why would she have been hanging around in the woods in our domain? I don't remember seeing her among the various search parties we assembled, although to be fair I haven't been able to oversee even half of them myself. Tristan's domain is only about an hour's carriage ride from the Heart, so it wouldn't be unexpected for him to send manpower to help with the search.

Something about it just itches at me in a way I can't explain. So I prowl onward, tracking her scent.

It isn't easy. So many other wolves have passed through this forest that once I leave the spot where she lingered behind, the distinct aspects of her smell mingle with dozens more until there's no longer a clear trail. But I continue in the same direction and pick up a faint whiff of it at close enough intervals to stay on course.

My investigation leads me out of the woods to a short span of fields. My back prickles with the new openness and the knowledge that I'd be easily spotted. I can't see any sign of my fellow fae in the fields.

I hesitate there for a minute and then decide to circle around the open ground, keeping to the shelter of the trees and tasting the air for any sign of where Jax went after she crossed them.

I'm a little more than halfway through my circling when a different odor reaches my nose—a whiff of smoke, seeping from deeper into the woods near me, just beyond the official border of Hearth-by-the-Heart. The breeze has me downwind, so I slink into it, knowing whoever might be up ahead shouldn't be able to sense my arrival.

The leaves rustle overhead. I set my paws quietly, barely disturbing a twig. Subterfuge might be Whitt's domain, but any skilled warrior needs the ability to be stealthy when necessary.

I've crossed maybe half a mile when the faintest murmur of voices reaches my ears. I can't make out the words yet, but I catch another hint of Jax's scent mixed with the smoke from the fire. The breeze shifts, and I ease to the side so I can stay downwind as I creep closer.

When I'm near enough that the voices form audible words, I stop and crouch low to the ground. I can just pick up the flicker of the fire in the distance through the trees.

A figure moves past it—not Jax, but a taller, bulkier man I've also seen among Tristan's close pack-kin. The wavering light dances across a wooden structure behind them. They've conjured at least one building to set up a temporary campsite here.

There's nothing forbidding them from doing so. This unclaimed strip of land lies between a few different domains, not officially belonging to any of them—and even if it did, we Seelie are generally tolerant of temporary visitors as long as they don't bother our packs. But why have they settled in here when they could be home in an hour?

The first part of the conversation doesn't offer much enlightenment.

"I thought the hare would be better if we cooked it, but it hasn't helped much," the bulky man mutters.

I recognize the reply as Jax's voice. "No one's stopping you from hunting down something else."

The man grunts and digs into his meal with the sound of torn flesh. There's a faint thump as if something heavy has been moved. They talk briefly about the state of the game in these woods and how much better the hunting was when Tristan's cousin Ambrose oversaw this area as arch-lord. My hackles rise in annoyance, but their remarks are nowhere close to treason.

I wait, debating how much longer I should stay in the hopes of overhearing something useful, risking another shift in the wind that might alert them to my presence. I'd like to have something more to report back to Sylas than I do so far.

I *could* simply walk up to them and ask them what their business here is, but somehow I doubt I'd get a true answer.

Then the man says, "Do you think the delivery tomorrow will be enough?"

"Maybe we'll want another," Jax says. "We'll see how it goes."

He chuckles to himself with a dark note I don't like at all. "Weapons to protect *Lady Talia* and destroy the Murk. Ha."

I don't like the sneer in his voice when he refers to Talia either. And he sounds as if he's mocking the idea that they'd be protecting her. Is he saying they're bringing weapons for some other reason?

"May as well destroy them, the filthy vermin," Jax says, which reassures me for just a moment before she adds, "They did offer an excellent opening, though, I'll give them that."

My body stiffens. An opening to do *what*?

I strain my ears harder, but the man simply lets out one more chuckle and goes back to his meal. Jax shifts something with another thump. The next time they exchange words, it's to debate who'll keep the first watch. I don't hear anything else that sounds odd.

The wind starts to shift, and I reluctantly retreat. I don't have much, but I need to tell Sylas what I *have* heard.

As if he needs to be dealing with worries over Tristan's pack-kin on top of Talia's loss.

My heart thumps heavy in my chest as I lope up the hill toward the castle. I didn't keep close enough watch over Talia—have I missed even more, a threat to our entire pack, as well?

CHAPTER THIRTEEN

Talia

The iron bars drag at my hands and leave a faintly gritty residue on my skin. My nose has filled with a smell that's far too close to the stink of dried blood. But I can't deny that Orion found the perfect job for a human in the midst of his fae subjects.

The Murk who are working alongside me, using a large machine to melt down the bars and then pour the liquid metal into molds, have to switch off regularly as their faces pale and sweat breaks out on their skin. The Murk's Heart doesn't have the same aversion to iron as the Heart of the Mists does, and its power helps the fae drawing on it resist the usual ill effects they'd experience from being close to the metal they find toxic, which must be how they were able to create that iron-laced smoke in the summer realm. But being near the substance still wears on them after a while.

It doesn't affect me at all, at least not physically. So here I am, feeding the bars into the furnace, knowing that all this work is going toward tools that'll help the Murk attack the other fae.

At least I'm getting a close look at their tactics. When the first batch of molds have set, one of the Murk women working in this alcove calls me over. “Could you move them from the original molds into these?” she says, pointing to another row of contraptions on a table along the concrete wall.

I’d appreciate the fact that she asked rather than ordered more if it wasn’t obvious now what I’m making. The Murk are creating cuffs and collars like the one Arch-Lord Celia once subdued Corwin’s magic with—constructed with other metals they can handle without harming themselves on the outside around an iron core to turn any fae they lock those bindings around helpless. I wonder if the collar Celia found in Ambrose’s things was originally Murk-made too.

I lift the iron cores out of the smaller molds and set them in the center of the larger rings, weighing my next words. “You’d have to get pretty close to someone to get one of these things on them,” I say to the fae who are readying the lead they’re going to pour around the iron. “How are we going to manage that?” Celia was only able to get the collar around Corwin’s neck by taking him by surprise and overwhelming him before he knew what was happening. That won’t work on a larger scale.

What else does Orion have planned? The whole reason I’m pretending to want to join their invasion is so I can find that out.

One of the men gives me a fierce-looking smile. “We’ve got many other uses for the iron, and Orion is working on spells to let us repel the effects more easily and for longer. We’ll have smoke and arrows and darts.”

The other rubs his hands together. “I look forward to seeing them suffer a tiny bit as much as they’ve hurt our kind.”

“You’ve had bad run-ins with the fae of the seasons?” I ask.

The first one nods. “Haven’t we all? I lost my mother to them.”

“My cousin,” the second one mutters with a twitch of his tail.

And what were those fae doing when they were “lost”? Somehow I suspect they were causing trouble, and the other fae were only defending themselves. But I can’t expect these ones to open up to me more if I point that out.

“You’ll still need to get pretty close even for smoke and projectiles to reach them,” I say instead, running my thumb over my mouth as if contemplating the problem. “It’s a long way from the fringes to any of the important domains." The other fae would have to notice a huge force of Murk heading their way with all this equipment long before the Murk got anywhere near the Heart of the Mists—unless they have some secret strategy.

"Oh, they'll never see us coming," says the woman who beckoned me over, letting out a harsh chuckle. "Soon we'll have full 'carriages' of our own, and we're only getting more adept at hiding ourselves. All we'll need—"

A voice from behind me interrupts, light but firm. "I think Orion would appreciate more work and a little less talking."

My pulse stutters. I glance over to see that Madoc has come into the workshop alcove. His heavy-lidded eyes linger on me for a moment longer than the others, studying me. Does he suspect that I'm here specifically to hear their talk and not because I really want to be making weapons?

I'm itching to ask what exactly the Murk will "need" to hide a mass of carriages, but it feels too risky to push the subject with Orion's close associate looking on. I set the last iron core in its new mold and go back to the furnace where more of the bars need to be added to the melting vat.

Madoc follows, dismissing the man who was pouring the melted metal into the molds and taking over that job himself. Despite his position with the Murk king, he obviously doesn't mind getting his hands dirty.

Does Orion himself ever come and help with the work? Or does he just give orders and dispense judgment while lounging around his throne?

"So, you decided to take up the cause, did you?" Madoc says to me, his expression tightening only slightly as he sets his hands close to the liquid iron to adjust the angle of the spout.

I wonder what his aversion to the metal feels like, just how much the Murk's Heart is able to shield them. Would these collars work against their makers if we found a way to turn the tables on them?

I'm not sure how much Orion might have told him about the conversation that led to me taking this job. The last time I talked to Madoc, I was criticizing his king's methods.

"I think all fae have a right to the Mists," I say, which is reasonably true. "And maybe the ones who'd have liked to see me locked up deserve some of the same treatment themselves."

The woman near me snorts. "That'd be all of them. If you don't meet their standards, they want you dead or enslaved to them—and we'd never agree to the latter."

"The humans trapped in the Mists don't get much choice," Madoc remarks. "They can't fight back. We'll see them freed too."

My gut twists, thinking of how I'd just started to fight for the rights of the other humans in the summer and winter realms before I was stolen away. I want to see them get their free will back, but not by having all the other fae slaughtered or enchained instead.

One of the men by the lead vat harrumphs. "We don't have any need for mortal servants running around doing our own work for us." He halts and glances at me. "Not that we'd turn away your voluntary help, of course."

His hasty clarification doesn't erase the disdain I heard in his voice. I'm not actually surprised that at least some of the Murk look down on humans just like their Seelie and Unseelie counterparts do. I guess it'd be hard for them not to when we are so much less powerful and so short-lived. But Orion and Madoc have liked to paint a picture of me being treated as an equal here.

I'm probably respected only for how I inadvertently supported their war. How would they talk to me if I wasn't their king's creation?

The thought of Orion's meddling with my body and spirit sends a shudder through me I can't quite suppress. Madoc's gaze latches onto me again. "Are you all right?"

I can't tell whether he's concerned or suspicious. Maybe both.

I chuck another iron bar into the furnace. "I don't like remembering how those fae treated me in the Mists. It's bad enough that they've damaged my body permanently. They shouldn't get to hold onto my mind too."

The man Madoc took over from, who's hung back in the doorway, lets out a sound of agreement. "Orion says they've infected us all with a sense of inadequacy and failure. That we'd have accomplished so much more if not for all those millennia of being shoved to the fringes and treated like vermin. Many of us they've outright killed or hobbled, but they've marred all our souls. Our new Heart is only just starting to heal them."

No wonder they hate the fae of the seasons so much when Orion is spouting proclamations like that. No responsibility taken for the way the Murk have treated the other fae all this time. How many of the Murk here have really dealt with the Seelie or Unseelie face-to-face in good faith to know what they're actually like?

"It's good that you're finally getting a chance to overcome their bullying," I say, seeing a chance to subtly get at the information I want. "And incredibly impressive that you've come up with so many strategies to put them in their place. The fae I was with had no idea how often you were coming into the Mists. It must be a very clever trick to disguise your presence so completely."

I'm hoping that my praise will encourage some bragging, but all I get are a few chuckles. "That it is," says one of the men.

"The pack and flock you call yours must have stepped up protections after the incidents we arranged with the Unseelie village, the smoke, and the rest," Madoc says in a casual tone I don't totally believe. "What did they think would manage to stop us?"

He's talking as if he's only looking for an amusing conversation, mocking the other fae's efforts, but he's also trying to get at *their* strategy, whether purposefully or not. I nibble at my lower lip nervously, but the truth is I don't know much I could tell him anyway.

"I think it was mostly just a matter of more," I say with a light laugh as if I'm buying into the idea that we're just poking fun at them. "More guards, more sentries. Obviously that wasn't enough, or I wouldn't be here."

Too bad for me.

"And we're all glad for that," Madoc says, shooting me another smile. "The many crimes of the fae of the seasons will soon be repaid in full."

Another waft of the iron scent fills my nose, and suddenly I can't bear to keep up this façade any longer. A burn tickles the back of my eyes, threatening to spill over into tears.

I don't want to be here. I don't want to have to worry about seeing the men I love destroyed by these people—to be helping prepare the tools to do it. I've been hanging in there, keeping up the best front I can, but inside I can feel my strength starting to crumble.

I can't show my true feelings in front of the Murk around me, though. Hefting another iron bar, I let my arms wobble, not totally for show. After I toss that one in, I rub my biceps. "I'm not sure I can keep this up for much longer. My muscles aren't used to this much physical labor."

"Of course," Madoc says. "There are plenty who can take over. We appreciate your help. If you'd like me to bring you to the healer to have the soreness addressed—"

I shake my head quickly. "No, that's all right. I think it's better if my body adjusts without any supernatural intervention. I'll just go take a nap."

I stop in the bathroom to wash as much of the metallic stink off my hands as I can. It remains on my clothes after I leave, little whiffs reaching my nose at random intervals, but one of the Murk took the other outfit they've given me this morning to clean it and I don't have anything to change into right now.

Ignoring the smell as well as I can, I head toward my hovel, but then wander on past it as if I've changed my mind and want to stretch my legs some more. I keep a careful eye on the tracks around me as I drift through the tunnels toward the maintenance area.

No one appears to pay me much mind. My show of helping with the war preparations might at least have earned me a little more trust from my captors.

I still wait in the maintenance area for several minutes, faking an injury to test for unseen watchers, before I risk using the true name to reshape my bracelet.

This time, it only takes two tries to get the conjured wrench to the right size. But it turns out I wasn't totally lying about my arms being tired. I yank and strain at the second bolt I've picked for what feels like an hour, sweat trickling down my back, and by the end of all that effort I'm not sure I've budged it more than one full rotation.

I lower the wrench, a dull but deep ache radiating through my arms into my shoulders and back. I don't think I can make any more progress today—I barely made any as it is.

My free hand clenches with the urge to slam it into the vent cover in frustration, but that won't give me anything but bruised knuckles. I let out a breath in a ragged sigh.

I thought I might be able to arrange my escape in a week. What if it takes so much longer?

What if the strengths I have aren't enough to get me out of here at all?

There has to be another way I can find a chance to escape.

CHAPTER FOURTEEN

Talia

The first several times I've encountered Madoc, he came up on me out of nowhere. Now I find myself trying to turn the same trick on him.

I've meandered along the passage by the stairs to his telescope room several times before my strategy works out. From far away, I see the station lights catch on his pale hair just before he strides into the darker space of the tunnel. I limp toward him, attempting to keep a casual pace as if I just happened to be walking this way while still approaching fast enough that I'll catch him before he heads up to his private room.

When I'm a little closer, I pretend to just have noticed him. "Madoc?" I call out, raising my hand to catch his attention.

He pauses and then ambles over to me. His mouth forms an offhand smile that today looks a little stiff to me.

Alarm prickles through me. Did he realize I lied about where I was going after my work in the weapons workshop this morning?

He doesn't say anything accusing, though, only nods to me. "Talia. Did you need something?"

"I—" I bite my lip as if I'm nervous about what I'm going to ask, which doesn't require any acting. I'm just nervous for different reasons than I want to let on. "All that talk around the weapon forges earlier made me realize there's so much I don't know about the history between your people and the fae of the seasons. I thought *some* of them were kind, and it's been hard to get totally invested in attacking them with that idea still in my head."

Madoc lets out a rough chuckle. "They're kind when they think it benefits them, not as a matter of character. It's understandable that you were confused, though. Given how badly the first fae you encountered treated you, even a little kindness must have felt like a lot in contrast."

"Yes. Well..." I look down at my feet and then back at him. "I feel like I need to see more for it to really sink in—how important this uprising is, how much I need to set aside all the things I believed before. I don't want to stand with you if I'm giving less than my full commitment. Everyone here in the Refuge seems to be doing all right. Are there other Murk colonies that the other fae have assaulted or something like that, that I could see to drive home just how bad things have gotten for you?"

To let me step beyond the walls of this place and hopefully reach out to Corwin, even if only for a moment? Hell, just getting a glimpse of the outside world might help me convey to Whitt where the Refuge is. And if I can get some of the rat shifters worked up about their hatred of the fae of the seasons, they might give away more about their plans for revenge.

If I could get just one useful thing out of this gambit, I'd be happy.

Madoc contemplates me with a serious expression that sends a pang of guilt through my stomach alongside the tension. Does he believe me? Is it kind of horrible for me to lie to him so blatantly?

It can't be more horrible than the fate they're arranging for the fae of the seasons. I can't imagine any way everyone back in the Mists could deserve the torment the Murk are planning.

"We keep our colonies scattered," Madoc says after a long moment. "Specifically so that if the other fae track down any one of them, it's unlikely to lead them to others. And there's no way we could keep your bond to your soul-twined mate shielded to make that journey. But there is something within the Refuge that I could show you. It won't be pretty. You have to be prepared for that."

A twinge of disappointment ripples through me, but I knew that getting out of this place immediately was a long shot. If there are more parts of the Refuge I haven't stumbled on before, it can't hurt to see them too.

I'll take whatever scraps of hope I can get.

"Of course," I say. "I know firsthand how savage the fae can be." My hand rises automatically to my scarred shoulder. The long-sleeved shirt I'm wearing covers all the marks, but from the tightening of Madoc's jaw, he knows what I'm thinking of.

Those scars are no secret, but abruptly I find myself wondering just how long he's been watching me. The Murk must have set up Aerik and his cadre to come across me and my family while in the grips of the curse—it was part of their plan that some vicious Seelie would discover the power of my blood.

"Were you there?" I blurt out. "The night I was attacked. Did you help with that part of the plan?" Have I just been feeling guilty about deceiving one of the people most directly responsible for the worst moments in my entire life?

But Madoc is shaking his head. I'm more relieved than I probably should be.

"I don't do much work for Orion above in the human world," he says, and touches his ears with their slight but obvious point. "He prefers to use the many Murk who could pass for human without a spell for those missions."

"That makes sense. The—" I cut myself off before I finish mentioning that the fae of the seasons used similar reasoning when sending people to the human world. I don't think Madoc would appreciate being compared to them, and I still want him to show me what I've been missing here.

Is his larger portion of fae blood in comparison to most of the Murk what earned him his spot in Orion's inner circle? But at least a couple of the other men I've seen the Murk king consulting with had ears as rounded as any human's.

"Come along then," Madoc says into my silence, looking as if he'd prefer we change the subject too. He motions for me to follow him farther down the tunnel, keeping a slow pace for my benefit, and I fall into step beside him.

My earlier thoughts are still spinning through my head, though. "It is true that the Murk have mingled more with humans than the fae of the seasons generally do, isn't it?" I venture. Most of the rat shifters around here lack pointed ears, for all their tails make it impossible not to know they're something other than human. And that dilution of their fae heritage is part of the reason they needed to make their own Heart to draw magic from.

"Yes. We don't choose our leaders based on the supposed purity of their blood here."

"But Orion looks almost true-blooded," I can't help pointing out. I'm surprised there were any Murk with enough fae heritage to produce a child that obviously fae.

I don't say that bit out loud either, but Madoc must pick up on my line of thinking.

"His parents and grandparents and perhaps more before that wanted to help us rise above the position we've been forced into, and purposefully sought out mates who were more… fae-inclined," he says. "You could almost say he was born for this, to be powerful enough to accomplish everything we needed."

And because of that lineage, he's also arrogant enough to think everyone should follow his whims, no matter how horrifying, I guess. I grit my teeth against that observation, remembering how well my criticism went over with Madoc last time.

"What exactly are you going to show me?" I ask instead.

Madoc just shakes his head. "It'll be easier to explain when I can show you. It isn't that far." He pauses and glances down. "Is your foot hurting you?"

I've been limping the entire time I've been living in the Refuge, so it isn't as if he could think it's a new injury. But he sounds honestly concerned—and maybe even a little chagrinned that he hasn't thought to check before. An unwelcome warmth flickers in my chest.

"No worse than usual," I say. "The longer I stay on it, the achier it gets, but I never have to walk too far around here."

"All right. If it becomes a problem, or if you need a replacement for the brace in your boot, let me know. I'm sure we can replicate it."

I don't know what to say to him after that. Does my minor discomfort really matter at all to him?

It's too confusing trying to untangle his motives, so I focus on setting my feet one after the other alongside him.

We walk all the way to the last station in this direction and clamber onto the platform there. Madoc walks up to a set of steel doors that I assumed went nowhere important, since I never saw anyone going in or out of them. He unlocks them with a few murmured words and a series of swift gestures I can't follow and pushes one wide for me to walk in past him.

On the other side, a linoleum floor leads down a short hall to a single door, this one unlocked.

Madoc rests his hand on the knob. "We're not sure what the humans who built this place meant to use this area for, but they never finished it. The air doesn't pass through easily, so it's not suitable for spending large periods of time in it. We've dedicated it to days past instead."

"What do you mean?" I ask.

He opens the door and ushers me in.

Right away, I can see what he meant about the unfinished part. The room is large, nearly half again the size of the station we just left, but the walls are rough concrete mixed with patches of bare bedrock, and the craggy ceiling adds to the cave-like impression. Only the floor has been sanded smooth.

A magical light drifts down from one glowing source in the middle of the ceiling. It catches on a line of metal chairs along the walls, stretching all the way around the room. More chairs form a series of concentric rings moving toward the center of the space, with gaps here and there where a person can step between them.

But the strangest thing is the clots of fog that hang over nearly every chair. They're like little dark clouds, churning in place a few inches above the seats. They remind me a little of the shifting light inside a Seelie's soul stone, but they aren't contained in any other object and they give off no light at all.

We aren't alone in the room. A Murk woman is sitting on one of the chairs at the far end of the room, the patch of fog there wrapped around her chest. Her jaw is set firmly, but a few tears have trickled down her cheeks.

"What is this place?" I say, my voice dropping to a whisper. The woman gives no sign that she's noticed our arrival.

"The vault of memories," Madoc says simply. "A way of keeping a record of the crimes done to us. Any Murk who's lost something to the fae of the seasons may offer up his memories here so that what was lost is never forgotten."

A shiver runs over my skin. The air in here is very still but cooler than the rest of the Refuge. "And what happens when you sit in one of the chairs?"

"You're absorbed into the memory left there until the part offered up ends or someone shakes you out of it." He gestures to the rings of chairs. "You can see whatever you'd like. Every memory in here shows how little the other fae think of us."

I can just… step into other people's memories? Traumatic memories, from the sounds of it. My legs balk. "I don't want to intrude on something private."

"We all have access to everything in the vault," Madoc says. "You'd be honoring the events by witnessing them and recognizing what was done to us."

"Can you tell me what I'd be seeing ahead of time?" I ask.

He shrugs, an oddly sheepish expression creeping over his face. "If I tell you which to view, encourage or discourage you from any of them, you won't trust that whatever you see is really representative of what we've faced. Pick a few at random, and you'll get a fair sampling."

He has a point there. I still find it hard to propel myself forward.

I walk along the line of chairs against the wall, peering at each of the churning dark patches in turn. They all look essentially the same, none bleaker or more violent than another. There's really no way of telling what each might hold—to my senses, at least. From what Madoc said, there must be some sort of magical trace the Murk can pick up on that gives an idea of the contents.

I said I wanted to see what the Murk have actually been put through by the other fae—and I can't see how I'm going to get anything else of use out of this place. There could still be information in one of these memories that'll get me closer to escape.

Madoc has hung back by the door as if to ensure there's no chance of me thinking he's influencing my decision. When I look back at him, his mouth has formed a crooked line, as if he's not totally happy I'm here.

It was his idea. But then, these are his people's deepest wounds.

Has he left a memory here?

I set aside that question and force myself to pick a chair at random, halfway along the room. Bracing myself, I sink into the chair.

As I settle into the seat, a chilly tingling sensation wraps around my torso and flows up to my head with my next exhaled breath. The world around me tilts, and I close my eyes instinctively.

And then I'm there.

A fire is blazing all across a small wooden cabin. The smell of smoke fills my nose. A man lies dead in front of the building, his torso slashed through from shoulder to waist so deeply the edges of his ribs glint against the bloody flesh.

As I watch from the perspective of whoever this memory belongs to, a woman runs toward me, shooing at me to run ahead of her. I shake my head, but the panic etched on her face convinces me. My view swings around as I turn. I glance back a moment later just in time to see a wolf lunge out of the shadows to tackle the woman to the ground. It plunges its claws into her chest with a savage grin.

I jolt awake to find myself clutching the sides of the chair, my breath coming short. For a second, the smoky smell lingers in my lungs. The still air cools the sweat that's broken out on my forehead.

Madoc watches me silently from near the door. The woman who was here before has left.

That memory doesn't tell me much, though. Who knows why the Seelie attacked those Murk? Maybe they'd already hurt the summer fae. It's easy to look like the victim when you're controlling what anyone sees of the story.

I push myself off of the chair, wavering as I catch my balance, and stride deeper into the room to one of the chairs closer to the center. Dragging in a breath, I sit down.

The chill wraps around me, I close my eyes—

And now I'm swinging high above an icy plain. There's a pain in my behind from an appendage I don't have in real life. The wind ruffles my fur, and I realize the memory is of a Murk in rat form.

A rat clutched by a raven. The black wings flap overhead, and the talons clutching my tail give me a shake so hard my bones rattle. Then the bird dives downward, plummeting toward the ground. It tosses me just as it lands, a few of those bones snapping as I hit the ice.

The raven shifts into an Unseelie woman. She jabs something I can't see into the base of my tail to stop me from running, though I'm too dizzy to be likely to anyway.

"Show yourself," she snaps. "I have questions."

Pain hazes my mind as I leave behind my animal form—other than my tail, which enlarges but remains pinned.

"What do you want?" I stammer. "I wasn't hurting anyone. I was only foraging—those woods belong to no domain, I'm sure of it—my mate is close to having our child; she needs—"

"Enough lies," the woman snaps, even though I can tell the Murk whose memory I'm in meant every word he said. Nothing but fear and anguish runs through his frame—and a pinch of hunger in his belly. "You don't belong in the winter realm at all. What tricks were you up to?"

"I swear, I only came through to the fringelands because I thought something grown in the land of the Heart might fill her more," the man says. "I don't want anything except to gather a few morsels of food and leave."

"We'll just have to pick you apart until we discover the truth, then."

The Unseelie woman turns as if expecting someone else, and a flare of panicked certainty shoots through my chest—I won't make it through this alive. My mate will never know what's happened to me. She'll be all alone.

In that moment of desperation, I spit out a string of syllables. Pain sears through my bottom—but I'm free. I leap away from the tail I've severed from my body, shifting into rat form at the same time, and dash into the shelter of the nearby woods even though every step is agony.

When I come out of that memory, I'm shaking. Madoc has come closer, standing over me as if he was considering snapping me out of it early. He peers into my eyes. "Have you seen enough?"

I swallow thickly. The man whose memory I just inhabited didn't deserve that treatment. But after all the Murk have done—so much the fae of the seasons haven't deserved either—I'm not going to say they deserve to be slaughtered over a few overly vicious sentries.

"I'll look at another," I say, annoyed that my voice wobbles.

Madoc frowns, but he doesn't stop me. He hangs back as I weave through the chairs again. But when I stop and swivel to sit down on the next one I've chosen, he clears his throat urgently. "Maybe not that one. That's… That's a particularly wrenching one."

I hold his gaze. "Shouldn't you want me to see it, then?"

He opens his mouth and then closes it again with a sickly smile. "You're right. I should. Just—be prepared. If you react too strongly, I'll pull you out."

Is he putting on a show because he doesn't want me to see what this memory contains for some other reason? I sit in the chair, even more determined than before, and shut my eyes.

This time, I fall into a dimly lit tunnel that stinks of sewage. Because it's a sewer, I realize as I take in my surroundings. It's hard to focus on any details because my heart is pounding so hard. I'm standing braced in front of a doorway on a ledge that runs alongside the channel of sludge.

Several fae are approaching. I can't tell whether they're Seelie or Unseelie at first, but then a few bare their teeth to show wolfish fangs. "We'll take her for questioning," the one in the lead says. "Destroy the rest."

"No, please!" I cry, throwing my arms wide as if I can stop them with my body. "They're only—"

One of the fae punches me in the throat so hard my voice turns into a croak. Another yanks my arms behind me and snaps a magical binding around me as he carries me with his colleagues into the room I was trying to defend.

It's… It's full of children. Young fae ranging from toddlers to kids who don't look older than five or six in human years. They all freeze and stare at the sight of the intruders.

The few adult Murk who're standing among the children rush forward, letting loose their own rat claws, but the wolf shifters slice through their throats and bash their heads in a matter of seconds. Then they turn on the kids, some of whom are staring in stunned horror, others starting to wail or shriek.

The summer fae warriors barge through the room, catching every Murk child in their path with their fangs or claws. Blood splatters the little faces. Bodies slump like toppled, dismembered dolls across the blankets spread on the floor. And one of the Seelie—one of them *laughs*.

"This many fewer to grow up and become thorns in our side," another mutters, grabbing a toddler who was scrambling away from him with a whimper and slashing the poor little body right down the middle.

A scream of protest finally bursts from my damaged throat. The man holding me wallops me across the head—and I whip back into the vault of memories.

I double over in the chair, vomit burning up my throat before I have a chance to even try to rein in my nausea. Madoc springs forward, grasping my shoulder, pulling my hair back from the spray that spills from my mouth. I gag and sputter, those horrible images flashing through my mind on repeat. I can't shut them out, eyes open or closed.

"I'm sorry," Madoc says raggedly. "I shouldn't have let you anyway."

I stay hunched over for several seconds longer until I'm sure my stomach is done heaving. Then I bring my hands to my face. "That—who were all those kids? What were the Seelie doing there?"

Madoc eases back. "We have… what you'd call orphanages. For the Murk who aren't yet old enough to fend for themselves, who've been left parentless for a variety of reasons." His mouth twists. "I spent some time in one of those, though thankfully not that one, obviously. As far as what the Seelie meant to do, you saw it. One of them must have noticed the Murk living there when they were in the human world for some other reason, and they took the opportunity to exterminate as many of us as they could."

I don't want to believe it. Does Sylas know that kind of thing goes on? Do any of my mates? No matter how many spiteful pranks the Murk have played, no matter how many deaths they've caused, to rip apart tiny children who'd never done *anything*…

My stomach lurches again, and I wait until I've gotten it under control before I speak again. "I can see why you hate them so much."

Madoc sighs and helps me out of the chair. My legs tremble. He keeps his hand on my elbow to steady me and murmurs a few quick phrases. The dinner I threw up crumbles into dust that wisps away.

My cheeks flush with embarrassment that he not only saw me in that state but cleaned up after me too. He isn't acting disdainful of my reaction, though, the way I can so easily imagine fae like Celia or Laoni behaving.

He looks me over as if confirming I really am okay and then says, "It isn't so much about hate. I do hate the fae of the seasons for the things they've done—don't get me wrong. But I don't stand with Orion to punish them. I stand with him to make sure Murk like the ones you saw never have to be punished again."

He hesitates, and then adds, "The woman whose memory you were just in came to the orphanage where I was living next. She managed to get away from the Seelie who captured her, but she lost one of her arms in the process. She never told us what happened to the children she'd looked after before us, though. I didn't know until I came here and sensed her presence in that memory."

I shiver. "I don't regret seeing it. I needed to know. But it was horrible."

"It was. And for her, and the other children like me, and every other Murk who's had to live in constant fear of the fae of the seasons stumbling on us at the wrong moment and deciding to rain their vicious judgment down on us all, I want us to have a real home. I want us to be able to walk around freely without that shadow hanging over us. Hell, I want us to be able to partake in the Heart of the Mist's magic again, if it'll have us, even if that's a pipe dream. We're fae… We shouldn't have to live as if we're only rats."

He averts his gaze as if he's ashamed of how much emotion he's shown. His frustration rang through his voice.

I want to tell him I understand, that I respect him more for the compassion and resolve he's just shown. But how can I when seeing that resolve through would mean destroy everything in the worlds that *I've* come to care about?

CHAPTER FIFTEEN

Madoc

The sun is bright overhead and the grass soft under my back, but for some reason no jolt of apprehension passes through me. Some part of me knows that right now, I'm perfectly safe.

I close my eyes, and a soft touch brushes across my cheek. When I look up, Talia is leaning over me. The waves of her vivid pink-and-purple hair frame her pretty face, her green eyes brighter than I've ever seen them up close—but then, the only times I've seen them up close before are in the dark of night or the artificial light of the Refuge.

She belongs out here in daylight. It gleams off her like some kind of magic.

But even more magical are the sparks that light up all through my body when she strokes her fingers over my cheek again and along my jaw. I don't even think about it; I just reach for her. As I push myself up on one elbow, she lowers her head to meet me.

That first kiss is pure, glowing joy. Her mouth is sweet, and her breath hitches with a hint of a needy whimper. Just like that, I'm on fire with my own desire.

I pull her down over me, kissing her harder, delving my fingers into her silky hair. Exploring every inch of that hot, sweet mouth with my tongue. Reveling in the way her body fits against mine, smaller and softer with curves that nestle against me in all the right places.

I slide my hand down over her breast, swiveling my palm against the peak through the fabric covering it, and she gasps. She pushes upright, straddling me, and I realize for the first time that she's wearing that lacy, rosy dress she had on when I whisked her away from the summer realm. It's unmarked by the trip now, which some distant part of me recognizes is odd, but the rest of me doesn't give a shit.

Especially when Talia raises her hands to the neckline and tugs. The fabric slips down over her shoulders and chest, baring her to the waist. Her small breasts sway with the movement, peach-pink nipples hardening in the open air.

She tilts forward as if offering them to me, and how can I possibly resist?

I take one nipple and then the other into my mouth, working them over with my tongue until Talia is moaning and writhing against me. The shifting of her body against my groin is the most excruciating torture.

I can't wait any longer. I shove up the skirt of her dress and rip off her panties.

"Madoc," she pants, so full of wanting I nearly explode just like that. I fumble to free my cock, and then I'm plunging into her slick heat as if I'm meant to be nowhere else.

Talia clutches my shoulders, riding me with rolls of her hips. Pleasure like I've never known pulses through me with every thrust. My head tips back into the grass with a groan. I grip her hips to pull her into an even better angle—

And my eyes pop open for real.

I blink, unsatisfied hunger coursing all through my body. I'm staring up at the dark ceiling of my little room, sprawled on the inflatable mattress I set up there, my body flushed and my dick unbearably hard. Alone.

I rub my hand over my face, fighting to get my urges under control. Of course I'm alone. As far as Talia's concerned, I'm just the prick who stole her from her supposed mates and dragged her away from the sunlight. She has no interest in my actual prick. Even if *it* can't help noticing how appealing her lovely face and lithe body are.

But I don't think it's her good looks that provoked this dream. I haven't had one like it about her before. My thoughts travel back automatically to the past day, to our excursion to the vault of memories. To the way she looked at me after I told her about the woman from the orphanage, as if she wanted to take up a sword and fight to the death for me right there and then.

She felt our anguish. I'm not sure if she truly was turning against the fae of the seasons before then or if she was only digging for information the same way I have with her, but in that moment, she hated them too. She wanted to stand with me.

She let me hold her arm all the way to the door until I was sure she was steady, staying so close the warmth of her body grazed mine in the chilly air. And when she looked up at me after we left, so many unspoken words shone in her eyes that I wanted to drink them from her lips.

Maybe it's not surprising that not just the soul-twined mate Orion tied her to but three other high-ranking fae besides have fallen for her. There's a fierceness to her, an inner strength that burns inside her even now, even after everything she's discovered.

She *would* fight for whatever she feels is just, even against creatures with far more power than her, all the way to her death. I've seen that, clear as day.

I sit up, shaking my head to clear it. That fire also makes her dangerous, because it might be us she decides to fight. I've also seen enough of her, spoken enough with her, to be sure her interest in her mates was more than just fickle hero worship. She might be angry on our behalf for the crimes done to us, but I don't think her loyalty to those specific men has wavered. No matter how I've prodded, she's never said a word against them.

And there are times when I don't think she realizes that anyone's watching her when a sadness comes over her face that pricks at my heart more than it should.

Right now the only thing aching is my unattended erection, though. The lust the dream stirred up in me is refusing to leave me. With a hiss of frustration, I reach for myself through my clothes and shut my eyes, calling up the naked figures of other women I've actually bedded behind my eyelids.

As I stroke myself, the images keep shifting back into Talia's slim body, her pale face with its frame of vibrant hair. But she feels too ephemeral. I can't quite give myself over completely.

Muttering curses under my breath, I jerk my clothes into place and head down the stairs. My shoes make only the faintest rustling sound over the gravel.

Talia's new house is the closest to this end of the station where I built it. I don't even get up off the tracks, just walk until I'm level with it. The door flap is shut, but I don't need to see her. I take a long, slow breath, letting the tart scent of her, like freshly grown leaves, fill my lungs. I listen to her own breaths, the faint rhythmic wisp as she sleeps.

After several seconds, I know I've drunk in enough to get where I want to go. I scramble onto the opposite platform and duck into one of the bathroom stalls. Now, focusing on the false images of her from my dream and her very real scent, I come in less than a minute.

It's only a basic bodily urge now satisfied, but I feel absurdly uncomfortable afterward, as if I've somehow defiled Talia even though she wasn't really involved at all. As if it's such a horrible thing that a Murk like me might direct any lust her way. She's a human—a human who was shaped by my own king. She isn't *better* than me.

I've mostly pushed the uneasy feelings inside when I head back to the tunnel. I slip down onto the tracks—and the flap on Talia's house pushes open. I freeze.

"Madoc?" she whispers in her clear voice, which holds none of the passion it did in my dream but enough concern to bring back a pang of guilt. As she peers out at me, she swipes her hand across her eyes, obviously still sleepy. "Just getting another middle of the night snack?"

Did my thoughts manage to wake her up after all, or is she sleeping so badly in her new home that the simple act of my walking by pulled her out?

Either way, she doesn't appear to have any idea what I was actually doing, thank all that's holy.

"That's all," I say. "Nothing important. You look like you should get some more sleep."

She mumbles in agreement and lets the flap drop. I should set off, but I can't quite will my feet to move. I stand there as if guarding over her until I hear her breaths even out with sleep again.

She has no idea what went on in my head. And it doesn't matter anyway. Animals rut at each other. Whatever physical desire I've felt, it doesn't mean anything beyond my having a working dick.

I remind myself of all those things, but when I finally do make it back to my room, I don't get much more sleep myself. The images of Talia that haunt my mind now have nothing lustful about them.

She peers out at me from the shadows of her makeshift home. She thanks me for easing the pain of her headache. She answers Orion's questions in front of me, clearly nervous but refusing to be cowed.

She stares off toward the ceiling in a rare private moment, as if hoping she'll be able to peel back the layers of cement and asphalt with her hopes alone to see through to the world above.

She looks at me, pale and sickly but full of righteous horror, and says, *I needed to know.*

I finally get up when the rest of my people will be stirring, though my nerves are brittle from my fragmented sleep. Maybe the simple fact of the matter is that I know something isn't exactly right here. Talia might not be Murk, but in most ways that matter, she's one of my people too.

It's early enough that I can hope not too many people are hassling Orion yet. I catch up with the fae bringing his breakfast and help myself to a few tidbits on the way to his audience room. They know my standing with him well enough not to protest.

I fought hard for that standing. I've earned our king's ear. I don't think I'm really going to ask for all that much.

But when I come up on the platform that holds his throne and watch him get up from it with all his feral yet regal poise, my chest constricts.

I smile and take a seat across from him at his motion. He accepts a mug of coffee from another servant and sips it with great enthusiasm before digging into the food. "Well, then, my busy friend. Any progress?"

I've already told him about taking Talia to the vault of memories. "There hasn't been much time for new developments," I say dryly.

"Who knows what may happen while others are sleeping?" he says with a flippant wave of his hand, oblivious to the uneasy twinge his remark sends through me.

I choose my next words carefully. "I have been thinking more about my observations. It's obvious that Talia is coming around to fully support our efforts to claim the Mists. But it also makes sense that she's had a little trouble adapting to spending all her time down here after such a… different life before."

Orion hums and licks yolk from a soft-boiled egg off his fingers. "I hear what you're saying and ask you to get on with the point."

"I know we have to be careful of the soul-twined bond," I say. "But it would only take a small amount of energy to temporarily expand the shield a little, wouldn't it? If we could give her an hour or two above, outside or even in a building with windows—she couldn't see anything that could lead back to the Refuge's actual location anyway, and she'd have no way to communicate what she does see to anyone regardless…"

I trail off at the arch of Orion's eyebrows. He snickers to himself. "You want to coddle her? She's barely given us anything. She must know all kinds of inner workings of the arch-lords' courts, and she's keeping it all close to the chest."

I resist the impulse to bristle. "I don't see it as coddling. She's done a lot for us already, and we've *used* her a lot. Offering her a little kindness would be strategic, making her feel even more that we're on her side and that she should be on ours."

My king makes a dismissive sound and shakes his head. "Of course we've used her. She's *mine.* I made her. That's what she's for. And she has more use in her yet if she wasn't so stubborn." He picks up a cherry danish. "I think we should take the opposite approach."

I study him warily. "What do you mean?"

"She obviously doesn't trust either of us enough to open up. There's an easy way to shift the dynamic. What is it humans call it—good cop, bad cop?" Orion smirks. "I'll get meaner to give you the chance to play her champion. Let's see what we get out of her once you've earned her full devotion."

Doubt winds around my gut, making the bits of breakfast I ate churn. This isn't how I wanted the conversation to go at all.

I've seen how close Talia already is to believing in us. But I can tell from Orion's tone that if I contradict him, he'll go from amused to scathing in an instant. I might make things even worse for her if he thinks he needs to teach me a lesson too.

Talia's voice rises up from my memory. *As far as I can tell, Orion is more interested in hurting fae—and not just the fae of the Mists.*

I shove that thought aside and focus on the present. "What exactly did you have in mind?" I force myself to ask.

"Oh, you'll see," Orion says with delight sparkling in his eyes. "Just make sure you swoop in and 'save' her thoroughly afterward."

CHAPTER SIXTEEN

Talia

The moment I step into the throne room, I can tell something has shifted in the atmosphere. Orion is poised on his throne, his tail slung over one arm and flicking idly but the rest of him absolutely still. His usual close companions, including Madoc, are standing as if at attention on the dais around him rather than lounging in their typical casual poses.

There are only a few other fae around, hanging back by the walls, tensed but with hints of anticipation in their faces. And the twitching orange glow of their Heart washes over them all.

I pause just inside the room, abruptly uncertain. When one of the Murk told me the king wanted to see me, I assumed Orion was going to offer to share another meal with me and chat a little like he has before. Or maybe suggest another job he thinks I could help with. This… feels very different, in a way that makes my skin crawl.

Orion beckons me closer. "Come along, my pet," he says in a tone much more mocking than affectionate. "I don't want to be yelling across the room to talk to you."

I limp forward, even though every particle in my body is

clanging with alarm. What good would running away do? It's not as if there's anywhere I could flee to that he wouldn't find me. My fingers itch to reach for my bronze bracelet, to rub the cool metal to remind myself I have that one secret tool, but I'm afraid of drawing attention to it.

"What did you want to talk about?" I ask, keeping my voice as steady as I can. He can probably pick up on my nervousness with his sharp senses, but I don't want to make it any more obvious than I have to. My gaze darts to Madoc of its own accord, and his mouth moves just slightly. I can't tell whether he wants to reassure me or warn me—or maybe it's neither.

"We're fine-tuning our plans for our invasion of the Mists," Orion says. He pauses until I've come to a stop right at the edge of the dais and motions for me to step up so I'm right in front of him. "We've been able to gather plenty of information, but our methods do still have a few limitations. I think it's time I saw through the rest of your purpose there."

A chill prickles through my nerves. I hold myself stiffly, just a couple of steps from his chair. "What do you mean?"

The Murk king gives me a narrow smirk. "You've spent a lot of time among the highest ranking fae of the Mists. You've had access to an Unseelie arch-lord's entire mind. I'm sure you know all kinds of details about their habits and strategies that we couldn't glimpse otherwise."

My pulse stutters. Both he and Madoc have nudged me about my knowledge of the other fae from time to time over the past few days, but they've never demanded information. I assumed it was because they didn't think I'd necessarily learned all that much that would be useful to them. Apparently they were only biding their time, hoping I'd volunteer more than I have.

I can still attempt to play the ignorance card. I offer a sheepish smile. "There weren't any invasions or wars when I was with them. I don't think I know very much that would help you prepare, or I'd have mentioned it already. Mostly… Mostly we talked about more personal things."

I duck my head as if I'm embarrassed by the reference to the intimacy of my relationship with most of the fae who told me much of anything.

Orion's tail keeps flicking, his smirk still in place, his eyes glittering coldly. "*I* think you still have some loyalties to the fae who took you as their mate, and that's keeping you quiet. As if they aren't just as bad as the others when it suits them. Why do you think I chose a human to shape rather than one of my own kind? If you'd been a Murk, you'd never have made it out of that first cage."

Is that true? My gut twists with the question, but there's really no way of knowing.

And it doesn't change the fact that I believe the fae I trusted back home would be willing to consider that the Murk might deserve more than the lot they've been given. That they'd be horrified by the violence I witnessed in the vault of memories yesterday.

"That might be true," I say, the lie heavy on my tongue, "but I still don't know what I could say that would help you."

"And that is why I've gotten tired of waiting for you to get your head on straight and fully embrace your true loyalties."

In one swift movement, so sudden I have no chance to react, Orion shoots forward to the edge of his seat and snatches my wrist. As he yanks me right up to him with a strength I wasn't prepared for, my warped foot stumbles. I nearly fall right into his lap.

But maybe he wouldn't have minded that, because the next second, he's swept out his own foot to knock my legs out from under me. My knees hit the surface of the dais, leaving me kneeling in front of him, my breath locked in my throat. When I open my mouth to protest, he grasps a clump of my hair and hauls my head back so I'm staring up to meet his gaze. His claws have come out, pricking my scalp like needles.

There's a rustling beside us. "Orion," Madoc starts, with a rough note in his voice.

But if he was going to speak on my behalf, his king doesn't want to hear it. Orion waves him off with his other hand. "It's time she understood who exactly is in control here, and just how much control I can wield." He grins at me, his face full of wicked amusement even as the pain of his grip radiates through my head.

I don't want to beg, and I don't expect it to do me any good, but the words spill out anyway. "Please. Ask me whatever you want, and I'll tell you what I can. I don't want—"

He jerks my head back and forth, sending another jab of pain through my wrenched neck. "I don't care what you want, little girl. You are mine. I made you. And now I'll take what *I* want."

He intones a few harsh words of magic, and the dissonant energy of the Heart hits me even harder. A burning sensation flares deep in my mind, spreading through my awareness as if my brain has caught fire.

I gasp, tears springing to my eyes. I try to blink them away, but something in Orion's spell holds my eyelids open as he peers into me as if seeing right inside my mind.

Which maybe he is. My thoughts jumble and whirl, and I nearly choke on the realization of how many things I *do* know that I'd hate for him to find out. But the burning is heightening into a full-out blaze, and I can't focus on anything except those gleaming yellow eyes pinning me in place.

However much he's dragging from my mind into his, he mustn't be able to control it perfectly. His pupils flicker back and forth like he's reading a book, and he snaps out a demanding question. "The illegal artifact collection the former arch-lord was keeping—your Arch-Lord Sylas didn't dispose of all of it?"

The answer tears up my throat as if dredged up by a barbed net. I can't hold it in. "I—I think he and the other arch-lords got rid of everything they thought was dangerous. But there might still be some things left." Has Celia held onto anything along with the collar she used on Corwin? I try to swallow down the words, but more crawl from my lungs. "I don't know where it would be, though."

Orion gives my head another brisk shake, but he seems satisfied that I've told him enough about that subject. "The magic used to create your new castle on the border. How did the opposing realms come together on it?"

I don't know much about that either, but what I do comes searing across my tongue. "They said they—they just had to appeal to the Heart of the Mists, and it accepted their intentions. And the border vow had to stay in place."

I can't feel my limbs anymore, not even my knees braced against the dais—only the scorching agony and the piercing of the Murk king's gaze. "What exactly did you say to convince Arch-Lord Laoni to back off on destroying that castle when she called you to attend to her alone?"

"I'm not sure," I gasp out. "She—she'd come down with the curse, and I reminded her that I didn't have to heal her. That it would probably be easier for me if I didn't. But I told her that she and her people mattered enough to me that I'd cure her even though she'd been attacking me. I think—I think she finally realized I didn't have any intention of hurting her."

But I am anyway. Nausea twines with the pain inside me. I'm betraying every one of the fae of the seasons right now, and I don't know how to stop myself.

The burning sensation is starting to ease back, though it still hurts like hell. I don't know if Orion is exhausting his powers or if he's simply winding down on purpose. "What did your mates do to make the Heart of the Mists flare the way it did at your mating ceremony?"

My voice comes out in a croak. "I don't know. I had no idea that was going to happen. They didn't mention it before or after."

He lets go. My bones have turned to jelly. I collapse at his feet, my nerves jittering as if I've been stabbed by a thousand splinters all over my body. A dull ache fills my head.

"That's enough for now," Orion says, nudging me with the toe of his shoe. "Bring her back to her house and let her sleep it off."

I don't know who he's spoken to until firm but gentle hands slide over my shoulders and a familiar voice murmurs close to my ear, "I'm going to help you up now. Can you walk at all?"

Madoc eases my arm around him for support and lifts me to my feet. I wobble on my legs, my sense of the room around me still hazy. Orion has already turned to converse with his other men as if he doesn't care whether I even make it out of the room.

When I stumble with my first step, Madoc lets out a soft noise of consternation and hefts me right up into his arms. His thunderstorm scent fills my nose.

I don't want to be carried—I don't want to be handled like an invalid—but I can't convince any part of my body to move to my will.

Madoc strides out of the throne room with me. As we head down the tunnel toward the station where he built my hovel, his voice drops even lower than before, his chin grazing my forehead. "I'm sorry. I didn't know he was going to do that."

What could Madoc have done about it if he had known? What would he even have wanted to do about it? It was all in the service of his cause, wasn't it?

How much did Orion see that will help the Murk ruin every part of the life I came to love in the Mists? How many fae are going to *die* because I didn't have the power to fight him off? Fresh tears well up behind my eyes.

"I'll talk to him, tell him you want to help, that he doesn't have to go about it that way," Madoc continues. "He'll see reason—he's just impatient now that we're so close to the goal. That doesn't excuse —" His voice goes raw. "You didn't deserve this."

Maybe not, but it happened anyway. And I have no doubt it'll happen again if I'm still here—maybe even tomorrow. I have the urge to crawl away inside myself as if that's even possible, as if Orion couldn't drag me out with his awful magic anyway.

Madoc sets me down in front of my "house." He speaks a few magical words, and the already fading pain pulls back even more. My head is starting to clear, but being able to think about what just happened only makes me more miserable.

"If I can do anything else for you," Madoc starts.

I shake my head before he can go on, not meeting his eyes. "Let me just be alone, please," I rasp.

My arms and legs have recovered enough that I can crawl inside the hovel. I have the sense of Madoc lingering outside for a few minutes longer as if to make sure I don't change my mind and call out to him after all. Then he's gone.

I curl up on the blankets, staring vacantly at my hands. I have no idea how much Orion saw in my head that he could turn into a weapon against the men I love. I don't think he saw some of the worst things I could have given away, like my ability with true names or the fact that Whitt gave me his, maybe because it didn't occur to him to search for that. Surely he'd have remarked on it if he'd noticed.

But that doesn't mean he won't dig that out of me later. Soon. He could turn *me* into an outright weapon. In some ways he already has.

My gaze narrows in on the bronze bracelet. A wild, desperate impulse floods me.

I can make sure he never uses me again, that he can't steal one more thought from my head. The Murk haven't left any sharp weapons in my reach, but I could transform that bracelet into a knife right now and slash it across my own throat like I once threatened to in front of Ambrose.

Every awful thing Orion wants from me would drain away with my blood gushing over the floor. It'd all be done.

I sit up and touch the bracelet. "*Fee-doom-ace-own,*" I hiss, pouring all my fear and guilt into the words.

The band releases my wrist and straightens into a razor-sharp blade.

Staring down at it, I run my fingers over the warmed bronze. I should just do it. It would be definite, final… and easy. An immediate escape.

Something in me balks at that.

How much would I be leaving behind? I'd destroy any chance of Orion getting more information out of me—if there's all that much more he *can* get now—but also any chance that I could escape the way I meant to before, to warn the men I love of all the things *they* don't know. I'd be abandoning them to a curse their enemy conjured and a war they don't even know is on the horizon.

For several minutes, I grapple with myself. I bring the bronze edge to my throat to see how the pressure feels. My heart lurches, and I lower my hands again.

Something stronger than my panic rises up from deep inside me.

I've gotten through so much. I've faced so much and refused to give in. And part of me still believes that I can do more by staying in this world than leaving it, as much as I might want to flee the horror of what Orion's done to me.

I close my eyes for a moment, and the resolve solidifies. I'll get back to my home and my mates one way or another. The Murk won't break me.

I'll just have to fight even harder in the few ways I know how.

Heart help me, let it work.

CHAPTER SEVENTEEN

August

As I walk across the polished stone bank to the still, glassy water of the Pool of the Clouded Past, my heart sinks. I'm not sure if I'm more worried that I'll spot something I should have noticed earlier, some mistake I made the night Talia vanished, or that it'll be clear the situation was hopeless from the start.

I kneel down at the edge of the bank. My reflection shines back at me, framed by the stark blue of the sky. I look… tired, my forehead creased, redness creeping into my eyes. I've barely slept more than a couple of hours at a time since the Murk stole Talia from us. When that letter arrived with her blood staining the paper, mocking us for losing something so precious to us…

The Murk could have no concept of just how precious she is to me, my brothers, and Corwin. What in the lands do they know about love?

And now we have other challenges too. The full moon is approaching, seemingly faster every day. We've started preparing the pack for undergoing the shift and discussing strategies to share with other domains, but the truth is, none of us are really sure what it might look like. How badly it might go.

On top of that, Sylas hasn't been able to confirm any wrongdoing on Tristan's part. His pack-kin gave a perfectly reasonable-sounding explanation for their activities near Hearth-by-the-Heart, claiming it was all precautions to help fend off a possible Murk attack on the Heart. We have extra guards keeping an eye on that area, but with it being free land, we can't force them to leave without a valid excuse.

Which naturally they know.

I catch myself gritting my teeth and force my jaw to relax. Right now I have to stay focused on what's in front of me—that is, my chance to take a glimpse into the past. I didn't have Sylas extend the request for the visit to our father only to sit around stewing over things I can't control.

"Show me the night of my mating ceremony," I say. "From the moment I left Talia at the platform to go get some refreshments."

The water shimmers. An image forms of a crowd of dancing fae. There's so much joy in their faces that my chest clenches up.

I watch myself moving through that crowd toward the refreshment table, my brothers on either side of me, Corwin just behind. Back then, I was only thinking of how happy I was to finally be able to say Talia was my mate in every possible way—and what sort of tart I wanted to eat first. Now, I scan the revelers around us, watching for any sign of ill intent.

Our pack-kin and the few Unseelie celebrating among them look totally innocent in their reveling. I don't catch a single hostile glance or conspiratorial murmur, not even a flicker of a frown. And I don't spot any suspicious figures among them who don't belong to either realm.

I guess we can hope that whatever magic the Murk have found, it hasn't let them mingle with us that closely undetected. The ones who took Talia did arrange to get her well away from the rest of the crowd before making off with her.

Of course, that means the pool won't be able to offer any clues at all. It can't show me what was far beyond my view.

I keep watching anyway.

We stop by the table and quickly pick out a few delicacies, none of us wanting to be away from Talia's side for very long. As Sylas turns back toward the platform, Whitt moves to the wine table, and I'm momentarily diverted by a couple of the guards I've been training with the longest, who clap me on the back and offer more congratulations. Their faces are ruddy with the alcohol they've already downed, but I don't see any malicious magic in them.

Then, as the me of the past moves to weave through the crowd, I spot a face that makes my gut tighten. Not because it's anything to do with the Murk, but because it's the cause of my other worries.

Tristan was standing maybe ten feet away from me at that moment, his cadre-chosen Jax beside him. He's saying something to her that the pool doesn't convey, but his lips curl with a sneer right before my view of him is blocked by the dancers.

His reaction isn't exactly a surprise, but it's a little disheartening to see that he couldn't summon any positive feelings about the occasion even on a night when so many other fae were full of happiness. But then, he's never seen Talia as anything other than a means to political power and a cure for the curse.

At least I can rest assured that he'd never have helped the rats take her *farther* from him and his interests than Sylas already had.

I peer at the pool as the rest of the scene plays out: the discovery of Talia's disappearance, the frantic initial search, the sight of Donovan's pack-kin unconscious in the woods. The Murk who carried out the crime must have been long gone by the time we made it there. I don't see anything I wasn't already aware of.

I sit back on my haunches, exhaling in a huff of frustration. There's been no further word from Talia. She hasn't reached out to Whitt again—the knowledge that he shared his true name with her without mentioning it to me until now sends a jab through my stomach, even if I understand the reasoning. Why didn't I think to do the same? And her connection with Corwin has stayed silent. He's sure she's still alive, but beyond that…

I wish the pool could show me *her* memories or what she's going through right now, as horrible as it might be.

My hands ball into fists. At the same moment, footsteps rasp across the rocky terrain behind me.

I stand and turn, my back stiffening when I take in my father approaching. I purposefully avoided flying my small carriage within view of the castle so that I wouldn't need to speak to Lord Eldris, since Sylas had already cleared my visit with him. Why he's insisted on seeking me out, I have no idea. I doubt it's for anything good.

"Did you find everything you were looking for?" he asks, offering one of his thin smiles. No hello, no acknowledgment of our relation to each other. He crosses his arms over his chest and lifts his chin imperiously.

"I'm managing just fine," I say. "If I'd needed assistance, I'd have reached out to your pack-kin. You needn't have troubled yourself."

The words themselves are as polite as I can manage, but a bit of bite might have crept into my tone. My father's eyes darken. "I don't need any guests telling me what I can do or where I should go in my own domain."

I'm not just a guest, I'm your blasted son! I want to snap at him, but I hold my annoyance in check. We have enough problems without my temper getting away from me.

"I would never think of doing so," I reply evenly. "I only meant that I had no intention of disturbing you."

He ignores that remark and comes up beside me, stopping a few paces away along the edge of the pool. "You're looking for answers to do with that human girl of yours."

"Lady Talia," I say, with emphasis on her title. "Yes. As you must be able to imagine, we're very concerned with getting her back quickly and safely."

My father grunts, gazing across the pool rather than at me. "Such a shame a resource so important to our kind is tied up in a fragile mortal body."

I can't help bristling at that remark. "She's more than just her body and more than just a resource as well."

He glances sideways at me with a patronizing air that sets my nerves even more on edge. "You always were quick to emotion. It would have been better for you to have tied yourself to a proper mate, but I suppose there's no helping it now. You'll have plenty of time to choose more wisely when the dust takes her."

His tone is so matter-of-fact, as if he's discussing nothing more disturbing than the sunny weather, that it takes all my self-control not to lunge at him and slam his head into the water until he's drowned. My muscles flex all through my shoulders. "Would you say the same to your son the arch-lord?" I ask, a growl slipping into my voice.

Lord Eldris doesn't look remotely concerned by my anger. If anything, his expression only gets more disdainful. "Of course not. An arch-lord is allowed his whims. But I'm allowed my opinions, and there's no reason I shouldn't impart them to you. You obviously have too much of your mother in you."

In that second, I can only see red. He's lucky I don't tear his head right off his body. How *dare* he speak of my mother—the loving, kind woman he had brutally slaughtered in front of me on one of *his* whims—so callously.

I take a step toward him, and the breeze brushes over me. The wisp of it over my bare forearms brings the ghost of Talia's touch. I can almost feel her here, grasping my hand, reassuring me that she's here with me no matter what this bastard says to me. That he can't poison what we share.

And she would be right, wouldn't she? The pathetic, bitter man in front of me doesn't have to matter at all. I've left him behind; he has no more control over me. Once we get Talia back and she continues her campaign on behalf of the humans in the fae world, he won't even be able to control the people like my mother he still rules over either.

I don't have to worry one bit what he thinks of me. I don't have to give him a speck of emotional energy. He doesn't even deserve my rage, because that would mean I care.

My anger simmers down beneath a cool wave of soothing calm. I stare back at my father the way I've seen Talia face hostile arch-lords before. "I'm glad for every part of me that came from my mother, because I doubt what I inherited from you is worth anything. You're no longer my family. As far as I'm concerned, you stopped truly being my father when you ripped the one parent who actually parented me out of my life. So you can keep your advice to yourself. I have no interest in so much as speaking to you again."

I swivel on my heel and stride off without giving him a chance to answer. Even after I've leapt into my carriage, I don't look back. His pride may be slightly stung, but I doubt he cares much what I think of *him* either.

As the carriage soars over the land, whisking me far away from him, it's as if a huge weight has washed off of me with the rushing of the wind. I've felt lost without Talia by my side, but she's still here in a way. All her sweetness and light have touched me and stayed with me.

I just need to keep being the man she fell in love with.

I don't have any new answers, but when I reach Hearth-by-the-Heart, I summon all the pack-kin who are currently present that I started training in combat back when we were less sure of our footing among the other lords. I've slacked off on that practice a little since we founded our alliance with the winter fae, but in this moment, taking it up again feels like the most productive thing I can do.

"We'll start with the warm-up exercises and move on to defensive forms," I say, walking around the group assembled by the pack village. "We know we have more enemies than we suspected we'd have to deal with, and that they're more powerful than we'd have anticipated. I want to be sure that you're all ready for them."

I may have let Talia down, but I won't let the rest of my pack down in my distress over her kidnapping. The best way I can protect them is to make sure they're prepared to protect themselves—against whatever threats might descend on us next.

CHAPTER EIGHTEEN

Talia

Few of the Murk were around to witness Orion's assault on my mind, but I suspect word about it has gotten around. When I approach the ones stocking the food table the next morning, they accept my help but shoot me quick glances with what feels like a mix of wariness and pity. My skin tightens at the thought of what they might be wondering about me, but I'm not going to bring up the subject if they don't.

Instead, I pay close attention to the food they've brought. Most of it looks like it was nabbed from restaurant kitchens or even dumpsters, leftover catering trays maybe, nothing labeled. Some of the fruit has stickers on it, but knowing they originally came from Mexico or Ecuador doesn't tell me much when I know those countries export produce all over the world.

I'm not even sure I can draw any conclusions from the fact that there's quite a bit of breakfast food in the mix. My view from Madoc's telescope suggested that the world above the Refuge is on the opposite day-night schedule from how the Murk operate down here, but I don't know how close its source really is to our actual location.

Or this could be food that was prepared hours ago that the thieves have simply reheated after waiting until it's the appropriate mealtime. Hell, they could even be slipping through a couple of portals to some other part of the world completely, someplace where it is breakfast time even if it's not directly above us.

Even the boxes they're using are unlabeled, not giving anything away. Are they normally this cautious, or has Orion specifically ordered everyone to avoid bringing in anything that could give me a clue about where I am? The types of food don't give much away—there's always a mix of more familiar North American type items alongside dishes with Mediterranean or Asian or other influences I can't place with my limited human-world experience.

"It must be tiring, carrying so much stuff all the way here," I say in a casual tone as I rearrange a few apples on the table, just trying to look like I'm still pitching in.

The fae woman across from me shrugs. "Between all of us who work together, it's a pretty simple job. We all need to eat."

Which neither confirms nor denies that they're traveling a long way. I search for another tactic and then sigh. "I understand why I need to stay down here, but I do miss going outside. What's the weather like today? Maybe if I could picture it, it'd be easier not to be able to see it myself."

One of the other fae lets out a sound like a muffled snicker. The woman gives me a look that I suspect is all pity now. Not that her pity does me any good.

"I didn't pay that much attention," she says. "We have to be focused on steering clear of the humans and getting around locked doors and all the rest rather than what's going on in the sky."

And she's probably been warned not to tell me anything about the outside world anyway. "That's okay," I say with forced brightness, as if it doesn't matter that much to me anyway.

Just then, Bren saunters up to the table. He nudges aside a couple of other Murk who were picking out their breakfast and heaps several choice items on his plate, including the last four of the very popular sesame seed-dusted rice balls. The fae he displaced hang back until he's gone, glance mournfully at the now-empty plate, and take what they want from the rest of the offerings.

"Nearly disgraced and now he's rising in the ranks fast," one of the men mutters to the woman near me when Bren is gone.

"Because of the fight," I say.

He shoots me a cautious glance but nods. "He proved how far he'll go for the king. Orion rewards loyalty."

The woman shrugs. "I don't mind sticking to food duty if it means there's no risk of getting my guts clawed out."

"True. But once you've survived that, no one can touch you outside the king's circle."

"Do those kind of fights happen a lot?" I ask, not because it helps my escape but just out of queasy curiosity.

"Now and then," the woman says, not sounding at all disturbed by the fact. "Orion has plenty of ways of testing the ones who want to stand close to him. And some he trusts more than others to begin with. Or less. That Madoc." She shakes her head and then seems to decide not to say whatever she was going to follow up with.

My curiosity is immediately caught. "What happened with Madoc?"

"Better not to tell tales about anyone who stands with the king," the man mutters, and starts filling the now emptied plates with different food.

"It isn't 'tales' if it's true," the woman says, and turns back to me. "He was really just a boy when he made it here, and no one knew who his family had been. Orion and his close circle didn't make it easy for him. But Madoc was determined to show what he was made of, and he did. One of the fiercest battles I've ever seen, in the end. At one point I thought he was lost. He earned the spot he's got now more than some of them did, that's all I'll say about it."

She bustles off, leaving me wondering just what not making it "easy" for someone looks like around here, when fights to the death are a common event. What more has Madoc gone through to earn his spot?

I don't have to ask why he'd have put himself through

anything. I heard how committed he is to helping the rest of the Murk have better lives. Every word he said to me in the vault of memories has stuck with me, adding to the uneasiness twined through my chest.

I linger by the food table for a while longer, nibbling on one thing or another even though I don't feel remotely hungry, listening to the pieces of conversation I catch as the Murk pass by and grab their own meals. Then I watch where they go. There's a doorway at the far end of this station that has a few fae coming and going fairly regularly. I see them each press their hands to a specific spot on the door before it opens though, so presumably it's tied to some kind of magic.

I don't think I'm going to convince the door that I'm Murk too. Talking any of the Murk into opening it for me seems even farther out of reach.

Orion hasn't called on me yet today. How much of a reprieve is he going to give me before he rakes through my mind again? I haven't gotten anywhere with the close-lipped Murk. I have to go back to the one sort-of solid plan I have.

I amble through the tunnels toward the maintenance room, pretending I'm just stretching my legs and looking around. Like in the past, no Murk are hanging around all the way down that final tunnel. I hesitate for several minutes, wondering if Orion will be able to pick this plan out of my head too. But I've already started it, so it isn't as if not continuing would stop him from finding out if that's the case.

I told myself I'd keep going, keep trying, so now I have to do that, or I might as well have slit my throat yesterday.

My muscles seem to be adjusting to the routine, at least. Clambering onto the machine below the vent isn't as much of a strain. I even manage to shape my bracelet into the right size of wrench on my first attempt.

I get to work on the bolt I started last time, heaving with all the strength in my arms. Imagining every twist is locking Orion and his hateful methods away as well as freeing me.

My shoulders start to throb, but I get a good enough rhythm

going that I don't mind. Reposition and yank, reposition and yank, over and over until the bolt finally loosens enough to slip out.

A grin spreads across my face. I swipe at the sweat on my brow, poke the bolt back into its hole for appearances, and move on to the next one. Maybe I'll even get another fully out today.

I'm so caught up in that hope and the work that I don't register voices approaching until they're close enough that I make out actual words.

"—always so grimy out this way."

I jolt to a halt, my fingers freezing around the handle of the wrench. The chuckle that answers the remark sounds distant, but the rasp of footsteps is coming closer. Have they already heard my efforts?

My heart thudding, I mumble the true name for bronze as quickly as I can. With my focus scattered, the wrench doesn't bulge. I gulp a few breaths to steady myself and try again, keeping my voice as low as I can.

The tool wavers and curves around my wrist. I need to repeat the true name once more to fully smooth it out, my pulse hammering away the whole time. The voices sound like they're nearly at the entrance now.

I slide down the side of the machine, landing a little too hard on my warped foot. I have to clap my hand over my mouth to hold back a hiss of pain. With my limp more pronounced than usual and fighting a wince, I make my way through the machines toward the tunnel.

I'm about halfway through the maze of old equipment when the voices stop. Then one calls out, "Is someone there?"

"It's just me," I say quickly, hurrying into view as quickly as I can. "I was taking a look at all the machines here, wondering if there's something we can use for taking back the Mists. No such luck."

The two Murk who've wandered this way eye me, but neither questions my story. "It's all a bunch of junk," one says. "Orion's already had us scavenge what we can from here."

“I guess that makes sense,” I say with a weak laugh. “I’ll see how else I can help out. Did you need anything?”

“We’re fine,” the other fae replies, a little sharply.

I limp on toward the nearest station, but after several steps my foot hurts badly enough that I need to stop and give it a rest. I perk my ears, hoping I might catch a little more conversation from back down the tunnel.

The two fae who passed me have gone silent. That’s odd. I stand there for a while, slipping my foot out of my braced boot to massage it, and I don’t hear another peep from them, not so much as a rustle.

Then it occurs to me—that’s because they aren’t in the tunnel anymore. There must be another exit down there, one they’ve used to leave the Refuge.

Maybe it’ll be just as locked to me as the others, but the next chance I get, I need to find out.

CHAPTER NINETEEN

Talia

By lunchtime, my foot is still sore. When one of the Murk stops by my hovel to tell me that Orion wants to see me, I limp over on wobblier legs than usual, both because of the pain and my apprehension.

The Murk king is sitting off to the side of the dais with a spread of food and Madoc beside him. Orion doesn't seem to pay much attention to me as I make my way slowly over, but Madoc's gaze tracks my movements.

"Did you hurt yourself?" he asks in the low, hoarse voice that often has a strange gentleness to it.

It's hard to appreciate that gentleness when he's sitting next to the man who tormented me so gleefully yesterday.

I sink down at the edge of the platform a careful distance from both of them. "Just the same old hurt, acting up a little more than usual today. It happens sometimes." Definitely not because I was interrupted in the middle of arranging my escape.

Orion looks at me then, but only to nod in acknowledgment as if nothing at all horrible has passed between us. He motions to the food. "Help yourself. We don't want you wasting away."

Why, because then he wouldn't be able to pick any more thoughts out of my brain?

I bite back the snarky remark and pick up a stuffed pepper that fits easily in my hand. I'm not feeling particularly hungry, but I'll eat if it stops him thinking about other things he'd want me to do… and ways of forcing me into doing them.

I keep waiting for the other shoe to drop, for Orion to reveal his reason for calling me here, but he simply makes casual conversation about the day-to-day activities in the Refuge with Madoc and a couple of other fae who pass by. Maybe he simply wanted to confirm that I *would* come when called.

And to observe me up close. Is he checking for signs of hostility or rebellion after yesterday's spectacle? Waiting to see if I'll volunteer more information to try to avoid it happening again?

Is there anything I can volunteer that wouldn't hurt anyone but would put on a show of cooperating to buy me more time? I mull it over as I eat in wary bites, but I'm afraid even the details that seem innocuous to me might turn out to hurt the fae of the seasons in the long run. I've already inadvertently helped this vicious king far more than I'd ever have wanted to.

As I get to the point where I'm not sure I can force myself to swallow anything else, Orion turns to me abruptly with an audible sniff and a twitch of his tail where it's curved across the platform at his side. "You're getting pretty rank," he says in an offhand tone. "You haven't had a proper wash since you got here, have you?"

Shame prickles across my face even as my hackles rise. It's not my fault the only bathroom I have access to is a public-style restroom without any bathing equipment. I've been making do the best I can wiping myself down by the sinks.

"No," I say stiffly. "I didn't know there was anywhere where I could."

Orion snaps his fingers at Madoc. "You're not so fresh yourself. Why don't you take her down to the waterfall, and you can both get the grime off you. I've got to keep some kind of standards for the company I keep." He smirks, and I can't tell how much he's actually bothered by our state of cleanliness and how much he's just enjoying badgering us about it.

Madoc seems to study his king for a moment before offering a mild smile in return. "Of course. The waterfall shouldn't be busy at this time of day."

A waterfall… down here? That doesn't make much sense. Does this mean I'm actually getting to go outside? Is Orion giving me more leeway now that he's searched my mind?

I don't dare appear too eager about the prospect in case they pick up on my ulterior motives. When Madoc motions for me to follow him, I limp along, still slowed by the ache in my foot. He glances down at my boots as we reach the tunnel. "You're sure you're all right to walk?"

"What's the alternative?" I ask. "I don't need to be carted around like I'm helpless. As long as I *can* walk, I will."

"Fair enough."

We walk through the station and into the next tunnel. A few other fae pass us. When they've moved on far enough that I can no longer hear them, Madoc speaks again, in a lower voice even softer than usual.

"How are you doing otherwise? Are you having any lingering effects from the magic Orion used on you yesterday?"

A lump rises in my throat before I can catch it. I don't like how much relief I get from the concern in his voice, from the possibility that *someone* here might give a crap what happens to me beyond my usefulness to their war. That relief doesn't do me any good.

Maybe Madoc has gone out of his way to help me settle in and understand things more than the rest of his kind, but that doesn't mean I can trust him. He's still on Orion's side.

My head and really everything except my foot and my emotions feel just fine now. "No," I say. "But it wasn't exactly enjoyable while it was happening." I hesitate. "Is he going to do it again?"

I'm not sure whether Madoc would tell me the truth even if he knew. He glances away, swiping his hand across his mouth with an uncomfortable expression. "If he thinks he needs to. I've been talking to him about it, encouraging him to give you space to open up more… naturally. Like I've said, he sees his goals so close within his grasp, and he's gotten impatient. I'll do what I can."

Which might be not much at all. I swallow thickly and resist the urge to hug myself.

I have to get out of here. If this waterfall doesn't help with that, then maybe I can find another moment to work on the air vent today. I could go in the middle of the Murk's "night" while they're sleeping. Whatever it takes, as much as my arms can handle.

Partway down another tunnel, Madoc pushes open the door on a hovel built against the wall that I took for another house. Instead, it leads to a passage that was clearly fae-made rather than human.

The cement of the walls gives way to natural rock in a winding passage that rises a little upward and then dips down again, my hopes lifting and falling with it. The air is chillier here, the few specks of artificial light that glimmer on at our movements showing me only the outline of Madoc's form a couple of steps ahead of me.

Then the passage widens abruptly with a warble of sound. Water tumbles down into a sort of trough along a stretch of wall maybe twenty feet long. Shelves carved into the opposite wall hold folded towels and bars of soap. There's a bin in the corner heaped with used towels that I guess Murk from the Refuge must launder periodically like they have my clothes.

There are a few fae standing on the dry side of the room, just finishing getting dressed. At the sight of Madoc and maybe some gesture from him I don't pick up on, they toss their towels into the bin and scurry away at once.

I tread farther into the room cautiously. Warmth wafts off the falling water, its spray almost pleasant where it flecks my skin. A drain at ankle height sucks away the water in the trough before it can get close to overflowing.

"Where does this all come from?" I ask.

"There's an underground stream," Madoc explains. "It runs alongside one of the active subway lines, close enough for the heating systems to warm the water in this area. We simply diverted it a little."

He shoots me a smile as if hoping to see I'm as pleased with that fact as he is.

I'd like it more if it wasn't just one more feature of what to me is a prison. "Definitely useful," I say, since he seems to expect a response.

"We won't be disturbed while we're here. You can take as long as you'd like. A warm soak might do your foot some good too."

Madoc says that and then kicks off his shoes. He goes through the motions so casually but quickly that I don't totally register that he's undressing until he's tugged off his socks as well and is reaching for the hem of his shirt.

I back up a step, my face flaring. "I, ah—I'd rather wash alone."

Madoc blinks at me as if it hadn't occurred to him that I'd object. "You can leave your undergarments on. I will too. It won't be any more exposed than if you were at a swimming pool."

The mention of swimming pools makes me think of the saunas in Sylas's castles—where I wore absolutely no clothes, and where I enjoyed August's company very much. Those memories make me feel more uncomfortable about this situation rather than less.

When I still don't move, Madoc's mouth forms an apologetic grimace. "I'm sorry. Orion wouldn't want you this far from the main areas of the Refuge unmonitored. I have no intention of gawking."

As if to emphasize that statement, he turns his back to me and continues stripping. I turn away from him too before I see any more skin exposed. I walk a little farther down the room, putting a good ten feet between us.

It won't be that bad, will it? I'll leave my bra and panties on like he said; I won't be anywhere near him. We'll just ignore each other and get clean, and then this will be over with. I can pretend he isn't even here.

I might not trust him, but since I've arrived here, he's never imposed on me physically, and he's had plenty of opportunities when he could have if he'd wanted to. I have to admit that even if I don't trust him in general, I can't picture the man who just apologized for the lack of privacy forcing himself on me in any way.

My nerves start to settle. I pull off my boots and take off the borrowed shirt and sweatpants. After my work on the bolts in the air vent cover, my arms look wirier than I'm used to, the thin muscles a little more defined.

Grabbing a bar of soap, I walk over to the falling water. The abrupt hiss of it to my right tells me Madoc has already stepped under it. Without glancing his way, I clamber into the trough and duck my head under the torrent.

Despite my situation and how many fears I'm holding in, there's something amazing about the rush of warm water over my mostly bare skin. It feels so comforting and almost normal. I lean into it, closing my eyes and just absorbing the heat and the soothing flow for a minute.

But I don't want to linger here very long. Wielding the soap, I scrub my face and body as quickly as I can. It gives off a light floral scent that reminds me of the summer realm with a jab of homesickness. As the bubbles are sucked away into the drain, I work more foam into my hair. I haven't been able to do much with it in the sinks, and the feeling of the strands turning squeaky clean is a relief all on its own.

Is it wrong to get any enjoyment out of this place? I have to think I need to take whatever strength I can from the few parts that aren't horrible. If having this moment makes it easier for me to focus on escape afterward, then it's working in my favor even if I'm here on Orion's orders.

As I stand in the water for several more seconds after the soap has all been washed away, Madoc's voice reaches me. "I'm glad you got to see that we do have a few luxuries here."

My eyes pop open. He's still standing several feet across the room from me, out of the water now with a towel he's rubbing over his pale hair, his back to me like before. But he must have picked up on my relaxed state one way or another.

I hadn't meant to look at him at all while he was partly undressed, but something about his comment—about the idea that even the highest Murk see something like this room as a *luxury* rather than a basic necessity, and what that says about the lives they've been forced to lead—sharpens my attention just for that moment.

The toned muscles flex all across his shoulders and back, but I don't find myself admiring them. No, the moment I focus on his body, my gaze is drawn to the flecks and lines—some white enough to stand out against his already pale skin, some a deeper pink—that mark nearly every inch of him. It takes a moment before understanding clicks in my head.

They're scars. He must have a few dozen of them just on his back and arms, which I've never seen before either thanks to the long-sleeved shirts he's always worn around me. More scars mottle his calves and knees beneath his damp boxer shorts. I'd noticed a few around his face in the past, but maybe he used to have more there too and simply put more work into healing the cuts and scratches that would be most visible when he was clothed.

The question spills out. "What *happened* to you?"

Madoc jerks around, dropping the towel to his shoulders. The folds of fabric partly cover his well-built chest, but what I can see of it has plenty of scars too, including a long, wide one that makes it look as if someone nearly carved through his ribs.

"What do you mean?" he asks, his stance tensing.

I step out of the water and feel abruptly naked. As I hurry to grab a towel of my own, I motion toward him, averting my eyes before I've stared for too long. "All those scars. How did you get them?"

It occurs to me a second later that the question is pretty personal, but I can't bring myself to care. I've been forced to have my mind wrenched right open for his king to stare at—he can forgive a few prying questions in return.

Madoc wipes the towel across his torso and grabs his shirt. "I don't see how it matters."

That answer tells me immediately that the fae of the seasons weren't responsible. If he could blame it on their cruelty, he would have in an instant.

My mind trips back to the conversation I had with the Murk woman at the food table this morning.

"I heard that Orion put you through a lot when you were working your way up to being one of his main 'knights'," I say. "What exactly did he do to you? Is *that* where the scars came from?"

"I said it doesn't matter," Madoc replies, the hoarseness in his voice thickening.

I wrap the towel around myself like a dress, covering me from my chest to my knees, and turn to face him. "It matters to me. You want me to support him and his war. You want me to help all the fae here. How am I supposed to trust you if you're going to clam up the second I ask anything hard?"

Madoc glowers at me in his shirt and boxers. It's the first time I've seen him aim any negative emotion my way since our first conversation when I woke up in the Refuge. My back stiffens, but then he's glancing away. A ragged sigh slips out of him.

He drags his gaze back to me, crossing his arms. "It wasn't anything all that unusual. Orion tests the loyalty of anyone who wants to play a larger role at his side. You've already seen that."

"And testing your loyalty meant cutting you up all over your body?"

"I tried too young," Madoc says. "I didn't know what I was doing, and I had to be taken down a peg more than once. They needed to be sure of me. But I could have left any time I decided to. I didn't have to take on the dangerous jobs, or put up with being shoved around, or fight when I was called on to. I *wanted* to, so that he'd see I was stronger than all of that."

"And you really think that's okay?" I demand. "To beat up on—what—a teenager? To send you off to get hurt, just because he could? He probably laughed the whole time, watching you take it. He made you *kill* someone like he did with Bren the other day, didn't he? Rip apart another Murk, just because he likes seeing people being torn to pieces."

Madoc's eyes flash. "You want to talk about enjoying ripping people apart? Do you know why I was fending for myself like that at all? What you'd see if you found my chair in the vault of memories? The fae of the Mists you still want to protect, that you seem to think are somehow better than the man you're complaining about—a squad of the raven shifters tore my *parents* to pieces."

My frustration flames out. "What?"

He turns away, raking his hand through his hair, but the pain is clear in his voice. "All we were doing was living on the fringes of the Mists. It wasn't easy—there wasn't much food to scavenge and there were beasts to fend off—but it was nice being a bit nearer to the Heart. My parents could use a little magic. I remember being able to feel it, distant but… *there*."

The hint of awe in his tone at the memory makes my own heart squeeze. He misses it, even with the monstrous Heart that Orion has created right here.

"And then one day my parents came running," Madoc goes on. "A sentry had spotted them—a squad of Unseelie was on the way. We ran for the portals, but there wasn't enough time. I watched one of the ravens chop my father's head right off his body and ram it into a tree branch like a trophy. My mother managed to push me through to the human world a second before they caught her too. The way she screamed…"

My stomach lurches. I can picture the scene far too clearly. My voice comes out thin. "I'm sorry."

Madoc just shrugs. "I'm lucky they didn't kill me too. I had no idea where I was, and I was a child and all tangled up in fear and guilt over leaving my parents—I stumbled into a carnival that was going on in with all kinds of humans around. If the ravens came looking for me there, I was lucky that a Murk who was passing by happened to notice me first. She brought me to the orphanage. I stayed there until I was old enough that I could convince them to let me leave, and then I traveled straight here. I'd heard about Orion and what he was trying to do. I wanted to be part of it."

Silence falls between us. I don't know what to say. I'm aching from throat to gut, and Madoc doesn't look as if he's feeling much better.

How much of that did he even want to tell me? He's avoided mentioning it before.

"I've never denied that the Seelie and the Unseelie can be awful,"

I say finally. "That doesn't mean I can't hate seeing Orion treat you or the other Murk awfully too."

"It isn't all awful," Madoc says. "You know that. And it'll be amazing when we've seen his plans through. There always has to be some sacrifice along the way."

"But… this much?"

"What exactly would you have me do differently?" he demands. "Walk away? I spent decades proving myself—what the hell was the point in enduring all that if I'm only going to toss the reward aside?"

I pause and then venture, "It just doesn't always seem to me like getting to stand beside him is such a reward."

We stare at each other for a long moment. Madoc is the one who breaks away first.

"Get dressed," he says brusquely, reaching for his pants. "We should get you back to the Refuge, where you'll find there are hundreds of fae who're a lot better off having Orion ruling over them than we ever were before."

CHAPTER TWENTY

Corwin

The Hall of the Heart isn't exactly where I want to be right now, while each passing hour without any sense or news of my mate weighs heavier on me. But the rest of life in the winter realm goes on even if I wish I could pause it.

And some of that life is ending.

"We've lost four to the curse since your mate vanished, with two more fading away as we speak," Laoni says, her hands braced on the top of the gleaming marble table. I wonder if the others can guess at the full reason for the glimmer of panic in the back of her eyes. "It's only coming on faster."

"It should taper off some once—once those who are undergoing it for the second or third time are no longer included in that number," Terisse points out, but she sounds pained. None of us want to think about those who got their second chance succumbing to the curse after all… least of all Laoni.

Uzziah frowns. "If we settle the matter within the next few weeks, it shouldn't come to that. Have you had no contact with your mate through your bond still, Corwin?"

"None," I say, with the jab of anguish that comes with the admission. I'd never tell them that Whitt has, but we haven't learned anything useful that way regardless. "You can be sure we've tried every other strategy we can think of to track down the Murk responsible. I actually have a proposal to make that might speed up that process."

Laoni raps her knuckles on the table. "Well, then, let's have it."

She wouldn't be so eager if she knew what I was going to suggest.

I prepare myself for the arguments I expect to come. "Talia was stolen on Seelie land. It seems most likely that her captors would have gone for the nearest portals to escape into the human world. One of Arch-Lord Sylas's cadre-chosen and I have made discoveries about the sort of magic the Murk have been using to cover their presence, but it's very subtle. Still, it may be able to lead us to the area where they left the Mists—and where their new spies are traveling from."

"Excellent," Uzziah says. "What are we waiting for then?"

I draw myself up a little straighter. "I think our best chance is to combine forces with the Seelie. A large squadron of our strongest sentries and soldiers alongside theirs, searching the fringelands and collaborating with our magic to draw out the traces of the Murk's passage. Sylas and I could oversee it together. We'd only need whatever manpower you can provide."

Laoni's lips twist as I suspected they would. "We send our people over to their realm to make up for their failings?"

I fix her with a hard stare. I'm past the point of being intimidated by her disapproval. "Laying blame is less important than recovering Talia, wouldn't you say?"

"It's not so much the laying of blame." Her hand clenches and then flexes as she forces her fingers to uncurl. "You know I want to see our people healed. But we can't sacrifice their future safety either. I'm only concerned about the precedent it might set—that the Seelie will feel we'll be at their beck and call in other situations as well."

"There must be ways to mitigate that risk," Uzziah says.

Terisse's head droops, her expression clouded. I can't tell what she thinks of any of this.

"I don't think it's risk at all," I say. "The Seelie understand as well as we do that these are extreme and unexpected circumstances. Is this an urgent matter or not? Coming up with vows or whatever else to try to offset any possible future entitlement will only delay our chances of success—and give the Murk more time to switch up their strategies."

Neve stirs at the far end of the table. It's never clear how much she's listening to these discussions, but her voice rings out perfectly clear if dry. "We must protect our people now. We've managed to find peace with the Seelie. I don't see why we shouldn't work with them on this. I agree."

I offer her a quick smile, but Laoni is shifting her weight on her feet. "I'm not saying we *shouldn't* do it. I only want to be sure we don't commit to more than we're comfortable with."

I will the edge out of my tone. "We won't be committing to anything. It'll be a one-time operation, albeit on a large scale. This is the time when we need to decide what really matters. You've balked at and challenged the alliance with the summer realm plenty of times." I glance around the table at all three of my colleagues who've contributed to those challenges. "You've gone as far as deceiving our people to try to prove your point. None of that has exposed any true problems. Hasn't this resistance gone on long enough? Now our entire realm is threatened by your reluctance."

Laoni's eyes flash, but Terisse's shoulder's stiffen. Maybe she's thinking, like I was, of the moment during my confirmation ceremony with Talia when she pretended to be cursed. She speaks before Laoni can.

"Corwin is right. We've stretched out the conflict so long, and maybe that's why we lost the cure in the first place. Perhaps if we'd been more coordinated before, Lady Talia would have been better protected that night. If the Seelie will work alongside us, then I say we take all the help we can get."

She glances at me then with a look I think I can read an apology in, and my heart lifts just a little despite all that's weighing on it.

Uzziah lets out a huff, but he can't seem to find any argument to offer the three of us. And we could carry the majority if we wanted anyway. "All right," he says after another pause. "If we're going to do it, we should get on with it and make this happen now."

Laoni's lips have flattened, but then her shoulders come down. She looks more defeated than accepting as she nods to me. "So be it. I have people adept at seeking spells whom I can ask to join the effort. Are there any other sorts of magical affinity that would be helpful?"

At least she's asking practical questions now that she's done balking at the idea. "Yes," I say. "The Murk's primary method of disguise seems to involve a reflective element. Skill with detecting illusions or rebounded light would be particularly welcome."

Terisse snaps her fingers, the clouds that appeared to be hanging over before having departed with her newfound conviction. "I have just the man who'd be an excellent addition. Shall we all confer with our flocks and then send along those who'll be participating?"

Everything's proceeding faster than I'd dared to hope, but I can't complain about that. "I want to put word out to the nearest flocks as well so we can gather as large a group as possible, and I'll need to inform Arch-Lord Sylas so he can do the same, but we do want to act quickly. Have your people head to Heart's Cadence within the next two hours. We'll set off then."

We disperse from the Hall, my steps toward my palace much lighter than they were entering. Zelpha and Verik join me before I've made it halfway there.

"We're going ahead," I say before they need to ask. "I'll see to our own flock folk. You and the others reach out to any nearby domains you think will contribute."

Zelpha's lips curl with a tense smile. "I'd imagine they all will, if it's toward bringing Lady Talia back. And we *will* bring her back." She gives my arm a companionable bump with her elbow that's the most reassurance she can offer while maintaining her professional demeanor in public view. Then the two of them leap from the ground in raven form.

By the time the two hours I asked for is up, I've gathered two dozen of the most adept magic-users from my own flock, and a couple hundred fae from other flocks have assembled around the palace. They've already been at work conjuring carriages.

I leap into my own carriage, Verik and half of my flock folk accompanying me in that one, and motion to the others. "Follow my route. We'll meet up with the Seelie forces on the other side of the border and head to the fringelands as swiftly as we're able to."

On the summer side, the warm air washes over me with a rush of leafy scents I'm coming to appreciate. Sylas is waiting with his own squadron of wooden carriages, containing nearly twice as many fae as I'm bringing. Whitt stands by his side. We exchange quick nods of encouragement and set off without another word. There's no argument between the three of us about how urgent this mission is, both for our people and for ourselves.

Taking in all the vehicles soaring across the summery landscape, a little more hope blooms in my chest. With all of us put to the task, combining our talents, surely we'll get closer to rescuing the woman we lost.

I just have to try not to focus on worrying about what state we'll find her in when we do. I will not be crippled by my grief. I'll take all the love I have for my mate and turn it into the strength to get her back.

During the journey to the fringelands, my coterie and I take to raven form to fly from carriage to carriage and make sure all of the fae with us are clear on our strategy. All the gazes that meet mine are bright with determination. I may feel the loss of my mate deeply, but I'm not alone in missing her.

The weather grows hotter and muggier as we near the hazy forests at the very edge of the Mists, the opposite of what we'd face on the winter side. The heat turns my stomach, and many of my fellow Unseelie look uncomfortable, but no one complains. I pass on the suggestion to adjust the warming charms on our clothes to cooling ones, which eases the discomfort a little.

Deep within the fringe forests, where the portals glimmer with their dark sheen here and there just up ahead, we halt the carriages and disembark. Normally even when we've assembled together, the summer and winter fae have kept to their own kind. Now, Sylas urges everyone to mingle.

"We want to make full use of our varied skills," he says. "We can't fully collaborate if we're still keeping ourselves separate."

I step up beside him to show I'll be working closely with my own Seelie counterpart. After a few hesitant murmurs, the two groups of fae merge, until it's hard to pick out who's wolf and who's raven at a glance. Then we set off.

Sylas and I chant the first spells, and the others raise their voices to match ours. The Heart's reach is thinner here, but between all of us, magic thrums through the air. It ripples over my skin and across the landscape. I walk slowly amid the crowd, every sense alert for the slightest hint of one of the lingering spells we're scanning for.

We're starting the search with a relatively small area to condense the power of our efforts. When one stretch of forest turns up nothing, we move on, continuing our chant. Sweat beads on my face and trickles down my back, but I ignore it.

The first shout comes after perhaps half an hour. There's a trace of a shadowy illusion at the base of one tree, with an odd quaver to the magical energy that sits uneasily with me. We mark that spot and tramp onward. My spirits are lifting, but one hint isn't enough to be sure it's more than random chance.

Then another call rises up, and another, and I taste a prickle on my tongue that leads me to the faintest glimmer where a few beams of sun seep through the fog. We mark all of those as well. Then, across a few more miles, we find nothing.

Sylas calls a halt to the search and tells everyone to refresh themselves with the drinks and food we're all carrying. He turns to me, his expression both pleased and serious.

"It's still a somewhat large span, especially considering how the portals shift around."

"It is." I inhale slowly, and a small smile crosses my lips. "But we've narrowed it down. More than one of the Murk have passed through that stretch, and none nearby elsewhere. Many of them must be coming through one of the portals in that general area. At least now we have a starting point instead of wandering the human world aimlessly."

"Indeed." Sylas looks toward the portals. "Now the real search can begin."

CHAPTER TWENTY-ONE

Talia

Silky sheets slide across my limbs. They feel like a warm breeze licking over my skin.

I roll over on the bed, and Corwin is there beside me. He slips his arm around my waist and tugs me to him, love shining in his dark eyes.

My heart swells with joy and longing. I hug him to me, abruptly choked up.

He's here. My soul-twined mate, with me again. It's been so long. I started to wonder if I'd *ever*—

The thought shivers up from some distant part of me that this doesn't make sense. How *can* I be with him? Where even are we? There was— I'd been—

The doubts wash away with another rush of warmth and a deeper longing. I can't focus on anything except the hunger to get closer to the man I'm lying next to.

The same desire echoes into me from Corwin. He grasps the sides of my face and pulls me into a kiss.

Our lips meld together, our tongues tangling, and heat flares low in my belly. I want to be with him in every possible way, to feel him around me and inside me, to have him flood my body with all the amazing sensations I know he can bring.

As if in answer, Corwin wrenches down the sheets. I'm nearly naked underneath, only my panties on. He dips his head to suck one of my nipples into his mouth, and the pleasure I was seeking rushes through me. I press my head into the pillow with a gasp.

He works me over with strokes of his tongue that draw the tip of my breast to a hardened peak and squeezes my other nipple between his fingers. Giddy sparks shoot through me straight to my sex. I squirm against him, whimpering, eager for more.

"Please," I mumble. "Please."

With an urgent noise, Corwin pushes up to kiss me hard on the mouth. At the same time, he yanks at my panties. They whip off me with a snap of torn fabric. Then the hard length of him is pressing against me. I lift toward him, bliss throbbing through my core where he's rubbing against my slickness, encouraging him on. An instant later, he's thrusting right into me, stretching me, filling me.

I'm so wet already that he slides in deep with a burn that's nothing but welcome. A moan escapes my lips. I buck to meet his thrusts, claiming every ounce of pleasure he can bring to my body. We're here in this together, passion searing between us, and nothing will ever break us apart again.

My release comes with such force that I shudder and cry out, my back bowing up against the sheets. As Corwin reaches his peak with a stuttered breath, three more figures gather around us.

All my mates have come to me. Sylas's mismatched gaze raises more heat as it travels over my naked curves. Whitt licks his lips, which have curved into a wicked grin. August's strong hands descend to pull my face to his.

In a matter of moments, I'm lost between them, kissing one and then another, arching into their caresses, more whimpers and gasps tumbling out of my mouth. Whitt enters me with one quick thrust while Sylas works me over from behind to prepare my other opening. August fondles my breasts. It's all so much I can barely catch my breath.

Bliss rolls over my body in waves. I writhe between them, tipping over the peak only to be tossed up toward it again, soaring higher and higher with every burst of heady delight—

And then a raucous laugh rips through the haze of pleasure. I flinch, and my eyes snap open. The cocoon of passion and love I was wrapped in an instant ago vanishes, though my body is still throbbing with desire.

The sight around me snuffs out any lingering hunger like a bucket of icy water dumped over my head. I'm lying on my side at the edge of Orion's dais, the erratic orange light of the Murk's Heart wavering over me. A small crowd of fae has gathered in the throne room around the platform, all their eyes fixed on me. Many are leering, several are chuckling. It's one of them whose laugh woke me up.

From a dream. My hands drop to my sides, with a surge of relief to confirm that unlike in that dream, I'm fully dressed. But I— Did I fall asleep here?

My head feels muddled—I don't remember the last moments before I drifted off. It's hard to imagine being relaxed enough to doze off here. Did Orion carry me from my house… to put me on display…

As I push myself into a sitting position, my heart beating wildly, the king steps up beside me. He grins down at me with a twinkle of vicious amusement in his yellow eyes. "Thank you for that lovely performance, my pet. My people have found it very entertaining—and provoking."

Performance? Provoking?

A few of the watching fae make gestures that mimic sex, and my stomach plummets even as scorching heat shoots to my cheeks. There's nothing lustful in that heat now, only shame.

I might not be naked, but I must have been making some of the sounds from my dream in reality, maybe even moving my body without realizing it. And they all watched…

"I—I—" I stammer, but I don't know what to say. My face burns even hotter. I pull my legs up in front of me as if to shield me from all those stares.

"All right," Orion calls out. "The show's over. Get back to work—or if you haven't got work to do, maybe you'll be inspired to enjoy each other as much as my pet enjoyed her dream."

The fae around the room start to turn, drifting toward the entrance, but their leaving doesn't give me much relief. A shiver wracks my body.

Orion crouches next to me, still with a sharp smile on his face, and speaks low enough that no one else will be able to hear. "Nothing in your mind is safe from me. This is only one of many demonstrations I could offer."

I cringe away from him and bump into the legs of someone who's come up at my other side.

"I think she's gotten the message," Madoc says, his voice casual but with a thread of tension running through it. "Maybe we should let her get some proper rest now?"

Orion straightens up and waves his hand dismissively. "Do what you like with her. I've had my fun. For now."

He saunters away with his tail swinging as if I'm a toy he's done playing with. I can't contain another tremor that races through me.

Madoc peers down at me, a frown tugging at his mouth. *He* saw all that too. He saw me moaning and squirming with desire in my sleep…

Another rush of embarrassment nearly suffocates me. I rub my hands over my face. I just want to curl up into a ball tiny enough to drop through a crack in the floor and never be seen again.

But that's not an option. Madoc waits without speaking as I gather myself. Part of me wants to ask just how bad it was, how much of the dream I acted out in front of the audience of Murk, but I can't bring myself to even mention the topic with him.

He probably thinks it's awful that I'd still want my mates at all, even in a dream, after everything I've seen and heard about the fae of the seasons.

Slowly, I pick myself to my feet and limp alongside him toward the door. I'm not sleepy—and from the glow of the magical lights, it seems to be daytime by Murk standards—but my sense of time has been upended. Still, I'm exhausted in a way that has nothing to do with wanting sleep. The uncertainty and fear I've been living with, amplified over the past few days, has been wearing away at my inner strength. I hate how weak I feel.

"No one will remember it in a day or two," Madoc says in an obvious attempt at being reassuring. "They don't really care. It was just Orion wanting to remind everyone of his power."

"Especially me," I mutter.

Madoc pauses as we come out into the tunnel. The fae who watched my humiliation have totally dispersed—there's no one nearby. He ducks his head. "It was a horrible way to do it. Do you need anything? Food, or something to distract you?"

The fact that he's trying to help in his hesitant way only makes me feel worse. He *can't* do anything for me. Would he even want to try anything that would actually get me out of this nightmare when it'd bring Orion's rage down on him—destroy everything he went through so much already to gain? I doubt it.

It's probably a risk even admitting he doesn't agree with his king's tactics.

I glance up at him, a strange mix of affection and anger twisting in my chest. I'm glad he's at least trying and frustrated that he won't do more all at the same time. He offers me a pained smile, which brightens the planes of his not-at-all-unpleasant face just a little, and an even more horrifying thought strikes me.

If Orion can peer inside my head and manipulate my dreams, what else could he compel me to think? To feel? To *do*? He'd probably delight in the idea of forcing me to betray my mates with one of his inner circle—or maybe even with himself?

My skin crawls at the idea. I step a little farther away from Madoc. I don't know if there's any real chance of what I've just imagined happening, but even considering it is making me jumpy. I don't want to be near any of them right now.

"I think—I think I just need to walk a bit and clear my head," I say. "On my own."

Madoc opens his mouth as if to say something and then closes it again. After a moment, he nods. "Of course. If there is anything I can do, just seek me out."

At the nearest station, he moves away from me to speak to a few of the fae carrying boxes through a doorway. My gaze lingers on the entrance for a moment, my memories stirring.

I have to get out of here before I find out just how far Orion is willing to go. Is there a way I haven't tried yet that would be even easier than the air vent?

As innocently as I can manage, I wander around in the other direction and head toward the far end of the Refuge where the maintenance room is.

As I step into the final tunnel, voices ahead of me catch my ears. I creep closer, staying close to the wall. A glimmer of light illuminates a fae face for just a moment before the three shadowy figures at the far end of the tunnel vanish.

I wait a few minutes to be sure they're really gone and that no one else is coming, and then slink over to check the end of the tunnel. There *is* a doorway there, one I thought was just part of the tiled wall that closes off this section of the Refuge. When I run my fingers over the grout, I can now feel a thin seam around one chunk of them that must open up.

But it won't open for me, no matter how I press and pry at it. I can't get any grip with my fingers at all. Even if I could, it's most likely sealed with magic as well.

Hugging myself, I step back before anyone can come through or otherwise stumble on me tugging at it. Orion might enjoy terrorizing me, but that doesn't mean he'd want to know I've gotten so desperate I'm trying to leave. How would he punish me for that infraction?

I can't just stand around doing nothing, though. My restlessness drives me over to the air vent. But as I scramble up onto the machine beneath it, I catch a rustling sound somewhere nearby.

I freeze, my pulse hitching. The rustling comes again—not so close I'm worried anyone's seen me, but it could be right near the entrance to the room. A Murk in rat form patrolling the borders of the Refuge?

Hell, it might even be a normal, not-at-all-fae rat, not that I'd be able to tell the difference.

I crouch by the machine for several minutes, but the rustling continues. It starts to get a little louder, coming this way. If it is a sentry, what will they think of me hanging around here? How closely might they examine this place if they suspect I have a special interest in it?

Gritting my teeth in frustration, I push away from the machine and meander back to the tunnel.

Isn't there *anything* I can do to get closer to escape? With every passing minute, the darkness feels more constricting, the air thinner. My heart is still beating fast, and sweat is forming beneath my shirt even though I'm far from hot.

I limp onward, desperation nipping at my heels. If I could even just get a few seconds when I was sure I was completely alone, that no one would hear me…

Halfway down the next tunnel over, I pass a workshop room that's currently unused. The furnace is still running, its crackling thrum filling the room. A smoky, metallic scent trickles into my lungs, but a flicker of hope rises up at the same time.

I dart into the room and squeeze behind the furnace where I can't be seen from the tunnel and where I can hope its noise will cover any hint of my voice even to fae ears. There's no one nearby right now, but someone might come along at any moment. I have to be fast.

I cup my hands over my mouth, picture Whitt's bright eyes, and whisper, "*Wye-con-ell,*" with all the hope and anguish in me.

An ache opens up down the center of my skull, but a glimmer of my mate's presence catches in my awareness at the same time. *Whitt,* I think at him, ignoring the quickly building pain. *Whitt, hear me. Speak to me.*

His voice carries to me from so very far away. *Talia! We're trying — —think we've narrowed— Are you—*

The connection I've been able to forge is so tenuous his words are already fragmenting. I have no idea how clearly he'll be able to hear me. *I'm trying to find a way to escape. Still no clues about where I am. Be careful. The Murk have a Heart. They have so much more magic than we thought. I—*

Anything else I'd have conveyed to him is lost in a sharper sear of agony that feels as if my scalp is literally peeling away from my skull. A choked gasp breaks from my throat. I drop my head, pressing the heels of my hands to my forehead.

Whitt's voice and any sense of him I had vanish. There's nothing in my head but a thrashing pain. It's all I can do to hold back a sob.

Tears trickle from my eyes anyway. Even this physical distress isn't enough to drown out the anguish swelling through me.

Did I manage to tell him anything useful at all? Why couldn't my magical abilities be just a *little* stronger?

I wrap my arms around my knees and bury my face against them, my tears soaking into my pants. I don't know what to do. I don't know how to get out of here.

What if I never can?

CHAPTER TWENTY-TWO

Whitt

Talia's voice quavers through my mind, splintering and fading in and out despite my best efforts to hold it in focus. *—trying to find— —no clues about where— Be careful. —a heart. They have so much—*

And then she's gone, with a jolt of agony that radiates from her into me, lingering even after I've lost any hint of her.

My fingers clench against the map I'd spread on my desk as if I can catch her and pull her back to me. An even deeper anguish digs into my gut.

So much urgency and turmoil reached me even in that brief, frail connection. She was upset, maybe even desperate. And I don't even know what it is she was trying to tell me.

I slam both my fists down on the desk, my frustration cracking the outward nonchalance I've gotten so adept at putting on. In the privacy of my study, it hardly matters, although I'd have teased August about such a show of temper. My fangs have leapt from my gums, as if there's anything in front of me I can tear apart to save my mate.

All I have are the same books and scrolls and other bits of aged paper I had before.

I glare down at the specific piece of aged paper spread out in front of me, the map I was studying when Talia called on my true name. It isn't giving me answers anywhere near quickly enough.

With a combination of magic and ink, the map holds as accurate a record as we can maintain of the main portals to the human world from the Mists. Of course, those portals do move around some and so need frequent updating, and minor ones regularly emerge into being or vanish. It's a partial picture at best.

Still, I've been making note of the most longstanding portals in the area where Corwin and Sylas found consistent traces of Murk presence along the fringes and comparing them to our sentries' observations from the human lands on the other side to see if any place jumps out as a hotbed of rat activity. The pests are likely to be less careful in the human world, where most of those around them can be easily deceived.

So far I haven't found any evidence from past reports that would make one spot or another seem like a particularly good target to focus on, though.

We have other sentries investigating every portal currently there in the meantime, not to mention stalking through those distant woods hoping to catch one of the vermin on their way through. We've worked out traps that should be sprung by the magic they're typically using. But there's no way of knowing if it'll be enough.

And Talia may be running out of time. What are the blasted vermin putting her through?

I scan several more pages of old notes and then shove back my chair with a sigh and the start of a headache prickling at my temples.

Is there something better I could be doing with my time? The part of me most aware of my role as Sylas's cadre-chosen nags that I should be making more plans for how we'll deal with the curse when the full moon arrives in less than a week's time, but to the rest of me, that feels like defeat. Like acknowledging that there's no way we'll have brought Talia home before then.

How can the mangy rats have gotten the better of us so thoroughly?

I'm about to go out so I can meet the most recent sentries as soon as they return from the fringelands when one of the castle attendants knocks on my study door. When I open it, he cringes a bit, and I school my expression into something less fierce. It won't do any good going around looking as if everyone I encounter is a rat I'm planning to eviscerate.

"My apologies for interrupting," the attendant says quickly. "One of Lord Tristan's cadre-chosen wishes to speak with you. She's waiting outside."

She is, is she? My senses automatically go on high alert. Tristan only has one female cadre-chosen, that woman named Jax, and I haven't been happy about their odd but not explicitly imposing activities near our domain either. What does she want with me specifically, and why now?

"Thank you," I say with a brisk nod, and go down to find out.

Jax is indeed standing several paces from the castle's front door, her toned frame clothed in a casual but form-fitting dress that seems more appropriate for a revel than a business call. She flicks her black hair over her shoulder and fixes her heavy-lidded eyes on me with a small, sly smile that raises my hackles.

Why is she looking at me as if we're in on some kind of secret together when I've barely spoken to her before today?

"Whitt," she says smoothly. "I'm glad you were able to meet with me on such short notice."

"If there's trouble or a new development involving the Murk, I'd want to hear about it at once," I say, keeping my tone coolly polite. "What is this about?"

"Walk with me, and I'll explain."

I'd rather she spit it out right here, but I do have to maintain more decorum than saying as much. She's probably enjoying the thought that she'll irritate me by drawing out her report. So I'll just have to irritate her right back by showing as little annoyance as possible.

She walks toward the woods that lead to the edge of the hill—

toward the small outpost she and a few of her pack-kin have set up on the unclaimed land beyond Hearth-by-the-Heart. She doesn't expect me to go all the way down there with her just to find out what she wants, does she?

I keep pace with her, taking no pleasure from the bright mid-morning sun. "Feel free to begin explaining at any time."

"To be honest," she says, "I'm mostly concerned about you. You've been running yourself ragged over these past several days, haven't you?"

As we step into the shadows of the forest, I shoot her a puzzled look. "Of course I've been working hard. My mate has been stolen by the blasted Murk, who pose who knows how many other threats to the rest of us as well. It'd hardly make sense for me to be taking it easy."

One corner of her lips curls upward as if she finds my statement amusing. Abruptly, I find I *would* like to eviscerate her, rat or not.

She speaks smoothly but lightly. "And is your lord working himself quite as hard as you, or is he leaning on you to do the heavy lifting, as lords so often do? Not that I'm speaking from experience or anything."

Her wry tone implies the opposite. Is she suggesting she's unhappy with Tristan's leadership? Perhaps this unexpected overture will be useful to us after all, if she's going to reveal something that he wouldn't want us knowing.

I'm not going to besmirch Sylas to draw her out, though. "I'm quite satisfied with my pack's leadership," I say evenly. "But I'm sure such situations do arise in other packs more often than is ideal."

"I'm glad to hear you haven't encountered that problem yourself. I've often thought it must be difficult for you, being so close to true-blooded and yet reduced to little more than a servant simply because of a younger brother's birth." She tsks her tongue.

It takes a concentrated effort to hold in my wince at her words. The rancor I've felt in the past toward Sylas has faded a great deal since we've gotten any misunderstandings and missteps between us out in the open, but she isn't wrong to have guessed at it. I suppose it isn't *difficult* to guess, though. Most fae in the same position would probably have resented it more than I did, considering I have very little interest in taking on Sylas's responsibilities anyway.

I shrug. "It leaves me more time for revelling and requires less stern adherence to duty, which suits me just fine. I'd hate to see what chaos any pack I ran would end up falling into."

Jax lets out a soft laugh and pats my arm, her hand lingering by my elbow just long enough for a renewed sense of uneasiness to wash over me. She isn't trying to lead up to any confession about her own feelings with this line of conversation—her family isn't high enough that she could ever have had a lordship in her sights. I can see how far she is from true-blooded in the shell of her ears, only slightly more pointed than August's human-like ones.

"I suspect you sell yourself short," she says. "I've seen how well your pack responds to you. They're at least as much yours as Sylas's."

I don't like the direction she's heading in at all now. "Is that all you brought me out here for?" I ask. "To compliment my rapport with my pack-kin?"

Jax stops in a small clearing, turning toward me as I stop with her. She touches my arm again, letting her fingers rest on my wrist as she peers up at me through her eyelashes. "I came to speak to you out of a fellow cadre-chosen's concern and the respect I've formed for you across our dealings with your pack. I didn't think you'd want to admit to any difficulties with your pack-kin around, but we all need our chances to shed the pressures on us and enjoy a little escape."

She reaches into the folds of her skirt and draws out a small bottle. "I gather you're a particular fan of absinthe. We got quite a fine vintage brought in not long ago—consider it a gift and a recognition of your worth."

As I stare at the bottle in her hand, I can't stop my spine from going rigid. Bile has risen in my throat. Images of another woman in a different forest crash through my thoughts, scattering every impulse but the urge to destroy the threat in front of me as quickly and thoroughly as I can.

It isn't my worth or respect she's focused on. The scheming woman is trying to *seduce* me. Like Isleen, with the flirty touches and the wine—is it only absinthe in that bottle or did Jax think she could blot out my self-control just like that snake of a—

My claws and fangs have already sprung free before I get a hold of myself enough to realize how I'm reacting. I catch myself just shy of lunging for Jax's throat—and not with a love bite. The only lust her overtures have stirred up is a desire to see her dead and strewn across the forest floor.

That can't be the reaction she was hoping to provoke, I realize. I cough and step back, trying to cover the rage that's still searing through my veins. She can't have any idea what happened between Isleen and me, let alone how the encounter ate at me and nearly destroyed my relationship with both my brothers and the woman I love. She's simply using common tactics toward a goal she doesn't know has already been accomplished in a much more dire way.

That may very well be only regular absinthe in that bottle. She may simply have hoped to shatter my faithfulness to my mate.

But the shame and fury over that encounter with Isleen haven't totally healed, I can see now. I'm still itching to gut the woman in front of me for even suggesting I betray Talia like that. I drag in a breath, forcing more of the vitriol in me down.

Lashing out at Jax might not have been the response she was expecting, but it could have harmed me and my pack even more than if I'd succumbed to her advances. The cadre-chosen of an arch-lord's pack savaging that of another lord over offering him a beverage? Imagine all the concerns about my stability and unfairly hostile intentions toward Tristan's pack he could raise.

She has no idea how close she came to unraveling me in entirely the wrong way.

"I appreciate your offer," I say, managing to clear all but a little gruffness from my voice. "I'm afraid I can't indulge right now, as I'm keeping my head as clear as possible given the current threat."

Jax peers at me, no doubt picking up on some trace of my intense reaction and puzzling over it. She twirls the bottle between her fingers. "Well, it's a gift for whenever you'd want to enjoy it. Take it with you, and I hope you'll find yourself a moment to relax before too long."

She hands the bottle to me, so I take it. Then she taps my chest. "If you should feel you'd like to talk to someone with no ties to your own pack, I'll be just down the hill tonight."

I doubt she imagines I'm likely to take her up on *that* offer after the way I just recoiled, but perhaps she feels she has to make the attempt just in case. I give her a brief nod, and she saunters away with a sway of her hips designed to draw the eye.

As I head back toward the castle, the last shreds of my horrified rage subsiding, a deeper discomfort wraps around my gut.

Why did she come to me and make this proposition *now*? Is it random, or is there something in particular she'd be aiming to achieve with the timing?

Sylas and August are home at the moment, getting fae from our pack and others organized for another search effort, but both of them planned to make excursions later in the day that would take them away from the domain until well into tomorrow. Astrid has already gone to supervise our sentries traveling around and out of the fringelands. Tonight, for the first time since Talia's disappearance, I'd be the only member of the cadre present at Hearth-by-the-Heart.

How interesting that Tristan's cadre-chosen seemed intent on distracting me at this precise moment.

Even as my stomach twists uneasily, my thoughts sharpen at the sense of a scheme. I spring forward into wolf form and lope off to inform my lord of this ominous development while we still have time to respond.

CHAPTER TWENTY-THREE

Talia

When the ache in my head eases back enough that I can move without falling over, I make my slow, wobbly way back to the station that holds my hovel. As I pull myself onto the platform near it, a couple of Murk amble by. They shoot me a quick glance and chuckle to themselves, their tails twitching with amusement.

My stomach sinks. I can guess pretty easily what they find funny. Even if those two didn't witness my humiliation earlier today, the fae who did have probably passed on the story all through the Refuge by now.

I glance around the station and catch several more piercing glances, some of which jerk away when I notice them, others that linger for a few seconds in what's close to a leer. My gut knots even more. I crawl into my "house" and huddle there, waiting for more of the ache in my skull to subside.

I haven't eaten anything yet today. After a while, my head starts to spin more than throb, and my stomach pinches with enough hunger to cut through my other discomforts. I grit my teeth and head over to the meal table.

The two fae who've just brought a fresh load of food aren't ones I've spoken to before. The woman sees me coming and arches her eyebrows with a hint of a sneer to her lips. She mutters something to the man, who glances over and grins in a way that makes me want to run right back to my hovel.

I grab a few items that are the easiest to carry and hustle away without a word. One of the Murk on the tracks brushes close to me, murmuring, "Maybe you could dream about me sometime."

I don't answer, dashing the rest of the way to my house. Inside, I pull the door flap tightly shut and crouch against one hard plastic wall. I have to force down the dumplings and pear I grabbed, and my stomach doesn't feel much better afterward.

Simply lying there doesn't help me relax. My whole body may as well be a live wire. Nervous energy thrums through it, sparking occasional fresh bursts of pain in my head.

The small space starts to feel suffocating. I don't know what's going on outside, what new horror could be descending on me.

I ease back the flap just a bit and watch the fae passing by outside. Seeing them doesn't exactly reassure me, but it takes the edge off my panic.

What am I going to do if I can't get into the air vent in time? Are there any other escape routes I might not have noticed? I'm not sure how to find that out, though. It'll look suspicious if I start poking around at the walls and structures here more than I already have.

As I'm mulling that problem over, Madoc's familiar form comes into view. He's picked up a tortilla wrap from the table, and he's walking along the tracks past me as he swallows his first bite.

I'm momentarily torn in two directions, but trying *something* seems better than staying shut away in here doing nothing. I push myself out of the hovel and hobble over to catch up with him.

"Madoc!" I call, careful not to pitch my voice too loud. I don't really want to draw anyone else's attention if I can help it.

He glances over and stops so I can catch up. My frayed state must show more than I realize, because he frowns, his brow knitting with concern. "Are you all right, Talia?" His gaze darts through the station, mainly in the direction of the throne room. "He hasn't—"

"Nothing else has happened," I say quickly. Nothing worth mentioning, anyway. I fall into step with him, and he continues on toward the tunnel, keeping a slower pace to account for my limp. "I just—I was wondering, are there many other little side passages and rooms in the Refuge like that one you have?" Maybe one of those would have some kind of vent or crevice a slim human woman could fit into that's escaped Orion's consideration.

Madoc nods, his expression still worried. "A few, here and there. Why do you ask?"

"I—" I need a good excuse. A couple of Murk pass us as we enter the shadows of the tunnel, and their smirks provide enough inspiration. "I was just feeling like I need to get away from everyone here for a little while. Farther away than just in my house. Maybe it sounds silly, but—"

"No," Madoc says, in the gentle tone that always surprises me a little even though his hoarse voice falls into it so easily. "I can understand. But those hideaways have all been claimed by one fae or another. You wouldn't be guaranteed privacy." He pauses. "If you wanted, you could make use of mine. I was going to pick up something there, but then you'd have it to yourself for at least a few hours."

That isn't what I was hoping for, but it's at least more of an opportunity than I had before. If Madoc has kept anything related to his work for Orion in his private space, I'll have a chance to find it.

And maybe if I play up how unsettled I am by Orion's treatment, I'll earn even more of his sympathy. Not that I need to do much playing up. I just have to resist the urge to hide my discomfort.

"That would be great," I say. "If you really don't mind."

"Not at all." He gives me a smile that looks a little sad. "I'm glad I can do something to make things easier for you."

"Thank you."

Just as we're coming up on the entrance to his room, another Murk saunters toward us. The fae man's eyes travel over me, and just as he passes me, he reaches out to grope my breast.

I yelp, jerking away with a flinch, and Madoc leaps in so quickly his tail lashes through the air.

He slams the fae man against the wall of the tunnel. There's nothing gentle about his voice now. "She isn't a toy for you to play with. Don't you dare treat her like that again."

The other man stammers, his eyes growing wide. "I—I'm sorry, I thought— Of course, she's Orion's. I would never— I'm sorry."

Madoc steps back with a look of disgust, his stance still tensed, and motions to me. "Apologize to *her*."

The groper meets my eyes much more warily this time. "I'm sorry for touching you." He scurries off down the tunnel without a backward glance.

Madoc scowls after him. When he looks at me, his expression somehow softens even as something fierce lights in his eyes. "Has that been happening a lot?"

I hug myself. "Not—not like that. Not actually grabbing me. But people are definitely looking at me differently."

He mutters a curse under his breath and stands there a moment, as if he feels he needs to do something else but doesn't know what. Finally, he ushers me on into the passage with the stairs, keeping a respectful distance behind me.

Is he upset because he thinks the other fae are going to mess with what Orion obviously considers his property, or because of how it affects *me*? His insistence on the apology to me seems to suggest the latter.

But how much does it really matter if he can't—or won't—do anything to protect me from his king?

At least his obvious horror at anyone else manhandling me eases any anxiety I might have had about being alone with him in his private space. I sink onto one of the pillows scattered along the wall, and Madoc sits on an overturned crate on the other side of the room. He studies his mostly uneaten wrap and sets it aside as if he isn't hungry after all.

"You can spend as much time in here as you need to," he says. "I can bring you food and escort you anywhere you need to go in the rest of the Refuge. I know that's probably not how you'd want to live, but—it'll get better, it's just that the… events from this morning are still fresh in everyone's minds."

I rub my forehead. "Until he does something else to me."

Madoc knows who I mean without me needing to name him. He sighs. "I don't agree with all of Orion's tactics, but he's handling things the way that's worked for him for centuries before now. It isn't about you personally, I promise you."

Does he really believe that? I gaze back at him steadily. "But it is. I'm not fae. I'm hardly even human to him. He calls me his 'pet.' As far as he's concerned, he made me and I belong to him. There's no way of knowing how far he'll go, how much worse he might treat me than anyone else here, is there?"

Madoc's mouth twists. "I *have* been talking to him. I'll bring up the current situation too—that it's affecting the respect the others should have for you after the way you've helped us. And—if you'd open up to him, he'd see you more as an equal collaborator. Tell him everything you saw in the Mists, anything that might help us. He just needs to be sure he can trust you to be on our side."

I recoil from the idea inwardly, my back going rigid. "You expect me to betray my mates to a man who's enjoyed torturing me more than once in the past few days."

Madoc looks away, his jaw working. When he brings his gaze back to me, his eyes have hardened. "You've seen how the fae of the seasons have treated us. We're only defending ourselves from a continuing existence of being hunted down and slaughtered at every turn. Would you still rather side with *them*?"

"It's not about picking sides," I snap, my nerves finally fraying completely. "There are plenty of horrible Seelie and Unseelie, and I've never denied that. Back when I was in the Mists, I was doing everything I could to change things to help everyone they're being horrible to. But it isn't all of them. I know my mates, I fell in love with them for a reason, and I haven't seen one thing that's made me question my faith in *them*."

"They're all part of the same system," Madoc says, sounding frustrated, but I don't want to hear any more.

"And so are you. Trying to tell me that I should just give in to whatever Orion wants so he won't hurt me, that I can't expect any better because your war is so much more important. You know what? I can admit that I was wrong to assume that the Murk were all as awful as the other fae said. I know now that you've got reasons for being angry, and lots of you aren't just looking to make other people miserable."

"Of course we aren't."

"Right," I say without slowing down. "It isn't fair to judge an entire people based on what some of them do. And if you think I should recognize that when it comes to the Murk, then maybe you should realize it applies to the rest of the fae too."

Madoc stares at me, apparently lost for words. "I—" he starts, and cuts himself off. He seems to gather himself, but there's something awkward in his posture, as if he's no longer comfortable in the room. "I'm sorry," he says, not quite meeting my eyes. "I meant to give you some space and instead I've upset you. I'll go."

He picks up a couple of papers that were on the floor by his telescope and slips down the stairs without waiting for my response. Not that I have any idea what I'd say next. My throat is aching now, with all the anguish that leaked into my voice with my last words.

Maybe it's too much to hope that anyone here would ever see my point of view. It was hard enough getting the summer and winter fae to relax their guards enough to recognize that they didn't have to be enemies, and they'd only been in real conflict with each other for a few decades. It seems like they've been at odds with the Murk for pretty much forever.

A sense of hopelessness rolls over me, making me want to curl up and wallow in it, but I gather my resolve. Ignoring the heaviness in my heart, I get up and examine every inch of Madoc's room, rifling through his snack stash, checking under the blankets of his makeshift bed, peering at the star diagrams stuck to the walls.

I don't find anything else that feels like a clue I can use. Another wave of hopelessness hits me, thickened by my growing exhaustion. I sink down on the pillows again, thinking I'll just rest and recover for a little bit.

But I must fall asleep, because sometime later I find myself blinking awake with a jolt of adrenaline, my mind taking a moment to remember why I'm waking up in a different place from usual.

The artificial light overhead has dimmed to the faintest of glows. I can barely make out Madoc's form across from me, mostly covered by blankets. His breath rasps in and out in the slow rhythm of sleep.

I must have been here for hours. He came back, found me sleeping, and didn't want to disturb me even though he needed to get his own rest.

I sit up carefully, not wanting to ruin his sleep either. Then I notice the plate of food he's left for me next to the pillows: some kind of flaky pastry that gives off a meaty scent when I inspect it, an orange, and a powdered donut. Even though he was probably annoyed with me after the way I talked back to him earlier, he didn't want me going hungry or to have to navigate the tunnels outside on my own to get a meal.

A strange sensation squeezes around my heart. I look at the vague shape of the fae man across from me and wish I knew the right way to thank him. The right thing to say to make him understand.

Because I meant it when I said that I don't think the Murk are all evil. *He* isn't evil, even if he's gotten caught up in Orion's awfulness. After what I've seen, I'm not sure I can blame him for assuming that's the only way to get a better life for him and all the other Murk. What other options have presented themselves?

I don't want to let Orion get away with his plans for the Mists, but I don't like the thought of Madoc suffering because of his king's choices either.

I can't do anything about that in my current situation, though. The sleep has given my emotions a chance to reset, and the thought of venturing out into the rest of the Refuge is no longer quite so intimidating. Especially considering that it seems to be the Murk's "night" now, so almost everyone will be asleep.

That makes it the perfect time to get back to work on my escape plan, doesn't it?

Taking the meat-filled pastry with me and filled with a rising sense of purpose, I creep down the stairs and through the tunnels toward the maintenance room. As I expected, the Refuge is dark and silent. I have to step carefully to avoid stubbing my toes when I can barely see a few inches ahead of me.

I gulp down the pastry, which turns out to be stuffed with spiced chicken and some kind of dried fruit, and am just wiping the crumbs from my fingers when I reach the collection of abandoned machines. I make my way to the one by the vent, clamber up, and whisper the well-practiced true name. The bracelet reshapes in my hands. Balancing myself on the machine's sloping top, I get to work on the next bolt.

This one seems to come easier, or maybe that's just because of my renewed surge of energy and determination. I twist the wrench with all my strength, picturing myself managing to loosen not just one but two or maybe even three tonight. Then I'd be more than halfway to my goal.

I've just heaved on the wrench one last time, feeling the bolt give completely, when a skittering sound reaches my ears. It's so unexpected that I startle. My hands jerk on the wrench—and the tool tugs the bolt right out of its hole. The metal cylinder clinks off the top of the machine and falls to the concrete floor with a louder clatter.

My pulse lurches. I freeze instinctively, and footsteps thump toward me. Down—I have to get down so they don't see what I was doing. With no time to transform it, I toss my wrench behind the machine and start to slide off.

Before my feet have even reached the ground, a Murk woman who must be one of Orion's sentries darts into view. She takes in me and my guilty pose. Her eyes, better suited to the dark than mine, lower to inspect the ground. She leaps forward and plucks the bolt off the floor.

When she straightens up, she's just a foot away from me. I'm afraid to move.

She holds the bolt up between us. "I think Orion needs to hear about this right away."

My voice tumbles out of me. "Please, I was only— I wasn't hurting anyone—"

The fae woman mutters a few magical words, and the words die in my throat. I feel as if my mouth is stuffed with some invisible substance. My limbs have gone rigid too. I couldn't move now if I wanted to.

She prods me and nods with a look of vicious satisfaction with her spell. "You stay right here, and we'll see what my king makes of this disobedience."

CHAPTER TWENTY-FOUR

Talia

From when I first woke up in the Refuge of the Murk, I've done my best to keep my composure, to hide how terrified I am, to put on a show of resilience. The moment I see the cage, that self-control flies out the window.

My legs stiffen, my heels attempting to dig into the ground to stop the two fae men escorting me from dragging me any closer. My pulse lurches and starts to rattle through my veins. My body shakes with the frantic rhythm.

It isn't exactly like the cage Aerik held me in. The bars look like steel rather than bronze, and there's no door, just an entire side that's folded down to make room to shove me in. But it's even smaller than that one, only a little bigger than I am. There'll be no room to pull away from any of the walls, no way to do more than sit in a crouched position.

The cage is set off to one side of the dais. Orion stands over it, grinning eagerly as his men haul me the rest of the way over. Even though it's still very early in the morning by Murk standards, a couple of his close associates have arrived to stand around him. A few dozen regular Murk have drifted into the throne room after hearing of the commotion.

Not one set of eyes I meet holds a trace of friendliness. Madoc hasn't appeared—I don't know if he's even aware of what happened.

I don't know if there's anything he could do if he is.

"In you go," Orion says briskly with a clap of his hands. "If you can't be trusted to roam free, we have to make some adjustments to your living situation."

"I wasn't going to run away," I lie, unable to stop my voice from quavering. I've tried these arguments before when the king first confronted me in the maintenance room, and he didn't believe me then, but I can't give up on the tiny chance that they might sway someone else who'll speak up for me. "I just missed the fresh air. I only wanted to get a taste of it and then I'd have come right back."

Orion snorts. No one else makes a sound except the huff of the guards as they toss me into the cage. I sprawl on my hands and knees, and someone shoves the side of the cage up to close it. A lock snaps into place. Orion seals it with a tap of his hand and a few words of magic.

There are bars all around me, everywhere I look. The smell of the newly forged metal clogs my nose. The orange glow of the Murk Heart flickers over me, the quaking pulse of its energy feeling somehow mocking.

I wrap my hands around my knees, my chest constricting. My heart is thumping so fast I'm half afraid it'll fly right up my throat.

I squeeze my eyes shut, but images of the past flash through my mind regardless. Aerik's disdainful stare. Icy Cole jabbing me with his sharp fingers and elbows. The stink of my own filth all around me, the endless days without a glimmer of hope. The snap of my warped foot.

I've conquered those fears. I've held the panic at bay before, getting better at it every time. But since then, I've never been thrown into a cage by fae who are my enemies. This isn't just a reminder of past horrors—it's the same horror repeated.

It could become even more horrifying. Orion has no reason to care about keeping me alive and reasonably healthy like Aerik did.

My lungs clench tighter. My breath squeezes in and out with a painful wheeze.

"Look at her shudder," the Murk king says in a mocking tone. "Pitiful little human girl thought she could get the better of us. Of me." He cackles and smacks the top of the cage, making the bars and my nerves jangle. "What were you using to loosen those bolts, pet? I know those spindly fingers wouldn't be strong enough on their own."

Pain pierces my skull like it did when he questioned me before. He's trying to wear me down—but I've already told him the truth. The words tear out of me like they did the last time he raked through my mind. "I made a wrench. I used that."

The spell he's put on me doesn't seem to force me to give more details as long as the statement itself is truthful. And whatever powers Orion possesses to reach inside my thoughts, he hasn't been able to determine that I *am* being truthful—or that I used a true name's magic—so far. Maybe the possibility is so far-fetched to him that he'd never recognize it.

"*Made* a wrench?" he sneers. "Someone here made it for you or maybe with you, you mean. Who helped you with your little plan?"

"No one," I say truthfully. "I did it on my own."

"Then someone's going to have to pay for not keeping a close enough eye on the workshops, I suppose." Orion peers over the growing crowd as if he thinks he's going to spot someone to blame right now. Even in my muddled state, I notice a few of the nearer fae cringe.

I close my eyes again, tuning out the Murk king, our audience, and my panic as well as I can.

Focus on something else, I tell myself. *Focus on something better.*

The tickling of the sweet-smelling grass in the fields of Hearth-by-the-Heart. The sweep of Corwin's wings when he carries me through the chilly winter air. August shooting me a smile across the kitchen as we cook together. Whitt, spinning me slowly in a dance during one of the revels. Sylas's powerful hands caressing my body as he kisses me.

I am more than a pitiful human. I'm more than a pet. I have to hold on to all those other parts of me and not let this setback shatter my spirit completely.

Even if I can't think of any way I could possibly get out of this.

My pulse evens out enough that I'm no longer dizzy. I draw a breath into my chest and then another. My ribs still feel as if they're closing around my lungs, but not quite as painfully as before.

When I open my eyes again, my gaze catches on Madoc's pale hair where he's moving toward the dais through the gathered fae. When he spots me, the tendons around his jaw tighten. I think he nearly stumbles. His gaze darts from me to Orion, and he walks the rest of the way to the platform even faster.

I doubt he'll be able to convince Orion to let me out, at least not any time soon, but knowing he's here, knowing he's bothered by what's happening to me, gives me a shred of comfort.

Orion stalks away from the cage across the platform, pacing from one end to the other and back again. He rubs his hands together. A manic gleam has sparked in his eyes that makes my skin crawl in uneasy anticipation.

"I shaped this girl as a tool of our own," he says, "and it seems she doesn't appreciate the special role I gave her. But there are other ways we can still use her against our enemies, hmmm."

"What did you have in mind?" one of his other associates asks with a broad grin.

"Let me see." Orion comes to a stop by my cage again and taps his lips. "So many of the fae of the seasons have staked all their hopes on this fragile human. They see her as the answer to all their problems, as some kind of blessed being sent by their Heart to protect them. How much do you think it would crush their spirits to watch us crush her?"

Twittering laughter spreads through the crowd. A chill of starker fear seeps through me to pool in my gut. What's he talking about?

Orion smirks down at me. I get the impression he can tell just how much he's unnerving me and enjoying every hint of my discomfort.

"Yes, that would be perfect," he says. "We'll make a show of it. String her up for them all to see, let them watch as we snap every bone and slice through her skull. It won't do to kill her, of course, because then they'll be able to mourn her loss. We'll leave her paralyzed and lobotomized, a broken shell they'll still be scrambling to reclaim. And in the middle of their distress, we'll sweep in and slaughter them as if we're the wolves and they're nothing but lambs and lame ducks."

A cheer rises up, but I barely hear it, I've gone so numb with horror.

No. To be locked inside my body even more fully than I'm trapped in this cage, to have my mind cleaved apart so I can barely form a coherent thought—to be made utterly helpless, nothing more than a doll he's dangling as bait—and for my mates and all the other fae who've come to support me to have to watch—to know I'm being used to bring about their doom—

Tears are streaming down my cheeks before I even realize I'm crying. I press my hands to my eyes, but nothing will hold them in. I'm starting to wheeze again with the contracting of my lungs.

Oh, God, maybe I should have slit my own throat while I had the chance. My bracelet is gone now; I've got nothing at all here in this cage.

How can I stop this from happening? How will I not go insane waiting for him to carry out his awful plan?

I swipe at my tears and grasp the bars of my cage. "Please," I say in a ragged voice. "I could help in other ways—there's so much else I could do—" If I could just buy myself a little more time…

But Orion only scoffs, his yellow eyes offering nothing but vicious amusement. Instinctively, I look to Madoc, who's come up beside the throne. His pale face has turned almost sickly, but he hasn't said a word yet. *Please*, I think at him.

His king follows my gaze. Orion snorts and pats his hand on the top of the cage again, sending another vibration through it. "Looking to my faithful servant for help, are you, pet? Do you really think he gives a damn what happens to you as long as you serve our cause? He did well then, if you fell for his act. Excellent work, Madoc."

Madoc… dips his head in acknowledgment of the praise. When

he lifts it again, he's focused completely on his king, as if I'm not there at all. The bottom of my stomach falls out.

Orion strokes the top of the cage as if petting a cat. "I choose who stands beside me carefully, little girl. You obviously didn't realize that. Has he seemed to dote on you, to be there for you when you needed it? Anything he offered you, it's because I ordered him to win you over. You're a tool to him as much as you are to me. He doesn't care about you any more than he does a bar of lead. But illusions are his speciality, and from the expression on your face, he wove quite a good one."

I try to swallow, but my throat won't work. There's a sob lodged in it. Madoc gives no sign that contradicts anything his king said.

And why would I expect him to contradict it? That all makes sense, doesn't it? Throughout all the kindnesses he's shown me, he's never stopped trying to convince me to join their war, to turn against the fae of the seasons and tell Orion everything I can. Even last night, he was encouraging me to betray my mates.

I'm as alone here as I was when I first arrived. I never should have allowed myself to imagine I'd gained even a partial ally.

Despair descends over me again, wrapping around me like a suffocatingly thick blanket. I lean my face against my knees and focus on only the pressure of my arms hugging my legs, the hard floor of the cage beneath me, and the coolness of the air.

In their eyes, I'm nothing, and I've never felt more like that's true than in this moment.

"Well, then," Orion says, apparently satisfied that he's traumatized me as much as he possibly can, "let's leave my pet to reflect on her many mistakes and get to work on finalizing our invasion."

He steps away from the cage. Footsteps scrape across the dais, and lowered voices fall into discussion at the other side of the room. There's a rustling and an excited murmuring as the gathered fae go back to their work.

And I'm left with nothing to do but hold onto myself as hard as I can.

CHAPTER TWENTY-FIVE

Madoc

I didn't know it was possible for me to feel the same anguish now as I did on the day the Unseelie warriors slaughtered my parents. I was a child then, and I've had decades upon decades to harden myself since. I've seen and heard of so many horrific acts. They fuel my determination, but they don't shake me anymore.

Until this moment, watching an act dealt by the hands of my own king.

I already had the sense that something was wrong from the energy in the air as I hurried to the throne room. When I emerged from my rooms after waking and finding Talia gone, there were murmurs of "traitor" all through the tunnels.

I hadn't realized they meant her, though. I walked into the throne room not at all prepared to find the woman who's come to haunt both my dreams and my waking hours hunched in a cage, shivering in terror.

As I make my way to the dais, the voices around me blur into a wordless din. I keep my head high and my strides steady, because if Orion catches any hint that I disagree with his approach, that she's won any loyalty over what I feel for him, it might be even worse for her as well as for me. But inside I'm aware of little other than her slim form contorted by the size of the cage, the panic in her wide green eyes, the effort I can tell she's making to try to hide her distress —and the agony the sight provokes in me, twisting through me from throat to gut.

What has she done? What could she *possibly* have done that would require a punishment like this? She hardly had the means to commit any major betrayal.

But what she said to me yesterday is true. Orion doesn't see her as one of his people but as one of his belongings, a pet. Caging her after she's stepped out of line probably makes perfect sense to him.

My king is pacing the dais now with an air more like a lion than a rat. I can't ask him what she's done or say anything on her behalf while he's putting on this display for the audience that's gathered. Hopefully I can draw him aside soon after he's done with his spectacle and convince him that outright traumatizing her is only going to make it harder for any of us to earn her support.

Not that I think there's much chance of getting her to completely abandon her devotion to her former home after the way she spoke to me yesterday. But it's an argument Orion will understand. We can at least allow her to be comfortable while we keep her cooped up in the Refuge, until we can finally move in on the Mists.

"I shaped this human as a tool of our own," Orion says now, "and it seems she doesn't appreciate the special role I gave her. But there are other ways we can still use her against our enemies, hmmm."

My body tenses. Does he mean to take this punishment even further?

What *did* she do—try to kill him? That's the only crime I can think of that would warrant this kind of viciousness.

Ridiculously, I both can't believe Talia would resort to that kind of violence, and also wouldn't entirely blame her if she had. I wouldn't want her to succeed, of course, but it'd be understandable for her to want to after the way he's mistreated her already.

My king has stopped by her cage, putting on a show of

contemplating his options when I'm sure he knew exactly what he planned before he even ordered that cage constructed.

His voice comes out with a lilt that's both playful and cutting. "So many of the fae of the Mists have staked all their hopes on this fragile creature. They see her as the answer to all their problems, as some kind of blessed being sent by their Heart to protect them. How much do you think it would crush their spirits to watch us crush her?"

My hands start to clench before I catch them. He can't really—after all the ways she's advanced our goals, even if she didn't know what she was doing—she's been more instrumental in paving the way for our victory than anyone in this room other than Orion, and I have to admit that includes me.

But there's no respect or even pity in his gaze as he peers down at her, only sadistic glee.

"Yes, that would be perfect," he says. "We'll make a show of it. String her up for them all to see, let them watch as we snap every bone and slice through that skull. It won't do to kill her, of course, because then they'll be able to mourn her loss. We'll leave her paralyzed and lobotomized, a broken shell they'll still be scrambling to reclaim. And in the middle of their distress, we'll sweep in and slaughter them as if we're the wolves and they're nothing but lambs and lame ducks."

What? My stomach flips, sending bile up my throat. Nausea clamps around my gut.

The memory flickers through my head of the ravens cackling as they rammed my father's severed head on that branch, echoing into the cheer that's lifted up around me. For just a second, the world tilts.

The orange light of the Heart catches on the tears that've dampened Talia's cheeks. As she presses her hands to her face, her shoulders shake. When she reaches out again, grasping the bars of the cage, there's nothing but blank panic in her eyes.

"Please," she says to Orion. Her voice spills out in a babble, offering other help, other contributions, anything to save herself from the fate worse than death he just described.

How can he just smirk at her as if this is all a game?

And then she looks at me. She doesn't speak—for fuck's sake, she cares enough about me and the position I'm maintaining here not to call out to me overtly, even now—but the desperate plea in her gaze is unmistakeable.

Which means Orion doesn't miss it either. He laughs and taps the top of her cage, and just when I thought the moment couldn't get any more horrifying, he aims his smirk at me. "Looking to my faithful servant for help, are you, pet? Do you really think he gives a damn what happens to you as long as you serve our cause? He did well then, if you fell for his act. Excellent work, Madoc."

Oh, no. At the crumpling of Talia's face, misery written all through her expression, I feel as if he's stabbed a knife right into my chest.

It isn't true, I want to tell her. *It wasn't an act—not all of it.* If I'm being honest, in the past few days I've had to do more acting to *avoid* showing how much I'm coming to care rather than how much I don't.

But Orion is grinning at me in the wake of his compliment. How can I throw it back in his face? I nod just slightly, fixing my gaze on him, keeping my posture as still as I can. If I look at her now, I'm not sure I can hold onto my self-control.

Some part of *me* wants to kill him now.

Orion glances down at Talia again and speaks in a croon. "I choose who stands beside me carefully, Talia. You obviously didn't realize that. Has he seemed to dote on you, to be there for you when you needed it? Anything he offered you, it's because I ordered him to win you over. You're a tool to him as much as you are to me. He doesn't care about you any more than he does a bar of lead. But illusions are his speciality, and from the expression on your face, he wove quite a good one."

With every word, he drives the knife deeper—into both my chest and Talia's, from her reaction, which I can't help marking. Her whole body folds in on itself even tighter than before. The panic in her eyes dulls, but only because it's shifted into a sort of dazed hopelessness that brings my claws prickling to the tips of my fingers.

She looks like that fierce spirit of hers has already died.

I drag my gaze back to my king as he says a few dismissive remarks. He waves off the crowd and motions for me and a few of his other knights to join him at the other end of the dais. My feet move of their own accord, carrying me away from the wounded figure in the cage.

It takes a minute before I'm sure enough of my voice to speak. The conversation has started around me, but I've barely heard it. As soon as there's a lull, I tip my head to Orion and then toward Talia. "What's the reason for all this? Did she hurt someone?"

Orion guffaws, as if the notion of Talia managing to harm one of us is absurd—which it actually kind of is, knowing her to the extent I do now. I don't think he's assuming that based on his knowledge of her personal values, though.

"She thought she'd flee," he says in a derisive tone. "Got her hands on some kind of tool and was working at the bolts on an air vent in the maintenance room that someone missed as a possible exit. Now she's seen what her lies and her commitment to the fae of the seasons earn her."

He goes back to discussing the best timing for his gory demonstration and our attack to follow. Should we launch it while the Seelie are wild with the curse, when they'll have little control but won't understand what's happening, or afterward, to amplify their helplessness? Are the other colonies prepared to march within the week? Have we stockpiled enough equipment?

Practical considerations in the lead-up to destroying the woman crouched just twenty feet from us, bit by painful bit. All because she wanted to get away from this place, to return to the mates she loves. *That* is the treachery Orion objects to so violently.

I'm standing right next to him, but I watch him as if from a great distance, adding little to the conversation other than occasional nods and noncommittal murmurs. I note the way he cuffs one of the young fae who comes with a report across the ears, for no reason except the girl stutters a little. I observe as Bren enters the room, and Orion jokes to the others about the scars that the fight he incited will leave behind. And all the while, Talia's clear, soft voice filters through my thoughts.

There's no way of knowing how far he'll go, how much worse he might treat me than anyone else here, is there?

He made you kill someone like Bren the other day, didn't he? Just another Murk, just because he likes seeing people being torn apart.

You want to save your people. As far as I can tell, Orion is more interested in hurting fae—and not just the fae of the Mists.

I told her she was wrong. I told her he only wanted to make us as strong as we could be, that his methods were necessary to have brought us the power to win against the other fae. But she's chipped at my certainty, and now…

Now I'm not so sure she wasn't seeing things more clearly than I ever have, when I was so focused on both the vengeance and the brighter future Orion promised.

Our king has done amazing things. No one could deny that. The Heart blazing away beside us is the clearest possible testament. But is this what I want a new era for my people to look like? Celebrating torture, reveling in violence and pain…

Are we really better than what the fae of the seasons think if we'll stand back and even cheer Orion on while he breaks every part of the woman in that cage, who's done nothing worse than try to live her own life? Who's managed to care about at least some of us regardless of what we've put her through and what she's heard about us before?

Although it's hard to imagine she cares after this latest assault. We've just proven everything the fae of the seasons would say about us true, haven't we?

And I helped, by standing there saying nothing to challenge it. By acting as if I appreciated Orion's praise and his plan.

Nausea grips me all over again. I said to Talia once that all the tests I went through were worth nothing if I threw away what I won with them. But what are they worth if I don't use the position I won to fight for a future where we really aren't living in fear—of the wolves and the ravens, and of each other? Of this man who calls himself our king?

I go through the rest of the conversation and then my other

duties of the day as if sleepwalking, most of my focus inward. There is a line I'm not willing to cross, and my king has just drawn it for me. So what am I going to do about it?

The pieces of a plan of my own start to come together in my mind alongside a growing resolve.

Every time I enter the throne room, Orion is there, but that's not unexpected. I have to wait just a little longer, even though that means more time for Talia to dwell on the threats and the claims he made.

When the lights dim, I head off to my room as if I mean to turn in for the night. I know Orion will do the same soon, down the tunnel to the large chamber carved into the rock beyond the throne room walls. He casts enough magic around its entrance that he doesn't bother posting guards there. He trusts his skills more than any of us.

After I'm sure he'll be asleep, I intone the words of one of the illusion spells I helped perfect around me. Orion didn't lie when he said that kind of magic is a particular affinity of mine, and it'll hide me from my fellow Murk as well as any other fae. Then I shift into rat form and slip down the stairs and through the tunnels.

Talia has lain down on the floor of the cage, curled into a ball. There isn't room for her to extend her limbs much more than that anyway. Her eyes are closed, her face blotchy with past tears and present stress. Seeing her like that wrenches at my heart all over again.

She's stayed so strong through so much… He hasn't finally broken her, has he?

I glance around the throne room once more to confirm that there's no one here before shedding my rat form. Then I weave a more detailed illusion, one that'll reflect the image of Talia I'm seeing now to anyone who glances this way. It doesn't do any good to keep myself hidden if a random passerby could notice she's talking to someone.

I ease within that illusion and pull back the one that was hiding only me. Reaching through the bars, I brush my fingers over Talia's hand.

She jerks awake in an instant, faster than I expected. All at once she's scrambling as upright as she can get, shoving herself against the far side of the cage.

"What do you want?" she asks, but the fierceness I'd have expected in her voice has faded. It wobbles with a trace of fear.

She thinks I might have come to inflict some new torture on her.

Staring into her strained but still pretty face, taking in the distrust in the eyes I never meant to admire, I have trouble remembering what I wanted to say. My hesitation dredges up a wash of shame. *She's* adjusted her opinions about the Murk after the things I've shown and told her, admitted to being wrong. How can I still balk at doing the same for her, after all the suffering she's faced since I brought her here?

"I want to help you," I say. "I don't agree with what Orion's done to you or anything he talked about doing to you."

Talia makes a noise of disbelief. "Are you still trying to trick me into trusting you, after he's already told me that was all his idea? How stupid do you think I am?"

I swallow thickly. "Not stupid at all. Smarter than me in many ways, I've come to realize." I glance away and then back at her, not knowing how to convince her. "It's true that he ordered me to be friendly with you to try to get you to open up about your knowledge of the Mists. But the rest of the things he said aren't."

Her gaze is still full of doubt. I force myself to go on.

"I might not agree with all your allegiances, but there's so much I respect about you. Your bravery, your resilience, your compassion, your willingness to listen…" We won't get into the emotions I've felt that went beyond respect, but the thought of those compels me to add, "Even your loyalty to your mates. You're not just a pet, and you don't belong to Orion. You're your own person. I *have* come to care about you, and you don't deserve this."

"But somehow Orion isn't aware of any of that," she says.

"Orion is… Orion. He wouldn't have appreciated me feeling conflicted over the job he'd given me, so I've let him continue thinking I was only spending time with you on his orders. But I can't stand with him if this is how he's going to rule. I'm drawing that line."

Talia studies me through the bars. Her expression doesn't give away any clue of how much she believes me. When she speaks, her tone is skeptical. "And how are you drawing that line? By coming to talk to me? Because you talked to me plenty before, and it didn't stop this from happening."

"No, it didn't." I rub my hand over my face. "I didn't think it'd come to this—maybe I should have realized. Maybe I was too caught up in my own hopes for the future to see clearly. But I see now."

"What does that even mean?" she asks.

"I—" There are things I still need to be sure of. It's not just Orion but all of the Murk I have to consider. "If you went back to your mates, what would you say to them about the Murk? Would you tell them to slaughter us all?"

Talia frowns. "Is this some trick to get me to reveal something about how they work or what their strategies are? I'm not falling for it. Why don't you just go away, if all you're looking to do is ask me more questions?"

She turns her head, leaning her cheek against the bars and closing her eyes, shutting me out the only way she can.

I sit there, torn. But the answer isn't really all that difficult to arrive at, is it?

She's taken more than one leap of faith for me. I can't expect her to make another if I won't offer one of my own. And deep down, I do know what her answer would be, don't I? It's only selfishness that makes me want to hear her say it in so many words before I trust it.

I trust her. I trust the love and determination I've seen burning in her soul.

"That's not all I'm looking to do," I say, summoning all the firmness I can into my voice. "I'm here to help you leave the Refuge."

Then I reach up to the top of the cage and mutter the words to bring the side of it swinging down, opening up the way to her freedom.

CHAPTER TWENTY-SIX

Talia

The wall of the cage hits the ground with a faint clink. My eyes have already popped open at the shift in the air with the movement of the bars. I stare at the lowered wall and then at Madoc poised next to me on the edge of the dais, now visible without any barrier between us.

He's letting me out. He really—

My first surge of relief snaps away with another flare of suspicion. This could still be some kind of trap. He's trying to lure me into betraying Orion all over again to give Orion an excuse to torture me even more.

I never should have believed a single word that came out of his mouth.

He's watching me expectantly. I turn away, leaning my head against the bars on the opposite side. "Go away. Whatever you're trying to do, I'm not falling for it."

"Talia." There's an edge of frustration in Madoc's voice. Did he really think I'd fall for his conflicted supporter act that easily a second time?

He inhales roughly and releases the breath in a rush. "Fine. I understand that you don't trust me. I can't really blame you. But if you don't come with me now, I don't know if we'll get another chance. Orion's talking about making his move after the next full moon, which is in just a few days. I don't—I don't know what else he might do to you in the meantime. What could I possibly be leading you to that'd be *worse* than what he's already planning?"

His words and the rawness in his voice sink in slowly through the numbness of my despair. It's true that Orion couldn't really hurt me worse than he's already declared he's going to. He's said he's going to break every part of my body and deaden my mind in front of all the fae of the seasons—what could be more awful than that?

If there's even the slightest chance that Madoc really does mean to let me escape, that he isn't as loyal as Orion thinks, wouldn't it be better to take that chance than to throw it away when I don't have any others? I know for sure no one else in this place is going to help me, and I've got no tools that'll open this cage on my own.

The only advantage I have left is whatever difference the things I've said to Madoc might have made in the way he sees me and his king.

I look at him warily, taking in the urgency in his gray eyes, turned thundercloud-dark in the dimness of the room. The pallor of his face, still a little sickly. His hand, gripping the side of the cage so tightly the knuckles have whitened.

He's giving every appearance of being desperate to get me out of here. But I just don't know whether I should believe it.

Maybe it doesn't matter whether I believe it or not, only whether I'm willing to let my uncertainty keep me here where I know my situation is hopeless or to take whatever tiny chance I might have with him.

But I can't stop myself from asking, in a steadier voice than before, "Why would you help me escape? Aren't you worried that I'll bring the fae of the seasons down on the Refuge, destroy all those dreams you have about making a better life for the Murk?"

It might not be the wisest idea to remind him of just how badly this situation could go for him, but I need to hear his answer. I need to understand how he could see this betrayal of his king—and possibly his entire people—as a reasonable option.

Madoc's throat bobs, but he holds my gaze. "No, I'm not," he says. "The way into the Refuge isn't that easy; we'll be safe here regardless of what you tell your mates. Am I worried about how it'll affect our chances of getting a better life in general? Of course. But—I think I know you well enough now to say that you aren't going to go back to the Mists and tell them we should all be butchered. You'll do whatever you can to avoid bloodshed on both sides. And maybe by getting you back to them, I'll have shown enough proof for *them* to trust that there are at least a few of us who deserve better than the brutality they've aimed at us."

A touch of emotion passes through my chest, like a feather brushing between my ribs. It takes me a moment to recognize it as a flicker of the hope I thought I'd lost.

I still don't know what Madoc's full intentions are, but he has been listening to me, and not just for strategic information he can pass on to his king. He understands what matters to me.

He maybe even believes I could pull off a miracle beyond any magic I've possessed so far.

"You'd want that?" I say. "You'd rather settle things with negotiations and treaties, if that's even possible, than with a war where you'd get to rule over all of the Mists if you won?"

"If there's a way to end the attacks on us and to give us a proper home in the Mists without even more of us dying, without us resorting to savaging people who don't deserve it, then I'll take it," Madoc says. "I didn't think it *was* possible. But from what I've seen while I watched you in the Mists and now here… I trust that if anyone *can* make it possible, it's you."

A strange note comes into his voice with those last words, one I can't decipher but that sends a wobble through my pulse. I don't trust him, but then, I never did, not completely. But he's said enough that the chance I'm taking doesn't feel quite as precarious. That's enough.

I didn't slit my throat the other day because I refused to give up. I'm not going to roll over and die on Orion's whim now either.

I ease forward out of the cage, and Madoc pulls back to make room. His gaze darts around the throne room. He doesn't look all that reassured by the fact that he's convinced me, which reassures *me* that this isn't some gambit just to trick me.

"The one other thing Orion said that's true is that I'm good with illusions," he murmurs. When I've crept free of the cage, he closes the side again. "I can make it look as if you're still in there to anyone who doesn't come too close. But as soon as Orion is up for the day, he'll check on you. I'll have to dispel the illusion before then, which means you'll need to be well on your way at that point."

I'll need to be well on my way—which means Madoc isn't coming all the way to the Mists with me. In spite of everything, my pulse stutters with concern. "Isn't he going to know you helped me? What's he going to do to *you*?"

Madoc smiles tightly. "I'll be laying down more than one kind of illusion. I think I can cover my tracks well enough. He already knows you've been able to surpass his assumptions of what you're capable of —and one benefit to his single-mindedness is that I don't think it'd even occur to him that someone who's worked as hard to earn his favor as I have would ever throw it away. Come on. We need to go to the maintenance room first."

I follow him out of the throne room and through the tunnels, sticking close behind him, walking as quickly as my warped foot will allow. My legs and back ache with stiffness from being cramped in the cage all day, but stretching them in motion brings some relief along with the soreness.

Once, my toe hits a bit of gravel that rattles against the tracks, and I freeze. But no one comes running our way, and Madoc urges me onward. A little while later, a small furry body scurries past us on the opposite side of the tunnel, briefly lit by one of the few dimmed bits of illumination still on for the night. The rat-shifted Murk doesn't pause or even glance toward us.

Madoc must have one of his illusions wrapped around us even now. At least I've got proof that he's as good as he said.

When we reach the maintenance room, he peers around the walls and points to the vent. "That's the one you were working on?"

I nod. He walks over and climbs onto the machine below much more easily than I ever did. With a few muttered words, he's loosened all of the bolts and let them fall to the floor. He sets the vent cover on top of the machine. Then he beckons me closer.

Is he sending me out by that route after all? Now that I've spent nearly a full day in a cage, the thought of squeezing myself into the small opening makes my chest clench up.

But when I step over, Madoc just reaches to take a strand of my hair between his fingers. "I need to use this to make sure they believe you went this way. It'll keep them off your trail for longer—hopefully long enough for your soul-twined mate to get to you once he can hear you again. All right?"

All he wants is to pull out a hair, for my own protection—and he's asking my permission rather than simply taking it. Some part of me that was still a little afraid that he was leading me into a trap relaxes, and my heart thumps faster.

This is really happening. He's getting me out of here. I *will* speak to Corwin again, soon.

"Go ahead," I whisper.

There's only a brief pinch in my scalp when he tugs out the hair. Madoc turns to the vent and holds the root of the hair in front of his mouth. He speaks a few magic-laced syllables and then blows into the tunnel.

I'm not sure exactly what effect he's conjuring, but a moment later he snags the hair in the corner of the opening and hops back down. "That's done. Now for our actual route."

He leads me away from the maintenance room to the nearest station, and then to a doorway locked with magic in one corner. I'm not sure what illusion he draws with his murmured words, but the sentry stationed just a few feet away doesn't so much as blink when Madoc opens the door and motions me through.

I find myself in an even darker, mildew-smelling space. I can barely make out the walls around me, which I find by stretching out my hands—the space is just wide enough that I can touch both with my arms completely extended. Madoc is little more than a blur in front of me.

"I can't see," I say.

The air shifts. I think he's going to offer his hand and balk at the idea of taking it, but instead he simply steps a little closer. "Hold onto the back of my shirt. Try to adjust. This is the easiest part of this route."

Wonderful. I grope through the darkness and curl my fingers into the fabric of his shirt. Something brushes my ankle and then jerks away—his tail, I realize.

He moves forward slowly enough for me to follow behind him, gradually picking up the pace when I show I can keep up. My boots tap against uneven bits on the floor, some of which slide at the contact, but I can't tell what we're walking over. I don't even have a sense of how far this hallway stretches. Madoc stays silent, so I do too.

How many fae travel this way regularly? What are the chances we'll run into some?

How far do we have to go before I can reach out to my mates?

Those questions whirl in my head as I tramp on, essentially blind. The darkness starts to close in on me, shortening my breaths. I drag air deep into my lungs to steady myself.

Madoc slows before he comes to a complete halt, so I don't walk right into him. As I let go of his shirt, there's a grating sound like something mechanical turning. He speaks a few more words of magic under his breath. Then, with a soft creak, a door swings open. A waft of cool, damp air washes over us.

There's a little more light on the other side, a faint glow that seeps down from somewhere above. The passage ahead of us appears to slant upward and then veer to the side through solid rock, roughly carved into a narrow tunnel.

This isn't part of the original station, clearly, but a route of the Murk's own making.

The rocky floor gleams with a hint of moisture. A faint trickling sound reaches my ears. I hesitate, staring into the passage. "How much farther?"

"It's a long route, and a little twisted," Madoc says. "The shape of it is a spell in itself—to prevent discovery. I'll lead you all the way to the surface."

There really isn't any way to go but forward, is there?

I square my shoulders. "Then let's get going."

CHAPTER TWENTY-SEVEN

Talia

Madoc was right when he said the first hallway was the easiest part. The rocky passage may be slightly better lit, but my feet wobble on the uneven ground. Any place that's smooth is also slick with dribbles of water. When I brace my hands against the walls to catch my balance, the rough stone there scrapes my palms.

He doesn't hurry me, even though he has so much more on the line than I do. I was going to be worse than killed anyway. His entire standing among the Murk hangs in the balance right now, probably his life as well.

But he stops every few steps to check that I'm coming along all right. A few times he opens his mouth as if he's going to offer to carry me over the tricky terrain, but then he shuts it, maybe guessing —correctly—that I'd rather stumble along than have his hands on me. He keeps his tail tucked close to his legs so it doesn't risk tripping me.

"We can talk in here," he says. "I still have a spell on us to deflect any notice of our presence, and it's unlikely anyone will be coming through this passage at this time anyway."

That makes sense, or why would he have chosen it? I nod, clambering over a particularly steep bump in the floor. "I guess this isn't a route you'd generally be bringing cargo through." I can't imagine trying to carry boxes of lead or whatever while constantly stubbing your toes and risking tumbling on your face.

The corners of Madoc's lips twitch upward. "No, we have other passages for that. This one is typically used by travelers who'll be bringing back information and observations rather than supplies."

Spies, he means. Like he was in the Mists. Like other Murk must be right now, watching over my mates and our people.

I wet my lips, abruptly noticing the pang of thirst in my throat. I haven't eaten or drank anything except a few scraps Orion tossed to me several hours ago, and my nervousness isn't helping.

Madoc must catch the motion or something in my expression, because he digs a small bottle of water out of his pocket. "I thought you might need this. I have a few bags of snacks as well. Nothing especially filling, but the dinner spread didn't offer any items I could easily store for later."

"That's okay." I accept the water with a gratitude I'm not totally comfortable with. My gaze slides over the contents, which look perfectly clear. The seal on the lid is still in place—but of course that doesn't mean much when you're dealing with magic.

Being suspicious of the drink is kind of ridiculous at this point, though, isn't it? What could Madoc have gained by bringing me all the way out here only to drug me that he couldn't have achieved much easier? I twist open the lid and take a few gulps.

When I glance at Madoc again, a shadow has crossed his face. He's noted my hesitation too. "I am sorry," he says, looking awkward. I'm guessing he's not very accustomed to apologizing. "For —for not being able to step in sooner. For not doing more before it got to this point. I didn't think it *would* get to this point. He's never — It isn't—" He doesn't seem to know how to go on.

There's something heart-wrenching about the fact that he sees the scars that Orion and his followers left all over his body as *normal*, so much more acceptable than the way his king treated me. But I suppose it is different in plenty of ways, even if I don't think what I've been through is that much more awful.

"He's never had a human whose genetic code he altered around to toy with," I say. "He's still the same person he was before. You just gave him a pass because of what he could do for you."

Madoc's mouth twists. "It seemed necessary—the way he ran the Refuge, the way he pushed us to prove ourselves. War isn't a kind thing, and that's what we've been preparing for. But you paved our way toward victory so much, and all you wanted was to go home..."

He pauses. "I can understand why you'd want to go back, and it worries me that Orion apparently can't. I thought that's what the war was about—reclaiming our home. But if he could torment you like this for wanting the same thing, then maybe you're right. Maybe causing pain is more important to him than anything else."

He starts walking again, and I shuffle after him, watching his careful, steady paces over the undulations in the stone floor. I feel like I have to offer something in return for his admission.

"After what happened to your parents, it might be understandable if you'd want to cause the other fae a lot of pain too," I say, not really sure what I'm getting at. I just want to understand, to get a sense of what I'm leaving behind, what I can tell the other fae when I reach them.

Madoc shrugs without looking back at me. "Many times, I've imagined inflicting a *lot* of pain on the savages that tore my family apart. I'd bet you're not completely immune from those kinds of thoughts either."

I think of Aerik and his cadre, of the blood that splattered the forest on the edge of my childhood town and the scars marking Jamie's face, and have to admit, "I'm not. I wouldn't toy with them if they were helpless in front of me, but I've been glad to see them get put in their places as well as we've managed so far." Every time I see Aerik's cruel face, I'd like to punch it or stab him in the gut. I can own that.

"There've been a lot of crimes committed against my people," Madoc goes on. "There are a lot of Seelie and Unseelie I'd like to make pay. But… I can't say it doesn't ring true to me, what you said about not judging everyone by the actions of some. I can accept that it wasn't fair of me to assume your mates didn't care about you for who you are, just as you do them. You're obviously very good at inspiring emotions one wouldn't necessarily expect."

There's a sort of self-deprecating wryness to his tone, but it's the weariness underneath that niggles at me. "What are you going to do after I'm gone?" I ask.

"I'll pretend to help with the search that'll no doubt go out for you, and maybe lay a few more misleading clues to confuse matters. Then we'll get back to planning the war. Without the spectacle Orion was planning and knowing that you'll be able to prevent the full-moon curse from taking the Seelie, I'd imagine he'll delay the attack he was hoping to carry out a little longer. Hopefully for long enough for you to make some progress encouraging the wolves and the ravens to consider negotiations."

"I'll do what I can." It's hard to think beyond reaching my mates again, setting my feet back on familiar ground. I have no idea what *they've* been through while I've been missing. And… "I can't see telling them that Orion is worth bargaining with. I wouldn't trust him to mean a single word he says. We can't even count on him sticking to the letter of an oath he gives when he's not governed by the Heart of the Mists, can we?"

"No." Madoc rubs his mouth. "We'll take it as it comes. I can feel out others subtly and see who might be inclined to support a peaceful change rather than full-out war. And maybe there'll still need to be some fighting, just… not quite as much as otherwise."

"If we can resolve this without all of any kind of fae ending up dead, that'll be better than what he's planned," I mutter.

"And if it comes to that, then it comes to that. I can't say I'm all that optimistic about the fae of the seasons caring one bit about how we feel about anything." A trace of bitterness comes into Madoc's voice. He shakes himself. "That isn't the point of this. The point of this is *you* don't deserve the fate he had in mind for you. That one thing I can change."

A lump rises in my throat. "And if I can't make any arrangements quickly enough, or there aren't enough Murk who'll compromise? Will you be with them fighting to slaughter all of the other fae, trying to rule over the entire Mists?"

Madoc is silent for a long moment. When he stops and turns toward me, the expression on his face echoes the hopelessness I felt locked up in that cage. "I won't strike out at anyone who isn't striking at us," he says firmly. "I can promise you that much. The rest is up to them."

Staring back at him, I feel as if I can suddenly see the bars that have snapped into place around *him*—maybe back when his parents were killed in front of him, maybe from the moment he was born. He's been caged in his own way by the hostility toward the Murk, by the way the leaders he had stoked the urge for violent vengeance.

Is it any wonder he has trouble seeing another way?

Neither of us has been dealt a good hand among the fae. But he's trying to do something better with it now anyway. That does count for something.

"I hope it goes much better than that," I say, but I can't say I have all that *much* hope myself.

Just about anything would be better than the picture his king painted of our near future, though.

Another thought hits me with a sudden chill. "Do you know—when Orion reached into my head and was searching through my mind—did he find anything he was planning to use against the other fae that he didn't mention in his questions?" Just how much did I end up betraying my mates yet again?

Madoc blinks as if confused before understanding flickers through his expression. "You don't have to worry about that. He didn't search your mind at all. He only wanted you to think he had—that he *could*—to intimidate you. The questions he asked were based on observations we've made in the Mists, and he used a spell to force you to answer truthfully, but he can't actually see right inside anyone's head."

"Oh." An unsettling mix of relief and embarrassment trickles through me. There's yet another trick I fell for. But at least that means I can be sure Orion doesn't know any of my few remaining secrets.

We walk on in silence for a time. The passage veers one way and then another, seeming to double back on itself at least twice, sometimes sloping downward again before it heads back up. My warped foot is starting to ache. I feel as if I've walked at least a couple of miles.

Then we take another turn, and the passage widens—well, the space between the walls does, anyway. The floor, not so much. A deep chasm appears to have pushed the wall on the right a few feet farther away, leaving a strip of stone just wide enough for us to comfortably walk along next to the perilous drop.

My legs balk. I peer down into the chasm, unable to see the bottom, only total blackness.

"We're almost there," Madoc says. "Stick close to the wall, and you'll be fine." He has his own hand resting against the wall at our left, the end of his tail braced against the ground by his feet.

I gather my resolve and limp after him, setting my own feet as far from the chasm as I can. At least this section of the path is pretty straight.

"You said the passage is a spell," I say. "That's why it's so long and twisted. What kind of a spell?"

I'm actually only asking out of curiosity, no thought of scheming left in my head other than the desire to get out of this place, but Madoc tenses a bit before he answers in a careful tone. "Only to ensure that those entering this way don't reach the Refuge unless they actually know where they're going."

That's why he isn't concerned about me bringing an army down on the Refuge. The fae of the seasons won't know "where they're going" even if I lead them to the place where I exit. There must be some kind of incantation or similar you need to make sure the path leads you right. It makes sense as a security precaution.

It also explains why it'd be *very* difficult for the other fae to have found me, even if I'd managed to give Whitt any real clues.

"How long have I—" I start to ask, just to break up the gnawing silence before it descends too heavily again.

Madoc cuts me off with a jerk of his hand. He freezes in front of me, staring at the passage ahead of us. Apprehension washes over me.

Then I hear it too. A metallic squeak like unoiled hinges, carrying down through the dim space.

Someone's coming.

They're coming quickly. Just a couple of heartbeats after I caught the squeak, distant but audible voices reach my ears. I can't see the figures who're talking yet, but I have the sense it's only a matter of seconds before they turn the bend to come into view.

Madoc's head swivels sharply, taking in the passage around us. He scrambles several paces farther up and leaps across the chasm to a small ledge that barely juts out far enough to support his feet. He motions to me. "My illusions can stop them from seeing and hearing us, but it won't let them walk right through us. We have to get off the path."

I hurry after him, my heart hammering. As I come up across from him, the two figures step into sight at the top of this section of the path. They're hustling toward me, one behind the other, talking in excited voices.

But not so excited that they'd miss running straight into a solid body, whether they can see me or not.

My gaze whips back to Madoc and the ledge he's braced on. There's room for another person to stand there next to him, but only just—and I'd still have to *make* it to that spot. Jumping over a fathomless crevice with a crooked foot that's now outright throbbing.

The image flashes through my mind of me careening down into the vast darkness below. My pulse hiccups and thumps even harder.

"I don't think I can do it," I whisper. "My foot—I'll fall."

Madoc stretches out his arm. "You just need to get close enough for me to catch you. *Quickly.*"

My focus narrows in on his open hand. He wants me to trust him with my safety, to put all my faith in him…

Haven't I already done that by coming this far with him anyway?

The Murk sentries are coming up on us fast. I don't let myself second-guess my last thought. With a gulp of air, I step backward to give me a bit of a running start, and then throw myself toward the ledge.

For a second, with nothing solid beneath my feet, my stomach starts to plummet as if I'm going to fall with it. My eyes have squeezed shut of their own accord.

Then Madoc's hand clamps around my elbow, yanking me the rest of the way to him so his other arm can slide around my back and swivel me toward the wall. He holds me there, just inches from his body, his thunderstorm scent wrapping around me too.

My feet wobble and settle on the ledge, but I don't dare nudge him away. He's become my entire sense of balance. I can feel the faint, nervous thump of his own pulse echoing through his embrace into me.

The two fae dash on past us. Their voices are drowned out by the pounding of my heartbeat in my ears. Madoc and I stay there, locked in place and perfectly still, until I can't hear them at all.

Tentatively, I dare to look over my shoulder. I can't even see them now—they've gone around the turn at the bottom.

Madoc adjusts his grip on me, and a jolt of panic shoots through my veins. But he keeps the same firm but gentle hold he's offered from the start.

"I should leap back across first, and then you jump to me like before," he says in a low voice, his breath tickling over my forehead. "Can you find a position where you feel steady?"

I swallow hard and manage a nod. Gradually, he eases his arms back and I lean against the wall, keeping most of my weight on my good foot. Madoc watches me closely, making sure I'm okay.

He pushes off the wall and lands solidly on the path with a swish of his tail to help steady himself. When he turns and holds out his hands to me, my pulse still skips a beat at the thought of the drop between us, but I don't hesitate as long as before.

Going back to safety is easier. And I already know he can catch me.

I fling myself toward Madoc, and he grasps my waist for just long enough to set me fully on the stone floor. I exhale shakily. "Let's skip that part next time."

Madoc lets out a startled laugh. He gazes down at me for a moment with an expression I can't read and then points me toward the top of the path. "Let's hope there isn't a next time."

Despite the pain in my foot creeping up into my calf, I pick up my pace, knowing escape is close but that we can't be sure no other Murk will show up unexpectedly. Thank God, we make it to the top of that steeper strip and leave the chasm behind without incident. Madoc directs me along a couple more brief passages to reach a short ladder that leads up to a circular panel in the ceiling.

He climbs up the ladder, murmurs a little magic, and shoves the panel to the side. Air fresher than anything I've breathed in over a week washes down over me, and a gasp escapes my lips. Madoc peers down at me, an emotion I don't recognize flitting through his eyes again.

He isn't reconsidering letting me go, is he?

But he leaves the panel open, coming back down the ladder to where I'm standing. He touches my shoulder so lightly I barely feel the press of his fingers through my shirt.

"Talia," he says, his gaze so intense I get worried about what he's going to say all over again.

Before he can go any further, he stiffens, his attention flicking away. He spits out a curse and turns back to me with so much more urgency than before.

"They've already noticed you're gone," he says. "They'll be searching all the passages. I have to get back to divert them. Move fast as soon as you get outside. Get away from the entrance, stay hidden, and call your raven. I'll do what I can to keep them off your trail. And—thank you."

I'd ask what he's thanking me for, but he dips his head to graze his mouth against mine in the most fleeting of kisses. It's there and then gone before I can react to that either. The instant he pulls back, he nudges me toward the ladder. "*Go!*"

There's no time to say anything at all. I spin toward the ladder, grasp the rungs, and haul myself toward the world outside as fast as my muscles will move me.

CHAPTER TWENTY-EIGHT

Sylas

"Nothing yet," August mutters under his breath, as if I can't see that nothingness just as well as he can. He shifts on his feet next to me, his boots rustling against the dry needles scattered on the forest floor.

Even at this late hour, long after sundown, the summer air is warm against our skin, laced with a sweet cedar scent. I don't find that smell as soothing as I normally would, not when we're braced for a treacherous attack.

All around us, dozens of our warriors and other pack-kin August has trained up to competency are waiting with us. With Whitt's help, we've devised a variation on the deflection spells the Murk have been using to avoid notice, ensuring that no one can tell we never ventured much beyond the bottom of the hill when we gave the appearance of setting off this afternoon. We've been lurking hidden in one of Hearth-by-the-Heart's forests with a view of the castle for hours.

"Maybe they've thought better of it," Astrid murmurs at my other side. "Or we've misread their intentions."

I incline my head in acknowledgment. I'm not sure whether I'd rather either of those possibilities were true than see us launch ourselves into battle tonight.

We held back from the larger search effort I'd planned for yesterday after Whitt gave his warning, concerned about an attack from Tristan's pack. When nothing came of that, we decided to lay this trap.

By all appearances, my castle is currently vulnerable, most of my pack's warriors absent, only my strategist who's a fine but not extraordinary fighter as a figure of authority. Whitt even made a show of walking around the fields outside pretending to take swigs from his gifted bottle of absinthe after we left.

If Tristan's pack means to attack, now would be the ideal time. And if they do, then I need to be here to prevent the violent uprising from succeeding. No doubt Tristan thinks he can slaughter all those of my pack who remain and then catch me and the rest of my cadre by surprise on our return, making it easy for him to claim the domain that was once his cousin's for his own.

But if they don't, then we've wasted nearly two days that might have brought us closer to finding my mate over nothing.

My gaze slips away from the castle toward the edges of the pack houses that I can make out through the trees. We instructed those who can't fight to shore up their entrances with magic and stay inside if they hear sounds of a battle tonight. I hope that's enough to protect them. If Tristan's forces arrive, they should tangle with our sentries first, but I wouldn't put it past him to send warriors to quickly deal with our weakest kin who might raise the alarm.

We had the sentries draw back from their typical patrols to remain within our hearing. I have no doubt that any attackers would aim to dispatch them as swiftly and brutally as possible for the same reason they might target the village.

The minutes slip by. An owl lets out a low hoot from a nearby tree. Our warriors stand still and on guard around us, not letting the impatience and uneasiness I'm sure they feel show. Despite my own apprehension, a flare of pride fills me at what an admirable force we've nurtured within our pack.

I only have a moment to enjoy that sensation when a scuffling sound reaches my perked ears. There's a faint noise like a yelp cut off, barely audible unless you were listening for it.

My fangs spring from my gums in an instant. I jerk my hand toward the castle, and we charge forward as one being, leaping into wolf form to make the sprint at a faster pace.

At least a dozen attackers have surrounded the nearest sentry—he might already be cut down. More sounds of a struggle carry from the far side of the castle. There's already the crunch of splintering wood as the doors are forced down. Rage sears through my veins, pulling my lips back from my teeth in a snarl.

That wretched mangy traitor of a lord. But he misjudged me if he thought I'd make this easy a target. He'll regret ever threatening my pack, taking advantage of the harrowing situation we're in. I'm already itching to tear him to pieces myself.

Half of our fighting force, led by August, splits off to fall on the intruders on this side of the castle. Some slash at the warriors in wolf form while others rise up as men and women to fend them off with swords.

I race with Astrid and the rest around the side of the castle, pushing my limbs as fast as I can go. There will be blood spilled here tonight, but I'll do whatever I can to ensure most of it is on Tristan's side.

Instead of surprising us, we've turned the surprise around on them. The attackers who marched on the front of the castle whirl around and flash fangs and claws, but they're surrounded in an instant. We plow into them without giving them more of a chance to react.

For the first several minutes in the fray, I remain in wolf form, lunging this way and that, ripping through a throat here and carving open a belly there. When one of Tristan's cadre-chosen advances on me with sword swinging, I shift with a violent stretch of my limbs, snatching up my own blade from my belt and plunging it into his chest before he can do more than nick my cheek.

One more small scar to add to my existing assortment.

I spin around, panting and gripping the hilt of my sword tight in my hand. Bodies are littered across the field in front of the castle I so painstakingly built. The sight sends a pang through my heart, but there's no time for regrets now. More of my brethren are still struggling between those bodies.

Tristan brought more warriors than I expected—but I haven't left anything to chance. As I spring at a woman about to skewer one of my guards, a fierce cry rises up from the lands to the south. A moment later, a brigade of Donovan's pack-kin rushes in to help us defend our home as I did once for him. The messenger I instructed to race to his castle and raise the alarm made the journey even faster than I'd hoped.

But where is Tristan in all this? I know the assault is his doing because I recognize many of the attackers from his pack, but I haven't seen the lord himself. Surely he didn't send forward this offensive without even being here to oversee it?

That would make him not just a traitor but a coward as well.

The scent of blood is thick in my nose, and growls and the clang of blades fill my ears, but as I topple one more warrior, an even more alarming noise pierces through the din. It's a bark of pain that sounds distinctly like my older brother, coming from inside the castle.

I knew a few of Tristan's pack had breached the walls, but I'd assumed we'd caught most of them before they'd made it inside and that the guards stationed within could deal with those who slipped past us. As I burst past the front doors, I realize I've been at least partly mistaken.

Bodies of both my warriors and Tristan's lie slumped in the entrance hall, and more sounds of a commotion filter from deeper within the castle. There's another grunt that I'm sure now is Whitt, followed by a dark chuckle that makes my blood run cold.

"With me!" I holler, summoning any warrior who can break from the battle outside to follow me, and race down the hall toward the fighting.

There are a few more bodies in the rooms beyond. One of my guards is struggling with a fae man who's slashing out with a dagger in one hand and clawed fingertips on the other. I barrel into him before he has time to register my presence, and my guard stabs him in the heart the second he's knocked to the ground.

"Thank you," she gasps, clapping her hand to a wound on her side that's bleeding.

"More help is coming," I tell her. "Find a healer as soon as you can." I have to get to my brother before even a healer won't be enough.

Blood dapples the wooden floor, mixed with larger smears here and there. I dash along that trail, worry clenching my chest. Then there's a loud metallic clatter up ahead, and I know exactly where I'll find them.

I hurtle into the kitchen in time to watch Whitt hurl one of the pots he knocked off their hooks at Tristan's head. The lord dodges with a sneering laugh, but he stops in mid-step at my entrance, his sword still held at the ready.

August will not be pleased with the mess our intruders have made of his favorite room. Shards of broken glass and china litter the floor. A few of the cupboard doors are bashed in. And there's blood streaked all over the place.

Perhaps a little is from Tristan, a few small wounds leaking through his clothes on his forearm and thigh, but I have to think most of it is Whitt's. He's favoring one leg, his trousers stained crimson from a gouge by his hip, and his opposite arm—his dominant one—hangs limp, the shoulder carved open to the bone. More blood colors his vest from somewhere on his abdomen.

He's holding himself upright, his teeth bared and his eyes sharply determined, but his forehead gleams with a sheen of sweat. He's barely holding himself together.

I step forward, brandishing my own sword. "It's over, Tristan. We saw through your plot. Most of your pack-kin have already fallen. Back away, and you might leave here with your life if not much else."

Tristan meets my gaze with a wild, vicious light in his eyes, as if the curse has come over him three nights early. But he's fully coherent when he speaks. "You killed my cousin; you stole his domain. You sent my entire family into disarray—for what? Some dust-destined dung-body with a few pretty tricks?"

I don't think there's any reasoning with him, but he's closer to Whitt than I am to either of them, and I don't like those odds. I move carefully forward, pressing my advantage without any sudden moves to provoke him.

"Your cousin was scheming to murder one of his fellow arch-lords, as you no doubt well know, since most likely *you* were the one he meant to put in Donovan's place," I have to point out. "Talia had nothing to do with it. Don't blame me or her for the fact that he faced the rightful consequence for his crime."

Tristan laughs again, this time more of a sputter. "See it however you want. If I can't have the throne Ambrose meant to give me, I think I'll take at least one of *your* family down on my way out."

Without any more warning than that, he springs at Whitt.

I fling myself around the island that's standing between us. Whitt has grasped a heavy pan, which he swings at Tristan's temple. But this time the lord doesn't even bother to dodge. He takes the blow with a sharp exhalation and stabs his sword toward Whitt's chest.

My brother could try to wrench himself backward. But he sees me coming, and he has all the faith in me I could possibly ask for. Instead, he blocks the strike with his good arm, hissing as it chops into his flesh, and shoves Tristan toward me in the same instant.

I slam into the lord and tackle him to the floor. With one harsh smack, Tristan's sword goes spinning away. Whitt slumps against the cupboards. I bring my own blade to the traitor's throat.

"You have me at your mercy," Tristan says with a sickly grin, pinned beneath me. "But what if I say I—"

I plunge my sword straight through his neck before he can say the word *yield.*

His head rolls back to thump against the tiles. The blood that spurts up and flows out to puddle beneath him looks like justice—for all the ways he's betrayed our people, for all the harm he's tried to do to those I care about. Not a speck of guilt settles in my gut.

Whitt makes a choked sound that I think might have been an attempt at a chuckle. If that's the best he can do, then he's even worse off than I realized.

I push away from Tristan to kneel by my brother's side. He's nearly as bloody as the man I just killed—Heart help me, maybe even more so.

"Technically you should have given him his lawful opportunity to surrender," my strategist says, somehow taking on his usual wry tone even with the strain in his voice.

"*Technically* the bastard met a better end than he deserved as it was," I retort, and get to work muttering what spells I can to stem the bleeding.

"I have no complaints myself, to be clear," Whitt mutters, and then lapses into silence. He's starting to fade.

I grit my teeth, speaking the spell words faster, drawing as much of the Heart's energy through me as I can. Then the sound of pounding feet reaches my ears.

Several of my pack-kin and a few of Donovan's burst into the room. With a rush of relief, I spot my best healer among them. He's probably come worried he'd need to tend to me, but I can't say I feel any better about it being Whitt who needs him instead.

"Quick!" I wave him over. "And anyone else with any strength in bodily magic as well. He's bleeding out fast."

"I'll be fine," Whitt says, but it's more of a mumble now.

When I've done what I can and have drawn back to let those more skilled do their work, I pace the kitchen, worried it won't be enough. I have the urge to stab Tristan a few more times for nearly taking my brother from me, not that the treacherous lord would feel it.

But it turns out Whitt was right, as he so often is. By the time the rest of my pack and those of Donovan's who came to our aid are gathering in the castle, the rest of the attackers now dealt with, all of Whitt's wounds are sealed, and the healer has rejuvenated him enough for him to look clear-eyed around the kitchen and remark, "You'd better get me to my room to finish recovering, or August is going to finish the job Tristan started."

"It's better you don't move at all for at least an hour or two," the healer informs him. "Take your rest here."

And so Whitt sprawls out with a pillow and blanket I have a

guard fetch, dozing for a while, as the rest of us deal with the bodies and the damage done.

Tristan and his men we heap at the edge of the forest for the rest of his pack or his extended family to claim. Our own, the fourteen who took fatal wounds in the defense of our domain, we clean as well as we can and lay out by the pack village for their families to say their final farewells through the day. In the next evening, we'll hold the funeral ceremonies.

Dawn light is just peeking over the horizon when I step back, looking down at the row of the fallen. So many good men and women we've lost over that family's greedy quest for power. The sight weighs on me, all the heavier with the knowledge of how much else we still have to face.

"Come on," August says to me softly, and leads me back to the kitchen, which looks remarkably like it did before other than Whitt still snoozing in the corner. I suppose the pack-kin August trained know how much this space means to him and took particular care setting it right.

He gets out the fixings for a hot drink, and Whitt stirs from his sleep. Our older brother glances around the room with a smile. "Excellent, I got to skip all the clean-up."

August snorts, and I shake my head, and for a second the moment feels normal, all the loss we've experienced far in the distance.

Then there's a flutter of feathers by the window. A raven swoops inside, transforming into a man the second he's entered. Corwin's eyes are bright with a mix of hope and worry.

"I can sense her again," he says in a rush. "Talia. It's not totally clear yet, but—I'm going to her now."

CHAPTER TWENTY-NINE

Talia

The second I scramble out into the thin light of what's either early morning or evening, Madoc jerks the lid shut over the passage behind me. I sway on my feet, overwhelmed by the rush of sensations.

The fresh air gushes into my lungs like a drug. The open space around me feels eerily vast compared to the narrow tunnels I've spent most of the past several days in. And then comes a jolt of awareness inside me, the abrupt recognition of Corwin's presence somewhere distant but filled with hurried joy.

My soul! Can you hear me?

I can, I think back at him, nearly choking on my relief. *I can. I'm here.*

I'm coming as quickly as I can, Talia. I was by the Heart—it'll take a little time to reach the fringes. Where *are you?*

That… is a very good question. I stare around me, taking a few hesitant steps and struggling through the mental upheaval of my sudden change in surroundings to take in the details of the space around me.

I've come out into a courtyard of stone tiles in what appears to be a park. A few stone benches border the wide circle, and grassy fields and small hills dotted with occasional trees spread out around it. I spot a playground with a slide and climbing equipment in the distance.

None of that tells me where *here* is, though.

Another jolt races through my chest, this one less pleasant. Madoc told me to get away from here, to hide. How quickly will the Murk reach this spot to search for me? Will his attempt at diverting them work at all?

I set off as fast as I can limp, hugging myself. There's a path winding between the trees, and I make out the rooftops of buildings in the near distance. If I can check street signs or a map or a local newspaper, I should be able to figure out where I am.

I should have asked Madoc before he sent me out here so I'd know right away—but it's too late for that now.

Corwin can read my impressions and the emotions they stir up as well as he always could. *Even at my fastest, it'll take a few hours. Get yourself to safety and you can confirm exactly where you are afterward.*

I'm not totally sure where is safe. Where might the rat shifters be lurking in the human world? Are there others around—would they recognize me?

I wish I had some way to at least cover my hair, my most distinctive feature.

I hustle faster, ignoring the reawakened pain in my foot. A rustling sound makes me jump, but it's only a shift in the wind rippling through the branches of the nearby trees.

No one else is around. The light is gradually brightening, a pinkish tint hazing the sky. It must be very early in the morning here—no one's really up and about yet.

As I get closer to the edge of the park, I make out a wrought-iron gate up ahead and a road beyond it. Occasional cars are already cruising by. Even though I'm no longer used to the rumble of engines that was so familiar when I was a kid, seeing them gives me a flash of reassurance.

I'm not totally alone here, even if I can't ask any of the people in those cars where exactly I am.

As long as I can reach you, you're never alone at all, Corwin says through our bond, with an impression of his arms wrapping around me.

My heart tugs with a desperate longing to be in those arms for real. It's been too long since I was with my soul-twined mate—with any of them, really, but the bond between Corwin and me makes the pain particularly acute. My skin is quivering with the need to fully reconnect with him. The same urgency ripples from him into me.

If I could be there in an instant—oh, my soul, I've missed you so much.

I've missed you too. Thoughts of all the things I've been through without him start to rise up, but I shove them down. He's worried enough without knowing how the Murk treated me or the reason they stole me away. I'll be able to explain everything better and more coherently when we can talk face to face—and all the other arch-lords need to know too.

But there's one warning I have to give him now. *When you get here, you'll need to be careful. The Murk have a lot more magic than we thought. It's hard to explain, but they may be able to overpower even a true-blooded fae like you when you're so far from the Heart of the Mists.*

I can feel the truth of what you're saying, even if I can't understand how it's possible, he responds. *But we can deal with the Murk themselves later—once you're safely home. I'll avoid tangling with them. I only want to reach you and bring you back.*

Yes. The start of a sob clogs my throat. *Yes, I want that too.*

As I come up on the gate, the thought of one specific other arch-lord and his cadre grips me. *Are my other mates okay? Has the next full moon already passed? I lost track of the days…*

Corwin's voice washes over me, managing to be soothing even in its urgency. *Don't worry about any of that. Nothing matters until you're back with us. But the full moon hasn't arrived yet, and the others are—*

There's a moment's hesitation, and I can tell he's muffling impressions he doesn't want to pass on to me. Enough slips through for me to get the sense of an injury. *Were they hurt?* I ask with a flare of panic. *What—*

Focus on making sure you're *not hurt for now,* Corwin says firmly. *Sylas, August, and Whitt are all well—they're following behind me as quickly as they were able to get themselves together. There was only a... brief conflict that's now dealt with, which did no lasting harm to any of them.*

I know he's not lying, but that there's a lot more he isn't saying as well. Unfortunately, he's also right that this isn't the best time to discuss what's been going on in the Mists any more than it is for chatting about everything I've experienced.

I step through the park's gate and glance around. The street signs on the corner don't reveal anything about my larger location other than the names appear to be in a language I don't know. I wait for a break in the sparse traffic, dart across the road, and start glancing through the windows of the shops and restaurants lining the other side of the street.

Their names are all in that other language and so are the smaller signs hanging in some of the windows. But a café on the far corner has a laminated newspaper clipping pasted next to the door that includes an English quote: "The best croissants in Munich!"

Germany, Corwin says, catching my observation before I need to purposefully pass it on. *I know which portal to look for. It won't take long at all once I've reached the fringelands. Can you find somewhere you'll be out of danger to wait?*

I don't know. I dart a glance around and hurry onward, my heart thumping. Where can I go that I'll be sure the Murk won't track me down in the hours it's going to take Corwin to make it here? I don't know how to speak the local language—even if I did, the humans around me can't fend off fae magic.

I've got a head start, at least. That's something. As long as I can stay ahead of them...

But now that the initial burst of adrenaline is wearing off, I can't help noticing how tired I am. I'd barely gotten any sleep when Madoc woke me up to help me escape. My warped foot is aching, and my other limbs are starting to stiffen from all the walking and climbing and the stress that's gripped me for much longer than that.

Besides, as long as I'm out wandering the streets, there's *more* chance of a search party spotting me. I need somewhere I can take shelter and stay out of view. Somewhere I won't get kicked out of by the local citizens either.

I hobble onward, looking over a bus shelter, an alley, a coffee shop that's just opening for the day. None of them seem like ideal options. I can't shake the sense that I'm running out of time.

I turn one corner and then another, taking a weaving path so at least I'm not directly down the street from the park. How well will the Murk be able to sniff me out and know which route I took? Is there a bus I can hop on to give myself more distance?

How can I when I don't have any money to pay for the ride?

That thought has just passed through my mind when footsteps tap against the sidewalk somewhere nearby. Instinctively, I throw myself down behind the low wall around the patio of a restaurant that's currently closed.

I reacted not a moment too soon. As I peek through a small gap between panels in the wall, two figures come around a bend at the other end of the block—perfectly human-looking, but with a feral glint in their gazes that makes my muscles tense. One of them sniffs the air and heads my way. That and the intensity of their stares as they scan the street convinces me that they're Murk.

How did they get here so quickly? Or does Orion just have so many followers that they're everywhere? They clearly are sniffing me out, though. In a matter of seconds, they'll be on top of me.

I scramble for a solution and abruptly remember Madoc taking my hair and blowing his magic into the vent.

Can I push my scent away from me? I know the true name for air. I've used it to carry sound to me, so why not smells away from me?

It's the only real chance I have.

"*Briss-gow-aft,*" I murmur in as quiet a voice as I can manage, summoning the memories of leaping to August as he taught me the syllables.

The breeze stirs around me. I whisper the word again, compelling the current away from me, to wash over the ground where I walked and waft across the street in the opposite direction. Pick up every trace of my presence and disperse it elsewhere. Carry it away. Please.

The Murk keep walking toward me. I risk one more hissed repetition, putting all the mental energy I can into the magic—and they hesitate.

The one who sniffed before raises his nose. "That way," he says, pointing away from me in the direction I sent the breeze. They trot across the road and hustle around the next corner.

You did so well, my soul, Corwin says, with a tremor of distraught emotion that he isn't here to protect me.

But he's coming. I just have to hold out a little longer.

I don't know how long my trick with the air will divert my pursuers. I wait only a minute, until I'm sure they're well on their way, and then I backtrack the way I came, hoping any fresh scent I leave behind will mingle with the old and confuse my trail. I also mumble "*Briss-gow-aft*" under my breath at regular intervals, washing away whatever traces I can.

What else do I know about the Murk that might help? They're used to enclosed spaces, like I was starting to become… They're used to slinking through dimness and darkness, avoiding the full light of day, which is creeping up on us even now. That might help me.

And maybe they'd be less likely to look *up* rather than along the streets at the level where they're in the habit of finding things.

I spot a building with a metal staircase running up the brick wall to a side door on the third floor and scramble over to it. Wincing at every soft clink of my boots against the metal steps, I make my way up to the highest point and tuck myself behind a solid wall in one section of the landing that hides me from view.

I murmur the true name for air over and over, dispelling any trace of my scent from the area, until my throat starts to get hoarse and an ache spreads through my skull. Surely I've blown away enough traces of my path by now?

My head droops against the metal wall.

I'm almost there, Talia, Corwin says. *Hold on just a little longer.*

I can do that. I can. I fight back my weariness, scanning the terrain below for any sign of pursuers.

A yawn stretches my jaw. The sun beams down over me, draping me in more warmth than I've felt in days. My head lists to the side again, my eyelids drooping—

And a raven dives out of the sky.

Corwin lands next to me, shifting into the form of a man with his wings still spread, and pulls me into his arms. My hands shoot up to cling to him. The sob I've been holding in for what feels like days now tumbles out of me.

"I've got you, my soul," he says out loud, the same sentiment echoing through our inner connection. "We're going home."

CHAPTER THIRTY

Talia

Corwin must have cast one of the fae spells to hide us from human eyes, because he carries me away from the stairway where he found me with a flap of his wings and no concern at all about who might see us below. I cling to his shirt, tucking my body as closely against him as I can, but it doesn't feel like enough.

Even though he's right here, both physically and within me through our inner connection, the bond demands more. I'm burning to meld right into him, as if I can get close enough to make up for the days and days when we were much too far apart, when even our bond was muted.

And it isn't just me. The same need sears through him, making his arms tighten around me.

Soon, he says, even his inner voice ragged with urgency. His wings flap harder, the speed of his flight making the wind whip through my hair and tousle his dark curls. *We're almost there, almost away from them.*

I sense it when he spots the portal he arrived through. He dives with a warble of the wind and careens through it so quickly the passage is little more than a brief blurring of my vision and flip of my stomach. Then we're whooshing through into the fog of the Mists' fringelands.

Corwin spins, still holding me tightly, and snaps several magically charged syllables at the portal we've just come through. It wavers and contracts to a much smaller shimmering surface, and I can tell from the impressions that trickle through him to me that he's sealed it off to ensure no Murk follow us. It'll only hold a day or two, but they have no hope of reaching me right now.

Relief washes over me, with a sharper surge of desire right on its heels. I lift my head, and Corwin is already dipping his to meet me.

The impact of our first kiss after so long apart sizzles both of us like an electric shock. I find myself twisting in his arms, wrapping my own around his neck and my legs around his waist, kissing him harder.

I need, I *need* to reinforce the bond that was nearly severed by confirming just how entwined we are in every possible way. I've never felt this kind of carnal longing before, ringing through every nerve and amplified by the answering desire radiating through my mate, as powerful as the lightning bolt that first bound us together.

No coherent thoughts pass between us now, only that flaring of emotions and errant words. *You… My soul… So long…*

As our lips crash together, tongues tangling, I'm only vaguely aware of Corwin moving us until he's laying me down on the floor of the carriage he must have ridden here in. His wings are still spread above us like a dark canopy.

He devours my mouth and then kisses my jaw and my neck. Everywhere his hands and his hot breath touches me, my skin lights up with giddy quivers.

The twist of need between my thighs burns deeper. I wrench at his pants, and he tugs down mine as he kicks his the rest of the way off. His shaft slides against my core, setting off a pulse of pleasure so intense I moan.

Corwin buries his face in the crook of my neck as he lines

himself up. My hips arch to meet him, but he hesitates just for a second, with a wild spark of recognition. *It's your time. You're fertile.*

I've avoided full sex with all of my mates during those days of the month before, but not a single particle of my being can bear to wait now. *I don't care. I* need *you.*

And I need you, he replies with a strangled sound, and plunges into me.

Another moan escapes me with the heady rush of being filled so swiftly and completely. My knees lift to grip Corwin's thighs. I sway into his thrusts, urging him as deep as he can go. As the pleasure and pure joy of being completely connected again swells through me and flows between us through our bond, our mouths collide with more frantic kisses. Our hands roam all over each other's bodies. The muscled planes of my mate's body flex beneath my fingers.

My mate, Corwin thinks with a shudder of breath. *My soul. Mine.*

Mine, I echo back to him, clutching him with all my strength. The wave of ecstasy builds and builds, carrying me higher with every gasp and rocking of our bodies. My fingernails dig into his shoulders, and he groans at the delight that sparks with the pinch of pain.

I'll never let them take you from me again. Never.

Corwin bucks into me, his rigid length finding that perfect spot inside me again, and again, and—

My release blazes through me, tossing me over the peak and leaving every nerve tingling, spurred higher by the burst of bliss as my soul-twined mate follows me.

In the shaky aftermath, Corwin hugs me to him, as if we really could melt into one being. I inhale his cool, foresty scent, letting it wash any remaining hint of the Refuge's dank tunnels from my lungs. Then my mate raises his head.

We're no longer alone. Sometime in the middle of the mad collision of our bodies, my other mates reached the fringes. Sylas, Whitt, and August have come up by the side of the carriage. August looks awkward, but his expression is bright with love and relief. Whitt's lips are curled in an amused smile, and the intensity of his gaze heats my skin all over again. And Sylas…

I've never seen my Seelie arch-lord so overcome with emotion. He holds himself as tall and noble as always, but I don't need a soul-twined bond to recognize the mix of anguish and elation in his mismatched eyes.

We're bound together too, me and the three of them, in every way *we* possibly can be. We swore ourselves to each other what now feels like years ago—but we never had the chance to even start to consummate that official commitment.

A fresh surge of longing rushes through me. I need all of my mates—I need them with me; I need them *in* me.

Corwin recognizes my hunger, and perhaps my Seelie mates do too, even with only sight and scent to go by. Without a word, he draws back, giving them a soft smile and a nod. As I sit up on the lightly padded floor, I reach for them. They leap in to join me.

"You're all right?" August says, nuzzling my shoulder, trailing his fingers down my back.

Sylas strokes his firm hand over my hair with a growl. "If those mangy rats hurt you—"

They did, but not in any way that seems to matter right now. "I'm okay," I say, my voice quavering. "I just—being so far away from you—not knowing if I'd ever—" My throat chokes up. I catch Whitt's gaze where he's knelt in front of me. "I'm sorry I couldn't reach out to you better."

Before I can say any more, he touches my cheek. I can see all the same love glowing in his eyes as when he gave me his true name. "You did everything you could. It killed me not being able to reach out to *you*. But you're back with us now, and that's what matters."

He tugs me in for a kiss, nearly as urgent as the ones I just shared with Corwin. A hum of approval resonates from Sylas's chest, and he dips his head to nibble my earlobe. August switches from nuzzling to marking my shoulder with his mouth. The same need buzzing through me thrums in the air between us.

My body seems to move of its own accord. I can't resist the yearning in me any more than I could with Corwin. I yank Whitt closer, run my fingers into the thick waves of Sylas's hair where they fall to his shoulders, and lean into August's embrace.

In the haze of passion, I'm not totally sure who's stroking their hands over my breasts, who's lifting my shirt to kiss a path down my spine, who's delving deft fingers between my thighs where I'm still slick from my first homecoming. All that matters is the growing inferno we're caught up in. Even Corwin, watching from the bow of the carriage, gives off nothing but approval and a sense of rightness.

I unfasten Whitt's slacks first. As his hardness springs free, he groans and pulls me onto his lap to straddle him. His mouth reclaims mine, one hand braced against the floor of the carriage for balance, but I can't help noticing that his other arm moves stiffly as he reaches to tug my shirt right off.

I pull back just an inch, remembering the vague answer I got from Corwin about what my other mates have dealt with while I've been gone. "Are you hurt? What happen—"

Whitt cuts me off with another desperate kiss. His answer spills across my lips. "Nothing that isn't already healing, mighty one. And being with you makes me feel as if it's all already behind me."

I can't help kissing him again, making a note in the back of my mind that I need more answers later. That thought is swept away a second later by the thrust of Whitt's shaft into me.

I whimper and sink into him, wanting all of him. He kisses me hard, cupping my breast as he rocks me up and down on him, my other lovers caressing me everywhere else.

"I love you," he murmurs between kisses. "My mate."

When I choke up this time, it's with nothing but happiness. "I love you too. All of you. So much."

He slides his hand down to fondle the sensitive nub just above where we're joined, and my second release surges over me. I tip back my head, and my cry is swallowed by Sylas's lips. The giddy wave crashes over me.

Whitt sits me down on one of the side benches, panting in the aftermath of his own finish, and August is there in front of me in an instant. My gentlest lover dapples kisses across my lips, cheek, and neck until I'm whimpering for more. When I grip him through his pants, he lets out a strangled sound.

"Oh, my sweetness," he says roughly. "Nothing was right without you."

"I'm here now," I say. "I never want to be apart from you again."

His next words come out fierce. "We won't give them a chance." Then he's kissing me with ardor to match, stealing my breath.

The moment his pants are loosened, he enters me, filling me to the brim, his tongue delving between my lips at the same time. I'm so sensitized now, so adrift on the pleasure of this moment and the moments before, that I'm spiraling toward my peak with just his first few thrusts.

I try to hold on, reveling in the exquisite stretch of August's hardness inside me, in the tender words that tumble from his mouth, but it's a losing battle. I clench around him, and he joins me with a ragged grunt.

August caresses my cheek as he gives me one last, lingering kiss, so sweet my heart aches with it. Then he eases back to make room for Sylas, who's been stroking his fingers over my naked skin.

The Seelie arch-lord gathers me against him. He steals a quick kiss before pulling back to meet my eyes. "Will you welcome one more of your mates, my love?" he asks hoarsely.

As if he needs to protect me from himself. As if I don't want him, need him, just as much as the others.

"I couldn't want anything more," I say, tugging him back to me. I didn't realize how just empty I felt trapped among the Murk until now, with all my mates around me.

Sylas lies me back down on the floor of the carriage, his powerful frame braced over me. He kisses my mouth and down my neck to my chest, where he sucks one nipple and then the other into his mouth. I squirm with the sparks of pleasure, my sex throbbing again for this final act of completion. My chest hitches. "I need you."

Sylas growls, and if he meant to take this slower, that intention must vanish with my plea. I raise my knees, and he presses forward to meet me, filling me slowly but steadily until I'm gasping with the blaze of sensation. At this point, it's all I can do to cling onto him and ride the maelstrom, spinning into bliss with every pump of his hips into mine, losing myself with a shudder that spreads even more delight all through my body.

The Seelie arch-lord comes in me with a fresh flood of heat. Then he rolls off me and eases my body up into a sitting position again, so all of my mates can gather around me.

In their ring of heat and adoration, I let my muscles go slack. Now that the wrenching compulsion for connection has been satisfied, my previous exhaustion is rolling back in.

But it doesn't pull me completely under. As my mates murmur more words of affection and fond caresses, memories of everything beyond this moment start creeping back in.

The impending war. The curse. Orion and his horrible Heart.

I jerk back into alertness. "We have to get back. There must—in the winter realm, the curse, it's taken more people. And the full moon is in two days?"

Corwin kisses my temple. "You needed this closeness to be yourself again," he says. "We'll speed back—if you're up for the journey now? It won't help anyone to push yourself after the ordeal you've already experienced."

I squeeze his hand. "I think I'm up to a carriage ride." I can nap during the trip back. And then—

Another thought strikes me, so hard and piercing I flinch. My mates ease back. "What's wrong?" August asks, his body already tensing to leap to my defense.

"I—" I don't know how to tell them this. I've just realized that they don't know the facts I've come to accept over the past several days—they don't know how entangled both I and my powers are with the leader of the Murk and the magic he wields.

Would they even have wanted to share this interlude with me if they did?

My expression brings a shadow across Sylas's face. "Whatever you're facing, we'll see it through with you. You can tell us."

How can I admit to them that I'm the tool of their greatest enemy, an instrument meant to bring about their downfall?

But I have to. I can't hide this from them. The fear of what could happen to *them* is already gnawing at me with every moment I stay silent.

"There's a lot I have to tell all of you," I say, the words stinging my throat on the way up. "But we should go back to the Heart as quickly as we can. I'll tell you on the way there."

Whitt glances across the hazy forest toward a wooden carriage that he and his half-brothers must have arrived in. "Why don't we take our craft, then? It's larger."

"Of course." Corwin glances at me with curiosity and concern, but he doesn't press for me to speak right away.

We pull our clothes back into order and clamber out of the gleaming winter carriage. The Unseelie arch-lord dismisses it with a few words and gestures, leaving a sheen of frost on the ground that melts within seconds. We settle into the summer carriage without delay.

I sit in the widest middle seat with August and Whitt on either side of me, Corwin across from me, and Sylas setting the vehicle into motion from the helm. As it weaves between the trees, he moves to lean against the starboard side between the two benches, watching me.

Whitt gives my knee a gentle squeeze. "Go ahead, mite."

My throat constricts. All at once, my eyes are burning with tears.

I force the words out before my mates get too caught up in worrying about me to really listen. "I—I found out where my powers come from, and why I can heal the curse. It's all because of the Murk."

My mates stay still and silent as I lay out everything important that happened and everything I learned, from the moment Donovan's pack-kin led me into the woods through to my escape from the Refuge. When I stumble over some parts, August grasps my hand, and Whitt slips his arm behind my back.

I can sense the tension in all of their stances, but they don't withdraw from me. Not yet, anyway.

When I finish, there's another long moment of silence. Corwin extends a tendril of affection and horror at my mistreatment my way, but I can tell he's disturbed by more than just that.

He glances at Sylas. "Can we trust the cure she offers, then? The Murk may have worked something worse into it, something that'll harm us more in the long run."

"Orion didn't mention anything about it working that way," I say. "He said the point of the curse was so that all the fae of the Mists would start counting on me, so it'd hurt you when he took me away. But… there could be more to it that he didn't talk about."

"It could all have been lies," August says abruptly. "There's nothing *stopping* them from lying. Even if they've made some kind of false Heart, for it to give them enough power that they could cast a spell that huge… It's impossible, isn't it?" He sounds more hopeful than certain.

Sylas shakes his head. "I don't know. I'd have thought an awful lot of things we've seen the Murk do in the past few months were impossible, but yet they happened. And it explains a lot of things that I didn't fully understand before." He pauses. "Aerik even told me that the reason he and his cadre came out of the Mists the night they stumbled on Talia, they were hunting down a rat. One of the Murk led them right to her."

A shiver passes through me, even though it's only confirmation of what I already knew. "I thought I was connected to the Heart of the Mists—everyone was saying I was blessed. But it's not that at all. It was the Murk's magic all along." The power in me comes from that horrible orange mass with its jittering light. Just the memory of it makes my skin crawl.

"That might not be true," Whitt says thoughtfully, still running his hand up and down my back in a soothing motion. "You said this Orion and the other Murk didn't show any sign of suspecting you could use true names. They left the bracelet on you and had no idea you might have used it to form a wrench. *That* power didn't come from them. Perhaps the Heart of the Mists recognized what you could do for us and welcomed you regardless of the Murk's intentions."

"Its powers do work in inexplicable ways," Corwin says.

"So what do we do now?" I have to ask.

Sylas rubs his jaw. "I think we'll return to the Heart of the Mists as quickly as we can and consult with our fellow arch-lords. Talia is ours far more than the Murk's now. We'll let nothing challenge that. But how to proceed with the curse—we should come to a consensus that the entire rulership is satisfied with."

I don't know what's worse: the thought that people might die while I stand back because the arch-lords are too suspicious of the source of my cure, or the thought that I might hurt the sickening fae worse if I do cure them. But the rest of Sylas's words and the obvious agreement from my other mates reassures me. They're not casting me aside.

Tears well up anyway, all the emotions that've been churning inside me spilling over. August hugs me to him and grabs a folded blanket they had ready, tucking it around me.

"You've been through a lot," he says. "And you met it with as much courage as I could expect from any of our warriors. Get some rest. You're not on your own anymore."

I'm tired enough that I manage to sleep cuddled up against him for the rest of the brisk flight home. When we reach the Heart, I wake up just enough to walk groggily to my bedroom in the border castle. The last thing I remember is August lowering me onto the bed.

When I wake up next, I'm alone in the room, unsure how much time has passed. My head still feels muddled, my chest heavy, but I can't bear to doze any longer.

I push myself onto my feet and limp through the halls to a room on the summer side with a balcony. As I step out, fresh sweet air tickles over my skin. I breathe it in deeply, savoring it, but it doesn't release much of the tension inside me.

In the distance, my pack-kin are moving around the pack village and the castle of Hearth-by-the-Heart. I turn toward the true Heart itself. The glowing white mass, like a ball of pure sunlight, pulses in its steady rhythm just south of the balcony.

The ripples of its energy flow over me with the warm breeze, momentarily soothing. But do they feel quite as strong as they used to?

I frown, stepping all the way to that side of the balcony. It's hard to remember exactly how big the Heart of the Mists was before, exactly how potent its magic. Maybe I'm imagining things. Still, cold fingers close around my gut inside of the summer heat.

This Heart may have embraced me. My mates may have happily welcomed me back. But Orion is still out there with the Heart of his own making, and I'm connected to him too whether I like it or not.

The one thing I know for sure is that he'll stop at nothing to use me to destroy everyone and everything here I care about.

LIES OF MURK - BONUS SCENE

Why did Madoc steal that kiss from Talia before he let her leave—and what was waiting for him back in the Refuge? This bonus scene shows the events in chapter 27 from his point of view.

Madoc

With every step I take along the passage out of the Refuge, I'm starkly aware of Talia behind me. The scuff of her footsteps as she limps along as carefully as she can manage. The definite distance she's keeping between us, staying nearby but never letting herself get close enough that my tail might brush up against her.

I should be asking myself whether this is really worth it. I should be wondering if I've gone mad to risk everything that's mattered to me for this woman who still sees me as the enemy. But the fact is, after what she's seen and heard, I can't blame her for holding that opinion… and there's not a single doubt left in me.

She asked about the magic of this passage, the way it prevents intruders from reaching my people's home. When traveling down the path from above, heading toward the Refuge, those like me who are familiar with the twists and turns don't even need to think about it anymore. I barely see any route but the true one, it stretches out so clearly in front me.

Helping Talia escape feels the same way right now. A certain path without a single other option my mind will consider.

She draws in a breath in the silence. "How long have I—"

Even as she speaks, a different sound reaches my ears from the opposite direction. I jerk to a halt, whipping up my hand to cut off her words.

Talia is aware enough of the potential danger we're in to freeze alongside me at the edge of the chasm that lines this part of the passage. We both stand in rigid silence as a faint mechanical squeak carries from the not-so-distant hatch to the world above.

In a matter of seconds, we'll have company. Company we can't hope to avoid while we're standing on this path.

As a murmur of voices reaches my ears, my gaze darts over our surroundings. There. On the other side of the chasm a little farther up, there's a ledge just big enough to hold the two of us. My body moves on pure instinct, propelling me until I'm level with it and leaping across. I catch myself against the wall and spin around toward Talia with my hand already beckoning her.

"My illusions can stop them from seeing and hearing us, but it won't let them walk right through us. We have to get off the path."

Talia lurches up the rocky surface with a nervous hitch of breath. At the same moment, the two approaching figures come into view up ahead. They mutter to each other, coming on fast.

Talia sees them too. Her gaze whips to mine, her green eyes unbearably wide with fear. She shifts her weight, favoring her deformed foot, and swallows audibly. "I don't think I can do it. My foot—I'll fall."

The terror on her face wrenches at my heart. I haven't brought her all this way only to lose her to a couple of clueless sentries—who are closing the distance far too swiftly.

I fling my arm toward her. "You just need to get close enough for me to catch you. *Quickly*."

Her hesitation pains me almost as much as her distress. Have I lost so much of the good will I gained with her over the past several days that she'd rather be caught and thrown back into Orion's cage than trust me?

But then she moves. She shuffles backward and scurries forward to throw herself toward me.

Her aim is good. All I have to do is clasp her elbow and heave her straight to me, swinging her around so that we're standing face to face with our shoulders against the wall. She trembles against me, her eyelids tightly shut.

I can't back away. There isn't room. I have to stand there with my body all but pressed against hers, the tangy sweet scent of her filling my nose, my heartbeat kicking up a notch at her closeness. Her skin is so soft beneath my fingers. An ache spreads through my chest, stretching down to my groin and up to my lips.

All the things I'd like to do with this woman. All the ways I'd like to feel her. But I can't have any of it. She isn't mine.

Even if she wasn't already so attached to those fucking fae of the seasons she calls her mates, she'd probably never consider any rat that way.

Strangely, the thought doesn't come with the resentment I might have expected, only a dull sense of resignation and a pang of loss. As if I ever had her anyway. I'm about to send her back to those mates. That's what this escape is all about.

They deserve her more than Orion does. I'm sure of that much.

I'm vaguely aware of the sentries rushing by. Their voices and footsteps fade away as they veer along the path below. I gradually exhale.

"I should leap back across first, and then you jump to me like before," I say to Talia under my breath. "Can you find a position where you feel steady?"

She dips her head slightly. As I release her, she leans more of her weight against the wall. I eye her until I can tell she's got her bearings, and then I spring back to the path.

This time, when I offer my hands to her, she barely hesitates at all. I catch her slim waist in my grasp and set her firmly on the path before releasing her.

A shudder runs through her frame. "Let's skip that part next time."

A laugh tumbles out of me—that she's strong enough to still make a joke about the situation despite her obvious panic, that she can talk about doing this *again* so easily. My humor dries up in my throat with the recognition of how much I wish there could be a next time, just… not like this. Not here.

When I say my goodbyes at the end of this path, most likely I'll never see her again.

But that's the outcome she'd want, and it's better than leaving her under Orion's heel. I gesture toward the top of the path and force myself to say, "Let's hope there isn't a next time."

Talia is still limping as she always does, but she manages to scramble along faster after that near-disaster. Past the top of the chasm, there are only a couple of short hallways before we reach the exit.

I clamber up the ladder, speak the true names to activate the locks, and open up the hatch. The outside air gusts over us, and Talia gasps. There's so much longing in the sound that my gaze snaps back to her face.

As she focuses on me, her expression turns uncertain. I ease back down the ladder, my pulse stuttering. Is she afraid to go out into an unknown place alone?

What would happen if I went with her?

A part of me twangs with the urge to find out. But too much of my life is still tied to the people living down below, the people I've sworn to bring to freedom just as I have for the woman in front of me. I can't abandon them.

Maybe seeing Talia make her escape is the first step toward that freedom, though. A freedom that doesn't require so much bloodshed on both sides. I never would have believed it was possible a week ago, and I'm still far from confident, but this fragile yet determined woman has lit a wavering flame of hope inside my chest.

I find myself resting my fingers lightly against her shoulder. "Talia," I say, not totally sure how I want to follow her name but gripped by the need to say *something* to express the clash of emotion inside me—

And then the call comes, as if I've been yanked by a leash attached to my gut. The sense of my true name being spoken resonates through my mind, followed by Orion's voice in a furious hiss. *Find the girl. She's gone!*

I can't ignore the call. I've fulfilled its command in an instant—I don't need to "find" Talia when she's right in front of me—but my king has discovered her disappearance much sooner than I'd hoped. I have to get down there before he realizes *I've* disappeared too.

A curse lurches over my tongue. I catch Talia's gaze again. "They've already noticed you're gone. They'll be searching all the passages. I have to get back to divert them. Move fast as soon as you get outside. Get away from the entrance, stay hidden, and call your raven. I'll do what I can to keep them off your trail. And—thank you."

I can't help adding that last expression of gratitude—and somehow as the words slip out of me, I'm leaning forward and pressing my mouth against hers for just an instant. I need… I need to leave her with some trace of me to remember, a particle of our time together to carry with her into the open air above.

A hint of her taste crosses my lips, and I'm already tearing myself away, prodding her toward the ladder at the same time. "*Go!*"

She jerks away and climbs up the rungs with more speed than most would have believed she was capable of after watching her uneven gait. She pulls herself out through the opening, and I dart up the rungs for just long enough to slam the hatch shut behind her. Then I'm racing back down the path as fast as my own feet can carry me.

My illusion still disguises me. No one will see or hear my hasty retreat back to the Refuge. I just have to make home there before Orion starts to wonder why I haven't touched base with him yet.

I navigate the twists and turns without a second thought, the walls blurring together. By the time I reach the doorway into the

Refuge proper, my breath is burning in my heaving lungs. I take as few moments as I can get away with to gather myself and then sprint down the last passage into the nearest tunnel.

My fellow Murk are running this way and that with murmurs and twitching eyes. There's no way to tell whether they're more anxious about the loss of our human or Orion's wrath over that loss. I merge into the chaos and head toward the mechanical room with the grate where we left our red herring.

I find a couple of the lower guards already there, examining it. "What did you find?" I bark at them as if I don't know, as if I need their answer urgently.

"She might have gotten out this way," one says with a hint of a cringe. "There's a strand of pink hair, but—"

"Well, go after her then," I snap with a wave of my hand. Both of them shrink into their rat forms and scuttle off down the passage on their hopeless quest.

I dash from one station to another, making sure at least a few people take note of me in each spot, and then return to the throne room. Orion is pacing back and forth on the dais, his tail slashing through the air, his expression rigid with fury.

"I've checked all through the Refuge, my king," I say, coming to a stop at the foot of the dais. "There's some sign of her by the air vent she was attempting to get into earlier. I sent men down it to search for her. Has there been any other word?"

He shakes his head with a sharp motion and swivels toward me. "I've been betrayed, Madoc. She couldn't have done this alone. One of our own got her out of that cage. It's impossible that she could have opened it herself."

I choose my next words carefully. The last thing I want is punishment for my crime to fall on anyone else's shoulders. "She has surprised us before."

Orion snorts. "Your mind is a little too open. No, there is a traitor in our midst. And we are going to find him… and make him pay."

CHAINED SOUL

BOUND TO THE FAE #8

CHAPTER ONE

Talia

The Unseelie woman stands stooped in front of me, her stance rigid and her skin tinged blue. She's the seventh winter fae I've healed in the week and a half since I escaped the Murk and made it back to the Mists, but somehow the process still feels different.

Not every part of that difference is necessarily bad. My tears well up faster these days, taking almost no effort at all. But that's because I can't help thinking about the several cursed fae I *couldn't* save while I was trapped by the rat shifters in the human world. The Unseelie men and women who waited, hoping for my return, while the curse's icy claws gripped them tighter and tighter until their bodies shut down completely.

As I brush my tear-damp fingers over the woman's cheek, her wan face lights up with relief. I wish I could feel the same thing. Even knowing that I'm saving her life, that no more lives need to be lost right now, I can't help remembering the worst of the things I learned while the Murk held me.

This curse is their doing. Their king, Orion, has managed to infect all of the Mists with the horrible magic of the false Heart he created. And every bit of the fear and distress his curse provokes has been flowing out of the Mists to add to the Murk Heart's power. The thought of its erratic orange glow sends a shudder down my spine.

I know how I'm connected to the curse and the Murk now. I escaped them in some ways, but in others, I'm still tied to Orion and his magic. I can't let the curse overcome the fae around me—that would only add to the distress that fuels his Heart—but with every healing I carry out, they rely on me more. Which means if Orion manages to tear me away from them again, they'd *hurt* even more.

The woman beams at me, the frost fading from her hair, and I manage to smile back at her. I can't think about all those things now. Orion *won't* tear me away from my home again—my mates are taking every step to ensure that's not possible.

Whether he brings his Murk forces here to attempt to tear all of us to pieces is a totally different consideration.

Which is why, when I step back from the woman and her mate helps her walk back to their carriage with the few flock folk who came along to witness the healing, I have to brace myself for a different sort of confrontation. When the cursed woman arrived, we'd already been preparing for a meeting of all the arch-lords in the border castle that's become my real home between the winter and summer realms.

They'll have delayed, waiting for me to return, but I'm not looking forward to another of these conversations that involve at least as much arguing as planning.

Corwin and a couple of his coterie members accompanied me to the spot by the Heart of the Mists where I always offer my cure. They stand poised in a half-circle around me like a protective detail. It seems unlikely that the Murk would spring at me right here, with the rhythmic pulse of the Heart's energy washing over me from just a few feet away, but the rat shifters did kidnap me from one of the domains by the Heart before. No one's taking the slightest chance with my safety now.

I turn to face the Heart for a moment, soaking in the brilliant glow that feels like the warmest beams of sunlight. My hand reaches automatically to my opposite arm, where a new bronze bracelet grips my wrist. August tied the magic in it to the matching bracelet he gave my brother when we made a quick trip to check in on him after my return. Jamie's okay. I'm okay. How can I ask for more?

I made it through Orion's cruel treatment. I have the tools to defend myself as well as I can. And the true Heart shines on me in ways he never guessed. Weirdly, I feel closer to it now that I know it didn't give me all my powers.

The bits of magic I can wield used to seem like they might be random chance, a fluke of nature. But really, Orion arranged for my power to cure and my ability to form a soul-twined bond. And even though I have the Murk's horrible influence twisted all through me, the Heart of the Mists welcomed me and offered me some of its own power. Without the true names I can call on in some small way, I might not have made it this far.

When I set off for the castle, Corwin comes up beside me, Zelpha and Olander keeping their positions ahead and behind us. My soul-twined mate slips his hand around mine.

It will get easier again, he says through our inner connection. *Healing the curse, I mean. You're still recovering.*

My mouth twists. *I don't think I'll ever be able to stop thinking about how the Murk have used me until the threat is over and the curse is ended. At least your colleagues decided to trust me enough to let me keep curing people instead of leaving them to die.*

That was one of the earlier arguments after I got back, out of concern that the Murk might have worked some surreptitious evil into the cure itself. But the winter arch-lords quickly decided that some unknown harm was less of a problem than their people literally dying in front of them.

I suspect their decision was helped along by the fact that the arch-lord who's been most opposed to my involvement with her people, Laoni, is going to need a second cure herself any day now.

As we come up on the winter entrance to the castle, a wave of weariness sweeps through me. I stop for a moment to gather myself and restrain a yawn.

Are you all right, my soul? Corwin asks, worry furrowing his brow. *You've seemed more tired than usual today. Was your sleep interrupted?*

A little, I admit. I rarely have dreams of my initial captivity among the summer fae anymore, but since my return, images of the things I saw among the Murk have haunted my sleep. The steel cage Orion tossed me into. The pain that seared through my mind when he forced me to respond to his interrogation.

And also violence dealt to the Murk by the fae I consider my own. Every few nights, I find myself back in the sewer orphanage, watching several wolfish warriors tear apart Murk toddlers like bloody dolls.

Not all the crimes committed have been on the Murk's side.

I *have* been feeling especially worn down the past few days, for no reason I can point to. Maybe it's just taken some time for the weight of everything I've discovered to catch up with me after the initial relief of being home. I've hidden it from Corwin's awareness of me as well as I can because he has enough other things to worry about, and me being a bit tired is hardly comparable to an impending war. Today I just want to crawl back into bed and sleep for the rest of the day, though.

I'll take a nap after this meeting, I tell Corwin, rolling my shoulders to gather my strength, and limp on into our castle.

The rest of the arch-lords, both the four others of winter and the three of summer, are already gathered around the long meeting table in a room in the center of the castle. Several cadre and coterie members stand poised along the walls. I take a seat with Corwin at my left at the head of the table and Sylas at my right. Whitt, who's poised with August behind his lord, reaches to give my hair a playfully affectionate tug, as if just to remind me that they're all here for me.

"All right," Laoni says briskly, as if she's more in charge here than anyone else. "Now we can get on with things. The first order of business…" She fixes her piercing gaze on me. "Have you sensed any sign of the Murk's influence acting on you since our last meeting?"

Of course that's her first priority. "No," I say, keeping my voice even. "If I had, you'd already know about it."

Celia, the most senior of the summer arch-lords, clears her throat. "Well, then, let's discuss the progress we've made in our efforts at locating this 'refuge' where their king is hiding as well as the other Murk colonies. The scouting parties under my cadre's supervision haven't discovered any larger habitations of the vermin yet, although they did come across a building in Oslo that appeared recently vacated of rats. What about the rest of you?"

I'm tired enough that I can't stop my mind from drifting as the other arch-lords give their reports, snapping back to attention when one or another asks for my opinion on a specific observation they've made. That's why I'm joining this meeting at all when no one else's mates are present—I'm the only one with direct knowledge of the Murk's current status and habits. But no one seems to have encountered much of the enemy at all.

"They must realize that I'll have told you everything I learned as soon as I got back to you," I say after all of the arch-lords are finished. "They're laying low because they know how thoroughly you'll be searching." But that doesn't mean the Murk aren't working just as hard on their war efforts as before. Orion's people were accomplishing plenty just within their underground home of abandoned subway stations.

"They're still attempting to spy on us," Uzziah mutters. The dour winter arch-lord scowls. "One of the patrols reporting to me caught a rat near the fringes last night and dealt with it as appropriate."

He means they killed it. My stomach knots, and I sit up in my chair a little straighter. My mind darts to the story Madoc told me about his parents, brutally slaughtered simply for daring to try to make a life for themselves and their son on the fringes of the Unseelie realm.

A protest rises in my throat, but I'm not sure what to say. I've already appealed to the fae around me that they shouldn't assume every rat shifter they come across is out to harm us, but at the first suggestion that I had sympathy for any of the Murk, even my mates tensed. Laoni accused me of being brainwashed by them.

It took another few days and several spells and conversations before they let me rejoin the meetings afterward, and even now, only

Corwin and Sylas seem to understand my concerns. If I'm going to get the agreement of enough of the others to swing the balance toward a different policy, I know I have to approach it from a more practical rather than emotional angle.

Madoc, the Murk man who helped me escape his king, hoped that by helping me he'd give me the opportunity to push back against the fae of the seasons' hatred of the Murk, to encourage them to open some kind of dialogue so that the conflict might not come to outright war. So far, I've failed in that. But then, even Madoc made it clear he knew it was a long shot.

Mostly he helped me escape because he believed saving me from a fate worse than death was more important than his loyalty to his king. And that right there is how I know not all the Murk are spiteful villains.

"Did the patrol try to question the Murk they found?" I ask.

Uzziah turns his scowl toward me. "What do you mean?"

"What I said. Did they try to question the Murk and see if they could find out anything about what the rats are planning now, or did they go straight to killing? We need to learn everything we can, don't we? And they'll know more about what their own people are up to than anyone here does, including me."

Uzziah's scowl deepens. He probably suspects I'm concerned about more than just uncovering the Murk's schemes, but he can suspect all he wants. He can't argue with what I've actually said.

Not much, anyway. Celia gives it a shot. "We've already seen how quick the Murk are to end their own lives rather than risk giving anything away—and how much magic they can wield if they're given a chance to. When it isn't likely we'd get anything out of them anyway, it seems safer to simply dispose of them before they have a chance to attack our own people."

"Everyone should be prepared for their magic now," I say. "And when it's a patrol of several of you against one or two of them, I can't see how they'd get away with much. When we're not having much success with our own searches, shouldn't we at least *try* to get some information from them?"

Or to make sure they're even part of the enemy forces and not just random fae passing by, I think but don't say.

Sylas leans forward. "I agree with Talia. It's worth the risk for the chance that they'll give away something useful. We can't win a war by avoiding all danger to ourselves."

"Even if they told us something, we couldn't trust it to be true," Laoni says. "That false Heart of theirs obviously doesn't take issue with lying."

"Then we discuss what they do say and decide for ourselves how to proceed," Donovan speaks up. "We can't discuss it at all if we don't have the information."

Corwin nods. "Agreed. I've already instructed my own patrols to question any intruders as well as they can."

Terisse, who seems to have come around to Corwin's side somewhat after long supporting Laoni, inclines her head too. "I think that's reasonable. We've been acting in anger, wanting to destroy them, when we must keep our heads cool and handle the problem rationally. They've been counting on manipulating us through our emotions all along."

"All right," Laoni grumbles, and Uzziah sighs but nods. Celia grimaces a bit but offers her own acceptance.

I wouldn't be surprised if the orders they give still encourage the patrols under their watch to switch to violence with little provocation, but maybe I've managed to soften the viciousness a little.

The rest of the conversation doesn't have much to do with me. When we all get up at the end of the meeting, I have to suppress another yawn. I definitely need that nap. But first I hang back with my mates as our guests head out of the room in the directions of their own realms.

August tugs me against him from behind and presses a kiss to the top of my head. "You spoke well," he says.

"Only because I didn't say half of what I wanted to," I mutter, and pause. "Do you think there's any real chance that we could work toward finding some sort of common ground with the Murk?"

I catch a flicker of skepticism through my bond with Corwin that echoes the expressions on my other mates' faces.

"I'm still not convinced there *is* much of a common ground to be found," Whitt says, leaning against the table. "Yes, that one rat helped you get free, but there was plenty of self-interest in that gesture in the grand scheme of things. He's expecting you to help the Murk in return—as you are."

"He knew it might not work, and he was risking his life going against Orion," I protest.

Corwin rests his hand on my shoulder. "What I've seen in your mind of your interactions with Madoc appear genuine, but he's an admitted expert at illusions. I don't think it's wise to trust any of the Murk without further proof, especially when we have plenty of proof that so many of them want to destroy us all."

My mind feels too bleary for me to come up with a coherent argument to that point. Maybe there isn't one; maybe he's right. I just can't shake off the horror of the scenes I saw, the ways the Seelie and Unseelie have fanned the flames of the Murk's hatred by treating them like, well, vermin.

"We'll attempt to talk rather than do battle where we can," Sylas says in his reassuringly steady baritone. "We simply have to be more wary than ever of the threat they pose."

"I know." I exhale slowly, and a yawn finally stretches my jaw before I can hold it back.

August nudges me toward the doorway. "Get some rest. You've been spreading yourself thin."

"I'm all right," I say, but as I take the first few uneven steps past the table, a rush of dizziness washes over me. I sway, snatching at the nearest chair for balance, and my stomach flips over with a twinge of queasiness.

Corwin is at my side in an instant. As he peers into my eyes, a quiver of anxiety pierces my heart. What if I'm not just tired—what if something's wrong with me?

But he leans a little closer with an intake of breath, and when he pulls back so I can see his face clearly again, the smile that's appeared there is nothing short of dazzling.

"My soul," he says in a voice soft with awe, "it's no wonder you're feeling out of sorts. It must have only just taken root—you're with child."

CHAPTER TWO

Madoc

The sentry reaches me just as I've emerged from my private room. "Orion wants you," she says, her tail twitching nervously, and darts on down the shadowed tunnel.

I was heading to the throne room to check in with my king anyway, but the fact that he's specifically called for me, and this early in the day, sends a ripple of tension through my body. Willing my muscles to loosen, I set off to find out what news he has to share.

The everyday work of the Refuge carries on around me. I don't catch any excited murmurs or notice any unusual movement in the same direction I'm heading.

If Orion had somehow gotten Talia back into his clutches, *that* news would already be buzzing through the Refuge, wouldn't it?

I tell myself as much, but I can't help bracing for the worst as I step through the throne room's broad doorway, controlling my reaction in case I come face to face with the woman Orion considers his "pet" back in a cage. When I see only my king pacing the dais, no one else around other than a couple of his other knights lounging nearby and a few petitioners lingering by the walls waiting to be heard, relief washes over me. It doesn't wipe away all of my apprehension, though.

There are other horrible developments I could encounter here. For example, Orion might have discovered proof that I'm the one who allowed Talia to flee the Refuge in the first place.

As I approach the dais, Orion keeps pacing, his tail lashing from side to side and a manic gleam in his yellow eyes that puts me even more on the alert. The other knights are keeping casual poses, but they watch our king with subtle wariness.

In the two weeks since Talia's disappearance, with what he's rightly assumed was the help of at least one of his subjects, Orion's temper has been even more unpredictable than usual. To reach him, I have to walk over fresh blood stains on the floor from the servant he dispatched yesterday for not having quite a fast enough answer when questioned about Talia's escape.

So far not just that one but five others of my fellow Murk have died instead of me for my crime. With a lot of blood spilled in the process too, although Orion's torture didn't convince any of them to own up to opening Talia's cage or offering her tools. I didn't point at any of them, but the guilt weighs on me almost as heavily as if I had.

I'd have owned up to my part and accepted my punishment if I didn't think life would be so much worse for all the rest of our people without me here to be a voice of reason if Talia convinces the fae of the seasons to make overtures of peace.

Of course, that *if* is seeming increasingly unlikely. As far as I know, we haven't received any sort of message from the Mists in those two weeks. The Seelie and Unseelie squadrons we've observed prowling through the human world have looked much more menacing than friendly.

Maybe it's overly optimistic to expect Talia to sway any of the fae of the seasons out of millennia of prejudice and animosity. Maybe she never intended to speak up for us at all. It could be that all her claims of caring about the atrocities the other fae have carried out against us were a trick of her own, designed to win my sympathies so that I'd end up helping her.

My experience with the world has left me jaded enough that I've entertained the thought for a few minutes here and there. My sense of the woman who convinced me to take her side against my king has faded over the days without her presence. Can I really be so sure she was as genuine as I thought at the time?

But then I remember her retching as she came out of the vaulted memory of the orphanage slaughter, the defiant tremor in her voice when she told me she was willing to give the Murk the benefit of the doubt—but I should extend the same to the fae of the Mists in turn. She didn't think she was winning me over. She thought I'd be angry that she was daring to speak honestly about her feelings.

And even if she had been manipulating me, would she really have deserved the torment Orion had planned for her?

No. I did what was right, even if my king wouldn't see it that way. She'll have needed time to recover and to persuade the other fae. Even her mates will probably find the idea of associating with any of the Murk a difficult pill to swallow. I can't criticize her for not making it happen faster. How much progress have *I* made toward preparing my people for the possibility of negotiating a truce rather than waging war?

None at all.

I come to a halt at the base of the dais near the throne, peering up at Orion. "I was already on my way here when I heard your call. What do you need?"

Orion continues his restless trek back and forth across the platform for a few more iterations before he finally stops and turns toward me. He runs his thumb over his lips. His claws are out, and he draws a thin line that beads with blood along his mouth without seeming to notice it. Or maybe he does, and he enjoys the sensation. It's hard to tell with Orion at the best of times, which are definitely not now.

"That Bren," he says in his coolly offhand way. "I've been thinking. He made quite the disruption while we were settling my pet in. Could there have been an ulterior motive? Have you seen any reason to be suspicious of him?"

I carefully avoid mentioning that Bren didn't cause the

disruption he was involved in anywhere near as much as a couple of Orion's lackeys set it in motion and Orion himself fanned the flames. I doubt that the young fae wanted to end up fighting to the death with one of his colleagues, even if he's happy with the reward he earned.

A memory flickers through my mind—harsh breaths rushing from my lungs, limbs striking out to claw and snap, a fist hitting me in the throat so hard a hint of that ache remains now, even decades later. I resist the urge to touch the spot. Orion will know what I'm thinking about.

"Nothing I've seen from him has made me suspect he was helping her," I say. "Do you think more of our people were involved than those you've already dealt with? I'd imagine by now the problem is solved."

And you can stop slaughtering your own people out of nothing but paranoia and the sadistic enjoyment of watching them beg.

How had it taken me so long to see just how toxic Orion's leadership is? How he breaks us as often as he builds us up? And what he's building is a community in his image, far too close to the vicious vermin the other fae make us out to be for my comfort.

After I went through so much to earn my place in his inner circle, I never let myself look at the reality all that closely. I let myself believe this was the only way and that it would be better once we'd won back our home.

Now, with Talia's words in the back of my head and clearer eyes, I can see that's not true. Orion will always be as he is: a man who could gather enough power to take on the fae of the Mists and who delights in the suffering that power can bring as much as he does the hope. Possibly more in the suffering.

My king lets out a huff of breath. "I haven't gotten concrete acknowledgement from any of the traitors. Maybe I've got the bastard—or bastards—that the girl twisted around her finger somehow, but maybe I haven't. We all need to stay on guard." He shakes a bony finger at me.

I dip my head. "Of course. I've been keeping my eyes peeled for any sign of rebellion. If I catch any, I'll obviously bring the perpetrator straight to you. So far, from what I've seen, everyone's hard at work preparing for the next steps in the war."

I was hoping that statement might prompt Orion to comment on what those next steps will be now that his original plan of using Talia in our initial offense has been foiled. Instead, he wanders away from me, his gaze going distant. His Heart's orange glow dances on the white spikes of his hair, turning them into flames.

"We'll have the Mists," he mutters. "We'll crush all of them, even the little girl who'd rather be among those monsters than with us."

I decide to prompt a little more overtly. "How soon do you expect we'll move on the Mists? Are there any other supplies you'd like me to have our people and the other colonies gathering or making?"

Orion shakes his head. "Everything can proceed as it is. My pet's escape changes things a little, but that only means we'll have to wait a short while longer before the time is ripe for our attack."

He spins abruptly toward me with another wave of his finger. "I've set that in motion—I've just sent someone to press the trigger. It should start to kick in soon. I want you to go back to your former duties, watching over the girl and the fae around her in the Mists. You may need to be there for some time, so take a day or two to prepare accordingly. You can report back as the situation evolves. We want to be ready to strike as soon as they're at their most vulnerable."

A chill creeps through my chest. What has he triggered? "Have you launched some early attack already?" I venture.

A sharp chuckle tumbles out of Orion. "In a way. You will need to be more cautious than ever before. They're patrolling the fringelands much more avidly these days. There've already been a couple of men who haven't made it back. But with your skills, I'm sure you can manage."

"I've always been able to dodge the wolves and ravens before, even coming into the arch-lords' domains," I say. "I'm not worried about that. But what exactly do you want me to be watching for? Is there some sign I should anticipate?"

Orion laughs again and goes back to his pacing. "I want those pricks totally wrecked before we attack. Carved up on the inside before we slice into them from the outside. Carving *her* up in front of them would have done the job nice and quick, but this way should be equally effective, if slower." He swings around toward me, his eyes even brighter than before. "The best word of advice I can give you, Madoc, is always have at least one backup plan."

CHAPTER THREE

Talia

I hadn't thought my mates could get more protective than they already were. It turns out I was wrong.

"You really didn't need to do this," I tell August as he sets a tray with a full, extravagant lunch on my lap where I'm sitting up in bed. "I'm already feeling better. I could have walked down to the dining room no problem."

August tucks himself next to me against the pillows propped along the headboard and kisses the side of my forehead. "But it was even easier for me to bring the food up to you. There's no reason you shouldn't get to relax."

I'm a little afraid he's going to start trying to spoon-feed me next. I grab the spoon before he can attempt to and dig it into the thick stew, which gives off a meaty smell laced with cinnamon and cloves. It makes my mouth water even though my stomach is still a bit queasy.

The little chunks of meat and vegetables practically melt in my mouth. I close my eyes, enjoying the flavor, but then open them again to give August a pointed look. "It's very sweet of you, but I don't think it'll be good for me if I do nothing except lie in bed for the next nine months."

"I know." He nuzzles my hair and slips his hand across my waist to give my belly a gentle stroke. "But you're only just getting used to the physical changes. You can give yourself a break and let me look after you for a little while."

I'm so early on that there's no outward sign of the life that's growing inside me. It's definitely had an impact internally. For the past few days, waves of fatigue have continued to hit me at random moments, and I've been sleeping more than usual in general. The nausea comes and goes. It's never gotten too bad, other than yesterday when the smell of frying eggs had me running out of the kitchen on the verge of vomiting.

I'm pretty sure August has since scoured every trace of egg from the entire castle.

But even in my frequently tired state, there's a giddy energy to my spirits. I haven't given much thought to having children with my mates before, other than avoiding it happening by abstaining when I'm fertile. There's been so much going on in our lives that's put all of us in danger, it's hardly seemed like the right time to consider starting a larger family. Now that it's happened, though, a smile immediately springs to my mouth every time I imagine bringing a baby into the world that's partly me and partly one of my men.

I was with all four of them during our urgent interlude right after I escaped the Murk. There'll be no way of knowing which is the father until the baby's born, although my mates have said they might be able to tell whether it'll be Seelie or Unseelie by my scent as it grows. None of them seems particularly bothered by the fact that the child might not be genetically theirs. I can already tell that whoever this baby owes its heritage to most closely, it'll have not one but four devoted fathers watching over it.

Just like I have all four of those men watching over me right now.

As I cuddle next to August's brawny frame and get on with devouring the stew as well as the buttered roll, sugared berries, and lemon tart he's brought me, Sylas strides into the room. A soft gleam comes into his mismatched eyes as soon as they settle on me, sparking a flutter of warmth in my chest. The Seelie lord has always been kind to me, and I've never doubted how much he loves me from the first moment he told me he did, but there's a new quality to his affection that gives me an even cozier sensation.

Is it like this in human families too? I was only four years old when Jamie was born, so I don't have any clear memories of how Dad might have treated Mom differently when she was pregnant. And maybe it'd be different with a first child compared to the second.

The fae don't have children easily. I know it's particularly special to them to have one on the way, more than I can fully understand even with the direct access I have to Corwin's joyful reactions.

Sylas comes over and leans past August to give me a quick kiss. "You're well?" he asks as he draws back.

"I'd have a hard time not being well with all the coddling I'm getting," I say, raising my eyebrows.

He chuckles, but a hint of a shadow crosses his expression. "Have you felt anything unusual at all—different today from the other days?"

I shake my head, frowning. "No, not that I've noticed. Why?"

Sylas exhales with relief, and his smile returns. "One of our patrols caught a Murk spy last night. She'd made it past the fringelands—we're not sure exactly how long she's been lurking around. They managed to subdue her and have brought her to Hearth-by-the-Heart for questioning, but so far we haven't gotten anything out of her. I just wanted to be sure, knowing one of them has been on the loose within the Mists."

A twinge of my own protectiveness runs through my gut, and my hand moves to my belly automatically. I was ready to do whatever I could to stop the war and defend the place I call home as it was, but now—now I feel like I could knock aside trees and blast down walls if that's what it takes to make sure the new life inside me stays safe.

From here on, it's not just about my mates and the rest of the fae. We're growing our family. I *can't* let this war touch that.

Sylas catches my defensive response. "We aren't holding the

woman anywhere near this castle—or Hearth-by-the-Heart's castle either. She'll be kept at a careful distance from the entire pack and especially you."

"Okay." I let out my breath, but my appetite has faded. It's an uncomfortable feeling, both being glad that Sylas's warriors held themselves back from outright slaughtering the Murk woman on sight and unnerved by the thought of her existing anywhere near me. "Are you sure she's working with Orion?"

Sylas nods. "She's made no attempt to deny it, and she was using the same sorts of illusion spells we've seen from the others."

The illusion spells Madoc might very well have taught them, or at least helped perfect their strategies for. My stomach twists a little more. "I'll let you know if anything changes, but I really am totally fine right now."

"Then I'll leave you to your meal." The Seelie arch-lord gives me one last tender glance and heads out.

I eat a little more of the stew and some berries, but I find I'm too unsettled now to gulp down the entire feast. Thankfully, August doesn't take offense.

"The tart will be just as enjoyable later on if you want it then," he says, leaving its small plate on the side table. "And let me know as soon as you're at all hungry again."

I'd ask him if next he's going to set up a bell so I can ring for him, but I suspect he might actually do that if I gave him the idea. I stretch my arms over my head and wiggle my legs beneath the covers. "I think I've done enough resting. You can't argue with me getting some fresh air, can you?"

"You do whatever makes you happy, Sweetness," August says. "Just don't leave the castle unless you've got company."

"I know, I know." I don't actually mind *that* precaution, considering I have been kidnapped from under my mates' noses once.

August bustles out to return the dishes to the kitchen. I'm just sliding off the bed when Corwin's and Whitt's voices reach me from the hall outside. Corwin has been keeping a wall partly raised against our connection so I'm not bombarded with impressions from his often stressful preparations for war, but a flicker of his apprehension touches me now as their words become clearer.

"—don't think this is the best time for that kind of experiment," he's saying.

"It's the perfect time," Whitt retorts. "Anything we can do to improve our chances, we have to jump on as quickly as possible. It isn't as if it'll hurt her." He sounds offended that Corwin would even imply that anything he'd suggest might harm me.

"Even involving her in any of this…" Corwin trails off as they come up on the doorway. They both come in with an air that's both tense and vaguely sheepish, as if they're embarrassed to realize I must have heard them arguing.

"What's going on?" I ask. "What am I maybe getting involved in?"

Corwin catches my eye with a tendril of fondness mixed with resignation. He knows that I'm not going to back away from the opportunity to help, no matter how much he'd like to shield me from the harsher parts of the conflict.

Whitt gives me one of his typical crooked grins, but the good humor in it doesn't quite reach his ocean-blue eyes. No matter what he said to Corwin, he's hesitant about asking anything of me too.

"I had an idea," he says. "A way we might be able to more easily track down the Murk or be alerted if they come into the Mists."

I perk up immediately. Searching for Murk presence by scanning for traces of their magic hasn't been easy—the fact that the woman Sylas's patrol caught made it out of the fringelands can attest to that. Finding their colonies in the human world has been even harder. If we had a way to locate Orion and his Refuge, deal with him directly… that would end the war right there, wouldn't it?

"That's wonderful," I say. "What's the idea?"

Whitt and Corwin exchange a glance. Whitt goes on, his voice softening. "I got the idea after Corwin noticed your… current state the other day." His eyes twinkle at the mention of my pregnancy. "We can scent the new life energy forming inside you through its presence in your blood. But that isn't the *only* energy you have running through you. The Murk king used a lot of magic to shape you, to make it so that your blood and tears could heal our curse and your soul could bind with Corwin's."

I resist the urge to hug myself at the reminder. "I know. How does that fit in to your plan, though?"

"Like can call to like. I suspect that with a tiny sample of your blood—or perhaps even something as small as a bit of skin or hair—we could create a tracking spell by having the Murk influence in your blood reach out to any of the rats present within the spell's range."

The thought that my body contains so much Murk "influence" that a spell like that would work makes my skin crawl. But I can understand what Whitt's saying. And it *wouldn't* hurt me at all. Corwin was only trying to spare me the pressure of thinking about it.

I might be more tired than usual, but I'm not going to fall apart, I say to him gently through our bond. *I still want to contribute everything I can.*

Of course you do. I just—

A wordless surge of emotion passes to me, but I know him well enough to understand his uneasiness. He thought he was going to have a child once before, only to discover the woman he'd been with was lying to him. He has no fears that I've deceived him in any way, but as far as I know, he's the only one of my mates who's previously had the possibility of a child and then lost it. Even when he's aware the baby might not be his, genetically speaking, it makes sense that he'd have the most trouble reining in his protective impulses.

It's okay, I say, sending him the impression of an embrace. *Just remember that I'll feel worse if I'm left in the dark or if something bad happens that I could have helped prevent but didn't get the chance to.*

As he inclines his head with an apologetic grimace, I focus back on Whitt. "I don't see why we shouldn't at least try it. What do you need from me right now?"

"We have the means for an easy test," the strategist says. "I believe Sylas told you about the Murk woman we captured? She's being held on the outskirts of the domain. With a drop of your blood, I can cast the spell and we can see if it'll lead us to her."

That sounds simple enough. I hold out my hand, and Whitt

takes it, dipping his head to brush a kiss to my knuckles in thank you.

He produces a small glass disc from his pocket and murmurs a quick word to split the skin of my forefinger. The second a drop of blood wells up, he presses it to the middle of the disc. Then he closes the tiny cut with another intoned true name. I barely feel the slight sting before it's over.

"All right." Whitt studies the blotch of blood on the disc with obvious concentration. Gathering himself, he closes his eyes and mutters several more syllables under his breath that are beyond my comprehension. When he looks at me again, his expression has lit with hope. "I obviously haven't had the opportunity to try the spell out yet, but I think that should work."

I guess he's been working on the idea for the past few days, not wanting to disturb me with the request until he had an easy way to perform a trial run. Now that the trial is underway, an unexpectedly eager sense of anticipation shivers through me.

When my mates turn toward the door, I move to pull on my boots, the brace fitting snuggly around my warped foot. "I want to come with you—I want to see if it works."

Corwin stiffens. "We can't be sure the rat won't attack you if she gets you in her sights."

I give him a baleful look. "Haven't Sylas's warriors restrained her better than that? If she could attack *anyone*, I have to think she'd be doing it already."

Whitt rubs his mouth, his gaze flicking from me to the disc and back. "I can't say I love the idea of you getting all that close to her, but I don't see how it'd hurt for you to come at least far enough to be sure the spell is effective. The two of us will be there to defend you if need be."

We both look at Corwin, who sighs and grazes his fingers over my cheek. "If you must, my soul. I suppose I should know better than to try to rein you in."

"I'm just barely starting to be pregnant, not a total invalid," I remind him, and peer at the ruddy blotch. "Is it supposed to do anything?"

A smile curls Whitt's lips. "It already is. Look there." He points to the edge of the smear. It's vaguely circular and fairly even all around—but that one edge protrudes just a little farther. As I watch closely, it creeps a tiny bit more toward the edge of the disc.

Even after all the fae magic I've seen before, it's kind of amazing. A little laugh spills out of me. "Wow. Is that the *right* direction?"

"I don't actually know," Whitt says with obvious amusement. "I asked Sylas not to tell me where they set up the holding cell so that I'd be able to run this experiment if you agreed. If I know where we're supposed to be heading, I might accidentally steer the spell. Why don't we go find out?"

The three of us hurry through the castle, our pace only slowed by my limp. Once we've come out the front door, Whitt studies the disc again and motions to the right, toward the field that leads to the northern forests.

As we walk on, I take peeks at the bloody blotch. The edge that protruded before is pointing even more obviously in the direction we're going. Whitt tests it by turning the disc in his hand, and the original bulge contracts while another forms, aimed at the path we were already following.

In the shadows between the trees, Corwin's apprehension wavers from him into me through our bond. He eyes the terrain in front of us pensively. "I'll go ahead," he suggests. "If the holding cell is over here, I'll confirm and meet you a safe distance away."

Whitt waves him away, and Corwin springs into the air in his raven form. He flies off through the woods.

The spymaster contemplates the disc and adjusts our path just a smidge to the left. "It can't be too much farther. Sylas said he was keeping her within the boundaries of the domain. How's your foot?"

I'm not limping any worse than normal, but I guess the question is part of the increased attentiveness I can expect from now on. "The same as usual," I say. "Don't you start worrying about me too. If I need help, I'll say so."

Whitt shoots me a slyly affectionate glance. "I know how stoic you like to be. It can't hurt to check."

We tramp farther through the brush, following a trail few people have traveled before, judging by the natural debris that's scattered across the forest floor there. Twigs crackle under our feet, and bushes tug at our clothes. The ground veers downward as we reach the slope of the hill.

We've been walking a few minutes longer when Corwin appears in a spot of sunlight up ahead. His expression is still tensed, but there's a hint of satisfaction in the set of his lips. "Your trick worked. They're holding her just at the base of the hill—if you kept going this way, you'd run right into her."

We have a solid way of tracking down the Murk. Whitt and I exchange a grin, and then Whitt strides ahead. "I'd like to see how it responds when I'm closer."

When I move to follow him, Corwin steps to intercept me. "I think you'd better not— As restrained as she is, it wouldn't be pleasant for you."

I'm about to protest when a ragged voice filters through the trees from farther down the hill. "You're all cunts and bastards. I look forward to seeing the bunch of you filleted and dumped in a pit."

I wince, drawing up short. The fury in the Murk woman's tone doesn't leave any room for talk of negotiation. I can't imagine how anyone could even raise the subject with her.

She only wants to hurt us… like so many of the fae who follow Orion still do. What if Madoc is a rare exception?

But at the same time I can't help wondering just what she went through to fuel her hatred toward the fae of the seasons.

I doubt she'd tell me if I asked. And seeing me might incite her anger even more.

I hesitate and then reach to take Corwin's hand. "Let's go back to the palace."

And hope that the war won't end up following us there no matter what we do.

CHAPTER FOUR

August

The portals out of the Mists always point to the most peaceful parts of the human world. I've led my assorted group of fae warriors out onto the shore of a small, gleaming lake, this section sheltered from the rest of the shoreline by a thick stand of trees. The sounds—and smells—of occasional nearby traffic carry on the cool breeze, and with just a couple of steps, I can see the buildings along the city streets a short walk away.

Dawn light is only just creeping across the sky, the shadows still long and the sunlight dim around us. We timed this venture as well as we could in the hopes of finding more Murk activity while most humans are still sleeping—and reducing the chances that any humans might be caught in the fray if we get the opportunity to attack.

As we pause to confirm that our concealing spells have held solid during the trip through the portal, Kesral comes up beside me. Sylas asked the winter arch-lords to contribute some of their people to this mission so that we'd have a full range of skills to draw on. If this goes well, we might find ourselves tangling with more rats than we ever have before, and closer to their home turf than our own.

The Unseelie warrior peers at the glass disc I'm holding. "That little thing is going to find the Murk for us when nothing else did?"

I can't blame him for being skeptical. I gave Whitt an odd look of my own when he started explaining his new tool to me.

"I've seen it in action," I tell him. "Only on a much smaller scale than this, though. And we'll need to keep all our senses on the alert the whole time for any other sign of the rats. Our goal is to see if we can locate any sort of colony here, and if we have the upper hand in numbers, we'll take as many rats back for questioning as we can. It'll be easier if we notice them before they notice us."

Kesral nods, and I study the smudge of Talia's blood that marks the disc. We have every reason to believe there should be some Murk presence in this city. The rat shifter who helped Talia escape let her out onto these streets from their main colony, the one she said they call the King's Refuge. Even if the Refuge itself isn't here, because of the magical tricks they use to warp the paths between it and the world above ground, this is a location that's tied to it at least some of the time. We've caught hints of the Murk here and there during our past expeditions.

If we can find even one who could take us to the Refuge itself, we'll be within reach of a much bigger victory.

The urge grips me to tear straight through the city, savaging any of the vermin I stumble on—the horrible creatures that stole my mate away and tormented her. To protect both her and the child growing in her in the most immediate and thorough way I can. Just the thought of the pain they caused her brings up a fresh flare of defensive anger into my chest, alongside a twinge of affection even headier than any I've felt before.

We haven't spoken about it, and I don't see any need to, but it's most likely the child is mine. The one benefit to having much less fae in my blood than my true-blooded and nearly true-blooded brothers and Unseelie counterpart is that I won't suffer as much trouble having children as they will. My seed would have taken root more easily than any of theirs.

As happy as the knowledge makes me, Talia's current state makes *her* more vulnerable. I will not let her meet the same fate as so many humans caught up in fae passions. She deserves much better. And right now, the Murk are by far the greatest threat to her safety and happiness.

But as much as my fangs tingle in my gums, I know Talia is right about holding back our violence. I might not trust one hair on a rat's ass, but they're planning something bigger than what a single rampage of wolves could prevent. We need to find out more to be fully prepared, to hit them where it'll really hurt.

And that means keeping the bastards alive long enough to drag some information out of them.

My entire squadron knows the drill. As I set off toward the city streets, they fall into a loose formation behind me. The smear of blood offers an increasingly definite point to the south.

I keep my attention focused on it, knowing my companions will be scanning for any other signs of Murk presence while I can't. Every minute or two, I stop and give the smear a chance to shift. When the angle changes slightly, I head down a different street and then cross a broad courtyard.

A few human early-risers meander down the streets past us obliviously, our spells nudging them to avoid us without them even realizing they're being influenced. The smell of fresh bread with a rich nuttiness tickles into my nose from a nearby bakery just getting started for the day, and my mouth waters. If we weren't on such an urgent mission, I'd stop to steal a little for sampling. Instead, I walk on.

At my next stop, the pointed part of the blood doesn't adjust at all. The Murk must be close ahead.

One of my pack-kin sniffs the air and grins sharply. "I catch a whiff of rat. We're almost on them."

"Proceed slowly, watching for any hint of their presence," I remind the others. "We don't want them to know we're coming until we're ready to strike."

We murmur our concealing spells thicker around us and tread onward, eyes sharpening and ears pricking. I shift more of my concentration to our surroundings, already knowing where Talia's blood is directing us.

Up ahead lies a narrow street lined with buildings three and four stories tall. With the sun so low, the shadows they cast cover the entire road. The windows are dark, all the inhabitants no doubt still in bed.

At the far end of the street, I can make out a larger structure that has a grand look to it—maybe a government building or a museum of some sort? Have the Murk managed to take over some part of that as their own?

My hackles rise. We're protecting not just ourselves and my mate but all the humans the rats would play their vicious tricks on too. Both worlds will be a better place if we can clear out the worst of the vermin.

Talia says they're not all horrible, but the sweetness in her that always sees the best in people is part of the reason I fell in love with her. *I've* never encountered a rat worth spitting on if it were on fire. But I guess once we've captured a few to talk with, we'll find out whether any will prove themselves worthy of her compassion.

My warriors spread out across the streets in a wider formation, checking doorways and the few tight alleys between the buildings. Talia's blood still points straight ahead. I don't think we're close enough to discover the rats yet, but I don't see how it'll hurt anything to make a quick inspection here regardless. We don't have to be fully braced for battle until we're nearly on top of them. How could they know we'd be tracking them so easily now?

But maybe I should have considered all I know about the Murk and their tricks a little more.

We're nearly at the end of the street when I glance down at the glass disc again and jerk to a halt, frowning at it. The most obvious point is aimed forward like before, but… has the entire smear gotten *larger*?

My squadron stops around me, waiting for my instructions. I stare at the disc and then press my thumb against the other side, framing the splotch of blood. At least, framing it at first. Now that I have another shape for comparison, I can see how the ruddy mark is expanding, creeping ever so slowly to match the width of my thumb. And the original point is starting to contract—

Understanding hits me with a chilling smack, a moment too late. "Back-to-back!" I shout. "They're surrounding us!"

But even as the words burst from my lips, a flurry of bodies spring at us from the thickest shadows along the edge of the buildings, all around us. The Murk tackle several of the warriors closest to them to the ground, blades flashing in their hands, needle-sharp claws glinting.

My own claws erupt along with my fangs. I lunge at the nearest flailing bodies, snatching my sword from its hilt as I go.

The Murk attackers managed to surround us—so quickly and discreetly we didn't pick up any trace of them even in our search. As I wrench a rat shifter away from one of my comrades and ram my sword into his gut before he can stab his knife at my throat, the pieces click together somewhere in the back of my mind.

We thought we knew what we were up against. We thought we'd prepared for the Murk to be stronger and slyer than we'd ever have anticipated before. But we underestimated them all the same.

They must have had a scout watching the portal where we came through who ran ahead to warn the others nearby. Either that one observed my new tool, or they've been able to spy on us so closely in our own world that they found out about our new use for Talia's blood ahead of time. They grouped together so that we'd be drawn on a clear course, and then surrounded us at just the right pace so that the movement didn't show up clearly on the disc. And they concealed themselves even more cleverly than I thought they could manage with us right here next to them.

The Murk aren't just the worst of the current threats we're facing. They might now be the worst threat we've *ever* faced.

It's not just their stealth and cunning that's allowed them to momentarily overwhelm us either. As well as the slash of blades and claws, the fae who've launched themselves at us are snapping out words of magic. One opens a deep cut in a Seelie warrior's arm without even touching her. Another makes an Unseelie fighter's feet fly out from under him so she can leap onto him and stab him in the back.

As I slam and slice through one rat shifter and then another, I register that there are more of us than them. The Murk probably didn't expect to completely overpower us, only to take down as many of us as they could before they were cut down themselves. My warriors are rallying, but the surprise of the attack got the better of some. Several of my comrades are sprawled in the street between the fallen rat shifters, a few struggling with their wounds, others gone limp, possibly dead.

I don't have the chance to help any of them right now. Yet another Murk dives at me from an unexpected angle, and his claws dig deep into my shoulder before I manage to drive my sword through his heart. As he crumples, a pained grunt catches in my ears. I spin to see two of the rat shifters lunging at Kesral from both sides.

The Unseelie warrior who's joined Talia and me on past trips to the human world is no slouch. He batters one of the desperate attackers away with the flat of his sword and then plunges the blade into the Murk woman's chest. But the smack of his other arm isn't enough to deflect the second attacker. The Murk man rams his knife right into the side of Kesral's neck.

I'm already dashing toward him. As he crumples, a roar of rage rips from my lungs. My wolf surges free automatically, my furred frame crashing into the vermin. My fangs sink into his own neck to tear open his throat.

The sickly metallic flavor of the Murk man's blood floods my mouth. There's nothing appetizing about it. I shove his slackening body away, sputtering, and shift back into the form of a man.

When I drop at Kesral's side, his eyes are already staring blankly at the sky. The blood spurting from the severed artery is slowing into a fainter pulse as the last shreds of his life drain out of him. There's nothing I can do for him.

Looking up at the scene around me, anguish squeezes my heart. The fighting is over. The last of the Murk are dead. But too many of my own people lie slumped between them. A few of the warriors who have particular skill at healing are leaning over those who haven't succumbed to their wounds yet, but I can tell at least a couple of them are fading.

Kesral is gone. I have to help those there's still hope for.

With a lump in my throat, I leave him and hurry to an Unseelie man who's intoning panicked words over one of my pack-kin who has a gash across her stomach. I join him, adding my own true names to the chorus.

We manage to bind her flesh to seal her wound, but the blood she's already lost drenches her clothes. Her eyes flutter shut, and her head lolls. I can't tell whether she'll survive the trauma she's been through.

None of the Murk have. I should be able to take some grim satisfaction from their dead bodies. But as I rush to the next injured warrior, the knowledge drags on my spirits instead.

The Murk have already discovered our new strategy against them and used it against *us*. We've lost several of our people in a horrible way. And we didn't even manage to take *one* of the blasted vermin captive for questioning like we'd planned. In every way, this mission was a failure.

When I've done what I can for those who are gravely injured, I straighten up and catch the eyes of my comrades who are still relatively unharmed. I will the roughness of grief and frustration out of my voice, but only barely.

"Carry the dead and those who can't walk with whatever magic you can most easily use. We'll bring them home."

And then I'll face the judgment I deserve.

CHAPTER FIVE

Talia

As the sky darkens to shades of purple with the deepening evening, the pack steps back from where they've gathered around their two fallen kin. I slip through the gathering to where I can watch Sylas begin the funeral ceremony I first saw him carry out for his brother-in-law, Kellan.

For both of the murdered fae, a couple of family members or friends join the arch-lord in chanting the magic-laced words and moving through the gestures. The herbal scent that rises off the leafy fronds placed around the shrouded bodies takes me back to that past ceremony more vividly than I like.

Kellan was the first fae I ever saw die. There've been so many more since then. I've found a lot of happiness here in the Mists, but there's no way to deny that it's come with a lot of danger and violence as well.

I didn't know either of my pack-kin being honored tonight well. As part of the pack's contingent of warriors, they were often out on patrols, not hanging out around the pack village for the more domestic tasks I've helped with. But I can tell from the words Sylas and their loved ones say in their honor that they were well-respected and will be missed a great deal.

As Sylas raises the goblet with its shimmering liquid and asks that the summer sun embrace the dead woman at his feet "with all its warmth," a shiver runs through me. How much more will the Murk steal from all of us before they're finished?

Sylas pours the liquid over the body, and the shroud glimmers for a few moments before absorbing it. The other fae ease back as he falls into a more intent chant, the one that will transform the woman into her soulstone, a sparkling representation of the being she once was.

He finishes with a stretch of his hands over her body, and the flare of light washes over us all. I know to expect it this time, but it takes my breath away all the same.

When he's completed her ritual, Sylas moves on to the shrouded man next to her. Whitt brings him a fresh goblet of the ceremonial liquid. Even the spymaster with his normally impervious good humor looks grim this evening.

He thought he'd given us a huge advantage with the new tracking strategy he came up with. Instead it led to several deaths across the arch-lords' domains. I didn't see the body, but August said Kesral was killed too.

My gaze flicks toward the glinting haze along the border between the realms. How is Laoni coping with his loss, when she fought so hard against admitting she cared about him while he was alive?

Kesral might have supported his lady over me, but I can't blame him for that. He was kind to me and willing to open up the few times we traveled to the human world together. I might have liked to attend his funeral too, to honor him in my own small way, but I doubt Laoni would approve of my presence.

I didn't even ask Corwin. He's kept himself partly shielded from me as he carries out a funeral for one of his flock folk, the impressions that do seep through tinged with so much sorrow and fury that I can understand why he's trying to shelter me from them even though he doesn't need to.

August shifts his weight where he's standing at the front of the gathering just a few steps from Sylas, his head bowed low. I haven't managed to talk to him much either since he returned this afternoon, bearing the dead. The anguish I can read in his posture and his expression jerks at my heart. Knowing him, he's taking the full weight of the blame for himself. As if the rat shifters haven't taken so many of us by surprise so many times.

When Sylas has completed the second ritual, the families step forward to collect the soulstones. Then the pack drifts away, many of them gathering by the houses to grieve together.

Sylas nods to me and turns toward the castle of Hearth-by-the-Heart with Whitt flanking him. I'll stay with them there until everything's settled on both sides of the border. Both they and Corwin are worried about keeping our joint castle well-protected while everyone's distracted by the funerals.

August turns on his heel, stretches out into wolf form, and lopes toward the woods, his ruddy fur sparking with the last bits of sunlight before the shadows between the trees swallow him up.

I know sometimes he goes for a run on his own when he's grappling with his emotions. I hope he'll come back soon.

In the castle, I find myself drifting down to the basement. The leather sofa in the entertainment room holds a hint of August's musky scent from his many stints on the video game console. Maybe he'll come down here or to the gym once he's back to work off some tension in other ways.

I nestle against the arm of the sofa and wait, keeping my ears pricked. When footsteps rasp over the stairs, I raise my head in anticipation. But they stop just after they hit the smooth floor of the hall. I wait for several seconds and then limp over to the doorway.

It is August. He's standing motionless in the middle of the hallway at the base of the steps, the brighter light that streams down the staircase deepening the contrast of shadows on his brawny body. He seems to be staring at the wall, or at nothing—or maybe at something he can only see in his mind, drawn from his memories.

It isn't hard to guess what he might be remembering that has him looking so upset.

I walk over to him. He shakes himself out of his daze and turns toward me as I reach him, and I wrap my arms around his solid chest. He hugs me back, but something about his embrace feels more hesitant than I'm used to.

"It isn't your fault," I tell him, my words partly muffled against his shirt. "I know I've said we need to give some of the Murk the benefit of the doubt… but a lot of them do hate the other fae and are willing to be totally vicious to hurt you. And there's still so much we don't understand about their new kind of magic or how organized they are."

August sighs, his chin coming to rest on the top of my head. "I let down my squad. I led them into a trap, even if it was accidentally. I didn't respond quickly enough to prevent all those deaths. And I let *you* down by killing all the Murk too. I didn't even think about trying to capture them in the thick of it—I just ripped into them."

I hug him tighter. "You were defending yourself and your people. I'm not upset at you for that. If you'd tried to go easier on the ones attacking you, maybe more fae on our side would have died. It wasn't like you had much choice."

"I just…" He pauses, and his voice dips lower, as if he's not totally sure he wants me to hear what he's going to say. "I call you Sweetness because that's what you are—you're strong, but you're always caring and compassionate; you'd never hurt anyone unless you absolutely had to. And I have this beast inside me. There's a part of me that thinks of violence *first* when my temper sparks. How can you ever really be safe…"

He trails off again.

I ease back and touch his face with a noise of consternation. "Do you honestly think I have any worries at all about you hurting *me*? Because I don't. Nothing about you scares me; it's been a long time since it has."

"You haven't had to see me fight, not really, not all that much," August says. "If I came toward you like Aerik and his cadre did that night, you'd still panic."

"You *wouldn't* come at me like they did," I point out. "And if you just mean your wolf, I'm not scared of that either. I've been up close to it and others before. I know the difference."

"I'm just saying it might not be so different if you saw me in certain states."

The determination to show him just how much I trust him swells inside me. I step back, toward the longer end of the hall that leads to the gym. "Why don't we find out? Let me see your wolf now."

August gives me a questioning look, but because he's August, he drops down at my request, shifting into wolfish form with the motion. There's a grace to the transformation that I appreciate more every time I see it.

He stands before me on all fours, golden eyes glinting within his ruddy fur, his tail swishing from side to side. His head comes all the way to my shoulder. A prickle runs through the scars embedded in my skin there, but it doesn't reach any deeper. I know the man in front of me, even when he's in the shape of an animal. All I feel for him is love.

At the thought of what I'm going to do next, my heart does skip a beat. But I gaze at my mate a few moments longer, letting the emotion settle. Then I turn on my heel. "Come catch me!"

I say the words lightly and with a dare in my voice, and then I start jogging down the hall as quickly as my warped foot allows.

August's wolf lets out a huff of confusion, and for a second I think he won't play the game I've instigated. But then his paws thump against the floor behind me at a slow lope, not really chasing me yet but following.

The sound provokes a quiver of panic that just as quickly turns into an excited jolt. "Is that the best you can do?" I call over my shoulder with a breathless laugh. "You're never going to claim your mate like that."

With a sound almost like a chuckle, August picks up his pace. He charges after me. I glance behind me, seeing his furred form closing in, and everything about his muscular stride echoes the man I love. The man I know would never run after me like this in anything *other* than a game.

Another giggle slips from my mouth. I push myself a little faster and manage to dive through the gym doorway with August at my heels. As I spin around, he pounces on me, shifting back into a man in time to brace his arm beneath me before I hit the padded mats that cushion the ground.

His expression is still a bit tense, but his eyes dance with exhilaration. The same giddiness lights up in me all the way to my core. Before he can say anything, I run my fingers into his hair and yank his mouth to mine.

August kisses me deeply, his pulse thrumming in his chest even faster than mine. But it's a good energy, a sense of scoffing in the face of danger together, which sets my nerves even more alight.

I trust this man, and I love him, and right now I *want* him more than I know how to express.

August tears his mouth away for just an instant, his voice rasping. "You're sure you're okay?"

I tug at him insistently. "I'll be more okay if you keep kissing me."

The remaining tension finally melts from his stance. He meets my lips with a laugh that spills his breath hot across my mouth.

I haven't come together this urgently with any of my men in days. They've all been treating me so delicately since they found out I'm pregnant. But I don't feel at all tired or sick while the adrenaline hums through my body. With every kiss and caress, August wakes me up into sharper alertness—and desire.

I want to be loved in *every* possible way, not just the gentler ones.

My fingers fumble with the hem of his shirt. With a groan, August helps me pull it off him. He looms over me, his eyes darkening as I trail my hands over the muscular planes from his shoulders down across his torso. His abs flex as I graze the top of his slacks.

He kisses me again and finds the zipper on the side of my dress. With a few hasty jerks and a little squirming, I'm tossing it aside. My mate gazes down at me, nothing but hungry adoration in his eyes.

He claims my mouth once more, and then the corner of my jaw, and then my neck, sucking hard enough that I gasp. As he charts that path downward, he cups my breast, swiveling his thumb closer and closer to the peak until I'm pressing into his touch. With an approving growl, he sucks the other nipple into his mouth at the same time as he pinches the first.

I arch into him, reveling in the pleasure that's quivering through my chest and throbbing between my legs for more. Thankfully, August picks up on my impatience, and he's never been one to deny me for long. With a pleased grin, he dips lower, hooking his fingers around the sides of my panties at the same time.

He pauses over my belly, still flat at this early stage, and kisses around my belly button so tenderly my throat constricts with emotion. I tease my fingers into the short strands of his auburn hair, and he dips even lower with a yank of my panties.

The second he's bared my sex, he's pressing his mouth to it. His tongue flicks over my opening, his lip sliding over the sensitive nub above, and a rush of bliss floods me.

I grip his hair harder, and he laps at me even more eagerly. It's all I can do to ride the storm of passion he's summoning inside me with each swipe of his tongue. I whimper and buck toward him, and he groans.

"So sweet inside and out," he murmurs, and dives back in.

My body starts to tremble with the sensations racing through it. My hips sway up, August grazes his teeth over my nub, and I come with a violent quaking, possibly wrenching his scalp with my grip on his hair.

August doesn't show any sign of minding. As my limbs sag in the aftermath of my orgasm, he looms back over me with a beaming smile and captures my lips, passing my tart taste on to me.

My hips bow up to meet his again, seeking that even deeper pleasure. I pull at his trousers.

August's breath stutters out of him. He kicks his pants off, and I'm already wrapping my fingers around his thick erection. It twitches in my grasp, so hard I have to swallow a moan at the feel of it.

"I want you inside me," I say, meeting his eyes. "I love you tame and I also love you wild. I'm not going to break."

August growls eagerly and pushes into me, stealing another kiss as he does. I raise my knees to let him plunge in deeper, unable to stop the moan that reverberates up from my chest now. We rock to meet each other, urgent but still tender, his lips dappling kisses across my face and neck. He keeps one hand braced against me while the other strokes more pleasure across my curves.

As the feeling of fullness inside me drives me toward my second peak, I push myself toward him more forcefully. August slides his hand beneath my bottom and lifts me up. At the new angle, his thrusts spark a hotter blaze of bliss that sweeps through my whole body. I whimper, pressing into him once, twice, and then cry out as I tip over that ecstatic edge again.

August's pace turns more erratic. As I clench around him, his chest hitches. He burrows his face against my shoulder and grunts as his heat fills me.

He sinks down beside me, wrapping his arm around me to tuck me close. I nestle myself in his embrace. For a few minutes, we just lie there, coming down, enjoying the lingering heat we generated between us.

"No more worries," I say, turning my head so I can look at him straight on. "Not about how I feel about you. We've got plenty of other things to worry about without adding that to the list. You're my mate, and nothing can change that."

August sighs, but it's more a sound of release than of resignation. He kisses my hair just above my ear. "You do know how to make a point, Sweetness," he says with a fond glint in his eyes. "I'll try to remember this one."

"You'd better," I mutter teasingly, and snuggle against him again, wishing there *weren't* quite so many other worries to take up the space in both our heads.

CHAPTER SIX

Talia

When the thumping on my bedroom door jolts me out of sleep the following night, the darkness outside my window shows that it's barely morning yet. As I roll over next to Sylas, who stayed with me in the border castle tonight, the voice of one of the castle's many guards on duty filters through.

"My lord, there's news from Tumble-by-the-Heart that I think you should hear right away."

Tumble-by-the-Heart is Celia's domain. Sylas sits up immediately. "Just a moment." He brushes a quick kiss to my lips before grabbing his clothes. "You go back to sleep," he murmurs to me.

I'm feeling that extra weight of exhaustion again, so I let my head sink back into the pillow, but my mind has started buzzing too much for me to drift off. I try until after Sylas has strode out into the hall and finally grab my thin robe to pull over my nightgown and pad over to the door. I'll feel better if I know what's going on.

I've just eased the door open when my own name reaches my

ears. My pulse stutters. I hurry out. At the sight of me, Sylas and the guard fall silent where they were talking farther down the hall.

"What about me?" I ask. "What's happened?"

Sylas opens his mouth and closes it again with a pained expression. He obviously doesn't want to get me involved. But then he sighs. He knows me well enough to realize I'm not going to let go of the subject until he explains.

"One of Celia's patrols caught a Murk man not far from her domain," he says. "He's saying he only came to pass on a message… to you."

My heart outright stops for a second. I limp over, hugging myself. "They didn't *kill* him, did they? It could be Madoc—he might really want to help us." I hate to think what the Murk man who arranged my escape would have had to find out that was bad enough for him to risk coming here to tell me about it. Somehow I can't imagine he's bringing news that Orion's agreed to negotiate a peace treaty.

No, whatever it is, it's almost definitely awful.

The guard gives me an odd look, but says, "He's still alive, as far as I know. Arch-Lord Celia is holding him at the base of the hill on her side, like we did with the woman we captured." He turns back to Sylas. "She wants to know how you'd like to proceed."

I draw my posture up straight and firm before Sylas can answer. "I'll go see what he wants to tell me, of course."

Sylas frowns. "We don't know for sure it *is* the Murk who came to your aid before—and even if it is, we can't be sure of his intentions now. I don't want you coming within range of their magic. If he has something to say, he can pass the message on through me."

I cross my arms over my chest. "I think it's a little late to be worrying about me getting affected by Murk magic. If he was willing to pass on the message to anyone other than me, he'd probably have done it already. Madoc doesn't exactly trust the rest of you—I'm not sure how much he even trusts me." Enough to think I deserved not to be tortured, but that's a pretty low bar.

"That's assuming it's even him," Sylas reminds me. "A lot of

Murk are aware of your name and the fact that you've come back to us, I'd imagine. This could be one of their tricks to lure you into a more vulnerable position."

I let out my breath in a huff, but he's right. We need to be careful. "Fine. I'll describe him to you and give you a couple of questions to ask that only Madoc should be able to answer. If you're convinced that it's him, then we have less to worry about." I pause. "But even if it isn't, I think we should give whoever it is some chance to show what they came for."

Sylas lets out a disconcerted growl, but he doesn't outright refuse. "We'll cross that bridge if we come to it." His gaze skims over my nightclothes. "Why don't you get yourself dressed, and I'll see who else I can rouse at this hour to accompany us? I'm going to take every precaution."

As I limp back to my bedroom, Corwin's voice emerges through our bond, slightly groggy with interrupted sleep. *What's all this commotion so early in the morning, my soul? Are you all right?*

Yes, other than a little tired, as you'd expect, I answer as I tug the first dress my hands fall on out of my wardrobe. *I'm sorry I woke you up. It seems one of the Murk has been captured near Celia's domain, and he claims he has a message to pass on to me. It might be Madoc. We're going to go confirm.*

My sense of my soul-twined mate snaps into sharper alertness in an instant. *I can be there too, if the Seelie won't object.*

I don't see what reason they'd have to complain. It'd probably be good for someone from the winter realm to witness what happens too.

I shed my nightclothes and pull on the dress, which is simple enough that it doesn't require much fussing to get it lying right but significantly more ladylike than my nightie. I am going to be presenting myself in front of a bunch of Celia's pack-kin and maybe the arch-lord herself as well as fae I'm more comfortable around.

And possibly this rat shifter, whoever he is.

By the time I make it downstairs to the summer entrance to the palace, Corwin has already joined Sylas there—and so has Sylas's entire cadre, though Whitt looks a bit bleary-eyed. August is already tensed in a defensive stance, and Astrid has her short sword in her hand. She muffles a yawn and then shakes herself.

"I don't think you *all* need to be there just to protect me," I say with a twinge of guilt at the thought of them being tugged out of their beds.

Whitt shoots me a breezy grin. "Who says it's for you?" he teases. "I want to hear what the rat has to say." He stretches his arms over his head, no longer favoring his injuries from Tristan's attack on Hearth-by-the-Heart weeks ago. "And more eyes and ears never hurt anyone. He won't touch one hair on your head."

I suspect if I wasn't coming with them, they'd have shifted to take the relatively short trip at a wolfish lope. Instead, we step out into the warm night air to a carriage that's already been conjured. I settle onto one of the benches, restraining a yawn of my own, and consider what Sylas could ask the Murk man. Something only Madoc and I would know.

"If he says he's Madoc, and he looks right"—I glance at Corwin—"you should be able to recognize him from my memories, although I guess it could be an illusion. Ask him about the three scenes I watched in the vault of memories. There was the burning house, the man who was caught by the Unseelie while he was looking for food for his mate, and… and the kids in the orphanage."

I've told my mates about what I saw before, and their faces all turn somber at the reminder. "Is there anything else we could check?" Sylas asks gently.

I can't think of why Madoc would have mentioned all three of those memories from the vault to anyone else, but just in case… "You could ask him what he needed to reassure me about—a lie Orion told me—when we were leaving the Refuge. I thought Orion might have been able to read my thoughts, but Madoc said he was only pretending to."

Will he even remember that? I hope so. But if he doesn't, he can simply say so and I'll have to think of some other proof.

The carriage glides across the open plains around the Heart and between the smaller stands of trees. As we reach Celia's castle, a sentry is waiting there. He waves his arm to us and motions for us to follow him into the thicker forest on the slope of the hill.

I figure we're about halfway down when Sylas draws the carriage to a halt. "You'll wait here with Astrid and August," he tells me. "Corwin, Whitt, and I will see to the captive. We'll return as soon as we have a better idea who he is."

They spring out of the carriage, the Seelie men immediately taking on their wolf forms and Corwin soaring after them as a raven. The Unseelie arch-lord raises his mental barriers again, with a tendril of apology. He doesn't want me being disturbed by what the Murk man might say or do when we're still so unsure of what we're dealing with.

August tucks his arm around me, and I lean against him, letting my eyes slide shut for a little while. I'm too wound up to have any hope of sleeping deeply right now, but I do doze a bit.

The next thing I know, Whitt is standing at the side of the carriage with a wary expression.

"It's your man, as far as we can tell," he says. "This Madoc. He answered everything to our satisfaction. Celia has a dozen guards staked out maintaining the holding cell—apparently they were pretty concerned by the fact that he managed to get this close to the Heart before anyone caught him, so they suspect he's rather powerful. Which tracks with what you learned about his skill with illusions too."

"How *did* they catch him?" I ask as August helps me out of the carriage.

The corner of the spymaster's mouth quirks upward. "It was one of the blood trackers you helped me make. It seems the Murk haven't learned how to avoid them completely, or else this one didn't hear the news."

The thought that I was responsible in a roundabout way for bringing about Madoc's capture makes my stomach twist, but it's done now. I need to find out why he's come—and make sure Celia's guards don't hurt him.

August and Astrid flank me for the last short tramp through the thicker woods, where it'd have been difficult to navigate a carriage anyway. We emerge into a large clearing. A few magical globes cast an amber glow over the space. Sylas and Corwin are poised by the edge of the ring of trees. The guards Whitt mentioned stand at attention all around them.

And in the middle of the clearing, surrounded by a translucent wall of light that shifts and whirls like oil in water—

"Madoc!" His name jolts from my lips, and I'm darting forward before I can really think about it.

My impulse is to run right to him, to check him over and make sure he's okay, but August sweeps me up before I can make it even to the glowing barrier around him.

"Careful still, Sweetness," he murmurs.

I stare at the man within the shimmering cage. Madoc has straightened up from the crouched posture he had before, his heavy-lidded eyes fixed on me, the amber light turning his straight, straw-pale hair faintly orange. My gaze darts lower, automatically looking for the long, thinly furred tail I got used to seeing on him. It's strange to find it missing, even though I know the fae tend not to show their animal aspects unnecessarily. It was only a quirk of the way Orion ran the Refuge that he wanted everyone to display theirs.

An angry bruise marks Madoc's left cheekbone, and a cut that runs from his right temple almost to his jaw is still seeping blood. Now that he's moving, I notice that he's favoring one side, as if he's got some other, unseen injury as well. My gut lurches.

"What did you do to him?" I demand as August's grip loosens enough to put me back on my feet, though he keeps his hands on my shoulders. I glare around the clearing at the guards. "You didn't need to attack him."

The one who must be the squadron leader scowls at me. "It wasn't us. He arrived like this. And the patrol wouldn't have known how hard they needed to come down on him when they spotted him. Why would we give the vermin a chance to get the upper hand?"

I guess that makes sense, but it doesn't stop me from feeling sick. I yank my attention back to Madoc, who offers me a tight smile.

"I'll survive," he says in the lightly hoarse voice that guided me through so many of the horrors I faced in the Refuge. "You could say it's my fault for getting caught. I meant to pass on my message in some way not quite so hands-on, but I'll take what I can get. I'm glad to see your defiant spirit hasn't gone anywhere just because you found your freedom."

An ache forms around my heart that he's taking this setback so calmly, unshaken even with fae who wouldn't hesitate to kill him all around. As if all that matters is seeing through his mission. But that's how he's always been, isn't it? Dedicated and determined, sometimes to the point that it frustrated me.

The fact that he's here at all is proof that he's capable of adjusting his resolve, though. I doubt Orion approved of him reaching out to me like this. He hasn't let his commitment to his people blot out every other consideration of what's right.

"Of course it hasn't," I say to his remark about my spirit. "I'll have them bring a healer." I spin toward Sylas. "You can get Celia to agree to that, can't you?"

Sylas inclines his head, but his gaze remains on Madoc. "First I'd like to know what brought our unexpected visitor here at all. What's the message? What did you want to tell Talia?"

Madoc's eyes narrow as he takes in the fae men around me. Then he focuses on me instead of Sylas. "Your mates are very careful about ensuring your protection, I'll give you that. Let's hope they can continue to be."

"Is that a threat?" August growls before the Murk man can go on.

Madoc's gaze hardens into a glower. "No," he snaps. "It's a warning, one I risked a lot to come here to deliver, so maybe you can give me a chance to actually tell you." He drags in a breath and meets my eyes again. "With all the magic Orion cast on you, there was one spell lying dormant that he was keeping in reserve as a backup plan. From what I understand, he sent someone into the Mists to trigger it about two days ago."

Two days ago? A chill washes over my skin. I don't remember anything unusual happening then. It's been a bit of a blur since we realized I was pregnant, but that was almost a week ago.

My hand rises to my belly instinctively. Orion's spell doesn't have anything to do with *that*, does it?

"What exactly did he trigger?" I ask, hardly wanting the answer but knowing I need to hear it.

Madoc grimaces. "From what he told me, it's a curse on *you*. It'll start by simply weakening you and causing you some pain. But it'll get increasingly worse within a matter of days, until—until it kills you."

CHAPTER SEVEN

Sylas

I lean against the carriage's hull, gazing down at my sleeping mate. She refused to go any farther from the holding cell than this, even though her exhaustion was obviously catching up with her. We arranged as comfortable a bed as we could nestled between two of the carriage's benches, and she drifted off almost immediately.

The early dawn light that filters through the foliage overhead catches in her vibrant hair. I murmur a few words to create a sunshade so the rays won't wake her as they brighten. Then I look at my lead warrior—and chief healer.

"You haven't sensed any signs of illness in her?" I ask August. He didn't show any indication that Madoc's claims fit with his observations, but he might not have wanted to say anything in front of the company. He may not even have wanted to speak to Talia about it yet until we've discussed it ourselves, so as not to worry her unnecessarily.

My brother shakes his head with a smile much tighter than his usual. "Nothing—and I've checked her over for any reasons for concern every day since we discovered the pregnancy. Other than the child forming inside her, I haven't picked up on anything about her physical presence that's changed since before her kidnapping."

"You don't think the pregnancy could be related to the curse, do you?" The thought makes my gut sink.

August's smile disappears completely. A frown creeps into its place as he studies Talia's sleeping form. "We knew she was fertile when we were all with her after she escaped the Murk. The timing of Corwin first noticing the pregnancy and the energy she's giving off fit that as the date of conception. I've specifically searched for any hint of Murk influence tied to the new life, and there's none of that either. But I guess we can't know absolutely for sure. They've hidden a lot from us."

"Yes." I stifle a frown of my own. "We'll have to keep a close eye on her and the progress of the pregnancy. It might be best if you do a physical scan of her twice a day now so we can catch any new developments as early as possible."

"Maybe Madoc is wrong," August suggests. "Or maybe the trigger Orion told him about didn't work. Talia's foiled them in other ways before. The Heart of the Mists has supported her."

"I'd like to believe that, but we can't count on that being true. Our own curse doesn't show itself except one night every month. The Unseelie's strikes at random. It wouldn't be all that unexpected for whatever the Murk king has placed in our mate to take some time showing itself."

With that grim statement hanging over us, I turn toward the slope that'll lead me back to Madoc's holding cell. "I need to question the rat more. You stay here and watch over her, and I'll send Astrid up to join you." After everything Talia's been through, I don't feel comfortable leaving her without at least two trusted guards, even this deep in our territory and so close to our Heart. Corwin has gone off to fly around the nearby lands, watching for any hint that Madoc didn't come alone.

August inclines his head in acceptance of my orders, and I stride on down the hill to the clearing where I left my other two cadre-chosen—and the Murk man who's supposedly looking out for Talia's best interests.

I wouldn't trust *him* to guard her from his own kind, but it was easy to see how his demeanor changed in her presence—the difference in his expression and posture when he was focused on her compared to the rest of us. She's won some sort of victory with him, as she's won over so many other fae. But is it enough to overcome his obvious contempt for Seelie and Unseelie alike?

I'm interested to see how he'll talk when he doesn't have her presence to keep his more hostile impulses in check. Perhaps I'll learn something he'd only let slip when it's just us fae.

Nuldar's words come back to me from the last time I visited the sage, when I asked him about how we could end the curse. He said the answer was on its way to us… and that we needed a "snare" to catch that answer. *If it can capture a single heart, it will bring all you need to know back to you.*

Could Talia be that snare—and Madoc the heart she's captured? So far he hasn't told us anything that would help us eliminate the curse, nothing we hadn't already learned from Talia after her time in the hands of the Murk. But then, she might not have come back to us at all if she hadn't made an ally of him.

We'll have to wait and see how that plays out as well.

As I come up on the clearing where Celia's guards are maintaining their solemn vigil, Whitt and Astrid both move to rejoin me. "How's our mighty mate?" Whitt asks, the playful note in his voice unusually subdued.

"Getting her much needed rest," I say, and nod to Astrid. "You should join August in watching over her. Alert me of anything at all worrying."

"Of course, my lord," the wiry woman says, and springs into her wolf form nearly as nimbly as if she were several centuries younger. She was the most faithful and capable of my guards, and she's proven an excellent addition to my cadre. I should have thought of inviting her into it sooner.

Whitt walks with me back to the holding cell. He may have some questions to contribute to the interrogation too. Stopping closer than the guards are standing but still a few feet from the glowing walls, I peer at Madoc through the shifting barrier.

He isn't as musclebound as my own frame or August's, but he could just about match Whitt's physical build. And both the fact that he made it so close to our inner domains and Talia's reports have made it clear his magical talent is one to be reckoned with as well. He could be a formidable ally if he's willing to remain one—or a formidable enemy if he's not.

He gazes back at me, his expression wary. He's dropped down into a crouch, leaning slightly forward with his forearms resting on his knees, but I can tell he's ready to leap from that pose in an instant should he see an opening. He definitely isn't happy about staying among us in captivity.

"I have more questions for you," I say, crossing my arms over my chest.

"Of course you do." He straightens up so we're closer to the same level. I have a few inches on him, but no more than that. "What else is it you want to know, arch-lord?"

He says my title with a hint of a sneer, as if it's more an insult than an honor. I grit my teeth automatically but keep my mind focused on the interrogation. I can't let him distract *me* with his attempts to provoke my temper.

"This curse your king supposedly put on Talia—you said he mentioned having sent someone to trigger it just a couple of days ago. Did he give any indication of when the curse itself was laid?"

Madoc's eyes flicker, and I suspect he's debating whether he wants to tell me even that much. But after a moment, he draws in a breath. "I asked him a few questions as if out of curiosity. As far as I could tell from his answers, which aren't always all that concrete, it was part of the initial spell he worked on her when she was a newborn."

The thought of Talia as an infant brings up all my apprehension about her current state. "But he didn't offer any details about what the curse on her would entail?"

"I told you that already," Madoc says shortly. "All he said was that she'd suffer and waste away, and he expected to see you all panicking and distraught because there'd be nothing you could do to stop it. I couldn't press all that hard without making him wonder why I was so concerned about the specifics. Believe me, if I'd been able to find out anything that would help you—help *her*—prepare better, I wouldn't be keeping it to myself."

I can't say I'm convinced of that claim, but I let his answer stand. Whitt has obviously been thinking along similar lines, though. As I pause to consider my next question, he clears his throat. "Did he say anything at all that hinted at the curse involving her being with child?"

So many emotions dart across Madoc's face, it's almost impressive to behold. From the shadow that crosses his eyes and the twitch of his muscles that's almost a flinch, the only thing I'm sure of is that the idea comes as a complete surprise—and he doesn't like it at all. Which might be enough of an answer in itself.

"No," he says, the hoarseness of his voice thickening a little. "I can't think of anything he said that would suggest… *Is* she? With child?" There's an oddly hesitant note in his voice, as if he isn't sure he wants to know after all.

"I'm simply covering every eventuality," Whitt says smoothly. "It seems a reasonable potential ploy."

Madoc regards him suspiciously but says nothing.

"Why *did* you come to pass on this warning to Talia?" I ask, bringing his attention back to me. "You pointed out that you've put your life at risk doing so. What made it important enough to take that risk?"

His gaze turns into a glower. "I already risked my life once getting her away from Orion in the hopes of saving hers. Obviously there wouldn't have been much point in that if I was just going to let her die anyway."

"I think the question still stands," Whitt says breezily, cocking his head. "Why help her at all?"

Madoc flexes his fingers, and for a second I think I catch a glint of claws emerging. But they vanish just as quickly. He scowls at both of us. "I wouldn't think I'd need to tell either of you that she's a pretty extraordinary woman. She managed to convince me that there might be some hope of this conflict ending in ways other than a bloody war. And regardless of that, no matter what you think of the Murk, I don't happen to enjoy watching someone who doesn't deserve it suffer."

I have the feeling he doesn't count us among those who don't deserve to suffer. I focus on the other part of his answer. "Is that what you'd want—an end to this conflict that doesn't include war? It was your people who started the war. It seems you've been waging it against us for decades without us even knowing."

"*We* started it?" Madoc sputters in disbelief, but then he shakes his head. "It doesn't matter. I don't think it'd be good for *my* people if we have to resort to that kind of combat. Talia sees something worthwhile in the lot of you, so maybe there are a few of you it'd be better to have sticking around too." He doesn't bother to hide his skepticism.

My eyebrows rise just slightly. "You value my mate's input quite a lot."

I purposefully referred to Talia by her relationship to me to check his reaction. Madoc doesn't show any additional animosity, but then, there's plenty between us already. His lips curl back just slightly. "I hope you do too."

I can't see any point in continuing to badger him. Other than being a little more open in his dislike of us, he hasn't given away anything useful, and the only things he's been able to tell us overtly, we already knew. I'm no closer to being sure of what we should do with him.

"You know the way to your Refuge where your king has his false Heart," I say carefully. "If we dealt with that—"

Madoc's gaze sharpens into a glare. "I'm not leading you back there to carry out what I have to assume would be a slaughter. *That* wouldn't do my people any good either. I came in the hopes of sparing Talia some pain, not to bring down heaps more on the Murk."

I'd expected it was a long-shot anyway. "I can understand that." Easing back, I dip my head to him—nothing like a bow, but a brief indication of respect. Regardless of how I feel about his people or him about mine, he's sacrificed a lot on behalf of my mate. I can recognize that generosity.

"That's enough for now," I say. "I'll leave you be."

As I head toward the trees, there's a rustle as Madoc steps forward. His voice drops. "Is she—is she all right? The curse really hasn't affected her at all yet?"

I glance over my shoulder at him. The anguish that seeped into his tone and the consternation on his face, as if he hates asking me for reassurance but can't help himself anyway, disarm my wariness in a way nothing else he's said before has.

He does care about her, not just about the role she might play in getting the Murk to their goals.

I still don't have much faith in anything else he's said, but the realization brings down my hackles enough for me to answer honestly. "Nothing. As far as we can tell, she's in perfectly normal health—and my healer has a lot of experience with all forms of bodily magic."

"Good," Madoc says, his shoulders sagging. "Thank you."

Whitt and I walk several paces into the shelter of the woods before my brother catches my arm. He murmurs a quick spell to the air around us to muffle our conversation from distant ears. "What do you make of him?"

"I was going to ask you the same thing." I rub my jaw. "He doesn't like talking to us, but I didn't get the impression he was holding back anything significant either."

"Neither did I." Whitt gazes back the way we came. "But what do we do with him now? We can't ask Celia to release him and let him run free simply because he's made friends with our mate."

"No." I pause. "But perhaps we could come to a more formal agreement with him after we've held him a little longer, had more chance to feel out his intentions. It might help to let Talia speak to him on our behalf. If we could count on him revealing more about the Murk's preparations, that would be worth a lot."

"It would." Whitt lets out a restrained snarl and meets my eyes. "But for all we know, this whole tale of a curse could be a lie. Just how far are we willing to trust him, no matter what he says?"

CHAPTER EIGHT

Talia

A tingle passes over my skin and into my flesh with each soft true name August murmurs. He seems to be casting his magic over every part of my body, starting from my head and working his way down. I hold still, fighting the urge to fidget.

What are we going to do if he *does* find something wrong? I might be the cure for the fae's curse, but Madoc indicated that there is no cure for the one Orion planted in me.

My stomach twists, but August finishes his examination with a smile and a squeeze of my shoulder. "I still can't see anything out of the ordinary. I'd say you're stronger than that rat king bargained for, Sweetness."

I smile back at him, only partly relieved. It's easier for him to say that when he never had to deal with Orion face to face or stand in the unnerving glow of the Murk's Heart.

All's well? Corwin asks through our bond in a hopeful tone. He's been checking in on me even more than usual during the times when his duties take him from my side.

As far as August can tell, and bodily magic is his specialty, I reply.

Maybe we'll be able to find out more about what I need to watch out for after I talk to Madoc again.

My mention of the Murk man provokes a ripple of uneasiness from my soul-twined mate, but he doesn't argue against it. He already knew that was the plan. I'm supposed to go to Madoc and try to negotiate some kind of deal, his help in exchange for his freedom. I don't think it's exactly the kind of negotiation he wanted to be having, but I can't blame the fae of the Mists for being even warier of the Murk after the attack a few days ago and now this news of a fatal curse in me.

"Ready to go downstairs?" August asks. "If you need more time, they'll wait, arch-lords or no."

I square my shoulders and turn toward my bedroom mirror, taking in my reflection. August has touched up the pink and purple in my hair again since I returned from the Refuge. The turquoise dress I've picked, formally long but not particularly ornate, brings out both those vivid hues and the green in my eyes.

I'm Lady Talia. My opinion matters too. I will not let myself be bullied into saying anything I don't agree with.

At least I'm less worried about that from the Seelie arch-lords than I would be if it was someone like Laoni who'd captured Madoc. I'm not sure he'd even have stayed alive long enough to deliver his message if her warriors had come across him.

The thought of him slaughtered makes my stomach twist tighter. I shake off my discomfort and nod to August. "I'm fine. As good as I'm going to be." My broken sleep has left my mind a little bleary, even with catching up on some in Sylas's carriage this morning, but I've been equally tired in the past week just from being pregnant. If I've got eight more months of this ahead of me, I'd better get used to working around it.

It'll be worth it. As August walks with me into the hall, my hand drifts to my belly. It'll be worth it for him… or her… I wonder if some fae magic will tell me whether I'm expecting a son or a daughter before the birth.

Those warmer thoughts fall away as we step into the border castle's main meeting room. Sylas and Whitt are already there, Astrid having stayed behind with Madoc to keep an eye on how he's treated. Donovan and Celia are waiting for me as well, standing by one end of the long table, each with a cadre member of their own. Donovan's eyes glint, bright with what looks like excitement at the possibilities we're going to discuss, but Celia is much more solemn. The oldest of the Seelie arch-lords is always the most pessimistic of the trio.

"All right," I say. "I'm here. I think this is going to be pretty straightforward, though, isn't it? I'll explain to Madoc that if he'll agree to pass on more news to us about Orion's plans, we'll let him go. I think he'll agree to that." It isn't as if he wants to stay locked up here.

Celia looks at Sylas instead of me. "Does she have no sense of the necessary precautions?"

Sylas gazes steadily back at her. "That's why we're having this discussion, is it not? To come to an agreement on what precautions are necessary?"

I frown at Celia. "What are you talking about? Obviously I'm not going to put myself in harm's way or say anything that could hurt anyone here in the Mists. I'm not an idiot."

She finally turns to me. "Offering this vermin his freedom could hurt us greatly in itself. We'll have no guarantee of him giving us any aid at all. And who knows what he might have discovered before my guards caught him that he'd run off to report to his 'king'?"

I bristle automatically at her disdainful tone. "He's already proven that he isn't totally loyal to Orion by coming here in the first place, hasn't he? If you treat him like he's attacked us instead of helped us, which is all he's done so far, you'll just be encouraging him not to trust the fae of the Mists."

Her eyes narrow. "It isn't our fault if the rats want to blame us for a natural wariness founded on their own horrible actions for centuries upon centuries past."

Before I can point out the horrible actions the other fae have taken against the Murk as well, Sylas breaks in. "This Madoc *has* helped us, or at least attempted to, and he's helped Talia in the past at great risk to himself. I don't fully trust him either, not only because of his divided loyalties but also because we can't know what greater sway his king may force on him later on. But I agree with Talia that we have to appeal to his *better* nature at least as much as the aspects we fear."

"It's not a matter of fear," Celia mutters, and then sighs. "We do need to have some kind of failsafe in place. I won't order my people to free him otherwise."

"Of course," Donovan says, his eagerness brightening his voice as well. "But it is an excellent opportunity we're getting. We've never had a rat on our side, a way of finding out what's going on within the Murk community. No matter how much magic they have, we couldn't ask for a better advantage than that."

Celia gives him a cool glance. "Assuming we don't end up double-crossed. And an even better advantage would be if he'd point the way straight to his king so we can cut off this rebellion at the root."

Sylas clears his throat. "He's already made it quite clear he won't betray his people to that extent. Pushing him will only make him more resistant to offering us anything at all."

"Fine. But we still need some guarantee of his loyalty, however little of it he's going to offer."

I wasn't feeling queasy before, but all this tense back-and-forth has brought out a twinge of nausea. I sink into one of the chairs. "What do you even mean by a failsafe? We can't enforce a vow or anything like that, can we, when the Murk aren't tied to the Heart out there anymore?" I motion toward the Heart of the Mists, its resonant energy humming through the air even with the walls hiding it from view.

"I've been thinking on that," Celia says. "You've mentioned that the Murk king lashes out against any of his subjects if provoked, haven't you? Does that mean this one would face severe punishment for a misstep despite his high status in their false court?"

I can only imagine what Orion would do to Madoc if he found out how his knight had betrayed him, and I don't want to. "Yes. His position wouldn't guarantee any protection. He'd probably face worse punishment so Orion could make an example of him to discourage anyone else from turning traitor."

Sylas is nodding, apparently having picked up on the direction Celia is heading in. "Then we have some leverage over him in the fact that he's come to us at all."

Her eyes gleam. "Exactly. All we need is some basic proof of his complicity. Perhaps we could ask him to mark an object in a clearly identifiable way or cast magic into it—something he wouldn't have done as part of his regular missions and that we couldn't have obtained without his cooperation. If he makes any move to harm us after we release him, then we can reveal the proof to the rest of the Murk. It sounds as though that should give him plenty of motivation to keep his word."

I can see her logic, but the idea doesn't sit totally right with me anyway. Maybe because it's essentially threatening the man who's looked out for me more than once—and relying on that threat rather than trust to ensure his continuing help.

But how can I blame the fae around me for not being willing to fully trust one of their long-time enemies, one who clearly still doesn't like them particularly? I'm not sure *I* even trust him to come back after they've held him captive once, no matter what he hears from Orion next.

"He wouldn't *have* to come back, right?" I say slowly. "If he hears nothing he feels we need to know, he'd have no reason to. I wouldn't want us to destroy his life just because we got antsy about a long period of silence."

"That's a fair point," Sylas says. "We'd strike against him only if he actively struck against us."

Celia looks as if she's going to argue, but Donovan jumps in first. "And we could test that pretty easily. Let him see one thing that he'd think was damaging before he goes, something that would suggest an obvious target or tactic to the Murk. Then we wait and see if they make use of that opportunity. If they don't, then we know he didn't pass the information on to his king."

I don't love the idea of setting Madoc up for a fall either, but… if he *would* use his time here to help Orion attack us, then he isn't any kind of ally or friend to me, not really.

"I'd agree with that," I say.

Celia purses her lips. I don't think she considers my opinion on the same level as her own and her colleagues', but at least she doesn't make that as obvious as some of the winter arch-lords have. "All right. We can work out the exact details while Talia speaks to the man. If we're going to make use of him, we should do it quickly. The longer he's here, the more suspicious his king might become of his absence."

Whitt rests his hand on my shoulder. "I'll take you to speak with him, mite. I'll hang back so I'm not obviously part of the conversation, but I'd like to listen in so I can judge his answers for myself."

I drag in a breath, suddenly not sure *I'm* ready for this conversation after all. "Okay."

Whitt leads me out to a small carriage. "No wolf-back riding today?" I tease.

The spymaster arches an eyebrow at me. "I wouldn't have thought that much jostling would be ideal in your current state."

My hand drifts to my belly again. It's true that I have been getting queasy in general much more easily than usual. "I never had a problem with it before, but maybe it's better to be careful."

As he guides the carriage toward the woods where Madoc is being held, Whitt lowers his voice. "Celia has agreed that the guards will draw back out of hearing while still monitoring the holding cell magically. We want Madoc to feel he's speaking just to you, since you're the only one he seems to trust at all. But I'd like you to use my true name to ask me to hear what you hear, so I can follow the conversation completely without being close myself. It won't be as smooth as your conversations with your soul-twined mate, but the outcome is similar."

"Of course." I reach for his hand and squeeze it, abruptly needing that contact. I haven't used Whitt's true name since the second time I tried to reach out to him from the Refuge. It still sends a flare of happiness through me that he shared something so intimate with me to begin with.

Now I have to see whether I can convince Madoc to trust me even a fraction that much.

As before, we get out of the carriage farther up the hill where the forest starts to thicken and walk the rest of the short distance to the clearing on foot. As we come into view of the holding cell, Whitt motions to the leader of the guards. They all fade back into the trees as if they were never there.

I pause, and bob up on my toes to whisper Whitt's true name right into his ear. "*Wye-con-ell.* Hear what I hear." A giddy shiver travels through my chest, and he smiles before pressing a kiss to the top of my head. Then he escorts me the rest of the way to the shimmering wall before turning and walking away to give us our space.

Madoc sits up on the mat he's been given to rest on. Someone's brought him a small pillow and a blanket too. The cut on his face has been healed, only a faint pink mark showing where the skin was broken before. His expression doesn't exactly brighten at the sight of me, but the shadows darkening it draw back a little.

I sit down on the other side of the shimmering barrier so I'm not looming over him, which would feel uncomfortable. "Sorry it's taken so long for me to come back. I'm glad to see they've made you more comfortable at least."

"It hasn't been that long as far as I can tell," Madoc says with a hint of wryness. "Am I right in assuming I can thank you for this incredible generosity?"

I did insist to Sylas that he needed to get Celia to show a little consideration to our prisoner. I shrug awkwardly, not wanting to make a big deal of it, and have to ask, "Have they brought you any food?"

"Oh, yes, I'm not going to starve." He chuckles darkly.

But no doubt being locked up in this holding cell is only confirming his beliefs about how the fae of the Mists see the Murk. I swallow thickly. I know I need to be cautious of him still, that my mates all feel he could still have some ulterior motive up his sleeve, but I can't help wishing this could be a proper conversation across a table in a regular room, like the one I just had with the Seelie arch-lords.

"I'm sorry about all of this," I say. "I don't like seeing you locked up like a criminal."

Madoc shrugs. "I know it wouldn't have been your doing. And I know it'd be asking a lot for the fae of the Mists to see me as anything *other* than a criminal."

"Still… I know what it's like being in a cage, and I wouldn't wish that on anyone."

We look at each other for a moment, and I can tell he's remembering the night he opened up Orion's cage for me too. His tone softens. "At least this one is more spacious than the ones you've had to suffer. And it is a little relief to see they haven't decided to kill me just yet."

There's more truth than teasing in that statement. I meet his cloud-gray gaze, my stomach knotting all over again. I *need* him to listen to me, for both our benefits.

"They don't want to kill you at all," I say. "They're hoping we can come to a deal, which would mean not just keeping you alive but releasing you."

Madoc blinks at me, genuinely startled. "What could they possibly think was worth letting one of the dreaded vermin run free after they've caught him?"

I gather my words and my resolve. "You want to see the Murk get a better life without war if you can, don't you?"

"You know I do," he says, his voice roughening with the passionate determination I have to admire. "That's why I'm here."

"Well then… The Seelie—and the Unseelie too, I'd imagine—would find it easier to trust the Murk, and you as their representative, if they see that you're willing to work with us. They'd let you go back to Orion under the condition that if you heard about any plans he's making that would hurt us—something like the curse you say he's tried to spark in me, or an attack or an ambush—you'd warn us ahead of time."

Madoc doesn't look unwilling, only skeptical. "I won't tell them anything that would harm *my* people."

"Of course not. And if there wasn't any news to pass on at all, that would be fine too, although I guess then we'd be at a standstill."

I pause. "I think this could be a solid step in the right direction. You'd have a chance to talk more with the other Murk who might be willing to negotiate and let us know about any progress there as well."

"And that's it? No catch?"

I grimace. "They do want a show of faith to give us some security that you wouldn't turn against us." I explain about Celia's suggestion as quickly as I can. "But if you don't instigate anything, none of the Murk will ever know. I'll—I'll make the arch-lords all take a vow to that effect before you agree to anything if I have to."

Madoc is silent for a long moment. He studies me, his expression unreadable. "What do you think?" he asks abruptly. "Do you honestly believe that going through with this deal would be better for all of us—not just the fae of the Mists?"

"Yes," I say without hesitation. "I wouldn't be here talking to you about it if I didn't. I argued with *them* about what was reasonable to propose before I even got here."

The corner of his mouth twitches upward. His expression may be shadowed and his cheek bruised, but that hint of a smile shows how handsome that face can be in unexpected ways.

"I can imagine you doing that," he says. He leans back on his hands, the hint of a smile falling into a pensive frown. "I'll need to think about it. I won't take too long, but—it's a lot to decide on."

"I'll tell them that. Thank you for at least considering it."

His smile doesn't come back, but a glint that's almost playful comes into his eyes. "It's a good thing for them they've got you on their side."

I get up, and he lies down on his back to gaze up at the sky as he does his thinking. How often has he gotten such a clear view of that sunlit expanse while living in the Refuge?

Can he even enjoy it while he's trapped in that cell?

A deeper urge grips me, to offer him even a fraction of what he's offered me by coming here. I wet my lips. "I have to report to the arch-lords, but I'll come back. I could bring a book if the guards will let me give that to you, or we could just talk. If you'd want."

Madoc pauses, tipping his head to the side to consider me. For a second, he looks so uncertain I want to reach right through the magical barrier and squeeze his hand. He really isn't sure what to make of my kindness either, is he?

The sudden vulnerability fades away behind an impassive front, but I know he means it when he says, "I'd like that."

As he leans his head back again, I limp toward the trees, watching for Whitt to come to meet me. The guards draw forward first. They must have been tracking my movements well enough to realize the conversation is over.

I've nearly reached the edge of the clearing when an odd prickling sensation races through my chest. I keep walking, not paying it too much mind after all the other twinges I've experienced with the pregnancy, but as my foot hits the ground with my next step, the prickle explodes into a lance of pain.

I gasp, my lungs seizing as if they've been stabbed through with a spear. My legs wobble. I grope for something to catch my balance, but the rush of agony has stiffened my arms and blurred my vision.

"Talia?" Madoc calls in alarm from behind me with the thump of him leaping to his feet.

I can't form words to answer him, to cry out to Whitt, anything. Two of Celia's guards rush to my side, but I crumple before they can reach me.

CHAPTER NINE

Talia

I don't remember much of the hustle back to the castle, most of it in Whitt's arms. The pain washes through my nerves in waves, always sharpest in my chest. In the moments between waves, I feel utterly weak, my muscles refusing to move, my limbs gone slack. And through it all courses a deepening fear.

I haven't escaped Orion's curse after all. It just took its time kicking in. And this is only the beginning. Who knows how horrible it might get from here when it was dreamt up in the mind of that brutal tyrant?

After a while, I can hardly think at all. I'm vaguely aware of being settled onto soft sheets in the amber light of my bedroom's glow orb. Words are murmured over me, but all they do is numb the barest edges off the pain. Whatever spells are being cast on me, they can't quite reach into the center of me where the attack seems to be coming from.

For I don't know how long, I'm lost in a daze. Then gradually the agony eases back. When it's dulled to the point that it's only a constant but faint prickling behind my breastbone, I open my eyes and look around.

All four of my mates are in the bedroom with me now. Sylas, Whitt, and Corwin are standing in quiet, anxious conversation off in the corner. August paces by the foot of my bed. Corwin turns with a flicker of relief through our bond at the realization that I'm more aware now, but August speaks before my soul-twined mate can say anything.

"I don't know how—it couldn't have been more than an hour beforehand that I checked her. There wasn't even a hint that anything was wrong. I don't see how I could have missed it… but I must have."

"The Murk appear to specialize in magic that catches us off-guard," Whitt says. He and Sylas follow Corwin around the bed.

Corwin grasps my hand. "I'm glad to feel you in a more comfortable state now, my soul. We're going to do everything we can to stop any future fits." He glances at Whitt, his jaw tightening. "What exactly did the rat say to her before the pain came over her?"

Whitt opens his mouth, but I get there first, my voice croaking a bit as I push the words from my throat. "It wasn't Madoc. He didn't do anything to me."

Corwin frowns. "You can't be sure of it. You were near him when this curse or whatever it is hit you. *He* could be the trigger."

I push myself into a sitting position, ignoring August's noise of consternation. "I was near him for just as long yesterday night, and nothing happened then. I was walking *away* from him when it happened. I don't think we have any reason to blame him."

Whitt clears his throat. "I'm not saying we should remove the rat from all suspicion, but to my eyes he appeared very honestly distressed by Talia's collapse."

"If he is some kind of trigger, he may not even know it himself," Sylas says. "His king may have used him without him knowing."

"But how would Orion even be sure that Madoc would be able to get close enough to me to trigger anything, if that's what was needed?" I ask. "Even when he kidnapped me after the mating ceremony, he didn't dare come too close to the celebration, and that was before we were quite as guarded against the Murk. He obviously couldn't count on going undetected. I don't think that makes any sense either."

Sylas exhales roughly. "That may well be true, my love. And it's true that you suffered no ill effects from being in his presence earlier. Still, I think we need to proceed even more cautiously than before. He didn't agree to the conditions you offered him. He clearly thinks we're more the enemy than his king is."

I don't think there's anything else I can say—and to be honest, I wouldn't put it past Orion to have come up with some cruel scheme that would punish both Madoc and me. I just can't imagine him leaving a task that important so much to chance: the chances of Madoc getting so close without being caught, the chances that if he was caught, the fae who had him wouldn't kill him outright or refuse to let me anywhere near him.

The Murk king never believed the other fae really respected my opinions on anything. *He* certainly didn't when push came to shove. Even if he realized I'd want to defend Madoc, he'd have trouble imagining my mates allowing me to.

I pull my knees up under the sheets and tuck my arms around them. "So what happens now? I do feel reasonably all right." I glance at August. "Did that 'fit' do any actual damage to me?"

August's mouth twists. "I can pick up on a few traces of very minor internal injuries to your lungs and heart. Not so much that they wouldn't heal on their own given time, but if you continue to suffer from spells like that—if they get worse…"

"There has to be a way to tackle it," Whitt says firmly, though his eyes are dark with worry. "No magic exists that doesn't have a counter spell. It's only a matter of finding it. We can call in the best healers in both realms—and there's always places like the Serene Springs too."

But we've gone this long without finding a real cure to the other curses plaguing the fae of the Mists. I bite my lip.

The unexpected knock on the door makes all of us startle. Sylas goes over to answer it.

One of his staff stands outside. "My lord, Arch-Lord Celia has come to speak with you. She has news about the prisoner."

I tense on the bed. She hasn't decided Madoc was responsible for my curse activating and taken matters into her own hands, has she?

"Tell her to come up," Sylas says. "My mate will want to hear whatever she has to say and to have the chance to weigh in too."

The woman hesitates as if she's afraid of Celia's reaction to that order, but only for a second. Then she darts off down the hall.

I pull back the sheets and slide to the edge of the bed, though I'm not in any hurry to try standing up. My mates look ready to spring to stop me if I did. I'm still wearing the same dress from before, so I'll look reasonably put together in front of the other arch-lord, even if I am technically now an invalid.

A shiver runs through me. I push my worries about the future away. The one thing I do know for sure is that the men around me will stop at nothing to protect me from this and every other threat I might face.

Celia arrives at the doorway looking typically stern but a little puzzled as well. She takes in the five of us and offers me a small dip of her head in acknowledgment. "It's good to see you somewhat recovered, Lady Talia."

I'm not sure what prompted that gesture of respect—maybe her thoughts about what her people would face if I didn't recover—but I'll take it.

"What's the urgent news?" Sylas asks.

Celia turns to him, her jaw working for a second as if she doesn't totally want to tell him. "The rat shifter. Madoc, or whatever his name is. He's agreed to the deal."

My heart skips a beat. Whitt raises his eyebrows. "Just like that?"

Celia smiles thinly at him and then me. "I believe we may owe the credit to your mate. Not only did she pitch the terms to him well enough, but he seems motivated to see what else he might be able to find out from his king about her ailment. If he's to be believed."

A swell of tender emotion momentarily numbs the lingering prickle of discomfort in my chest. Madoc is willing to put his future safety in the hands of the people he hates so that he can help me yet again.

"We still need his proof," August says, flexing his shoulders as if he thinks he'll need to march over and demand it right now. "We can't assume—"

"He's already given it," Celia interrupts. "I wouldn't have come to report his decision to you unless it was firm. I arranged a clay tablet for him to mark, and he's done so. I only wanted to speak with you before I tell my guards to actually release him."

There's a pause between my mates. I suspect now that they're faced with the reality of letting a rat shifter loose, they can't help being unsettled, no matter how much this one has proven himself. I'm preparing to speak up in Madoc's favor again when Corwin slips his arm around my shoulders.

"The deal was made with the Seelie, so I can't speak to that. I don't object to him going free if he's committed to terms you feel will ensure he sticks to that deal. But before he leaves for however long he may be back with his kin for, I think we should speak to him about Talia's curse now that it's started to act on her. Perhaps he'll be able to observe something about it that we wouldn't, since he's much more familiar with the new magic of the Murk, or to suggest treatments we wouldn't normally make use of."

Whitt nods, a faint grin crossing his face. "Lord Bird is no feather-brain."

Celia considers the suggestion with a tilt of her head. "You'd let him get close enough to Lady Talia to examine her?"

Sylas hums. "We could start at more of a distance. We are putting a lot of trust in him as it is. I say we should extend that trust at least somewhat to this urgent situation. Show him that we'll keep *our* end of the deal before we ask more of him." He looks at Celia. "Can you have your guards escort him to the field just outside the summer entrance to this castle?"

"Are you sure?" she asks.

"We won't throw caution utterly to the wind. If he can offer any insight, it'll be worth the attempt."

Corwin supports me as I rise onto my feet. I test my balance with a couple of typically uneven steps and find I can walk like normal, no additional pain waking up inside me and no weakness gripping me. I squeeze his arm. "I think I'm okay for now."

My mates all stay within easy reach as we head down to the summer-side entrance. Corwin is monitoring my internal state so closely I can practically feel his attention brushing through me.

We'll get through this, I tell him. *We've gotten through so much else. One little curse isn't going to stop me now.*

But for the first time since I started reassuring myself that way in the face of the various threats I've encountered among the fae, I don't know that I totally believe it myself.

Sylas leads us to a spot about halfway between the border castle and the pack village of Hearth-by-the-Heart, as if he doesn't want Madoc getting too close to either of those sites. He and Whitt quickly conjure a narrow wooden table and chairs, so it'll even feel like a proper meeting—although from the words they continue to murmur around the furniture afterward, I suspect they're also building in protections against whatever they're worried the Murk man might do.

They arrange it so that there are five seats along one side, with our backs to the castle, and one chair on the other. The setup gives the sense of an interrogation, but it's a big step for them to accept Madoc this near our homes to begin with, so I don't complain.

Sylas has me sit at the far right of the table. He sits in the middle where he'll be most directly facing the rat shifter, with August between him and me, Corwin at his other side, and Whitt at the far end.

We've only just sorted that out when a cluster of figures comes into view, emerging from the path that leads into the nearest stretch of forest. Five of Celia's guards stand in a ring several feet wide with Madoc in the center, swords in their hands, a shimmer in the air that suggests they've brought some of the holding cell's barrier with them.

Madoc looks uneasy, but when his gaze veers from us to the pulsing glow of the Heart just down the border, something in his face softens. I can see even at a distance that the source of magic he either rejected or lost so long ago still stirs awe in him.

When they reach us, Sylas motions to the guards. "You can leave him in our care. He's soon to be completely released regardless."

The guards stiffen a bit at that order, but they bow and remove the magical barrier around Madoc before shifting into wolf form to lope back to their own domain. Madoc stands tensed with his hands braced against the back of the chair, taking us all in.

His gaze stops on me. "You're all right," he says, relief and horror warring in his tone. "I was afraid—it came on you so quickly—"

"I get the impression that your king enjoys drawing out his torments rather than seeing them to the end immediately," Whitt remarks dryly from the other end of the table.

Madoc's mouth tightens. "He does indeed."

Sylas inclines his head toward the chair. "I hope you'll take a seat. I understand you've accepted our terms and confirmed our deal through Arch-Lord Celia. We were only hoping to have a short discussion before you're on your way—since you seem concerned about our mate's wellbeing."

Madoc's stance relaxes just a bit. I can't tell whether it's because Sylas has confirmed that he's being released or because of the realization that this meeting is about me. He tugs back the chair and sinks into it, keeping a careful pose as if he might need to leap away quickly. I guess he can't help his instinctive guardedness.

"If there's any way I can help you ensure Talia's safety, I'd be happy to do it," he says. "That was the only reason I came here in the first place. I won't be able to question Orion too insistently or he'll get suspicious, but I'm sure I can find out *more* about what the curse entails, maybe even some hint about curing it."

"There's one obvious way," August says. "I know you dismissed this idea before, but it's more pressing now. If we could get at that false Heart of yours and destroy it, then all the magic that came from it would vanish too."

"Yes," Corwin agrees. "And that would end our curses as well. It seems a simple solution."

I didn't know they were going to make that argument, but the vibe along my side of the table tells me it was planned. They must have discussed it earlier while I was too out of it to pay attention.

Madoc grimaces. "That depends on what you mean by simple. It took Orion decades to develop the magic to create our Heart and over a century to build its power. I have no idea how you'd destroy it. You'd have a hard enough time getting to it, even if I was willing to show you the way to the Refuge. You'd better believe Orion has sentries all over watching for any sign of Seelie or Unseelie presence through any portal within reasonable traveling distance."

"*If* you were willing," Sylas repeats.

Madoc narrows his stormy eyes at the Seelie arch-lord. "I thought I made it clear that I'm not willing to throw so many of my people to be slaughtered by yours over one ruler who's taken things a step too far. I swore to report back any information that might protect your people and Talia's, and if there's a chance to remove just Orion, I'll inform you of that. But if we can find a way to end the curses that doesn't touch the Heart, I'd rather we used that."

Whitt raises his eyebrows. "Awfully attached to it, are you?"

"You don't understand." Madoc's gaze drifts to the Heart of the Mists again. He jerks it back to my mates. "Most of us can't reach *your* Heart anymore. Orion's is the only source of magic we can draw on. We've used it to grow things and heal and all sorts of other purposes that have nothing to do with hurting anything. There's nothing harmful about the Heart itself."

"It sounds as if we need to table that possibility for the moment anyway, until we can be sure of getting the upper hand," Sylas says. "The magic acting on Talia comes from that Heart, from the powers you're much more familiar with than we are. I know you aren't aware of any definite cure right now, but we want to hear any ideas you have about healing or dispelling strategies that are common among your kind."

Madoc studies me. "I'm not sure. We don't typically curse each other or lift the curses we cast on others. The curser sets the conditions." He pauses. "We make a lot of use of shielding—to stop bleeding, to section off wounded or sickly parts of the body so they don't affect the rest… It's possible something like that would at least slow down the progression."

I'm tired of sitting here being talked about as if I'm in a coma, unable to contribute. "Can you sense anything about the curse now that it's active—what it'll do, how it'll affect me?"

His gaze becomes more intent. Then he shakes his head. "Not from here."

I resist the urge to roll my eyes. "You can come closer."

Sylas coughs. "I'm not certain—"

He cuts himself off, taking in the Murk man's reaction. Madoc has gone even more tense in his chair, his shoulders rigid. Sylas's brow furrows. "*You* don't want to get closer to her."

Madoc seems to grapple with his words before he speaks. He doesn't look at me. "It's occurred to me that it might not be a coincidence that she got sick right after she spoke to me. I don't have any awareness of anything in or around me affecting her, but if there's any risk at all—"

"Oh my God, enough!" I burst out. "Between the bunch of you, you'll end up missing the cure because you're too afraid of doing anything." I push to my feet and limp around the table as forcefully as I can. The men all leap up too, Madoc included. Before he can back away, I snatch his wrist and pull his hand toward me so his palm rests against my dress over my breastbone.

He freezes, not jerking out of my grasp but looking utterly miserable. "Talia, if there's a chance that I—"

"If there's any chance that you being near me is going to set off another fit, then we might as well find that out in the early stages, don't you think?" I fix him with my firmest look and then glance at my mates, who don't look all that much happier about the situation than Madoc does, but have settled for coming up around us at a short distance in case they need to intervene.

Madoc gradually relaxes again, letting his hand rest against me. The warmth of his palm, a little more potent than the pleasant summer air around us, seeps through the fabric into my skin. He adjusts his fingers a tad and murmurs a few words, his gaze darting briefly to our audience as if worried my mates will pounce on him. A tingle carries through my chest that doesn't feel particularly different from when August has checked me over.

Madoc's mouth slants downward. "I can feel the spell. I can feel

Orion's influence in it." He closes his eyes and intones a couple more syllables.

Nothing changes inside me except that brief tingling sensation. The prickling patch between my lungs remains, but it doesn't expand or intensify. That only makes me surer that Madoc wasn't the trigger.

If we let paranoia like that interfere with how much we trust each other—or ourselves—then Orion will have already won.

"I've never encountered anything quite like that," Madoc says after a moment. "I don't know—the barrier suggestion I made earlier would be difficult to attempt even at this stage, with the lingering energy of it being so close to her vital organs. But maybe, now that I have a clearer sense of the curse, I'll come across something that would point me in the right direction once I'm home."

He opens his eyes, moving to withdraw his hand. I release his wrist. As his fingers and their warmth leave my chest, his gaze catches mine from where he's standing over me, just a couple of feet away. His fleeting touch brings me back to the brief brush of his lips against mine just before I left the Refuge—and stirs up a sudden curiosity about how it would feel to have him claim my mouth more thoroughly.

My cheeks flush. I step back toward my chair, willing away those thoughts as fast as I can.

He didn't hurt you, my soul? Corwin asks through our bond, with no sign that he's noticed the odd direction my emotions momentarily veered in.

No, I feel perfectly fine. "Madoc didn't have anything to do with setting off the curse," I say out loud. "So let's stop worrying about that and focus on finding a real solution."

Whitt chuckles. "You are adept as always at putting us in our places, mighty one."

"I suppose I should go and see what I can learn, then?" Madoc says with a doubtful note in his voice. Is he still waiting for the other fae to reveal this was all a ploy and he can't leave after all?

Sylas nods. "Yes. Report back with anything you hear that it'd benefit us to know as soon as you can."

"It's likely that Orion will send me back here of his own accord once I make my report to *him*. But I can't promise I'll have come across anything all that useful in the meantime." Madoc turns from them to focus on me again. "I'll do as much as I can. If there's any way I can help you, I will."

"I know," I say quietly, still grappling with the unexpected feelings stirred up by his nearness. "Thank you."

"Thank *you*," he says. "For being willing to believe in us despite what the man ruling us has done to you."

Without hesitation now, he nods to my mates and walks away toward the forest. One moment he's a man, striding along, and the next he's vanished—or almost. All that's left is a small, pale-furred shape darting through the grass.

Back to his home and to the king who'll destroy us all if he has his way.

CHAPTER TEN

Corwin

I've always been an early riser, and that tendency has only deepened while my worries for Talia dog me. The sun is barely painting the horizon gold when I cross from the palace of Heart's Cadence to the border castle to check on her. When I stop outside her bedroom, I can tell from the muted impressions through our bond and the rasp of subdued breaths filtering through the door that both she and Whitt, who stayed by her side tonight, are still sleeping.

I have no interest in waking her from her much-needed respite, but I don't find I can sit calmly in the common rooms or my own bedroom waiting for her to awake. My restless feet carry me back through the halls and out the door to wander in the briskly cool breeze that dances across the icy plain. Not even the melody that breeze summons in the diamond walls of my own palace soothe my nerves.

A couple of healers arrived last night and tried a few spells on Talia, and she hasn't lapsed into the same pained state that took her yesterday morning so far. But it might have been days from the curse being triggered until she first showed symptoms. Who knows how it'll pace itself? The healers couldn't discern those kinds of details in their examination of my mate.

A few more, the most skilled fae in the healing arts from across all the domains of the Mists, will be arriving throughout the day as the messengers we sent reach them. Heart willing, we won't even need them. But after everything I've seen from the Murk and their wretched king at this point, I'm not feeling particularly optimistic.

Our best chance may lie in the rat who came bearing the warning. A rat Talia has softened to more than I'm sure I like. She cares so deeply and is willing to forgive so much, my kind-hearted love. It worked to my benefit when she and I barely knew each other, but now…

There was a flicker of something deeper than gratitude in her after he checked her curse. And I may not be the most experienced in romantic relationships out of all fae kind, but his response to her strikes me as more devoted than simple compassion.

If *he* ends up hurting her…

As I shake that thought away, one of my colleagues who's perhaps even less successful in her personal relationships than I've been soars into view. I recognize Laoni from the turquoise tint to her feathers and the quality of her movement before she lands, transforming into her usual form an instant later.

She swipes her hand over her thick hair that's a lighter shade of the same hue as her feathers and tips her head in acknowledgment. "I thought… I'd see how you're faring, with the new developments."

I'd informed my fellow arch-lords of Madoc's claim about the curse shortly after I heard it, of course, and of the fact that it appeared to be taking hold the first time I forced myself to leave my mate's side after her fit. Talia's fate affects the entire fae world. I can't help wishing just this once that I could set aside my duties as ruler and focus only on her, though.

"It's distressing, of course," I say to Laoni, who's probably inspecting me for signs of my mother's sort of grief-stricken deterioration as we speak. "But we're tackling the problem every way we know how, quickly and decisively. If there's a solution within our grasp, we'll find it."

If there's not… I'm not thinking about that yet.

Laoni rubs her mouth. For a moment, she just gazes off across the glittering landscape alongside me as if we're contemplating the same topic together. I haven't typically seen her this pensive. I'm not sure whether to be relieved or concerned by her new demeanor.

"I'm sorry you're having to face yet another threat to your mate," she says finally, without looking at me. "I can only imagine how difficult it must be to have her right there and yet not be sure of how to save her."

I blink at her, taken aback by the unexpected condolences. Of all the fae I might encounter, Laoni is the *last* I'd have expected to express any sympathy. She's spent most of the few months since Talia joined us doing everything she can to undermine my mate and our union.

But things have changed. Talia became Laoni's savior as well as that of so many of our people. Just a few days ago, she delivered her cure to my fellow arch-lord a second time—at Laoni's palace, keeping it secret as Laoni prefers.

And perhaps my colleague *can* imagine how I feel better than she might have before. She lost someone in a much more final way—someone she wasn't there to save.

"The rats have a lot to answer for," I say tentatively, knowing how she reacted to Talia's gentle overtures on this subject. "Including one of your long-time guards, I know."

Laoni keeps her gaze fixed on the distant mountains, but I've worked alongside her long enough to know from the flex of the muscles in her broad neck that the remark affects her. She lets out a huff, and her voice turns just a little ragged. "We should have exterminated all those vermin ages ago before it could get to this point."

She still won't acknowledge the feelings she held for Kesral or even the childhood friendship they once shared. What did her father say to her, how did he push her over the years, for her to get to the point where she'd distance herself so much from a man she cared about deeply, simply because one of his birth parents was human?

I hardly think she'd answer that question, so I speak to the actual words she said. "I believe we were slaughtering as many of them as we encountered. It does get difficult to interfere much with those living in the human world without exposing ourselves to mortals more than is wise."

"We should have cut them all down before they fled there from the Mists." Her expression hardens. "We may need to make some compromises on our typical rules about exposure. I want to see that king of theirs, his Heart, and everyone who stands with him torn to shreds."

The furious vehemence in her voice resonates with my own inner turmoil. A picture flashes through my head of a horde of ravens descending on the swarming rats, slicing through them with our talons, tossing them into their false Heart until it suffocates with their bodies.

The thought brings a twinge of satisfaction into my chest, but it's a sickly sensation that turns my stomach as well. If Talia were awake and aware of me, she'd recoil from the images. I know she hates what Orion stands for and she wouldn't regret seeing him fall, but she doesn't want this to turn into a full-out war on either side if she can help it.

After the blood she's already seen spilled, her parents' and her brother's, and how much she's had to give of herself, I can't say I blame her.

"I want to see those who'd harm us dead too," I tell Laoni. "But I think we need to proceed with moderation. We once thought the Seelie were all villains, and clearly that isn't the case. None of us has really had a conversation with one of the Murk in centuries. Madoc seems reasonable enough."

Laoni scoffs. "Because it benefitted him to appear that way."

"It's because of him we have Talia back with us at all," I remind her and myself at the same time.

"Well, some people *can't* be brought back," she mutters. Then her gaze flicks to me finally, with a hint of anxiety. "Your mate had some specific ideas about my associations with my staff that—"

Is she going to outright deny it even after she's been calling for the blood of the ones who killed her old friend?

I shake my head before she can go on. "I know about the conversations you had. I make no judgments of you based on them. I'm still sorry that you've had to experience the loss. We need say no more about it."

Laoni's mouth tightens. I get the impression she feels she should thank me for how I've handled the situation but also doesn't want to acknowledge there was anything to handle. She settles for sighing. "I will stick to the agreement we came to that we will question any Murk caught venturing into our territory or by the patrols in the human world. But only because I want to squeeze every clue I can out of them that might allow us to wipe them from existence."

She takes off as a raven before I have a chance to answer her last proclamation. There wasn't much I could have said in response anyway.

A sense of groggy movement passes through my awareness—Talia is emerging from sleep. I'm about to turn to go in and greet her for the morning, to take some small pleasure in the fact that she's still well, when a carriage comes into view against the backdrop of the mountains. My heart sinks.

Of course, the other curses we face haven't disappeared just because a new one has emerged.

I head over to meet the vehicle as soon as it reaches the plateau. Since Talia's kidnapping, our brethren have been more frugal in how many flock-folk they send to accompany a curse victim. As the carriage slows, I make out just four figures—the man who's the afflicted one from the bluish pallor of his face, a woman sitting close to him who appears to be his mate, a younger man with similar features who's probably a son, and an older woman who's directing the craft while the others are distracted by their loved one's illness.

"I'm sorry to see you but glad you've made it here before the worst," I tell them. "Make your way over to the area in front of the

Heart, and Lady Talia will be out to perform the healing as soon as she's able."

My mate has already picked up on the activity, though her thoughts still feel a little muddled from the earliness of the hour. *I'll get dressed and come right down.*

You'll eat something first, I insist as I head to the border castle to make sure that happens. *He isn't going to freeze in the next hour. You need to look after yourself now more than ever.*

I'll eat a quick *breakfast,* Talia retorts. *I definitely don't need an hour. I'm not going to leave that man and his family in misery any longer than I have to.*

By the time I reach the castle, I can hear her and Whitt chattering in the kitchen already. I find them digging into stuffed rolls that August prepared in advance alongside dinner last night. He wanted to be sure of Talia having a breakfast that met his stringent approval while he was overseeing some of the current patrols this morning.

I pick up one myself and can't help savoring the crisp pastry as it melts in my mouth around the center of softened vegetables and fried meat in their tangy sauce. One reason not to mind my mate having three others: it's somehow brought even better meals into my life. Not that I'd mention that to Charles and Beth, whose offerings are still quite impressive as well.

"Is everything all right?" Talia asks me, maybe picking up on the lingering uneasiness from my conversation with Laoni.

"Laoni came to speak to me briefly," I say, deciding no more detail is needed. "She does tend to have a rather… chilling effect on my mood."

Whitt guffaws and then coughs when he nearly chokes on his bite of roll. "I like your sense of humor when you choose to bring it out, my feathered friend."

I half-heartedly glower at him, and Talia swats him. "You need to come up with some better nicknames for him. If 'mite' could become 'mighty one,' you're obviously capable of it."

Whitt smirks and tugs Talia close to press a kiss to the side of her neck. "You're still my mite, no matter how mighty you become."

"Well, your mite needs to go cure one of the curses I *can* tackle." She leans over to kiss him quickly on the mouth and hops off her stool. "I'm ready. Let's see to them."

Whitt follows us across the icy landscape to the Heart where the four petitioners and their carriage are waiting. His keen eyes skim over the snowy plains, and I know he's searching for any hint of rats or their illusions.

Talia smiles at the hunched man, bending a little to bring herself level with his face. "You'll feel better soon. It barely takes any time at all."

She drags in a breath and closes her eyes, raising her inner wall at the same time. She doesn't like having me see the horrible memories she has to bring up to provoke her tears, ones I've witnessed through her before but that it pains me to be reminded of. I'd share them with her if she wanted, but I won't demand it.

It takes a minute or so before the first tears streak down her cheeks. She swivels away from the cursed man to pretend to hide them, covers her eyes, and then turns back to him with damp fingers. As she strokes those fingers down the side of his face, the curse retreats like a light going on inside of him. His body starts to relax—

And Talia's seizes up.

The pain lances through her so abruptly that I double over with it too. I stagger, throwing myself the few steps between us as Whitt also rushes to her side.

Her whole body is shaking, and I can feel why in the agony that radiates from her into me.

"What's wrong?" the now-cured man asks, his voice rasping but steady, his eyes wide.

I wrap my arms around my mate, not knowing what to tell him. She's sick too, no matter what those first healers did for her.

And we don't know if there's a single person in the world who can cure her the way she just cured him.

CHAPTER ELEVEN

Talia

The newest healer frowns and tweaks her bulbous nose the way she has a dozen times already, as if it's a switch that'll activate more of her skills. She murmurs a few more magic-laced words with her hands hovering above my chest.

I don't feel anything except a faint tingle of energy passing through me, the same as during all her other attempts. I can tell she hasn't noticed any difference either from the way she knits her brow afterward.

"I'll do some more searching of the records and meditation with the Heart, and return when I have more ideas," she tells me.

I nod my thanks and hold myself still and somewhat regal on the bed until she's stepped outside. Then I flop back into the pillows with a groan.

Corwin's voice flits into my head in an instant. *All right?*

Yes, I reply quickly. *Just no progress either. I know they're all trying to help, but I'm starting to feel like a test subject in a lab.*

Corwin sends a tendril of apologetic sympathy my way. *That's the last healer we've called on. I believe Sylas and Whitt should be returning soon with the results of their investigations. In the meantime, I'm sending someone up who will hopefully make you feel more like a person again.*

I sit back up, my curiosity piqued. *Who?*

All I get from my soul-twined mate is mischievous silence. I don't totally mind, seeing that he's been able to find a little good humor in spite of the situation.

It's only a minute before a soft knock sounds on the door and a cautious voice travels through. "Talia?"

A smile springs to my face. It's Harper. I haven't seen my best friend from the pack in days with all the upheaval.

"Come in," I say, scooting to the edge of the bed.

Harper slips inside, her slim form as graceful as ever. She takes me in with her over-large eyes, looking as if she's a little worried that I might collapse right in front of her at any moment.

"I'm fine," I say, my smile softening. "For now, anyway. It's good to see you." My gaze drops to the bundle of fabric she's hugging against her. I don't even need to ask the avid dressmaker what that is. My cheeks flush in sheepish embarrassment. "You didn't have to bring me any presents."

"It's not because you've been sick," Harper insists, relaxing enough to hop onto the bed next to me. She pinches the shoulders of the new gown and gives it a shake to unfurl it. "I started working on it as soon as Sylas announced that you're with child. An expecting mother deserves the clothes to honor that fact." She grins at me.

As my gaze slides over the dress, I have to catch my breath. "It'll be an honor to wear something that gorgeous."

Harper's work is always impressive, but this... She's combined sections of deep green and rosy pink so that the wearer will look as if they're embraced by vibrant brambles bearing roses. A line of the delicate blooms arcs along the belly area as if to cradle the growing child. I can see in it how much any new life matters to the fae, how much the entire pack will be celebrating the baby growing inside me.

I rest my hand over the spot where it's growing, even if there's no outward sign of it yet just a few weeks in, and add, "Thank you. I love it." Now I just need to get my men to come up with an occasion for me to wear it. It's way too fine to act as a nightgown.

Harper grins even wider. She folds the dress with a few swift gestures, sets it farther back on the bed, and leans over to give me a quick hug. "I want to see you in it so many times on your way to becoming a mother and afterward."

There's an unspoken wish underlying those words. She wants me to survive long enough to wear it all those times.

I swallow hard. "I intend to," I say with all the confidence I can summon. I bring my legs up and turn to sit cross-legged against the headboard. "I haven't had much chance to see the rest of the pack lately. How's everyone doing? Anything interesting to report?"

I don't need to tell Harper that I'm looking for light-hearted news because there've been so many serious developments I'm already very aware of. She tucks the smooth strands of her flaxen hair behind her ear and tips her head to the side with a thoughtful smile.

"Well, the sheep made a break from their pen, and Elliot had to chase a few of them all the way onto Arch-Lord Donovan's domain. The way they were bleating when he brought them back, you'd think he was going to carve them up for dinner instead of just milk them to make cheese." She lets out a giggle. "And a couple of women from Arch-Lord Celia's pack asked me to make them matching dresses. You won't believe the theme they wanted…"

She chatters on about the day-to-day activity in the domains around the Heart, and I mostly sit back and listen. A bittersweet ache forms around my own heart that despite the possibility of impending war, normal life is still carrying on as well as it can—but I can't really take part in it.

Is Whitt still holding revels? I can't imagine him being in much of a partying mood these days, but I should encourage him to host one. The pack needs a chance to unwind and be happy even while we're guarding our home so carefully.

Harper is just finishing an animated recreation of a silly argument between Brigit and Pomya when footsteps sound in the hall outside. When the door swings open, Harper's mouth snaps shut. She pulls her posture straighter as Sylas and Whitt come in. She's always a little awkward around the ruler of the pack, maybe remembering how close he came to banishing her after a few of Ambrose's pack-kin caught her up in a scheme against me.

Sylas shows no lingering animosity, though. He nods to her. "It was good of you to come. I can see my mate has been enjoying your visit." He gives me one of his quiet but warm little smiles.

"I'll come back again soon," Harper says to him and to me, giving me another quick hug, and hops off the bed. "I don't want to get in the way, though." She dips into a low bow, waves good-bye to me, and leaves me with my mates.

For a little while as she and I talked, I'd been able to avoid thinking about the reason Sylas and Whitt were out "investigating." Now, taking in their relatively somber expressions, my spirits sink. Everything isn't normal, especially with me.

"Was there nothing?" I ask. They'd been following up on a few mentions of rare curative plants from Whitt's records, but they hadn't been sure how accurate the brief details were or, in at least one case, whether the plant even existed to begin with.

Sylas sits down on the edge of the bed by my tucked feet and nods to Whitt, who detaches a leather pouch from his belt. "We were able to track down a couple of the herbs we were seeking. Neither of them gives off an aura that's particularly potent, but they show no sign of being harmful either, so we may as well see what they do."

The first sprig Whitt pulls out has shiny round leaves and puffy blue flowers. He pulls off one of the flowers and starts to crush it between his thumb and his opposite palm. "One story suggested that skybloom might dispel hostile magic if the mashed petals of the flower are rubbed over the afflicted area. It's only noted in one place, so it obviously hasn't been tested much."

I loosen the bodice of my dress so I can tug it down over my shoulders, letting the neckline settle against the slope of my breasts. Whitt swipes the blue paste across my sternum with some murmured words. The stuff absorbs into my skin over the next few minutes, leaving behind only a pale blue tint.

"Do you feel any different?" the spymaster asks.

I concentrate deeply, but I can't pretend the prickling sensation that's been with me since the curse first struck me has disappeared. It remains as always between my lungs. "No," I admit reluctantly. "As far as I can tell, the curse is still there the same as before."

"Well, the effect may take some time to kick in. In the meantime, we also managed to dig up a clayvin root." He brandishes something that looks like a knobby yellow carrot.

"*I* managed to dig it up, you mean," Sylas says with a hint of a teasing tone.

Whitt holds up his hands in mock self defense. "It's not my fault clayvin only grows in the deepest of crevices and you're a significantly better climber than I am. If I'd gone down, I'd never have come back up. It was my spell that found it, though."

Sylas chuckles. "I'll give you that."

Seeing their easy banter, hearing the way they worked together on their mission, brings a welcome warmth into my chest. I tip my head toward the root. "So what do we do with that one?"

Whitt waggles it. "This is meant to be made into a tea that you'll drink. But it's supposed to be brewed at sunset and drunk at midnight for the best effect. We've got a bit of a wait to try that one out."

"So much to look forward to," I joke, but my own laugh falls flat.

A cloud of gloom passes over both my mates again, and the warmth that formed before tightens into an ache. We *should* have so many things to look forward to: the newfound peace between the realms, our lives together as mates, the child I'll be bringing into that union. But the threat of the Murk has cast a shadow over all the joy we should be sharing.

We should celebrate anyway—because who knows if we'll have the opportunity to later.

I slip across the bed to tuck my arm around Sylas, leaning my head against his shoulder. He hums happily and hugs me to him. Whitt takes the opening to sit down at my other side, giving my shoulder a quick peck.

It's all very gentle and comforting, but being enveloped between their bodies and their contrasting scents, a spark of deeper heat flares low in my belly. I don't question the urge, just push myself up to plant a kiss on Sylas's mouth.

He kisses me back tenderly, his hand stroking over my hair, but when I move to swing my leg over his lap, he catches me around the waist. "I don't think we should push the limits of your body right now."

I tug at his shirt. "I think we've discovered plenty of things my body is definitely capable of that wouldn't require pushing it to any limits."

"That was when you were well."

I balk at accepting the concern that's turned his brown eye even darker. I'm still their mate, and I want the full benefits of that relationship, thank you very much.

Keeping my fingers curled in the front of Sylas's shirt, I glance at Whitt and then back to the arch-lord. "I feel fine right now, other than missing getting properly close with my mates. It sounds like you two worked very well together finding me possible cures. There are lots of *other* ways I enjoy having you work together."

I do my best coy gaze through my eyelashes, but I'm not sure it works. I'm not exactly an expert at flirting. Sylas hesitates. Whitt teases his fingers over my outer thigh, but he doesn't move his hand any farther. I don't think he'll take me up on my invitation if his lord won't.

With a determined huff, I grip Sylas's shirt harder and straddle him before he can stop me again. I stare firmly into his mismatched eyes. "I want the men I'm mated with. The Murk are trying to take everything from me, and I'm not letting them take this away too. Don't you dare help them do it."

Then I press my mouth to his.

Whether it was my speech or the fierceness of my kiss or both, Sylas's reluctance flies out the window. He kisses me back with a growl, hard and hot, the hand on my waist sliding down to my bottom to pull me closer against him. I rock into him, gasping against his lips as I feel his shaft hardening beneath his trousers.

Yes. I want this. I want him, and Whitt, and all my mates when I have the chance.

I'm still alive. Orion hasn't broken me. We're together, and we'll celebrate that, no matter what other troubles come our way.

Another hand travels across my shoulders, brushing aside my hair. Then Whitt's skillful mouth is branding the side of my neck. As I continue kissing Sylas, the spymaster nibbles a path up to the crook of my jaw and then nips my earlobe with a jolt of pleasure that propels another gasp from my throat.

"I think our mighty mate should have what she wants when she's asking for it so very clearly," he murmurs, nuzzling my hair before marking another trail of heat down to my bared shoulder blade.

Sylas lets out a sound somewhere between a grumble and a groan. He tugs the bodice of my dress farther down, the neckline flicking over my nipples, and cups one of my breasts. The swipe of his thumb over the peak mimics the sweep of his tongue into my mouth to tangle with mine.

Whitt strokes his deft fingers over my other breast until my chest is awash with quivers of bliss. They drown out the faint prickling sensation completely. I arch into my mates' combined touch, kissing Sylas even harder and then turning my head to seek out Whitt's mouth as well.

How lucky I am to have this at all, to have found not one but four mates who can take me to such heights and who're happy to do so alongside each other.

I grasp Whitt's shirt and pull back just enough to meet his eyes and then Sylas's. The declaration sears up from deep inside me. "Whatever happens, whatever Orion puts me through, I'm glad I'm here. I'd rather be here with you even with his magic in me than living a normal life in the human world. Even if giving you up would cure me, I wouldn't do it."

"Talia," Sylas says in a strained voice. He kisses me again, roughly, as if he doesn't know how else to express his response.

Whitt wraps his arm tight around me in the joint embrace. "The only way I'd ever give you up is if it was the only way to save you. But we won't let it come to that. And right now, all I want to do is see you writhing with all the ecstasy we're going to bring you."

The promise in his heated words sets off a giddy tingling over my skin. I yank at his shirt in an effort to hurry us on toward the writhing in ecstasy part. Chuckling, Whitt pulls it over his head.

I turn to him, sliding off Sylas's lap to mount my other lover in turn. As I trail my hands and my mouth over the toned planes of muscle defining Whitt's chest, he tips his head back with a strangled but pleased sound. I lap my tongue over one of his nipples, and then he's cupping the back of my head, drawing me up to claim my mouth as thoroughly as he can.

Sylas tosses aside his shirt and leans in, his bare skin scorching against my back. He kisses the back of my neck and down my spine, his hands teasing around my hips and between my legs, just shy of the spot now throbbing for contact.

I push Whitt down on the bed, unable to stop myself from grinding against him. He hisses through his teeth. Through some silent communication, he and Sylas lift me up to peel my dress and my panties off me. I tug at their trousers.

"So impatient, mite," Whitt teases, stealing another kiss as he unfastens his pants. While he kicks them off, Sylas tucks his hand right over my core.

I moan at the rush of delight. For a few seconds, all I can do is lean back into Sylas and ride his hand. When he pulls his fingers away, I whimper in protest, but it's only an instant before Whitt's hardness settles against me.

My mouth waters with the deepest kind of hunger I know. I shift forward over Whitt, knowing his body so well now that I can line myself up without even thinking. He caresses my cheek, his eyes alight with both desire and adoration, and thrusts up into me.

Pleasure sweeps through my sex and up into my torso. I sway over Whitt, meeting the rolls of his hips as my hands brace against his chest, adrift in the haze of sensation.

As Whitt pushes himself up to bring my breast to his mouth, Sylas traces my other opening with magically slickened fingers. My body trembles with eagerness. I reach back with one hand to squeeze his arm encouragingly, and he lets out a rumble that sounds almost desperate with his own hunger.

"My love," he murmurs as he stretches me with one finger and then two. An embarrassingly needy cry tumbles out of me. "You deserve every pleasure we can give you. Never be afraid to ask for what you want."

I ask now with the motions of my body, pressing back into his touch over and over as I rock with Whitt. An intoxicating heat spreads all through my abdomen. Then the head of Sylas's thick shaft tests me. He pushes inside slowly, a little farther with each bob of my hips over Whitt. The blissful burn of my stretching muscles nearly shatters me apart right there.

"Mmm," Whitt says. "This is indeed an excellent cooperative effort. We'll have to come up with them more frequently, I think."

He winks at me, and my breathless giggle is lost in a moan as both men plunge into me together. I clutch Sylas's arm braced next to me and Whitt's shoulder beneath me, riding the wave of ecstasy they've conjured inside me higher and higher.

With each gasp and whimper that slips out of me, they speed up their pace, their muscles flexing with the effort. Our skin dampens with sweat where our bodies brush against each other.

Whitt pinches my nipple and swivels his thumb over my nub at the same time, and I feel the wave start to break. The tremor shakes me, pleasure whirling through every nerve before it bursts like the flare of a bonfire.

Sparks fill my vision. As I cry out, my inner muscles clenching, both of my men groan. Sylas comes with me, Whitt following at his heels.

We collapse together in a jumble of sweaty limbs and sated breaths. I tug my mates closer on either side of me, seeking as much of their heat as I can get as my body coasts in the afterglow.

But even that contentment can't completely mute the faint, inescapable prickle that rises up through my chest once more.

CHAPTER TWELVE

Whitt

When word comes at night that our rat of divided loyalties has returned to us, Sylas has him escorted to one of the meeting rooms in the castle of Hearth-by-the-Heart. We want our privacy for the discussion to come, but none of us wants the Murk man in the same building as Talia if we can help it.

The fact that he's returned so quickly, and not leading an army—at least not any we've spotted so far—bodes well. No Murk has acted on the bait Donovan arranged, a stray comment one of his pack-kin ensured Madoc overheard about a vulnerable town we're supposedly relying on for weapons, so it appears the rat shifter didn't pass that information on to his king. But I'm hardly going to throw caution to the wind.

Corwin and one of his older coterie men, Verik, join the three of us in the broad room with its gleaming wooden table, the two Unseelie looking a little out of place in the summery space. August, Astrid, and a couple others of Corwin's people have remained back in the border castle along with the usual assortment of guards. I kissed Talia good night there just an hour ago.

Madoc comes in escorted by four of our pack warriors. He looks a bit peeved about the level of security we're still enforcing, but he should just be glad that we arranged a signal for him to use to alert us that he was arriving, so it'd be our warriors going to bring him in and not Celia's or some other more hostile lord who might not care for the deal we made.

The rat shifter sits down at the end of the table we've left open for him. The guards hesitate behind his chair, glancing at Sylas for instruction. Even when he waves them off with a thank you for their service, they appear to balk momentarily before leaving us alone.

But I think two arch-lords and one near true-blooded fae are up to dealing with one Murk, no matter how good he is with illusions. I've already cast a spell that's now subtly humming through this space that will warn us if any magic is enacted by anyone other than the three of us.

"You returned quickly," Sylas says, leaning his elbows on the tabletop where he's sitting a few feet from the rat shifter. He keeps his tone as even as always, his expression a mask of authoritative confidence, but I recognize the keenness in his eyes. He's as eager as I am to hear what news our theoretical ally has brought from his fellow vermin.

"Yes," Madoc says, his gaze sliding from one to another of us before settling back on Sylas. He flexes his hands as if confirming that they're not bound. "During my assignments, I typically spend long periods of time in this realm with only brief trips back to report to Orion. I couldn't linger in the Refuge for long without him questioning it. I told him that the curse had started to act on Talia and that all of the fae were concerned, because that's what he'd want to hear, and he sent me back here to monitor how the situation progresses."

He pauses, and his gaze darts around the table again. The wary edge leaves his voice. "Is she still all right? I'd hoped—is she not well enough to leave her room?"

He expected Talia to be here when we spoke with him. I suppose that's not surprising, seeing as she played by far the largest role in making this deal happen. I can't stop a little dryness from creeping into my tone when I respond. "She's perfectly well at the moment, other than future concerns, but seeing as it's the middle of the night, she's asleep. You aren't so important that we were going to disturb her rest just because you showed up."

I anticipate a sharp reply, but instead Madoc looks a bit chagrinned. He does care about my mate in his own odd way, doesn't he? I'm not totally sure what to make of that or how to feel about it.

"Of course," he says. "I wasn't thinking—we're typically awake all night and sleeping most of the day unless there's something specific to take care of." His jaw works. "What exactly does 'perfectly well' mean? Has she had any more bad spells from the curse?"

The three of us exchange a glance over the table, debating how much to tell him. Corwin clears his throat, and I figure he's the most cautious of us, so I'll accept whatever he feels is an acceptable level of detail.

"She's had two more fits since you left," he says. "They seem to come over her relatively briefly about once a day, though the timing hasn't been at all predictable." He stops there, and from the shadow that crosses his face, I suspect he's remembering how she crumpled during our dinner together in the joint castle just hours ago.

"Were you able to learn anything more about the curse in the short time you spent back in the Refuge?" Sylas asks, bringing us back to the most important subject. "I assume you have something to share with us, or you wouldn't have announced your arrival."

Before he even speaks, the twist of Madoc's mouth reveals that he hasn't got much. "I thought it'd be best if I came straight to you in case there's any way I can contribute. Orion will think it's strange if I return home again too quickly with no major news, so I might as well be here offering what I can." He exhales roughly. "I did press him as much as I felt I could get away with about the nature of the curse. He indicated that the pattern you've seen of short attacks and then seeming recovery was normal. It's his way of jerking around your hopes."

"Wonderful," Sylas mutters. "Anything else?"

"He seems very sure that nothing you could attempt to cure her with will work," Madoc says grimly. "Which is another reason it seems better for me to be here than wandering around accomplishing nothing. He thinks the Seelie and the Unseelie don't have the powers or knowledge, but he doesn't know there are any Murk willing to help."

How much is he here because he doesn't want to see Talia suffer and how much because he's worried that if he can't come up with some other cure, we'll find a way to destroy his false Heart, the source of his people's magic? I could tell how much *that* means to him from his protest about destroying it.

I suppose his motivations don't really matter as long as we can make her well again in the end.

Corwin's head droops for a moment, and I can't help feeling a pang of sympathy for the man who's experiencing Talia's curse nearly as vividly as she herself is. He knows exactly how much agony it's already put her through.

"It's true that none of our attempts so far have appeared to make any difference to her condition," he says. "Nor have we been able to work with the barrier magic you mentioned to prevent the fits—as you suggested, the curse appears to be in too close contact with her essential organs to be sectioned off."

Madoc frowns. "I wish I was better at the healing arts myself. This far from my own Heart… And we can't exactly call on the Murk medics I know."

He halts there, and his gaze goes momentarily distant. My senses spring to the alert. He shakes himself and doesn't add anything to that thought, but he was obviously remembering *something* relevant. I file that knowledge away for later.

"What about your king's preparations for war?" I ask. "Did you get a sense of how soon he intends to move on us?"

Madoc inclines his head. "He's continuing to stockpile equipment and gather as many Murk as are willing to fight. He hasn't mentioned any specific plans to launch an attack soon. From what he's said, I believe he's waiting until Talia's curse has gotten significantly worse—or perhaps even reached its… end. So that you'll be distracted by your worries or your grief."

My lips curl back at the vileness of the strategy. We're working on a timeline directly connected to Talia's wellbeing, then. Keep her well, stave off the war.

If only it were so easy.

"Well, at least we don't have to be concerned about an immediate offensive," I mutter.

Madoc turns to the arch-lords. "I also know that Orion is trying to make it as painful as possible for you to intrude on the human world. He's had sentries observing the portals your patrols are most frequently coming through and has put out the word that any Murk who can bring back the heads of fae of the Mists will be well-rewarded. If you want to protect your people, you may want to stick to defending your borders on this side of the divide."

Corwin gives him a pointed look. "Which would also mean it'd be much harder for us to keep track of most of the Murk activity ourselves."

Madoc spreads his hands. "I can only tell you what I know. It's up to you what you do with the information. If you think it's worth getting into who knows how many skirmishes and potentially losing a bunch of your soldiers before the war's even really begun, have at it."

I think of August returning from his foray in Munich with the corpses of several loyal warriors and wince inwardly.

"We'll discuss the best strategy in more detail among ourselves," Sylas says. "Do you have anything more to add?"

"Those are the only things I picked up that I thought might be useful to you," Madoc says. "If I notice anything while I'm here that makes me think I have other information that's relevant, I'll tell you then."

My brother looks as if he's restraining a frown, but he simply nods and pushes back his chair. "Then I'd suggest we all get some sleep of our own and discuss the situation further in the morning—at which point you can also speak to Talia, as I'm sure she'll want to see you. I've set up a small cabin for your use in my domain. I hope you'll understand that for the time being we'll continue to have it guarded and magically secured when none of us is around to accompany you elsewhere."

Madoc's mouth flattens, but he seems to be putting forth his best behavior too. "I hope that in time you'll determine that those precautions aren't necessary, but considering it's a step up from the hospitality offered before, I'll take it."

As he stands, I follow suit, raising my hand. "Actually, I'd like to speak with our Murk companion a little more. You two don't have to wait up."

Sylas hesitates, and I can practically feel Corwin's apprehension radiating off him, but they both trust *me* enough now to sense that I have a private conversation in mind. The rat may reveal more when he doesn't have two menacing arch-lords breathing down his neck. They bob their heads in acknowledgment and leave the two of us.

Madoc sits back down as I do, eyeing me with twice as much suspicion than before. "What else do you want to talk about? I've answered all of your questions as well as I can."

I hum to myself. "Perhaps, but I'm not sure you've shared all the answers to questions you came up with yourself. You had an idea when you talked about the Murk healers you know, didn't you?"

Madoc tenses in his seat. "If I thought it was worth bringing up, I would have."

"Why don't you let me decide what's worthwhile and what's not? I'm the strategist here—don't put me out of a job."

Obviously despite himself, Madoc's lips twitch with a hint of a smile. It disappears as quickly as it showed itself. "Even if you'd want to do something with this information, I'm not sure *I'd* want to pursue it. And you'd need my cooperation."

"I accept those terms," I say. "Let's see what we can hash out. You're used to working around obstacles and tackling challenges in unexpected ways, aren't you? That's what Murk are known for. Add in a little wolfish wisdom, and we'll see where that gets us."

My nonchalant demeanor appears to put the rat shifter a little more at ease. He sighs and rolls his shoulders. "I only— There is a Murk woman I've heard of who's very powerful with magic. I don't know if she has any specific affinity for healing, but there've been rumors that she's second only to Orion in power. Which is a good thing for Orion—that he's still on top—because she doesn't like him much. She has her own small colony that she's refused to unite with his empire."

I tap my mouth. "Interesting. And you think we might appeal to her to see if she can break his curse on Talia, on the grounds that she'd get to really piss him off by doing so."

Madoc's mouth twitches again, how much because he's surprised that I followed his train of thought and how much because my phrasing amuses him, I'm not certain. "That's the gist of it, yeah. But I only know *of* her—I've never met her myself. I have a basic idea of where and how I could reach out to her, but I'd also need to ensure that no one associated with Orion ever finds out I did, or I won't be around to help anymore. It's also possible that she hates the fae of the Mists even more than she dislikes Orion."

"Reasonable concerns." I set my hands on the table, clasping them together. "Let's see if we can address them. I wouldn't think hiding yourself would be so hard. Are you a master of illusions or aren't you?"

Madoc grimaces at me. "My magic will definitely help me avoid notice. It won't help me convince her to speak to me."

I shrug. "From the sounds of things, she'll be more inclined to talk to you if she *doesn't* know who you are than if she's aware you're one of Orion's 'knights.'"

"All right, you have a point there." Madoc lets out a short chuckle. His eyes narrow, not at me but at the problem he's picturing, and all at once I can see the schemer in him, a mind that could align with my own.

"What would probably be *even* better is if I put an illusion on one of your people to help you reach her unnoticed by any spies. Then you could present your case directly along with a reward to encourage her to listen…" He pauses, and one of his eyebrows lifts. "I hear she's particularly fond of barbtooths and duskapple wine. We don't get much of either in the human world."

"I'd suppose not." I laugh and let a smile cross my face. I may not trust the man in front of me farther than I could spit him, but weaving a plan with him might actually be enjoyable. "Now how would we get her attention in the first place…"

CHAPTER THIRTEEN

Talia

I stop outside the cabin hidden away in the woods just beyond Hearth-by-the-Heart's castle, not sure whether to be more grateful to see that Madoc's living quarters here are significantly more private and comfortable than the holding cell he was stuck in last time, or unsettled by the guards and the hum of magic that still hold him captive. I understand Sylas's need for caution, but how long will my mates continue treating Madoc like an intruder rather than an ally?

August speaks to one of the guards, who at least does Madoc the courtesy of knocking on the door before opening it. "You've got visitors," she says gruffly. "You can come out."

The Murk man appears in the doorway with the wary expression that's his primary mode around the fae of the Mists, but when he finds me there, it relaxes a little with the start of a smile. "I wasn't sure they were actually going to let you come see me."

"My lord keeps his word," August says with a hint of a growl.

Madoc holds up his hands. "No criticism intended. You're

protecting your mate from the disreputable rats. It's very admirable." His tone walks the line between sympathy and sarcasm.

August frowns as if he's not sure which way to take the remark and seems to decide he'll just ignore it altogether. He sets his hand on the small of my back as if *I* need reassurance. "She's here. If there's anything you want to say to her, you can now."

Madoc's stormy gaze takes me in, and his voice gentles. "They said you've been mostly all right other than a couple more short spells of the curse."

It isn't exactly a question, but I hear the need for confirmation in it. "That's right," I said. "I feel pretty much fine most of the time. Just every now and then…" I shrug as if it's no big deal, as if my stomach doesn't clench up with the worry about when another attack might hit me, how it'll be if they intensify or start coming closer together—or both.

Madoc's mouth twists. "I suppose they've told you that I haven't been able to bring much news. Orion likes to keep his cards close to his chest."

"I know. I'd rather you stayed cautious than made him suspicious of you. Whitt did say that the two of you have come up with a possible plan."

He lets out a rough chuckle. "We'll see how that goes. He's supposed to come around later to work out the rest of the details. After he's consulted with his colleagues who aren't rats, I guess, to make sure I'm not leading you all astray."

I fix him with a firm look that I hope conveys as much confidence as I want it to. "It'll take some time, but they'll see that you really do want to help. It isn't as if you're all that happy to be working with them either."

"Fair point." He exhales in a rush, and I notice the shift of his weight on his feet, from one side to the other and back again. He's been stuck in the little cabin for hours.

"Do you want to take a walk while we talk more?" I ask with a twinge of concern. "Stretch your legs, enjoy the fresh air…?"

Something flickers in Madoc's eyes before his small smile returns. "I'd like that very much if my keepers will agree."

I glance at August, who knits his brow and then motions to the guards. "We'll give you some space," he says, "but I'm not letting you out of my sight."

"I wouldn't expect you to," Madoc says before I need to reply. He studies the guards as if making sure this isn't some kind of trick and then steps over the threshold.

It's still odd seeing him walk around without his tail, as if he's missing an essential limb. But having it out would *definitely* draw the wrong kind of attention around here. I wonder if it bothers him to hide it away after spending so much time with it out in the open in the Refuge. But then, he must be used to sticking to his purely man form when he's on his missions to the Mists.

The thought of all the times he spied on us in the past with nothing but hostility in his heart makes my gut knot. But he didn't know me then, just as we didn't know him. A lot can change in not much time at all.

I let him direct our path, and he ambles through the trees in the general direction of Hearth-by-the-Heart's castle. August and the guards follow several paces behind us. I can't see her, but I know Astrid is standing guard somewhere nearby too. Corwin is a constant presence inside me, watching through my eyes.

"No one's been too hard on you since you came back, have they?" I ask, not knowing if Madoc would even admit it to me if they had been. Whatever the fae of the Mists might say about the Murk, they do have their pride.

"No," Madoc says, in a tone that's bemused enough that I believe him. "Your pack has been downright gracious compared to my reception last time." He sucks in a deep breath, and his eyelids dip for a moment as if he's savoring the warm forest air with its tang of pine and spruce. Then his gaze veers to me again. "If you don't mind talking about it, what exactly are you feeling from the curse? I got my own sense of it, but knowing the 'symptoms' might help."

My hand rises to my chest automatically, settling on the spot right over my breastbone where I guided his hand a few days ago. "Most of the time it's just a faint sort of prickling sensation that feels like it's right between my lungs. When it's bad, it's like that spot…

bursts, with no warning at all, into a bunch of knives jabbing into me from the inside." I wince at the memories. "Sharp pain, and a lot of it. It's hard for me to think or really pay attention to anything more specific than that while it's happening."

Madoc's jaw has tightened. "But it doesn't last very long?"

I shake my head. "About a half hour, I think, all three times so far." Will it affect me *longer* the next time? I'm probably going to have another fit sometime today… I swallow hard and push that thought away. "I'm managing. It could definitely be worse."

"There's nothing very surprising about your description," Madoc says grimly. "Orion does like to be unpredictable and keep his enemies on their toes. I wish he hadn't decided you counted among those enemies."

"Well, the alternative was becoming his ally, and I definitely wasn't going to do *that*."

"I know." Madoc falls silent. As we emerge from the trees into the sunlight, he tips his face to the brighter warmth. An odd hunger crosses his expression, and it occurs to me that while he might have gotten plenty of fresh air during his missions into the Mists, he probably spent most of that time staying concealed in the darkness.

He glances toward my feet as if checking whether my limp has worsened and slows just slightly, heading across the fields at an angle that'll give both the castle and the pack village a wide berth, which is probably wise. Those little gestures—the recognition of where both I and my pack are vulnerable and the consideration to those factors—bring an ache into my chest that has nothing to do with the curse.

My mates *have* to see that this man has no interest in harming us. All he wants is to be treated as an equal, his ideas and goals worthy of consideration.

I can relate to that struggle on a bone-deep level. I'm *still* fighting to get all of the arch-lords to give my opinions their due. In some ways, as a human, I have more in common with the Murk than the rest of the fae. And I know how set in their ways they can be.

But I've made progress. I have to make sure Madoc can too. He's definitely determined enough, as long as he doesn't give up on the fae of the Mists completely.

He might have no intention of hurting us, but he's under threat himself because of his deal with the Seelie. I swallow hard and then ask, "You don't think Orion suspects anything at all, do you? He hasn't shown any sign that he's skeptical of your reports or whatever?"

Madoc shakes his head. "No, not that I've noticed. I don't think he trusts *anyone* completely, but he's mentioned things in my presence that I can't imagine him saying if he thought I might pass them on. It just may become increasingly difficult keeping his suspicions off me as I get more involved."

I have the urge to take his hand and squeeze it, but I'm not sure if he'd appreciate the gesture. "If you feel like you're no longer safe with him—or he shows that you're not—you can come here. You don't have to face it alone."

Madoc gives a raw laugh, maybe thinking about the irony of turning for protection to the fae he was recently planning war against —and still might wage war against if the fledgling alliance between him and the Seelie arch-lords falls apart. Then he looks ahead of us, to the glowing mass of the Heart of the Mists that's just come into view.

That's where he's been headed this whole time, I realize. He's taken us on a course almost straight toward it. The soft pulse of its energy over my skin is so familiar to me now that I only notice it when I focus on it, but he won't have been quite this close to it… maybe in all his time before he was captured the other day.

"Do you feel any connection to it at all?" I ask quietly.

Madoc's gaze jerks to me, startled and then sheepish. He turns back toward the Heart, which looms a little higher with every step we take toward it and the haze of the border. "No," he says, the admission sounding as if it wrenches at something deep inside him. "I—no."

And yet he wants it so badly. He wants to bring all of his people back here where they can be embraced by that light again, whether they can make use of its energies or not. Whatever you could say about the means he was willing to resort to, there aren't many dreams more noble than that.

I hesitate before saying anything else, afraid I might offend him by bringing up the tragedy he went through in the Mists so long ago. "You said when you lived with your parents on the fringes of the summer realm that they could use the Heart's magic a little."

Madoc comes to a stop about fifty feet away from the Heart, still facing it. We're close enough now that the glow touches him, bringing a warmer tone to his pale skin and turning his straw-blond hair into gold. He looks like he's wavering between crossing the short distance to walk right up to it and staying here where it can't wash over him quite so intensely.

"They could," he says. "Not very well, but they had a small connection. I could feel it a little myself then, but I hadn't learned any magic I could actually cast. But—when any of us start drawing on the Heart Orion made, it fills in all the places where that old connection would have been if we'd kept closer to the Heart of the Mists all along. Whatever shreds of a connection I had left, it overwhelmed them."

He shakes himself and swivels toward me with a crooked smile. "But it's worth it. I can do much more with our Heart than I'd ever have been able to with the feeble scraps that one would still allow us. *It* dismissed us ages ago."

I'm not sure the dismissal was so one-sided. From what my mates have said, certain actions—lying, unjustified killing—weaken the connection to the Heart for any kind of fae. At least some of the Murk in the past choose to separate themselves from its power so that they had more freedom to carry out their schemes.

It doesn't seem fair that their decisions carried on to their offspring, though. How many generations made their own decisions that dwindled the magic of the Mists in their family line before Madoc was born with the choice between barely any magic and magic from a different source?

"I know you have a lot of reasons to hate the fae of the Mists," I say, "but I don't think the Heart is that vindictive. Maybe you could find your way back to it if you opened yourself up to it. The Murk haven't really had the chance to try to get closer to it in a long time, and that's something we should change."

Madoc's next smile is bittersweet. "Of course you would say that.

It isn't that easy, Talia. Believe me, the Heart doesn't want anything to do with me or anyone else among the Murk."

"It hasn't turned *me* away," I argue. "Even though I'm only here because of Orion. Even though I've got Murk magic all twisted up inside me, and I'm tied to the curse that's been draining its strength."

"Well, it isn't going to shove you through a portal. But what has it *done* for you?"

A sudden resolve swells inside me. He needs to see—he needs to know. He *deserves* it, to know that he could bring an even better future to his people than he's been able to imagine.

Corwin, sensing my decision even from out of view, extends a waft of concern. *Talia, we still don't know if he might tell his king—*

It's okay, I insist before he can finish his protest. *I know Madoc. I think he needs to hear this. And even if he did tell Orion, it wouldn't change much now.*

Holding Madoc's gaze, I lift my hands with a little space cupped between them. "The powers Orion gave me—it's just the ability to heal the curse on the fae of the Mists and the soul-twined bond with Corwin, right?"

Madoc peers at me, obviously puzzled. "Yes, which is plenty. Why?"

"Then it's the Heart of the Mists that gave me this." I draw in a breath, think back to the joy of being snuggled between Sylas and Whitt yesterday after the passion we shared, and say the true name for light. "*Sole-un-straw.*"

A glowing ball flares into being between my palms. Madoc blinks, staring and then staring harder. "You—how did you—?"

I dismiss the glow with a flick of my fingers and reach for my new bracelet. "How do you think I was working on the bolts on the air vent? No one gave me a tool. I *made* it. Orion just didn't believe me." I grasp the warm bronze, remembering the panic of the moment when the Murk sentry caught me in the act, and murmur the first true name I ever learned. "*Fee-doom-ace-own.*"

The bracelet splits and straightens into a wrench in my hand. Madoc's eyes widen even more.

"That power didn't come from Orion or his Heart, did it?" I say, clutching the wrench. "He had no idea."

"He didn't," Madoc says faintly. "But—"

I point to the Heart of the Mists with a rush of affection for the presence that has been on my side for so long without me even knowing it. "*That* Heart decided I deserved a little magic of my own. Even though I was a tool for someone who wants to destroy everything in the Mists. If it could see something worthy in me, then there's no reason you or any of the other Murk should give up on it. It hasn't given up on you."

Madoc's throat bobs. He looks from me to the Heart and back again. So many emotions are warring on his face that I can't pick them apart, but I don't think I'm mistaking the flare of hope that shows briefly. It's followed by something warmer that seems to send a wash of heat straight from his gaze over my skin.

Before he can say anything else, a guard comes loping over from the castle, breaking the moment we were sharing.

"Whitt is ready to speak with you," he tells Madoc. "He'd like you to come right away."

"Of course he would," Madoc mutters, but there's a lot less edge in his voice than there might have been earlier. He shoots me one last bewildered glance and follows the man toward the castle. Whitt has appeared in the doorway, waiting.

The guards from the cabin fall into step behind Madoc. I limp over to August, feeling abruptly drained, even though I didn't cast all that much magic. With a quick murmur, I fix the bronze back in its bracelet form around my wrist.

August slips his arm around my shoulders, ruffling my hair. He looks down at the bracelet. "Are you sure that was a good idea, Sweetness?"

I watch Madoc disappear into the castle. Another ache twines through my chest, thinking of how hard it was for him to accept what I was telling him, to believe he could ever draw on the Heart of the Mists again, even when he's shown more honor than a whole lot of the summer and winter fae I've encountered in my time here.

Am I sure? Maybe not one hundred percent. But—

"At some point," I say, "we have to open our arms like the Heart did for me. I'd rather take the risk than not."

CHAPTER FOURTEEN

Madoc

I don't remember ever noticing grass being quite so soft. Or maybe it only is this close to the massive form that powers all life in the Mists. Either way, the blades cushion my body like a welcome bed at the end of a long day, tickling the back of my neck and my bare forearms. I'm not used to this comfortable warmth either.

But it isn't the end of a long day, only the very beginning of one —and I'm not sure just how long it's going to get. I'm lucky that Whitt allowed me this brief reprieve to "collect myself" as he put it, before we set off for the fringes to see if Delta will meet us for the parlay one of Whitt's scouts was able to arrange after plying her with the gifts I suggested.

The sunlight beams through my closed eyelids with a muted glow. It wavers faintly with the rhythm of the other nearby light source. I'm lying within several paces of the Heart of the Mists, and its energy washes over me, tingling across my skin. I can't decide whether the sensation is a pleasurable reminder of what could have been or a wrenching reminder of what isn't. None of that energy seeps right to the center of me where it could help me spark any magic.

It's just a few feet from here that Talia stood with her Seelie men when they officially claimed her as their mate. I saw only a snippet of the ceremony before I made my preparations to draw her away, and even that snippet was from a distance, perched in my rat form on a partly obscured branch halfway up a tree. The memory rises up all the same of the joy that lit her face.

At the time, that joy only angered me—that she'd throw herself in so completely with the fae who've savaged my people so brutally. Having spent a little time in their presence, I can admit that her choice wasn't totally horrible.

The men she's taken as mates clearly adore her and are willing to stop at nothing to protect her. It's only too bad they all seem so convinced they still need to protect her from me. Whitt, with his sharp mind that many of the Murk would admire if it wasn't in a wolf, has at least offered me enough respect to listen to my input. I guess I should give him a little grudging credit for that, and for not prowling around quite as imposingly as the others while I shared my thoughts.

Of course, a few days ago even *I* wasn't completely sure they didn't need to defend Talia from my mere presence. Who's to say her association with me won't still hurt her in ways I can't predict or control?

Footsteps whisper across the grass from the direction of Hearth-by-the-Heart. I open my eyes and raise my head, expecting to see Whitt or one of his pack-kin coming over to call me to the carriages.

Instead, it's Talia. The sunlight beams around her vibrant hair like a shimmering halo, and my heart flips over. The images flash through my mind of a dream I had weeks ago, lying in the grass and her sinking over me, baring her body to me.

My cock twitches, and I push myself upright, both confirming that I'm not dreaming now and willing away the imaginary encounter.

"Hey," she says, stopping a few feet away from me. She looks hesitant, as if even *she's* wary of me right now. My throat constricts.

"Felt like another walk?" I ask her.

"I just—I saw you out here. Are you all right? I know going to this woman and seeing through the meeting could put you in a lot of danger."

Oh. Her hesitation wasn't concern for herself but for me. I should have known her well enough to realize that.

A pang echoes through my chest. I'm not all right. I'm walking a thin line between saving and betraying my people, I'm still not sure whether I've kept to the right side of it so far, and…

And I'm falling for a woman I can never have. My heart aches with the urge to reach up and draw her to me like I did in that dream, to discover the sweetness of her mouth with more than just a fleeting kiss, to press into her until she's moaning with so much pleasure she can't contain it.

But I don't for a second think even the slightest overture I could make would be welcome. She hasn't mentioned the quick kiss I couldn't resist giving her on her way out of the Refuge, and definitely hasn't encouraged another. With her habit of assuming the best of people, she's probably decided it was a random impulse in a desperate situation that no real meaning should be attributed to.

She'd never betray the men she's already devoted to. And what exactly could I offer that would tempt her to anyway?

Besides, I wouldn't want her if she was the kind of woman who'd so easily turn her back on those she loved.

I'm hardly going to tell her any of that, so I manage a smile. "I'll be taking all kinds of precautions and sticking to the sidelines. None of the Murk involved will have any idea what my part was." I glance back toward the Heart and get to my feet. "I just wanted to enjoy the atmosphere while I can."

A smile of her own tugs at the corners of Talia's lips. "Even you have to admit the scenery here is a *little* nicer than an abandoned subway tunnel."

I hum. "Subway tunnels have a lot to recommend about them." I inhale the scent of the grass in the air and find myself acknowledging, because she's the only person I can admit it to, "I might be a bit nervous about this parlay. I've never done any kind of business with Delta before—and to encourage a collision between the Murk and the Seelie…"

"It won't be a collision," Talia says with typical optimistic determination. "It's the beginning of a larger alliance. The more the Murk see that we're willing to work with them, and the more the fae of the Mists see that the Murk can keep their word, the easier it'll be to find some kind of compromise that doesn't mean attacking each other."

I think she's being *overly* optimistic there. Orion isn't going down without a fight, and there are plenty of my people who'll stick with him to the end no matter what. But I suspect Talia's aware of that too. It's just her nature to put a positive spin on dire situations.

"I'd very much like to see that," I say, which is true, and spot several figures beginning to assemble over by Sylas's castle. "It looks like my reprieve is over. Time to get going."

I'm trying to ignore the uneasy sinking of my stomach, but maybe it shows through anyway. Talia offers me another smile. "Thank you for doing this—for everything you've been doing. I know how hard it must be when you have so many reasons to distrust us. I promise you the fae appreciate your contributions too, even if they're still being cautious around you."

She moves forward suddenly, slipping her arms around me in what must have been meant as a hug. But the second her body brushes mine, my stance goes completely rigid, my pulse stuttering. The heat of her, the soft swell of her chest—the fae watching, will they think I compelled her, that I'll hurt her—?

Talia jerks back as if burned. Her face flushes, and I'm immediately kicking myself for my instinctive defensive reaction.

"Sorry," she says hastily. "I didn't mean to make you uncomfortable. I just—I want you to know it's important to me that you make it back safe too."

Her apology makes me feel even worse than I already did. I could have gotten to hold her close for just a few seconds, breathing in her scent and knowing *she* trusts me enough not to be afraid of me. But how awkward would it be to try to re-enact the moment now?

"It's all right," I assure her as emphatically as I can. "I wasn't uncomfortable, just surprised. We Murk aren't generally much for friendly gestures of affection, so I'm out of practice with the whole hugs thing."

My dry tone at the end seems to put her at ease, so at least I can keep the possibility of future hugs if she dares to try me again. I'm going to try not to dwell on that potential future too much after we part ways.

Whitt has appeared among the other gathering fae now. He waves to me, and I dip my head to Talia. "I hope you stay well while I'm gone, and that we can come back with good news."

"So do I," she says softly. I walk away with more reluctance than is probably healthy, the image of her bright figure lingering behind my eyes.

Whitt beckons me with a grin that's just shy of friendly. I don't think he's totally warmed up to me, but I won some kind of points by being willing to mention this strategy at all.

The fae around him watch me with much more hostile gazes. And there are quite a lot of them too. They've conjured five carriages, each big enough to hold at least ten fae.

I go straight to Whitt, ignoring the eyes that follow me with suspicion. "I'm not sure we need such a large delegation for the initial meeting. We look like we're prepared for battle."

"We are," Sylas says, just coming out of the castle. His gaze is still plenty wary when it comes to rest on me, his posture all arch-lordly dominance. "From what I understand, you said yourself that this Murk sorceress may see us as enemies rather than potential allies. We don't know what kind of force she'll have at her disposal if she comes. I think it's best to be prepared for the worst."

"If you bring them all through, she isn't likely to stick around at all," I have to point out.

"We're going to leave most of them on the other side of the portal with a spell to alert them if they're needed," Whitt says with no sign of concern. "It's only a precaution."

Like the guards and the magic around the cabin where I've spent the last two nights. Like the gazes trained on me no matter where I go in the Seelie's domains.

Maybe it's ridiculous of me to think there's any point in attempting negotiations. If the fae of the Mists can't see me as a true ally even after the lengths I've already gone to for them, what are the chances they'll fully accept any of the other Murk?

But that's another matter. What we're doing today is for Talia most of all. If Delta can dispel Orion's curse, that's enough of a victory for me. The rest I can decide later.

Sylas has me join him in his carriage, which includes a few warriors I'm familiar with from my rotating guard detail, and Whitt takes another. I guess they've already done all the strategizing they need to. I sink onto my end of the bench and spend most of the journey watching the landscape whip by, the wind ruffling my hair.

What would they think of the vehicles some of my people have been able to conjure? We've traveled through this realm many times in them without being spotted, but somehow I think the fae around me would turn up their noses at anything less elegant than their own crafts, no matter how well-constructed.

Sylas doesn't attempt any conversation, but I can sense him monitoring me and the fae around me. At one point a couple of his warriors mutter something between themselves, and he clears his throat with a sharp look.

Maybe he's watching us all for my defense as well as theirs. It's a strange thought, and not enough to let me relax in their presence. I doubt he sees any value in me as more than a tool to help build this potential alliance.

The fog and hunched trees of the fringelands come into view in what feels like no time at all. I tug at the collar of my shirt, the fabric starting to stick to my back with sweat. I definitely prefer the sharp chill of the winter-side fringe area to the sweltering humidity here, especially when this atmosphere brings back distant memories of my childhood and the violence that destroyed my family.

As we disembark, the horde of warriors gathering together, anxiety pinches my gut again. Have I been instrumental in setting up a parlay that could benefit both the Murk and these fae—or have I set the stage for yet another slaughter of my people? I might be insane to trust any of the fae of the seasons.

The man who came out here yesterday with my illusion spell cloaking him wasn't able to speak to Delta directly. He left the gifts and the request of the parlay, and one of her kin dropped off a reply. For all we know, we'll step through the portal where we asked her to meet us and find no one there at all. She might have changed her mind about trusting the message or about wanting to associate with the fae of the Mists even if she believes they're genuine.

Sylas assembles a significant portion of the warriors in a squad stationed around the portal in question, but it looks like we're still bringing through about twenty with us. My teeth grit against another complaint.

I said my piece. If I keep badgering them about it, for all I know they'll take that to mean I've set them up and decide to bring even more.

"Ready to go through?" Whitt asks me. "Your illusion looks solid to me."

I spent the last several minutes in the carriage constructing the magic to give a different impression of my appearance. Delta will expect to see a Murk man among the fae of the Mists for this parlay, but I don't want her or anyone looking on to recognize me. I nod and let my tail lash free from the base of my spine like a signal of my heritage. If any of the wolves around me have a problem with it, let them sneer.

As we pass through the portal one after another, my nerves stay on edge. In the sheltered cove on the other side, which contains a narrow strip of little-touched beach framed by a semi-circle of craggy rock, I step off to the side of the main Seelie force where I'll be visible but not the main focus of the discussion.

Waves lap at the sand. Salt laces the air from the ocean, stinging my eyes and burning in my throat. It's no wonder this pathway to the Mists is rarely used, but that also makes it an ideal spot for particularly secretive meetings.

The fae around me grimace and grunt in their discomfort. But they're disciplined enough to jerk stiffly still, erasing all signs of complaint, at the sight of a woman clambering over the jagged rocks to meet us.

Delta's face is a deep gold like the sand, burgundy curls falling around it to her narrow shoulders. She picks her way partway down the rocky outcropping with nimble hands and feet. There's nothing particularly impressive about her clothes, what looks like three tattered dresses of different faded colors layered on top of each other. But I know it's her from the moment she stops and draws herself up straight, still several paces above the beach. Her presence emanates confidence and power.

More figures pop their heads over the top of the rocks, watching over the ruler of their colony. The Seelie warriors study them, a few hands moving to rest on the hilts of their swords. My body tenses, but they make no further move.

"You wished to speak with me, wolf," Delta says, crossing her arms. "What could you possibly have to say that might be of interest to me?"

Sylas steps toward her, his head held high. "I think we have a common enemy. I wondered if you'd like the chance to undermine King Orion's plans."

"*King*," Delta sneers. The stories I've heard of her disdain for Orion obviously didn't lie.

But my attention snags on some of the Seelie near the back of our formation who are easing away from the others, closer to the rocks. They aren't getting into position to strike at the Murk, are they?

"I understand that's what he calls himself, at least," Sylas says with a chuckle, and at the same moment, a few of the warriors I'm watching start moving their mouths with a quiet incantation.

My heart lurches with the sudden certainty that I've been wrong—I've led this woman and her followers into a trap. With no thought in my head other than interrupting the guards however I need to, I dart around the delegation toward them.

My sudden movement must put the Murk on the alert. As I scramble along the edge of the rocks, dozens more figures leap up on top of the rocks, braced for an attack.

The Seelie warriors whip around, taking in the Murk force that's abruptly tripled in size, and must conclude that the colony is already launching an attack. With snarls, several snap out spells and draw their swords, others pulling in close around Sylas.

The rest happens so fast I can barely follow it. I'm not sure any of the spells are more than shields, but the Murk shout and start hurling needle-like knives and spells of their own down on the Seelie. Most bounce off the defensive barriers, but a few slice across the warriors' limbs.

A roar goes up, the Seelie warriors charging toward the rocks, Sylas hollering for order—and Delta springs up the ledges to vanish behind her people in the blink of an eye.

"Wait!" I holler. I clamber up the rocks to try to speak to the Murk from closer by. The next second, they're flooding down over the rocks to meet the Seelie's charge. I manage to dodge the ones that rush right by me, one of their blades cutting my cheek open.

In a matter of moments, blades are hissing and voices crying out in pain all around the cove. Sylas calls for the Seelie to retreat through the portal. A few Murk lie bloody on the sand, but the others jeer at the retreating wolf shifters.

I duck low into a crevice. The only way to reach the fae I arrived with is to push through the crowd of Murk who may see me as just as much a threat as they decided the Seelie were. It seems better to stay out of the way entirely. They're obviously not in any mood to listen to an explanation.

And why should I try to make one? I'm not totally sure what did happen there, whether the Seelie were on the verge of launching an attack and the Murk caught them at it or whether all of us misread the situation.

Do I even *want* to follow Sylas's people? What exactly were they up to before everything went to hell? Maybe if I hadn't made a move at all, there'd be ten times as many Murk corpses sprawled around the cove.

I weave another illusion around me, hiding me from the eyes and noses of Delta's colony. They linger in the cove for several minutes after the last Seelie has vanished, but they don't follow the wolf shifters into the Mists.

Finally, Delta's voice rises in a brisk summons from somewhere beyond my view, followed by a snarky remark about the treachery of wolves. Her people quickly scale the rocks and follow her back to their colony.

I stay where I am, wedged between two rough walls of stone, my stomach knotting. That meeting couldn't have gone much worse, and I don't even know who to blame for its failure. The one thing for sure is that the Seelie started throwing around magic and waving their weapons before the Murk had done more than *look* at them.

Why had I trusted them even enough to attempt to arrange this parlay? I should have known they'd never trust *us* enough to deal with us fairly.

The only one back there who deserves any consideration from me is Talia.

That thought weighs heavily on me. I want to spit in the Seelie's faces and turn my back on them, but am I really going to abandon her too, after all the faith she's shown in me?

I remain crouched among the rocks for over an hour, grappling with myself. Then I squeeze out of the crevice and push on into the jungle terrain beyond, leaving the noxious salt of the ocean behind.

There's another portal in this area that's closer to civilization, one that'll let me travel back to the fringes to the doorway I need without me risking ending up in Sylas's company again.

If there's anything I can do for Talia, I can't manage it back there in the Mists, surrounded by jackasses who hate me for what I am. I have to go back to Orion.

CHAPTER FIFTEEN

Talia

The tension in the border castle's meeting room thickens with each new arrival. The arch-lords barely speak other than to mutter to their cadres and coteries, but everyone looks grim.

I brace myself on my chair near the head of the table, willing myself to stay focused. Another fit of pain came over me just a couple of hours ago, and I feel exhausted now. I can't tell how much it's left over from the curse's effects and how much it's the fatigue of early pregnancy.

Sitting next to me, Corwin wraps his fingers around mine with a waft of reassurance through our bond. Every other emotion I can sense from him is unsettled, though. Sylas has taken the head of the table, and frustration seeps through his normally composed expression. Behind him, Whitt's expression is similarly gloomy.

When the last of the arch-lords, Neve, arrives and takes her seat, gazing around at us as if she isn't totally sure why she's there, Laoni clears her throat and leans forward. "So, from what I understand the rat you took into your confidence stayed true to his nature. He led you into a trap, did he?"

My heart skips a beat. "That's not what happened!" My gaze darts to Sylas. "That *isn't* what happened, is it?" He called this meeting so quickly after his return that I've barely had a chance to find out what went on after he, Whitt, and Madoc headed to their parlay, but no one said that Madoc betrayed them.

Sylas's mouth flattens into a taut line before he speaks. "We aren't entirely sure where things went wrong, but they did go very wrong. Our Murk collaborator may have played a role in that."

"He appeared to incite the other Murk," Whitt puts in, his tone even but hard. The flex of his jaw tells me he's angry with himself as much as anyone else. "And he didn't return with us. He appeared genuine when we worked out the plan, but I could have made an error in judgment."

Celia sighs. "It was always going to be a risky move. We have to dismiss everything else he's told us then too."

"And send out orders to kill him on sight if he tries to return," Uzziah adds with a menacing edge to his normally dour voice.

"If his own people don't take care of that for us," Celia says. "We can send proof of his duplicity to his king as planned and—"

"Hold on," I burst out, smacking my free hand on the table for emphasis. "We haven't even talked about exactly what happened. How did Madoc 'appear' to incite anyone? What did the Murk do? What did our warriors do? You all made it back safely." I fix my gaze on Sylas in an appeal. "We can't make life and death decisions without knowing the whole story."

He exhales roughly. "You're right, we shouldn't. The account we can give may not clarify the situation all that much, though."

"Let's hear it all the same," Terisse says in a tone I can't read. She's sided with my men and their more moderate views recently, but she was loyal to Laoni not long before that. I'm not sure how strongly she resents the Murk.

Sylas folds his hands on the tabletop. "We went out to the fringelands and through a portal to the agreed-upon meeting spot. The Murk woman that Madoc had arranged for us to parlay with did arrive, with what seemed to be a small contingent of her followers. We'd only just started speaking when Madoc, who was with us, made a sudden move, hurrying toward some of our warriors at the back of the formation. The sight seemed to provoke the other Murk, and many more converged on us. They attacked, and we fended them off while making for safety through the portal. None of them followed us—including Madoc. I don't know whether he stayed with them or went off on his own elsewhere in the human world."

"Probably running back to his 'king,'" Donovan growls. Even the normally mild-mannered Seelie arch-lord has his hackles up about this disaster.

I swallow hard, thinking through Sylas's story, noticing the gaps. I can't believe Madoc would have set up him and so many others of our people to be attacked. He gave every impression of thinking they might come back with a potential cure for me. I didn't see the slightest hint of guilt in him when we spoke right before he left.

I might not be as adept at reading people as Whitt, but the spymaster trusted him enough to go through with the plan too. There must be something more to the situation.

"What were the warriors Madoc ran toward doing?" I ask. "Do you have any idea why he reacted like that?"

"They'd stepped a little apart from the rest of us to cast additional spells we'd want to have at the ready in case we *were* attacked," Sylas says. "It was only a precaution. They didn't make a spectacle of it or aim the magic at anyone."

"Madoc obviously noticed it, though. Didn't he know they were going to be casting spells?"

Sylas pauses, and Whitt speaks up into his silence. "It didn't seem wise to inform him of every aspect of our plans ahead of time. If he was conspiring with the other Murk, we'd have lost any potential advantage. But if he was acting in good faith, he should have realized we weren't about to do harm to anyone who didn't provoke it."

"Why?" I have to ask. I don't like arguing with my mates, but I don't seem to have much choice. They hate the Murk so much they can't even see how unfair they're being. "If you didn't trust *him* not to be setting up an ambush, why would you expect him to have more trust in you? It sounds like you're the ones who made the first unexpected move."

Whitt opens his mouth and closes it again. He looks briefly chagrinned.

Sylas steps in. “That shouldn’t have been enough reason for the other Murk to attack us. It was as if they were taking their cues from him.”

I shift my gaze back to him. “Why wouldn’t they? He was the only Murk with you—of course they’d be watching him to make sure everything was okay. Did they really attack the second he reacted to the spell-casting?”

Sylas frowns and rubs his temple. “My attention was mainly focused on the supposed sorceress. I saw a sudden surge of rat shifters appear along the ridge behind us—”

“They were all around us,” Whitt puts in. “A huge force they’d been keeping in hiding.”

“—but we’d done something similar,” Sylas acknowledges, glancing back at his strategist. “So I suppose we can’t fault them for that. Our warriors who were present responded to the sudden onslaught by casting shielding spells around us, and it’s a good thing they did, because they got them up just in time to fend off the worst of the initial attack.”

“Had any of the Murk actually tried to hurt our people *before* ours started conjuring those shields?”

Both Sylas and Whitt appear to consider, the rest of the table watching us in silence as our conversation plays out.

“I don’t believe they had,” Whitt says finally, slowly, “but it was almost simultaneous.”

“Then it’s possible that they were already worried because of Madoc’s obvious concern, and then they saw a whole bunch of you casting more magic and assumed *you* were about to attack them?”

He grimaces. “I’ll acknowledge that could be true. We can’t know whether that’s the case or they meant to turn to violence all along, though.”

“And since we can’t know, we have to assume the worst for the security of our people,” Celia says, drawing her slim form up even straighter. “We gave them a chance, and they betrayed us.”

"Or they gave *us* a chance, and as far as they're concerned, we betrayed *them*," I protest.

Laoni scowls. "If that's the case, then why hasn't the rat who's supposedly allied himself with you given any explanation?"

I glare at her. "Maybe because he's afraid you'll kill him the second you see him just like it looks like you tried to kill all the other Murk he brought to talk to you—like you were just talking about doing to him a few minutes ago." A sound of frustration escapes me, and another wave of exhaustion rolls through my body.

Corwin's hand comes up to grip my shoulder, keeping me steady. "We're all upset about what happened, and we clearly can't determine the motivations of anyone other than ourselves," he says to the table at large. "Talia is speaking from a good place, making sure we consider every factor. But…" He squeezes my shoulder. "I'm not sure how much more risk it'd be reasonable for us to take in the hopes that any of the Murk will really work with us."

"Exactly," Uzziah says. "We have the ability to track them down with her blood now. Maybe the first attempt didn't go perfectly, but we learn from our mistakes. I say we track down every one of those vermin we can and end them, and their Heart too. Then we'll have peace and all the curses hanging over us will be cured."

The murmur that goes around the table sounds far too appreciative of that suggestion. Even inside me, there's a tiny twinge of relief at the thought of taking a simple route, what could be the fastest and surest way to ensure all of us are safe so that I can live on and my child keep growing inside me.

But will it really be that simple? Orion has outmaneuvered us often enough that I can't believe it.

And even if we could be sure that a widespread massacre of every rat in existence would lead us to victory, it's not just simple but brutal—so brutal it turns my stomach.

The images from the Murk memories I witnessed flash through my mind—the violence, the bloodshed, the horror. Madoc told me he didn't want to win Orion's vicious, sadistic way… and I don't want us to win that way either. I don't want to see all the fae around me turn as vicious as the fae who savaged my parents and shoved me into a cage, as the ones who tore apart Madoc's family or the children in that orphanage long ago.

Shaking off Corwin's hand, I shove my chair back and push to my feet. Every head around the table snaps toward me.

"No," I say, as if I can make that call. Maybe if I speak as if I can, that'll be enough for them to listen to me. "I would rather *die* than get my cure like that. You think the Murk like Orion and his followers are horrible, vicious animals. What do you think *you'll* be if you massacre every fae who happens to have been born a rat shifter? Why *should* any of them trust you if you jump straight to that solution?"

"Talia," Sylas says gently, but I'm not done.

"They have some good in them," I say. "Maybe not Orion, but there are horrible Seelie and Unseelie too. Most of the Murk I talked to were angry, but they felt a lot of other things. They cared about their families and their friends. They supported each other and defended each other. They had hopes for a future where they *didn't* have to worry about the fae of the Mists descending on them with claws or talons at any moment.

"Attack Orion and anyone who insists on standing with him. Destroy their Heart. But if you're going to support killing Murk who won't ever raise so much as a finger against you, then I'd rather go back to their Refuge than stay here."

The declaration takes the last of my energy out of me. I slump back into my seat. Everyone is staring at me, Whitt's face gone sickly pale, horror trickling through my bond with Corwin.

Sylas recovers first. "I agree with Talia that we can't lower ourselves to the same baseness as the worst of the rats. We owe ourselves and our people more than that. But we obviously can't stand by and hope any of the Murk will advise us either. We should start sending out more search parties to track down the Refuge."

Laoni draws in a breath. I wince inwardly in anticipation of a caustic remark, but to my surprise, her voice comes out measured. "There are ways we could draw out the Murk who mean us ill to ensure we stay focused on destroying our primary enemies. They believe they can outsmart us—we can play into their assumptions, lay traps where we look like easy targets but can turn the tables on those who take the opportunity to attack."

Her fellow Unseelie arch-lords nod, slowly but without argument. Celia wets her lips. "Fine. For now. But we can't go easy on any intruding on our lands. We imprison and interrogate those we easily can; any who fight back will get what they deserve."

My hands clench on my lap. They still talk as if the Mists belong only to them, when obviously this is the world all the fae came from. Madoc isn't wrong that the other fae shoved the Murk out.

"What about Madoc?" I ask quietly, my chest constricting at the thought of him. "If he comes back, shouldn't we give him the chance to give his side? As far as I can tell, he hasn't violated the terms of the deal. *He* didn't attack anyone, did he?" I look at Sylas and Whitt.

"Not that anyone's reported witnessing," Whitt admits. "I lost track of him in the chaos, but I didn't see him so much as draw a weapon or speak a spell."

"Then all we know that he's done is hurry over to see what some of the warriors were doing. We can't destroy his life over that."

There's another silence. Corwin breaks it. "I'd say it depends on *how* he comes back. If he strikes out at us or joins others doing so, we'd obviously assume the alliance is over. If he makes a show of peacefulness but can't adequately explain his actions, the same. I do think he's earned the right to be heard after getting Talia back to us and then warning us of Orion's new assault on her."

The faces around the table don't exactly look happy about his proposal, but one by one, the arch-lords incline their heads. I wrap my arms around myself, wishing I felt more reassured.

I can't help suspecting that we're teetering on the edge of becoming monsters ourselves, and I'm afraid of how little it might take to push the rulers around me over that line.

CHAPTER SIXTEEN

Talia

The first of the new kind of fit hits me when I'm walking across the wintry plain between the border castle and the palace of Heart's Cadence, meaning to have a quick visit with Charles and Beth in the kitchen. I haven't spoken to them in ages. Even with everything going on around me—and inside me—I have to hold on to a few pieces of normalcy.

But I've only made it about halfway there when pain spikes between my lungs. My legs buckle beneath me, and Corwin, who was walking with me, catches me just before my knees smack into the icy terrain.

"Talia," he says, his voice tight with the strain of the agony I'm too wrapped up in to shield him from. "Focus on me. Ignore it as well as you can. I'll get you back to your room."

"Is there anything I can do?" Zelpha asks, hovering behind him. My mates have continued to insist that at least two trusted protectors are with me any time I venture outside one of our castles.

Corwin scoops me up into his arms with a ragged breath. "We

haven't found any spells that do much to dull the pain. At least I can bring her to where she'll be most comfortable."

Before he's taken two steps toward the border, though, the searing sensation that tore through my chest subsides. I gasp and tuck myself closer against him, shaken. Can it really be over already?

Corwin pauses, looking down at me, registering the change at the same time as me. "It hasn't let up anywhere near that quickly before, has it?"

I shake my head. "Maybe—maybe something we've tried has worked to weaken the curse after all?"

A flicker of hope crosses his face—and in the same instant, another vicious blade of pain slices through me, as if I'm being carved open from the inside out.

I cough and sputter, my muscles clenching up. A shudder runs through my body. Corwin hugs me close, his emotions as agonized as my body is. I know how much he wants to shield me from this pain and how deeply it wrenches at him that he can't.

"The pattern has shifted," he says to Zelpha. "Get Sylas—he should be at Hearth-by-the-Heart. Have him meet us in the border castle."

I don't see Zelpha's response, only feel the waft of air as she flaps away as a raven. Corwin extends his own wings in their larger form, the rest of him remaining a man as he soars across the frozen terrain the fastest way he's capable of.

As he lands on the doorstep of the winter entrance, the pain eases again. I don't trust the reprieve this time. I take shallow breaths, testing my lungs, still huddled in my soul-twined mate's embrace.

"You can endure this," he murmurs to me, sounding a little choked. "You're stronger than any Murk king's magic."

Maybe I am, but that doesn't mean it's any joy living through it.

Halfway down the hall, the next attack seizes me, with a slamming sensation as if not one but several knives are plunging between my ribs. I can't help crying out.

Corwin swallows thickly and hustles up the stairs toward my bedroom. The knives keep digging in until a moment before he's laying me on the bed covers.

I pant, my whole body aching in a duller but still distressing way. Every time the pain comes on me, I tense up, and the back and forth is wearing me out faster than if I were riding out a continuing wave. You'd think getting breaks would make it easier, but I can't appreciate them when I'm tangled up in the apprehension of wondering how long I'll get before it happens again.

How will I know for sure when this fit is even really over? *Will* it ever be over, or is this the new normal: switching between relief and pain over and over every couple of minutes?

Don't think like that, Corwin says through our bond, but I can tell he's worried about the exact same thing.

Sylas pushes past the door a moment later with Whitt close at his heels. "What—" he starts.

And then the pain is in me again, blaring through my awareness, drowning out every other sensation. I hug myself, pressing the side of my head into the pillow.

I can get through this. I am stronger. But oh God, I wish I didn't have to.

When I come back to myself, Corwin and Sylas are speaking in hushed, urgent voices. Corwin has walled off some of his impressions so I can't read them or hear what they're saying through his ears.

They're *arguing* about something… I can't tell what. Corwin seems worried. Sylas's jaw is tight with resolve.

Whitt catches my eye, his own expression fraught with concern. "I think we should let Talia decide," he says abruptly.

Despite the horrible state I'm in, a swell of love for him fills my chest. I even manage to smile.

"Let me decide what?" I ask in a croak.

Then I'm gone. The pain somehow spreads and shrinks at the same time—not several knives but dozens of piercing needles. My lungs are going to puncture and deflate like dying balloons.

I return to reality with tears stinging the corners of my eyes and a sob caught in my throat. Corwin sinks onto the edge of the bed next to me and swipes the moisture away. He looks at Sylas. "How can we put her through that stress when she's already suffering like this?"

Sylas frowns. "How can we not try when there's a possibility he could help? You know what she'd say—you heard her yesterday."

It takes me a second to gather myself enough to use my voice. "Whatever it is, I—"

Another searing wave, another spell of disorientation. After that, I give up on trying to have any kind of conversation, and I think my mates do too. Corwin murmurs soft words over me, conjuring a cool tingle that distracts from the pain the tiniest bit. Whitt sits down by the head of the bed and strokes my hair.

"If I could take this on for you, mite, you know I would," he says.

Sylas paces. In one clear moment, I think he's going to leave, but he doesn't. When a break in the fits lasts long enough that I start to relax into the mattress, he's still there.

My hair is sticking to my forehead with sweat. Whitt brushes it aside too. Corwin grips my hand. We wait, all of us anticipating another round…

But it doesn't come. The minutes tick by, and the memory of the agony fades. There's nothing left but the prickle behind my breastbone.

A laugh sputters out of me. "It's over."

For now. Until the next time.

Whitt gives Sylas a pointed look, and the Seelie arch-lord gazes down at me, his mouth twisting.

"Madoc has returned," he says.

I jerk upright, and Corwin tightens his grip on my hand. I sway with momentary dizziness before refocusing on Sylas. "What? When? What's he said?"

"A few hours ago," Whitt admits. "We wanted to question him thoroughly before we proceeded any further."

Before they told me he was here, they mean. I grimace.

Before I can complain about their secrecy, Sylas goes on. "I'm not sure he meant to engage with us any more than the first time he came. August and a few of our pack-kin caught him lurking in the woods near the castle. He *says* he was waiting for the chance to speak to you directly, that he doesn't want to deal with the rest of us."

"And how can we trust him if that's how he's approaching the situation?" Corwin demands, all protective ire.

Whitt shakes his head. "You haven't seen him. He's clearly furious with us because he thinks *we* ruined the parlay."

"Or maybe he's angry because his attempt at betraying us didn't work as well as he'd hoped."

Whitt raises his eyebrows at the Unseelie man. "I'll admit that using one's actual emotions in a deception can be an excellent tactic, and putting your opponent on the defensive is one as well. But he tried to avoid speaking to us at all. And he's brought several items that show no harmful properties that he says he gathered back in the human world—remedies the Murk use for various ailments. He simply wanted to give them to Talia."

"Which doesn't mean we should necessarily let him anywhere near our mate," Sylas puts in. "But we could bring what he's offered and see whether it helps her at all."

Corwin frowns. "Before anything of his comes near her, I'd like to—"

"Stop!" I break in. My chest is wrenching in a totally different way at the thought of the treatment Madoc must have gone through in the past few hours without my knowing. "I want to see him. What can he do to me that's worse than what I'm already going through anyway? Do you think Orion needs to send someone to double-curse me?"

I narrow my eyes at all three of the men around me. "If Madoc was trying to manipulate you, he wouldn't be antagonizing you. So stop antagonizing him and each other, and let's get on with seeing what he brought."

Whitt's mouth twitches into a tight smile. "She does know her own mind," he says to Sylas.

"She does." The Seelie arch-lord turns to Corwin.

I squeeze my soul-twined mate's hand, and he sighs before pressing a kiss to my temple. "All right. I don't like it, but… it's true that I can't see what he'd gain by specifically speaking to Talia." He pauses. "I'm not sure we want him having access to this castle, though. Talia, are you well enough to come down?"

I test my feet on the floor and nod. "I'll be fine."

Sylas and Whitt go ahead to collect Madoc from wherever August is watching over him. Corwin stays with me for the trek down to the entrance. My legs do hold me just fine, but partway down the steps, a whiff of broiled fish reaches my noise from the kitchen, and my stomach starts churning. Most food hasn't bothered me so far, but every now and then some odor brings out a rush of queasiness.

"There's nothing you can do to get rid of the smell fast enough for it to help," I tell Corwin. "Let's just get out of here quickly."

The scent is thicker in the hallway below. My jaw clamps tight against my rising nausea. The effort isn't quite successful, though. I've just made it out the door, about to take my first deep breath of fresh summer air, when my gut twists and I find myself vomiting what's left of my breakfast into the grass at the base of the wall.

Footsteps come hustling over, and I look up to see my Seelie mates, Astrid, and a couple of other guards hurrying toward me with Madoc in their midst. So wonderful to have an audience for this.

I swipe at my mouth, the lingering nausea subsiding, as Corwin rubs my back and intones a quick spell to remove the mess. Refusing to let the embarrassment hold me back, I step forward to meet the coming entourage.

"Has it gotten worse?" Madoc asks the second he's close enough for me to hear him, worry clouding his eyes. It doesn't look as if the guards who caught him hurt him, thank goodness. "If it's progressed to your stomach—"

I hold up my hand to stop him. Weirdly, the sight of his crookedly handsome face soothes my spirits even more. I can tell just looking at him, at the way he's looking at me, that I was right to argue on his behalf. I have the unexpected urge to try to hug him again, to feel those well-muscled arms wrap around me like when he hid me on our way out of the Refuge, to—

I jerk my mind away from those rambling thoughts, squashing down the flash of heat that came with them, and focus on his questions. "I think that was being pregnant, not the curse. A much happier reason to be sick but not great having both in combination."

The Murk man pauses, and I realize I hadn't told him that particular piece of news. It hadn't seemed relevant.

His gaze darts to Whitt and then back to me. "I wondered, after certain questions—" He doesn't seem to know how to go on. Finally, he settles on, "I'm sorry Orion's managed to ruin even more happiness than he could have intended."

"It isn't totally ruined yet," I say. "And it's the curse that matters. I hear that you've brought back some things that might help?"

"Yes, some medicines we use and a couple of charms… None of it's specifically for a curse like this, but they're at least different from what you'll have already tried. We combine a lot of human products with our healing creations, so maybe they'll have a stronger effect on you." He hesitates again, studying me. "You're going to accept them, just like that? Not run me through another round of questions about how the parlay went to hell?"

He sounds so uncertain of my reaction that something twists in my chest. Without letting myself second-guess the impulse, I step across the short distance between us. Corwin makes a sharp noise in his throat, but Sylas motions for the guards to stay where they are.

It's probably better if I don't actually hug Madoc, considering every time I even think about it, other emotions stir that I shouldn't be feeling. But I can offer at least this much. I touch his forearm, giving it a light squeeze as I gaze up into his eyes. He stares back at me, the storminess in his gaze simmering down into something warmer, and the feelings I hadn't meant to provoke flutter inside me anyway.

I have to focus on the matter at hand. "Did you *want* the parlay to go to hell?" I ask.

Madoc frowns. "Of course not," he says, his eyes flashing as they dart toward the men around us again. "I didn't want the Murk attacking your people. But although this fact is apparently a problem for some of them, I also didn't want *them* attacking any of the Murk there."

"Which none of us did until we were attacked first," Sylas says evenly.

"What counts as an 'attack' is obviously debatable," Madoc

mutters, and turns back to me. "They don't trust me, and I don't trust them, and it seems that's just how it is. So I won't arrange any more parlays. But even if they all want to be dicks about it, that doesn't mean I'm going to abandon you."

And there's the passionate defiance that allowed him to shake off his loyalty to his king on our behalf before. Always trying to do what's right for the people he cares about, even though it must be harder than ever for him to tell right now what that is.

I can't help thinking I'm lucky to have become one of those people.

I pull myself back a step, dropping my hand, before the conflicted sensations inside me rise up too far. He's an ally and maybe even a friend, but I definitely shouldn't feel any inclinations beyond that.

Even if I set aside my instinct to believe the man in front of me and look at the signs more logically, I have to agree with Whitt's assessment that Madoc doesn't appear to be trying to win any points or pull the wool over our eyes. His anger actually sounds more genuine than the restrained wariness he let show around the other fae before when he was trying to keep some kind of peace.

"That's good enough for me," I say, and glance around at my mates. "And that means it's going to be good enough for all of you too."

CHAPTER SEVENTEEN

Corwin

I've always done my best to allow Talia all the freedom she could want, to show I respect her opinions and believe in her strength. It's never been quite so hard to see those intentions through as it is right now.

She's sitting in the grass next to Madoc, just a few steps from the border castle and with several fae who could leap to her defense in a split-second watching over them. Still, my hackles rise as the rat shifter offers her a small nugget of molded powder that's one of his people's "medicines." I want to leap in there right now and tear it from her hands.

But she's been firm that she trusts him at least in this, and her arguments have been sound. I can't imagine how her situation *could* get any worse than it already is. And I can't say the Murk man has ever shown the slightest hint of wanting to hurt her. If anything, it's been the opposite.

The rest of us is another story.

I tamp down on those thoughts, not letting my uneasy emotions travel through our bond. I don't want to cause her more distress, and

I'm a little ashamed of how much my emotions are affecting me right now. Between all of us here, I'm supposed to be the level-headed raven, and I feel as wild as if there's a wolf underneath my skin.

"You'll want to chew it quickly," Madoc is saying. "Hopefully it won't upset your stomach."

Sylas clears his throat. "What exactly is in that thing?"

The Murk man glances up at him. "Various herbs, magic to bring out their healing properties, and stuff the humans call penicillin."

"Oh," Talia says with a soft laugh. "I had to take that once when I was a kid—when I had an ear infection." She looks at the nugget with amusement and then pops it into her mouth. Her throat bobs with her swallow. "It doesn't taste too bad. Not sure this curse works quite the same as bacteria in the ear drum, though."

Madoc gives her a crooked smile. "We don't typically use it for curses. Or for bacteria. But magically speaking, bringing out the gist of a material's properties can increase a similar effect you're going for."

"That's solid magical theory," Whitt agrees, if grudgingly.

"I guess it makes sense that your magic is much more entwined with human things than the spells the other fae use are," Talia says to Madoc. "Since you live so much closer to them. I've forgotten about a lot of what seemed so normal to me before I was brought here."

Her voice fades out, and I catch the flicker of concern in Madoc's eyes. He quickly produces another object from the inner pockets on the leather vest he arrived wearing. The item looks like a flower, silky purple petals with a small cloth bundle sewn into the center. He hands it to Talia, who brightens again.

"Very pretty," she says. "How does it work?"

"It's supposed to deflect hostile energies," Madoc says. "Not the most likely strategy to work when a lot of that energy is already in you, but again, I figured it couldn't hurt to try everything. It's got its own human component too."

He motions to the underside of the flower, and she flips it over. A giggle spills out of her. She beams at him with a rush of fondness that carries through her connection with me. Then she holds it up so we can see the symbol stitched to the base of the bundle. "It's the emblem for a squad of heroes from a TV show. I watched it all the time with Jamie. I didn't know it was still popular."

"Humans get very attached to their stories," Madoc says, smiling back at her. Then the smile tightens a bit around the edges. "As I suppose we fae do too."

I don't have to ask what sort of stories he's thinking of. Certainly we Unseelie and the Seelie have told plenty of horrifying tales about the Murk over the centuries. I haven't seen proof yet that those weren't warranted, though.

His remark reminds me of another sort of storytelling *he'll* have been doing recently. "You must have needed to give your king some kind of report when you returned to your home. He wasn't expecting you back so early, was he? What did you tell him?"

Madoc meets my gaze steadily. His wariness has eased a little with Talia's acceptance of his presence. "I had a perfectly good excuse. You don't think he'd have heard that a scuffle went down between Murk and fae of the Mists? And it wouldn't take much for him to guess *why* you might have tried to meet with Delta. He might be unhinged, but he's not an idiot. Now, if you'd managed to carry out the parlay peacefully, it could have been kept much more quiet."

"That doesn't answer the question," August says with a hint of a growl. "I'd like to know exactly what you told him too."

Madoc shifts his attention to the warrior. "I said that from what I'd gathered, the lot of you were getting desperate enough about Talia's situation to turn to Murk for help, but that being how you are, you obviously couldn't help screwing it up."

Talia frowns. "Isn't he going to realize that someone from the Murk side must already be helping us? How else would we have known to approach Delta—that she'd be a good choice to go against Orion?"

The rat shifter shrugs as if to try to hide the tension that's come into his stance at the question. "No doubt he'd already put those pieces together as soon as he heard there was some commotion with Delta's colony. It only means I have to keep being every bit as careful as I have been so far."

Talia glances around. "You don't have to worry—if he has other spies, and you're seen here with us—?"

Madoc snorts. "Even I couldn't manage to dodge all the protections around these domains, and I'm better with our concealing spells than anyone else Orion has working for him. I'd only be worried closer to the fringes."

Perhaps that's another reason he's come back to us—to keep him out of his king's sight. Although the moment that thought crosses through my head, I recognize the unfairness of it. Even if he dismisses the possibility, he knows that every moment he spends in our presence, he risks discovery.

And if his association with us is discovered, he won't be able to return home at all.

I may be too hard on him, too skeptical of his intentions. But I can't stop another rush of protectiveness from flaring inside me when his fingers brush Talia's as he hands her a small jar with a salve he's brought, or when he studies her so intently as she examines it.

It might not be all protectiveness. I can admit there's also a twinge of jealousy woven in because of the way she smiles back at him. Because of her laugh when he explains that the substance combines another human-sourced ingredient, this one a popular brand of soap.

She leans toward him just a little as she thanks him. And there's a joy humming through her at their conversation, at getting to talk with someone who understands that side of her old life in ways the rest of us never can.

"Did you ever see that commercial with the talking cat that ends up eating it?" she asks, and Madoc chuckles at the memory.

"We're pretty sensitive to anything that involves cats," he tells her with a quirk of his eyebrow. "That one definitely stuck with me. Thankfully I don't think any cats are required for the cleansing properties to come into effect."

Talia turns away to rub some of the salve into her skin over the spot between her breasts where she feels the curse even between the bad fits, and Madoc averts his gaze for her modesty. Somehow his courtesy niggles at me more than if he leered at her.

At least then I'd have a good excuse to want to peck him to death.

Talia tucks the jar into the pouch on her belt where she's also stored the flower charm. As she turns back to face him, Madoc studies her. "Are you feeling any different at all? I know it's early."

But he can't help hoping, just like the rest of us. The recognition of that hope and how the expression on his face aligns with my own sends an odd twist of emotion through me.

Talia touches the spot through her dress and appears to concentrate for a long moment. Her mouth slants downward. I can tell that she's as much sorry to disappoint us as disappointed herself. "Not that I can notice. But maybe it'll just take some time."

Madoc ducks his head with a grimace. "It was a long shot. I just didn't want to come back empty-handed."

"It's all right. *No one's* been able to affect the curse, so you can't beat yourself up that you can't either." Talia reaches out and rests her hand gently on his forearm like she did when he asked her if she trusted his offerings at all, determined to reassure him.

Madoc swipes his other hand over his face. "I know." But his voice comes out raw, and his expression has tightened.

I wish I could appreciate how much he cares about my mate's well-being. It's getting harder to believe it's an act. Talia doesn't think so, and her concern for him jabs through me.

"If that's everything, Talia should get some rest," Sylas says. "She's had a rough morning, and it'll give more of a chance for your potential cures to work."

Talia nods reluctantly and gets up. "What about Madoc?" she asks. "Are you going to shove him back into that little cabin for the rest of the day?"

Madoc speaks up before any of us has to. "It's actually for my benefit as well, Talia. If a spy did manage to make it this far by some miracle, they're less likely to notice I'm around if I'm hidden away in there. I was prepared this time, brought a couple of books." He pats the other side of his vest and looks at the rest of us. "You'll let me know if you think of any other way I can try to help Talia?"

Just Talia. Not the war effort, not our defenses against his people, not our own curse. Only her. He couldn't have made it clearer since he returned that he's given up on the rest of us.

Can I truly blame him for that?

Talia recognizes that part of his statement too, and a pang of distress shoots through her—both for us and the alliance she'd hoped we were building with him. She believes we've let him down too.

August helps her through the doorway toward her bedroom, and the guards move to escort Madoc to the cabin. As they leave, I motion to Sylas and Whitt. "A word?"

We gather in one of the border castle's smaller sitting rooms. I wait until August rejoins us a few minutes later. The cheerful expression I've come to expect from him has been gloomy more often than not in recent days.

"I can't see that anything he's done has hurt her any, but we'll have to keep a close eye on her," he says.

"Despite my earlier hesitations, I don't think he wants to harm her," I say. "I think she's the only person in the Mists he has any interest in defending at the moment."

"I'd have to agree," Whitt says with a sigh. "Which makes me more certain that what happened in the cove was an accident. We were reaching out to Delta mainly to see if she could cure Talia. Any assistance she might have offered in a war with Orion was a secondary concern at the time. I can't see the rat wanting to jeopardize that unless he honestly believed we weren't going to stick to *our* word."

Sylas considers me. "Is that what you wanted to talk about?"

I shake my head, but I have to dredge up the words. "I've also noticed how fond of him Talia's becoming."

Whitt's eyebrows leap up. "What are you suggesting?"

I spread my hands. "She feels a connection with him, and she's grateful for the ways he's helped her. She also sympathizes with the tragedies he's faced and his devotion to his people. He's continued to prove himself a loyal ally and even friend to *her*… It's not surprising that she'd come to care about him quite a bit too, is it?"

August bares his teeth. "If that rat even tries to lay his grubby paws on her—"

"I don't think there's much chance of that," Whitt breaks in. "I've watched them together—I think he's quite charmed by her, but he holds himself back. He knows how devoted *she* is to us, I've no doubt." He pauses, meeting my gaze. "But I have seen a little of what you're talking about, now that I think about it, and obviously you have more direct insight into her emotions."

"But a rat…" August mutters.

"She managed to give me a chance even when she saw me as the enemy, even when the bond was forced on her in a way she found terrifying," I remind them, my stomach knotting. "And you all accepted my place in her life, by her side, as well. I only thought we should have the subject out in the open between us, and possibly come to some sort of tentative understanding of how we'll handle their attachment to each other if her feelings continue to develop."

Silence settles over us. Sylas gazes off toward the window and then returns his attention to me. "She won't step outside the bonds of our relationship. She only revealed the deeper affections she'd come to feel for Whitt to him after August and I had assured her that it wouldn't be a betrayal—it was the same with you. She has one of the deepest senses of loyalty I've ever seen. If we don't mention it, she never will. She'll simply put her feelings aside."

"And that's what you think we should do?" I ask. "Ignore it?"

"We can't trust him," August says. "Whether he cares about her or not, he'd like to see the rest of us dead in the ground."

The corner of Sylas's mouth crooks upward. "I'm not sure that's true, if only because he knows how much losing us would hurt Talia. But I do feel it's too early to make any calls, and as long as we don't intervene, nothing significant about the situation is going to change. We have time to see how deep *his* loyalty runs, especially once war looms. Any affection she feels for him will shatter quickly if he shows he's willing to attack the rest of our people."

He's right. Of course he's right. That's undoubtedly how it'll play out: for all his doting, push will come to shove, and he'll take up arms alongside the rest of his people. Talia will never forgive him for giving up on the hope of peace.

And then nothing that's been eating at me will matter.

"I do think there's one part of his strategy we should consider taking up ourselves," Whitt remarks with a faint grin. "Try every possible cure, no matter how unlikely? There are options we haven't pursued yet because we assumed they'd have no effect. But I'd like to show our mighty mate that we aren't giving up either. She could probably use some time away from languishing around one castle or another day in and day out."

Our problems are hardly solved, but his suggestion lightens my spirits just slightly. I offer him a smile. "What do you have in mind?"

CHAPTER EIGHTEEN

Talia

"So, this spring is supposed to heal people?" I ask, peering over the bow of the carriage at the terrain ahead. Only the faintest gleam of water shows in the distance.

"Not specifically from curses," Sylas says from where he's standing next to me, guiding the vehicle. "And like much of the natural magic in this world, it isn't entirely consistent. But many fae have reported severe ailments that were washed away by a soak in the waters. We don't want to leave any stone unturned."

Because nothing my mates thought had a better chance of working has accomplished anything so far. Because despite everything they and Madoc have done for me, I woke up this morning feeling weaker than ever before.

The prickling sensation in my chest has expanded and sharpened. It's not as unbearable as the worst fits, several more of which struck me last night in quick succession, but harsh enough that I hesitate to breathe too deeply, avoiding the jab of discomfort that'll come. My heartbeat stutters at odd moments for no clear reason. And every now and then a splinter of pain pokes down to my gut.

I feel like I have a jagged-edged creature growing inside me, getting more restless by the hour.

Corwin can tell because he can sense quite a bit of that through our bond. I don't have the energy to shield him from much. I haven't told my other mates more than the briefest of details about my worsening condition, though.

They already know the situation is dire. They're already worried enough. The fact that we're taking this trip even with war on the horizon proves it.

"Even if it doesn't help anything, a good soak is always enjoyable for its own sake," Whitt says in a more typical wry tone, though I can hear the tension creeping through underneath. "I fully intend to take advantage of it."

"We can't have Talia in the spring on her own anyway," August points out. "If a fit came over her while she was bathing, she wouldn't be able to concentrate on keeping her head out of the water."

Corwin hums in agreement, and I restrain a grimace. So many considerations I never expected them to have to make. It wasn't that long ago that I told them to stop hovering over me because being pregnant didn't make me an invalid. I *am* an invalid now, thanks to the curse.

The questions that've haunted me more and more since the curse's effect intensified gnaw at me again. What if we can't cure it? What if I only have a few weeks left? A few days?

I swallow hard. I knew I wouldn't have a full fae lifespan with my mates, but I thought I'd at least get a full human one. I meant to reach out to Jamie when I didn't have to worry as much about the tensions of the fae world harming him—but even if I can't wait that long, how can I appear in his life out of the blue if I'm just going to really die on him right after?

Corwin steps closer and brushes a comforting hand over my head, sending a rush of devotion through our bond at the same time. *We'll find a way. Whatever it takes. It won't come to that.*

He can't be sure of those words, but I shove the grim thoughts away anyway. They don't do me any good. They only add to how much awfulness the curse can make me feel.

I will not lose hope like I almost did in the cage in Orion's throne room. I will not let the Murk king win.

A stretch of dark stone comes into view up ahead. As the carriage slows, passing into that area, I can see it's not just dark but pure black. But there's something soft about the blackness that gives the impression of a thick blanket or coat of fur, not the polished chill of the obsidian stones that made up the old castle at what's now Hearth-by-the-Heart.

Just looking at the darkly opaque surface calms something deep inside me. When Whitt and August help me out of the carriage, I find the ground is lightly spongy under my feet.

"It's a type of moss," Whitt tells me, observing my curious reaction. "It grows all over the stone here except right in the spring itself—and this is the only place in the realms it grows. Some have speculated that it's what gives the water its healing properties, but no one's really sure. Taking the moss away and trying to make a cure out of it elsewhere has never worked."

There are so many mysteries in the fae world. I find that somehow reassuring—that it isn't so odd that we'd have trouble unraveling my curse, that it's just the way many things work here. And overall, this world hasn't turned out so terrible, so maybe this situation won't either.

My mates lead me to the water. At the other end of the springs, a stream spills down a shallow, slick slope where the moss-covered rocks rise a few feet in the air. Then it courses into five separate pools, the one in the middle as large as my bedroom back home and the others less than half that size.

"I just… get in?" I say.

Sylas nods. "To ensure the full effect, if you're going to get any effect at all, it's best to soak for an hour or so. But I understand it's quite pleasant. If you start to feel unwell, just tell us."

I nod and start to pull off my dress. Whitt chucks his clothes aside with no apparent concern for modesty, which doesn't surprise me, and the others follow suit more slowly.

Corwin leaves on his boxer-like undergarments and sits at the edge of the pool. "It seems wise for one of us to be observing from outside the water."

"Hmm," Whitt says. "Don't want to get your feathers wet?" He winks and jumps into the gently flowing water.

I slip in more carefully, August sliding into the water next to me and holding my arm to make sure I'm steady. The moss might only reach the edge of the pool, but the rock surface my feet come to rest on has a rippled texture that makes it easy to grip.

The water, warm enough to immediately relax my muscles but not steaming hot, glides against my skin and around my shoulders. A sigh slips out of me, and I lean back against the wall, not really feeling up to doing more than that.

Corwin eases over so I can rest my head against his knee. He glances at Whitt, who's making a slow circuit of the pool, and I catch a flicker of good humor through our connection. "What's that you're doing, then?" he asks. "The dog paddle?"

"Oh!" Whitt clutches his chest as if wounded, his eyes sparkling. "Shots fired across the bow by Lord Bird."

August laughs, and Sylas shakes his head at all of them, sinking into the water up to his chin. Then he makes a gesture beneath the surface alongside a quick movement of his lips, and a little wave rises up to splash over Whitt's head.

As a giggle tumbles out of me, the spymaster mock-glowers at his brother. "Now I'm getting ganged up on by two arch-lords. I see how it is. But you forget that it's never wise to tangle with an expert in strategy."

He hasn't even finished speaking when a wave of his own shoots out of the water. Sylas dodges it—right into the path of a sudden larger one that completely douses his dark hair.

Swiping the wet strands away from his face, Sylas chuckles. August takes the moment of his distraction to aim a well-placed swell of water at the back of his brother's head.

"Now who's getting ganged up on?" the Seelie arch-lord asks with an amused glint in his dark eye.

The three of them swim, feint, and dodge around the pool, each getting drenched by one of the others in turn. A smile stays on my lips, watching them horse around like, well, wolf pups at play. How long has it been since *they* could really relax?

August ends up ducking past me, and I can't resist taking the opportunity to splash water over his ruddy hair with my cupped hands. He swivels with a grin and gives me a quick peck with his slick lips.

And I realize that I can fully enjoy the moment. The jabs of pain inside me have retreated. The prickle is still there, but dulled to its previous intensity. I don't know if that means much of anything, but it's enough of a relief that my smile widens.

I nudge myself away from the side of the pool. "I want to float," I announce.

"And what the mite wants, she'll have," Whitt says.

He catches my shoulder, making sure I'm steady in the water as I stretch out on the surface. Rivulets stream over the mounds of my breasts, and a flicker of desire reaches me from Corwin watching, but he reins it in.

The water holds me up in its warm embrace. I drift along, each of my Seelie mates guiding my path in turn with a tender touch to my head, my side, my hip. The sky stretches out above me, perfectly blue.

In that moment, I want to float like this forever, as if the world itself is holding me up, as if nothing could drag me down beneath the surface.

After a while I feel the urge to move again. I paddle around a bit and then come to a stop by the edge again. "I am feeling better," I tell my mates.

"That's wonderful." August swims over and tugs me into an embrace.

I nestle against him, but with the pain retreating, the feel of his naked skin against mine sets off a spark of my own desire. I tip my head, seeking a longer kiss.

August obliges with a pleased growl low in his throat.

A headier heat floods me with the meeting of our lips. My limbs slide against his, and he cups my breast beneath the water. The slow rotation of his thumb over the peak has me whimpering against him in an instant.

I can feel all my other mates' gazes on us, but they don't rush to join in. Corwin gives off a sense of caution, wanting to be sure I don't end up overwhelmed. They're going to let me take the lead.

I want this so much while I can enjoy it. I kiss August harder, arching into his touch. Another growl reverberates through his chest.

He holds me against the wall, careful not to press too tightly, and tucks his knee between my legs. The movement of it against my sex makes me gasp into his mouth. His tongue teases over mine, and he shifts the attentions of his hand to my other breast.

For a while, I just rock there, floating on pleasure as much as the buoyancy of the water, each graze of his thigh against me taking me farther from the worries of the present. Just as I'm starting to tremble with the sensations spiking toward my release, August pulls back.

"I can do better than this," he murmurs.

Hoisting me up, he sets me on the edge of the pool with my legs still splayed. Then he presses his face where his thigh was before, lapping his tongue over my opening and flicking it across the sensitive nub above.

Bliss ricochets through my body. I lean back on my hands with a cry, unable to stop myself from swaying my hips toward him, urging him on.

A dripping form crouches beside me, and Whitt's voice reaches my ear with a tickle of heated breath. "Can I help take you to even greater heights, mighty one?"

I manage a nod, punctuating it with a whimper as August eases a finger inside me. He pulses it inside me in time with the rhythmic swipes of his tongue, and Whitt trails his fingers over my damp skin. The spymaster strokes down my spine and across my belly, then up to circle my breasts.

My head tips farther back, and Whitt leans in to support it. His fingers swirl closer and closer to my pebbled nipples as August suckles me harder. Then, just as the final surge of pleasure crashes over me, Whitt squeezes the tips of my breasts.

The extra jolt of delight sends me careening even higher. I moan, clutching his arm, my other hand grasping at August's hair.

As I come down from the high, Sylas gets out of the pool next to us. Watching the water stream over his massive, muscular form sends a renewed flare of hunger through me.

I reach for him, and he smiles, scooping me up as if I weigh nothing at all. It's like floating in the pool, this sense of being totally supported above the ground… except in Sylas's arms, I can also do *this.*

I twist against him, tucking my hand behind his neck to tangle my fingers in his hair and tugging his mouth to mine. With a groan, he claims my lips. My hip brushes the hard length of his shaft, already fully erect, and a pang forms between my legs—a longing to be filled.

But I can still feel Corwin watching all this, restraining himself. The passion inside me needs all my mates with me for it to be fully satisfied.

I beckon the Unseelie arch-lord through our bond, and he rises. "Perhaps our mate needs to see just how well we can support her," he says as he walks over to us, with an unexpectedly husky note in his voice that makes me twice as eager as before.

The raven shifter grips my thighs, and Sylas loosens his hold so that Corwin can adjust me against him, spreading my legs. He teases his fingers over my sex before positioning me over Sylas's rigid length. A strained sound of impatience escapes me, but he has to know this isn't all I need from him.

I want you in me too. If—if you *want too…* He's never taken that role before.

The only response I need is the rush of desire that careens into me through our connection. Corwin lowers his head to nip my shoulder as I sink down onto Sylas. He eases one hand away for just long enough to wrench down his boxers. Then he brushes his fingers over my other entrance with a soft murmuring that turns his touch silky with conjured slickness.

Sylas nuzzles my cheek and my neck, dappling my jaw and throat with tiny kisses and grazes of his fangs. His hardness seems to swell even more inside me, filling me with a giddy burn. Then Corwin is sliding into me too, inch by inch, until I'm suspended between the two of them, held up by the potent mix of love and lust *we've* conjured together.

They move together as if they've worked in unison their whole lives, as if no border or animosity has ever divided them. Corwin's enjoyment of our closeness and the carnal delight brought by the squeeze of my muscles around him flows into me in a continuing current. All I can do is ride the growing surge, propelled higher and higher between them, weightless amid the torrent of pleasure.

Heat sparks all through my torso and sizzles through my veins. *Oh, my love,* Corwin says silently, his breath ragged against my spine. *Oh, my soul.* Sylas steals another kiss, his groan carrying into it, and Corwin bites down on my shoulder.

I come so hard it's as if I'm literally flying, soaring up into that endless blue of the sky. Quivers radiate through every nerve in my body.

The searing bliss of Corwin's release flings me even higher. I lose my breath, shuddering and then gripping Sylas even tighter as I feel him tense and jerk with his own peak.

How could anything be wrong when we can feel this way together?

Exhaustion rolls back over me as the two arch-lords lower me to the ground. I reach for Whitt and August to join me too, and my four mates sit in a ring around me, supporting me on the ground just as two of them did in the air just minutes ago.

My breath evens out, my muscles going slack. I wish I could go to sleep right here, and maybe not wake up until the nightmares of my waking hours are over.

But those horrors aren't going to leave of their own accord. After a short rest, I force myself to stir. "We should get back. Whatever the spring can do for me, it's already done, right?"

Sylas kisses my temple and meets my gaze with his mismatched eyes. "We can spare more time if you want to relax here a little longer."

Can they really spare it, though? *I* won't be able to relax if I start worrying that I'm keeping them from everything else they need to be focused on for too long.

I ease to my feet. "I can relax in the carriage. I do feel a lot better. Maybe this was what I needed all along."

The hope in those words stays with me for the first several minutes after we set off toward the Heart. I snuggle in between Whitt and August on a cushion they've set on the carriage floor and drift into a doze.

I'm half asleep when the next attack of the curse hits me, cutting through me so deeply and sharply a scream bursts from my lips.

CHAPTER NINETEEN

Whitt

My voice spills out into the silence of my study, intoning the last few magically charged words that will bind the pieces of my spell together—and to the item I'm attaching it to. Energy tingles through me, thrumming in my throat. Then I lean back in my chair, contemplating the duskapple tart on its plain plate.

What would August have thought of my request to nab one of these if he'd known what I was going to do with it? Well, I suppose I'll find out soon enough. I'll set the process in motion, and the knowledge that it's already done should help ease any qualms he has about dishonesty.

He won't be deceiving anyone else, only making use of a pre-existing trick.

No, I don't actually feel any guilt about going ahead with this without August's preapproval. I'm simply doing my job. What makes me hesitate is the thought of how I'm going to present it to our mate.

I know what Talia would say if I told her my full intentions.

She'd refuse to have any part in my plan. The blasted rat has won her over enough that she'd put his rights over the possibility of saving her and ending this war—and he's possibly won more than I'd like of her heart as well. If Corwin is picking up on other emotions brewing inside her…

I set that thought aside and tuck the tart into a cloth pouch before looping the drawstring cord around my wrist. My mate is ill, and it's also my job to protect her. If I could go far enough to erase her screams of pain from her past as well her future, I would. Whatever anger she might feel toward me afterward will be mine to bear.

I'll bear it happily if she's well enough to lay it into me.

When I step out of the study, the hall is quiet. No screams or groans carry through the air now. After the bad series of fits on our way back from the Serene Springs, which gripped her on and off for most of the journey, she had another wrenching spell that kept her up a significant part of the night. Nothing we attempted appeared to lessen her agony at all.

By the end of it, the whites of her eyes were ruddy and her nose had started to bleed. The Murk king's destruction is seeping right through her body now.

We have to end this curse before it tears her apart completely.

Nudging open Talia's bedroom door, I find her subdued but awake, nestled against Corwin on the bed. The raven shifter nods to me in acknowledgment and kisses the top of Talia's head. She eases her arms away from him, knowing we're changing "shifts." Corwin has business to attend to in his domain, as much as I know he wants to spend every minute at our mate's side.

Technically it isn't my turn to watch over her. Sylas intended to come by in an hour or two. I'm simply getting my work done in the meantime, and I can't say I mind being in Talia's presence while I do.

As Corwin gets up, I sit down at her other side. She leans into me, a tremor running through her body against mine as if it was taking a huge amount of energy just to sit up on her own for the few moments she did. Another twist of concern winds around my gut.

We may not have much time at all. Orion wants to draw out her torment and our distress alongside hers, but he also wants to see us crushed sooner rather than later. And even if she'll survive for weeks longer, I'm afraid the curse is starting to damage her in ways we won't be able to fix even if we can free her from its continuing grasp.

I leave the pouch with the tart at the end of the bed and wrap my arms around Talia, taking all of her weight. She sags into me with a sigh that speaks of exhaustion and frustration.

"I hate feeling like this," she mutters. "So wrung out but like I can't really relax. It hurts a little bit *everywhere*."

I nuzzle her temple, my throat constricting. If my plan works, I remind myself, she won't have to feel this way for much longer.

"We're still exploring possible cures," I say. "And searching for a way to get at the source of Orion's power. Perhaps our rat shifter friend will come through with another inspiration."

I brought up Madoc on purpose to get us started on that subject. Talia reaches toward her pillow and picks up the flower-shaped charm the Murk man brought her. I hadn't realized she was keeping it so close to her.

She traces its petals, gazing down at it as if she's hoping to find some kind of answer in its stitching. The thought of her having this present from him next to her as she sleeps twists me up inside in a totally different way. I have to hold back my fangs from emerging.

Talia glances up at me. "Is Madoc all right? You've been letting him leave the cabin now and then, haven't you? And he'll have to go back to check in with Orion again at some point."

She's worried about him even when she's in such a bad state. I swallow down the knowledge that if all goes as I intend, he'll be scampering back to his king much sooner than expected.

"As far as I know, he's faring just fine," I say. "He's a rat; he must be used to holing up in tight spaces."

Sick as she is, Talia manages to shoot me a chiding look. I run my fingers up and down her back, tamping down on my guilt. "Would you like to go have a visit with him? We could have him come over to the castle like he did before so you don't have to strain yourself much."

And then I'll offer her the tart to present to him, and of course he'll take any gift she offers without the suspicion he'd level at a similar gesture from one of us fae. When he eats it, my spell will take hold all through his body without him even noticing it. And after they've spoken, I'll take him aside and "reveal" that we've discovered the location of his Refuge. That we're going to launch an attack as soon as we've gathered our forces.

Then August and I will decide on arranging a convenient moment when he can escape. Madoc will dash right back to warn his king—and my spell will let us track him there. We'll descend on the Refuge right at his heels and destroy both his king and the false Heart that's powering all our curses.

Simple, elegant, and quick—the best sort of plan. If Madoc won't help us confront his king directly, then why shouldn't I force his hand?

Maybe he'll even thank me in the end.

Talia rubs her mouth. "I would like to spend time with him, just to give him some company. But I don't want him to feel bad when he sees me and can tell nothing he brought really helped."

Oh, my mighty, tender-hearted mate. I gently kiss the side of her head. "I think he'll be more worried if he doesn't hear from you, and that he'll appreciate spending the time with you enough to offset the rest."

Talia raises her eyebrows. "Are you starting to believe that helping me really does matter to him and that it's not all some kind of trick?"

I let out a soft laugh and answer totally honestly, "It's not very hard to believe that, the way he's stuck his neck out for you."

The way he talks to her. The way he looks at her.

Talia tucks her hand around mine, twining our fingers. "I'm glad. It was good, seeing the two of you working together. Maybe you'll be able to come up with another plan like that. Thank you for giving him a chance. I know it isn't easy with all the history between the Seelie and the Murk."

Her gratitude sends a sharper jab of guilt right through my chest. I have to force my smile. "I'm willing to keep an open mind if it makes it easier for us to protect you and the rest of the Mists."

"Good. You know…" She pauses as if it's taking a moment for

her to get her thoughts in order. "It isn't really fair that the Murk lost so much. So what if a lot of them liked to lie and trick people, and that weakened their connection to the real Heart? Why should Madoc or any of the others have had to start out already so distant from it when they hadn't done anything yet? And—*you* and the other fae of the Mists find all kinds of ways of tricking each other and giving the wrong impression by talking around the truth, but as long as you stick to the letter of the law, the Heart's given you a pass. At least… at least the Murk are upfront in their lies instead of acting like they're being truthful when they're not."

She lapses into silence again, leaving me struggling for words. She can't know what I was thinking. The unfairness she just commented on has obviously been on her mind for a while.

But I can't say she's wrong, can I? I *have* deceived my fellow fae, more times than I can count even since I've known her. I mean to do the same with Madoc just minutes from now—laying out just the right words to make him think what I want him to without actually saying anything that's strictly untrue.

Is that really so much better? Does it make me so much more deserving?

As far as the Heart is concerned, apparently so. But to Talia…

A knot forms in my stomach. She just thanked me for being someone I'm not, someone much more open and generous. And, blast it all, I want to be the man she sees me as. She's always found the goodness in me even when I had trouble believing in myself.

My other hand reaches for the pouch with the tart, but I don't mention it to her, only carry it with me as I help her downstairs to the summer-side entrance. A quick word to one of the castle guards sends him off to fetch Madoc. Talia settles into the grass, and I magically summon a few pillows from inside the castle so she can lean back against them to better preserve her strength.

I can still go through with my plan. I haven't backed out of it. I simply want to observe Madoc once more to be sure of my resolve before I make the final arrangements.

I find myself watching my mate as much as the direction where Madoc will appear. The moment he comes into view, her face brightens, her posture steadying just a little. Seeing him *reassures* her in a way I can't explain.

Or maybe I don't want to because of the jealousy that flares at the same time.

She isn't wrong about his reaction to her obviously weakened state. The pleased light that gleams in his eyes at the sight of her dims as he gets closer, his expression clouding over with concern. He sits down across from her gingerly as if he's afraid even moving near her might cause her pain.

He doesn't comment on it directly, but the first words out of his mouth are, "I've been thinking over all the healing spells I've witnessed, everything I've heard or seen about curses… and ways that maybe I could get more information out of Orion when I go back. As soon as—"

Talia holds up her hand with a gentle smile that I'd swear could melt the hardest heart. "I know. It's okay. It is what it is. I'd rather talk about something happier. Have you been enjoying the books you brought?"

The corner of Madoc's mouth quirks up at a bittersweet angle. In that moment, there isn't one part of me that can deny the devotion with which he's gazing at her.

It's a pity he isn't especially skilled in the healing arts. I have no doubt he'd stretch himself to the limits of his magic if he believed he could cure Talia on his own. He obviously has plenty of that Murk magic at his disposal, given his skill with illusions. If only it could be channeled—

An idea sparks in my head so abruptly that for a second it blots out everything else. I blink, testing the edges of the inspiration, reining in my eagerness in case I spot some flaw. But the more I prod at it, the more excitement swells inside me.

I should have considered this earlier. But I didn't—because I didn't really trust Madoc enough to open my mind that much.

It still might not work. But it feels like a much more solid possibility than our trip to the springs or Madoc's little cures.

And it doesn't require me betraying my mate's hard-won trust.

My mind keeps spinning, working through the details, as Talia and Madoc discuss his recent reads and then other favorite books, a few they're both familiar with. It's far too soon that my mate's energy begins to flag. I notice the drooping of her shoulders, and Madoc glances at me in the same instant.

He turns back to Talia, giving her the respect of addressing her rather than calling on me to make the decision. "You look like you could use some more rest. As much as I enjoy getting a break from the cabin, I'll feel better knowing you're keeping your strength up as much as you can."

Talia sighs, but she accepts his point with a dip of her head—which tells me she's faltering even more than she's letting show. The guards converge around Madoc to escort him away, and Sylas comes striding over from the castle of Hearth-by-the-Heart to meet us.

My brother gives me a quizzical glance, and I shoot him a smile that promises more explanation later. "I thought the mite could use a little fresh air and social stimulation," I say out loud.

Sylas hums to himself and gathers Talia up. I brush a kiss to her knuckles before heading after the guards.

I catch up with them at the edge of the woods. "Hold on a moment," I say, and they stop immediately. A cadre-chosen's words are worth that much.

Madoc's quizzical glance is much more suspicious than Sylas's was, but given what I intended to be saying to him when I first imagined this conversation, I suppose I can't blame him.

The smile I offer him I mean just as much as the one I gave my lord. "Our last collaboration didn't end up going so well, but maybe that's because there were too many conflicting factors in the mix," I say. "I have an idea for another way we could work together that might be just what Talia needs to set her free from your king's curse."

CHAPTER TWENTY

Talia

I've usually enjoyed carriage rides—the rush of the landscape sweeping by, the wash of the breeze. Today, every tiny hitch of the vehicle with the shifting currents in the air sends a splinter of pain through my ribs or my gut.

It hurts more if I'm holding myself at all upright. My mates created a sort of nest for me out of pillows on the floor of the carriage, where I can sit with my back resting against the bench by the stern, totally cushioned and out of the reach of the wind. I don't really like being down here where I can't see much except the sky and the upper branches of any trees we pass, but I like the pain even less.

I know there are two other carriages around us even though I can't see them. Sylas is directing one and Corwin the other. Each carries the skilled healers my arch-lords already assembled for my care as well as several warriors in case we need their protection. August and Whitt are in charge of the vehicle I'm in, which also holds Madoc and his now-typical contingent of four guards, as well as a couple of others who are scanning the landscape around us rather than the Murk man.

August has spent most of the ride sitting on the bench opposite me while Madoc and Whitt consult on our exact course. We're heading to the area of the fringelands that contains the portal that connects to the spot closest to the Refuge and the Murk Heart. Madoc hesitated to give full directions ahead of time, even though there are dozens of other portals in the same area and no way for us to know which is the key one without him specifying.

He was probably afraid that my mates would change their mind about their current strategy and attempt an invasion instead. I'm not sure he was wrong to worry about that. The wary alertness in August's glances around us suggest he's prepared for a battle.

But mostly he's focused on me. He's set his legs to one side of me so I can lean my head against his knee, appreciating the warmth of his body. Any time I wince, he tenses. He brought a sack full of delicacies that he put together in the kitchen before we left, but I haven't had any appetite. My stomach feels like it's stuffed full already—with needles and jagged gravel.

"We would have done this back in Hearth-by-the-Heart, but we didn't want to drain whatever power Madoc has left if it didn't work there," he says with a note of apology in his tone. "We might only get one real chance. We won't risk bringing you right through to the human world, and there our magic might not be up to the challenge anyway. But Madoc's component is the most important since he's the only one who can tackle the Murk aspects of the curse. He says he should be able to draw a little on their Heart just being close to the portal."

I nod. Most of that my mates have already explained to me in bits and pieces—or maybe more coherently, and I just haven't been able to hold my attention well enough to realize. How much is August reminding me to reassure me and how much for himself?

"Do you really think there's much chance it'll work?" I can't help asking, studying his expression. August is the most earnest of my mates; he isn't in the habit of using subterfuge. I'll get the most accurate sense of the odds from his reaction.

He smiles, and it looks genuine enough to lift my spirits despite my discomfort.

"I think it's the best chance we've gotten," he says. "We should have tried it earlier—if it didn't rely so much on Madoc's contribution… But mingling magical affinities is a longstanding if not all that common practice. There are lots of accounts of it working. We just need to get the balance right and to give him enough of a boost of energy to work through the trickier parts of his king's magic."

I thanked Whitt earlier for being willing to work together with our Murk ally, and now he's taken that alliance a step farther. I don't totally understand the magical theory of how it all works, but they're going to combine August and the other healers' medical magic with Madoc's Murk-based power to try to unravel the curse. The way Whitt described it to me, they'll be able to construct an effect kind of like the bunch of them are actually one super powerful Murk healer.

If this strategy doesn't work, I can't imagine what would… other than managing to destroy the Murk Heart itself. Which we'll probably still have to do to end the other curses afflicting the Mists. But I know as well as my mates do that it's going to be difficult fighting Orion on his own turf. I may not have enough time left for them to save me by winning that war.

My view may be too restricted for me to see much from my nest of pillows, but I can tell we're getting close to the fringes from the rising humidity in the air, turning it hot and sticky against my skin. My head starts to burn as if the weather has provoked a fever. August murmurs a cooling spell over me that provides a little relief, and then Whitt calls him over to discuss something.

As I lean back on my cushions, gazing up at the sky that's now streaked with clouds, Madoc picks his way across the benches to join me. He moves tentatively, as if expecting to be called back by the guards at any second. Was he waiting until August left to come over to me at all? I guess it'd make sense that he wouldn't feel terribly welcome around my mates.

No one hollers at him, though. He stops for a moment when he reaches me, the wind licking through his pale hair and turning it even more tousled than usual, and then sinks down on the bench next to where I'm leaning. He's careful not to sit too close, leaving enough space between us that we don't touch.

The pensive look on his face makes me want to reach out and squeeze his hand, to reassure him that I'm happy to have his company even if the other fae are still unsure of his loyalties, but I'm afraid of the reaction that large a movement will provoke in my body. So I simply adjust my position a little so I'm angled to face him, still tucked against my pillows.

Even that small movement provokes a wince, and Madoc flinches as if he feels responsible. "It's gotten worse again, hasn't it?" he says, looking me over.

"I'm managing," I say automatically.

He gives me a tight smile. "You're good at covering it up, but I've had a lot of practice at keeping things hidden myself. I can recognize the signs. You don't have to hide it with me to spare *my* feelings."

A sigh tumbles out of me. "What if it's easier for *me* to deal with it if I'm pretending it's not so bad?"

"Then that's fair enough." Madoc pauses, his gaze lifting to the landscape around us. "Do you want to be left alone, or would talking help too?"

I'm not sure how much talking *I* want to do, but listening to him could be a welcome distraction. Not just from the pains of the curse, but from all the other worries hanging over us as well. I look up at the Murk man, thinking of the glimpses of his life I got in the Refuge, the pieces he's shared with me since, all the weight I know he's carrying.

I want to know him—know what drives the complicated but brave and devoted man I've slowly come to understand. But I don't think I can handle anything too serious right now.

"Tell me about the things that've made you happiest in your life," I say. "I want to hear about something good."

Madoc blinks as if surprised by the request or maybe by the idea that anything in his life has been all that happy. But then he settles more solidly into his seat, his heavy-lidded eyes going distant with thought.

"I told you I spent most of my childhood in an orphanage," he says. "That one was under a street that had a popular candy shop on it. Once a week, the fae running the orphanage would let us go up in the middle of the night while the shop was closed and pick one treat to eat then or save for later. I think I ended up trying just about everything that store carried, getting a little thrill out of what flavors I'd stumble on next week by week."

The curls of my mouth twitch upward. "So that's how you got your taste for human snacks."

"It must be, although they had pretty different types back then. The best night, though, was when we found the shop had held some kind of party and no one had cleaned up yet. There was part of a cake left, and streamers and fancier snacks—we romped around like it was all of our birthdays at once. It felt like some higher power must care what happened to us, if it'd give us a gift like that."

The bittersweet thread that's crept into his voice tells me he doesn't see the joyful night that way anymore, but it's clearly still a fond memory. It's hard to imagine the man next to me as an excited child, delighting in something so simple that I'd have taken for granted when I was little.

"What else?" I nudge.

He hums to himself. "The first time I drew a star chart and really saw the meaning in the patterns there—that was exciting. There was an old Murk woman who taught me a lot of the skills, and I always enjoyed going to see her. She had a voice like crisp autumn leaves. It could spark images right in your head if you listened right."

"You'll have to show me how it all works sometime."

He glances at me, startled, and then smiles. "I'd like to see what you make of it. And there's also…" He draws in a breath and hesitates.

"What?" I ask when he doesn't go on, flicking my hand to tap his lower leg.

Madoc's smile twists. "A lot of my happy memories aren't things you're likely to be happy hearing about. Meeting Orion, taking in the power of his Heart, realizing that there was a real chance the Murk could get the home we deserve. Seeing the same hope in so many others around me. Taking steps to get us closer to that goal, knowing I was helping make up for all the things so many of us have lost…" He trails off, a shadow crossing his face.

My throat tightens. "I can understand why those things made you happy. I know… I know everything you've done with Orion has been because of how much you care about the rest of the Murk. I *like* that you care so much about them and that you've worked so hard to make things better for them, not just yourself. It's only the way Orion wants you to get your home back that's a problem."

"His way used to be how *I* wanted it to happen too, so maybe you're overly generous." Madoc lets out a rough laugh, his gaze drifting away from me again. "I just was so caught up in the dream of having all the Mists for us to roam freely through, and so angry with the fae who ran us out—"

He meets my eyes again. "The anger clouded my vision, and even when I was out there watching to see how you fared, I didn't *really* see. I should have realized it wasn't right, the way he was using you. I should have warned you sooner, not dragged you off to put you under his power even more."

The anguish of his admission turns his voice even hoarser than usual. I rest my hand against his leg again, an ache closing around my heart. "It probably wouldn't have made any difference. It might even have been worse that way. I don't know if any of us would have believed how much power he's built up if I hadn't witnessed it myself. No one would have trusted you at all. And he could still have triggered the curse in me. It's not like you could have saved me from that."

"I guess not. But all the same, I'm sorry." Madoc's throat bobs. "I'm not sure you even should forgive me. I'll do whatever I can to reverse the damage I helped him do to you, today and every day after."

I don't know what to say to answer the emotion in his words, and then a sharper pain shoots down my spine. A gasp escapes me. I pull my legs closer, hugging them, bracing myself to ride out the next onslaught of agony.

It doesn't escalate just yet, though. I close my eyes, but I feel Madoc's fingers brush over my hair in the lightest of caresses.

When I don't pull away, he repeats the gesture of comfort a little less cautiously. His touch sends a pleasant quiver through my nerves that I can't look at too closely right now. Not when another jab of pain slices through my stomach. I grit my teeth.

Then the carriage eases to a halt. Madoc stands.

August's voice reaches me as if from much farther away. "The others are going ahead to make sure the area is safe. We'll join them in a moment."

He comes over to me, but Madoc doesn't move away. I'm aware of him still standing over me as if guarding me as August crouches in front of me. "Will you need me to carry you over, Sweetness?" my mate asks with heart-breaking tenderness.

The pain has subsided a little. My thoughts have jumbled, but I know that I want to stand on my own two feet as long as I can. "I'll be okay," I murmur. "I might just need a little help getting out of the carriage."

"Of course."

While we wait to follow the others, there's a span of time where my thoughts are blurred by another pain that's not as sharp but digs in deeper, longer, with an insistent throbbing. I'm starting to think I won't be able to walk after all when Whitt calls over, "There's the signal. Let's get over there and begin."

The fae guards disembark around me with thumps of their boots hitting the ground. Madoc stays with me, steadying my balance with August as the two of them guide me out of the vehicle. As the Murk jumps down beside me, I sway and catch his arm to stop myself from falling—

And a harsh cry rings out up ahead where the fog is thicker between the trees. Footsteps thunder; bodies dart through the haze.

"Everyone, to me, *now*!" Sylas shouts from beyond my view. "We're under attack."

CHAPTER TWENTY-ONE

Talia

At his lord and brother's call, August jolts forward a step before he glances at me, his eyes wide, torn between staying with me and defending the rest of his people. The guards are already dashing to Sylas's aid. August's lips pull back in a snarl of frustration.

"Stay here," he orders both Madoc and me. "Keep out of sight." Then he charges into the fog with the others.

He reaches them not a moment too soon, from what I can tell. Grunts and groans and snarls are filtering through the haze—the battle already sounds desperate.

I strain my neck to see around the side of the carriage, but even that tiny motion sets off a wave of pain through my body. It condenses in the middle of my abdomen, right between my heart and my stomach, and continues to radiate in a steady, searing pulse.

"What's going on?" I ask, my voice coming out ragged.

Madoc frowns, peering into the fog. "I don't know." At a yelp and a raven-ish shriek that carries from the fray, he winces. His fingers tighten where he's still gripping my arm.

All at once, he tugs me farther around the back of the carriage, where I won't be able to see anything at all. His breath is coming fast.

Panic lances through the pain inside me. "Are they heading this way?"

"Not yet, but if they can cut through your fae to get to you, they will." His eyes dart to the trees around us, his mouth pressing flat, and my muddled mind pieces together one clear thought.

It's the Murk. My mates and their warriors have been ambushed by rat shifters. Who else *could* it be? Why would any of the fae of the Mists want to prevent me from being healed?

"They'll look for you at the carriage first," Madoc says, his expression hardening as if he's made a difficult decision. "We can't stay here—we can't take the chance."

He wraps his arm right around me, easing my own arm across his shoulders so that he can support my weight. I stumble across the ground next to him, barely able to control my steps. Every press of my feet against the forest floor sends fresh knives up through my thighs and belly.

I grit my teeth against a cry that might bring the attackers straight to us. A hiss still escapes me.

"I'm sorry," Madoc mutters. Then he scoops me right off the ground, tucking me close against his chest. His stormy scent fills my nose, matching the furor in his eyes.

He hurries several paces away from the carriage to a spot where a few trees stand close enough together to provide a decent amount of shelter. There, he lowers me so I can lean against the trunks. He pauses for a moment to touch my cheek, gazing into my eyes as if trying to read just how much distress I'm in.

"I'll get you away from here—back to your Heart," he says. "I won't let them hurt you more. I wish— That's the only thing I *can* do."

He turns and starts to intone magical words under his breath, spreading his hands over the damp earth. Pebbles and twigs jitter and dart across the ground to combine into a heap beneath his palms. More and more come, along with clumps of mud and bits of bark—a mess of debris that makes no sense to me.

Pain stabs through my gut, and I muffle another gasp. My jaw is aching from how tightly I'm clenching it. I close my eyes, trying to think myself away from the growing agony, to run somewhere inside myself where I can avoid the need to scream and sob with it.

A shudder wracks my body. I start to slump to the side, my muscles refusing to hold me up. My back scrapes across the trunk as I topple.

At the squeak that slips from my lips, Madoc whirls around. He catches me just before my head smacks into the dirt. As he eases me upright, his arms slide around me again, and for a moment he just hugs me. I tip my head against his shoulder, a whimper working its way up my throat despite my best efforts.

"I've got you," he says, his voice raw. "You'll get through this. You're too fucking strong for Orion to get the better of you—I *know* it."

In that moment, I can't say *I* know it. I feel as if I'm already unraveling, sheared into slivers of myself as I do.

Madoc keeps me nestled against his body as he swivels back to his work. I tense and shiver with a sharper hail of pain, and he alternates between the words of magic he's chanting and murmurs of reassurance.

When the agony eases back briefly, I manage to glance over to the heap he was conjuring. Except now I can see it's not just a heap or a mess.

The pebbles and twigs and the rest have assembled into the vague shape of a boat—so narrow only one person could sit in any part, only maybe five feet long but growing as Madoc continues working his magic.

Of course. He wouldn't be able to direct the Seelie carriage or Corwin's Unseelie vehicle with his magic, so he's making one of his own. The Murk I talked to in the Refuge did say they'd found their own way of traveling quickly through the Mists.

"It'll only take another minute or two before it'll fly," Madoc says before taking up his incantation again. The strain the hasty magic is taking on him carries through his tone and the flexing of his muscles where I'm pressed against his solid frame.

He's barely added to his carriage when footsteps and shouts ring out closer behind us. I flinch in Madoc's arms instinctively before I recognize August's voice, rough with worry. "Talia! Talia, where are you?"

"We're here!" I call back, the words coming out more a croak than anything else. But August hears me. He races over, twigs crackling in his wake.

Madoc stands to meet him, setting me on my feet but keeping me close against him for support. He's just straightened up when August reaches us, my other mates and a few of the guards right behind him.

August's eyes are wild, blood streaking past one of them from a cut on his forehead. Corwin is bleeding too, from a wound on his shoulder that I only catch the ache of now that I'm seeing it, I was so lost in my own pains. That's all I have time to take in before Whitt is springing at us, wrenching me from Madoc's grasp.

As he gathers me against him, the other men stalk toward Madoc, who backs away with his hands raised and his face paling.

"You set them up to be ready for us," Sylas growls. "And then you thought you'd steal away our mate?"

No, that isn't what happened at all. I try to speak, but as I open my mouth, the curse erupts through my torso, and all that comes out is a squeal of pain.

My mates are already lunging at Madoc. He shoots a frantic glance at me and then springs away, transforming into his rat form in midair and dashing between the trees to vanish into the haze. August moves to sprint after him, his shoulders hunching with the start of his transformation, but just then one of the Seelie carriages soars into view.

"My lord," one of the warriors on it calls out, his arm hanging limp at his side.

"We have to go," Sylas barks, and August draws up short. The Seelie arch-lord raises his voice to echo through the hazy woods. "But the treacherous rat should know that if he shows one whisker around my domain again, he'll be torn to pieces, along with any others of his kind."

No. This isn't right. I shake my head against Whitt's chest as he hefts me into the carriage, but he doesn't understand.

"It's all right now, mite," he whispers in my ear in a soothing tone. "We've got to get you out of here before the Murk follow us. They won't venture far from the fringes." He looks past me to the arch-lords who've just climbed in, the carriage jolting forward the second they're inside. "He was fashioning a vehicle of his own, did you see?" he says to them, his tone sharpening. "Heart only knows where he was planning on taking her."

Home, I think. *He was only going to take me home where I'd be safe.* But the pain is jumbling my mind too much for me to form any kind of coherent speech. I can barely even follow what's happening around me.

The Murk attacked. My mates and the guards fended them off—but not completely. Only enough to come for me and escape? *All* of them are bleeding here and there—there's a warrior slumped in the bottom of the carriage with one of the healers murmuring hastily over her—a few snarls still echo out of the fog. Are we leaving people behind? That's not right. That's not—

The next searing blade cuts right through my chest down to my core, and a scorching blaze of agony explodes in my belly. The scream I've been bottling up for so long rips out of me. I double over in Whitt's arms, my muscles quaking, cramps burning all through my abdomen. They throb on and on and—

Whitt makes a choked sound, his arms going rigid around me. "We need the healers with Talia. *Right now*. Please…"

There's something horrifyingly desperate in his voice, but I don't really understand. Nothing's changed—nothing's *worse* than it was before, is it? He only hates seeing me in so much agony. He only—

The world tilts as gentle hands come to rest on my belly and my thighs. I become vaguely aware that something down there is… wet. The fabric of my dress, sticking damply to my skin. What—?

As my eyes pop open, the three healers who made it onto this carriage weave their voices together in a single chorus. I stare at the place where they're touching me, where the pain rakes its claws through me again—and all I can think is that I might as well already be dead, the way I look. How can they fix this?

There's blood on *me*. So much blood, spreading all through the skirt of my dress even as I watch, pooling beneath me on the cushions.

How can— No one cut *me*. Has the curse slashed through something deep inside me?

Then, as the healers' increasingly ragged voices swell around us, as August reaches to squeeze my shoulder with a shaking hand and stark horror reverberates through my bond with Corwin, understanding hits me.

I'm not dead. I'm losing the other life I was growing inside me.

No. No! I rally against the realization with everything I have in me—but almost everything in me is agony.

The curse's endless blades pierce my lungs, my heart, and then my mind, and the world around me blinks away into nothingness.

CHAPTER TWENTY-TWO

Sylas

I'm not sure how many hours we've all been gathered around Talia's bedside when I notice that Corwin has left us. I raise my head from where I've been gazing down at my unconscious mate and realize only my brothers remain around me.

My hand stills where I've been stroking her hair continuously, as if the gesture will eventually summon her back to us. "Where did Corwin go?"

Whitt shrugs where he's sitting at Talia's other side, caressing her hand. "I can't say I was paying that much attention to Lord Bird."

There's no hostility in the nickname, but he can't give it any humor either. I suspect he feels just as broken as I do, watching Talia lie there, unable to rouse her from this new stage of the curse. Not knowing if we've only lost the child we expected to welcome or our mate as well.

This is exactly what the Murk king wanted: all of us struggling with terror for her and a sense of impending mourning. Distracted from whatever plans he's shaping. I can't let him accomplish the rest of his evil ends, but I couldn't walk away from my mate right after the tragedy. My fellow arch-lords are capable of handling the security of the realms for a short while.

The soft, erratic patter of Talia's pulse that my wolfish ears can pick up only reassures me slightly. She's still alive for now, but the curse hasn't stopped its horrible progression. If there's more ahead while she's still living, I have no doubt it'll be even worse, as hard as that is to imagine.

August stirs where he's been massaging one of Talia's feet, looking as if he's trying to coax wellness into her with the press of his thumbs. His lips pull back with one of the fits of fierceness that come over him whenever he glances at Talia's face, probably thinking of the vermin who did this to her. He manages to retract his fangs before answering. "He didn't say where he was going, just walked out."

The knowledge sits uncomfortably with me. Corwin has been most affected out of all of us. He's barely spoken in the hours since we returned to the border castle. I haven't seen him drink so much as a sip of water, let alone eat. Once I glanced at him and my deadened eye picked up a faded image of a raven's head imposed over his own, thrown back with its beak open in a wrenching cry.

The Unseelie arch-lord holds his emotions close. He started to shut down when Talia was missing too. I don't want to leave our mate even now, but I do have other responsibilities that will protect her and her happiness as well as the rest of the fae world.

I don't think she'd want me to ignore her soul-twined mate's distress.

"I'll find him and speak to him," I say. "And we'll need to regroup and put all the energy we can into finding the Refuge and destroying the Murk's false Heart."

I don't care about Madoc's warnings about the foolhardiness of attempting to challenge Orion in his home so far from our own. That rat was as treacherous as the rest of them, leading us into an ambush so his people could overwhelm us. We barely made it out alive. Several of our warriors fell to give the rest of us a clear path back to the carriages. There were too many of the rats—we might have all fallen if we hadn't decided we needed to run for it as quickly as we did.

I hate having fled in the wake of an enemy, but I'd hate to have seen my brothers, my mate, and all the rest of my men carved up by rat claws even more.

Whitt nods. "Call for us if you need us, and we'll send word if anything changes with her."

I stalk out of the bedroom, my heart so heavy it seems to have sunk to my gut, and sniff out the raven's scent in the air. He's gone downstairs, into the winter side of the palace…

When I hear voices down the hall, I pause and walk the rest of the way on silent, stealthy feet, keeping close to the wall. Corwin is standing in the entrance room with the woman from his coterie whom Talia's become friendly with—Zelpha. It's obvious from her voice that she's upset.

"I shouldn't be the one giving those orders to the flock and everyone else," she says. "They'll want to hear it from you. They're already at a loss, knowing the state Talia's in, knowing—" She cuts herself off before her voice gets more ragged.

"I have other things to deal with," Corwin says, more sharply than I've ever heard him talk to his inner circle. "Between you, Olander, and Verik, you should be able to keep things in order for a little while. Meriol and Domhnall will be returning soon if you need extra support."

Something about his words sends a prickle of apprehension down my back, and Zelpha looks as if they've struck her the same way. She narrows her eyes. "How long exactly are you planning on being busy with 'other things'? What's going on, Corwin? I know that with Talia so—"

"We aren't talking about this," Corwin interrupts. "Please go carry out the orders you've been given."

I get the impression Zelpha might want to say more, but she shuts her mouth and turns on her heel, her expression in the glimpse I catch of it not at all happy.

Corwin shakes himself in a gesture that reminds me of a bird setting its feathers smooth, and my apprehension grows. I step out into the entrance room—and at the same moment his older coterie man, Verik, comes hustling in.

The gray-haired man bobs his head lower than usual at the sight of Corwin. "I'm sorry to interrupt you. A small party has arrived from Brambledown. Their lord's chief warrior has come down with the curse."

Corwin closes his eyes for a moment, looking as if there are a few curses *he'd* like to put into words. As I walk over to him and Verik, his stance turns even more rigid. "You'll need to inform them of my mate's current condition. Tell them we're doing everything we can to see her well again, but she's incapable of carrying out her healing ritual for the time being. And offer my deepest apologies."

Verik's mouth twists, but he bobs his head again and heads back out. Corwin lets out a long sigh and looks at me. I catch the briefest flicker of hope before he takes in my expression and it dies. He must be able to tell I haven't come with good news.

"She hasn't even woken, has she?" he says.

"No. But Whitt and August will alert us right away if she does." I glance toward the doorway. "Word hasn't spread all the way through the winter realm yet?" We've had several representatives from other domains arrive at Hearth-by-the-Heart and the summer side of the border castle already to express their condolences.

"I'd imagine most know by now that she's been faltering, but this latest— Brambledown is one of the more distant domains. It won't take long after this." He rubs his forehead. "Did you need something?"

"I was surprised that you left without speaking to any of us," I say. "And I'm more surprised to overhear that you apparently have business you're attending to that you haven't mentioned. We need to move against the Murk quickly and decisively—and that means planning our strategy together."

In that instant, there's a light in Corwin's eyes so furious and yet wounded it reminds me of a tuskcat caught in a snare. "My soul-twined mate is hovering on the verge of death after days of agony," he says in the same curt voice he used with Zelpha. "She's lost the child I'd have considered mine regardless of its exact parentage. If I need to take some time to myself, I think I'm owed it."

He spins on his heel as if he thinks that'll be the end of the discussion, and not just apprehension but alarm clangs through me with a creeping suspicion. He's only taken two steps toward the doorway before I spring into his path, blocking him.

"You can have all the moments to yourself that you need," I say in a low voice, "but I ask you for Talia's sake to tell me where you're going."

Corwin outright glares at me with a fury I've never seen cross his face before, even when he was telling off his colleagues for disrespecting Talia. "I'm doing what has to be done. Get out of my way."

He tries to step around me, but I side-step and snatch at his arm. Corwin jerks back before my fingers can catch hold and shifts in a blink, but I manage to grab one of his raven feet before he's flown high enough to escape my reach. With a furious squawk, he pecks at my hand and then shifts again, shoving me backward with the hands of his man.

I sprawl on the floor but whip around in time to knock his feet out from under him with my heel. Sputtering, Corwin thumps on the ground and rolls over. The next second, I've pounced on him. I stare down at him in wolf form, my lips curled back. But no growl fills my throat, only a dull ache of grief.

Before he can fight me any more, I shift again so I can speak, letting my greater weight hold him in place. "You are *not* going to go off there and try to take on the blasted Murk king all by yourself."

The flicker of Corwin's gaze tells me I'm right. "Who said anything about taking on the king?" he asks haughtily, but it's too late for him to dissemble.

I glower at him. "Do you think I don't want to as well? Every time I *think* of those wretched rats I—" I cut off that sentence with a gnash of my teeth, anger surging through my chest alongside my grief. "Maybe I don't feel it quite the same way you do with your bond, but I understand enough. And I know that neither of us has a hope of destroying the threat on our own. We're going to have a hard enough time with the full force of our warriors behind us."

"But that will take time," Corwin says, giving up on any pretense. "He won't be expecting anything yet—he won't be expecting a single raven. I could get to him and slash out his throat before he even realizes he's under attack. I know where to go—approximately. I saw which portal one of the vermin we injured darted back through."

My heart leaps at the thought that we're that close to finding the Refuge, but anguish for the man beneath me washes through the rest of me. "Maybe you're right. Maybe that part would work. But killing him won't end the curse. You need to destroy this Heart he's made. You have your raven's logic—you can't tell me you honestly believe you'll be able to banish that all by yourself with all of his supporters shrieking for your blood."

Corwin grits his teeth, but then he sags against the floor, the fight going completely out of him. "I don't know. I thought… maybe if I worked the right magic to tie it to him somehow… It wasn't a solid plan. I meant to figure it out on the way there. And if it didn't work, then at least I'd send the Murk into disarray with their king's death while our larger force moved in to finish the job I started."

"And while you'd die starting it," I have to point out. "You can't for one moment believe that's what Talia would want. And if you didn't even make it to Orion, then it'd all be for nothing. Worse than nothing, because then they'll know we've located them and we'll lose any other element of surprise."

"But she— If I lose her too…"

He sounds so hopeless I pull back—warily, in case he was waiting for an opening. But Corwin just sits up, rubbing his shoulder with a vaguely abashed expression. He doesn't quite meet my eyes. "I can see my idea might have been foolhardy, but I have to do something. I can't just leave her lying there like that—who knows what she might be going through that I can't even feel—" His breath rasps with unspoken emotion.

"I understand," I say. "And we aren't letting them get away with this. Starting with the traitor who led us into that trap."

Corwin's eyes flash. "Have your colleagues already sent the proof to turn his king against him? I'd like to see how much he likes the reward he'll get in return for his *loyalty*."

I shake my head, a weightier anger settling in my gut. "Not yet. I told them to wait until I'd had a chance to think on it. And what I think is this: we use it the same way Orion has meant to use Talia against us. We prepare as quickly as we can to strike, and the moment we're ready, we send the message on. Let *him* be distracted by the double-crosser in his ranks just when we descend on him."

Corwin smiles thinly. "I dislike borrowing a rat's tactics, but I do appreciate the poetic justice—and the strength of the strategy. Perhaps it'll be what turns the tide for us."

He pushes himself to his feet and looks down the hall toward Talia's room, then toward the entrance he meant to leave through on his suicidal quest. He squares his shoulders. "They *are* going to pay," he says in a quiet voice so laced with menace I'm sure I'd never want to be on this man's bad side. "Both the king and the traitor. There could still be a chance…"

He stops, swipes his hand across his eyes, and takes a deep breath. "But you're right. It isn't much of a chance, and our mate deserves more than a half-cocked effort that might do as much damage to us as it does to them. I'd have shown our hand too early. I—I apologize for my carelessness."

I cuff him lightly on the shoulder. "I admire your dedication to our mate. Knowing you'd go to such lengths to defend her only makes me more glad to stand by your side. You ravens spend so much time focused on staying even-handed and balanced in your reactions that it's no wonder you fly right off the handle when you give your emotions free rein. Let's put all our strengths together with our colleagues' and come up with the surest way of crushing those vermin so thoroughly they never see the light of day again."

And—Heart help us all, especially Talia—let it work.

CHAPTER TWENTY-THREE

Talia

Everything is melting together. I'm walking across the ice fields between the Unseelie arch-lords' domains, and with one step I'm picking my way through the forests around my pack's former home of Hearthshire. A reddish haze seeps through everything, thickening and then spinning me around.

I'm lost. I need to get back to—to somewhere. But every part of me aches, and my head keeps spinning. My feet stumble under me. A fever sears through my veins.

I blink, and I'm standing in the hazy woods of the fringelands. Madoc runs up to me and throws his arms around me.

I sink into his embrace automatically, seeking the solid steadiness of his body, the stormy scent that speaks of the fire inside him.

Even though I'm already burning up, I want to absorb that fire. I want to—I want to kiss him, tuck myself against him with no clothing between us, listen to his gently hoarse voice telling me of the grand future he wants to conjure for his people, for us…

No, that's not right. I can't—

I spin away from him, and just like that, he vanishes. I trip onto the grass outside the border castle.

This is my home. Where I live with the men I love. I shouldn't be thinking—I shouldn't be *feeling*—

But a different sort of ache has formed in my chest with Madoc's disappearance. There's something in him that calls to me, even if it shouldn't.

I just have to ignore it. Preventing this war, or at least preventing it from destroying my home—that's what matters. That and my mates—where are they?

A sob fills my throat, and I turn around only to sway and topple right onto my back. The sky spins overhead.

I've lost them all. I've lost so much. Even—

There's faint sunlight seeping past a curtain. A gentle hand drifts across my forehead, holding a soft cloth that wipes sweat away. I blink and manage to focus on the face above me, pale with overlarge eyes and framed by sleek, flaxen hair.

"Talia?" Harper says with a sharp intake of breath. Her head jerks around to look at someone else. "She's awake! At least more than before."

I wet my lips, still feeling dizzy even though I'm not moving at all. Is the bed spinning under me?

Astrid comes into view, the wizened fae warrior's face looking more worn than usual. A smile touches her lips when I meet her eyes. "There you are. You've been gone a while."

She doesn't say that they were worried I wouldn't come back, but I know they must have been. *I* was worried, somewhere deep beneath the delirium of fever dreams.

I inhale slowly, testing my lungs. I can only take in a little air before the curse starts to jab at them. The pain echoes all the way down to my feet now.

There's another burning sensation around my abdomen. My hand goes to my belly, and tears rush to my eyes with a jolt of memory. My throat chokes up so much it takes me a minute to force the words out. "The baby…"

Astrid's mouth twists, and Harper blinks hard. I already knew—

lost, so much I've lost—but the grief smacks into me as if I've been hit by a car.

I squeeze my eyes shut, taking one shallow breath after another, my fingers curling toward my palms. I want to tear and rip, I want to punch and claw… I can't even say what. I just want to unleash this horrible wrenching sensation inside me on something else.

"I'll get your mates," Astrid says, with a rustle as she moves from the bed. "They wanted to know as soon as you were lucid. They stayed with you for hours, but they couldn't cure you that way."

She slips out of the room. Harper grasps my hand, squeezing it.

My mates—they must be making plans for war. The only way they can cure me with Madoc gone and every other avenue exhausted is to destroy the Murk Heart.

But even if they manage that, even if I don't lose any of them in the attempt, it won't bring back the life we made together that had only just started to bloom.

A sob hitches out of me. The tears that collected in my eyes spill out. I turn my head to the pillow so it can soak them up, and Harper eases closer, rubbing my shoulder with her other hand.

"I'm so sorry," she says. "I know that doesn't help—I know there's nothing I can say or do that would help. But if there was, I'd do it. It isn't fair."

No, it isn't. Nothing in my life has been fair, from the moment Orion decided to plant the seed of his magic in my family line, from the moment he stole me away from my parents to unfurl that magic into something that took over my body and soul.

I had this one thing that was only mine, that wasn't touched by him at all, and he managed to rip it away from me anyway.

The next stabbing pain of the curse is almost a relief because it's a distraction from the anguish of mourning.

Harper brings a goblet of water to me, but I find I can't sit up to drink properly. I end up spilling it all over the sheets as I sip sideways while still lying down. My limbs won't cooperate with me—even the slightest movement brings a wave of fatigue and prickles of pain over me.

I'm dying. Really dying, closer than I've ever been before. The thought sinks in and just kind of settles there, as if I can't fully process it. There's been too much wrongness for me to take it all in.

There was so much more I wanted to do and see, so much I wanted to accomplish. Who'll stand up for the humans in the fae world if I die? Who'll watch over Jamie? Will my mates take up the causes that were important to me, or will they mourn and then move on, with all the centuries they still have ahead of them?

And what about the man I'm not totally sure where I stand with? The fever weaves through my mind again, and for a second I think I see Madoc standing there at the edge of my vision. When I turn my head, he vanishes.

Sylas thought it was a ploy, bringing me to the fringes where the Murk were waiting to ambush us. Is he right, and my mind is too addled for me to see the situation as clearly as he does?

Madoc didn't feel like an enemy when he held me through my shudders of agony. He didn't sound like an enemy when he swore to bring me home.

What am I abandoning him to if I don't make it? Will Orion kill him as horribly as the Murk king once threatened to mutilate me?

I should have said something more to him before… Before everything…

My gaze latches onto Harper again, and I'm jolted by another abrupt shift in my emotions. Resolve grips me. I can't control anything about what'll happen with the men in my life when I'm gone, but she—she still has chances—

"There's a true-blooded fae you're in love with," I say, tugging at her hand. "I know you don't want to admit it, but there is."

Harper twitches with surprise and then flushes. "You shouldn't be worrying about my romantic prospects right now. It doesn't matter anyway."

"It does," I say. "It does to me." In case I never get to talk to her again. She made one misstep with me, but otherwise she's been here for me so much, done so much for me. If I can help her in one small way before I'm gone… "Why won't you go after him? Maybe he'd want you too."

"Talia… I know he won't. It's all right."

I frown at her. "Even if you don't think there's hope, you should tell me who it is. Just to get it off your chest, to tell *someone*." A rough giggle slips from my throat. "It's not as if I'm going to have much chance to give away your secret."

Harper stiffens. "Don't talk like that," she chides me. "They're—they're going to destroy the Murk and their Heart and then you'll be fine."

My fever flares; my thoughts fragment. My eyes flutter shut for several seconds. Then I focus on her again. "We both know that might not be true. Let me do this for you. Let me listen. Maybe you'll figure some things out if you just say it out loud."

Harper bites her lip, but my insistence has obviously affected her. She looks down at her hands and back at me. "I don't need to say it out loud to know there's no point. He hasn't met his soul-twined mate yet, but I've been around him lots of times now, and it's definitely not me. And he could have so many other women—why he'd be at all interested in me…"

The way she's talking reminds me of how I once thought about my Seelie mates, so sure they couldn't want a serious relationship with a human woman once they'd returned to their former prominent position in fae society. A twinge of suspicion runs through me alongside a fresh lance of pain.

Who would be high enough for Harper to feel so much lower than, when she's part of an arch-lord's pack?

"It's Donovan, isn't it?" I say quietly, watching her expression. I've seen her get a bit flustered in his presence before, haven't I? But I thought it was just general awkwardness, since she hasn't gotten to experience much of the fae world until recently, let alone the company of its highest rulers.

Harper's face flushes darker, and she drops it into her hands. "Don't tell anyone. He's never given any indication—I've tried to talk to him a few times, and he's very polite, but he's not particularly interested either. It's just… What would you call it? A crush. I'll get over it and find someone I'd really have a chance with."

Now that she's admitted it, I wonder why it didn't occur to me earlier. They're suited for each other as far as I can see, though of course I don't know Donovan especially well. They've both got a sort of softness to them, which hides an iron will that can come out when something or someone they care about is threatened. They're both unsure of themselves but doing their best to find their footing among people more experienced than they are.

That's not enough to make someone fall in love, but maybe Donovan just hasn't seen enough of Harper yet.

I squeeze her hand. "Yes, yes, you will." I don't know if I should add that maybe the arch-lord will come around and start to admire her. Would that really be for the best if he's going to be distracted by a soul-twined mate later on?

But then, I don't love my chosen mates any less than I do Corwin. If I can manage that, then why couldn't a fae arch-lord?

"And who knows what will happen with Donovan?" I go on. "Things… don't always work out the way it looks like they will at first. I should know." I let out another weak laugh.

"That's right," Harper says. "We just wait and see and hope for the best."

I can tell she isn't talking about Donovan anymore. She keeps holding my hand and starts rubbing my shoulder again, and a sort of calm settles over me. My body still hurts and my heart still aches at the thought of what I've lost and how much more I might lose in the days ahead, but at the same time…

I got to have the love of four amazing men for at least a little while. I got to experience what it was like to carry a child inside me, at least the beginning of the process. Who am I to complain when there are others who've never gotten any of that at all?

I do want more. I want so much more—I want the rest of the life I thought I'd have. But I'm not going to lay that sorrow on my friends or my mates. I'm not going to make this harder for them as well as me.

If that's the last gift I can give them, reminding them of how happy they've made me rather than how sad I am to leave them, then so be it.

"Thank you," I say to Harper. It takes an effort to keep my voice audible. "For sitting with me and talking with me. You've been a great friend."

Harper turns her head away for a second to swipe at her eyes. Then she beams at me. "You've been an even better one."

The bedroom door swings open, and all four of my mates burst into the room. As they converge around the bed, Harper gives my fingers one last squeeze and then slips away with a bob of her head to her lord and his cadre.

The men seem to hesitate, braced around me, as if they're afraid they'll hurt me if they get any closer. Corwin's had his walls up against our bond this whole time, but now that he's close, a trickle of a frantic mix of relief and anxiety seeps through to me despite his best efforts.

I reach out to them, all of them, ignoring the fact that my vision has started to double, making the outlines of their forms waver and multiply. "I want you all with me. I love you so much."

"And we love you," Sylas says roughly. They move together, encircling me in a mass of warmth totally different from the burning of my fever. I nestle between them, hugging one and then another, murmuring words of affection until I can no longer string them together.

These are my men, my mates. I'm going to savour every last moment I get with them, even while I'm wishing I'd get more.

CHAPTER TWENTY-FOUR

Madoc

I don't like the look of the Refuge when I emerge from a passage into one of the stations. All of my fellow Murk are bustling around, carrying equipment or supplies, tussling with each other in mock skirmishes that are clearly for practice rather than play.

Normally a lot of them are relaxing at any given time. The increase in activity doesn't seem like a good sign.

But maybe it should. Why should I mind if Orion is gearing up to launch his war in the next few days? Any hope of a peaceful resolution went out the window the moment the few fae of the Mists who'd agreed to collaborate with me turned on me the second something went wrong.

I was *trying* to save their mate, for fuck's sake, but apparently they'd rather I left her sitting vulnerable to attack, blithely assuming there was no way the tide could shift against them.

I shouldn't have cooperated with them in the first place. I should have learned my lesson from the disaster with Delta.

I just assumed that when it was solely to benefit Talia, they at least trusted me not to want to harm *her*. How the hell was I supposed to know that a squadron of Murk would be hanging around just in case we showed up? Do they think I somehow passed on a message in the few hours between working out the plan with Whitt and leaving?

Yes, they probably do. Maybe I emphasized my skills with illusion too much. And really, I might have been able to send a message like that if I considered all the angles well enough. I had plenty of time to observe how the Seelie guards kept watch, what would catch their notice and what was likely to slip past it.

None of that excuses them thinking the worst of me based on nothing but the fact that their attackers happened to be the same kind of fae as me, though. Why not blame Sylas and his damned cadre for the sins of Seelie like Ambrose and Aerik then?

My bad mood follows me through the station. I pause in the tunnel by the stairs to my private room, but even though I've been traveling a long time since I fled the claws and fangs aimed at me yesterday, I don't think I'll be able to relax.

Orion has probably already gotten word of my arrival. His spies multiply by the day. He'll want me to report immediately.

Several of the Murk I pass on my way to the throne room raise their hands or tip their heads to me in respectful acknowledgment. That's reassuring. I've been watching the responses to my presence from the first sentry I sensed in the area around the entrance I used, and so far there haven't been any signs that my own people see me as the enemy. I don't think the fae of the Mists have gone as far as revealing my association with them to Orion… yet.

I've earned the respect my fellow Murk offered by standing by my king—and I nearly threw it away. My teeth grit again at the memory of the accusations Talia's mates had hurled at me. How long will I have before they try to present me as a traitor to turn everyone against me? I haven't figured out exactly how I'm going to explain away the proof they could offer. At least it'll help that Orion isn't inclined to believe any Seelie over his own proven knight.

Then I think of Talia, of how fragile she felt tucked against me while I tried to shield her from the pain inside her, and my stomach knots.

Is this what all our time together comes to? Will I be marching on her mates and the rest of the fae she considers kin in a matter of days?

Will she even be alive by then to see her hopes of peace shatter, with me at the front of the charge?

But what else am I supposed to do? Completely give up on bringing my people to the home they deserve? Talia can't force the fae of the Mists to negotiate with us. They've shown how little they're willing to give even me the benefit of the doubt. As much of a force to be reckoned with as she is, she can't change the impossible.

I just wish that turning my back on the hope of some kind of treaty didn't have to mean turning my back on her too.

Does *she* think I arranged the ambush? Will that be her last memory of me—the supposedly false comfort offered as I tried to destroy the people she loved most?

Just thinking about it makes my hands clench. I have to hold myself back from slamming a fist into the wall of the tunnel outside the throne room. Orion will definitely notice and ask about *that* fit of temper, even if he only hears about it second-hand.

I step through the broad opening and walk up to the dais. Orion is sitting in a typically casual pose on the arm of his throne, his tail flicking back and forth over to the seat, talking to a couple of my fellow knights. When he looks over at me, his yellow eyes narrow.

A prickle runs over my skin. Have the Seelie tipped him off after all? Or does he suspect something's odd for other reasons?

But he beckons me over, dismissing the others with a careless wave and standing up straighter. His movements might be nonchalant, but there's a soberness in his expression that I haven't often seen. He doesn't look exactly *sane*, but he does appear unusually focused in his fierceness.

"Here you are again, Madoc," he says. "After all those long stints in the Mists before, I can't keep you away from the Refuge these days."

Is that why he's irritated—he feels I'm shirking my duty a little? I raise my chin, putting on the appearance of confidence though not insolence. It's a fine line between strength and rebellion in his eyes.

"I thought you'd want to hear as soon as there were any major developments," I say. "From what I understand, Talia's mates and several other fae brought her out to the fringelands to attempt some sort of cure for your curse there, and they were set on by an ambush of our people that had them running off with their tails between their legs. They've made a proclamation against the Murk, swearing to destroy any that they spot in 'their' lands. If they were getting help from a traitor among us before, that alliance has ended now."

I didn't even have to lie to say all that.

Orion hums and lets his tail loop around his wrist, tapping its tapered end with his long fingers. "They're being pushed to the brink, then, in your estimation?"

I nod. "They wouldn't have been desperate enough to bring her so close to our territory otherwise. Like I mentioned before, from what I've observed they've been trying all sorts of cures—with no success, naturally. Preventing them from going through with their most recent plan will only have unsettled them more."

My king chuckles to himself and turns so the quavering orange light of the Heart flickers over his angular face. "It *is* good that you delivered your reports in time for us to arrange that ambush. I can thank you for giving me the information I needed."

A chill wraps around my gut. What is he talking about? I couldn't have reported that the fae of the Mists would be sending a party to the fringes there, because I didn't *know* they would be the last time I spoke to him.

I manage to keep my voice even. "I'm afraid I don't follow. I wasn't aware of the ambush until after it happened."

"Of course, of course. I decided on that method after you left the last time. But you gave your account of why the Seelie went to speak with Delta, as badly as that went for all involved, and made it clear they'd realized they had no hope of saving my pet on their own. Based on those facts, it was obvious that they'd try to make use of our powers again—and where better than along the fringes, as close to our Heart as they can get." His eyes gleam with satisfaction.

I feel the exact opposite. Any enjoyment I might have gotten out of the thought of putting the fae of the Mists in their places curdles in my stomach.

They were right. Not the way they thought, not that I'd purposefully betrayed them—but I did screw them over all the same. I must have said too much, gone overboard in emphasizing one thing or another, showed too much of my hand—I didn't mean to give Orion such an accurate sense of the approach the other fae were taking…

If I'd just shut my mouth a little sooner, skewed the details a little more or left more of them out, I might be sitting next to Talia right now, seeing her free of the curse we broke her out of together.

I force a smile, because Orion is watching me, intent as ever. "I'm glad that my insight gave you that advantage."

His Heart doesn't cringe away from my lie. If anything, the orange light flares briefly brighter. Staring into it after spending time so close to the Heart of the Mists, my skin recoils from its erratic energy.

Talia's mates called it a false Heart, and they weren't wrong. It's nothing like the mass of living, harmonious power that fuels *their* lives.

It's all we've got. It's the best we can count on. And it's slowly draining away the real thing, while killing Talia at the same time.

The sudden, wild urge comes over me to shove Orion right into the center of that orange mass, to scream out words to shatter that glowing monstrosity.

I could free her that way. I'd be some kind of hero, even if no one knew but me.

But I don't actually know what words would shatter our Heart, and I doubt getting that close would even injure Orion. It's his creation, after all. I'd only be showing my hand, and he'd cut me down, and there'd be no one left to speak for reason at all.

And could I really destroy it even if I knew? At the same time, I'd be obliterating the magic my people count on, leaving us utterly vulnerable to the fae of the Mists, who are more determined than ever to exterminate us all.

There are no good options here. The best I can do is protect the people who need it most.

A sense of resignation settles over me just as Orion clears his throat. "I'm sure you've noticed that we're ramping up for our first real assault. There's just one more thorn I want to dig into their sides before we make our move. That does mean I'm sending you off again."

"Of course," I say, crossing my arms over my chest. I can't tell him that the fae of the Mists directly threatened me with death on my return to the world they consider theirs. What does it matter anyway? They'd have pounced without hesitation on any other rat who crossed their paths. Now the risks are no different for me than for anyone else.

As long as I don't walk right up to one of them and tap them on the shoulder, I've seen enough to ensure they never know I'm there.

Orion simply smirks to himself, gazing into the glow of the Heart for long enough that I start to wonder if he's forgotten the task he was about to give me. "What is it you need me to do?" I ask.

He grins wider, baring his jagged teeth. "I think it's time the fae of the Mists find out exactly what their savior's cure requires—and how far beyond their reach it is. Let them agonize over that for a day or two, and then we'll cut them down at their most shaken. Perhaps they'll even cut one or another of each other down in a vain attempt to meet the conditions."

A quiver of excitement shoots through me, though I keep my expression carefully neutral. He's going to lay out for me what would cure Talia's curse? But if it's something impossible, maybe it doesn't even matter.

"I can see to it that the word is passed on," I say. "Conjure an illusion of a Murk for them to catch, perhaps, who'll gasp it out in his supposedly dying breath. What should I tell them?"

Orion brings his hands together, his fingers tapping against each other in an unsteady cadence that echoes the Heart's dissonant pulsing. "As soon as possible, have them hear that the only way to heal the girl is for one who loves her to drench her with their life's blood by their own hand. Voluntarily, of course."

I blink, not sure I heard him right. Tendrils of tension begin to wind around my chest. "By their own hand," I repeat. "They'd need to do it themselves."

"Exactly." Orion turns his grin on me. "Perfect, isn't it? Her supposed mates will be falling all over themselves to make the sacrifice to save her, but even if they do care about her enough to qualify, their ridiculous Heart won't let them go through with it. It should cause plenty of chaos as they try, though."

It is perfect, in a horrifically sickening way. I swallow hard, suddenly feeling miles distant from this room and the man in front of me. My voice comes out, still steady, but I hear it as if from far away. "Is that really the cure?"

Orion cackles. "Why not? Every curse requires one. The trick is to place it out of reach. I was very pleased with that particular brainstorm." He motions toward the doorway. "Go on, then. We have blood to spill and heads to roll. I've waited long enough."

He's waited. As if this war is all about fulfilling his thirst for blood and chaos.

But then, to him it is, isn't it? Talia saw that within just a few days in his company. I've known it deep down all along, even if I drowned out the observation, telling myself it didn't matter as long as the rest of the Murk get what we're owed in the end.

Is this really what I owe them, though? A lifetime under a vicious king turned even more brutal in his victory? Do I doubt that he'll aim his sadistic desires at the rest of us even more once he no longer has plans of war to occupy him?

I dip my head and stride out of the room toward the nearest entrance. My pulse thumps heavy through my veins. The queasiness that came over me when Orion first announced the cure is spreading, deepening, with every step I take.

Is it so impossible?

Could I even get the chance to find out? If the fae around her get the slightest wind of my presence, they'll be chopping *my* head off…

I have my orders and my loyalties and my conscience. In this moment, they're all leading me down the same dank tunnel toward the outside world. I'll follow them as far as I can, and hope that when I reach the point where they diverge, I know for sure where I stand.

And if I have a chance to save everyone who matters—then I'll take it. I'll take it without a second's regret.

CHAPTER TWENTY-FIVE

Talia

I think it's the click of the door that rouses me from my daze. What I've been doing for the past day can't really be called sleeping. Not that I've really been awake either. I seem to fade in and out of semi-alertness, never totally present nor totally gone.

Either I've adjusted to the pain so much that I'm not noticing it, or my body has gone numb in its increasingly weakened state. There's just a dull throbbing all through my torso and limbs, with an occasional sharper jab or twisting. My breath has stayed shallow, my skin hot with the fever that washes through me in waves, seeming to drain more energy out of me each time.

One or another of my men has been with me each time I've been aware enough to notice—until now. Whoever was watching over me last must have stepped away while I dozed again. They're making their plans, gathering an army of fae in the arch-lords' domains—I've caught flashes of the preparations through Corwin's eyes in moments where the wall he's holding up slips.

I don't know how soon they intend to march on the Refuge now that they've narrowed down its location, but there's a rising urgency in the air that I can sense even from here. I suspect it's only a matter of hours now.

I don't know if I'm going to make it long enough to see them return. I don't know if they *will* return. I tried to tell Sylas the last time he was here, with stumbling words and my hand clamped around his wrist, that they shouldn't rush in for me. That they should wait until they're fully prepared. I'd rather have them with me when I die than die alone, knowing they might die too because they ignored the danger in their attempt to save me.

He told me not to worry, that they'll be ready for whatever comes. That they will all come see me before they leave, and that they intend to see me well when they return. That I'm never alone, because their hearts are always with me.

So why is my heart aching?

I've had trouble stringing more than a few words together in the past few hours, though. What voice I have comes out ragged. I don't know what arguments I can make that they'd listen to.

I'm not sure *I'd* listen if our positions were reversed.

I wet my lips. My stomach pinches with a trace of hunger that's quickly swallowed by a swell of nausea. My body sinks even deeper into the bed as my muscles give up more strength.

And then a soft point of pressure touches my wrist.

I twitch, not capable of a full flinch in my current state. Slowly, I manage to tilt my head to peer down at my arm where it's lying on top of the covers. We've kept them half over me, half off, draped across my abdomen, for some kind of balance between the fever's flares of heat and the occasional chills.

There's nothing on the bed beside me. I blink a few times in case my vision is faltering, but while the details are a bit fuzzy, I'm definitely not seeing anything except my arm and the deep blue bedspread. Maybe it was just a tic of my nerves.

But then, even as I watch, I feel it again. A more deliberate nudge, still soft, with a tickling sensation and then a larger patch of gentle pressure, as if a furry body the length of my forearm has rested against it.

My pulse hiccups, and even though I still can't see anything at all, a picture forms in my mind's eye—a pointed nose, quivering whiskers, and the long, sleek shape of a rat's body, crouched beside my arm.

Madoc's voice comes back to me from weeks ago as he guided me through the paths away from the Refuge. *My illusions can stop them from seeing and hearing us, but it won't let them walk right through us.*

He's here, hidden from my sight but not my sense of touch with his magic. It has to be him, right? What other Murk knows the fae of the Mists and the working of illusions well enough to have managed to sneak right into the border castle undetected?

What other would come to me so tentatively, waiting to see how I'll respond?

A lump fills my throat. He came back, even after—even after everything. He must know how the other fae would react if they knew. He probably has no idea how *I'll* react. But if I had even the slightest doubt about whether he intended our foray to the fringes to go wrong, his presence here right now would dispel it.

He could be out there spying on the war preparations—or sabotaging them. Instead, he's come to me, offering whatever gesture of comfort he can.

I turn my hand, tracing the shape of him. The bumps of his shoulders and the curve of his haunches stay perfectly still as my fingers glide over his fur. I tuck my hand next to him, stroking my thumb over his side, hoping he understands what I'm trying to show him—that I'm glad he's here, that I'm not angry with him or scared of him.

He leans his head against my fingers with another tickle of his whiskers, and I manage to find my voice. "Thank you," I whisper roughly. "I know it was a big risk… coming to me. I won't… I won't let…"

My vocal cords tremor, and I lose my momentum. Madoc presses his nose against my hand as if to say it's all right. Then he moves away from me. A jolt of loss hits me in the moment before I understand why.

Abruptly, he's sitting on the edge of the bed as a man, gazing down at me. His blond hair lies in disarray, his gray eyes not so much stormy as overcast with pain. His mouth tightens. "He should never have brought you this low," he murmurs. "This isn't how you're meant to be at all."

I swallow hard, loosening my throat. "I—I'm sorry."

Madoc's gaze turns into a stare. "What the hell do *you* have to be sorry for?"

All the hopeful futures I imagined flit through my head. "I wanted… to help bring the Murk home… to make the other fae see… to help you…" My voice wavers, and my thoughts scatter. It's so hard to focus.

Madoc's jaw flexes as he clenches it. "Even now, when you're—I'm not sure we deserve you." He shakes his head and closes his eyes for a second before meeting my gaze again. His voice comes out even more ragged than mine. "You're a light that could brighten even the Murk. And you'll have that chance, if you still want to take it when all this is over. You'll have your mates and your child and—"

A sob lurches out of me. "No child."

Madoc goes rigid. "What?"

I squeeze my eyes shut against the renewed surge of grief. "I got… so sick… It's gone."

The Murk man hisses through his teeth and swears under his breath. "I'm so sorry. If I'd known—if I'd found out sooner—*damn* him." He pushes to his feet. "I have to be fast. I wish I could do more, but I can give you this. And may my people deserve you after all."

As my eyelids flutter open again, Madoc draws a small, thin knife from his pocket. I only have a second to register it, to wonder what in the world he's talking about, when the door bangs open and a blur of furious Seelie hurtles straight at the rat shifter.

"Get your filthy paws away from her," August snarls, slamming Madoc to the ground.

Astrid and a couple of the castle guards race in after him. The knife goes skittering across the floor; Astrid snatches it up and reduces it to a blob of metal with a hastily snapped true name. August raises his hand, claws flashing from his fingertips, to slash at the man pinned beneath him, and my heart nearly bursts with panic.

The words wrench out of me. "No! Don't hurt him!"

August's arm is already swinging, but at my voice, he catches it with a jerk. His claws must still slice Madoc's skin, because I hear a pained noise from beyond my view, but it isn't the fatal blow my mate meant it to be.

"I was only trying to—" Madoc sputters, but August moves to clamp his hand over the rat shifter's mouth. My mate peers over the side of the bed at me, his eyes wild with a mix of fury and bewilderment.

"He was going to *kill* you," he says. "He snuck in here—the knife — We can't give him another chance. I'll tear out his throat right now."

I know how the situation must look, especially when August blames Madoc for the ambush as well. But not one particle of my body can believe that Madoc meant to use that knife on me, not in any way that would harm me.

Why would he have been talking about the chances I'd have, about getting to be with my mates and my child, if he meant to end my life right now? Why would he have offered any comfort at all instead of stabbing the blade into me the first moment I was alone?

I don't totally understand what he was going to do, but I know it's not that. I know I don't want him dead because he risked everything to help me.

"He wasn't— You can't—"

But my words won't come together quickly enough, and August is tensing to deliver another blow. He isn't listening to me.

Horror sears all through my body, and with a gasp, I launch myself forward. I fling myself upright and toward the edge of the bed, toward August, with a surge of effort that tears at my lungs and floods me with agony. But I manage to sit up, swaying and dizzy but holding off a collapse.

August's head jerks toward me. Astrid rushes to my side, but when she tries to help me lie back down, I shake my head as firmly as I can. My breath comes out in broken pants.

"*No*," I say, holding August's golden gaze, not daring to break that connection to even glance at Madoc beneath him. I summon every shred of strength left in me from every dark crevice in my being, propelling it all up my throat to move my tongue. "He hasn't betrayed us—he never did. He's been trying to help all along. He came back—he came back even knowing you'd react like this—"

"Trying to finish what he started," August says with a growl, but he hasn't moved to strike Madoc again, not yet. I have his attention now. I have this one chance, maybe my last chance, to set one more thing right before I'm gone.

My fingers clench at the sheet. "What he started was a bond between the fae of the Mists and the Murk. A way to stop the worst of the fighting, a way to— You have to let him— You don't trust him, so trust me. I've seen him; I know him. Whatever he was going to do here, it was to save us, not to hurt us. Give him a chance to talk. *Listen* to him. Believe what he says. Please. For me. Believe *me*."

As those last words fall from my lips, a deeper tremor shakes my body. All the breath goes out of me. I try to clutch at the covers, but my fingers won't move.

I've used up all the energy I had left, and now my limbs are crumpling, my spine sagging.

Astrid inhales sharply and leaps to slow my fall. My head sinks into the pillow, the room spins, and then my mind goes totally blank.

CHAPTER TWENTY-SIX

August

All the color drains from Talia's face as she collapses on the bed. My muscles pang with the urge to spring to her side, but that would mean releasing the villain beneath me, the rat that stood over her failing body with a knife in his hand—

Astrid is closer anyway. She slips her arms around my mate just in time to guide her more gently onto her side. Talia's eyes roll back, and her limbs go slack. Her eyelids twitch and close.

My heart stops. "Is she—"

"She's still alive," Astrid says quickly, leaning over Talia. "But her pulse is very weak." She glances at me with worried eyes. I've rarely seen the seasoned warrior show fear.

The man beneath me tenses and flexes his muscles, but I've pinned him too firmly for him to have any hope of escape. I hold my clawed hand up, imagining how easily I could slice through his jugular. How satisfying it'd be to watch this treacherous creature's life spill out of him. Even now, he glowers at me, not even pretending to make a show of peace.

But Talia's words linger in my head. The words she pushed

herself so hard to speak. He was worth that much to her, worth expending the little strength she had left to defend him…

The guards gather closer around me, ready to assist. I close my eyes, struggling between anger and reason. I want so badly to destroy the man who represents everything that's hurt the woman I love…

I know my mate, though. Talia is sweetness personified, kind-hearted and compassionate, but she isn't *stupid*. She's never softened to the fae who've mistreated her—if anything, she's gotten more confident in standing up to the scornful arch-lords and the enemies of her past.

She wouldn't forgive Madoc—no, talk as if there was nothing to forgive him for in the first place—unless she understood something I didn't.

She asked me to listen to him. Heart help me, she *begged* me to trust her. What kind of mate would I be to her if I refused what might be the last request she ever makes of me?

I drag in a breath and glare down at the rat again. I wish we'd kept that iron-core collar Celia used on Corwin all those months ago. If Madoc still has the use of his magic, how can I be sure he won't shift and flee our grasp?

I'd rather have brought him before my brothers and Corwin for them to interrogate him. Warring with words is more their area than mine. But if I don't have the choice, I'll question him myself, right here, with my claws inches from his throat and my fangs ready to chomp on a fleeing rat.

His only way out would be the door. I jerk my head toward the others. "Shut the door and guard it. Don't stray from it until I give the command. Two of you, let out your wolves. Stay ready in case he tries to dash for it."

One of the guards gapes at me. "You're not going to kill him?"

I give him a stern look. "I'm going to find out if there's anything useful he can tell us before I kill him. It doesn't work so well the other way around. If there are more rats already on the way—or already here—we need to know."

That isn't the main reason I'm sparing him for the next few minutes, and maybe they realize that, but it's an explanation the warriors can accept. They step back in formation by the door, two standing directly in front of it and the other two dropping onto all fours to flank them, their wolfish eyes gleaming.

Astrid remains on the bed next to Talia. She murmurs a few words I recognize as an invigorating spell, designed to encourage the flow of blood and the rhythm of the lungs. I can't tell whether it helps.

Time is ticking away from us. I keep my legs planted over Madoc's, my forearm locking his crossed wrists to his chest, but ease my hand down just enough to rest my claws against his neck instead of covering his mouth. "She asked me to listen," I say with an edge of a snarl. "I can't promise how *long* I'll listen for. So talk fast."

The rat shifter swallows audibly and opens his mouth, but Astrid speaks before he can, her tone urgent. "August, she's fading. I don't know—nothing I'm doing is keeping her with us."

My lips pull back from my teeth as my gaze snaps back to Madoc. "You *did* hurt her—you did something to her without even needing that knife—"

"I was trying to save her!" he rasps out, twitching under me again in a futile effort to shake me off. "For fuck's sake—I know how to cure the curse."

The blood roaring in my ears seems to still. He—what? "You found out—" I start, but the details of how it happened don't matter. All that matters is— "*How?* What do we have to do?"

Madoc grimaces. "I have to show you. You need to let me get closer to her."

I bare my fangs again with a rush of suspicion. "I'm not letting you get anywhere near her ever again. Just tell me what she needs."

"That won't do any good," the rat shifter snaps. "You can't do it. None of you can do it. Are you going to let me save her, or are you going to watch her die because you're too much of a stubborn prick to give me the chance? Why the hell would I have come all the way back here to kill her when she's already dying, you idiot?"

He might have a point, but his insults aren't exactly increasing my faith in his good intentions. "Why in the lands should I trust you if you won't tell me what this cure *is*?"

Talia shivers on the bed. A series of spasms run through her limbs. I can sense without even looking right at her that the last sparks of life are spilling out of her.

Astrid tugs the covers back from my mate's body. She presses her hands to Talia's legs, her stomach, her chest, and then her head, gasping desperate words, but I can tell nothing's bringing Talia back.

Madoc's eyes widen at the sounds from above. "You won't believe me," he says, struggling again. "Or you will, and you'll do something stupid. There isn't time to argue about it. I don't even know if I believe I can do it, but I'm the only one who can. Let me try, please!"

A groan of frustration catches at the base of my throat. He sounds like he means it, but he's a master of illusions. What do I know about deciphering lies? This is Whitt's domain.

But I was by far the closest when the spell we set all through the castle to alert us to Murk presence sounded the alarm. The others will be coming, but I don't know if they'll be here fast enough.

A thin whine carries from Talia's parted lips, and Madoc winces, his expression taut with apparent agony. "I'll—I'll give you my true name," he spits out. "You can *order* me not to hurt her. Just hurry up and let me get to her."

I can't help staring at him for a second as his offer sinks in. Our true names are something tied to our souls. The Murk might have lost their ability to wield magic when they shunned the Heart of the Mists—until they made that false Heart of their own—but that hasn't changed anyone's ability to wield magic on them. He's offering up utter control over his mind and body.

Talia shudders again, and I make my decision. "Tell me then," I growl, leaning close.

Madoc drops his voice for my ears only, the softest of whispers. "*May-dim-goss.*"

The tingle that races through my mind with the syllables speaks to the power in those syllables. He isn't lying about this. "*May-dim-goss,*" I repeat under my breath, and add, louder, with magic crackling through my voice, "You will not take any action that would harm Talia."

"I won't," Madoc agrees, with a wince as my intent latches onto his mind.

"You won't attempt to harm any of the rest of us either," I add, willing the strands of the true name's control to lace even tighter between us.

"Of course not. I just want to save her life. Now let me up!"

As I pull back, footsteps thump in the hall outside. Madoc scrambles up, spinning toward Talia.

"Wait!" I say, panic shooting through me, and he stops in his tracks with a hiss of frustration. His true name's power holds him in place.

At Sylas's command from outside, the guards move from the doorway. He, Whitt, and Corwin burst into the room, their expressions fierce and frantic.

Whitt glances from me to Madoc and then Talia and sputters, "Heart save us, what are you—"

Sylas is already lunging forward. I throw out my arm, only managing to hold him back because he catches himself at the gesture.

"He says he knows how to cure the curse," I babble. "He's given me his true name—I made him swear not to hurt her or us. But I—" I swivel back toward the rat. "Before you do it, tell us what the cure is."

My use of his true name is still fresh enough that I drag the answer out of him even as I can see the defiance in his stance. "Someone who loves her needs to offer up his life's blood by his own hand and cover her in it."

I feel my brothers and Corwin freeze as I do, horror rippling through me from head to toe. My first instinct is to throw myself at the bed where Astrid is still murmuring frantic spell words over Talia's failing body, to cut myself open from chin to gut if that's what it'd take. But even as my legs itch to propel me forward, I know I can't.

The Heart won't let me make that sacrifice. The men behind me know that as well as I do.

I turn toward Sylas, my heart thumping painfully fast. "If you did it—I'd offer myself—"

Madoc cuts me off with a short, humorless laugh. "That's what Orion wanted. That's what he imagined when he cast the curse—all of you falling over yourselves to prove your devotion in a way your Heart will never let you, maybe even slaughtering each other—but that won't work. You don't think he thought of that? *By your own hand*, I said. You have to do it yourself, and you can't. So that leaves me."

It takes a moment for those last words to sink in, and by then he's already leapt onto the bed. Corwin lets out a sound of warning, I spring forward—

And Madoc slashes the narrow claw he's extended from his fingertip right across his throat, as deep as it'll go.

Blood sprays from the mortal wound, raining down over Talia and the bed around her. In an instant, red stains every inch of her uncovered skin, soaking into her hair, her nightgown, and the sheets she's lying on.

Madoc's dying body crumples over her, more and more of the scarlet fluid gushing out. Astrid flinches backward and then reaches for him, stopping with her hands hovering over his shoulders, her own face splashed red. Her gaze darts to us. She doesn't know whether it's safe to move him.

I don't know either.

How—why— *He* couldn't possibly—

The blood coating Talia's skin starts to fade. It's seeping into her, I realize with a rush of horrified fascination. Her body seems to be absorbing the ruddy liquid everywhere it touched her directly.

In a matter of seconds, every speck of it has vanished from her flesh, leaving only her clothes and her hair drenched with the stuff. I take a cautious step to the side of the bed.

Then Talia's chest heaves with a rush of breath deeper than any I've heard her take in days.

CHAPTER TWENTY-SEVEN

Talia

A sickly meaty scent fills my nose. My lips part, and I instinctively suck in the air—tainted with that sour smell but welcome all the same. I drink in more and more of it until my lungs are full.

For the first time in days there's no pain, no stabbing or throbbing or even that faint prickle that's been with me so long. The relief hits me so hard my eyes pop open.

I'm lying on my bed in my bedroom still. I have a vague memory of long hours spent here, growing weaker, but none of that exhaustion grips me now.

My mates are standing around me, August helping Astrid move a heavy weight off of my body. Corwin leans close by my head. *My soul*, he murmurs through our bond, awed and yet anguished for reasons I can't totally decipher.

Sylas's dark eye gleams as he comes up beside my soul-twined mate. "How are you feeling?" he asks, strangely careful with the words.

The sensations coming back to my body in the absence of the

weakness and agony are so overwhelming it's taking me a moment to catch up. "I'm… wet," I say, abruptly aware of the dampness sticking my nightgown to my skin. "What—what happened?"

Even as I ask, I push myself to sit up. Corwin jerks forward as if to stop me, but the movement comes so easily, without the slightest hint of the strain from the last few days, that a laugh tumbles from my mouth.

Then I see the carnage on the bed around me, and the sound dies in my throat. My jaw snaps shut.

The entire middle of my vast bed is drenched with red, all around me and on me—my clothes, my hair slipping wetly across my shoulders. With *blood.* That's what the horrible smell is.

And—the weight August and Astrid moved away from me—they're just easing a limp body off the bed and onto the floor. My gaze snags on the rumpled blond hair, then the gaping gash on the man's pale neck, and a cry bursts out of me.

"What—what did you *do* to him? He—"

"He did it to himself," Whitt breaks in, his voice tight and unreadable. "He did it to bring you back to us."

I push my hands back over my dripping hair, wincing at the feel of it. My mind scrambles to process my last fragmented memories.

I was in such a daze with the pain and the fever—I'm not totally sure what was a dream and what was real. But I remember Madoc being here, first as a furry body tucked against my hand and then as a man sitting on the edge of the bed. I remember him talking, and August rushing in…

I shake my head as if I can argue the sight in front of me away. "I don't understand. You have to—you have to save him! Isn't there some magic you can do to heal him, or…?"

The solemn expressions on all my mates' faces make my voice falter and my stomach clench up. A different sort of pain radiates through my chest to squeeze around my heart.

No.

"It seems he finally found out the cure for your curse from his king," Sylas says quietly. "One that was meant to be impossible, to confound and torment us even more. Orion obviously never considered—" He pauses. "You needed to be covered in the life's blood of someone who loved you, who gave it themselves."

His words sink in bit by bit. My thoughts dart first to Corwin's mother, to her frantic, futile attempts to end her own life so she can follow her husband into death. My throat closes up. "None of you could have—the Heart wouldn't let—" The rest clicks in my mind with a jolt of understanding. "Then *he*—"

I can't say the words out loud. Madoc loved me. He loved me enough to give his own life to save me. Maybe he did it for his people as well, for the faith he had that I might prevent a bloodier war, but I have to assume the cure wouldn't have worked if he hadn't loved me for my own sake too.

My heart squeezes tighter. Tears prick at my eyes. "It isn't right," I say raggedly. "Isn't there anything you can do—any chance—?"

August straightens up from where he's been crouched on the floor where he and Astrid laid Madoc. I can no longer see the Murk man who's become so entwined in my emotions—and me in his, apparently—but the image of his lifeless body lingers in the back of my head.

August is frowning. "He's already gone. No one can bring someone back when the spark has already left them."

My hands grip the sheets with a sudden flare of hope. "But it *hasn't* left him, has it? You do the funeral ceremony for the Seelie who've fallen—the energy that makes their soul-stone is still in them. Something's left. If you could—"

Sylas reaches to grasp my hand. "That part is already disconnected from the body by then. No one's ever been able to reattach it. Resurrection isn't a power the Heart grants us, and likely for good reason."

He's trying to talk me down, to make me see it's impossible, but instead my mind latches on to the one piece of his statement that shows me a way forward.

The men around me are some of the most powerful fae in this world, but their magic has a source, something that fuels every shred of their power and all life in both the realms. Something that outshines all of them.

Corwin rubs my shoulder. "We should get you cleaned up, and—"

"No," I interrupt, propelled by a clang of desperate hope. I push myself to the edge of the bed, ignoring the clinging of my blood-drenched nightgown to my limbs.

Sylas and Corwin move to stop me, but I shove their hands away, my gaze darting to Madoc's sprawled body. The drained pallor of his face and the gouge through his neck make my stomach turn and only strengthen my determination.

"Bring him to the Heart," I insist, pointing at him as I get to my feet. My legs hold me without a hint of shakiness. *He* did that for me; he gave me back the life Orion almost stole from me, and I can't sit back while there's still even the slightest chance of repaying him for that sacrifice. "Carry him down there—now. Please, hurry."

My mates stare at me. "Talia," August says gently, "I don't think—"

"You don't *know*," I cut in, my voice rising. "You didn't think I could use true names or have a soul-twined bond before it turned out I could either. There's a chance. We have to try. After everything he did for me, I can't just leave him. *Please*."

When they don't move immediately, I push past Sylas and Whitt toward Madoc's body. Whitt catches my arm. I whirl toward him, but before I can tell him off and yank myself away, he gives me a quick squeeze and moves to join me. "All right. If you feel there's a way, then we'll try. We owe him that much."

He and August heft Madoc between them, Astrid darting in to fold the Murk man's arms across his chest so they don't dangle. August supports the Murk man's head with his shoulder, but the lifeless loll of it against my mate's broad frame makes my stomach churn harder.

"Hurry," I say again, yanking the door wider open.

A few guards are standing in the hall. The ones who came with August when he first charged to my defense, I guess. They stare at me in my bloody nightgown and then at my mates emerging carrying Madoc's body. I must look like a horror, but I'm not going to waste precious minutes prettying myself up just for appearance's sake. I have no idea if this will work at all, but everything in me tells me that with each passing second, the chance is farther out of reach.

"Clear the area around the Heart," Sylas orders the guards. "Keep everyone away until I give another order."

The guards wrench their gazes to him with bobs of acknowledgment and then hustle down the hall ahead of us. August and Whitt heft Madoc along as quickly as they can, the rest of us keeping pace.

Corwin stays close by my side. "You're completely well? You don't feel any lingering effects at all?"

I have no inner walls up—he should be able to sense the painless strength flowing through me nearly as well as I can. But maybe after everything he's watched me go through, he needs that extra reassurance.

"Nothing hurts," I tell him. "I'm totally fine. Better than I felt half the time even before—"

Even before the curse. Especially right before it struck, when I was tired and sometimes dizzy or queasy from the pregnancy.

My hand drops to my belly with a fresh jab of loss. For a second, my legs wobble. Corwin grips my shoulder. "If it's too much—you haven't really had time to mourn—"

I grit my teeth and shake my head, forcing myself onward. I won't lose even more than I already have. The baby inside me had barely started to grow. The man I'm trying to save was a fully formed person with a tangled past and dreams for the future—so many dreams...

Now that I'm free of Orion's curse, there'll be many more chances to see a baby born into my new family with my mates. There'll never be another Madoc if I can't find a way to bring him back right now.

We march out on the summer side of the border and hurry toward the glowing mass of the Heart. Its energy pulses over me with the rhythm that's like an actual heartbeat. A silent plea starts to reverberate through me before we even reach it.

Please. Please. Please.

Whitt and August hesitate partway across the field around the

Heart. I motion them onward. "Right up to it. Lie him down on the grass as close as you can get."

Without argument, they walk the last several paces to the edge of the border. Following them, the glow becomes so bright it stings my eyes. They set Madoc down and back up a couple of steps, giving me room to kneel beside him.

It's almost like when I found him lounging on the grass not far from here days ago, soaking up the Heart's energy the only way he could. Except then his body was full of life, and now it sags into the grass.

Blood from his wound has smeared across his shirt. I don't shy away from it, resting my hands on his chest. I stare into the pulsing light of the Heart with eyes narrowed to cut down on the glare and switch to begging out loud.

"Please. You have so much power in you. You gave me the ability to use true names even though I'm only a human, even though I was being used as a weapon against the fae of the Mists. You shone brighter for me at my mating ceremony. Can you shine for him too? He doesn't deserve to die. He did everything he could to help me—to help all of us. He wanted *peace*. Isn't that what you want too?"

The Heart simply keeps up its steady, indomitable thrum. The energy tingles into my skin, raising the hairs on my arms, but Madoc doesn't so much as twitch.

I wet my lips, searching for the right words. "He was the first Murk to find a way to work with the fae of the Mists in centuries. That should count for something. He ended my curse—his help might be the key to ending the other curses on this world. Please bring him back, so he can have a chance to do all the good he could have done. So he doesn't have to lose everything just so I could live. *Please*."

I put all the force I can into that last word. My throat feels raw.

But nothing changes. The Heart beats on, with no more sign that it's heard me than it's ever given before. No sign that it makes any difference to it that I'm begging it on my knees in a nightgown drenched in this man's blood, wrenched back from the edge of death by his sacrifice.

A surge of anger fills me, so swift and sudden it overwhelms everything else.

I push myself to my feet, my hands clenching. I must look absurd in my gruesome clothes and blood-stained hair, but I don't give a damn. I just want the impenetrable mass of magic in front of me to *listen*. The words spill out faster and harsher than even I was prepared for.

"How the hell can you call yourself a Heart? Don't you care about anything? You cared enough to take away the Murk's magic over something as small as a lie here and there. *That* was important enough to punish them and their children and their children's children, but everything Madoc has done isn't enough to make him worth saving? Maybe we should all turn to the Heart that the Murk made if you're so vindictive."

A hand comes to rest on my back. "Talia," Sylas says softly, and I can feel Corwin monitoring me closely through our bond, grieving with me but anxious for me at the same time.

"No," I say to them, and turn back to the Heart. "It should hear this. Everyone around here is always talking about 'the Heart' this and 'the Heart' that as if it's such a wonderful thing, but it's been horrible to some of its people too." I jab my finger at it. "The Murk *are* your people; *you* gave them whatever magic they started with and made them fae, and then you took it away, and somehow it's *their* fault they got bitter and resentful? I don't think it's that simple."

I drop my hand to motion to Madoc. "This man rose above all that resentment. He saw that things could be better, that his people might be able to live happier lives without having to ruin anyone else's. All he wanted was a home for himself and the fae like him. You promised them that when you brought them into existence, and it's about time you did something to help them get it. If you could believe in me, then there's no reason at all you can't believe in him too."

My anger starts to deflate. I swallow hard, staring into the glow again. "He believed in you," I add, my voice rough now. "Didn't you see him coming out here just to be near you? He believed in *you*. He wanted to come back to you. You know he did. That should count for something."

I sink back to the grass next to Madoc, my head drooping. I lean over him, letting my face come to rest against his motionless chest. My eyes squeeze shut against a renewed burn of tears.

It wasn't good enough. I couldn't figure out the right words, the right angle—I couldn't call on all that power. How could I have thought I would? I must look so pathetic, even deranged...

But I'd do it again. I'd do it over and over if I thought there was any chance it'd work.

That thought has only just crossed my mind when a sharper glow flares through my eyelids. I jerk upright into a wave of light that's washing over the field and all of us in it. For a few seconds, my vision is only white.

The Heart's glow contracts in on itself again. I blink away the blotchy afterimages left in my vision—and hear a faint rasp below me.

My gaze snaps to Madoc. To the slight hitch of his chest as if with a breath. To his neck—

The gash in his throat is gone. The pale skin has sealed over as if it was never torn. His eyes have closed and his lips parted.

When I hover my hand over his mouth, a wisp of an exhalation grazes my hand.

My own heart thumps so hard with joy I think it might burst out of my chest. I grip Madoc's hand and tip my face toward the Heart of the Mists, the tears that prick at my eyes now only grateful. "Thank you."

My mates gather closer around us. Whitt lets out a low, awed whistle. "You do know how to get things done, don't you, mighty one?"

Pride flows from Corwin into me, although with a twinge of hesitation.

When I glance at him, puzzled, he crouches down next to me. For a moment, we both consider the still-unconscious Murk man, watching the rise and fall of his miraculous breaths.

"You spoke well for him," my soul-twined mate says. "For all of the Murk, but especially him."

"I had to," I say automatically.

"I know. Because you love him too."

I twist toward him, my gut lurching. The truth of his words rings through me, but at the same time, I can't bear that he—that any of my men—would think I'd betray them. "I love *you.* All of you. I—anything else I feel doesn't change that at all. You're my mates, and I'd never let anything threaten our bond."

"We know you wouldn't, Sweetness," August says, resting his hand on the top of my head.

Corwin nods. "I don't bring it up as an accusation. I—" His mouth twists, and he inhales deeply before going on. "Three rabid wolf shifters once agreed to share their beloved with a chilly raven. How can I accept that kind of generosity and not extend it in return when it's so earned?"

I blink at him, hardly daring to breathe myself. "What are you saying?"

His affection streams through our connection as he smiles back at me, enveloping me with tender, accepting warmth. "He's proven his love for you. I can feel how much he matters to you. If there's room for five in your heart, I won't ask you to hold back."

He glances at my Seelie mates, and I follow his gaze, not knowing what to say.

Whitt lets out a chuckle and shakes his head, his expression uncertain but his eyes gleaming when they meet mine. "A rat shifter. I wouldn't have thought. But then, there was once a stuffy Unseelie who managed to welcome not one but three feral wolves as his soul-twined mate's paramours, so I'd be an awful hypocrite if I balked, wouldn't I?"

Corwin's lips twitch into a wider smile. I catch Sylas's gaze next. His mismatched eyes contemplate me for a long moment.

"I think we all owe Madoc an apology," he says. "We thought the worst of him so many times when you saw the truth. I've never denied you the right to follow your heart, my love, and I'm not going to start now. We can make it work."

August brushes aside my damp hair and kisses my temple. “He was willing to die to protect you. I wouldn’t argue with that kind of devotion.”

I thought… I thought I had to carve out that part of my emotions and set it aside. But they see—they understand—

I can’t kid myself that it’s going to be easy. The wariness and the knee-jerk distrust aren’t going to completely vanish in an instant. But they’re willing to embrace Madoc’s role in my life—to welcome him into the makeshift family we’ve been forming.

A smile splits my face, so wide my cheeks ache with it. “I love you,” I say again, choked up, to all of them.

CHAPTER TWENTY-EIGHT

Talia

The next time I walk into my bedroom, it's clear that a lot of magic has been worked there. No trace of blood remains on the sheets or in the air. The only sign of how much has changed is how normal I feel—and the presence of the man lying on one side of the expansive bed.

Madoc is still unconscious but breathing more steadily than when I left him in my mates' care to get myself cleaned off. They agreed that my room was a reasonable place to let him rest and recover from the ordeal his body has been through.

With his blood-splashed shirt removed, the daylight streaming through the window catches on the toned planes of his bare chest, highlighting the stark lines of the scars that mottle his skin. I feel a little strange seeing him partly undressed, but then, I saw him in nothing but boxers when we showered in the Refuge, so maybe he wouldn't mind.

I've spent a lot of time lying in this bed in the past several days, but after my stand-off with the Heart and going out to offer tears to the winter fae who were waiting for me, one of them nearly totally frozen, I could use a little rest myself. My mates are conferring with the other arch-lords about how to best proceed with the conflict with the Murk now that destroying their Heart isn't quite so urgent. I won't be needed anywhere else for at least a little while.

And I'd like to be with Madoc when he wakes up.

I climb onto the bed and lie down on the other side, leaving enough space between us that I could only just graze his shoulder with my fingertips if I stretched my arm out straight. For a few minutes, I watch the rise and fall of the Murk man's chest, take in the softening of his face in a deeper state of relaxation than I've ever witnessed before. How will he feel about what I've done?

I don't really know, but I can't regret my decision to do whatever I could to save him.

After a little while, I drift off into a more peaceful doze than I've gotten to experience since the curse dug its claws into me. I'm drifting in a serene, dreamless current when the movement of the body next to me jerks me back into full awareness.

Madoc is blinking, his arms flexing at his sides. He stares at the ceiling and then raises his hands to stare at them too. His expression shows total bewilderment.

I sit up, tucking my legs close beneath the simple dress I put on after I got cleaned up. The Murk man's gaze snaps to me. He looks dazed, as if he wasn't totally woken up yet. Maybe he isn't sure that he really has.

"It worked," I say, figuring that's what he'd want to know first. "Your cure. As far as I can tell, the curse is gone. I can't feel its effects at all."

Madoc blinks at me, his eyes slowly clearing, a crease forming in his brow. He sits up too—quickly at first and then slowing, wobbling and catching his balance when he must realize he isn't totally recovered. He pushes himself the rest of the way up carefully and touches his neck, the place where the flesh was slashed through. Not even a tiny scar remains.

"Then how— I was supposed to *die* for the cure to work," he says, and I'm weirdly relieved to hear that the Heart's touch hasn't smoothed out the familiar hoarseness in his voice. "'The life's blood,' he said, and—it should have…"

He looks at me, a clashing interplay of emotions crossing his face, as if he's relieved and unsettled, pleased and concerned, all at the same time.

"It did," I say. "Kill you. But I—I wasn't willing to accept that ending." My mouth twists into an awkward smile. "I asked my mates to bring you in front of the Heart, and I pleaded with it to heal you. And then I yelled at it for a while too. I'm not totally sure which part worked. Maybe it was both together. But one way or another, it did listen in the end, which is what matters."

Madoc's eyes widen even more. "The Heart—" His gaze jerks to the window, and his hand flies to the spot on his chest over his own heart. He breathes in and out, and every other emotion on his face falls away in the wake of a rush of awe. "I can *feel* it. Inside. The magic, the energy—I could—"

He halts abruptly and murmurs what sounds like a true name. A gleaming metal ball the size of a marble forms on his palm. He studies it for a long moment and then meets my eyes again, something startled but elated shining in his gray ones. "You brought me back to it. You—"

His voice falters. He seems to focus onward, his gaze going distant. His throat bobs. "I can't feel Orion's Heart at all now. My connection must have severed when I died, and the Heart of the Mists filled it in."

I don't know if I should apologize for that. "I didn't know how it would happen," I say quietly. "I didn't know if it would work at all. I just couldn't give up after… after everything."

A moment of silence stretches between us. Madoc looks down at his hands and then back at me. His jaw works. "You know, don't you? They told you the conditions of the cure, why the rest of them couldn't have— Why it had to be me."

He sounds oddly nervous, as if he's braced for some kind of rejection. As if he thinks I'd have brought him back from the dead mainly to tell him he didn't stand a chance of winning my heart.

Even if my mates hadn't given their blessing, even if I'd been going to bury these feelings down and accept that I was lucky enough as it was, I think I'd have told him. He'd have deserved to know even then.

"They did," I say. "But it still means a lot—even if you were the only one who *could* do it, you didn't have to. You could have let me go."

"No," Madoc says immediately, "I couldn't have."

The corner of my mouth curls upward, an ache of affection forming at the base of my throat. "I still have to thank you. There aren't enough words to thank you. And in case it wasn't obvious from the fact that I scolded the Heart of the Mists into bringing you back to life, I love you too."

Apparently it wasn't obvious after all. Madoc stares at me even harder for a beat. His voice comes out ragged, strained yet full of so much longing it tugs at my heart. "Talia…" He shakes himself. "I know how you feel about your mates—I wasn't expecting anything. I mean, I expected to die." He laughs roughly. "And that's fine. Even that would have been enough."

I reach across the covers and wrap my fingers around his hand. "I think you and my mates have a lot of talking to do to understand each other better. But they recognize the sacrifice you made—they respect it. There won't be any more questions about your loyalty. And they've managed to accept each other's place in my life. They're willing to accept you too. I didn't even have to *ask*. They took it upon themselves to inform me that you were welcome into the family."

My lips twitch with a wider smile, but Madoc seems lost for words. He opens his mouth and closes it again, his brow furrowing. His gaze searches mine. "You're saying…"

"I'm saying this castle has plenty of space, and everyone's agreed there's room for one more mate in it." I hesitate, my stomach abruptly sinking. "I mean, if *you'd* want that. I know it's not what most of the fae would typically hope for—to be sharing their mate. I know everything has been complicated, and you haven't gotten a great welcome here to begin with. If you couldn't see yourself in that kind of arrangement, of course I'd understa—"

Madoc's fingers tighten around mine, and he hefts himself closer to me, close enough to bring his other hand to the side of my face and rest his forehead against mine. "Talia," he breathes, "I'd take any amount of you over none at all. I'm only having trouble wrapping my head around the fact that you'd want *me*."

Oh. I raise my hand to his cheek and trail my fingers along it to his jaw and then down his neck, feeling the thump of his pulse. His chest hitches at the contact. All at once I want to touch that too, the taut ridges of muscle all the way down to the waist of his jeans.

"You're brave and generous and one of the most honorable of the fae I've ever met," I tell him. "Even when it's hard. Even when it means going against things you've always believed. You have the same kind of dreams I do, and I've seen how far you'll go to see them through—for everyone who matters to you, not just yourself. So don't sell yourself short."

He swallows audibly and nuzzles my forehead. "And you're my bright one, my light in the darkness," he says, barely more than a whisper, and then his head is dipping and mine is rising, and somewhere in the middle our lips collide.

The kiss feels like being caught in a thunderstorm, electric and wild, a flood of heat washing over my skin. Madoc makes a noise low in his throat and pulls me closer. I wrap my arm around his neck and tease my fingers into his hair, my other hand tracing down his naked chest the way I imagined a few minutes ago. My fingertips skip over the tiny indents and ridges where the scars cross his otherwise smooth skin, but I don't shy away from them. They're a testament to the trials this man has been through to make it to this moment with me.

More desire than I realized I was holding in rushes up through me, filling me to the brim. We kiss and kiss again, until I can't tell where each ends and the next begins. Hard, soft, urgent, and lingering, flowing into each other one after another.

It isn't long before I'm breathless, clinging to him, wanting more. Wanting to get as close as I can to this man who literally split himself open for me and yet somehow still can't see himself as a hero.

Madoc pulls back, but not far. A noise of protest forms in the back of my mouth, but the hunger in his eyes stops me from voicing it. He's not done. He just rests his hands on the skirt of my dress in question. "I want to see you."

I nod and lift my arms and my hips. With a ragged inhalation, Madoc lifts the smooth fabric up over my head and sets it aside. His gaze roves over me, nothing but adoration in it, and any self-consciousness I might have felt flees.

"So beautiful," he murmurs. "My fierce little fighter. *Mine*." He lingers on the word as if testing it out, and a smile tugs at his lips.

Holding my gaze, he brings his hand to my breast, cupping it and then slowly sweeping his thumb across the peak. At the jolt of pleasure, my nipple pebbles instantly. He swivels his thumb over it again, sending more sparks shooting through me until a gasp slips out of me and my head tips back, my body swaying into the caress.

He growls and tips me back on the bed, kissing the crook of my jaw and then down my neck with gentle nibbles here and there. "You have no idea how many times I imagined doing this. It's like a miracle getting to touch you for real. It's a miracle I'm here at all." A chuckle tumbles from his mouth with a wash of breath. "The one woman who could boss around the Heart of the Mists."

I make an impatient sound, my fingers curling into his hair, and he drops his head lower to suck my unattended nipple into the heat of his mouth. At the flick of his tongue, I whimper, my fingers digging tighter. I trail my other hand over his shoulder and arm, caressing every inch of skin I can reach as he worships mine.

He dips lower, kissing his way down my sternum and across my abdomen. When he reaches the spot just below my belly button, he pauses and presses his most tender kiss yet there. He glances up at me, sorrow momentarily overcoming the desire in his expression.

"There will be more," he says, as if he can conjure the future he's talking about into being like a spell. "A wolf and a raven both. I know the Heart will shine on you."

A pang fills my chest at both my loss and the way he's left himself out, even now. I stroke my fingers down the side of his face. "One of each then. A wolf, a raven, and a rat."

His stormy eyes flare, and all at once he's rising back over me, claiming my mouth so passionately that every nerve in my body quivers with delight. His fingers hook around my panties, and I grope at his jeans. The knot of longing swelling in my core turns desperate with the need to be fulfilled.

As Madoc kicks off his jeans and boxers, a tremor runs through his arms where they're supporting his weight. He did die just a few hours ago—he isn't quite back to his usual strength. But he simply sinks onto his side and rolls me toward him, enveloping me in his embrace and capturing my lips with another kiss.

I reach between us and wrap my fingers around his shaft. It presses rigidly into my palm, so hard the sensation is giddying.

Madoc groans and kisses me harder, guiding my thigh up over his at the same time to spread me open. I tuck myself closer to him with a whimper when he grazes the head of his erection over my opening.

"So many things I want to do with you when I have all my strength back," he mutters. "But this is more than enough for now."

I arch toward him, and he sinks into me, slow and steady. Another gasp ripples up my throat. He grasps my hip, angling me to receive his next thrust with an even headier burst of bliss. His other hand closes over my breast. His mouth drinks in my whimpers and moans.

And something else, like a silky finger, traces over my bowed back, across my bottom, and down the back of my thigh.

My muscles twitch in surprise, and Madoc pauses. His tail sweeps up to stroke across my upper arm like a fifth limb. "I can stay totally human-like," he says, watching my expression, "if you'd prefer it that way. There's just… more I can do with more of me to work with."

A sly gleam comes into his eyes, but I can recognize the wariness there too. The fear of rejection he's still grappling with—and why not, after how the fae I've allied myself with have treated him because of what he is?

I rest my hand against his cheek, gazing back at him. "I want to enjoy every part of you."

That's clearly the right answer, because Madoc dives in for

another kiss. His fingers massage my hip in time with the building rhythm of his thrusts inside me, and his tail drifts down my back again.

When it dips, carefully, to tease across my other opening, the tingling pleasure brings a fresh gasp to my lips. I kiss him harder, in case there's any doubt about me enjoying *that*, and he starts to stroke up and down across that sensitive area in time with the rocking of his hips.

Bliss is radiating through every bit of my body now. It builds in an expanding rush. I'm awash with the giddy burn between my legs, the shivers of delight as Madoc fondles my breast, the deepening tingles with each caress of his tail, and his tongue twining with mine to draw out a moan.

When I start to tremble, he picks up the pace just a little, just enough to send me spiraling right over the edge.

I cry out and clutch onto him as if I'll soar away completely if I don't hold on. Madoc groans and buries himself even deeper inside me, shuddering with his own release. He kisses me and kisses me again, murmuring gentle sounds that aren't quite words, hugging me close against him.

I hug him back, the joyful ache inside me spreading until it fills me completely, as if I'd been missing something up until this moment and now I've finally found that lost piece.

CHAPTER TWENTY-NINE

Talia

I wish that we could lie amid the sheets and cuddle and continue exploring each other's bodies for hours more, then welcome my other mates into the bed and see what kind of unity we could start to build between us all there. But there's still a war looming over us. My interlude with Madoc was only a brief escape, a luxury I start to feel guilty about after we've sprawled a little longer in the bed.

"Are you feeling well enough to get up and walk around?" I ask, kissing Madoc's cheek. "We should see where my mates are with their plans—and they'll want to speak with you." Corwin has kept himself at a distance so their discussions didn't intrude on my rest… and everything else… but I know he's aware that the Murk man woke up.

Madoc lets out a tense guffaw. "Somehow I don't think it's the walking that's going to be the biggest challenge." But when he gazes into my eyes, his expression softens. "There is a lot we need to discuss, and not just about you."

I reach out to my soul-twined mate enough for him to recognize my intent. *We're just finishing up a talk with the other arch-lords,* he says through our bond as I ease back into my clothes. *We'll meet you downstairs in a few minutes.*

Madoc, of course, doesn't have any shirt at all, so I dig one out of the closet in Whitt's bedroom, since he's the best match for the rat shifter's build. Madoc eyes the silky collared tunic skeptically but accepts it, probably preferring to feel a little over-dressed than to have this conversation with the other men while half-naked.

I feel it when Corwin enters the castle alongside the others, his mood apprehensive and yet hopeful. With equal wariness, Madoc follows me downstairs to the sitting room where my mates have gathered. A nervous twinge races through my own gut.

My mates accepted the role Madoc could play in *my* life, but how easy is it going to be for him to fit in here among the fae of the Mists overall? In the rush of relief and released emotion, we haven't even talked about how he'd like the future to look.

Is he going to stay here with us? *Could* he even go back to so much as visit his people if he wanted to?

How long will it take for Orion to realize what's happened and send out a call for his no-longer-loyal knight's death? How will the other arch-lords react to Madoc's continued presence among us?

What if I've saved him only to lose him all over again?

As we step into the sitting room, I force myself to shove those worries to the side. We have to deal with one thing at a time. None of the rest matters if even my mates balk now that the Murk man is standing in front of them again.

Madoc stops just inside the doorway, and I halt alongside him. My other men have dispersed through the room. Whitt is leaning against the arm of a nearby sofa, his eyebrows arching slightly when he catches sight of Madoc's borrowed shirt. Corwin sits at the other end of that sofa near him. Sylas has been pacing by the window, but he stops and turns toward us at our entrance. And August is standing behind one of the armchairs, his elbows braced against the top of its upholstered frame.

The apprehension I sensed from Corwin permeates the entire room. No one speaks, the four pairs of eyes settling on Madoc, no doubt noting how close we're standing to each other and the new familiarity in that closeness.

I can't bear to let the silence stretch for long. I made my choices, I feel what I feel, and now I have to own all of it.

I reach up to touch Madoc's cheek. When he leans his head toward me, I bob up to give him a soft kiss. His posture goes rigid, but he kisses me back, his hand rising to my shoulder. I remember the day when I went to hug him and how he tensed up then.

It really wasn't a rejection of me. He must have been as nervous of the reactions my gesture would provoke as he is now.

A flicker of possessive resistance carries through my connection with Corwin, but I can't say it's any worse than similar feelings he had toward my Seelie men. And this moment isn't just about Madoc. It's about all of them.

I go to Whitt next, trailing my fingers along his neck and seeking his kiss. His lips twitch with one of his sly smiles, and he indulges me with a pleased hum.

From him I step toward Corwin, bending over him on the sofa and brushing my lips to his from above. My soul-twined mate sets a steadying hand on my waist, tender fondness rushing from him into me. *You don't have to prove anything.*

I just thought I should set the right tone for this conversation from the start.

When I ease back from him, there's a faint gleam of amusement in his eyes. *I suppose there's something to be said for that strategy.*

Having watched my progression through the room, Sylas moves forward to meet me next to the sofa. As he claims my mouth, he strokes his hand over my hair, his massive presence sheltering me as he always has.

August has straightened up by the chair. His mouth twists with a bittersweet expression before he gives me a quick kiss and wraps me in a hug. The tension in the flex of his muscles around me tells me he's still not quite over the horror of my own near death.

Madoc has tracked my circuit of the room without comment or complaint, but he still looks a little uncertain as I return to him. I tuck my hand around his, feeling he needs the extra support.

I meant to say something, but before I can decide on what, August strides forward. He stops a few paces from Madoc and clears his throat.

"I'm sorry," he says. "I thought the worst of you more than once —I almost stopped you from saving her." The anguish of that knowledge rings through his voice.

Madoc relaxes just a tad beside me. One corner of his mouth ticks upward. "To be fair, I was standing over her with a knife. I can understand that it didn't make the most innocent-looking picture."

"Talia knew you weren't going to hurt her," August goes on. "I trust her judgment, and I should have trusted her more about you."

Sylas nods. "I believe we all should have. It was an immense sacrifice, what you offered—one none of us could have made, as much as we might have wished to. Even with Talia's efforts to bring you back… I assume you won't be able to return to your home and your king now."

Madoc's jaw tightens. "No. As soon as Orion hears that Talia's curse has been cured—if he even needs to hear it, if he didn't sense it through his magic the moment it happened—he'll realize what happened, and I won't be remotely welcome there if I want to keep this second chance at staying alive."

He pauses and then inhales sharply. "I should tell you—the ambush in the fringelands—it was partly my fault. Accidentally, but all the same… I said too much to Orion in an earlier report, enough for him to guess that you'd take the tactic of coming to a portal close to his Heart and to prepare for your arrival. If I'd known—you can be sure I'd never have led Talia into that trap."

"The rest of us, though…" Whitt says in a dry tone, and holds up his hands when Madoc's and my eyes jerk to him. "A joke! There's been distrust and animosity on both sides, and I don't think it helps anything to keep score. The question is where we go from here."

He glances at Corwin, who pushes himself to the edge of his seat with increased alertness.

"The ambush did serve us well in one way," the Unseelie arch-lord says. "You brought us to an area with a portal that leads to your Refuge's true location. I was able to spot which portal one of our attackers traveled through. Even without your guidance, we could march on the Refuge now. But… we'd stand a better chance of surviving that battle *with* your guidance. And of saving those of the Murk who'd be willing to survive alongside us and forge some kind of peace."

"*You're* willing to believe that the Murk could live in the Mists with you peacefully?" Madoc asks in a challenging tone.

Corwin stares right back at him, unshaken. "I think you've provided ample proof that we've let prejudice sour relations between our peoples beyond the point of reason. Unless *you* don't believe it's possible, I'm willing to give a chance to anyone who wants it."

Madoc's gaze shifts from him to Sylas. "And what about your other rulers? How are they going to feel about bargaining with the rats?"

"That's something we've already been discussing with them, in light of recent events," Sylas says. "I won't lie and say there isn't hesitation—I'd imagine we're all going to find adjusting our attitudes difficult, on both sides—but we can find a way through. It'll be easier if you'll come and speak with them. Perhaps with Talia by your side as she is now." He shoots me one of his small, soft smiles that never fails to make my heart flutter.

Madoc stirs on his feet uneasily. I squeeze his hand. "The Heart itself accepted you and decided you were worthy of taking as its own," I remind him. "They'll have a hard time arguing with that."

He looks down at me and lets out a short chuckle. "And even the Heart didn't dare argue with you." The affection that gleams in his eyes provokes another flutter.

Then he looks toward the window. "I—there's a lot I need to think through. I want this conflict settled with as few people dying as possible, and I want a home here for the Murk without persecution or being relegated to the fringes… and I need to be sure *all* of your people are on board with that idea and not looking for a chance to strike us when we let our guards down. But I can see there's a chance, and that's enough to make it worth trying. If I could take a moment —I'd like to go out to the Heart. I think I owe it plenty of gratitude too."

Sylas inclines his head. "You've been through a lot and had your life completely upended. I can't demand that you know exactly what to make of your new circumstances in an instant."

For the first time, I feel Madoc totally relax, as if he's finally letting go of the anticipation of a potential attack. "Thank you," he says quietly but earnestly.

We all walk with him to the entrance and out into the summer air. Madoc's pace quickens when the Heart is in sight and then slows as he comes right up to its immense, pulsing glow. He looks up at it with its pure light washing over his body, as if searching for answers in its thrumming energy the way I did once.

I'm not sure if he finds any, but after a few minutes, he closes his eyes. A soft smile curves his lips.

An ache forms in my chest, knowing how much he's missed this connection and how long it's been since he last got the chance to truly experience it. Now he's reveling in it in a way he never had the chance to before.

We've all lost a lot—him, me, my mates… Everyone. But we've gained things too. We've found trust and understanding, friendship and love.

Will it be enough to overcome Orion's sadistic madness? None of us can really know. But Madoc is right. There's a chance, and that's all we need.

Madoc is just stepping back from the bright center of the Heart when a wolf comes sprinting across the field toward us. As the six of us turn to face him, a raven dives through the border haze at the same moment.

Both messengers transform almost simultaneously, the wolf looking to the Sylas and the raven to Corwin, their faces wearing matching expressions of panic. My body tenses before they even speak.

The wolf sputters his words out first. "My lord—the Murk have come. They're invading the Mists."

CHAINED SOUL - BONUS SCENE

When Madoc returned to the summer realm after the disastrous parlay with Delta, how was he received—and what did Whitt make of him? Find out in this bonus scene from the spymaster's point of view!

Whitt

I'm just returning from a prowl through the forest below the hill when I spot one of our warriors hustling toward the castle. Loping over, I let out a sharp bark to stop her. When I reach her, I straighten up out of my wolf form.

"What's the hurry?"

"The rat has returned," the woman says with disgust twined through her tone. "We've subdued him. August is with him now—I was coming to alert the arch-lord."

Madoc has come back here? After the catastrophe of our meeting with Delta? He has to know we'll have blamed him. Did he think to carry out some other sort of sabotage that we've interrupted?

But even as those suspicious thoughts pass through my mind, I remember the arguments Talia raised during the meeting of the arch-lords. I'm not actually convinced that the rat meant for the catastrophe to happen to begin with—that our actions didn't set it in motion every bit as much as his.

At the very least, he'll have come back with information that'll reveal more of his intentions either way.

"Where?" I demand.

The warrior motions toward the stretch of trees just beyond the clearing around the castle. "A little ways down the slope, not far from the cabin where we held him before."

I give her a brisk nod of thanks. "Let Arch-Lord Sylas know—and you can tell him I've gone ahead."

I release my wolf to bound across the terrain more swiftly. A muffled grunt reaches me before I see its source, a hint of rodent smell prickling in my nose a moment later.

When I pull myself upright at the edge of the grove where three more warriors are pinning Madoc down, I find him flat on his stomach with his face pressed to the earth and a fresh bruise blooming across the back of his neck. The warriors are glaring down at him, claws and fangs out. August crouches next to them, just finishing a growled question. "—after what you've done?"

"Fuck off," Madoc mutters, his voice muffled by the grass.

My brother glances up at me. "He won't talk—well, other than insults. He says he came to speak with Talia, and the rest of us can 'go to Hell.'"

I roll my eyes. "We'll see about that." I motion August farther away and then gesture to the warriors. "Flip him over. I want to see his face while I'm talking to him."

The warriors roll the Murk man onto his back while maintaining a firm grip on him. He doesn't struggle, just sprawls there glowering up at me with so much animosity in his gaze, I suspect I'd find myself incinerated if he had his way.

"So, this how it's going to be from now on?" he bites out. "Every rat is the enemy again?"

I prop myself against a nearby tree, folding my arms over my chest and gazing back at him with a mild expression. "Considering the fact that the last time we encountered any rats—in fact, the rats *you* arranged for us to meet—they attacked us, it seems like a fair assumption."

Madoc lets out a disdainful snort. "They attacked *you*? Your soldiers started casting true names around before the conversation had much time to even start. I should have known you'd all have your heads too far up your asses to actually see any kind of compromise through. You've lost our best chance at—" He cuts himself off with a rough sound of frustration.

"If that's the way you feel about us, then why did you come back here?"

He scowls. "I brought some things for Talia. I want nothing to do with the rest of you."

I cock my head. "What kind of things?"

"I'll discuss that with her when I see her. For all I know, you'll flush them down the toilet because they came from me."

"You were hoping to give them to her directly—that you'd catch her on her own out here," I suggest.

He doesn't deny it. And I'm not even sure I can blame him for taking that tactic. I let out my breath. "If you've brought something that could help her, then of course we'll consider it. But you can't blame us for wanting to take a look at it first. You can either hand it over, or our people will rip it from you, which might not be all that wonderful for your cargo. It's up to you."

The rat shifter tenses, but he clearly knows he isn't getting any more choice than that in the matter. With a ragged sigh, he tips his head back against the grass. "Everything's in the inner pockets of my vest. It's all medicines and charms we use among the Murk. I don't know how much any of them might work, but they won't harm her to try, at least. It's the best I could do."

At my nod, the warriors peel back Madoc's vest. August steps in to murmur magic-laced words over the various odd items he finds in the pockets. I stay focused on the Murk man's face. "You couldn't get any more information out of your 'king' about her illness?" I assume he went back to his colony before returning here.

Madoc's mouth presses flat. He's already told me more than he wanted to. Well, the fact that he hasn't presented additional information suggests he didn't find out anything useful. I can't see why he'd hide it from us.

"What was the plan?" I try again, changing the subject. "Find Talia out for a stroll, hand over your medicines, and vanish again?"

"Essentially," Madoc mutters. "It's obvious I'm not getting any help from the rest of you."

"Is that why you're so keen on healing her—because you figure she'll help your cause?"

His lips curl in a momentary flash of revulsion. "No. Because she's in pain and she doesn't deserve to be. Just because *you* were willing to let your prejudices stop her from potentially getting a cure doesn't mean I'm that petty, whatever you want to think about my kind."

Ah. That's what he almost said earlier—not that the disaster with the parley lost our chance at negotiating a peace, but at curing Talia's curse. I eye him more carefully, thinking of all the reactions I've observed since he first came among us, all the gestures he's made toward the woman I love.

His presence here has always been about her first. He's dedicated enough to protecting her that he risked his recapture, which he had to have foreseen was highly probable, in a last-ditch attempt.

Another wolf lopes over to join us. Sylas draws himself up to his full formidable height next to me, and as tense as the rat already was, his frame goes even more rigid at the sight of the arch-lord. But Sylas keeps any anger he might be feeling in check. He stares down at the Murk man and then turns to me without speaking to him. "What have you determined so far?"

"He came to bring some folk cures for Talia," I say. "And he's very pissed off at us for supposedly ruining the parley with Delta."

"'Supposedly'?" Madoc sneers.

At the same moment, August raises his head. "I don't know how effective any of these items might be in alleviating her illness, but I don't sense anything harmful in them."

Sylas looms over the rat shifter. "If you mean us no harm, then why did you bolt at the beginning of the parley? You appeared to be anticipating an attack to come."

Madoc gives a sputter of a chuckle. "Yes, the attack from *your* people. I saw your warriors getting into position and starting their spells before Delta had a chance to give you more than a greeting. I was trying to stop them from harming *my* people, you immense idiot."

Sylas's mouth twists. I don't think he appreciates the insult, but what the rat said is perfectly in line with the possible explanation we'd already come up with.

"What if I told you that I'd only instructed them to cast shielding spells as a protective measure?" he asks.

"Then I'd ask why they pulled their swords out just at the sight of more Murk."

My lordly brother sighs and rubs his brow. "I think the entire calamity comes down to assumptions and a failure of communication, and I can allow that a great deal of that failure was on our side. I should have informed you of all of our plans before we arrived so that you wouldn't have been startled. And we shouldn't have reacted so defensively to Delta's followers. That our response provoked them is perhaps… understandable."

It's a major admission. I'm not sure Madoc realizes quite how large. But he falls silent, peering up at Sylas as if trying to read his motivations through the arch-lord's expression.

"I only wanted to speak to Talia," he says finally, in a more subdued tone than before. "I'll set aside the rest of my complaints, for now at least, if you can too."

My brothers and I exchange a glance. I'm inclined to agree, but both Sylas and August look more hesitant.

Before we have the chance to discuss the matter, a raven soars down through the trees. It transforms into the shape of a woman as it lands—Zelpha from Corwin's coterie. Her gaze catches on Madoc with a flicker of surprise, but the matter she's come on is urgent enough that she doesn't spare him more than that brief glance. Her eyes snap back to us.

"Talia's having another fit—it's different from the ones before. Corwin asked for Sylas to meet him at the border castle."

My pulse lurches, but not loudly enough to drown out Madoc's sharp inhalation. The panic and anguish that dart across his face only amplify my own.

We can't deal with him any further right now. Our mate needs us.

Sylas clearly has the same thought. He catches August's eyes. "Stay with Madoc and continue questioning him as you see fit. If he admits anything useful, send word. Whitt and I will see to Talia."

I'm already springing away through the trees as a wolf.

The journey to the border castle passes in a blur. I'm barely aware of anything but my concern for my mate until we're striding through the door to her bedroom, where Corwin stands in vigil over her bed. Talia glances up at us from the mattress, her lips parting, her forehead shining with sweat—and then immediately twists up with a spasm of agony crossing her face. She clutches at herself, burying her face in her pillow with a ragged exhalation.

The sight wrenches at me, but there's nothing I can do. Not even August's healing spells have been able to touch the pain inside her.

"It started maybe half an hour ago," Corwin is saying to Sylas in a quiet but strained voice. "The pain comes on her quickly and intensely, fades, and then comes on her again. Short, sharper bursts instead of one longer bout. There've been several already—I don't know how long they'll keep coming for."

Sylas's jaw clenches. "Madoc is here. He's brought a few items—"

Corwin's eyes flash with anger. "Maybe he's caused the shift in the curse."

"I don't think so," I say, breaking into the arch-lords' conversation. "He heard your message about her—he looked upset, not like he was expecting it." And I have trouble believing the man would cause Talia any kind of pain if he could help it.

"We don't know for sure," Corwin says stubbornly.

"He has some possible treatments he wanted to offer her," Sylas goes on. "Maybe they would do some good for her."

As they argue back and forth, I notice Talia's body has gone slack.

Her eyelids flutter, and she peers over at us. Her brow knits. She won't be able to make out their hushed conversation.

A lump fills my throat. Who are we to be debating the best course of action when she's the one enduring the agony?

"I think we should let Talia decide," I say.

A hint of a smile touches her lips that could melt a heart of ice. "Let me decide what?" she manages to ask in a hoarse voice, and then her body jerks with another spasm.

It's an agony in itself, watching her go through this torment. I sink onto the side of the bed and offer whatever murmured comfort I can, as little good as I suspect it'll do. Tears form in Talia's eyes, and her breaths come more ragged in each interlude between.

Finally, we get a stretch of peace that goes on and on until we all start to relax. Talia sputters a laugh. "It's over."

Relief floods me, but it's tempered by the knowledge that this won't be the last time. Not when we've done nothing to stave off the curse. We haven't even made use of the newest options available to us.

I look over at Sylas. He knows we need to tell her. His mouth tightens, but he shifts his attention to Talia. "Madoc has returned."

The news is enough to make Talia push herself upright, swaying as she does. She's almost as concerned for the rat's wellbeing as he is for hers. And it's for her sake, not his, that I argue in his favor while Corwin continues to be his usual stick-in-the-mud self. I've come to respect the Unseelie arch-lord, but he can still be a featherbrain from time to time.

Our mate's stubbornness wins out as it tends to do, and Sylas and I go off to collect the Murk man, since we're not making our mate take the trek all the way over to where August is holding him. Madoc scrambles up hastily and hurries along with us without hesitation now that he's gotten what he asked for.

I study him as we tramp over to the summer side of the border castle. Suddenly I'm intensely interested in observing his most unguarded reaction on first seeing Talia. It's moments like that when you can cut closest to the truth.

The scene we witness as we reach the castle is almost as unsettling as when I saw her seizing on the bed. She stumbles through the doorway with Corwin next to her and immediately doubles over to vomit into the grass.

We all pick up our pace to rush over, worry winding through my gut. Madoc's eyes have widened with his own concern, which appears completely genuine.

"Has it gotten worse?" he blurts out before any of the rest of us can speak. "If it's progressed to your stomach—"

Talia has gathered herself, a little healthy flush already coming back into her cheeks. She raises her hand to cut off the rat shifter. Her gaze flicks over him, and I can tell she's assessing him for any damage we might have done to *him*. Her face brightens even more in the moment when she must determine he's perfectly fine.

"I think that was being pregnant, not the curse," she says with a hint of wryness. "A much happier reason to be sick but not great having both in combination."

She obviously intends to reassure him, but in that first moment as the words hit him, they do anything but. He blinks, his jaw twitching, and his hand balls into a fist by his side. I don't think Talia can see it, and he releases it a moment later as he hazards a response, but my mind has gone quiet with a realization I hadn't quite let myself come to before.

He cares about her *that* much—enough that knowing she's carrying a child from one of her mates disturbs him. His affections run deeper than he's ever let himself admit openly.

And I'm not quite sure whether that's to our benefit or yet another problem we'll need to solve.

HEART OF THE MISTS

BOUND TO THE FAE #9

CHAPTER ONE

Talia

Normally, the carriages Sylas constructs out of juniper wood and magic skim over the ground smoothly even at top speed. I can feel how hastily the one we're riding in now was conjured with every quiver that runs through the frame. There wasn't time for perfection—especially not when every fae capable of conjuring them needed to create not just one but many in that short span.

A force of a few dozen carriages speeds toward the fringelands around us, with more presumably on the way as other packs hear the call for aid. And all of the fae around me have much bigger concerns than how well the vehicles will hold up to the journey. We needed to get going as quickly as possible to face the incoming invasion of Murk.

If everyone hadn't been in such a rush, maybe my mates would have argued more about my coming along. But when Sylas tried to send me back to our castle, I insisted that I wanted to be a part of this, to see exactly what horrors Orion had brought to the Mists I call home, and he accepted my demand with only a growl of frustration and a nod.

All three of my wolfish Seelie mates are sharing this carriage, along with a retinue of their pack's warriors and the Murk man I claimed as my fifth mate just this morning. Madoc sits next to me near the stern, his hand clasped around mine, his gaze sweeping over the fae around us warily.

Does he anticipate suspicion from the Seelie he's found himself allied with? If so, I haven't seen any yet. The fae of Sylas's pack, and probably many others as well, have already heard how Madoc gave his life to save mine and free me from Orion's final curse—and how the Heart of the Mists brought him back to life after I gave it a stern talking to. When their eyes stray toward us, I see only a kind of startled awe.

My other mates glance back at us regularly, but mostly to check on me, I can tell. August adjusts his weight restlessly on his feet, looking as if he'd have considered carrying me back home right now if his fighting skills weren't so needed at our destination. Mostly, though, they're occupied with making plans for the battle ahead.

"So, that's three domains they struck at once," Whitt is saying, rubbing his jaw. The sly spymaster looks unusually grim.

"And more on the winter side," Sylas says. When he looks my way this time, it's to include me in the conversation. "Has Corwin reported anything further?"

I've been exchanging occasional thoughts with my Unseelie mate through our soul-twined bond while he races with his flock toward the fringes on the other side of the border. My sense of him right now is hazy because he partly blocked off our connection while he conferred with his coterie. I have a vague sense of worry and anger from him, and an awareness of the larger force of raven shifters who're converging to join him and the other Unseelie arch-lords, but that's all.

I shake my head. "So far, he doesn't know any more than the sentry reported—they attacked the three domains close to the border and the fringes on the winter side."

Astrid frowns. “It must be a massive force for the Murk to have been able to overwhelm that many domains so quickly.”

Madoc speaks up from where he’s leaned against the side of the carriage. He isn’t totally recovered from his death and resurrection yet, but he manages to keep his lightly hoarse voice steady. “Orion always planned on waiting until he could be sure of striking a definitive blow right away. He’s been building his army and their arsenal for decades. I’d imagine when he realized that Talia’s curse was lifted, he pulled them together in the hopes of moving on the Mists while you were still distracted by her recovery, since he couldn’t use her death against you anymore.”

A bitter note comes into his tone. There was a time not that long ago when he stood beside the Murk king as one of Orion’s knights. He wanted to be over there helping the Murk take the Mists for their own. But we’ve all realized that not everything we thought about the fae we stood with and the fae we opposed was accurate. And in particular, he’s come to terms with the fact that his king is more sadistic than heroic.

“We may not be able to engage with them right away, then,” August says to his brothers. “If we go in too outnumbered, we’ll only be setting ourselves up for unnecessary casualties. We’ll want as large a force as possible assembled before we go up against them.”

Sylas nods. “It shouldn’t take long to gather warriors from across the realm. Everyone will understand the urgency. And we wouldn’t want to rush in immediately anyway. As urgent as the situation is, the Murk have surprised us too many times in the past. We need to take stock and make sure we’re tackling them in the most effective way.”

Whitt turns to Madoc again. “I don’t suppose you have any thoughts on that subject—what tricks your king might have up his sleeve, or what strategies would be most useful for pushing him back?”

Madoc’s mouth twists as his gray eyes go distant with thought. “I wasn’t around much for the final preparations, so I don’t know anything specific about his current plans. But he does like to use his opponents’ emotions against them, so if he can find a way to startle or unnerve you, he will. And you shouldn't assume anything you see is real at first glance. I may have been the strongest with illusions among his supporters, but there are plenty others with skills along the same line."

Whitt tips his head in acknowledgment, and Madoc's gaze slides to August. I feel the hesitation in his grip around my hand and squeeze his fingers in case he needs the reassurance. He returns the gesture and clears his throat. "August, could I talk to you about another issue that could become urgent when we confront Orion… and could we discuss it somewhat privately?"

The warrior's brow knits, but he motions the nearby guards toward the front of the carriage and comes closer to perch on the edge of the bench across from us. The sunlight flashes off his auburn hair. With a few quick murmurs, he draws a wall of magic around us that muffles the warble of the breeze and the voices of the other fae in the carriage—as I assume it'll do for ours too.

I look at Madoc, my stomach knotting. "What's wrong?" I have no idea what he'd want to ask August specifically about.

Madoc's mouth stays tensed at its awkward angle. "I haven't had the chance to mention this to you yet. When you were fading—when I was going to offer my blood to cure your curse and August stopped me—I offered him my true name to give him more security that I wouldn't hurt you or anyone else. Well, other than myself." A hint of a wry smile briefly tugs at his lips.

My eyes widen, the understanding of just how big a sacrifice he made washing over me even more powerfully than before. Fae rarely admit their true names to anyone, even their lords or mates, because it essentially gives the other person total power over them. For him to offer it to a man he barely trusted… "You shouldn't have had to do that."

"Well, it is what it is. I didn't think it'd matter, since I didn't expect to be alive to be called by my true name within a few minutes anyway." His gaze travels from me to August. "But here we are."

To his credit, August looks uncomfortable about the whole thing, not the least bit triumphant. "I won't use it again. You don't need to worry that I'd order you around or anything like that."

Madoc lets out a raw chuckle. "Actually, I'm going to ask that you *do* use it again, on a regular basis. You see… Orion knows it too. It's one of his conditions for accepting anyone into his inner circle. He mostly uses it to summon us when he needs us particularly quickly, but obviously he can do more with it if he decides to."

My heart sinks. A memory flickers through my mind of my escape from the Murk colony they call the Refuge, where Orion rules. As Madoc was helping me out into the human world above, he suddenly knew that Orion had realized I'd escaped. He must have gotten that true-name call.

"His power over you wouldn't have ended when your connection to his false Heart was broken?" I ask.

Madoc shakes his head. "Our true names are a part of us, a magic that's tied to our spirits rather than any other source. He hasn't tried to use it yet. He probably assumes I'm dead, whether he can sense that I'm no longer bound to his Heart or because he tried when I was out of commission and got no reaction. But as soon as we confront his army, there'll be an increased chance that he'll either see me or someone else will who'll report it to him."

August's expression has turned even more serious than when he was simply preparing for war. "What do you need me to do?" he asks, simply and steadily.

Madoc blinks at him. Maybe it still surprises him that my other mates are willing to trust *him* now, as if he didn't demonstrate his loyalty in the most undeniable way just this morning.

"Opposing uses of a true name cancel each other out," he says. "You just need to order me not to obey any demands Orion makes of me. But since the effect will fade over time, and we can't be sure when he might attempt to give a command, you'll need to repeat the order regularly. I'd imagine once a day should be enough."

"Of course," August says. "As long as you need me to keep it up." His golden eyes darken. "I hope you don't mind me saying that if I have my way, Orion won't be around to make use of any words at all before many more days have passed."

Madoc's fingers tighten around mine as if he's thinking of all the ways his king tormented me. "I don't mind at all. In fact, I share the sentiment. I only hope that not too many others of my people become collateral damage in this war he's forced on us."

None of us can be sure how the conflict will play out. Madoc is proof that the Murk aren't all malicious villains the way the fae of the seasons have liked to claim. But from the time I spent in the Refuge, I know that a lot of them hate both the Seelie and Unseelie vehemently—and I can't blame them for it, considering the way the other fae have savaged them, even their children.

It was hard enough for Madoc to accept that he might be able to peacefully negotiate some kind of compromise with the fae of the seasons. I don't know how many others we'll be able to persuade to take a more peaceful approach.

But even if those who stand with Madoc now are beyond our reach, there are many other rat shifters who don't agree with Orion or haven't bothered to decide one way or another as they focus on their basic survival. We can at least give them the chance to have the sort of life and home that should have been theirs all along.

"We'll do our best," August says solemnly.

I gently detach my fingers from Madoc's grasp and raise my hands to my ears. "We must be getting close to the fringelands. Why don't you give him the true-name order now? I don't need to hear it." I catch Madoc's gaze. "I realize it's safer for you the fewer people know it."

He gives me a tender smile I've never seen him aim at anyone else, the one that brings a flutter to my chest. I don't think he'd mind me knowing this part of him, but I can tell he appreciates the privacy I'm offering him all the same.

It only takes a moment. I cover my ears and peer over the side of the carriage, August must give his instruction, and then Madoc brushes his knuckles against my arm to tell me it's done. But by then my attention has been captured by the scene up ahead.

Several carriages are soaring toward us from the fringes across the increasingly rugged terrain. The vehicles themselves don't appear to be in the best of condition, a few of them jerking unsteadily, one trailing sputters of violet smoke.

Sylas and the other arch-lords motion for our brigade to slow. We come to a complete stop when we meet the approaching fleet.

I spot several bodies slumped within the carriages and other fae with blood on their clothes. My throat constricts. I can guess what they're going to say before the woman at the prow of the foremost vehicle speaks.

"We've fled Amberrise. We tried to hold off the Murk that attacked us, but there were too many of them, with vicious powers… We stayed as long as we could, but more than half of my pack has fallen, some never to rise again."

Sylas nods with a look of tense sympathy. "I'm sure you fought honorably and well. I wish we could have reached you sooner to help you before you had to abandon your home." He catches the eyes of Donovan and Celia on their nearby carriages and must get enough of a sense of consensus to ask, "Will you join us now in fighting back with a larger force? We intend to return Amberrise to you as soon as we possibly can."

One of the men behind the lady swipes his hand across his dust-smeared forehead with a weary sag of his shoulders. But the lady raises her chin high. "We'll do what we can. You're almost on their forces. They came after us shortly after we fled—our carriages were faster, but they can't be more than ten minutes distant by now. Do you have healers with you who could see to our injured? My own are exhausted."

The arch-lords motion to a few of the skilled among the gathered packs, who use magic to leap from carriage to carriage until they reach the new arrivals. Sylas keeps August with us, I guess feeling his strength is better preserved for the fight ahead.

The others prepare for battle, most leaving the carriages to get into formation ahead of them. My mates cast a spell around my carriage to shield it from stray attacks before going to join the others, their worried eyes telling me they wish I wasn't here at all.

"They won't even be able to see you," Whitt tells me. "I don't want them targeting you."

I wish there was more I could do right now than sit here watching to see what will happen.

Madoc stays with me, looping his arm around my waist as if bracing himself to haul me away if need be.

"Are you all right?" I ask him quietly. I can't imagine how he feels about facing his people again like this, although I suppose they won't be able to see him right now either. That's probably for the best, since I also can't imagine how they'll react to seeing him on our side.

He exhales roughly. "As all right as I can be. I knew this day was going to come, but I'd have preferred to get more time to brace for it."

"That's why Orion made his move so quickly, isn't it?" I said. "Not because of you, but because all the fae of the seasons have had their mind on other things." Mostly my survival.

"Yes. But that doesn't mean I appreciate his strategy."

A vibration the shield can't deflect passes through the air. I make out a horde of figures in the distance, rushing toward us. All at once, a deluge of shimmering, sizzling bolts of magic rains down on the Seelie army.

Some of the summer fae snap out the words to form shields. Others simply dodge. But as they jerk out of the paths of the blazing spells, several seize up and crumple in on themselves with blood spouting from their limbs or chests.

I shoot forward from my seat, a cry of protest in my throat. Madoc grips my shoulder, but his posture is equally tensed.

"They're mingling illusions," he says, his voice gone ragged. "The spells you can see are nothing, with hidden attacks in between."

He drags in a breath as if to shout a warning, though I'm not sure the army will be able to hear us through the protective magic wrapped around our carriage any more than they can see us. But in the next moment, it becomes clear that the Seelie warriors have figured out the trick for themselves. The arch-lords, August, and Whitt holler instructions to the crowd that others pass on to the farthest reaches.

When the next hail of destructive energy pounds down on them, they all raise their voices in unison to form one huge shield that deflects all of it—the spells both seen and unseen. Seconds later, with another chorus, they hurl magic of their own toward the incoming invaders.

I don't know if it's part of a plan or simply everyone drawing on their strengths, but a chaos of effects erupts around the advancing army of Murk. Branches and vines burst from the ground to yank some off their feet. Whirlwinds knock others over. Waves of fire roar to the left while a vast torrent of water pummels those on the right.

But the Murk are ready. A few fall, yes, but most of them must snap out defensive spells to block the effects. Then they hurl more magic at our forces. Energy quavers through the air, thick enough to raise the hairs on the backs of my arms.

The fae armies whip their power at each other over and over, neither willing to relent. Cracks start to form in the muddy earth between the lines of soldiers. My heart thumps so hard I'm afraid it's going to leap from my throat.

We're holding them off, but we're not pushing them back—not one inch, from what I've seen. Our people have to be tiring. Are theirs?

I squint, not able to make out much through the clashes of magic and across the distance. The expressions on the faces of the Murk I manage to catch don't look particularly fatigued. But… I don't see the kind of eager furor I can easily imagine lighting up Orion's right now either.

The glimpses I see of narrowed eyes and bared teeth look *desperate.* Determined and fierce, but with an edge of despair. Not because they already doubt their chances, I think, but because they know what their fate will be if they can't pull off this takeover after all.

They all believe their only possible fate is to slaughter the Seelie or be slaughtered in turn.

An uneasy sensation coils around my gut. We have to reach those people somehow, show them there's another path where no blood has to be shed. I know many of them won't listen, but there must be at least a few who will. The more of them we can peel away from Orion's side, the harder it'll be for him to keep up his assault on the Mists.

As I think that, something new is rippling through the Seelie forces. Orders are being called out. The warriors disperse farther along the battle lines. Voices rise again, and a barrier so thick that I can see the glint of it forms along the cracked ground between us and the Murk, thrumming up toward the sky like a thinner version of the border haze.

My Seelie mates come back to the carriage, August's hair damp with sweat, Sylas's dark eye tired while his ghostly one peers into a space none of the rest of us can make out.

"What's happening?" I ask, standing up.

Whitt answers, sinking onto one of the benches with a huff. "We weren't organized enough—we can't take back the domains like this. For now, we're stopping the Murk from getting any farther into the Mists. A significant portion of our warriors will stay here and defend our lands, while the rest of us figure out how the hell we boot the rats off our territory for good."

"Or how to crush all of them where they stand," mutters one of the warriors hopping into the carriage after them, and my men don't even start to argue.

CHAPTER TWO

Talia

"We need to act decisively," Laoni insists, her voice echoing off the high ceiling of the border castle's meeting room. "Root them out and exterminate this menace."

Nothing about her comment surprises me, but Madoc tenses where he's sitting next to me at the long table. Most of his recent dealings with the fae of the seasons have been on the Seelie side. He's not as used to the typical Unseelie iciness as I am.

Other than the two of us, it's only arch-lords seated around us. The coterie and cadre members present stand behind their respective lords. But I've earned a place in the discussion by virtue of my experiences with the Murk and my connection to the curse they've inflicted on the Mists, and Madoc… well, Madoc is the closest thing we have to an actual Murk representative, as much as he can speak for his people now that he's cut off from them.

Before either of us has to say anything, Corwin speaks up while sending me a waft of reassurance through our bond. "Simply throwing all our might at them and hoping to smash through their defenses didn't get us very far the first time. I think it's clear that defending the Mists is going to require a more nuanced approach. Decisive, yes, but incisive as well."

The Unseelie faced similar problems to the wolf shifters on their side of the battle. They ended up taking the same tactic of magically walling off the Murk forces and leaving a large contingent of warriors to hold that boundary. But neither summer nor winter knows how long the warriors will be able to withstand the Murk, especially when the Murk may change their own tactics at any moment.

Laoni turns to Corwin with a flash of emotion that looks almost like betrayal in her chilly eyes, as if Corwin owes her any allegiance after the way she's undermined him so often in the past. "I'd expect you to be taking a harder line with the vermin, considering how much they've cost you and your mate."

Her gaze darts to me briefly, and my hand twitches toward my belly automatically. There's no avoiding the punch of grief that hits me at her words. Corwin stiffens in his chair, a similar rush of anguish traveling from him into me, and Sylas's lips draw back in a silent snarl where he's poised at the head of the table.

Because of Orion's curse, I lost what would have been our first child. It was so early I'd barely had a couple of weeks to start to dream about my future motherhood, but the loss is still a raw wound. My men don't know which of them would have been the father by blood, but they all saw it as their child in spirit. I know they mourn what could have been as deeply as I do.

My teeth set on edge, and my fingers curl toward my palm. I lean forward, catching Laoni's gaze with the movement. "Don't you dare use my pain to advance your agenda. It was my loss more than anyone else's, and *I* don't want to see this war end with an 'extermination.'"

Laoni's expression twitches at the rebuke in my tone. I'm not sure I've ever spoken to her quite so harshly before, but I'm out of patience.

"What would you suggest, then?" Celia asks, looking at both me and Madoc. "With your knowledge of the Murk, how can we hope to win the war and protect the Mists if not by destroying the fae who seek to destroy us?"

The most senior of the Seelie arch-lords isn't any friendlier to the Murk than Laoni is, I know, but at least she's managed to phrase her question politely. And her gaze as it rests on Madoc shows more measured curiosity than anything else, unlike the Unseelie arch-lords who are mostly watching him with eyes narrowed with suspicion.

"Some of them might be won over to our side," I say. "We have to give them the chance to make that decision. As far as they know right now, you'd kill them even if they *weren't* attacking you. To most of them, this war is self-defense for the way you've been slaughtering them whenever you come across them for centuries."

Madoc inclines his head. "What Talia's saying is true. Orion wants blood however he can get it, and I accept that this war won't end until *he's* ended. But many of my people want a real home more than anything else. They want the place in the Mists that's been denied to them for so long, and the ability to live in peace without having to fear wolves or ravens will descend on them at any moment. I think that's a reasonable aspiration."

One of the coterie members makes a faint scoffing sound, but I can't hear it well enough to tell who. I bristle on Madoc's behalf all the same.

"The Murk who've attacked us haven't exactly been in a listening mood," Terisse says, rubbing her mouth. "And it doesn't sound as if they'd be inclined to believe us no matter what we say."

She might have a point there. An idea that occurred to me on the carriage ride as we returned to the Heart bubbles to the surface. "We could go back to the Murk sorceress, Delta—the one who doesn't agree with Orion's rule. The first parlay went badly, but maybe—"

"*Badly*?" Uzziah says with a huff of disbelief. "From what I understand, they attacked the Seelie representatives who went to meet with them."

"Because they believed the Seelie were about to attack them," Madoc puts in. "An impression I can admit I inadvertently added to. I think there's a decent chance she'd listen if you made a solid appeal."

"What, beg this rat queen to come to our aid?" Laoni's nose wrinkles in distaste.

There was a little while when I thought she was coming around to see my side of things more. But that was only with relations between the Seelie and the Unseelie—and before the man she wouldn't let herself admit she loved fell beneath the Murk's claws. Convincing her to see the rat shifters as worthy of respect is obviously going to be a lot harder.

I turn to Sylas instead. He was the one who led the original parlay anyway. "If we could convince even one colony of the Murk to trust us—and prove ourselves worthy of that trust by making room for them here in the Mists—it would go so far toward showing the Murk there's another way to get what they want. Isn't that worth apologizing for? What does it cost you, really, to be humble, when there were plenty of mistakes made on our side too?"

My mate inhales sharply. "Talia, I understand what you're saying. But we do still have to maintain some air of authority. We don't know this colony of fae at all—even our Murk ally has never dealt with them directly before. We can't leave ourselves vulnerable."

I frown, my heart aching with my frustration that I don't know how to make him see. "Being humble doesn't have to make you vulnerable. Apologizing when you've actually been wrong shouldn't be a weakness. Doesn't it show how confident you are in your authority if you're willing to *admit* where you've misstepped instead of pretending you can never be wrong?"

Sylas pauses, his mismatched gaze searching mine. The scar that marks his face from his forehead to his cheek, bisecting his ghostly eye, was given to him by a Murk woman he underestimated. I can't blame him for hesitating. But now he knows that there's more to the rat shifters than hostility.

"You're right," he says after a moment, to my relief. "For peace in the Mists and for righting past wrongs, I should be willing to take that step—and I am."

"It isn't that simple," Celia points out. "Even if this sorceress agrees to give us a second chance, what land are we going to offer her?"

Donovan shrugged. "There's plenty of unclaimed territory throughout the Mists. I don't think that should be a problem."

"We'll have to be careful about it," Uzziah says. "We wouldn't want them too close to any areas of importance in case she changes her mind about which side she's supporting."

Madoc clears his throat. "It is going to need to be *good* territory. You can't expect any of us to see a peace offering as genuine if you're shunting us off to the fringelands from the start. My people need a chance to reconnect with the Heart of the Mists and enjoy the benefits these realms can offer. It isn't an equal alliance if we're only offered table scraps."

"Of course," Sylas says with a tip of his head. "Since I'll be making the proposal, my cadre and I will look into the possibilities."

"Is that how this works now?" Laoni says. "We're guided by a rat who until recently was working against us? What authority does he have to make these kinds of demands?"

Madoc glowers at her. "I have the authority of having lived among and gotten to know hundreds of my people, including the king you're currently facing off against."

Uzziah's hands fidget on the tabletop before he forces them to still. "We do need to discuss exactly what sort of role the Murk would play here even if some of them can be convinced to back off from their war. We aren't going to raise them up to equal standing with us in an instant, are we? The closest thing they have to an arch-lord is that mad king of theirs."

"Of course we won't rush into handing over power to them," Celia starts.

Corwin breaks in before she can go on. "I think that *is* what we need to be considering already. We have our disputes with the Murk, and they have their own with us. But they are fae, and there's no reason that the Mists shouldn't belong to them just as much as the rest of us if they can coexist with us peacefully. And that includes having control over how their territories are governed."

Laoni's lips curl with increasing disdain. "They haven't yet proven themselves to be more than vermin. They've tied themselves to a twisted copy of our Heart. For all we know, this one sitting at our table is going to go running to his king as soon as he's in a position to earn back his place there." She flings her hand toward Madoc, who goes rigid in his chair.

"Exactly," Uzziah says. "Nothing good can come—"

The frustration that's been building inside me boils over. I push to my feet with a smack of my hands against the table. "Nothing good can come of all this arguing!"

All of the arch-lords fall silent, staring at me. Laoni's mouth presses into a flat line. I focus on her first.

"*You* and the rest of the fae of the seasons haven't proven to the Murk that you're more than bullies and child-murderers yet," I remind her. "We're asking them to make at least as big a leap of faith in us as we are in them. And Madoc gave up his life to save me, so I won't hear any of you questioning whether he deserves to be here. Your own Heart brought him back to life. You couldn't ask for more proof than that."

I sweep my gaze over the rest of the assembled arch-lords. A tremor runs through me, but I hold my posture straight. The words tumble out. "For years, I've been the cure for the curse Orion cast on you. Now I can show you how to finally get a full cure so that you never have to worry about it again. And I say that cure is compassion. Turning on the Murk with nothing but violence and hatred is only going to make them hate *us* more. We *have* to find a way to work with those of them who don't already hate you all so much that they'll never trust you."

"Now look here," Uzziah starts, but I keep going, ignoring him.

"If you're not going to give coexisting a real shot and meet them as equals who have just as much right to the Mists as you do, then I'm not going to stick around here anyway. I'm tired of hearing you all bicker with each other about which fae are more worthy. I'd rather be back in the human world if fae aren't capable of acting better than squabbling kids."

With that, I sink back into my chair. Defiant energy continues to hum through my veins.

I mean it. I'll go back to the human world and stay with my

brother if I have to, if having me leave is what it'll take to snap the fae around me out of their old prejudices.

But maybe it won't be necessary for me to go that far. The faces around the table look chagrined.

Corwin speaks up first, with an impression like an embrace through our bond. "I'm sure we can demonstrate to my mate that we're far more reasonable than that."

Donovan looks at Madoc. "Will you be able to appeal to your people? Will they believe that the Heart has accepted you?"

Madoc offers him a crooked smile. "It's already starting to mark me with the true names I've used since it brought me back." He tugs up the sleeve of his shirt to show one of the black tattoo-like marks that's formed on his bicep.

My breath catches, seeing it. It's undeniable proof of the Heart's welcome. A deeper hush falls over the room as the arch-lords take in the sight.

"But I won't be enough on my own," Madoc goes on. "They could see me as a fluke. I'll speak to them and try to convince them to negotiate rather than fight, but we need to be able to show that I'm not the only Murk you've accepted into the Mists. I'll have a much better chance of winning some over if there's already at least one Murk colony settling in."

"Then I'll make my plans to re-establish contact with Delta as quickly as I can," Sylas says. "Our defenses against the current Murk forces appear to be holding well for now, from what I understand?"

Laoni nods and says in a more subdued tone, "We've already set up a rotation of soldiers so that those on the front don't become too exhausted, as well as sending out supplies."

"We're arranging the same for our forces," Celia says. "We've bought ourselves a little time. We do need to see to the refugees from the captured domains—find alternative accommodations for them—now that their most urgent needs have been seen to."

Corwin stands up with an air of authority he's grown over the months since I first met him. "Then I say we pass the rest of the day with Sylas preparing for his overtures and the rest of us taking care of and organizing our people—from our domains and beyond—so that we're ready for whatever else the Murk king might send at us."

To my relief, a murmur of agreement goes around the table, no further arguments raised. I don't for a second believe that I've totally won my own battle, but at least I've gotten a temporary accord.

CHAPTER THREE

Corwin

The continuing bustle of activity all around me sends an uneasy shiver over my skin. I stop at the edge of the plain where our troops and other Unseelie are gathering into a vast makeshift camp and inhale deeply to settle my nerves.

Next to me, Talia peers out at the vast stretch of icy land that was once vacant and is now dappled with rough buildings of a variety of materials, each cluster marking the specialties of a different flock. "I don't think I've ever seen part of the fae world look this crowded."

I nod. "We like to keep space between our domains so there's less chance of the activities of one flock—or pack, since I suppose the Seelie have a similar policy—conflicting with another's. But a problem on this scale brings us all together."

The fae assembled on the plain just beyond the plateau around the Heart are only about half of all those who've come to join the fight against the Murk. The other half are stationed along the defensive wall where we're holding the invasion at bay or traveling between there and here. Warriors, healers, and other skilled fae from domains across the winter realm have been gathering here since the call to arms came yesterday.

The energy in the air is fraught with tension. None of us expected to be facing a war like this—ever, and certainly not so suddenly.

Talia sucks in a breath. I can feel her own unsettled emotions through our bond. "You don't need to be here for this," I remind her. "They won't expect my mate to come with me."

She draws up her head with her usual stubbornness. "I'm part of this war. I want to understand what's happening as well as I can and to be there for everyone who needs it. And it seems to help people to see with their own eyes that I'm okay."

Word of her previous illness spread rather quickly through both realms as Orion's curse dug its claws into her. I can say I prefer the sense of tense anticipation that hangs over this haphazard settlement to the hopeless anguish that gripped many of my people when her fate was uncertain.

My soul-twined mate has touched huge numbers of the Unseelie with not just the cure she can offer but her compassion and thoughtfulness as well. Why shouldn't she extend her kindness to our displaced flocks too?

We've set up the rulers and folk of the three flocks whose homes the Murk overran in hastily constructed dwellings near the base of the plateau, where they're as sheltered as possible from the regular comings and goings of the military camp. Some of their folk are still able to fight, but many are healing from the initial assault. My colleagues and I have attempted to offer them as much tranquillity as we possibly can.

"I don't know either of the lords or the lady of these flocks well," I tell Talia as we weave through the buildings toward that more isolated spot. "For convenience's sake, those on the fringes tend to visit the domains of the Heart less frequently than others do, and I have to admit I may have neglected them some because of the distance. None of them have had any complaints in recent years that required a major intervention. It's mostly been my colleagues on this side of the plateau who oversaw their needs while I focused more on the side of the realm nearer to my flock, but this war involves all of us. I'd like them to know that all of their arch-lords have their interests in mind."

Talia looks down at the basket she's carrying of delicate pastries my human chef and his daughter whipped up. A larger cart of prepared food floats along behind us on a magical current. "I hope they're hungry," she says. "Charles and Beth went all out."

"I'm sure good food will give the flock folk some small comfort." It was the most concrete gift I could offer with the restoration of their homes still so far out of reach.

My gaze catches on Talia's limp, slight at this pace with her foot brace on but noticeable all the same. Part of me longs to snatch the basket out of her hands so she's putting less strain on herself, but I already know what she'd say about that reaction.

It was only yesterday morning that she was wasted away nearly beyond survival. Only the day before that, she lost the child we'd already celebrated with such joy. I know she isn't fragile, but it's difficult to restrain the urge to wrap her up in every protection I can offer.

She must pick up on some of my feelings, because she gives me a soft mental nudge. *Getting out here and being useful makes me feel way better than sitting around in my room would. We will make a life and a family free from Orion's influence, but we all have to do everything we can to work against him first, right?*

I can't argue with her, and the quiver of restrained anguish she doesn't quite manage to suppress brings a jab of guilt into my chest. She's dealing with her own losses and the struggles she's been through the best way she knows how. I wouldn't want to get in the way of that.

The activity around the displaced flocks' settlement is more subdued than in the larger military camp. A few of the flock folk are standing around the edges of their clusters of buildings as sentries. The precaution is hardly needed with so many other fae around, but I can't blame them for keeping it.

The nearest woman's face lights up at the sight of us—more at seeing Talia than me, I observe without resentment. "Arch-lord," she says with a bob of her head. "Lady Talia. It's good of you to check in on us. I'll get my lord."

"Thank you," I say, and she darts off.

Talia watches her go, a bemused expression crossing her face. "She knew who I was. You said that flock hasn't come to the Heart recently."

I smile and ruffle her vivid hair. "I'd imagine word about the woman who's cured so many of us has spread to every domain in the realm. And you're not exactly difficult to pick out of a crowd."

She lets out a little huff of a laugh and walks with me to greet the other sentries, a couple of whom dash off to notify their own lords. As we come to a stop in an open area between the three flocks' houses, several other folk approach to see what's going on and then to exclaim over my mate.

"You're totally well now?" an elderly man asks as she hands him a pastry.

"The curse on me is gone," Talia assures him. "One of the Murk found a way to cure it and risked a lot to accomplish that."

A flicker of apprehension shows in his eyes at the mention of the Murk, but he doesn't say anything against them to her face. "With the help of him and the others of their kind who don't want this war any more than we do, we hope to restore your domain to you soon," I add. "Those who've attacked us will face the full consequences for their crimes."

"May the Heart will it so," the old man says with a dip of his head.

Talia draws her posture a little straighter when a couple who are obviously regal in bearing enter the little clearing. I greet the lord and his mate and offer my condolences for the trauma his people have been through, and he has a few of his flock folk take around their portion of the food I brought. His mate gazes out over the plain beyond us and offers a sad smile. "So many have come to defend the realm. I know it's not only for our sake, but it's uplifting to see all the same."

"We're all doing everything we can to set things right," Talia says, with a tremor of nerves that only I can sense about speaking up unprompted. "Even those of us who can't join the actual fighting."

The lord gives her a little bow. "You've defended us in all sorts of other ways, Lady Talia. We're lucky to have received your blessing."

She smiles back at them, but a twist of regret carries from her into me. She knows her ability to cure the curse isn't a blessing from our Heart but part of Orion's cruel plan.

That doesn't change the fact that you've healed us in every way you can, I say silently. *He had nothing to do with you helping mend relations between summer and winter. And we'd have been much worse off without the cure you could offer, regardless of why you have that power.*

Another of the lords is walking over to us now, with his own mate and a young woman I'm guessing is their daughter from the similarities in their features and coloring. Like her mother, her hair is a deep auburn with strands of maroon and burgundy woven in, her skin pale and her nose pointed like her father's. She looks as though she's barely passed the threshold of adulthood—I have a vague memory of taking a tour around the domains throughout the realm shortly after I took my throne and being introduced to a young adolescent daughter in theirs all those years ago.

The lord exclaims over the food we've brought. "You didn't need to go to the trouble. I can only imagine how hard you're working with this threat encroaching on the Mists."

"It was my chef who went to most of the trouble, and this is the best help he can provide," I say. "You've been through more than anyone should already. Whatever we can do to ease that pain even slightly, I'm happy to offer."

My gaze slides from him to his mate and then their daughter. The daughter meets my eyes with an air of hesitant curiosity—and her posture abruptly stiffens.

I glance around me to ensure nothing startling has happened without my noticing. I can't see what she might have reacted to. But when I return my attention to her, she's still staring, her lips parted. I don't know how to respond.

Talia picks up on my confusion. She steps toward the young

woman, holding out a pastry from her basket. "You should try one of these. No one makes them quite like Charles does."

My mate is trying to make an overture of friendliness and set the woman more at ease, but the fae woman's stance only gets more rigid as her gaze flicks between Talia and me. Her parents have noticed now as well. Her mother sets a hand on her shoulder. "Is everything all right, Kara?"

"I—" The young woman blinks hard and focuses on me again. So much emotion whirls in her dark gaze—more than I can make any sense of. She peers at me intently and then says, in a shaky voice, "Can't you feel it?"

I frown. "I'm sorry. I can't say I understand what you're referring to."

"I—you—" She presses her hand to her breastbone, her fingers curling into a fist, and something about that gesture sets off a spark of unsettled recognition in me even though I'm still bewildered.

That spot—right where I felt the bond the moment my gaze caught Talia's that night months ago.

But I'm still not prepared when Kara sucks in a breath and says, "*I* can feel it. You're my soul-twined mate."

"What?" Talia bursts out, her eyes widening. But the icy crash of a realization washes through her at the same time it does me.

We know now that our soul-twined bond was created by Orion. He used his foul magic to create a connection I now cherish regardless of its origins. But by working that magic, he interrupted the natural order of things. Of course I'd have a soul-twined mate among my own people, as any true-blooded Unseelie would.

My bond with Talia drowns out any I might have felt with this woman, though. Nothing stirs in me at all except horror at the situation she's found herself in. I have my mate… and that means she can't have hers.

CHAPTER FOUR

Talia

When we finally get back to the border castle, Corwin escorts me to my bedroom. "Wait here," he says. "I know you're shaken by this, and we'll talk it through, but I want to speak to Verik to have him see what else might be done to reduce Kara's suffering as much as possible. I'll be back with you in a matter of minutes."

The strain of the situation rings through both his voice and our bond. Our *false* bond that's superseded the one the Heart actually meant for him to have. My own heart lurches all over again at the thought, but I know he means everything he just said. I know he isn't abandoning me, no matter how much the ache inside me is already quavering with the possibility.

I go to the bed and curl up on top of the soft covers. My other mates aren't around, all of them working out the best way to approach Delta—probably deep in conversation in Sylas's study right now. They have no idea how my world was just rocked.

I managed to keep it together in front of the flock leaders and the fae woman who claimed Corwin was supposed to be hers. I suspect we left them with more questions than answers, but there wasn't much Corwin *could* tell them. Through the unsettled haze in my head, I catch snippets of his conversation with Verik, asking him to look into any history of mismatched soul-twined bonds as well as methods for severing a bond that isn't returned.

I already know there isn't any easy way. My Seelie mates spent days searching for a solution when we first found out I was tied to Corwin and turned up nothing that wouldn't put us both through hell. It's so strange to think about that time when I was horrified by the idea of being so closely connected to the Unseelie arch-lord, and now I'm in agony over the possibility of losing our bond.

We worked so hard to find a way to make this relationship work. We've shared so much with each other, come to such a deep understanding. All of that was real, wasn't it, no matter how the bond came into being at the start? All of that should still count.

I'm only vaguely aware of Corwin making his way back to my room. He comes in with a faint click of the door and a rush of fresh concern when he sees my pose on the bed.

I move to push myself upright so I don't make such a pathetic figure, but before I can get very far, he's already there, pulling me into his arms. He even brings out his wings to wrap them around me as if I need the additional embrace.

Maybe I do.

I press my face to his lean chest, breathing in his cool, wintry scent. Tears prick at my eyes. Am I selfish for clinging to this bond so tightly when I have four other men and Kara has no mate at all?

Corwin's arms tighten around me. "No, you're not," he says in answer to the question I didn't voice out loud. "It doesn't matter how our bond was formed. It's *there*, we've been living it, and it's the deepest connection any two people can share. There's a reason it's almost unheard of for soul-twined mates to refuse each other. To be wrenched apart after the bond has already been confirmed and consummated—I only know of it happening through death."

And even that way can prove difficult to deal with, as his mother is clear evidence of.

"It isn't fair to Kara, though, is it?" I say raggedly. "Her whole life as she's been growing up, she's expected to find a soul-twined mate. That's what would have happened if Orion hadn't intervened."

"It can't be the same for her," Corwin says. "It isn't the same loss. She and I *don't* have a connection between our souls—I can't sense her inner state, and she can't sense mine. She just has the impression that she should be able to. She doesn't even know exactly what she's missing."

I'm not sure if that makes the situation better or worse.

Corwin pulls back and cups my face with his hands, angling it toward him so he can meet my gaze. His affection washes over me like a flood of warm sunlight. "Just so we're absolutely clear, I have no regrets about how my life has turned out. Not a single part of me wishes I could set aside our bond to form one with this woman. I feel sorry for how Orion's meddling has affected her life and happiness, but that's already done, and I have my mate."

I wet my lips, and the fear that's been slowly building in the back of my mind spills out of me. "When we defeat Orion—when we destroy his false Heart… we expect all the magic he's cast with it to be destroyed too, don't we? The curses and everything else too. That means… when that happens, the bond that he created…" The possibility makes me so miserable I can't quite force the rest of the words out.

Corwin can follow my train of thought. It could be he's already thought that far ahead himself with his logical mind. He strokes his thumb over my cheek, his eyes still fixed on mine. "You will be my mate no matter what happens. I love you, and I'll still love you whether our souls are bound or not."

"But if we're no longer tied together, then you and Kara…"

His mouth sets in a tense line. "We can't know what will happen until we get to that point. None of us can predict how the Heart of the Mists will shine on us. But I can swear right now on my soul and my throne that I will not turn my back on you. I love you for so much more than the intimate understanding we share. *Nothing* can change that."

He doesn't have to turn his back on me for Kara to become a part of his life. I have more than one mate, so there's no reason he shouldn't be allowed to do the same… as much as the idea makes me prickle with unfair jealousy. Especially if it happens because I lose the most intimate part of our connection and she gains it instead.

The other factor that's occurred to me brings a lump into my throat. "She'd be able to give you a true-blooded heir like you should—"

Corwin cuts off that comment with the press of his lips to mine and a wave of bittersweet emotion that rushes from him into me—sweet because of the love radiating through it, bitter because off the loss we've suffered. He kisses me firmly but tenderly, moving from my mouth to my cheek and my jaw, dappling my face with increasing gentleness. The adoration conveyed with each brush of his lips lights up something inside me despite my worries.

"I cherish you, my soul," he murmurs between kisses. "And I will cherish any child you bring into our family. You are *more* than just my soul. You showed me how to open myself up to my feelings, how to trust my judgment. You made me see that past mistakes don't define us. You are twined with my heart and my mind and every other part of me, and I will not give you up for anything." He pauses, bowing his head over mine. His tone turns softly wry. "Of course, it might be easier for *you* to have one fewer mate to keep track of."

Every particle in my body rejects that suggestion. "*No*," I say, more fervently than I realized the word would come out, and then I'm yanking his mouth back to mine.

I let the rest of my words travel to him silently so that I don't have to end this kiss. *You've made me feel like more than just your mate, like I really am your lady, your equal. You showed me how I could reach for all the happiness I can imagine regardless of what anyone else thinks. I love you so much. There's no part of my life that isn't better for having you in it.*

Then we're agreed, he replies, his hand caressing down my side. *No one and nothing will tear us apart.*

The emotions flaring in me and rippling between us through our bond are more than just affection now. I kiss Corwin harder, and he responds with equal ardor, easing me down on the bed. His wings continue to form a canopy over us as his tongue delves between my lips. The feathered tips curl in to stroke their soft surface along my arms, sending an eager shiver through me.

You are mine, he says as he teases his tongue into my mouth. *Mine, always.*

Yours, I agree. A fresh rush of needy heat washes over me, and all at once I need to be so much closer to him. To reaffirm our bond in every way I can.

I yank at his tunic, and Corwin pulls back from our kiss just long enough to toss it aside. As my fingers travel over the tattooed planes of his bronze skin, his chest reverberates with a pleased hum.

The desire rising in him turns me on even more. I can feel him reveling in my eagerness, in the curves of my body and the heat of my mouth, and his hunger sets me on fire.

He drops his head and tugs down the bodice of my dress. In one swift movement he's cupped one of my breasts and sucked the peak into his mouth. Pleasure races through me at the swipe of his tongue over my hardening nipple. My fingers tangle in his dark curls, a whimper escaping me.

Mine, he repeats through our bond like an incantation. *My soul. My love. My mate. Mine.*

His mouth worships every part of me: one breast and then the other, the lines of my collarbone, the arc of my rib cage, the slope of my stomach. He lingers just below my belly button, placing a curving line of the most delicate kisses there. A tendril of grief penetrates the lust that's gripped us.

There will be another, I tell him, willing it to be true. *If it could happen once, the one time we came together when I was fertile, it can't be too hard to make it happen again, right?*

Corwin looks up at me, his dark eyes fathomless. *I will wait as long as it takes, and should it never happen, I still wouldn't have a single regret about tying my life to yours.*

The lump comes back into my throat. Then he's peeling my dress the rest of the way off me and lowering his mouth to my sex, and there's no room left in me for anything but a surge of bliss.

I gasp, my hips lifting to meet his lips. He grazes his teeth over the sensitive spot above and then teases his tongue over my opening, and I outright moan. At the same moment, his wings sweep down to stroke across my shoulders and chest. The texture of the feathers sparks all kinds of delight in my already sensitized breasts.

Corwin picks up on every tremor of pleasure and adjust his position to heighten the sensations even more. I tip my head back into the pillow, rocking with the movements of his mouth, totally adrift on ecstasy. It only takes one sharper suck on that sensitive nub to have me careening over the edge of my release.

He laps at me again as if he isn't done devouring me, but I need so much more of him. I tug at his shoulders, and he eases up over me, anticipation thrumming through him alongside his joy at seeing me so satisfied.

I reach for him, curling my fingers around his rigid shaft. The bliss that jolts through him at my touch only makes me wetter down below. I pump my hand around him experimentally, but the groan that escapes him shatters what's left of my self-control. I push my hips up to meet him, and he sinks into me as if we were made to fit together this way.

Maybe we were. Maybe this is right even if it isn't exactly how fate would have intended it. How could it feel so perfect if it wasn't?

Corwin plunges in and out of me, taking me higher and higher as the pleasure builds again. Then he rolls us over so I'm on top, straddling him.

I brace my hands against his chest and ride him with all I have in me, taking him deeper, my breath stuttering as he hits that special giddying place within. Impressions of me through his eyes flit into my awareness—I soar over him, my hair flying wild and my face alight with happiness, as if I'm as much a raven as he is.

I can't hold on very long. The feeling of him thrusting so deep inside me has me racing toward my second release in a matter of seconds. Corwin grasps my hips and adjusts my angle just slightly, and then a sharper flare of delight sizzles through both of us. Our lust feeds off each other's pleasure until I can't tell which sensations belong to me and which to him.

I clutch his shoulders, he slams up into me, and it's as if my whole body shatters with bliss. I cry out, every muscle shaking. Corwin lets out a choked sound as he spills himself in me.

Staying impaled on his softening shaft, I lean down over him to sprawl against his chest. Corwin wraps his arms and his wings around me to nestle me in his embrace. Our sweat-damp skin clings together as if even it refuses to consider us ever being parted.

I wish I could believe our future is as certain as our passion is right now. I wish there was nothing to fear in the destruction of Orion's awful Heart. But none of us really chooses our fates. I've made my choices where I've been able to as well as I can, and there's nothing left to do but hope that those choices keep all my mates with me.

CHAPTER FIVE

Sylas

As we come to a stop by the portal, Whitt frowns. "Are you absolutely sure you're going to insist on doing this alone?"

I inhale the thickly humid air of the fringelands, trying not to let thoughts of the invasion of Murk miles away distract me from my current purpose. "I need a clear show of trust and humility. Last time we miscalculated by having too many men on hand who were too eager for a battle. I can't think of a better demonstration of my intentions than presenting myself without any guards at all, can you?"

My older brother grimaces, but for all his strategic smarts, he has no answer for that. We've been debating my decision on and off from the moment I came to it.

The few guards we did bring along, more for our security on the way to the fringes than for my trip to the human world, stir restlessly on their feet where they're stationed by our carriage. Their gazes scan the hazy forest for any sign of the enemy Murk. I hope I've emphasized to them enough how important it is that they not treat the rat shifters who might return with me like anything other than allies.

If my word as arch-lord isn't enough to get through to my own people, there may be no hope of an alliance at all.

But the proof that it is possible stands right next to me. Madoc considers the portal with his heavy-lidded eyes and then nods to me. "It is a risk, but I don't think Delta or her people have any interest in slaughtering an arch-lord. And she'll be intrigued."

"And I have you to call on to support my claims," I say, my tone going slightly wry. A Seelie arch-lord and the once right-hand man of the Murk king certainly make an odd pairing. Perhaps that will intrigue the sorceress too.

For now, though, I'm going in utterly alone to get my message across as emphatically as possible from the start.

I murmur a word to test the loose spell that temporarily ties Madoc to me so that I can quickly alert him when I need his presence on the other side of the portal. Then I tip my head to both him and Whitt. "We need this, or I wouldn't be taking the risk at all. Wish me luck."

"Heart help you," Whitt mutters, but there isn't much argument left in his voice. I think he was coming to respect Madoc's input even before the Murk man proved just how far he'd go for our mate.

Squaring my shoulders, I step into the wavering surface of the portal. A rush like a chilly wind whips over me, the uncomfortable smell of salt fills my nose, and I find myself standing at the edge of the secluded ocean bay that was the site of our first disastrous meeting with the Murk sorceress.

Delta has evidently been waiting for me, drawn by the message we sent ahead of my arrival but still wary. Rather than coming right down the low rocky cliff that circles the beach, she merely eases up to the top of it from where she was perched behind the craggy ridge. She grips the rough stone tightly, her eyes narrowed as she takes me in.

I can't see them, but I have no doubt that a full force of her warriors is poised just out of view, ready should she give them a signal. Why wouldn't they be after the way our last meeting played out?

I've only taken a couple of steps from the portal. I could dive back through it in an instant if the thought of those Murk warriors worried me too much. That would mean giving up all hope of even having a conversation, though. I hold myself rigidly still, letting her look me over.

"Arch-lord," Delta says after a minute, in a voice that's not exactly sneering but definitely skeptical. She flips her burgundy curls back from her golden-brown shoulders. "Am I supposed to consider this an honor after the reception we got at our last meeting?"

The pride in me wants to point out that the reception her people offered mine wasn't much friendlier. I rein in the impulse and duck my head. Talia encouraged me to be humble, and I can do that when the fate of my entire people rests in the balance.

"We acted in haste and unfairly," I say. "The first gesture I wanted to make on seeing you again was to apologize for how sorely we misjudged you. The fact that you've come at all shows your generosity. I hope that you're willing to hear me now that I'm prepared to lay out my proposal properly. As you can see, I've brought no guards with me. I've put my faith in your good will, as I should have before."

Delta hums under her breath. At a flick of her hand, my wolfish ears catch rasps of movement from beyond the rocky ridge. Her people must be taking steps to confirm I haven't brought any warriors with me who are concealed. They may also be surrounding me. I do my best to tamp down on the apprehension prickling over my skin.

Instead, I lower myself to my knees. It's a position that makes me even more unsettled, but at the same time, I know it's necessary. I think of the stories Talia's told us of the horrors she witnessed done to the Murk—of the parents and children slashed apart by Seelie claws. My stomach knots, but not out of fear for myself.

"There's much more I should apologize for, as much as I can when it comes to the entirety of the fae of the seasons," I say, still keeping my head low. "We have mistreated you and all of your kind at every turn in monstrous ways I had the luxury of remaining partly ignorant of until now. There's no excuse for that or for the way we've demonized the Murk. Even as others like you are attacking my home now, I freely admit your hatred is understandable. I'm here to see if we can make enough amends to create a more peaceful future for both sides."

Delta makes a soft scoffing sound, but she adjusts her position to one that looks more relaxed, sitting on a small outcropping with her hands resting on her thighs. "How unsurprising that you come making this appeal while the entire Mists are under threat from those I'd say are very little like me other than in the most basic sense of our animal natures."

I raise my head to offer her a grim smile. "That's a fair distinction. I wouldn't be reaching out to you if I didn't believe that the Murk have as many facets as any other fae—and that you're very different from the one who calls himself king."

Her dark eyes continue to scrutinize me. "I'm listening, arch-lord. What is this proposal you're so desperate to make?"

The "desperate" comment rankles my pride again, but it isn't inaccurate. I straighten up so I can face her with more authority, so that it'll seem more likely that I can deliver on the promises I'm making.

"Both I and my colleagues understand that the greatest injury done to the Murk has been their all-but banishment from the Mists, which is the rightful home of all fae. We recognize the injustice of this situation and believe the first step toward a more cooperative relationship between our peoples is to give you back that home. If you'll take it, we have a domain within the summer realm where you could relocate your colony. Within its boundaries, it'd be yours to govern as you see fit."

"And outside its boundaries?" Delta asks, although I think I catch a glimmer of more intense interest in her eyes. "How will we be treated there?"

"As long as you do no harm to any of the Seelie, we will insist that you and your colony be treated like any of our packs." My smile turns crooked. "I can't promise every overture will be friendly. We deal with animosities and disputes amongst ourselves on a regular basis. But any sign that someone is targeting you because of your nature will be punished. I believe that simply being exposed to Murk who are living their lives normally will help my people come to accept you as equals."

"So, we're to be an experimental test case and a lesson in proper etiquette as well."

I restrain a wince at her interpretation. "Unfortunately, a certain amount of learning is going to be necessary. I've had to go through it myself. But I don't think it'll be only on our side, will it? Your people will also need time to adjust to the idea that you can exist among Seelie who won't attack or degrade you."

Delta blows at a stray curl that's slid across her forehead. "I suppose that's true. If we moved into the Mists, though, we would be taking a far greater risk, placing ourselves essentially at your mercy. What reason do I have to trust that this offer is genuine and not an attempt to knock out another major power among the Murk while Orion is thwarting your efforts to defeat him?"

This is a moment I expected to come. "I have someone who can join me who I believe can speak to that matter. If you'll allow me to summon him, he'll come alone as I did."

The sorceress hesitates for a second and then nods, but I notice her stance tenses again. This is how it will be for quite some time, I expect: a small gesture of trust followed by a small request, and then the same in return, until we're no longer so cautiously feeling each other out. I can't criticize her for her wariness.

I say the word to trigger the spell that'll alert Madoc and step more to the side of the portal. It's only a matter of seconds before he eases out onto the beach next to me, the ocean breeze ruffling his pale hair.

His posture is tense too, and it occurs to me on a deeper level than it did before that this is the first time he's revealed himself to any of his people since he committed to siding with the fae of the seasons. From what he's said, he has little past connection to Delta, so it's unlikely she'd take the betrayal anywhere near as personally as his king will, but that doesn't mean she'll be happy about it either.

He hasn't cast an illusion over himself like he did last time. He *has* unfurled his tail before arriving. He stands tall with the thinly furred appendage curving across the ground next to his feet, announcing what he is in a way more definitive than any words could manage.

"Hello, Delta," he says, gazing up at her. "We've never met before, but I know you have scouts throughout this world. Maybe they've kept you well enough informed that you can recognize me."

The Murk woman hasn't moved, but her eyes have widened. She speaks a few magic-laced words that I manage not to flinch at. From the way Madoc's posture turns even more rigid, it's a spell testing for any magic laid over him. She's ensuring his appearance isn't an illusion.

"You're one of that megalomaniac's so-called knights," she spits out, with more hostility than she aimed even at me. "What are you doing here?" Her gaze darts to me. "What are *you* doing with him?"

Madoc answers, his voice going dry. "It seems we need to work on acceptance not just between the fae peoples but within our own. Yes, I used to stand beside Orion. But I've come to see him for what he is, and now I oppose his methods whole-heartedly. I'm only trying to make sure he doesn't take too many others down with him."

Delta still looks skeptical. I raise my eyebrows at her. "I'm not sure if I should be offended that you apparently think I'm so dim-witted I'd ally myself with a supporter of the man currently trying to destroy my people."

She gives herself a little shake, and for the first time, a smile crosses her own lips. The glint in her eyes is more mischievous than anything now. I suppose that will always be part of the Murk's nature no matter how nicely they promise to play.

"Fascinating," she says, studying Madoc for a little longer. "And *you* believe that our best chance at not being ruined by the mad dictator lies with types like this?" She motions haphazardly toward me.

Madoc's mouth curls into a smirk I decide not to be offended by either. "I think that for all Orion's power and fury, he's going to have trouble completely wiping the Mists clean of other fae. And I think

I'd rather not live in a society of Murk founded on so much death—on both sides—if there's a better way. If we're not exterminating them all, then the only way to coexist with the fae of the seasons on the lands we deserve is to find a way to work with them. But I haven't been letting them off easy."

"And you'll vouch that the offer they're making is genuine? They truly have lands they'd give to my colony without any hidden demands?"

Madoc shrugs. "This one definitely means it. We also have a major advocate in the human woman who's been the cure for their curse. She holds plenty of sway among the fae of the seasons and has forced them into plenty of other compromises they might not have agreed to without proper motivation."

He hasn't mentioned his newfound connection to the Heart of the Mists. From what he's said, Delta and her colony have never completely lost their own connection since they never fell in with Orion to bind themselves to his false Heart. We'll save that appeal for the Murk king's followers.

Delta hums again and returns her attention to me. "What exactly are the lands you'd offer us? I have no interest in the swamps or scrubby forests along the fringes."

I open my mouth to tell her about the spot Whitt and I picked out that my fellow arch-lords agreed to, a well-sized stretch of fields and forest about halfway between the fringes and the Heart that's not terribly close to any pack we feared might be particularly hostile. But something stops me.

Through my deadened eye, the ghostly impression comes of another version of Delta's face overlying the one before me. It's tipped to a stream of sunlight that dapples her cheeks with a pattern so familiar my breath catches in my chest.

Understanding comes to me like a spark flaring in the back of my mind. The place we chose is good *enough*, but it's hardly impressive. It's not much of a show of dedication to an alliance. I'm only going to get one chance to pitch this, and I'm getting the sense that Delta is going to need more.

I'm speaking before I give myself the chance to second-guess the impulse. "I'd say it's an excellent domain, but I may be biased. Until very recently, it was mine."

Madoc's head twitches as if he's caught himself from jerking around to stare at me. He knows I've diverted from our plans.

Delta's eyebrows jump up. "Yours?"

"Yes," I push onward. "I founded a domain in a bountiful forest not far from the Heart, one I called Hearthshire. It has plenty of space and natural resources, and you can make use of the buildings already there if you wish—or replace them with your own. It was my pride and joy for decades, and I only left it when I had to move my pack with my appointment as arch-lord. I couldn't offer a better home to anyone."

The Murk sorceress is silent for a long moment. I can't tell whether it's a good silence or a bad one. She rubs her hand across her mouth and another flicker of a smile touches her lips. It's then that I really start to hope.

"I recognize the generosity of your proposal," she says. "But I do still feel the need for some caution, as I'd imagine you can understand. I'll send a small envoy of my people to inspect this domain and observe how your people respond to their presence for a few days before reporting back to me. If I'm satisfied with their report, we can discuss the possibilities further."

I incline my head to her. "Thank you for hearing me and for giving this alliance a chance."

Delta chuckles lightly. "Let's hope you prove that it's worth my while."

CHAPTER SIX

Talia

The huge, round room in the center of the Bastion of the Heart is packed fuller than I've ever seen it. Seelie men and women swarm around the three thrones of their arch-lords. Sunlight beams over them from the high windows and catches on the veins of gold that stream through the sandstone walls. Sylas, Celia, and Donovan have drawn their grand seats together at one end of the room so they can speak in unison to the many lords and ladies who've gathered from domains all over the summer realm.

At the moment, though, they're only talking among themselves—in hushed voices in the small alcove formed behind the thrones. I can hear them because I'm perched on the arm of Sylas's throne, leaning close with August at my side.

"Offering Hearthshire was not what we agreed on," Celia says.

"I realize that," Sylas replies, keeping his voice even. "But it allowed me to give a more personal touch to the offer, and I think that's what persuaded Delta to trust me. As with the other spot we'd spoken about, there aren't any near neighbors who should cause major issues."

Donovan cocks his head with a pensive air. "It is prime territory, though. We've already gotten a few requests from emerging lords looking to set up a new pack there. The fact that it was established by a lord who went on to your esteemed position only makes it more appealing."

"Well, we'll just have to inform those lords that it's no longer available." Sylas glances around at his colleagues. "What's more important—ensuring our alliance with the Murk who aren't actively at war with us or gaining the favor of some minor lord who should be loyal to us regardless? There's plenty of land to go around, as you well know. The fact that this land is special is exactly why it made a good offering."

I can't help speaking up. "Arranging peace with the Murk isn't going to happen unless you can treat them like equals. Why shouldn't Delta and her colony deserve Hearthshire as much as any of the Seelie?"

"It's not entirely about *deserving*," Celia starts, but then she doesn't seem to know how to explain what else it'd be about. She sighs, and I can see that she's resigned herself. "Well, we can hardly go back on what you promised now without having her question the entire arrangement. I hope you've sent your own pack-kin to help her envoys settle in?"

"We expect them to arrive later today, and yes, I've already assigned two of my people as well as my cadre-chosen Astrid to overseeing the initial transition." Sylas motions to the horde of gathered fae waiting for the larger meeting. "Shall we get on with planning our next steps? Even if Delta decides to throw in her lot with us, that hardly wins us the war."

"Yes, yes." Celia moves to come around the thrones to take her seat, and the two men follow. I slip off the arm of Sylas's throne as he sinks onto it, but he catches my hand with a quick squeeze. August and Whitt stay close by, and Madoc draws up close behind me. My men are still particularly wary of any new attacks the Murk might attempt on me now that Orion's horrible curse has been foiled.

A lot of the gazes in the crowd linger on Madoc even in his sheltered position by the throne. The fae might have heard about his role in healing me and be overjoyed that I've survived, but I don't think all the lords are totally happy to see a rat shifter standing so close to their arch-lords.

My eyes snag on a few figures *I'd* rather have never seen again. My pulse lurches as I yank my gaze away.

Aerik and his two cadre-chosen, icy-haired Cole and the burly man whose name I've never bothered to learn, are standing near the thrones, waiting for the meeting to start. It's not surprising that the lord who murdered my parents, savaged my brother, and stole me from the human world is here when pretty much every lord in the summer realm is. I just hadn't thought about the fact that I might have to face my former captor.

August squeezes my shoulder. I nod to show I'm okay, even as concern flits into me from Corwin across the border after he's picked up on my momentary distress.

It was months ago that I helped my Seelie mates defeat Aerik and his cadre and sever any claim they had on me. They hold no power over my life. I won't let them shake my strength or distract me from what's really important.

"Let's come to order, please," Celia calls out from the central throne, and the voices echoing off the vaulted ceiling fade. Everyone turns to face the arch-lords.

Donovan raises his voice next. "We need to come to a consensus on our next course of action against the Murk forces that've captured domains on both sides of the border. Since this war requires all of your aid, we feel it's only right that you have a say in the course we take. So far, we've managed to hold off further incursion, but haven't been able to displace the rat shifters and their king from the lands they've taken."

"We're open to hearing any suggestions and offers of resources that might help us turn the tide," Sylas adds. "We *can* overcome them, but only with all of us working together."

Someone speaks up from the middle of the crowd. "What's this about Murk being invited to take up homes here in the summer realm? Why are we bringing them into our midst?"

The disgruntled murmur that follows those questions sends a

chill over my skin. We won't be able to work out any kind of alliance with Delta if too many of the fae object to her presence.

Sylas sits up a little taller in his throne. "As should have been explained to all of you, we've come to recognize that our understanding of the Murk is flawed. Many of them don't support this war or the king who's launched it, or only support it because they fear that we'll wipe them out completely if they don't strike back, which I have to say is a reasonable concern given our past aggression toward them. We'll stand a much better chance of ending this conflict with few lives lost if we can find a common ground with those who'd rather not be our enemies."

"But after all the ways they've attacked *us* over the years—and this curse—" someone else starts.

Donovan cuts him off, speaking just as firmly as Sylas did. "The curse was the doing of the Murk king. And I can't say that the Murk have attacked us more than we've even attacked each other. We're all fae, and we all belong to the Mists."

"I can assure you that every precaution is being taken to see to the safety of all our people as the Murk move among us," Celia puts in, with an imperious glower at the crowd that seems to dare anyone to accuse her of being careless. I have to admit that sometimes her authoritarian air works in our favor.

"I think we're ignoring another very obvious factor," a voice rings out, and my previous chill sinks right through to my bones.

It's Aerik speaking, in the same cool, bored tone he often took when instructing his cadre about how to deal with me. When my gaze darts to where I spotted him before, I find he's staring right at me. It's all I can do not to cringe against August as if I can hide in my mate's embrace.

I can't contain a shiver. August sets his hand on my shoulder with a reassuring grip, his lips drawing back with a hint of a snarl. From behind me, Madoc strokes a comforting hand down my back. He knows who Aerik is too, I remember. He watched over the lord's domain while Aerik held me captive, waiting to see how Orion's plan would play out.

Celia's eyes have narrowed. She may not be as warm to me as the other two Seelie arch-lords, but I don't think she cares for Aerik's tendency toward cruelty either. "And what factor is that, Lord Aerik?"

He lifts his chin toward me before turning to her. "The human girl. Our supposed cure. She's a tool of this Murk king, isn't she? Who's to say he isn't still weakening us and the Heart through her?"

I stiffen at the accusation, my heart thumping hard enough to dizzy me.

Menace glints in Sylas's eyes as he stares Aerik down. "I'll remind you once that you're speaking not just about the woman who's protected us from the curse for years but also my mate. We've found no indication that Orion is continuing to work any magic through her or that she presents any direct threat to the Mists."

Aerik doesn't shy from the arch-lord's glare. "All her relationship with you means is that you're hardly an unbiased judge of the danger she poses to us. The Murk king recently attempted to kill her, didn't he, as a way to distract you? We're also ignoring her value as bait or a bargaining chip. She means something to him, and we can use that against him as he tried to use her against us."

The sounds passing through the crowd now sound like protests, which should reassure me, but I'm still struggling just to hold myself together with Aerik's sharp words resonating in my ears. My breath has started to come short. I grope for the tricks I've learned to deal with the spells of panic that used to come on me much more frequently.

Whitt leans close, his breath grazing my ear alongside his voice. "He's nothing, mighty one, and you're so much more. We won't let him lay a finger on you."

His resolve steadies me. I focus on his assurance, on the warmth of August's and Madoc's hands, on the solid floor beneath me.

This man has taken too much from me. I *refuse* to give him any power over me.

Someone else raises their voice in the crowd. "We can't let any harm come to Lady Talia. She's the only one still holding back the Murk's curse."

"But will we even need her temporary cure if using her means we could conquer him completely and end all this?" Aerik's gaze snaps back to me. "If she's so concerned for all of us, perhaps she should offer that sacrifice of her own accord."

Maybe that's what he hoped to get at all along. He couldn't really have expected that his fellow Seelie would support throwing me to the rats, could he? Unless he's blocked out all the support that's been growing for the woman he treated so awfully. Or he honestly can't imagine that any of the fae could truly respect me as an equal and assumes they'd toss me aside for their own benefit if that was the easiest way to save themselves.

But I could see him scheming up some way to provoke my sense of responsibility and guilt, to push me toward giving myself up regardless of what the rest of the fae think.

From anyone else, that gambit might have had a chance of working. I might believe they really were concerned about finding a way to save all of their people—I might see myself as selfish for not being willing to offer up my life to save so many others.

But from this man, I know he's the selfish one. I doubt he's thinking about anyone other than himself, to keep him and his pack out of the fighting. As if his family won't have played at least as big a role in driving the Murk's resentment of the other fae as anyone else in this room. As if the war isn't their responsibility too.

Anger starts to stir inside me, burning away the quivers of panic. My hands clench at my sides.

"We've seen no reason to believe that Lady Talia would have that significant an impact on the outcome of the war," Donovan says.

"And we certainly aren't going to throw *any* of our people to our enemies to shield the rest of us, especially not one who's already given so much for all of the fae," Sylas adds with a growl.

Aerik shrugs with an air as if he feels they're all taking his suggestion with far too much offense. "Why not let her make that decision? Or does she no longer need to speak for herself now that she has an arch-lord and his cadre to hide behind?"

His gaze seeks me out again. I stare back at him, my skin tightening around my body. I feel like I might crack, but maybe not in a bad way.

He treated me like a helpless animal for years. He used me to advance his standing while leaving me in filth and breaking my body, and now he thinks he can use me again. How can I stand here and let him get away with it?

My chest constricts, but I step forward anyway, tugging free from August's grasp. My mate makes a discomforted sound, but he doesn't pull me back.

The fae between me and Aerik draw to the sides as if trying to steer clear of whatever's about to go down between us. I'm not sure whether they're at all intimidated by me or only worried about his response, but it gives me a clear view of the man who ripped my childhood and my family apart.

"I can speak," I say, my voice trembling but coming out loud enough to carry. "But I'm not sure you should be asking me to, when there's so much I can say. How can anyone trust your opinion about me after the way you had me living all those years you held me captive? Do they all know that you kept me in a cage so small I couldn't even stand up? That you barely gave me enough food to keep me alive? That you let your cadre bruise and batter me as if I were a punching bag for their amusement?"

The color starts to drain from Aerik's already sallow face. Apparently he didn't think I'd ever challenge him this openly. The hisses of disgust in the crowd make him stiffen.

"You fought us," he snaps. "You tried to break free. We needed you. No one should blame us for doing what we had to in order to hold on to our cure."

"And yet somehow the moment I joined Sylas's pack, I didn't need any cages to hold me or to be starved so I'd be too weak to move." I motion toward the arch-lord's throne, my gaze still fixed on Aerik, pain and fury searing up my throat. How dare he? How *dare* he still treat me like I'm nothing more than a tool? "Because I'm a thinking, feeling person, and I *wanted* to help the fae when I found out about the curse. You never even gave me a choice. So, I don't give a damn about your opinions now, especially when it comes to how I can 'help' you. I'd be happiest if I never had to see your face or hear your voice again."

None of the arch-lords interrupt, watching to see how the confrontation plays out. Aerik's gaze flicks to them as if he expects them to intervene on his behalf. I don't risk looking away from him, but from the clenching of his jaw, none of their expressions give him the support he was searching for.

Madoc steps up beside me, his head held high. He pitches his voice to bounce through the vast room, his tone scathing. "If anyone needs proof that spiteful and malicious behavior isn't confined to the Murk, they can look no further than this man. How strange that some of you would paint all of my kind as villains when monsters like him exist among the Seelie."

The rumbling of the other assembled lords is taking on a fiercer tone. A few lean close to Aerik with words that must be harsh given the way his face twitches. He motions to his cadre, and suddenly they're weaving away through the crowd toward the exits.

A strange sensation of lightness comes over me. He didn't acknowledge anything I said, didn't bother to say a word in response, but I'm glad I said it anyway. He might not care that he hurt me, but an awful lot of the fae around me do, and he cares what *they* think. That's good enough for me.

As the angry muttering starts to die down, Madoc raises his voice again, more calmly this time. "If we can get back to discussing strategy, I may be able to help. We've given Orion's army time to realize that taking the Mists will hardly be easy, and we've begun making overtures to the Murk who don't stand with him. I think it's time for me to reveal myself to the king's followers and show them there's another way."

My pulse hiccups. Presenting himself to Orion's forces means tipping Orion off to the fact that he survived—and I have no doubt at all that the Murk king will be baying for his former knight's blood the second he finds out.

I grope for Madoc's hand. "Are you sure?" I ask quietly.

He aims a tight smile at me. "It's what I'm here for. The sooner I speak up, the more of them I may be able to save."

CHAPTER SEVEN

Madoc

As the defensive wall of magic comes into view up ahead, the carriage slows. My heart thuds faster as if to make up for the change.

As far as I can see in both directions, hundreds of Seelie are gathered along the wall, maintaining the shield against Orion's army. The magical barrier is mostly transparent, but I can't make out all that much of the Murk forces on the other side. They've left a stretch of grassy field turned cracked and muddy by the fray as a buffer between them and the Seelie. As I watch, a few spots on the wall spark where an aggressive spell must have hit it.

The breeze that wraps around me is warm and increasingly humid this close to the fringes, the late afternoon sun overhead beaming brightly, but neither of those elements touch the cold, clammy sensation in my gut. I told Talia I was ready to face my people and reveal the full extent of my betrayal, but I don't feel totally prepared now.

I wish I could be sure I'll be able to convince any of them my desertion wasn't a betrayal but an act meant with their future in mind too. How can I explain to them that the Seelie don't have to be our enemies? That Orion poses a greater threat to their lives than most of the fae of the seasons do?

I'm still not completely sure how true that is myself. No one's approached me with any overt hostility since my resurrection by the Heart of the Mists, but my reception from most of the fae here hasn't exactly been joyful either. I trust Talia, and I'm going to trust her men, but I can't shake the niggling worry that their influence might not be enough.

It doesn't matter, though. Even if we end up struggling against the Seelie and Unseelie in one way or another, I *am* sure that the war Orion's leading so many Murk into will only make things worse. His dreams of grandeur weren't particularly accurate. He wasn't able to storm right through the realms and topple the fae of the seasons like dominos. Even if he can win, it'll be a drawn-out, brutal victory in which more Murk die than survive.

The carriage comes to a complete stop at the camp where some of the warriors are getting a break from the standoff while digging into a meal. I forced down a little food at the start of the journey to keep my energy up, and it sits heavy in my stomach. The smell of the hearty stew makes me a bit queasy.

Sylas comes up beside me where I'm still poised by the bow of the carriage. The fae who came with us, mostly pack-kin of his who are switching off with those who've been on the front for a while now, are already disembarking.

"We'll keep a shield around you the entire time," he says. "As long as you don't stray too far from the wall, you should be able to get back behind its protection quickly enough if they attack."

I nod. I'm going to have to step through the barrier in order to convey my message to my people. I have tricks up my sleeve to do it somewhat safely, but it's still going to be a dangerous task.

Sylas pauses and looks me up and down, his pale, blind eye seeming to see as much as his darkly alert one. Talia told me he got that injury from a Murk woman's spell. I never really know what to say to him with all his lordly airs.

He loves Talia, and he's accepted me because of the sacrifice I made for her. I have no idea what he makes of me beyond that.

"If you need a moment to ground yourself, there's no sense in rushing into it," he says. "You're doing a valiant thing here today, and I defy any of my fellow fae to claim otherwise."

My skin prickles with the suggestion that I've been some kind of hero. I don't feel like it.

"I'm doing it for them," I say, tipping my head toward the Murk in the distance. "Because I want them to have the best lives they can."

The corner of his mouth quirks upward just slightly. "I'm not going to criticize you for that. Why shouldn't they be your first priority? My kin are mine."

"Well, I hope your kin prove me right that this is the best course of action."

Sylas's expression turns serious again. He glances along the front at all the Seelie who've joined the fight, and for the first time, I can really see the burden of his role weighing on him. This is a man who's been through a lot and who's discovered that no plan is ever truly cut and dried, that you can always lose something no matter how well you think you've prepared.

I never saw that kind of gravity in Orion. He treated his rule like both a divine right and a game. I doubt my king ever questioned whether one cruel whim or another was justified.

And that's why I'm here, isn't it? In some ways, my people are as trapped as Talia once was, caged by flames of hatred that Orion is determined to fan past the point of no return.

"There will almost certainly be more turmoil ahead," Sylas says, "but after everything we've already weathered and all the changes for the better Talia's brought about, I have faith that it'll come out right in the end. For all of us." He glances at me again. "I can only imagine how difficult taking this step toward bridging the gap between our people's will be for you. If there's any other way I can help, don't hesitate to say so."

"For Talia's sake?" I can't help asking, my tone going dry.

Sylas considers me. "I hope you don't actually believe that's true.

It may have been a fraught journey getting to this point, but you're family now and a colleague besides. You've shown who you are at heart, and I admire that man quite a lot. Your king may not support you, but you have plenty of others who will now."

I hadn't expected a response anything like that. My stomach flips over, startled but also weirdly pleased. In that moment, for the first time, it hits me that I could be a full part of Talia's odd family and not just a hanger-on grudgingly accepted.

I open my mouth and close it again, abruptly awkward with the knowledge of how skeptical I've been about his intentions. "Thank you," I say finally. "I might not always be the best at keeping my snarky remarks to myself, but I do appreciate your trust and respect all the same."

Sylas turns toward the wall, his gaze fixing on the Murk. "They should extend the same. But it'll likely be a slow process." He moves to the edge of the carriage. "Give us a signal when you're ready to cross."

I'd been wavering, but something about the conversation has solidified my resolve. I may as well take advantage of my confidence while I have it.

"I'll go now," I say, hopping to the ground on the other side.

Sylas waves a few other Seelie over, and the four of them weave a shielding spell around me to protect me from any sudden attacks. As their magic tingles over me, I intone several words of my own, constructing the spell I'll put into action as soon as I've passed through the wall. I may not be much of a warrior, but illusions can get you pretty far when you're not looking to do damage, only to avoid it.

When the Seelie are finished building their protections around me, they escort me over to the wall and open a small section of the barrier so I can walk through. I know they'll keep it open the entire time so I have an escape route and so they can bolster their spells on me if they need to.

The landscape on the other side is exactly the same, even though at this point it feels like it should be a different world. I inhale the humid air deeply, restraining a grimace at the sour tang of hostile magic that hangs in it now after all the fighting, and focus my attention on the Murk forces about a mile away across the beat-up field.

With a few more quick words and energy directed with all my concentration, I project an illusion of myself across the distance to stand on a low lump of earth I've picked out. All at once, the swarm of Murk come into sharper focus, many of them startling at my sudden arrival and swiveling to face me. I can see them and hear their uneasy murmurs as if I really were standing just fifty feet away, with a jarring awareness of the spot where I'm projecting the image of myself superimposed over my real surroundings.

"My friends and comrades," I say, flicking my tail to the side to make sure it's fully in view. "I think many of you will recognize me. I've fought and worked alongside you for decades. I've given my all to support you and work toward the future we deserve in every way I can, so please, give me your ears now. I have something incredibly important to tell you."

My voice and the small gestures I make are echoed into the illusion just as the sights and sounds facing that conjured version of me echo back to my real eyes and ears. Several of the Murk have raised their hands with weapons or in preparation to cast spells, but someone else calls out, "It's Madoc! He's alive." The others gathered around outside the pack village they took over stir on their feet, restless with uncertainty.

I wish I could reach all of the Murk who are stationed across this realm and the winter side, but the best I can do is hope that my message sticks well enough that at least a few who believe me will pass it on. "That's right," I say. "I was Orion's knight, and I helped you all prepare for this war. But I've discovered that there's another way. A way we can have our home and not just that, but the power of the Heart of the Mists as well."

"How do we know it's really him?" a skeptical voice calls out of the crowd. "Maybe this is just a trick from the Seelie who killed him."

I train my illusionary eyes as well as I can on the figures in front of me. My vision is slightly blurred as it travels across the distance to the real me, but I can still identify a few fae whose names I remember.

"Dani," I say, nodding to one woman, "I found a space for your new home in the Refuge when you arrived with your son and got you set up in the weapons workshop." My gaze slides to an older man. "Cullen, I was always grateful for your scavenging runs because you'd find the freshest meats, as I thanked you for more than once." And to another man. "Lucah, I hope your leg isn't troubling you anymore after that clash we had with the Unseelie sentry in Stadtpark."

I *have* been there for my people, and I can tell from the widening eyes and the shift in the tone of their murmurings that they at least believe that I'm *me* now.

I pitch my voice to carry even farther. "Many of the fae of the seasons have savaged us over the years. We will not forgive the ones who carried out those crimes. But as I've spied on their leaders, I've come to realize that they aren't all the monsters we think of them as any more than we're all the vermin they've made us out to be. There are fae among them who can see reason and hold sway over the rest of their people. Even as I speak, the first Murk colony is taking up residence in the summer realm with no blood shed on either side and full autonomy to live as they please."

I catch a few gasps from the crowd. "You can't be serious," someone says. "The fucking wolves and ravens would never—"

"They would," I interrupt, raising my hands. "How do you think I'm here at all? I've been able to gain their trust and persuade them toward the future we deserve. And it's not just the fae on our side. The Heart of the Mists itself has welcomed me."

I tug open my shirt, revealing the multiple true-name marks that've formed on my chest and shoulders. An awed hush falls at the crowd's first glimpse, followed by a chorus of excited chattering.

"You could all find your way back to the true Heart with the full extent of its power too," I say. "I'll help guide you. You only need to step away from this war and join me in building a home for ourselves here without the slaughter. I swear on my soul and my magic that if you come to the fae of the seasons peacefully and call on my name, they'll bring you to me unharmed. The more of us stand together, the more we can win for ourselves without any more of us needing to die."

"Like you died," a crisp voice rings out. A shudder travels down my back at the sound of it before I even see the speaker.

Orion pushes through the crowd. I wonder how far away he was when he must have gotten word, how quickly he had to rush to get here to confront me. He steps a couple of steps ahead of the rest of his army, his arms folded over his chest, his yellow eyes narrowed, the sharp white tufts of his hair looking even more vicious than usual. The splotch of a magical burn marks his chin. He hasn't shied from the actual fighting, but then, I wouldn't have expected him to.

The sight of my king makes part of me want to turn tail and duck back through the wall. Ghosts of old pains wake up in the scars that crisscross my body between the true-name marks. But I hold firm, facing him, willing my stance to remain steady.

He might rule our people, but he isn't the leader they need. If Delta can dismiss him, then so can I.

"Yes," I say before he can go on. "I died. I died by my own free will saving the woman who's already given up so much herself to advance our cause, because *you* decided to repay her for her help with a torturous death. But the Heart of the Mists has touched her, and it brought me back to life when I saved her. Even your magic couldn't defy its will."

Orion's lips pull back in a sneer. "You think you know so much." He gestures carelessly at the crowd. "Don't listen to this traitor. I sent him to his death because his mind had gotten weak and his dedication shaky. He's nothing but a wolf in rat's clothing now."

"You sent me?" I retort. "You wanted me to torment her and her mates even more—"

His gaze snaps back to me. "Did you think I was so distracted I wouldn't notice how your loyalties were shifting? I only told you the cure because it ought to have been an easy way to get rid of you while she still met the same fate." He tuts with his tongue. "But of course the meddling Heart managed to get in the way of what should have been. It won't overshadow my power for much longer."

His words pierce my chest with a spear of ice. He noticed? He *meant* for me to sacrifice myself for Talia, as some kind of punishment for the loyalties he threw away more than I discarded?

I was playing into his plan all along.

For a second, I rock on my feet as the revelation sinks in. But it's chased by a certainty that steadies me again.

I *didn't* play into his plan—because he was wrong about me. He thought I'd die needlessly, and that Talia would follow me; he thought my cure wouldn't work. He assumed I was only delusional in imagining I loved her.

It isn't surprising, really. I doubt Orion is capable of that kind of feeling for anything outside of himself and his sadistic games. How could he wrap his head around anyone else truly being that devoted to another being?

I square my shoulders. "You're wrong. You're wrong now and you were wrong then. The Heart didn't save Talia—I did, because I love her. Just as I love my people, in a way you could never be capable of. If they let themselves admit it, everyone here knows that you care more about seeing blood spilled and pain dealt out than bringing anyone happiness. I can lead the way to a future that's *joyful* rather than—"

Before I can get any farther, Orion whips a spell toward me with a flick of his hand. It's so fast I barely have time to react—so fast that if I really were standing right in front of him, it'd likely kill me.

Instead, the searing, stabbing agony only grazes my real flesh before I'm yanking away from the shattered illusion. A holler goes up far away across the plain as my former king must be rallying his troops.

I don't stop to see what fate he has in store for me next. I leap through the gap in the Seelie's wall. The guards waiting there hastily speak the words to seal it again, just as a barrage of hostile magic batters the surface and the ground all around where I was standing a moment ago.

Sylas has stayed nearby in anticipation of my return too. He meets my eyes with a respectful dip of his head. "You spoke well."

I let out a shaky laugh I can't contain. "I hope so. The proof will be in how many of my people really took in my words."

We wait, joining the soldiers in their dinner despite my churning stomach. The blue of the sky deepens into evening and then night. The Murk continue bombarding the wall for hours before finally taking a break. They might have thought their efforts were futile, but the warriors along the wall breathe a sigh of relief, exhausted from reinforcing its magic.

We're just about to head back to the Heart when a wolfish messenger lopes past the warriors to Sylas. He straightens up into the form of a man, his expression an odd mix of eagerness and apprehension.

"My lord," he says. "We've had a few Murk cross over just now, asking for Madoc. Should we let them through?"

A smile stretches across my face as hope unfurls in my chest stronger than ever before.

"I think we should," I answer for the arch-lord. "I'll go talk to them right now."

CHAPTER EIGHT

Talia

I can't help thinking that the Unseelie who built this halfway house of sorts could have used more welcoming materials. The walls are a dark, chilly metal, the floor a lighter gray stone. They included one window, but it's so small it almost makes the room feel darker in contrast with the wintry sunlight outside. At least Zelpha was able to conjure a lantern orb to cast a warmer glow over the small space.

Five Murk are huddled together on the lightly padded bench that stretches along the far end of the room. They look ready to shift into rat form and bolt for the nearest hidey hole at the slightest suspicious move. I finally convinced the guards to hang back outside the doorway while I came in to talk to them, although Zelpha told me there was no way they weren't going to keep protective spells shielding me the whole time.

I guess it's possible that this bunch of Murk might decide killing me would help them somehow, but they don't look like malicious schemers. They look scared. And why not, when they've essentially thrown themselves on the mercy of the fae who've slaughtered so many of their kind in the past?

But they believe in Madoc. They came for him. That knowledge lights up a glow of fondness and pride in my chest.

I step toward them now, stopping in the middle of the room under the lantern. "Hi," I say. "I'm not sure—do you know who I am?" A couple of them look vaguely familiar, but I can't remember whether I crossed paths with them in the Refuge or not.

One of the women offers a tentative nod. "You're Orion's human. The one he tied into the curse."

I've heard that phrasing enough that I don't bristle, even though it makes me feel a little sick. "I don't belong to Orion. He worked magic on me that changed the course of my life, but I'm still my own person—which is why I came back to the Mists rather than staying and letting him use me to hurt the fae of the seasons. But I want to protect fae like *you* too. I've been working with Madoc to ensure you'll be treated fairly."

"Where is Madoc?" asks the man at the end of the bench.

"He's coming," I assure them. "We've had several Murk come over on the summer side, and he's been helping them get settled in. Arch-Lord Corwin—my soul-twined mate—has sent a messenger to him, and I'm sure he'll come as soon as he can. He's grateful for every one of you who've decided to try for peace instead of war. So am I."

The second woman shudders. "There are fae of the seasons who've attacked us, but… Orion killed my brother in front of everyone in the Refuge, just for asking for an explanation about one of Orion's plans that wasn't clear. Orion *smiled* while he was doing it and then had the body chopped up and stuck in a forge. I never really understood why that had to happen."

A lump rises in my throat. "It didn't have to. That's the kind of world Madoc *doesn't* want you to end up in. We think all of the fae can share the Mists in harmony, without so much violence between us."

"And the Heart…" Another of the men glances toward the wall in the direction of the glowing mass he can't see from here but that he can obviously sense, even though he has no connection to it yet. “We could draw on it again?”

“I’m sure you could,” I say. “It welcomed Madoc—I was there when it healed him.” It feels too self-aggrandizing to mention that I was the one who badgered it into restoring his life. “I don’t think… I don’t think it ever totally turned its back on you. I’m not sure how it all works, but it belongs to all of you just as much as the Mists do.”

The first woman tucks herself closer to the man next to her, who I’m guessing is her mate. “And the arch-lords—the Seelie and the Unseelie… They aren’t going to punish us for helping with the invasion?”

“They’ve agreed not to,” I say. “And some of them are looking forward to finding a common ground. If anyone treats you harshly, tell me or Madoc or anyone who works for Arch-Lord Corwin or Arch-Lord Sylas. They’ll make sure it doesn’t happen again.”

The second woman gazes out the window. “I’ve never been this far into the Mists before. It’s… it’s beautiful out here, even if it’s cold.”

A smile tugs at my lips. “Yes, it is.”

I spend the next half hour telling them about my favorite spots in both realms, describing the scenery and other features in as much awed detail as I can give as I see their rapt attention. By the time the door opens behind me, I’m wrung out of stories, but the five Murk have relaxed their stances.

Their faces brighten at the sight of the figure who’s just walked in. The first man springs to his feet. “Madoc! We—we heard about what you said to Orion. This war—it’s only just started, and it’s already nothing we’d have wanted.”

Madoc comes up beside me and sets a gentle hand on my shoulder, giving it a squeeze. “I’m happy to see you all and glad that Talia could keep you occupied while you waited for me. Did you want to stay in the winter realm? We’re building a small temporary village on the summer side not far from the Heart until we see how many Murk join us and can start to think about forming new colonies. I could have you join them, or we could set up something similar here.” He glances at me.

I nod. "I'm sure Corwin would be able to make that happen. Do you want me to talk to him?" My impression of my soul-twined mate is vague at the moment—he's gone out to the front, and he tries to avoid distracting me with his observations of the ongoing battle as much as possible—but he expected to return soon.

"I think the summer realm sounds nice," the second woman pipes up. "After all that time in the subway tunnels, I could use some summer warmth."

The others chuckle and mutter in agreement, and Madoc shoots me a quick smile before leading them off toward the border. I follow them out and stop by Zelpha where she's stayed with the guards.

"See," I say to Corwin's youngest coterie member. "They weren't interested in hurting me."

She clucks her tongue at me. "Can't be too careful. And I'd say that same about any Unseelie I didn't know too, just to be clear. We've had enough trouble from some of the ones we *do* know." She flicks her gaze not all that subtly toward Laoni's domain.

I can't really argue with her there.

I stretch my arms in front of me, and my gaze veers to the vast camp set up nearby, at the base of the plateau. "I think I'll go talk with the fae in the camp and see if there's anything I can do to make things easier for them. Unless there was something else you needed to get to?" My mates' insistence that I always have at least a couple of guards monitoring me does mean a few restrictions on my activities. I understand the need, but it can still be frustrating.

Thankfully, Zelpha shakes her head and sweeps her arm toward the camp. "Let's see what our assorted warriors are up to."

I head across the fields in my limping way, the thin layer of frost crunching under my boots, and Zelpha matches my slow pace without complaint. But before I've quite made it to the assorted buildings dotting the terrain, a slim figure with mottled maroon and burgundy hair slips around the nearest structures to walk over to join us.

My pulse stutters when I recognize the young woman as Kara—the true-blooded woman who pointed to Corwin as her supposed soul-twined mate.

I stop, waiting for her to reach us, my stomach twisting. I have no doubt about Corwin's dedication to me, especially after our interlude together where he affirmed his love so many times and I did the same for him. But that doesn't make this situation any simpler or less stressful.

What can Kara want to talk to me about? I have no idea what to say to her. I've essentially stolen her mate, though, so the least I can do is give her a little of my time and see what she wants.

Zelpha and the guard she brought with us hang back a few steps to give the fae woman and me a little space for our conversation. As Kara reaches me, her gaze darts to them and then back. She bobs her head in a meek gesture that contrasts with her almost regal lady-like bearing.

Part of me can't help thinking about how she'd look much more fitting at Corwin's side than I do. She was born into true-blooded fae royalty, even if only a small fringeland flock. This is her heritage. I was meant to be an ordinary human living my life with no idea that the fae even exist.

But we're here with things as they are now, and there's no turning back time to change any of it.

"Hi," I say awkwardly. "Was there something you needed?"

"I was just—" She hesitates and wets her lips, and I get the sense she's equally uncertain about how to have this conversion. That impression eases my nerves a little, although she's the one who sought me out, so I have no idea how to encourage her.

She glances at my guards again, and her mouth slants at a pained angle. "Could we… speak privately? Since really, our association is around a private matter."

I guess that's a fair statement. I know Zelpha isn't going to agree, though. When I check with her, she's frowning.

"You can cast a spell to keep us from hearing what you're saying," the coterie woman says. "But Lady Talia will stay close by and in our view. Arch-Lords' orders."

Kara's lips purse, and for the first time a hint of annoyance touches her expression. But she doesn't argue, just murmurs a few words that make the air hum and then go totally silent around us.

Her hands flit beside her body as if she isn't sure what to do with them. She settles for clasping them in front of her. "You were there—you know what Arch-Lord Corwin is to me."

I swallow hard. "Yes. I'm so sorry. I can't imagine how difficult it is to be in your position."

"Yes. Well." She unclasps her hands and fidgets with the skirt of her plum-purple dress. Her eyes narrow slightly as she considers me. "I was thinking, though, that if it was outside magic that created your bond with Arch-Lord Corwin, then it should be easier to dispel than an actual soul-twined bond."

My stomach starts to sink. "Maybe," I say. "But neither of us wants to dispel it. Corwin and I have bonded in many ways other than just through magic. There's more to being someone's mate than just having the internal connection." I should know, since I don't have any magical bond with the other four men who've worked their way into my heart.

"But the internal connection is what takes it beyond a regular mate-bond," Kara says. "I *should* have that connection with him. I can't have it with anyone else." She pauses. "And you have other mates as well, from what I've heard."

There's a faint derisive note in her tone that brings my hackles up despite my sympathy for her. "It just happened that way. I'm fully dedicated to all of them."

She hums to herself. "I heard you were generous, that you're always looking out for the fae and doing what you can to help us. Wouldn't you step out of the way of the soul-twined bond I was supposed to have?"

Her gaze turns so beseeching that guilt clamps around my gut, but I don't know any other way to answer her. "Corwin and I have already sworn our loyalty and love to each other. I don't know what's going to happen with the magical part of our bond as we continue to fight with the Murk, but the rest isn't going anywhere. I *am* incredibly sorry that it worked out this way, but there's no way to undo what we already feel for each other."

Something flares in the fae woman's eyes. Her voice sharpens. "Then you're stealing him from me. Stealing another woman's destined mate. How can you even look me in the face when you're ruining my life?"

My jaw goes slack at her abrupt transformation, even though I saw hints of her animosity before. "I—it's not like that," I stammer, but she barely seems to listen.

"It's exactly like that," she says, stepping closer so she can loom over me with her greater height. "You know he's meant to be mine, but you'll happily keep him wound around your finger. A *human.* A human full of Murk magic. He deserves so much better than you. If I could—"

The silencing spell around us fractures as Zelpha bursts through it, clamping her hand on my arm and positioning herself partly between me and Kara. She's a few inches shorter than the true-blooded woman, but she glares up at Kara with a flex of her muscles that gets a clear threat across. "You'll step away from Lady Talia and calm yourself," she says in a taut voice. "And you won't be having any more private conversations with her, that's for sure."

"*Lady* Talia," Kara says with a scoff, but she spins on her heel and marches off without another word.

I deflate a little in Zelpha's grasp. The coterie woman whirls toward me. "Are you all right? What did she say to you?"

"Nothing I can't understand, even if she was harsh about it," I say quietly, and hug myself. The words still ringing in my ears aren't about what I've done or what's done to me but the most fundamental piece of who I am: *A human.* Spoken with such disdain.

I'm more than that. I'm worth just as much as Kara or any other fae is. But it's hard to hold on to my certainty in that knowledge with her scorn still echoing through me.

CHAPTER NINE

Talia

"This really isn't necessary," Corwin assures me for what might be the fiftieth time. He's stayed close to me on the carriage for the entire journey out to the winter realm's front, poised by the side of the vehicle next to the bench where I'm perched. He hasn't expressed his worries for me any more overtly out loud, but his concern radiates through our bond.

I reach to grasp his hand. "I know. But we've seen how everyone—especially the Unseelie—has responded to me since I started curing the curse. I don't feel like a savior exactly, but if it lifts their spirits to see that I've come out to encourage them, then I think that's worth something." *More than sitting around back at the castle not knowing how else to contribute*, I add silently.

You've already given more than anyone could have asked, Corwin replies in the same way, his fingers tightening around mine. But he doesn't argue about my insistence on joining him on today's foray to the front again.

"I can always tell when you're talking in your heads," Madoc says from where he's sitting at my other side, in a tone that's more wry than offended.

I bump my shoulder against his. "It's just Corwin being his usual protective self."

"Hmm. That does seem to be a common theme." Madoc isn't yet comfortable making any obvious shows of physical affection in front of the other fae, but his tail tucks around my waist in a loose embrace. He's coming along for similar reasons to me, although by speaking up to the Murk on this side of the border, he's got a lot more chance of accomplishing something useful than I do.

The winter fringelands are basically the opposite of the summer ones, which I suppose makes sense. I can tell we're getting closer as the temperature dips from refreshingly crisp to bitingly cold and the limited vegetation vanishes completely, giving way to long stretches of jagged rock and ice. The only similarity is the growing haziness of the sky overhead, dulling the sunlight. On the summer side, that effect ramps up the humidity. Here, it deepens the chill.

I let go of Corwin's hand to wrap my arms around myself. I'm wearing a hooded wool coat over my Unseelie-style dress, with warming charms in both pieces of clothing as well as my boots, but the frigid air still makes me shiver. It's hard to imagine anyone wanting to live out here, but I guess that's why it's only less prominent lords who end up settling their flocks this far from the Heart. Maybe there are some minor benefits to being so close to the human world… when the Murk aren't launching an attack from that direction, anyway.

The squadron of warriors around us has mostly been sitting in quiet conversation for the trip, occasionally calling over to the several other carriages arriving with us. When one man suddenly leaps to his feet, I can't help startling.

"Something's wrong," he says, pointing toward the distant horizon.

My human eyes can't make out whatever he's seeing, but the second Corwin's head has jerked around to follow the man's gesture, his posture stiffens. He mutters a curse in his head that only I can hear and motions to the warriors around us, pitching his voice to carry to the nearest carriages. "It looks like the Murk have pressed forward with a fresh attack, and our people may be struggling. Push on as quickly as you can and prepare to enter the fray as soon as we arrive."

He shoots a frantic look my way. I tug my coat even tighter around myself and offer him a wavering smile. *We knew it was possible this would happen. You have to join them—we can't turn back now.*

I can't lose you either, he replies firmly. *I'll stop this carriage farther back and ensure every possible protection is placed around it.* He pauses. *I suppose our soldiers may need your encouragement now more than ever.*

I wish that were a happier thought.

Madoc stands so he can take a closer look. The carriage soars ahead so quickly the wind starts to whistle against its sides. I peer through the crystalline windshield that stops the air from stinging my eyes too much, and the scene that disturbed the Unseelie around me so much swims into view.

Light is flickering all along the horizon like tiny streaks of lightning. Conjured attacks, I have to assume. And they're flashing against a nearby castle of pale stone. My stomach knots.

Before, the front was well away from any domains other than the ones the Murk had already taken over. They've driven their offensive all the way to at least one that's deeper into the winter realm. How many more flock folk are dying right now?

A fae in raven form dives from the sky to land on human-like feet in an open spot in our carriage, her wings still out.

"My lord," the woman says in a rasp. "We hadn't been able to send word, we've been so busy. The Murk struck out at us unexpectedly less than an hour ago. We had to fall back or they'd have managed to surround us and slaughtered us all. We're trying to hold Silverspun, but— With the tricks of the Murk magic, it's hard to keep up with them."

Corwin's mouth sets in a grim line. Madoc raises his hand to catch the woman's attention. "What exactly are the Murk doing?"

She hesitates for a second but answers at Corwin's nod. "They used an illusion to give the impression that they were launching an attack farther along the front. As soon as we'd diverted significant manpower that way, they actually pressed forward in a spot no longer so well-defended. Quite a few managed to burrow into the earth far below the wall in rat form, which allowed them to come at us from both sides. And they've been manipulating the thick ice out here to their advantage: melting it beneath us, propelling it up into blades… We lost quite a few people as it was, even pulling back. The wall shattered, and we haven't had a chance to focus on rebuilding it, we've had to put so much effort into fending them off."

"We'll lend our strength to yours, of course," Corwin says. "I'll join the battle myself. I don't want to see them taking any more ground."

"We're trying our best."

"When their forces are on the move, always strike out at a few of them to test them before assuming anything you see is real," Madoc puts in.

The woman dips her head. "We've been doing that. But they had enough real fighters among the illusions that it was convincing." She grimaces. "We now think they had spells on them to draw any magical attacks toward the real figures rather than the illusionary ones."

Some of the Murk volunteered—or were bullied into—taking on a suicide mission. I wince inwardly.

We speed the rest of the short distance to the new line of fighting. Corwin motions the other carriages to form a barrier ahead of ours and has the warriors around him join him in constructing a swift but potent shield around this specific vehicle. "Stay here," he tells me. "If things take an even worse turn, we may need to leave in a hurry."

I nod reluctantly. There's nothing I can offer from back here, still nearly half a mile distant from the real fighting. But it's not as if the Unseelie army has time to really take in any encouraging words right now. They're caught up in a fight for their lives.

"I'll stay with her," Madoc says, running his fingers gently over my hair. "I won't be able to speak to my people properly while they're in the middle of a rampage. If you can temporarily subdue them, call me in."

"Thank you," Corwin says, and with a flurry of wings, he and the dozens of Unseelie around us soar off to meet our enemies.

I move to the bow of the carriage, but even from there, I can't make out much of the fighting. My gut has balled into a knot as hard as a stone. My men worry about me so much, but I have plenty of reasons to worry about them too.

"Will the Murk target Corwin specifically?" I ask Madoc without looking back. "Will they recognize that he's an arch-lord?"

"In the middle of the fray when they're all fighting as hard as they can? I doubt it." Madoc joins me, slipping his arm around me and pressing a careful kiss to my head now that we're alone. "I won't lie to you and say he isn't in danger, though. You know how fiercely the Murk are willing to fight for what a lot of them see as their only chance at real freedom."

"Yeah." I lean into him, an ache expanding through my chest. In that moment, the war ahead of us feels endless.

It seems as if the front is moving closer to us rather than farther away, meaning the Murk are still making headway. I'm racking my brain for anything I could do that might make a difference when an odd chorus of shouts goes up, loud enough for my ears to pick up on them even across the distance.

"What's going on?" I ask, straining my eyes. Corwin has blocked me out so I don't have to feel more than vague impressions of the danger he's facing.

Madoc leaps onto the edge of the carriage for a higher vantage point and murmurs a few words that must enhance his vision. His stance goes rigid. "Damn it, Orion." The words come out ragged.

My heart lurches. "*What?*"

Madoc is grappling with so much fury it takes a few moments before he manages to answer. "He's brought out children. All the Murk kids he could round up from the orphanages and wherever else, from the looks of it. He's pushing them ahead of the real warriors."

My stomach plummets. There's no way that choice won't end

badly for us. Either the Unseelie will balk at attacking while the children are in the way, in which case the Murk can press on even farther… or the Unseelie will cut them down like other Murk children have fallen to the fae of the seasons in the past, and their deaths will only fuel the other rat shifters' hatred.

If they take the latter route, I'm not sure there'll be any winning this war at all—not the way I hoped to see it end. The Murk won't be able to believe that any Unseelie would ever treat them with respect or kindness.

Before I can really think about it, I'm already scrambling out of the carriage. *Corwin*, I call out, as firmly as I dare for fear of distracting him at a bad moment. My voice hits the barrier in our bond, but I hope he can hear me at least a little. *Don't let anyone hurt the kids. Please. There has to be a way—*

Madoc catches me by the arm before I've made it more than a few limping steps toward the front. "Where are you going?" he asks, his face taut with panic.

I motion desperately toward the line of fighting. "I have to say something—I can't let them screw this up. If they start attacking the Murk children…"

We're doing our best, Corwin replies in a strained tone, and I catch a glimpse of the battle through his eyes: kids who look no older than five or six in human years scattered among older ones, all of them cringing while spells fly over their heads. Then he shuts me out again.

Madoc's mouth twists. "They aren't going to fall back all the way across the realm. At some point, Orion will force their hand."

"Isn't there something we can do to counteract this approach?" I ask. "Could you talk to the kids, convince them to retreat…?"

Even as I say it, hopelessness rushes through me. I doubt the kids want to be there anyway. If they had a real choice, they wouldn't be in the fray to begin with.

Madoc sucks in a rough breath, and then a glimmer of inspiration lights in his eyes. "Maybe not with words, but—our children are more sensitive to materials like iron and salt because they're not fully connected to Orion's Heart yet. If I could quickly slip through a portal farther down the fringes and bring back a sizeable amount—we could set up a different sort of protective boundary that the kids couldn't cross. The Unseelie couldn't either, but it'd at least force a stopping point."

"Yes," I say. "Go—as fast as you can." And then, when he hesitates, "I'll be fine. I won't get any closer until you come back."

He gives me a quick kiss and leaps into the carriage. Thankfully, my other mates taught him how to work their vehicles. They wanted to be sure he could quickly get me out of danger in a situation like this, but I think this use is just as important.

In a blink, the carriage vanishes from my view. He's cast an illusion over it. I slink close to the backs of the other carriages and duck down on the icy ground, praying for a safe and swift journey.

Of course, Madoc bringing back whatever he's able to quickly grab won't be enough of a strategy on its own. We have to get the materials onto the ground between the Unseelie and Murk armies somehow. Madoc will be able to handle a little with his reduced sensitivity while he's still forging his new bond with the Heart of the Mists, and I can help some if the fae shield me while I'm in range of our enemies, but will that be enough?

Corwin has picked up on our planning and opened the connection between us just enough to communicate. I can feel the strain behind his words. *What are you doing? Where's Madoc gone?*

I explain our tentative plan as succinctly as I can and then ask, *Are there other Murk who've come over to our side with the Unseelie now? Or any human servants who could help?*

My mate's reluctance to see *me* helping carries through, but he doesn't voice it. *I believe at least a few of the lords sent human servants to help with things like the meal preparation. I'll see if we can gather them and get ready to clear a strip of land where you can work. We won't be able to save this domain today.*

Then maybe that's our answer. If there's no way to push the Murk far enough back anyway, get ready to fall back yourselves, and we'll lay down the protections just outside the flock's village.

He replies with a sense of sorrowful agreement. I give him an affectionate mental nudge. *It's horrible, but it could be so much worse.*

Send any humans around back to the carriages.. I'll get them ready to act.

It takes what feels like ages before the first figures peel away from the crowd of Unseelie and hurry over to me. The sight of the dazed expressions on the several men and women who end up joining me makes me shudder inside, but I don't have time right now to badger the fae about their policies for human servants. I talk my new allies through the basics of what we're going to do—throwing down materials that'll ward off our enemies—and they seem to grasp enough of what's going on that I think they'll participate.

A crackling explosion sounds from over by the fighting. One of the turrets on the stone castle crumbles away amid sputters of flaring magic. I flinch.

Despair has just started creeping over me again when Madoc's carriage blinks into view right next to us. He's standing at the very front, as far from the sacks heaped at the back of the vehicle as he can get, but his face has turned a sickly shade.

"I didn't consider that *I* don't have the Murk Heart easing my reactions now either," he says, almost tumbling off the bow and staggering a little on the landing. "I had to 'convince' some humans into carrying the salt over… and the trip back wasn't exactly enjoyable."

"But you made it," I say with a rush of relief. "We can handle the rest." At least, we'd better be able to.

I beckon the other humans over and have everyone heave a sack over their shoulder. There's a tab at one end where we can rip them open. Sending word to Corwin that we've got our supplies, we hustle toward the fray.

Several Unseelie warriors hurry to meet us. One of them is Corwin's coterie member Olander, who was out here helping guide the battle before we arrived. Wings unfurled, they scoop us up in their arms with just a grunt at being so close to the noxious substance. "We'll make sure you spread it widely enough and quickly enough," Olander says in a terse voice, holding me carefully. "Corwin's orchestrating the rest of the plan."

We whip across the rest of the terrain so quickly I barely have time to think about what I'm doing. Searing energy sizzles through the air around us and smacks against shields suddenly thrown up. Just as we jar to a halt, the rest of the Unseelie army surges backward around us at a call from voices throughout the crowd.

"Now," Olander says, and I echo his command to my fellow humans as I tear open the bag.

Salt spills all across the frozen ground, the grains sparkling in the muted sunlight. A hiss goes up through the Murk nearby. With his breath rasping painfully as he flaps his wings, Olander sweeps us along the boundary they've chosen, spilling a thin layer of salt all the way across. The other warriors who hefted us do the same with their charges.

More voices shout out words of magic on both sides. A splinter of flame pierces a shield and slices across my temple. I ignore the pain, focusing on pouring out the salt steadily.

And then the sack goes limp in my hands. Olander hauls me away from the jeering Murk forces, but as we spin, I catch a glimpse of the rat shifters at the front of the fray. The children have fled backward, as we hoped. The others can't use them as a shield without drawing farther away themselves.

I don't know how long our gambit will hold, but as Olander sets me back on my feet at the back of the swarm of Unseelie warriors where Madoc is waiting, a new sense of conviction grips me.

There *is* more I can do in this war, more than had ever occurred to me. And now that I know it, I'm not backing down.

CHAPTER TEN

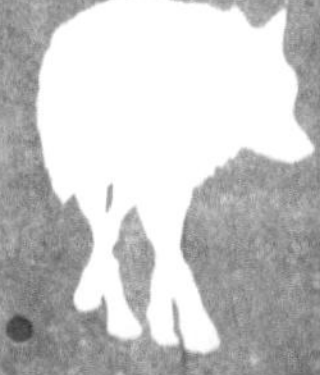

Whitt

I study my mate where she's perched in one of the chairs in my study, her legs drawn up next to her and her bright eyes even more alert than usual. Sometimes I find it difficult to wrap my head around what the woman I love is capable of.

"That was a crazy plan," I tell her. "Literally salting the earth? Sending the most vulnerable beings among us to the front of the battle? But somehow you pulled it off."

"We had the Unseelie protecting us the whole time," she points out in her typically stubborn way. "And it only worked temporarily. The Murk still gained ground. I was hoping you'd have some ideas for ways we can use similar strategies."

I lean back against my desk and raise my eyebrows at her. "We want to start seasoning the rats some more? Hold a barbeque, perhaps?"

Talia's lips twitch with a hint of a smile, and she rolls her eyes at me playfully. "No. The whole point is to try to *avoid* anyone getting barbequed unless it's totally necessary. Especially those kids."

A little shudder runs down her body that sends a pang through my chest. If Orion cared even a fraction as much about our people as she still does about his, we wouldn't be in this situation.

"It made me realize how much the humans who've been living among the fae can help," Talia goes on. "The Murk who're drawing their power from the false Heart might not be as sensitive to the usual materials as the rest of you, but it does bother them, especially over time. If we could find ways to expose them and weaken them, then it'd be easier to reclaim the territory they've taken over and stop them from taking more."

"But the only way we can use those materials is if we have people who aren't affected by them to carry out the hands-on work," I fill in. It's a clever approach, one I'm ashamed to say never occurred to me. For all I admire the woman in front of me, I often forget how human she is—and that the others like her may have nearly as much to offer. "Very sly. The difficult part will be how to expose the Murk to salt or iron or both without them catching our human allies first and destroying them."

"Yes." Talia's mouth slants at a pained angle. "I haven't figured that out yet. I decided that coming to the resident strategist was my best bet." She tips her head in a beseeching way that makes her look particularly lovely.

I decide there's no point in ignoring my desires while we have this conversation. I walk over, scoop her up, and flop down on the chair with her in my lap. A snort escapes her as my arms wrap around her, and she leans her head onto my shoulder. "A better position for thinking?"

"Much better." I nuzzle her soft hair. "Makes me even more inspired than usual to determine how to *not* put your neck on the line any more than we can possibly help."

Talia exhales slowly, her gaze going distant with thought even as she cuddles closer to me. "I guess there isn't any easy way to propel the materials toward the Murk forces, right? If the fae tried to cast their magic directly at the salt or iron, it'd affect them too badly for them to get very far."

I nod. "And somehow I can't picture you humans, as mighty as some of you are, managing to fling handfuls of salt far enough with just your muscles to make much of an impact. We'll need to rely at least partly on stealth."

"I don't think even Madoc could create a spell that would hide us well enough for us to walk right among the Murk without them catching on."

"No. And as soon as you started laying your trap, they'd sense it and attack you." I frown, my thoughts starting to whirl with possibilities. "Perhaps if you were in carriages, some kind of vehicle we could quickly yank back out of their range…"

"That did occur to me too," Talia says. "Raining it down on them from above somehow. If we were high enough up, would that work?"

"Perhaps. It still feels very risky to me. And there's a high chance of them being able to deflect falling materials toward *us* instead, which could even make it difficult for us to retrieve your carriages." Even the breeze could work against us in its temperamental state near the fringes.

"The Unseelie carried us while flying yesterday." Talia's brow knits. "But it was hard for them even only a couple of feet off the ground, being so close to the salt we were carrying. That would probably be dangerous too."

"Yes, I wouldn't consider that a reliable method." But the cogs in my mind are spinning toward a sense of eagerness I'm happy to be familiar with. I'm on the verge of something. If not from above, then…

The idea clicks together in my mind so abruptly and perfectly that it's hard to believe I wasn't planning it out all along. A grin stretches my lips. "We take the opposite tactic, then. Turn their own scheming around on them. They've tunneled toward us before, so why can't we do the same with them?"

"Tunnels?" Talia repeats.

"Larger ones than required to fit a rat," I say, adjusting her against me. "We have our barrier against the Murk army extending well into the ground now, so they'll have had to give up on that tactic for themselves. We can conjure tunnels beneath their camps. I don't think we could bring *our* whole army at them that way, but just a few here and there to lay the trap… Yes, it could work. Then you and the other humans carry the materials in and lay them down. The effect would gradually creep up over the rats through the soil. They shouldn't realize what's happening until they're already weakened, and then we can drive them back."

Talia's face brightens. "I like the sound of that. Do you think all the arch-lords will agree? We'd want to strike out all along the front at the same time, wouldn't we?"

"I'd imagine so. Once we've used the tactic once, we're not likely to get away with it again, so we need to give it our all the first time out. And what's there for the arch-lords *not* to like about getting their domains back?" I give her a quick hug and a peck to her forehead. "Clearly we're an excellent strategizing team."

"Well…" Talia pauses, her body tensing a little against mine. "I should be there with the other humans, helping prepare them ahead of time and guiding as many as I can when we go through with the plan. I'm the only human in the Mists who has much idea what's even going on. And I have one condition before I'll agree to take on that role."

"What's that, mite?" I ask, though I can already guess.

She peers up at me. "You know that before the war started, I was pushing for better treatment for the human servants here. If I'm going to help the fae win this war—if all the humans in the Mists are going to put their lives on the line like that—I want the arch-lords to vow that they'll give their servants more freedom of choice once the war with the Murk is over and ask the other lords to do the same. No more drugging them into obedience. No more controlling them through magic. No more preventing them from going home if that's what they want. I don't think the arch-lords are going to be very happy about that—well, some of them."

"I expect you'll have the full support of at least two," I say wryly, and consider the rest. "There's meant to be another meeting of the full host of arch-lords not long from now. I can propose the scheme—and your conditions—to them then. I think your request is perfectly reasonable… and I don't deserve my job title if I can't convince them of that too."

"They aren't always the most agreeable," Talia mutters.

"No, they aren't." I rub my jaw. "Why don't you sit this meeting out and let me handle it all myself. I suspect it'll go over better coming from me rather than them feeling like you're ordering them all around directly. And you deserve a break from all their squabbling."

Talia looks hesitant, but then she sighs. "Maybe you're right." She relaxes into me a tad more, and an ache wraps around my heart.

She's been through so much in her time in the Mists, and worse calamities than ever in the past month. I don't know what to do or say that could make up for what she's lost or the pain she's experienced.

But maybe there is no making up for it. There's only moving forward and showing her that we're there for her every step of the way.

"Go visit that dress-making friend of yours," I suggest, setting her on her feet so I can stand up. "I think she's getting restless with so much of the pack gone to join the fighting."

I'm not looking forward to this conversation with the arch-lords, but it's best dealt with quickly and cleanly. As Talia heads out, I let Sylas know I've got something to say to the bunch of them, and he gives me the go-ahead with a glint of amused anticipation in his dark eye. He can obviously tell from my energy that I'm ready to go on the offensive.

When the eight leaders have gathered around the long table in our meeting room with their associates nearby, most of them looking predictably gloomy, I don't give them any chance to get started on their own business. I step up to the table, rap my foot against the floor, and peer around at all of them. "Lady Talia and I have come up with a strategy to win back the territory we've lost from the Murk. But it's going to require some cooperation from the lot of you."

I'm met with a mix of curiosity and apprehension, the latter mostly from Corwin's Unseelie arch-lords. "Where is Lady Talia?" Laoni asks, as if that factors into what I said.

"Getting some much-needed rest after all the running around

she's been doing on our behalf," I say. "This is ultimately my plan, but she's fully ready to participate. And her participation will be required for it to work. But if we want to go ahead with it, there's a condition you need to agree to."

Uzziah coughs. "Asking for our agreement before we've even heard the plan?"

I narrow my eyes at him even as I smile. "I can give you the gist. We all know—you ravens more than anyone, I'd suppose—how your human servants contributed to pushing back the Murk and undermining their efforts to unnerve us with horrible tactics yesterday. Talia led that charge. She's willing to lead another one, one that will involve every human in the Mists who's able to take up the cause—and I believe this effort could win us back a significant portion of the ground we've lost."

"I'm waiting for the 'but' to come," Celia says, but her tone is more dry than cool.

I tip my head to her and let my gaze skim over the assembled arch-lords again. "You also know Talia's feelings about how the humans in our realms have been treated—stripped of free will and often of most of their minds as well. My lord and I and her other mates agree with her stance. If she's going to lead them in risking their lives to fend off the Murk, she wants you all to swear a vow that once Orion has fallen, the chemical and magical manipulations will end, and those humans will be given free choice about whether to continue serving you. Both your own servants and you'll also ask it of the rest of the lords."

The air of restrained outrage that emanates from our regular opponents doesn't surprise me at all. "And you'd let her get away with this kind of blackmail?" Laoni demands. "We're in the middle of the war—it's not time to be negotiating amongst ourselves when so many lives are at stake."

Sylas speaks up. "I'd imagine it's lives Talia is concerned about—the lives of all the humans in the Mists that many of us have treated so carelessly. This isn't *their* war. Why should they put themselves in danger on our behalf if we aren't even willing to give them their basic freedoms?"

"I'll agree to it," Donovan says easily, but then, he'd already essentially agreed to work with Talia on this subject before our concerns were diverted by the Murk.

"Our influence over the humans is how it's always been," Terisse says, looking torn.

"This demand is ridiculous," Uzziah mutters.

Oh, he doesn't like ridiculousness, does he? The feather-brained ravens take so much pride in their supposed reason. My spirits lift as I see the exact way to skewer that pride.

"What am I supposed to make of all these arguments?" I say, arching my eyebrows at the Unseelie crew in particular. "Here I thought the ravens had complete faith in their ability to rule. Are you so incapable of handling your flocks that you can't believe any of these human servants of yours would stick around unless you were forcing them to?" I tut under my breath.

Laoni's face flushes into a blotchy complexion. "It isn't about capability," she snaps, but then seems to realize she isn't doing herself any favors with her show of temper. She pauses for a moment to gather herself.

I take the opportunity to drive the point deeper home. "If you're not incapable, then it shouldn't be a problem. Unless it's actually that you're lazy, preferring to take shortcuts rather than put in real effort to maintain your authority."

The Unseelie arch-lord glares at me. Her voice comes out thinner than before. "Hardly. It's simply that we rely on them, and such a huge change would be a big adjustment."

"So would living under the Murk's tyranny, I'd imagine," Celia says, to my surprise. I'd expected her to resist too. She leans back in her seat with a resigned air. "It's an understandable request, and after all we've seen that Lady *Talia* is capable of… perhaps it's been too long coming."

Corwin nods. "Yes, I quite agree."

Uzziah shoots him a glare as if to say, *Of course you would*, but his animosity has deflated. "She's not exactly an average example of her kind," he says in one last-ditch attempt to hold on to his slaves.

"How would you know?" I ask mildly. "Have you ever given

them the opportunity to show just how much they're capable of? That smacks of not just inability and laziness but a failure to embrace your subjects' full potential as well. I really thought the winter fae were much more diligent than that."

His jaw flexes. "We didn't need more from them."

"Ah, but a truly efficient ruler should allow everyone within their domain to contribute to the best of their abilities, I should think. Forgive me if I'm wrong."

He frowns at me, and I gaze steadily back at him, keeping my expression affable. "I suppose we would manage," he grumbles, with a sideways glance at Laoni. "And perhaps we may have missed a few possible benefits."

The self-appointed head of the Unseelie arch-lords sighs. "Fine. It isn't as if we're so dependent on having a few humans around to clean and cook. Now let's hear the rest of this plan."

The corners of my lips curl upward with a sense of triumph I mostly hold inside. "It'll be my pleasure."

CHAPTER ELEVEN

Talia

The temporary Murk settlement not far beyond Hearth-by-the-Heart's borders has such a peaceful atmosphere that I feel my nerves unwind as I sit at the base of an oak in its midst. More tall trees loom over the several wooden houses that've been constructed there, the breeze whispering softly through their leaves. Streams of golden sunlight pool on the grassy ground from the gaps between the branches. A delicate floral scent drifts from the wildflowers dotting the edges of the clearing.

Do the Murk find this atmosphere as peaceful as I do after so many years living in whatever underground or otherwise hidden spaces they could make their own in the human world?

The ones Madoc is talking to right now keep gazing around them with an expression somewhere between awe and terror. I wouldn't blame them if they're still afraid that the fae of the seasons might descend on them at any moment with claws and talons out.

"I can feel it," says a young man named Flynn, whose scruffy brown hair nearly hides his pale hazel eyes. "I know it's there. But the energy isn't coming right inside me."

Madoc gives him a reassuring pat on the shoulder. "It'll take time for you to learn how to open yourself up to the Heart of the Mists and for it to accept you. I… took a pretty extreme route to getting there quickly, which I don't recommend trying on your own. But if it welcomed me, I'm sure it'll reach out to all of you in time. You just need to show you're willing to meet it halfway."

"And you've already taken a big step in that direction by coming to us at all," I pipe up.

The woman next to Flynn, whose name I haven't caught, is swaying a little with the breeze. "They're really going to just let us have all of this?"

Madoc nods. "The fae of the seasons have become increasingly committed to making cooperation between willing Murk and themselves work. And you can be sure I'm taking them to task whenever they balk." He grins, though his stance looks a bit awkward. "Have you gotten totally settled in? If there's anything else you need in your homes for now, I can arrange it. This won't be your permanent village—we're still working out the details of how the resettlement is going to work with the colonies so disrupted."

As he walks off with the woman and a couple of the other Murk, who start asking him questions about the nearby trees, Harper scoots closer to me from where she was poised under a neighboring tree. After we'd spent a little time discussing the state of the fae world and her latest fashion projects earlier today, I mentioned I wanted to see how the newest arrivals were fitting in, and she asked to come along.

"They really are a lot like us, aren't they?" she says now, her over-large eyes even wider than usual as she takes in the temporary settlement.

"More like you than I am," I remind her. "They're still fae. The relations between the groups have just gotten very… twisted and bitter over the centuries. I guess the same thing might have happened between summer and winter eventually if that conflict had kept going for a lot longer."

Harper sucks her lower lip under her teeth to worry at it for a moment. "I wonder how everything soured to begin with. There must have been some kind of falling out or dispute like there was between the Seelie and Unseelie."

"It's probably impossible to know now. And it doesn't really matter. No one involved would still be alive. Trying to figure it out would just give all the fae an excuse to point fingers at each other again."

"And we do seem to love doing that, don't we?" Flynn says in a flippant tone, sinking onto the grass near us. He studies me for a moment. "I know you're the human with the cure." His gaze slides to Harper. "But who are you?"

Harper sits up a little straighter, her mouth twitching as if she doesn't know how to take the question. "I'm Talia's friend," she says stiffly. "Harper of Hearth-by-the-Heart—that's Arch-Lord Sylas's pack."

"Oh, I've figured out *that* much." Flynn leans back on his hands casually. "So, you just came to gawk, then?"

Harper's mouth opens and closes before she answers. "No! I—Talia said she was going to visit. I thought there might be something I could do to help." She pauses, and I decide it's better to let her choose if she wants to say more rather than jumping in. She wets her lips. "I can imagine it must be hard leaving behind your home—I mean, even though the Mists should be your home. I'm sorry if any of the other Seelie have been rude to you."

Flynn snorts. "Rude? That's hardly what I'm worried about." But his shoulders have relaxed, a defensiveness seeping out of his posture that I hadn't noticed until now as it fades. "Well, thank you for saying that. What do you think of us so far?" With a flicker of movement, his tail swings into view as if trying to provoke her.

I'm proud to see that Harper appears not at all fazed by that aspect of him. "I don't know what to think. I haven't really gotten to know any of you. But I can see that Talia's right and the Murk aren't all bad."

"Managed to make a good impression, did I?"

A tiny smile curves her lips. "A little. You could still do some work on it."

A laugh sputters out of Flynn, and then Harper and I are

giggling too. It's a relief to find humor in the situation instead of the tension that's been weighing on us for so long.

"Maybe I'll swing by your fancy arch-lord domain sometime and you can give me the tour," Flynn says. "Really test your hospitality."

"Any time," Harper retorts, responding like it's a challenge, but I think I see a hint of a blush in her cheeks. Interesting.

Madoc ambles back over to us. He tips his head to Flynn. "I heard you're decently handy when it comes to food prep. Do you want me to walk you through the local flora and fauna it's easiest to make use of? I had to rely on that knowledge a lot during my missions while I was still spying for Orion."

"Sure." Flynn jumps up, but he aims a wink at Harper before he saunters over to the edge of the clearing with Madoc.

I look at Harper. "I think you made a new friend. And apparently he cooks. That's definitely a plus."

She makes a face at me. "We were just chatting a bit. I wanted him to feel welcome." But there was definitely a bantering tone to their conversation that I haven't really heard from Harper before—and her gaze follows him for a few seconds before she jerks it back to me.

It isn't long before Madoc rejoins us, and we hop in the carriage that's been waiting with two of Sylas's guards keeping watch over me. Madoc's expression has turned pensive, but I'm not sure what to say to him with the others around. He might be trusting the fae of the seasons more, but I doubt he'd want to share anything all that personal with relative strangers just yet.

He may not want to share what's on his mind even with me.

When we reach the pack village, I give Harper a quick hug before she heads off to her house. I might have gone to see what news Whitt has on the plan we're hoping to launch tomorrow, but my attention comes back to Madoc.

He's adrift here among the fae he spent so long hating. I don't want to leave him to work through whatever uneasiness he's dealing with alone.

"Hey," I say as he helps me out of the carriage. "You haven't really seen much of the border castle yet, have you? Other than the common rooms and, um, my bedroom." And the room of his own that my other mates furnished for him. I can't imagine it really feels like *his* to him yet.

Madoc gives me a crooked smile. "Is there more I've been missing out on?"

"Oh, yes. Come on, I'll show you."

Inside the border castle, the guards drift away and it's just the two of us. But I really did want to show Madoc that there's more for him here than responsibilities and expectations. I lead him down to the basement where August and Sylas have re-located their entertainment room now that we're spending at least as much time living here as in their castle back in Hearth-by-the-Heart. *And you never know,* August had teased as we brought his electronics over. *Maybe I'll even convince Corwin to have a go at a video game someday.*

It's admittedly hard to picture my Unseelie mate getting caught up in a digitized race or fighting match, but Madoc is more familiar with human entertainments than any of my other men. When we walk into the room, which is on the summer side with a wooden floor and walls that give off a light birch-y scent, he takes in the TV and game system and lets out a low whistle.

"Okay, another reminder that I misjudged your taste in men. Which of them lowers themselves to indulging in human pastimes like this?"

I swat his arm and walk over to the leather sofa. Its well-worn surface hugs my body as I sit down on it. "August's the main gamer, but Sylas joins in now and then. The movies are his."

Madoc takes in the DVDs on their built-in shelves at the other end of the room and chuckles.

"And you can use whatever you want down here too," I add. "The entertainment room is for all of us to share."

Madoc sinks down next to me. He tucks his hand around mine. "Is that why you wanted to show me this part of the castle—you're looking to challenge me to a gaming battle?"

I gaze up at him, taking in the heavy-lidded eyes and slightly crooked nose that make his handsome face particularly distinctive. We're still really feeling our way out with each other. Our lives have been chaos since the day we first committed to each other as mates, so there hasn't been much time for settling into any kind of new normal.

But I want that with him. I want us to have the same certainty and ease that's developed with my other mates over time.

"I thought it might be nice to have some time to ourselves to talk," I say. "You seemed like you had a lot on your mind after we visited with the Murk village. Do you think they're doing all right? Have any problems come up?"

"No, nothing like that." He gazes at the wall for a moment, seeing something in his mind's eye. "They're not totally convinced that I haven't roped them into some batshit scheme, but they're giving it a shot, and the Seelie have been… decent so far. That's what matters."

"It's going well, then."

"As well as I could have hoped." His attention slides back to me. "I don't have any specific concerns. It's just all a little much, I guess. I never—I gave orders on Orion's behalf, but he was always the one in charge. And now the Murk who've come over are looking to me as the ultimate authority on how we'll get by among the fae of the seasons, and I don't feel like any kind of supreme expert. I hardly know how I fit in yet. I just hope I don't lead them down the wrong path."

A rush of affection sweeps through me. I push myself up on my knees so I can more easily look him right in the eyes, bringing my hand to his cheek at the same time. "I know you won't, because you care about them even more than you care about yourself. You're doing everything you can to make their lives better for them. It might still be hard, but they're better off here than if they were still under Orion's rule."

Madoc brushes his fingers over my hair, meeting my gaze with a look so adoring it melts me. "At least I'll always have you on my side, my bright one."

The nickname sends a giddy quiver through me. "It's not just me," I say firmly. "Sylas and Corwin and the others will be standing with you the whole way too. You're part of our family now, on the same footing as them. We're all in this together."

In an attempt to emphasize that sentiment, I lean in and press my mouth to his.

Madoc lets out an approving hum and grasps my waist, tugging me to him. In a moment, I'm straddling him, my dress riding up my thighs, our chests pressed together in perfect cohesion. Madoc kisses me deep and slow, savoring my mouth until it's all I can do not to squirm against him to relieve the pressure forming between my legs.

"I don't know how I got this lucky," he says in his lightly hoarse voice, teasing his fingertips right over my scalp. "Not just to live beyond death but to have you as well."

We haven't really gotten to "have" each other all that much so far. I dip my head so my nose grazes his. My voice comes out in a sultry tone I'm not used to. "How do you want to have me right now?"

A strangled sound of need escapes Madoc's throat, and then he's pulling my mouth back to his. This kiss is more urgent but still tender, his tongue slipping between my lips to twine with my own. His hands circle my waist to rock me gently against him. When my core brushes the growing hardness behind his trousers, a whimper spills out of me.

"I want you," he murmurs between kisses, "every way… I can possibly have you." He pauses and peers up at me, his dark gray eyes lit with a glow of desire. "I imagined this, dreamed of this. You coming to me, wanting *me*. I never believed it could be real."

"We had a long way to go to find each other properly," I say. "Both of us." I yank at his shirt, and he lets me peel it off so I can trace the lines of the new true names now marked on his chest. "And I'm not the only thing you found your way to."

"No, but you're the most important."

My throat constricts with so much love I don't know how to put it into words. A memory rises up of a time when I had dreams I never expected to see fulfilled of my own, and Whitt showed me just how enjoyable it could be to have them made real.

I lean forward and press a soft kiss to Madoc's jaw, marking a path along it to just below his ear. "What did I do in your dreams?"

His throat bobs. "Usually I was lying out on the grass in the sun, and you'd kneel over me, and…" He traces a finger along the neckline of my dress. "And offer yourself to me, I guess you could say."

I can do that without any hesitation at all. I pull my dress up over my head and toss it over the arm of the sofa. As Madoc's gaze darkens with hunger, I nudge him around until he's lying on the cushions with me braced over him in only my panties. "Like this?" I murmur.

"Damn close," he says roughly.

I ease forward, kissing him eagerly as my naked breasts sway against his chest. With a growl, he brings his hands to them, caressing the soft curves. When he swivels his palms against my nipples in unison, I gasp at the shock of pleasure that races through me.

Crawling a little forward, I offer my breasts to his skillful mouth. Madoc grins and pushes up on his elbow to slick his tongue over one pebbled tip. As he works it over, I have to swallow a moan. My body starts to rock again, my panties dampening with my desire.

Madoc doesn't leave me hanging. A narrow line of pressure teases across my leg, and I realize he's brought his tail out to play. He flicks it all the way up to the apex of my thighs, and I hiss at the swell of pleasure as he sucks my breast deeper into his mouth at the same time as he caresses me between my legs.

"I love the sounds you make," he mutters as he moves to claim my other breast with his lips and tongue. "I love the way your body moves with mine. I love *you.*"

For a second, I choke up. I grip his hair, arching with the quickening strokes over my sex, but not too lost in the haze of bliss that I can't reply, "I love you too. So much."

With a rough sound, he pushes his body up and flips us over so I'm under him now. As he tugs at my panties, I lift my hips to help him along and then fumble with the clasp of the fae trousers that've replaced his old jeans.

His tail lashes from the air above us and then coils alongside me.

As he grazes his shaft over the slickness of my sex, the thinly furred length flicks over my nipples and traces around my belly button.

I'm panting with longing now. Madoc captures my mouth for one more passionate kiss and slides inside me, filling me until I'm quivering with the delight of the sensation. He thrusts in and out the same way he first kissed me, slow and savoring, like the most delicious sort of torture. I gasp and let out a very undignified whine that makes his gaze spark hotter.

"You'll have everything you could possibly need," he says like a promise. As he hefts my hips off the cushions, his tail slips beneath me and settles into the spot it offered so much pleasure the first time we came together. It rubs across my other opening as if I'm about to be penetrated in a way I've only ever experienced before with two men. Giddy heat blazes through me from both sides.

I moan and clutch the back of Madoc's neck. He bows over me, his breaths turning ragged, his thrusts speeding up in tandem with the rhythm of his tail between my cheeks. "Come for me," he whispers. "I want to see you come so hard that in that moment, there's nothing else."

His heated words send me careening over the edge. My head jerks back against the cushions; a tremor of ecstasy runs through my entire body, making me clench around him.

Madoc groans, watching me as he continues bucking inside me. With a few more erratic thrusts and a hitch of his chest, he floods my sex with his own release.

He eases down over me, covering me like a blanket but holding himself so he doesn't crush me with his weight. After he steals another kiss, he murmurs, "That's one sort of entertainment."

A laugh tumbles out of me, but I have to say, "Not just entertainment. It'll always be an act of love too."

"Yes." He lowers onto his side and wraps me in his embrace and his thunderstorm scent. "No matter what comes. Always."

CHAPTER TWELVE

Talia

I'm the first human to enter the tunnels. The fae skilled with earth and stone have been working for hours constructing passages from well behind the current battlefront to out beneath the current Murk camp.

We realized pretty early on that we weren't likely to drive the Murk out of the Mists completely, since if the Seelie and Unseelie linger too long in the areas where we've laid our trap, they'll weaken too. There's too much distance to cover. But we have hope we'll at least take back the domains the Murk most recently stole and shake their resolve.

After the initial influx of Murk crossing the border to speak to Madoc, no more have joined us. There are fewer than twenty living in the temporary settlement. I hope the setback we're going to create now will convince more of Orion's followers that their king isn't their best chance at a better life. Delta is bringing her colony to Hearthshire later today if all goes well, but I don't think she'll turn the tide. We need more than that.

Astrid descends into the tunnel with me, standing off to the side as I peer through the network of passages that veer off in several directions from the common starting point. The initial tunnel is broad, with enough room for maybe a couple dozen people to squeeze in together, but the rest are much narrower. Having seen them mapped out on paper before the construction began, I know they branch out even more at various points, ending in over a hundred different key spots where we'll place our materials.

The Unseelie have made a similar construction on the other side of the border. I've already talked with the humans on that side and given as much guidance as I can. Madoc will be overseeing them, since I can't be in both places at once.

I rest my hand against the earthen wall, finding it solid and cool but not unpleasantly so. Lantern orbs light up the tunnels off into the distance, but their amber glow gives the narrow spaces an atmosphere that's more eerie than comforting. We're far enough down to block out any sound from above, so there's nothing but silence and the faint wisp of our breaths.

Once we reach the end of these tunnels, we'll be right beneath the Murk most eager to slaughter us all. The fae who constructed the passages did their best to ensure we shouldn't be noticed before we can withdraw, but they can't protect us completely.

"All good?" Astrid asks, leaning against the wall opposite me.

"I think so." I inhale the air thick with the scent of disturbed soil and restrain a shiver. "I hope none of the humans who'll be helping turn out to be claustrophobic."

She hums to herself. "I believe Whitt and some of the others who helped prepare them checked for that possibility."

Right. I should have realized Whitt would think to take that factor into consideration.

"I guess there really isn't anything more to do except give it our best shot," I say, and then pause, studying the warrior's wiry form in the magical glow for a moment. She's lived a long time—more than a century—and knows her people way better than I do. I can't help asking, "Do you think this effort will make any difference? To how the fae see people like me, I mean? Or are they just going to think of it as servants doing their job?"

Astrid sighs and cocks her head. "I don't know. I've certainly been impressed seeing how the humans you've brought together have risen to the task, even though they don't totally understand it and most of them are still feeling some effect from drugs or magic or both. And *you've* proven how much strength and smarts a human can have. But we fae tend to be pretty stuck in our ways. It's at least a step in the right direction."

"Yeah." I glance toward the narrower tunnels again. "We're doing something none of the fae can. This might be the moment that turns the tide of the war in our favor. That should count for something."

"I think it will." Astrid grins. "Besides, you got all their vows to start treating humans right whether they think they deserve it or not. What they do matters more than what they're thinking for now."

I'd like to change both, but she has a point. I square my shoulders and turn back toward the earthen stairs that lead up to the surface. "All right. Let's get started."

The crowd of assembled human servants stands in a semi-circle near the opening. Most of the fae warriors are still in position along the front and throughout their camp, ready to make their move when the Murk show signs of faltering, but several have drawn closer to watch our plan play out. My Seelie mates and Donovan have been walking around the gathered humans, answering any questions and reminding them of the task ahead.

None of the fae gets too close to the inner part of the semi-circle, though. There lies a huge heap of bags of salt and iron filings. Madoc was able to persuade some of the rebel Murk to help him gather it. I can't sense anything from it, but the fae who come within several feet of the stash wince and start to pale before immediately retreating.

To make the materials as easy to carry as possible, my fellow humans and I spent much of the morning pouring them from their original containers into backpack-like sacks. Each holds a mix of salt and iron, as much as we could stuff them with before they got so heavy it'd be hard to carry the loads for miles beneath the surface. Thankfully we don't have to rely on only our physical strength for that.

"Has everyone received their quickening spells?" I ask.

Whitt nods, coming over to join me. "You're the only one left," he says. "Shall I do the honors?"

"Please." I hold myself still as he chants a few soft words. A tingle spreads over my feet. I test the spell the way he explained earlier, digging my heel into the ground to push off, and one step carries me several feet.

I land with a puff of air and a short laugh. "This must be what walking on the moon is like. Have they all tried it out?" I glance at my human companions.

"Yes, with varying degrees of success. We kept at it until we were sure they could all navigate well enough once they're in the tunnels. They have their badges with their numbers." He motions to a nearby woman who has a bracelet marked 73 on her wrist. The fae labeled the tunnels so everyone would know which passage they're supposed to end up in. "Do you want to give them their last pep talk, mighty one?"

"Of course." I drag in a breath and rub my own bracelet, the bronze one that connects me to my brother back in the human realm. Maybe when all this is over, I'll be able to properly reach out to him and find some place in his life. Then I step forward to where all the assembled humans will be able to see me.

"Hi, everyone!" I call out in as upbeat a tone as I can manage. "We're going to do an amazing thing today. It is going to be dangerous as well, so please keep in mind your instructions. I'll be right down there with you. Watch the numbers on the tunnels and walk to the one you've been assigned as fast as possible using your quickening spell. As soon as you get there, open your backpack and pour the contents along the trough near the ceiling—there'll be a ledge to stand on so you can reach it easily. As soon as you've done that, hurry back here and come back above ground. We should all be in and out in less than an hour. Is anyone confused?"

The expressions around the semi-circle do look dazed, but no one raises any concerns. My stomach knots.

I couldn't ask the fae to totally free their servants right away, because we couldn't predict how they might act otherwise, and if they make the wrong move during this operation, they could get themselves and all the others killed. I have to believe the trade-off is worth it. If I hadn't suggested this course of action, I wouldn't have had any bargaining chip to get the arch-lords' cooperation for afterward.

"Let's go, then!" I say, and heft my own pack over my shoulders. The other humans move without hesitation to grab theirs. With a little direction from the fae who are careful not to get too close, they assemble into a line two across. We tramp down the steps into the tunnels.

Once I'm inside, I slip into the corner where Astrid stood before to watch everyone go by and make sure no one seems uncertain. The others stream past me, pausing only to glance at the numbers marked by each passage. I even see several already pushing off and taking advantage of the spell attached to their feet. We have miles of territory to cover—and I want everyone back fast enough that they can stay safe.

When the last of them has marched by me, I set off for my own tunnel, which is the farthest of the bunch. I bound along through the glow of the orbs, the feeling of being momentarily in flight giddying but also disorienting. The straps of the pack start to dig into my shoulders. I hope none of the others are too uncomfortable.

Before the tunnels finish splitting off, I cross paths with a few of my fellow humans who are already on their way back to the Seelie camp. They don't look particularly triumphant, but they match the smiles I shoot them, which eases the knot of guilt inside me a little.

Those ones got out okay. The Murk clearly haven't noticed anything unusual yet.

Several minutes later, I reach the end of my passage. It's not even a room, just a dead end with the ledge I was expecting and a high trough built into the earth just over the level of my head. I hop up on the ledge, wobbling on my bad foot, and heave off the pack. In a matter of seconds, I've loosened the ties holding it shut. The mixture of salt and iron filings hisses out into the dark space.

The trough is still about five feet beneath the ground the Murk are walking on. It'll take time for the effects to seep through, but with so many of these toxic pockets spread out beneath them, we think the effect should be significant within a few hours.

In case it starts creeping over them sooner than that and they catch on, I hurry back the way I came, faster now without my load weighing me down.

I catch up with more of the other humans on my way out. "Thank you for your help," I say to them, urging them along. "We couldn't have done this without you." And the fae above had better keep that in mind going forward.

When I finally clamber back out into the fresh air above ground, the humid atmosphere near the fringes tastes extraordinarily fresh. I want to flop down on the grass and absorb the sunlight for a little while, but this isn't the time or place for that.

Carriages are already soaring off, conveying our human helpers back to their packs. The last of them are climbing into a few more vehicles that've been waiting for them. The Seelie warriors are all poised along the edge of their camp now, several of them sending out periodic murmurs of magic words. They're checking for any signs of weakening among the Murk across from us.

August must be in the middle of the army, ready to lead our pack's warriors in the coming battle, but Whitt spots me and hustles over. "We should get you out of here," he says.

I shake my head. I suspected my men would try to insist on my leaving. "No. It was partly my idea. I want to see how it goes. Obviously I'm not going to run in there and join the fighting, but I'd like the fae to know their cure is standing with them."

His mouth twitches, and I can't tell whether he's suppressed a smile or a frown. "Somehow I suspected you'd say that. Let me arrange a safe vantage point."

In the end, I find myself with Astrid again, sitting on a low knoll just beyond the camp. The terrain around us gives off a thrum from all the protective magic cast there, but I can't really argue about the necessity for that precaution.

"You don't mind having to play babysitter while the rest of them fight?" I ask the wizened warrior.

She shrugs. "I've had plenty of battles in my time. These old bones don't object to getting a break when there's other work to be done and plenty to take up swords in my place."

As the last words fall from her lips, her body goes still. She stares into the distance, her brow furrowing. "I think it's starting."

I peer across the landscape with my less acute sight. I can't make anything out clearly, but there does appear to be a little more movement—and more erratic movement—among the Murk forces in the distance. The Seelie are stirring too, probably gearing up for their charge.

And then it happens. Someone must give the word, because all the Seelie surge forward as one being, some in the form of men gripping swords and lances, others dashing in their midst as wolves. They've used the same quickening spell they offered us, racing across the no man's land between the camps in a matter of seconds.

My heart starts thudding so hard my ribs seem to shudder with it. My fingers curl into the grass as if I need them to hold me steady.

The Murk appear to rally against the coming onslaught, but with less precision and cohesion than the force rushing at them has. Flares of magic shoot out on both sides; the ground cracks in one place and heaves up in another. Rumbles fill the air. A tremor races through the earth all the way to where I'm sitting.

Tension grips my body. Every second matters. Every second the Seelie are fighting, the salt and iron will start to wear down their strength too. And there's nothing more I can do now to help them.

I'm not sure how long I sit there watching the battle from afar, my gut clenching harder with every passing minute, my fingernails now digging into my palms. But then there's a shift in the currents of movement. The Murk fall back, a little at first and then in a flood, pulling away from the attacking Seelie as quickly as they can.

Relief washes over me. I blink back tears that spring to my eyes with the wave of emotion. I still don't know how many of our own people have fallen, whether my men are okay—but we won. We forced them back. Seelie are already swarming into the nearest pack village to reclaim it.

I'm just getting to my feet, wanting to head down to meet the first messengers to report back the moment they arrive, when a voice

I know far too well echoes across the landscape, amplified by some sort of spell.

"You're proving just as tricky as the Murk you call villains, my pet," Orion says from wherever he's projecting his words. A shiver travels down my back, knowing he's addressing *me*. "Don't delude yourself into thinking we're beaten. You'll soon regret turning your back on the one who made you—and I suspect those who've taken you in will regret it too."

With those chilling words, his voice falls silent. I have no idea what he means or whether it's an empty threat, but abruptly my heart is thudding hard all over again.

Astrid reaches me and grasps my elbow. "We won't let him hurt you," she says firmly.

I believe she means that, but I also know that Orion has found many ways to hurt me in the past that none of my friends or mates could protect me from.

CHAPTER THIRTEEN

August

As the carriage passes through the entryway to Hearthshire's castle and the surrounding village, Madoc peers up at the immense, arching trees. "So, this was *your* home once upon a time, was it?"

I can't tell from the rat shifter's mild tone whether he's impressed or amused. But ever since I tackled him on the verge of saving our mate and nearly prevented him from making the sacrifice Talia needed, I've committed myself to giving him the benefit of the doubt.

Even if he is amused, so what? I'd imagine the grand entrance and the lush landscape in the clearing beyond it does seem a little over the top to someone whose last home was a subway station.

"Yes," I say. "Although not for all that long. I was here for a few decades with Sylas before we were banished to a fringe domain, and it was only a matter of weeks after we had Hearthshire restored to us that he was chosen as a new arch-lord." I pause. "There's a lot of complicated history there."

Madoc chuckles, but at least he doesn't sound mocking. "Talia has filled me in on a little of that. Is it strange, handing the place over to a bunch of rats?"

I'm not sure if there's a good way to answer that. I grapple with my words for a few moments before saying, "It would be strange seeing *anyone* take the place over. Sylas founded the domain—we encouraged the growth of the forests, built the castle from the ground up… And I guess it is particularly strange to have the new residents be Murk. I mean, it isn't as if we've had any Murk living among us at all for a long time—not openly, anyway."

"Fair." Madoc leans against the inner hull of the carriage as it comes to a stop several paces from the nearest homes and inhales deeply. The flicker of appreciation that crosses his face convinces me that he does actually admire the setting, even if he's not being effusive about his appreciation.

Regardless of what I said, my first look at the Murk slipping from the old houses, which they've mostly left as is, makes my skin crawl until I tamp down on my instinctive reaction. The rat shifters don't look so different from Seelie exactly, but they're still wearing the layers of worn clothing that seems to be the preferred style in Delta's colony, and they move with a stealthy, slinking quality rather than typical fae confidence. Or, typical *summer* fae confidence, I should call it. Since they're as much fae as I am.

A bunch of them stop near the edge of the village to study me, unspeaking. Then Delta strides out of the castle with no lack of assurance in *her* stride. Several more of her people emerge behind her and arrange themselves at her flanks.

"The arch-lord himself couldn't come?" she says, raising her eyebrows at me.

I will myself not to bristle. "He is a little busy with the current war," I point out. *I* was very busy with that war less than a day ago, rushing in on the weakened Murk forces and sending them running. If I twist at the waist too quickly, my side still stings a bit where I took a hard magical blow, but it was worth it. We recovered three of the domains the Murk had stolen. We've had to rebuild our defensive wall and spent hours neutralizing the salt and iron that's now on our land, but it was worth it.

Orion hasn't shown any sign of giving up, though. That's part of the reason I'm here, although I don't think Delta will appreciate me leading with that subject.

She doesn't appear to be overly offended by the fact that I've come instead of Sylas. "Well, I guess an arch-lord's… what do they call you? Cadre? Is a great honor in itself." Her tone is lightly teasing, but her smile is warm enough that it doesn't rankle. "Did you come to check up on us?"

"Yes," I say. "If there's anything you've had a problem with or resources you need help finding, or if any of the other Seelie have hassled you at all, we'll deal with the issue as quickly as we can."

"Hmm." She glances behind her at the castle. "Your lord isn't going to mind if we start rearranging the rooms and all that, is he? I assume he's relinquished all claim on this castle."

The thought of the kitchen I spent so many happy hours in being dismantled niggles at my heart, but I ignore the sensation. Between Hearth-by-the-Heart and the border castle, I have *two* very nice kitchens in my new home.

I sweep my arm in what I hope is a gesture of generosity. "This entire domain is yours now. It's up to you what you do with it. As long as nothing you do adversely affects any of your neighbors, of course."

"Of course," Delta says dryly. Her gaze flicks to Madoc. "How long do you think it's going to take before they stop feeling they have to remind us not to be a menace?"

Madoc's mouth twitches into a smile. "I'd give it at least a few decades."

She shrugs. "We have been a bit of a menace, so as long as they don't mind us reacting the same way to them, I suppose it doesn't matter." There's a gleam of mischief in her eyes when she meets my gaze again.

If she's trying to get a rise out of me, it won't work. I have my temper well in hand these days, if not quite as controlled as my older brothers can manage. "I'm sorry for phrasing it that way," I say. "It will probably take a while for old habits to die. And also, my lord wouldn't be very happy with me if I misrepresented expectations."

Delta laughs. "No doubt he wouldn't. Well, you could be some help, come to think of it. I can tell your pack had magical protections set up along the boundaries of the domain—warning signals and wards and the like. There are traces of the spells left, but not enough for me to work with. And I'm not used to dealing with quite so much plant life. Maybe we could take a stroll through the forest, and you could advise me on some typical techniques." She glances at Madoc again. "And you've spent quite a while adapting your magic to the Mists, haven't you? You might have some useful insights too."

"I'll do my best to provide them," Madoc replies.

We set off, still with the retinue of what I've now counted as eight other Murk trailing behind us. I'm not sure whether Delta wants them to learn whatever we end up teaching her too, or if she has them along because of her concerns about how menacing *we* might become.

She picks her way through the brush like it's an obstacle course, springing onto logs and skirting shrubs more nimbly than I bother with. Her sharp eyes dart across the terrain, and I don't think she misses very much. I'm impressed that she even picked up the traces of those protective spells that haven't been bolstered in months.

"I have to admit I'm pleasantly surprised," she says after a few minutes. "The guards Arch-Lord Sylas had escort us from the fringes kept any hostile thoughts they were harboring to themselves. I wouldn't say they were outright friendly, but no one came to blows, even though my people can be rather… cheeky at times." She flashes a grin at me that suggests it's not just her underlings who have that inclination.

Sylas was very strict with the pack-kin he chose for that job, and he selected them carefully based on their self-discipline as well as their open-mindedness. I think it's better not to mention how concerned he was about the proceedings, though.

"We're working hard at making a new balance between our peoples feasible," I say instead. "It might take time for everyone to come around, but I think we've made a good start of it."

Delta cocks her head at me. "You're still not totally convinced we won't turn around and attempt to murder you all in your sleep."

She doesn't sound offended with the comment, but I lose my hold on my tongue for a second anyway. "I—I'm not totally sure I'd blame you for trying, considering how many of the Murk the Seelie have murdered, often without real cause. It shames me that I didn't realize the full extent of our cruelty earlier."

It's hard to tell what Delta makes of my remark. She gambols onward, turning to Madoc now. "And you've been right in the thick of it. Have you managed to convert many of Orion's believers?"

"A small number so far," Madoc says. More crossed the border yesterday, and I know he was integrating them into their temporary lodgings well into the night. "Not enough to put a real dent in his forces, but we're whittling away at them."

Delta sighs. "He's going to drive them all to their deaths, and who will benefit for that other than him and his sadistic inclinations?"

Madoc grimaces. "Unfortunately, I've come to agree with that assessment. Maybe the reason I've found I can get along with the wolfish louts is that I have plenty of my own regrets." He shoots a wry glance my way.

The Murk man has grown in confidence since he first ventured openly into our midst. It's hard to connect the man ambling along beside me with the one who crouched defensively amid the magical cell Celia's guards had conjured around him the first time I met him. But then, the reception he's gotten has improved quite a bit too.

The more time I spend around Madoc, the more I can see how he earned Talia's affections. There is a kindness and honorableness to him despite his past associations, qualities she spotted much sooner than the rest of us did. But of course she would, when those are the features that call to her spirit so strongly.

I'm still getting used to the idea of the rat shifter being part of our collective of mates, but I can't say I resent his presence. I might even be coming to appreciate it.

Delta comes to a stop by a vine-laden tree. "This is one spot where I can still sense the wards, but I can't quite get a grip on how they were constructed. They feel more potent than what I'd typically conjure—especially when they've held on so long after you left."

Ah. It makes sense to me immediately why the practiced sorceress had trouble here. I step closer and pat my hand against the trunk of the tree. "This is a bracewood, with its typical begone vine around it. They have a special symbiosis where the vine gives off an aura that deflects pests from the tree and the tree offers some of the nourishment its leaves take from the sun to the vine here in the shadows. Where they're native to the land, it's typical for us to draw on their essence in creating our spells."

Delta examines the tree. "And how exactly does one do that? I'm not getting a sense of much energy off it."

"To really make use of the effect, you need to learn the vine's true name," I say, and pause. I know it myself. While Sylas is the plant expert among us, anything defensive falls into my purview as well. But something this specialized can't be taught as easily as passing on a true name—and it might not work for Delta if she doesn't come to it more naturally.

I can offer a tip I picked up on my own journey to earning that true name, though. "You can learn it faster if you—carefully—wrap some of the vine around yourself and meditate within its hold."

The Murk sorceress raises her eyebrows, but she doesn't scoff at the idea. She strokes her fingers over one of the leaves with a thoughtful air. "That's useful to know. Thank you."

Maybe now would be a good time to bring up the favor I'm supposed to ask of her. But I can't quite figure out how to broach the subject. Whitt should be here doing this. Except *I'm* the military leader.

As I waffle internally, Delta crosses her arms over her chest. "If there's something else on your mind, wolf, you should simply spit it out."

Yes, definitely they should have sent Whitt, who rarely gives away what he's feeling even when it isn't any great secret. I let out my breath in a rush and look at Madoc, who makes a bemused gesture. He knows what I'm supposed to ask, but he isn't going to bail me out. Really, he shouldn't.

"You should know this is a request, not an order, and your answer has no effect on your being welcome here," I start, figuring I should get that part out of the way upfront.

"Duly noted."

I can't see any way to continue other than barreling right onward. "We've made some good progress in pushing Orion's forces back, but he's been difficult to completely displace. You clearly don't like what he's doing any more than we do, even if it's for different reasons. If you or your colony would be willing to contribute at all to our efforts against him, whether in the fighting or simply suggesting strategies or spellwork… The more of us are working together on this, the faster we'll be able to defeat him."

"Ah." Delta's eyes narrow in a way that doesn't seem all that promising. But then she adds, "I've been expecting this. I should give you points for not leading with it."

I don't know if that means she's on board or not. I wait, trying not to look too beseeching. Madoc gives off the impression that he's restraining a smirk.

"I think," the Murk woman goes on after a long pause, "that we should take a little more time to get our bearings here before throwing our lot in too much with the Seelie. I don't mean that as an insult to you or your lord. But I have to look out for my people's safety first. I'm sure you can understand that."

My heart sinks, but I dip my head. "Of course I do. I'll just say that if you do think of anything that might improve our chances, we'd be immensely grateful if you let us know."

Delta smiles, and in that moment, my failure doesn't feel like quite so much of a loss. "Because you took my refusal so well, you can count on me doing that," she says. "Now let's see about another spot in these woods that's confounded me, and maybe I'll come up with some inspiration along the way."

CHAPTER FOURTEEN

Talia

From a high window in the border castle, I spot August and Madoc's carriage returning. By limping across the fields around Hearth-by-the-Heart, I reach them just after they've disembarked. Sylas has already joined them, his expression intent.

"Was the sorceress willing to offer any kind of aid?" he asks.

August's mouth slants at an awkward angle. "Not exactly. She isn't ready to put her people in the line of fire right now. But she didn't seem totally against the idea, and I think she was genuine when she said she'd do some thinking on tactics we might take against him."

"She was," Madoc says without preamble. "You might associate the Murk mainly with lying, but when we say a thing that plainly, we generally mean it. If she'd wanted to lie to get something out of you, she'd have made more of a show of what she was supposedly going to offer in return."

One corner of Sylas's mouth crooks upward. "And that's why I'm glad I sent you along too. We'll be meeting with the other arch-lords later this afternoon. I'd hoped we'd be able to bring Delta to the table as well, but if she needs more time, I—"

My attention is yanked from his words to my wrist by a quiver of the bronze bracelet that grips my skin. As I stare at the gleaming band, the quiver intensifies to an all-out shudder. Prickles of heat race into my flesh.

My mouth goes dry. "My bracelet," I croak. "It's connected to Jamie—it's supposed to warn me—I think something must be happening to him."

August and Sylas spring to my side in an instant. August touches the bracelet he enchanted, and his stance tenses. "Something's definitely wrong."

"Jamie?" Madoc says, and then understanding clicks in his expression. "Your brother. He's still in the human world, isn't he?"

As I nod, his eyes turn stormy. For a second, I can't speak through the constricting of my throat.

"It's Orion," I say. "It's got to be. He warned me, and now—"

"We don't know that for sure," August says quickly. "And the spell is meant to detect extreme emotional distress as well as physical. He isn't necessarily hurt. It could simply be something happened that upset him a lot."

It's sad that his reminder gives me some relief. Maybe the bracelet is alerting me because it's *only* that Jamie's girlfriend broke up with him in some horrible way, or our aunt and uncle kicked him out of their house, or he's found out he's failing all his classes. But any of those would be better than having him fall into Orion's hands.

I hadn't known Orion was even aware that Jamie existed, but it's not surprising that he would. His people have been keeping watch over me since I was an infant and he embedded his spells in my body. Madoc may even have reported to his king that I discovered my brother was still living.

I meet his gaze, and I can tell the Murk man has restrained a wince. "I didn't know your brother was alive until you told me," he says, as if he can guess what I'm thinking. "I did report to Orion about your abrupt interest in something in the human world when I noticed your travels there, but I didn't follow you, and I didn't know what you'd found. He'll have had other spies in the human world, though."

Clenching my hands, I pull myself together as well as I can. "It doesn't matter. What matters is protecting Jamie now. How quickly can we get to him? Is there any way we can defend him using the connection through the bracelet?"

August shakes his head. "Not at this distance, not when we have no idea what's happening to him. The portal that leads to his town isn't in the Murk's area of occupation, so we could go to it—at our fastest, it'd take a couple of hours, but that's unavoidable." He looks at his lord.

Sylas is frowning, but he nods. "You take her. I'll have Whitt join you. I should stay to continue the discussions around the war with the Murk." He touches my cheek. "I'm sorry, my love. If I thought my coming would make a significant difference, I'd be with you no matter what."

"It's all right," I say, meaning it. "If Orion *has* done something, then figuring out how to beat him will help Jamie too."

"I'll go as well," Madoc says. "The arch-lords have already heard everything useful I've had to say lately. I might be able to help interpret the signs if Orion's people have been involved with whatever happened."

Corwin's voice peals into my head, full of urgency. *What's the matter, my soul? What's upset you?*

Something's happened to Jamie, I reply as I scramble into the carriage that just returned from Hearthshire. *We're going to find out what. Sylas is staying back for the meeting with the other arch-lords, and you should too. No matter what Orion's done, the most important thing is defeating him.*

Corwin's anguish travels through our bond, but he can't argue with my reasoning. *Let me send Zelpha so you have additional support if you run into any danger out there. She can be with you in a minute.*

All right, I say, and a chill seeps through my skin. I was so worried about Jamie that I didn't even consider what might happen to *me* on the other side of that portal.

Is this more than just an attempt to hurt me through my

brother? Is Orion laying a trap? I'm not sure if he could know that I'd be warned so quickly about Jamie's situation, but it's always possible. We'll have to hurry but also go carefully. My stomach twists in on itself.

As Whitt hustles out of the castle at Sylas's summons, his eyes wide with worry, Zelpha drops out of the sky in raven form. August speaks the word to set the carriage in motion. In an instant, it's racing forward across the fields and down the forest path toward the fringes.

As the howl of the wind rises with the speed of our journey, August tugs me down into the lowest part of the carriage's floor. Whitt takes over steering, shooting concerned glances my way. Zelpha perches by the stern, keeping watch from there, and Madoc sinks down across from me, close enough that his raised knees lean against mine.

The sensations emanating from my bracelet fade away. It lies cool and still against my wrist. I touch it, swallowing hard. "I can't feel anything now. Does that mean—?"

"The worst of his distress might have passed, leaving him perfectly fine," August assures me. "Or he could have been knocked out."

Madoc rubs a comforting hand over my calf. "He'll still be alive. I know this much about Orion—if he's involved, he wouldn't waste a useful bargaining chip by destroying it right away." He grimaces. "Forgive my phrasing. That's only how he'd see it."

"I know." I stare up at the stark blue of the sky and try not to let my worries overwhelm me. There's no way to find out what's happened to my little brother until we get to his home… Even then, it might not be obvious. I have no idea where he even was when the bracelet activated. For all I know, the family went on a last-minute trip. He could be halfway around the world, as unlikely as that is.

I'll be able to help him better if I'm clear-headed and focused. Panicking is only going to make figuring out the problem and dealing with it harder.

I take slow, even breaths, girding myself as well as I can for whatever we might discover. August rubs my shoulders, and Madoc leaves his hand resting on my leg, his touch reassuring.

I'm not alone. My men and Zelpha will do whatever they can to protect Jamie too.

We just have to get to him.

The traces of humidity in the air can't thicken quickly enough. As the sky hazes overhead with the now-familiar fog, my heart thuds faster. It's all I can do to keep sitting on the floor of the carriage while Whitt guides it the last short distance to the right portal. Its slowing speed makes my muscles itch with restlessness.

When Whitt finally halts the carriage, we leap out and stop just long enough for him and Madoc to cast concealing spells over all of us. We're not only keeping ourselves out of view of the regular citizens of the human world now but any of Orion's lackeys who might be lurking around too. Then Zelpha takes a quick prowl around the portal while August and Whitt conduct a hasty magical search for any sign of Murk presence.

Zelpha returns to us with her brow knit. "I can't see any evidence that Murk are here now, but I thought I caught a whiff of rat over in the trees nearby. Someone may have come through this area recently."

We can't know if that had anything to do with my brother or if it was simply part of their ongoing war efforts. Biting my lip, I join the fae at the portal. August takes my hand and tugs me through with him.

In the park on the other side, my legs ache to run straight to Jamie's house. My men insist that we hold off for just a few minutes so they can check for Murk on this side too. When they don't turn up any sign of a waiting ambush, we hurry through the streets under what looks to be the thin light of early dawn. It's always a different time of day here than in the fae realm I've left.

The neighborhood where my aunt and uncle live is so peaceful at this hour that my nerves start to settle despite my uncertainty. It's hard to believe anything all that bad could happen here. My bracelet hasn't stirred again since that first warning signal.

Maybe it really was just a particularly bad emotional spell that

Jamie's worked through. Maybe the alert misfired, and nothing's been wrong at all.

Then we come around the corner onto the block where their house is, and my legs stall.

Two police cars are parked outside my aunt and uncle's house. A couple of officers are just walking back to their car, one of them shaking his head, his expression somber. My heart plummets.

The next thing I know, I'm running over in my limping way. My fae companions hurry after me, but they don't try to pull me back. They trust me not to do anything that'd reveal us.

All I can think of is finding out what's happened. I pause, panting, by the front porch. My aunt is talking to a police officer who's paused in the doorway. "I don't know what could have happened or what that could mean," she's saying in a wavery voice. "It doesn't make any sense. You didn't see any signs that he's been hurt?"

"There's no indication that there was a struggle or that he was injured in the room," the officer says. "It could be it's some kind of odd prank that he's in on?"

"He's never been the type to do anything like that."

The officer shrugs. "Teenagers. They can be unpredictable. I should know—I have two of my own. You can be assured we'll follow up on every lead, but take heart that there's a decent chance he'll turn up before the end of the day."

In the room, he said. Jamie's bedroom? I rush on around the side of the house to the window that looks into my brother's one private space in the house.

I stumble to a stop in front of it and whirl to peer inside, gripping the window frame. When my eyes catch on the scene inside, my head jerks forward so fast my nose bangs the glass.

Now I understand what my aunt was saying about "what that could mean." There's a message scrawled on the wall of Jamie's room over his bed in thin but deep gouge marks I can already imagine one of the Murk carving with their razor-sharp claws.

He'll be returned when you return to me, the ragged letters spell out.

Of course my aunt wouldn't know what that's talking about. The message isn't meant for her. It's for me.

My fae companions have gathered around me. August lets out a growl, and Madoc makes a strained sound in his throat.

Whitt sucks a harsh breath through gritted teeth. He's the one who speaks first. "He isn't having you."

"He has Jamie," I say faintly. I sway on my feet, and August and Zelpha catch my elbows on either side, steadying me.

"Orion wouldn't bring him back even if you went to him," Madoc says, gently but firmly. "He'd *enjoy* showing you that he doesn't have to keep his end of the deal. It'd be his punishment for you running away from him in the first place."

"Jamie has nothing to do with this." A sob clogs my throat. "He never should have been dragged into the war at all." The fae have already slashed up his face and left who knows how many other scars on his body, stolen his family from him as surely as they have from me. And after all the work he's done to rebuild his life, they'd smashed it apart all over again.

A vicious emotion flares deep inside me. In that moment I want to raze it all to the ground—every inch of the Murk colonies and the Mists too, until there's no one left who could torment people like me and my brother.

It's only for an instant, and then I come back to myself feeling even more helpless than before. I don't really want all the fae to die. I just want the horrors of my life to be behind me, not multiplying at every turn.

I glance at Madoc. "Is there any way of telling where he's brought Jamie?"

The Murk man shakes his head. "They'll have traveled through multiple portals. That's our standard tactic for muddying our tracks. They had at least a couple of hours head start on us. They could be anywhere by now."

"The Refuge…?"

He hesitates. "I don't think so. Orion knows I'm with you now, and I'm familiar with all the tricks for getting in there."

Whitt slips his arm around my shoulders. "Let's go back to the

Mists. We have scouts we can send to sniff out whatever trail there is to be found. You're vulnerable here—we aren't much of a force to protect you if it comes to that."

I don't want to leave without knowing how to help my brother, but I can see I'm not going to get the answers yet. Feeling like I'm trudging through a fog, I walk with them back to the portal.

Partway there, August scoops me into his arms like he's so fond of doing and cradles me against his chest. I press my face to his shoulder, tears welling in my eyes. I long to soak in the comfort he's offering, but at the same time, it's hard to believe I deserve it.

I brought this on my little brother, just like I did nine years ago that night when Aerik and his cadre tore through my family.

The cloud of despair sinks over me so thickly that I barely notice when we reach the portal. August carries me through. All of the fae around me stay in solemn silence as we march the short distance back to the carriage.

It isn't long after we've left the humidity and the haze of the fringelands behind when Whitt draws the carriage to an unexpected stop. Another, smaller vehicle is racing toward us with a single Seelie woman at the helm.

"I'm glad I caught you," she says in a rush as she swings around beside us. "Arch-Lord Sylas said you'd be traveling through this way. The Murk have launched another attack, and they're gaining ground. We need everyone who can come at the front, now."

CHAPTER FIFTEEN

Talia

I know how bad it is from the fact that Sylas doesn't assign any of the warriors to stay back with me as guards. All of my companions, even Madoc, leap out of the carriage the second we reach the battlefield with hasty instructions for me to stay there out of sight. I crouch on the floor near the bow, peeking up over the side of the vehicle and across the tops of the other carriages that've brought a renewed wave of warriors to the front.

From what the messenger who caught us reported, we've lost the domains we recovered yesterday. The Murk have already pushed forward beyond their previous gains. I'm not sure how they managed to overwhelm the Seelie this time—the woman didn't explain before she rushed back to rejoin the fighting—but whatever tactics they used, those were clearly effective.

Grunts, clangs, and cries ring out from where the fae are struggling against each other just a hundred feet away. Magic like lightning crackles across the sky. More sizzles back and forth between the warriors. The ground shudders. All I can make out is a mass of bodies swinging and twisting this way and that, some of them as men, some of them wolves.

The Seelie army must be trying to raise a new barrier to at least stop the Murk from advancing any further. I catch a shimmer in the air above the battlefield—but it's shattered apart a few seconds later by a blast of magical energy. A few slivers of the hostile spell fall to the ground around me like fragments of shooting stars. One hisses across the bow, leaving a burnt mark in its wake.

I scramble to the stern, putting a little more distance between me and the fighting. I think my men cast protective spells over the interior of the carriage, but I'm not sure how well those are holding. I can't blame them for rushing when there'll be no one to protect me at all if the Murk tear through the Seelie forces completely.

Slivers of similar urgency flash through my bond with Corwin. I'm guessing that as before, the Murk have launched their new offensive on both sides of the border. I'm afraid to reach out to my Unseelie mate to ask what's going on. He probably needs all his concentration to ensure he and his people survive.

Guilt winds around my gut and squeezes tight. What can *I* do to protect any of them? I've been held up like a savior for the cure I could offer for their curse, but now that the war has shifted to overt combat, I'm a liability, a weak link that needs to be defended.

No, that's not totally true. I managed to get the other humans involved to offer a strategy that turned the tables on the Murk for a little while. It obviously wasn't enough, though. And no humans can wade into this fray to lend a hand. We'd be cut down in a matter of seconds.

Is there anything I could do from a distance? I strain my mind, but nothing occurs to me. Even if I had some on hand, flinging salt or iron around wouldn't do any good when the two sides are in such close combat. I'd hurt my own people more than Orion's.

I can't save my men or the rest of the fae, and I can't save my brother either. I wrap my arms around myself, but I can't hug the growing despair out of me.

No matter what I do, Orion has always found some new way to torment me—and the people I care about. Maybe in some ways,

Aerik was right. My connection to the Murk king makes me a threat to everyone else. As long as I'm with the fae of the seasons, I'm a liability not just because of my physical and magical weakness but because of how much two of their arch-lords and others besides care about me. Because of how well Orion can hurt them through me.

As I worry at my lip with my teeth, an image flickers across the thin haze of clouds overhead. At first I don't even look up, assuming it's only more spells for the attack. But then I catch a glimpse of the shapes from the corner of my eye, and my gaze snaps upward.

It's Jamie. The Murk have cast a conjured projection onto the clouds—not just here, but at other intervals all along the front. They must be hoping I'll see it but unsure of where exactly I am.

I don't know how real the image is. It shows Jamie crouched in a corner with his knees drawn up to his chest, an angry scratch on his forearm and a bruise on his forehead, his eyes wide with confusion. I don't see any bracelet on his wrists. My hand shoots to my own, which is still inactive.

Is that because this picture they've conjured isn't real or because they took his off him, breaking the connection?

Maybe it doesn't matter whether this shows him as he really is right now. I know that the Murk took him. I know they aren't going to be kind to him. If he isn't huddled like this, he's in a similar position, experiencing similar emotions.

As I watch with horror clamping around my stomach, a shadowy figure moves at the edge of the projection. It kicks Jamie in the side, and he falls to the ground with a flinch. My posture jerks straighter, as if I could leap up into the sky to stop what they're doing to him.

But I can't. He's not really there. I have no idea where he even is.

A horrible understanding creeps up through my mind. I know it's true that Orion will have made a false promise. There's no way he'll free Jamie unless he's forced to. But that doesn't mean that me giving myself up to him would be pointless. He won't have any reason to torture Jamie if I've accepted his demands.

I can't put myself in the Murk king's control, of course. He'd only torture me to upset my mates and their people. But there was a time when I considered ending my life so that Orion couldn't use me any further. If I got close enough for his people to see and then went through with it… He wouldn't be able to hurt anyone else through me anymore. He wouldn't have any reason to hold on to Jamie.

I grapple with the idea for several minutes. The clash of magic is sending an increasingly acrid scent into the air. It mingles with a meaty, metallic odor I know is from all the blood being spilled.

How could I even give myself up if I decided that would be the best thing I have left to offer? I ease up on my knees to take in the view of the battlefield again, my body tensed to duck if I need to.

The battle is raging on. I think the Seelie have been pushed back a little closer to the carriages than they were the last time I took in the scene. The fray is so chaotic I can't tell where their forces end and the Murk's begin.

Is Orion himself anywhere near here, or is he overseeing the charge from some other point along the front?

There aren't exactly any gaps in the fighting where I could slip through. And as my gaze slides over the warriors, a more potent emotion rises up through my hopelessness.

The fae before me are throwing themselves into the battle with everything they have. I see blood streaming from wounds and flesh blackened from magical fire, yes. I see bodies fallen amid their comrades, limp and torn. But I also catch glimpses of the faces of those still living, their expressions taut with determination and defiance, their teeth pulled back in snarls as they refuse to back down.

They're fighting to the limits of their strength to hold on to their homes and defend their families. There's a certain desperation in it, but it's fierce and unrelenting. They won't give up unless the Murk completely overwhelm them, and they're putting every particle of energy they have into ensuring that doesn't happen.

There has to be more I can give, more I can do, than handing myself over. I'm not done yet, am I? There's so much more I wanted to have in this life.

And giving up might mean saving Jamie from further torture… but it might mean giving up on him too. Do I really believe it's impossible that we could manage to save him without my sacrificing myself, which might mean sacrificing him too anyway?

I have to protect my own family. I have to insist that the arch-lords lend people to help rescue Jamie as soon as we can stave off the most immediate threat to the entire Mists. I wish there was something I could do right now that would spare my brother any further pain, but there *isn't.* Not even losing my life would guarantee that outcome.

Orion might even torment Jamie more out of frustration that he didn't get to decide my fate after all.

But maybe there is a little something I can do even now for all the fae who're fighting for our home. I wanted to come out to the front and encourage them before. Here I am now. I need to make sure none of them succumb to the same despair that nearly dragged me under just minutes ago.

Ignoring the jittering of my nerves, I scramble back across the carriage to the bow. There, I pull myself onto the lip of the hull, which is just wide enough for me to steady my feet on it. Staying crouched for the time being, I cup my hands in front of my chest and close my eyes.

Joy. I need to summon all the joy I can find and create an image of my own to send out there.

My mind slips back to my interlude with Madoc in the basement lounge the other day. To Whitt's eagerness as we came up with our plan together. To Corwin's promises of unending love. To all the affection my mates have showered on me, all the promises we've made. To seeing Jamie happy with his girlfriend and his new family.

There'll come a time when that's all we have, when our worst troubles are so much smaller than our joys. I have to keep believing that.

The true name for light spills over my lips with a rush of energy. "*Sole-un-straw!*"

As I push myself upright, a golden glow blazes out from my hands. I raise them up to the sky and then stretch them to either side of me, casting the light all around me. Even this far from the Heart of the Mists, its power is with me. And I'm with the fae who are fighting for it.

"We can do this!" I call out, willing my voice to travel. "We can push them back. We can protect what's ours. This world belongs to the Heart, and the Heart shines through me and over all of you. Feel it in you now. Let it fend off those who want to break us."

I'm not sure how much sense I'm even making, the words tumbling out of me without much thought. But all through the fray, fae glance toward me and throw themselves back into the fight with what looks like renewed energy. More magic sings through the air from our side. More voices holler and growl. A surge of power hums through the air around me and through our army, and in that moment, I see the Murk start to falter.

"For the Heart!" a voice calls out, and I spot August raising his fist in the midst of the battle.

"For the Heart!" the chant rises up. "For the Heart!" More and more voices join in with each iteration.

More of the Seelie call out, casting their magic together, and a blast of wind knocks much of the Murk army backward. Before they can recover, the earth heaves up to topple more of them. They spit out their own spells, but the Seelie have managed to buy enough time to hastily build a new wall that deflects those first, less focused attacks. By the time the Murk are heaving the full force of their magic at us again, the barrier is thick enough to hold firm.

I sink back into the base of the carriage, my breath ragged and my head throbbing a bit from the amount of magic I managed to pull through me. This isn't a victory, but we held off a total loss, and that's enough for me—for now.

I only hope I can do the same for Jamie.

CHAPTER SIXTEEN

Madoc

The Seelie lord twists his hands together where he's standing at one end of his castle's meeting room. I suspect he didn't expect his complaint to be answered by both an arch-lord and one of the sort of fae he's complaining about.

Sylas has folded his arms over his broad chest. His voice stays even, but he doesn't bother to smooth a trace of annoyance from it. "If I'm hearing you correctly, you can't say there's anything specific that the Murk colony has done to disrupt your pack or your domain."

The lord grimaces. "No, not *yet*. But I—there's an energy to their presence—it's clear to me that they have suspicious intentions."

I raise my eyebrows at him. "I'd say your intentions are much more suspicious, considering you called us out here in the middle of a war with nothing to show for it except your impressions of 'energy.' You're the one who took your sentries close to the colony, aren't you? The Murk inhabitants haven't been near your domain?"

Something flashes in the lord's eyes. He definitely doesn't like being talked to that way by a rat. He turns to Sylas as if I haven't spoken. "You understand that given the history I needed to take precautions…"

Sylas lets out a skeptical rumble. "Given the history between the Seelie and the Murk, I think it's understandable that Delta's colony may not be giving off the friendliest impression. They're vastly outnumbered among us here, and they're fully aware that they're on precarious ground. When they haven't committed any actual crime, I ask that you leave them be."

"And if you start inventing crimes, you'd better believe we'll figure out who's really to blame," I add.

The lord's gaze flicks back to me. "Is that a threat?"

I offer him a thin smile. "No, it's just a statement of fact. I know about the animosities people like you hold toward people like me better than anyone, and I'm giving this peace my best shot for all our sakes."

"And I hope that you can look beyond your prejudices to work toward the same future peace, which all of your arch-lords wish for," Sylas puts in.

The lord hems and haws a bit but doesn't make any further complaints. I wait until he's seen us back to our carriage and we're well out of hearing before I say anything to Sylas.

"Do you think he's going to cause problems for the colony?"

The Seelie arch-lord sighs. I could pick up on his frustration with the unnecessary visit while he spoke to the lord, but it's a relief to see that wasn't just for show. He really does feel the prick was wasting our time.

"We'll keep a close watch," he says. "We anticipated that some of the packs might harass their new Murk neighbors. I suppose we can be thankful that he doesn't have enough manpower to make much of a strike, with so many of his warriors out at the front."

"Small blessings," I mutter.

Sylas tips his head to me. "You spoke well in spite of his attitude toward you. The more they see that the Murk can be both firm and reasonable, the harder it'll be for them to justify the idea that you're somehow less than us. It's simply going to take time to get there."

His praise warms me more than I'd have expected it to. I nod. "I know. I was prepared to never get there at all, so that one thing is going well. Now if only Orion wasn't continuing to be such a menace…"

"We have had another influx of Murk refugees from his army since the clash yesterday," Sylas points out. "While you're helping them adjust, perhaps you can find out something useful from them about his next plans, or the situation with Talia's brother—or any other factor we'd want to know about."

My heart aches at the thought of the latest attack Orion has made on Talia's happiness. The moment we returned from the front yesterday, she demanded that the arch-lords take action to rescue her brother—that at least a few pack members be spared to search for him and determine a viable plan. There was a lot of grumbling from some of the others, and I can tell she knows it isn't likely to happen quickly. Orion's giving us far too many other things to worry about at the same time.

"I'll see what I can get out of them," I say. "The Murk who've come over from Orion are particularly wary, and they see even me as a potential enemy because I've sided with the rest of you. Most of them aren't coming over out of any grand dream of peace but because they're getting the idea that they might be on the losing side. I'll freely admit we can't trust them not to switch back if the tide turns too far in Orion's favor."

"I'm not surprised to hear that, but I appreciate your candor."

He'd probably appreciate it more if I was able to honestly say something more optimistic, but I can't be too snarky about the man even in my thoughts. He's committed to this course of cooperating with as many of the Murk as will take us up on the offer, and he's seeing it through to the best of his ability.

It's a short trip back to the Heart, where no doubt the arch-lord is due to discuss our next steps with his colleagues any moment now. Corwin has come over to the summer side of the border castle in anticipation of our arrival. He glances from Sylas to me, aiming his question at both of us—a recognition I didn't know *I'd* appreciate until just now.

"We aren't facing yet another calamity, are we?" he says.

Sylas's mouth curves into a crooked smile. "No absolute disasters so far. One of the Seelie lords is getting restless about having a Murk colony a few domains over, trying to stir up doubts about them. The two of us were able to put him in his place solidly enough that I don't think he'll take any action, at least not while the war is still raging."

"I suppose that's some comfort," Corwin mutters, and sweeps his hand back through his blue-black curls. He pauses and focuses on me again. "I hope he wasn't too disrespectful to you."

I shrug, startled that the Unseelie arch-lord even bothered to ask, though maybe I shouldn't be. "I've had worse treatment. Mostly he tried to ignore me. I made that difficult for him."

A hint of a smile touches Corwin's lips. He catches Sylas's eye, and I have the sense that some unspoken communication passes between them, maybe something they've already discussed.

Sylas clears his throat. "It's obviously not an ideal time for making any major changes here while our people are stretched so thin, but something we will need to raise with our colleagues before too long—the Murk will need representatives here by the Heart. Whether you decide to call them arch-lords or some other title of your choosing."

"Not king," I grumble, and Corwin's mouth twitches again.

"That'll be up to the Murk," he says. "But we thought—at least three leaders would make for a good start. With three, you always have a tiebreaker. And it may be enough—the three Seelie arch-lords have held their own against the five of us ravens."

"That makes sense," I agree. "If you want me to watch for possible candidates among the refugees, I'll keep it in mind, but I don't think any of them are quite up to the task yet. They're barely up to coexisting with the Seelie at this early stage. Of course, there's Delta, if she's willing."

The two arch-lords exchange another look, one that makes the back of my neck prickle with apprehension. But then Sylas says, in a subdued tone that doesn't quite disguise a hint of amusement, "Yes,

Delta would be an obvious one to ask. But we were first thinking of *you.*"

Oh. *Oh.* I blink, startled much more deeply than before and embarrassingly so. It takes me a few moments to gather my words. "I—I hadn't really thought about setting myself up as some sort of figurehead—"

"You'd hardly be just a figurehead," Corwin says softly. "You've been instrumental in coordinating the efforts to bridge the gap between our peoples since before we even fully accepted you as an ally. You have enough sway with your people that many of them are choosing to trust you over Orion. There's no one it'd make more sense to appoint when the time comes."

I'm not sure what to do with the chaotic mix of emotions that's flooding me. I can't even tell whether I'm more awed or disturbed by the suggestion.

Me, a ruler of all Murk kind? Even with two colleagues, that seems like a stretch. And it'd mean dealing with the leaders of the fae of the seasons constantly.

But then, I'm doing that right now anyway, aren't I? And I know what Talia would say if I told her about this offer. She'd tell me that it's only natural they'd want me as a fellow arch-lord—or whatever—and that she's sure I'd be up to the task. My lovely mate with her unshakeable faith.

Thinking of her doesn't erase my doubts, but it does steady me enough for me to say, "I'm glad to know you see things that way, and even more glad I don't need to make any decisions on the subject just yet."

Sylas chuckles. "We felt it'd be good to mention it before relations between our peoples go much further." His gaze slides down the haze of the border to a spot somewhere beyond the gold-laced walls of the Seelie's Bastion. "Perhaps we'd build another border castle at the other side of the Heart, one the highest Murk leaders could call their own. Seeing as you don't belong to one specific season or another."

Suddenly I can see it—a towering structure created in the Murk style, multiple materials woven together into something odd but functional. A place where all of the rat shifters in the Mists would know that they can come and make an appeal if they run into trouble—know that the Murk who rule from there have just as much authority as their Seelie and Unseelie counterparts.

Yes, that would be a miraculous thing.

"Let's win this war first," I say. "Then we can have fun negotiating about new castles and Murk arch-lords with your colleagues."

Corwin gives me a wry smile. At the same moment, one of the sentries comes loping over in wolf form.

"We've had another small group of Murk arrive," he says when he's straightened up as a man. "They've been escorted to the temporary settlement. They're asking for Madoc—don't want to speak or even be near any of the rest of us."

I won't blame my fellow Murk for feeling that way. "I'll head right over." I tip my head in an awkward goodbye to the arch-lords and set off for the settlement.

It's only once I've passed into the shelter of the first stretch of forest that I sink down into rat form and dash along that way. I still don't feel totally comfortable showing just how rat-like I am too blatantly among the other fae. I guess that's something I'll have to get over eventually… but there's plenty of time to reach that point.

The temporary sort-of colony has doubled in size in the past few days, and these new arrivals will expand it even more. I shift again at the edge of the makeshift village, where a few of the more established Murk are conjuring new dwellings. It's good to see them taking some initiative to help the newcomers settle in.

I can easily spot the five who've just arrived. They're standing close together in the middle of the space, their stances defensive and their gazes twitching between the few Seelie guards keeping an eye on the place. In theory, the wolves are mostly here to assist if the displaced Murk need it, but I'm sure that's not how most of my fellow rats take their presence. I make a mental note to ask them to keep their posts a little farther off, out of view unless the Murk actually call on them.

There's another Seelie in our midst. Talia's friend, the one she's told me made her most elaborate dresses, is standing tentatively at one edge of the settlement. She's talking with a few of the more established fae, including the young guy named Flynn who's a little too cocky for his own good.

From the way he's grinning at her and flourishing with his hand alongside some remark he's made, I suspect he's flirting his ass off. He'd better make sure the wolf girl doesn't hand it back to him. She might not look like a fighter, but they've all got fangs and claws.

I head straight to the clump of newcomers, who relax only slightly at the sight of me. I recognize a couple as regulars from the Refuge.

"I'm glad to have you join us," I say, and motion toward the houses the other Murk are constructing. "Did you want to lend a hand with your new homes?"

The bunch of them all look uncertain. "We didn't realize those were for us," one woman admits. "The Seelie just… let you all build more houses whenever you want?"

I expand my gesture to take in the field around us. "They've given us plenty of room to set up camp while we're still figuring out how this whole cooperative existence thing is going to work. You can ask any of the others who've been here longer—we haven't had any trouble from the wolves. They recognize that you've already proven a lot just by leaving Orion to seek us out."

"To seek *you* out," one of the men I recognize clarifies, with a penetrating look I square my shoulders against. "Things have… things have gotten pretty troublesome over with Orion, even if a lot of the rest don't want to admit it."

"It's hard for anyone to acknowledge they've been wrong, even to themselves," I say. "I've been there."

The remark seems to set them more at ease. We drift over toward the houses-in-progress, and a couple of the newcomers join in with the casting, met with welcoming nods from the Murk who were on the job. I shoot them a smile and make another mental note to find some way to thank them well later.

I have other concerns at the front of my mind right now, though.

I glance at the man who spoke about the difficulties with Orion. "We could bring over so many more of our people sooner if Orion was toppled. You clearly know he isn't doing us any favors with this war."

The second man speaks up in a gruff voice. "He's keeping the pressure on the other fae. Maybe they wouldn't accept us like this if they didn't see they can't get away with cutting us all down on a whim anymore."

"We've had good reasons for being angry and wanting payback," the first man adds.

"Of course—I've wanted that too," I say. I'm going to have to walk a careful line here. "But they've seen that our actions have been justified now. And the longer this war is drawn out, the more of our own people are losing their lives. I wouldn't ask you to reveal anything you're uncomfortable talking about, but if you've found out details that could get us to the peace we all need sooner, I'd make sure the information is handled with proper care."

I won't let the Seelie run rabid with it, I'm trying to convey. The other Murk don't appear particularly convinced.

"We weren't as high up with Orion as you were, not by a mile," the first man says, hedging.

"Well, if you think of anything," I say, knowing it's better not to push too hard in a first conversation, as impatient for a resolution as I am. "Even about an aspect that's not all that crucial to Orion's plans, like where he's stashed the human boy he's kidnapped. Either way, you can settle in here, and we'll—"

The second man's snort cuts me off. "There's no retrieving that kid."

My spine stiffens, but I try not to let my reaction show. "Why would you say that?"

He opens his mouth and then closes it again, with a glance at his companions. I must have won enough points to earn this much trust, though, because the first man spreads his hands in a helpless gesture.

"We heard he's got him shut away in some pit in an old iron

mine. Tons of the ore still all around. It's hard enough for Orion's people to go in—no one connected to the Heart of the Mists is getting within half a mile of that place."

My spirits sink, but I don't let that show either. "I guess we'll see about that. Do you have any idea where exactly this mine is?"

CHAPTER SEVENTEEN

Talia

"An iron mine," Celia repeats. She braces one elbow against the table in the border castle's meeting room and pinches the bridge of her nose as if Madoc's report has given her a headache.

"Why not?" Laoni mutters from where she's sitting at the other end of the table. She shakes her head as if we've purposefully conspired to make this situation as difficult as possible.

Terisse frowns. "Do we have any idea where this specific iron mine is?"

Madoc exhales slowly. "It was hard enough dragging even a little information out of the newest Murk arrivals. They're still getting a sense of how they're going to fit in here among the rest of you. And I'm not sure how many more details they actually know. It's quite possible they were telling the truth that they had no idea."

"Are there a lot of iron mines in the human world?" Donovan asks. "How easily could we narrow it down?"

"It'd be like looking for a needle in a haystack, unfortunately," Whitt puts in from where he's standing just behind Sylas's seat. "But if we can find other methods to bring to bear—"

"We shouldn't even be discussing this!" Uzziah sputters. "How can we focus on one—*human*—boy when both of our realms are under threat?"

My hackles rise. For the first time since this meeting started, I lean forward and let out some of the emotion churning inside me. "It's not 'just' one human boy. He's my brother, and he's already nearly died once so you could have your cure. If we can get him away from the Murk, then we'll have screwed up Orion's latest plan. The more we undermine him, the less faith his followers will have in him—the more of them we'll win over."

"Talia raises a good point," Corwin says with a tendril of reassurance he extends through our connection. "We've made relatively little progress fighting the Murk head-to-head—and I'll point out that the one major victory we accomplished was based on Talia's inspiration and only possible with the hard work of her and many other humans. The rat shifters have been beating us when it comes to trickery, so if we can undercut their tricks, we're taking away their main advantage."

Thank you, I say to him silently, and he shoots me a quick smile.

Celia stirs in her chair. "I don't see how we'd be able to get at the boy when we're much more affected by iron than Orion's contingent of Murk is. We can hardly send a squadron of humans into this mine to face off against the rats alone."

I've already thought about that, and the knowledge sits heavy in my stomach. "We can't," I agree. "But if we could just take a little time to discuss the possibilities… Orion's managed to out-scheme us more than once. We should be able to challenge him on that level if we all put our minds together, right?"

"The first concern is obviously finding the correct mine," Sylas says. "We can't do anything for the boy if we don't know exactly where he is."

Donovan perks up. "We were able to track down Murk before using Talia's blood. She should have even stronger physical ties to her brother than to the rat shifters, shouldn't she? Could we make use of a similar strategy?"

Whitt, who masterminded the tracking spell, taps his forefinger against his lips. "Unfortunately, that spell worked on a localized level. We'd have to end up in approximately the right vicinity to have any hope of it picking up his presence. Without narrowing it down more, it'd be a fathomless task."

"We still have sentries attempting to monitor the Murk in the human world," Terisse says, glancing around the table. "Have any of them reported recent activity that might point us in the right direction?"

Laoni's mouth tightens. "One of mine never returned. I think she was caught by the Murk and killed. The other is due to report in tomorrow."

"I haven't heard anything useful from ours," Uzziah says grudgingly.

There's no guarantee any of the sentries who'll send back reports in the next few days will have discovered anything either, and with every passing hour, there's more chance that Orion will decide he doesn't need to keep Jamie alive.

I exhale sharply in frustration and run my fingers over my bronze bracelet. "It's too bad they took Jamie's bracelet off him. I had a connection to him that way even across the distance. Maybe it could have led us to him."

Whitt's eyebrows rise. "I hadn't thought about the specific magical approach August used with his spell. I'm not sure how easy it'd be to locate your brother in the physical world using similar means, but you *do* have strong blood ties to him. I think if we conducted magic through you the same way August charmed the bracelet to work, we could cast a spell to wherever he is. It might not be the most comfortable process..."

My spirits have already lifted. "I don't care. If it's a way to reach out to him, I can endure it. But... if the spell doesn't tell us where he is, what other magic could we cast that would help him?"

"The girl has more uses than that," a softly creaky voice says. It takes me a second to realize it's Neve, the elderly Unseelie arch-lord who seems to drift through most of these meetings without paying much attention to them. Her gaze has cleared a little, and it's fixed on me. "We can work metal, and she can handle iron."

Whitt claps his hands together. "Yes. You're right—that just might work."

Celia looks from one to the other, her expression as puzzled as I feel. "What do you mean?"

"Talia doesn't have any aversion to iron," Whitt says. "If we conduct metal-working magic *through* her, we may be able to manipulate the ore around her brother. With enough effort and expertise, I could see it being possible to create some kind of protective shell or similar around her brother that would shut out the Murk until we can get to him ourselves—until they're defeated and he's no longer guarded."

My heart leaps. "You really think so?"

He nods. "But we'll need the strongest metal-workers we've got. There's Sorling in our pack—he's very adept with bronze and copper. Metal tends to be more an interest of the Unseelie, though, isn't it? You birds and your eye for shiny objects." His own eyes twinkle with humor.

Laoni hesitates and then admits, "A skill with metals runs in my family. I can contribute."

I blink, startled that she'd offer, but maybe she realizes her colleagues would point her out if she didn't. She meets my gaze evenly. "I don't want this to take too much focus away from our other efforts, though," she adds.

"Of course not," I murmur.

"I'm sure we can round up a few more," Terisse says. "How quickly would you have the technique worked out?"

Sylas glances back at his strategist.

Whitt has started to pace the room. "I may be ready in a matter of hours. Perhaps we should convene in Corwin's palace, since this is more wintry magic. Gather your people, and I'll send word when I'm ready to direct the attempt. I need to consult my books." He stalks out into the hall without another word.

Uzziah huffs as he gets up, but he doesn't argue about the situation. I follow Sylas and the other Seelie back to the summer realm, figuring I might be able to help Whitt sort through his books—or at the very least, it might be useful for him to have me there to test out bits of techniques on. My pulse is thumping hard with the prospect of doing something for Jamie so soon.

Celia strides ahead of the rest of us, heading toward her own domain—and a figure steps into view in the distance, by the forest closer to the Bastion. At the sight of the sunlight glancing off his dandelion-yellow hair, my feet jar to a stop.

It's Aerik. He looks like he's waiting to speak to Celia. What does he want now?

The other men follow my gaze. Sylas lets out a restrained snarl.

Whatever Aerik says when Celia reaches him, she doesn't appear to listen for very long. She makes a dismissive gesture and then sets her hands on her hips when he starts talking again. Finally, he slinks off between the trees.

Sylas marches over, and I hustle along as quickly as I can after him, Madoc keeping pace beside me. Celia sees us coming and waits for us to reach her.

"What was that about?" Sylas demands.

Celia's gaze settles on me with an unusual amount of sympathy. "Word has gotten around that we're concerned with your brother's predicament. Your former captor was urging me not to be distracted by such 'minor matters,' as he put it. You don't need to worry. I informed him I don't see it the same way." She sighs. "I'm sorry you had to spend any time under that man's power. He isn't what the Seelie should be."

Her words can't change the past, but the sentiment in them loosens a little of the old pain that's lodged inside me. "I'm glad that most aren't as bad as him," I say quietly.

She waves me off. "Go with your mates and see to this scheme. The faster it's done, the better for all of us."

It *is* only a few hours later that I find myself sitting cross-legged on the floor in one of the grand diamond rooms in the palace of Heart's Cadence with several fae poised around me. Whitt outdid himself with his research, flying from book to book and scribbling furious notes on whatever papers he could lay his hands on.

He sent our pack-kin who are still on hand at Hearth-by-the-Heart into the woods to gather up a couple of different plants that are supposed to help open me to the magic that's going to flow through me. The leafy stems are now draped across my shoulders and pooled in my lap. They give off a sharp herbal scent that itches my nose.

"So, I don't have to *do* anything?" I ask him as he circles me, making one final inspection.

"Just sit still and keep your emotions as calm and your mind as open as possible," Whitt says. "I'll stay with you to help you relax, since the actual magical talents required aren't in my main repertoire." He glances around at the gathered fae, mostly Unseelie, including Laoni. His sharp gaze might rest a little longer on the arch-lord. "I trust that you all are totally clear on what's expected of you, or that you'll speak up now if you're not?"

When no one raises any issues, he turns to Corwin, standing directly in front of me. "Are you ready to guide the process?"

Corwin inclines his head, offering me a waft of affection and hope at the same time. "Absolutely. We'll make this work."

Whitt sinks onto the floor behind me and eases his arms around my waist. "Lean back against me and breathe slowly and deeply," he murmurs by my ear. "I've got you. The spellwork might feel confusing or even painful, but I won't let anything really hurt you. Do you trust me?"

"Of course," I say automatically. It's true. As I let my weight sink into Whitt's solid frame, the worst of my anxiety subsides. He's the cleverest person I know. He wouldn't be going through with this attempt if he wasn't sure it had a good chance of working—and no chance of going horribly wrong.

If we can protect Jamie, just about anything is worth it.

I close my eyes, letting my awareness narrow down to the cool floor beneath me, the warmth of Whitt's embrace from behind me, and the softly murmuring voices of the fae around me that start to spill out into the air. They're speaking in true names and other words of magic, so I can't understand them anyway, but a quiver of energy runs over my skin.

After several seconds, the quiver digs deeper, expanding into a tremor that travels through me from my breastbone down to my gut. I have to restrain a gasp. Whitt picks up on the tensing of my muscles and strokes his fingers over my arms in a soothing gesture. I let him lull me back into a sort of peace as the flow of magic passing into me continues to grow.

In a matter of minutes, it feels as if I'm lying beneath a waterfall that's pummeling my chest with a chilly torrent—if that torrent would pass right through my skin and flesh and out the other side of me. It takes concentrated will to keep my breaths steady. My nerves are singing in harmony with the deluge, both exhilarating and unnerving.

Images begin to flash through my mind alongside the stream of energy, giving me something else to focus on. I see my brother crouched in a darkened room with walls of packed dirt and wooden posts. I taste the metal woven all through the soil around me. Particles of it jitter free from the earth, my nerves twitching with every movement, and course into a current that flows around him.

At the same time, a colder wash of magic sweeps through me into him. Jamie's eyes roll up, and his body sags. My pulse stutters, but I simply inhale another slow breath.

We talked about this ahead of time. To make sure my brother doesn't starve to death or die of dehydration while locked away from Orion's malice, the fae are putting him into a sort of magical stasis. He won't be aware of anything, and his body will sustain itself without nourishment for days on end.

With luck, it won't be *too* many days before we can wake him up again.

As Jamie slumps onto the floor, the metal is already rippling across the ground beneath him. It coats the earth there with a thick layer and then rises up on every side of him.

Other impressions are trickling through the torrent of energy now. This work is putting a strain on all of the fae who are combining their talents. The feel of the iron at the other end of their casting nips and gnaws at them, gradually biting deeper. Twinges of pain echo into me.

I steer my mind away from those uneasy sensations toward the rhythm of Whitt's breaths against my back and his familiar scent, like sun-warmed sand. It doesn't matter if it hurts in the moment. I'm saving Jamie from so much more hurt. I can hold on for as long as it takes, just as the fae around me are.

In my mind's eye, I see the iron shield around my brother curve up over him and seal into a seamless structure. Then the fae summon more and more of the ore out of the earth to thicken the walls. We need them so sturdy and potent that not even Orion can throw enough magic at them to break them. We need to make sure it isn't worth it to him to try.

More discomfort radiates from the fae around me: clenched jaws, fisted hands, ragged breaths. I do my best to ride out the wave, but my concentration starts to waver. One more layer of iron smooths into place around Jamie's shield—and then everything falls away.

The images of my brother, the pain, and the flood of energy wash away in an instant.

My eyes pop open. I sit up straighter, looking at the fae around me, my gaze coming to rest on Corwin. "Do you think it's enough? Will he be okay?"

My soul-twined mate offers me a tentative smile. His brown skin has grayed with the effort, but a healthy flush is already seeping back into his face. "I believe Orion will find it quite impossible to inflict any harm on your brother now."

I can't imagine what the Murk king will make of the situation when the guards check on Jamie and find him encased like that. Thinking of Orion frustrated should give me some satisfaction, but instead it only sends a shiver through my stomach.

The sense of dread doesn't leave me as Corwin invites us all to stay and have dinner in his palace to refresh ourselves. The food is delicious as always, but after just a few bites, my stomach is churning. I flinch at the simple scrape of chair legs against the floor.

It's done, I tell myself. *It's done.* And I've almost convinced myself to believe it when Verik bursts into the room.

"My lord," he says, "my lady—you're needed to heal the curse. It's a child."

CHAPTER EIGHTEEN

Talia

As I reach the small group of Unseelie clustered together in the glow of the Heart, starker now as evening falls and the sky darkens, I can tell it won't take any work to summon the required tears. The sight of the small boy curled in the woman's arms is enough to bring a burn to the back of my eyes all on its own.

He doesn't look as if he could be more than two or three, however many years that translates into in fae terms. His body is already nearly blue from head to toe, his hair laced with frost, his fingers curled into rigid forms. It's hard to believe he's even alive.

The words tumble out of me in my horror. "Why did you wait so long to bring him?" The only fae I've seen this far gone with the curse have been suffering for at least a couple of days before they reached that point.

"We didn't," the woman says, her voice barely more than a faint rasp. "It started less than an hour ago. We set off as soon as we noticed—it's come on him so quickly." There's a hitch in her chest like she's suppressed a sob.

My horror grips me harder, with icy fingers. The curse has gone from its first signs to nearly fatal in the space of an hour? It's never been anywhere near that potent before.

I don't have the bandwidth to wonder too hard about that, though. The boy needs my help. I turn away, letting the tears that've been welling up spill down my cheeks and hiding my face with my hands.

These poor parents. I have only the vaguest experience in losing a child—one I never saw or got to hold in my arms to become that much more attached—and I know how painful even that loss was. And for the fae, with their limited fertility, every child is so much more precious.

More tears than I'm sure I need trickle from my eyes. I swipe at them a few times before turning back toward the couple and the few flock folk who've come with them. I stroke my damp fingers over the little boy's terrifyingly frigid cheek, braced for bad news.

It takes a few moments. At first, he doesn't stir. Then the blue starts to fade from his skin, and the frost melts from his hair. A breath of relief rushes out of me as he twitches and presses his face against his mother's chest with a whimper.

I cured him in time. It was close, but he's safe now.

Corwin comes up behind me and rests his hands on my shoulders. A similar crash of emotions is whirling through him—thinking of this child nearly lost and our child who was. He dips his head to the couple. "May he live long in the Heart's light."

The couple stammer their thanks, the woman squeezing my hand briefly with her own eyes flooded with tears, and then they head back to their carriage. I take Corwin's hand and turn back toward his palace.

Verik has been waiting farther to the side. The graying coterie member turns to follow us and stops in his tracks, peering toward the edge of the plateau. "There's another carriage coming."

My legs stall. Corwin stays next to me as we watch the vehicle come closer, the light of the lantern orb attached to its windshield expanding larger with its swift approach. A sickly sensation coils in my belly.

It must be a coincidence. Fae have been coming and going a lot since the war began. The carriage will probably swing to the side and go down to the camp at the base of the plateau…

But it doesn't. As the cool evening breeze licks through my hair, the new carriage pulls right up to where we're standing by the Heart. My own heart sinks even more at the sight of the fae scrambling over the side.

It's Fina, the pregnant woman I've healed from the curse more than once now, except she's not pregnant anymore. The bulge of her belly has shrunk, and she has a small bundle wrapped in her arms.

She and her mate hustle over to us, so frantic they don't even remark on the fact that we're already here. Fina is shaking so badly she can't seem to get words out.

Her mate keeps his arm tight around her shoulders. His voice comes out with a quaver too. "Please. I don't know if— It came on so quickly. She's so *cold*."

In that moment, I hate the playacting of the Unseelie cure, the fact that I have to go through the motions of not wanting to show my vulnerability for it to work. I want to spill tears right over the infant tucked against the fae woman's chest, her tiny face like ice when they peel back the blanket. But I need to turn away as the tears well up again, need to give them a moment to overflow, need to paw at them as if I want to get rid of them before returning my attention to the baby and tracing my fingers over the curve of her cheek.

She *feels* like ice as well as looking it. I have to restrain a shudder. It's hard to imagine there's any life left in the tiny body.

"We could feel her still breathing up until just before we reached here," the father babbles as if he can talk the possible tragedy away. "We pushed the carriage as fast as it would go."

Then the baby's lips part. A thin wail pierces the deepening dusk as the curse's chill releases it. Fina gasps and hugs her daughter even tighter. "Thank you," she says to me. "Thank you and thank the Heart."

My relief at seeing the cure work doesn't dislodge the dread that's thickened in my gut. I glance at Corwin, not wanting to say what I'm thinking out loud in front of them.

This couldn't be left over from her *curse. She'd have come down with it too. And for it to happen at almost the same time as another child…*

The same anguish twists through Corwin's silent words. *I think we should stay here by the Heart for a little longer. Just to be sure.*

I don't like the directions my thoughts go from there, but I have to say it. *Do you know how many Unseelie children there are in the realm right now? Which domains they're in?*

I know a few off the top of my head and could determine the rest with a quick glance at our records. But—if this is more than just a horrible coincidence—anyone else affected will already be on their way here. We can't go to any of them without missing all the others.

He's right. But as we watch Fina and her mate drift back to their carriage, I'm tormented by the fact that I can't do anything except wait and find out just how horrible this night is going to get.

A small flicker of hope has just lit in my chest when the sight of another traveling light in the distance douses it again. I grip Corwin's hand, my pulse thumping harder.

Other Unseelie are starting to gather in a loose ring around the Heart, coming over to see what's going on while giving us lots of space. They must have noticed the first two carriages and now this new one. Maybe sentries from the other arch-lords' domains who witnessed the two cursed children passed on word. I don't know what to say to them, so I stay silent.

This carriage is racing toward the plateau so quickly that its hull groans as it passes over the ridge. In the glow of the orb, I can make out mottled sections on the outer walls where bits appear to have fallen away in the driver's haste.

Four fae leap out, the man in the middle hefting a girl who looks around eight in his arms. Her limbs are folded at rigid angles. Her eyes are half-open, what I can see of them frosted over. Her hair has gone pure white with ice.

My throat closes up. She's dead. I can already see that.

But maybe Fina's baby was too, just not quite so far gone that my cure couldn't work. Maybe I can still heal this girl as well.

The man stumbles to me with a wildly desperate expression. "Please," he says raggedly.

I have to try.

I've vaguely aware of the crowd around us growing as I put on my performance of hiding my tears. They gush freely now, driven by grief and a deepening sense of helplessness. The second I think it's safe to turn back to the girl, I swivel and reach for her cheek.

The moisture from my fingers hardens into fresh trails of ice on her cheek. Her father bows his head over her body, murmuring prayers under his breath.

She doesn't move. She doesn't come back to life. We stand there as the seconds slip by torturously, and the girl remains solidly frozen. Her father clutches her tighter with a stifled groan.

Tears I can't use dribble down to my chin. I wipe at them with my sleeve, willing down the scream that wants to break from my throat. It isn't fair. It isn't *right.*

But in Orion's mind, this is probably a perfect sort of justice. I stole one child he wanted to victimize from him, so he twisted his curse to victimize who knows how many more.

I don't need any message carved in a wall to tell me that this is my punishment for protecting my brother. *My* punishment… that the Unseelie are having to bear much more than I am.

The carriages keep coming. Another and another, closer together as those from farther flung domains converge on the plateau. From the choked explanations a few of them manage to give Corwin, it sounds like the curse struck all the children at the same time. The two families who were close enough to the Heart to realize the urgency of the situation and make it here within an hour or so got lucky. The others…

I try to heal every one of those deathly cold bodies. I haven't totally stopped crying since the first I failed to revive, so it doesn't take any effort. At least not that part. With every child that stays still and stiff, with every parental face that crumples with the most hopeless sort of grief, it gets harder to push down the scream that's still clawing at my chest.

After the ninth child, the family returns to their carriage, and I can hear the mother attempting to muffle her weeping. An ache has crept through so much of my body that I think it might swallow me whole. There must be a couple hundred fae standing around the Heart in what's now full night, bearing solemn witness to this extended tragedy.

Corwin rubs my back. Agony thrums through all my impressions of his inner state too, both for me and for his people. I can feel how much he longs to wrap his arms around me and take comfort in my embrace while offering the same to me, but he doesn't want to show any weakness in front of the other fae.

We watch the horizon for more lantern lights. One minute slips by, and another. Despite the warming charms on my clothes, my fingertips are starting to go numb. We wait, and we wait… and no one else comes.

Nine children struck. Seven who didn't make it. Seven much, much too many.

Someone speaks up from the crowd. "The Murk did this, didn't they? We have to make them pay!"

A restless muttering spreads through the assembled fae. "Yes," someone else says. "Why are we trying to make any kind of peace with them? They're monsters—they should be slaughtered, all of them."

A figure steps close to the front of the crowd, and in my daze of grief, I realize it's Kara. She's wearing a cloak with a thick hood that shadows her face, but her gaze seems to pierce right through me.

"The rats sent their own children out with their army against us, I hear," she says in a voice that rings through the night. "We fell back to *save* those children. And now they couldn't make it clearer that they'll never extend the same compassion to us. While this human tries to tell us we should make friends with them!" She jabs her hand toward me.

Corwin's stance pulls even straighter than it already was. "Kara," he says, his tone rough but firm. "You don't know the full situation. Not all of the Murk agree with those tactics any more than all of the Unseelie share the exact same views."

She shrinks a little under his criticism, but the crowd has already been riled up by her words. "We can't show them any kindness."

"Tear them all apart like they deserve."

"What does a human know about how the fae really are, how they've always been?"

"We've let the rats get away with too much!"

The mass of fae falls silent at the arrival of two other arch-lords. Laoni and Terisse nod to Corwin, Laoni's expression exhausted and Terisse's miserable.

"We have more to speak about between us arch-lords," Laoni says, taking in the crowd. "The Murk will not get away with this crime—you can be sure of that. For now, please go back to your homes or your camps—and look after each other."

The other fae start to meander away, a few shooting glances at me that feel decidedly hostile. Now that I've failed to save the most treasured members of their society, I guess they don't see me as quite so much a savior. I'm not sure I can blame them for that.

I can't believe people like Madoc and Delta deserve to die simply for being Murk. But… what if Kara's a little right? What if I've been too soft, and we could have ended this war already otherwise?

If I hadn't protected my brother, would Orion have done this anyway just to hurt the Unseelie every way he could? Or is it all my fault?

CHAPTER NINETEEN

Whitt

I'm a little surprised to find August alone in the border castle's kitchen. I poke my head right through the doorway to get a better view of the room, but there's no sign of Talia, even though I can tell from the mouth-watering scents in the air that this late breakfast is nearly done. He's rarely without our mate as his helper on the mornings we're here.

"Talia hasn't come down?" I venture.

August shakes his head, his mouth twisting. "She's still in bed. It took her a long time to get to sleep last night, so I was careful not to disturb her when I got up. I figured she needed the rest."

I'd imagine she did—and not just physically. I can only imagine the emotional toll last night's events in the winter realm took on her. Corwin himself was choked up, more emotional than I've ever seen him, as he told us what happened while holding Talia close as if he could protect her from the tragedy with the force of his affection. I doubt he'd have left her side if he'd had any choice, but the Unseelie arch-lords have a lot on their plate now.

Our mate's eyes were red-rimmed from crying, and she barely

said anything on her way to her bedroom with August and Corwin. I wonder if she's still sleeping now or just having trouble facing the day ahead and all the fresh horrors it might bring.

"I'll check on her," I say. "She should get some food into her too."

I leave August to carry the plates over to the dining room and head upstairs, passing Sylas on the way. He tips his head to me in acknowledgment, clearly deciphering my intent. "Make sure she knows we all realize she did her best," he says.

My lips curl in a bittersweet smile. "I'll try." My mighty mite can be stubborn in many ways, not all of them to her benefit. She often has some trouble avoiding taking on more of a burden of responsibility than should really be hers.

I stop in the hall outside Talia's bedroom door and prick my ears. The rhythm of breaths I can make out tells me she's awake—and that she's been crying again. The pace is too rapid for sleep, with a soft hitch here and there as she struggles to get herself under control.

An ache squeezes my chest. I nudge open the door and walk over to the bed.

Talia is still bundled under the covers. She doesn't look up as I clamber onto the expansive mattress next to her, but when I tug her closer to me, she adjusts her position just slightly to nestle against me.

"Am I needed outside?" she asks in a tone that's trying so hard to be nothing but determined. "I can get dressed and come down."

"Right now, I'm not concerned about what anyone needs other than you," I inform her, nuzzling the back of her neck and breathing in her sap-sweet scent. "August has whipped up one of his masterpiece breakfasts. If you can't summon much enthusiasm for your own sake, think of how happy *he'll* be to see you enjoying it."

Talia lets out a grumble in response, but my ploy does work. She squirms out of my arms and slides off the bed. I track her movements through the room as she limps to the wardrobe and paws through it, noting the tension that appears to weigh on her limbs, as if she's pushing through sludge rather than air. Her face still looks worn with exhaustion, despite how long she's been in bed. When she turns to me after pulling on one of the Unseelie-style dresses Corwin has provided her with, the smile she offers me looks more pained than pleased.

The ache inside me digs deeper, but I don't know what to say to her to make this better. Maybe the best I can do is not focus on the horrible things at all but distract her with something totally different.

I prowl over to her and sweep her off the ground into my arms swiftly enough that she lets out a squeak of surprise. "What are you doing?" she demands, giving me a baleful look.

I press a peck to her forehead. "Auggie gets to cart you around like this all the time. Why shouldn't I get to as well?"

She lets out a faint harumph, but the slightest bit of humor has crept into it. "I don't love it when he does it either."

"Hmm. Then I'll just have to improve on his technique."

"That's not—" She cuts herself off with a soft huff and lets her head lean against my shoulder as I carry her down the stairs. I glance toward the room we've set up for Madoc, but only silence emanates from within. He's often been leaving in the mornings to check in on the temporary Murk settlement. I'd imagine he has particular concerns about their safety after last night's offensive against the Unseelie.

Orion certainly has a knack for stirring up hatred against his people.

When we reach the dining room, Sylas and August are already there. August has taken the liberty of dishing out a small portion of each of the delicacies on offer onto a plate at Talia's usual spot. "You can have more of anything you want, of course," he says quickly as I set her down there.

"I'm sure this will be plenty," Talia says, looking at the meal as if it's a bowling ball she's being asked to swallow down. She picks up her fork but then simply holds it in the air, her gaze darting between the three of us taking our seats around the table. "You'd have heard from the winter realm—there haven't been any more children, have there?" Her jaw tightens as she braces herself.

Thankfully, Sylas can shake his head. "No further cases of their curse have been reported," he says in the gentle voice I've only heard my lord and brother offer this one woman. "It appears that Orion was only able to amplify the curse in those nine victims."

"It must have taken an awful lot out of him even managing that," I say. "Up until now, he's ramped up the effects slowly, decreasing the time between victims and the speed they fell ill by tiny increments. To go from days to an hour or less in one go, and in not one but several fae… He's probably pushed himself to his limit. We may even see a respite from their curse for a week or more until it's recovered the energy he squeezed out of it."

Talia doesn't look as relieved by that suggestion as I'd have hoped. "It's still seven more children than should have died," she says faintly, staring at her plate.

"The Murk aren't the only ones who've crossed that line," Sylas says. "You've told us yourself about the fae who've slaughtered Murk children. I suppose they'd see it as fair turnabout."

"That doesn't make it better."

"No. But it does mean these sorts of things have happened through no influence of your own."

August jumps in. "For him to be able to put so much magic into the curse so quickly, he was probably already planning on using that strategy before you reached out to your brother. Maybe he sped up his timeline a little, but it was only a convenient excuse. You didn't *make* him do it."

"I know," Talia says, but she doesn't sound all that convinced. She stabs at a sausage patty and takes a bite. Even her chewing seems sluggish, as if it's taking more effort than it should.

The rest of us start to eat too, but all of us pay more attention to how our mate is doing with her meal than to our own. She works her way through half of her plate before she pauses again and looks up at us.

"The Unseelie last night—the ones who came and saw what was happening—they weren't happy that I couldn't heal everyone. Or that I've been speaking up for the Murk. Do you think… They seemed to accept me before, but now that I've let them down, what if—"

"You haven't let them down," I break in, with a flare of irritation at the Unseelie. I tamp down on that emotion. "They'd just witnessed something terrible, and they weren't in their right minds. *Their* reaction has very little to do with you either."

"But maybe they shouldn't have put so much faith in me to begin with," Talia says. "I'm not a savior—I could only cure anyone because Orion wanted to use me against you—there's nothing all that special about me or my ideas."

August lets out a growl of denial, and a sharper pang shoots through my heart. But at the same moment, a spark of inspiration lights in my head. I push back my chair. "Come with me."

Talia blinks at me, startled. "What? Where?"

"You'll see." I motion for my brothers to join us. "I think this is more important than breakfast. As much as we appreciate your culinary efforts, August, we can come back to them later."

August doesn't argue, looking more hopeful than anything else. Sylas stands as well, trusting me to know what I'm doing. I'm sure they're as agonized over Talia's self-doubt as I am.

I wrap my hand around Talia's and match her uneven gait down the hall to the summer entrance and out into the pleasant late morning sunlight. The area right along the border is quiet for the moment, no other Seelie tending to business nearby. I lead my mate and my brothers across the open plain, veering away from the glow of the Heart itself to step through one of the entrances of the Bastion.

I glance around, dredging up the right path from my memory, and head for one specific staircase. It spirals up to a landing in one of the building's side towers, where a small arched window offers a view over Hearth-by-the-Heart.

Talia steps to the window, gazing out over the view, and then turns to look at me again. A soft light had come into her face that wasn't there before, and I know she recognizes the significance of this place.

"You remember what happened here," I say.

"I came up here during Sylas's coronation celebration," she says quietly. "I was—I was worried that you'd all take mates from the other fae now that you had even more prestige than you ever did before."

I stroke my hand over her hair. "And we found you here, and each of us swore to you that there was no one else we wanted more. It was here that we first agreed we'd make you our mate in every possible way, publicly and officially. It took longer than we'd anticipated to get to that point, but we did make it there in the end."

She bites her lip. "But why…"

I ease my arm all the way around her, tucking her against my chest. "I wanted to remind you of how much faith *we* have always had in you and still do. There's no one more special in our eyes in the whole of the fae world. And you trust our judgment, don't you?"

A hint of a smile touches her mouth, even though her eyes still look sad. "You might be a *little* biased."

Sylas chuckles and rests his hand on her shoulder. "You've proven again and again how much strength and insight you possess. You've guided us and opened our eyes in so many ways. Maybe your approach to the conflict with the Murk isn't absolutely perfect, but I'm sure none of the rest of us have perfect ideas either. That doesn't mean they aren't valuable. *You* are valuable, and any fae who tries to say you shouldn't be contributing is only proving that they're a dolt."

"But when it's kids…"

"No one else could save them either," August says. "You saved two that wouldn't have made it otherwise. Who else could offer that much? Who else even tried? If there's one thing I know about you, it's that you won't back down. You'll keep giving your all and doing whatever you can to help the rest of us, whether we deserve it or not."

Talia releases a shaky breath. "I'm sure the three of you deserve it."

"And you deserve everything we can offer you, mighty one," I say, and draw her chin up so I can capture her mouth.

I mean it to be only a tender, reassuring kiss, but as she turns in my arms to embrace me more fully, a deeper heat stirs inside me. I pull her closer, reveling in the eager sound that carries from her chest, in the mix of softness and strength that flows all through her body.

She's our mate, and maybe what she needs more than anything right now is a full demonstration of how much we cherish her.

When Talia has melted into my arms, I draw out the kiss a little longer before bringing my mouth to her jaw and the side of her neck. Then I raise my head to glance at my brothers. "Perhaps we should ensure no one comes up this way to disturb us until we're done here."

A sly gleam has lit in Sylas's eyes. He and August murmur a few words to discourage any wanderers from venturing up this staircase, and I turn Talia in my arms so that she can receive more affection than I can offer on my own.

As I slide her hair to the side and nibble across the crook of her shoulder, August steps in to capture her lips. Talia keeps one hand clutched around a fold in my shirt and teases her other fingers into August's hair. Sylas moves in to complete our circle, trailing his fingers up from her belly to the neckline of her dress and along it, just above the swell of her breasts.

There was a time when I'd have felt jealous, seeing my brothers touch Talia this way. A time when I thought I couldn't have her because it would mean needing to share her like this. Those emotions couldn't be more distant now. Nothing but joy touches me at seeing the way she leans into Sylas's touch, hearing the whimper that escapes her as August deepens their kiss. Her body is made of heat against mine, pressed against my hardening cock like a brand, and I wouldn't have her any other way than so fully satisfied.

"I love you," I murmur by her ear, and nip her earlobe. "I'll always want you with me, want you sharing every idea that comes into your head. I can't imagine going without you."

Talia's grasp on my shirt tightens. She draws her mouth from August to kiss me again. Afterward, her voice comes out ragged, and not just with arousal. "I just want to be as good a mate as any fae could be."

August makes a rough sound. "You are that and more." He slips his fingers down over her bodice, provoking a gasp as his thumb skips over the peak of her breast.

"We couldn't have asked for a better mate," Sylas agrees. "*I* couldn't have asked for a better match while I rule as arch-lord. You're worthy of all the same awe our people offer me." He kisses her shoulder and starts to sink down to his knees. "But since they're not here, I'll offer all the worship I can—and happily."

When he eases up the skirt of her dress, Talia's eyelids flutter. She tips her head against my shoulder with a stuttered breath as Sylas's mouth grazes her sex through her panties. I know what a delight that experience is—and even if I'm not the one getting to enjoy her most potent flavor right now, I can make the moment even better for her.

I let her rest more weight against me as her body goes even more slack with the pleasure racing through her. As Sylas tugs down her panties and swipes his tongue right over her, skin to skin, a moan tumbles from her mouth. August leans in to drink the sound from her lips, and I dip my fingers under the neckline of her dress.

Her nipples have already stiffened beneath the fabric. I tease my fingertips in slow and then swifter flicks over one and then the other, until Talia is quivering against me, her hips rocking to meet Sylas's mouth, her breath coming in gasps. With a hasty motion, I loosen her dress and draw the cloth right down to bare her breast, cupping it in the same moment.

When I position it for him, August accepts my offer without hesitation. He lowers his head to suck the peak into his mouth. Talia's eyelids drift shut, nothing but a flush of bliss coloring her face now.

We're bringing her to these heights—the three of us, together. It feels like nothing short of a miracle.

My cock is straining against my slacks, but I do my best to tune its demands out until Talia gropes behind her, reaching for me. As her slim fingers close around my rigid shaft, a surge of pleasure flares from my groin. I can't hold back a groan.

She runs her hand up and down over me, her grip shaking with the eager tremors racking her body. Then she squeezes so hard I almost come just like that. A cry spills from her lips as she quakes and trembles with the force of the orgasm Sylas has brought her to.

It takes a moment for Talia to gather herself. Then she bends over in front of me, wrenching her skirt even higher with a glance over her shoulder.

I can't refuse her invitation. I yank my slacks open and run the head of my cock over her slick opening, reveling in the bliss of the motion, in the eager gasp that slips from her mouth. Sylas captures it with a kiss, and August kneels next to her, stroking her chest with his hands now.

My hunger for her grips me, and I can't hold back any longer. I plunge into her, the heat and the quiver of her channel around me flooding me with the headiest of pleasures.

Talia lets out a sound like a mewl. Then she's fumbling with my brothers' pants, taking Sylas into her mouth, August with her hand, switching between them as they both groan.

Even with the need for release blazing through me, I want to make her second peak even better than the first. I reach around her hips and massage her clit in time with my thrusts. Talia jerks against me, her sex clamping around my shaft. The second she starts coming, I follow her with a choked growl.

She doesn't neglect my brothers, relishing them with her hands and mouth even as she rides out the aftershock of her orgasm. I brace her against me to help her keep her balance as she brings them one after the other to satisfaction.

Then we all sink down on the stone floor. A little laugh spills out of Talia, the first fully joyful sound I've heard this morning.

I tip my head close to hers to kiss her temple, my heart still thumping hard. I can't think of anything I couldn't do, any length I wouldn't go to, if she needed it. I hope she never doubts that of any of her mates. And if I have my way, she'll have the full loyalty of every other fae in the realms for as long as she's here with us.

May that be much longer than Orion intends.

CHAPTER TWENTY

Talia

The Seelie camp at the base of the hill around the Heart is much more haphazard-looking than its equivalent on the winter side. Rather than orderly rows, the buildings in their various materials stand in irregular clusters. Fae are bustling to and from the several hubs of activity where supplies and food are being distributed. There's a clatter of pans in one direction and the hiss of a knife cutting through fruit in another.

Harper gazes around her with a typical wide-eyed expression. "So many fae from so many packs all here together. And I guess there are just as many out at the front."

Astrid, who's joined us for this visit along with another guard from our pack, nods. "A war is a big undertaking. You should hope you don't have to see it again in your lifetime."

I glance at her. "You've never seen anything this big, have you?"

"Thankfully no, and I wish I could have given this one a miss too." She shoots me a wry smile. "Although at least the ravens managed to work together with us instead of giving us an enemy to deal with on both sides."

We've brought freshly pressed cheese from Elliot's sheep and a huge basket full of loaves of bread that August baked. After handing those over at one of the eating areas, I start to wander through the camp somewhat at random, not totally sure what else I can do but wanting to be here to offer it if the fae around me have any ideas.

They're the ones taking on the most risk in this fight. I've put myself within reach of the Murk army once and only briefly. They've been rotating with their comrades on the front since the first attack.

Many of the fae who are out speaking with each other or grabbing a meal notice me and tip their heads in acknowledgment. Some call out to me by name. "Lady Talia, may the Heart shine on us with you."

"It's good to see you're well, Lady Talia."

"We'll beat the bastards soon, Lady Talia. You can count on that."

There's none of the derision I sensed from the Unseelie last night. I'm not sure how many of the summer fae even know what happened there so recently. And when I haven't let *them* down in any way, maybe it wouldn't matter to them regardless. But even after my thorough worshipping at the hands of my Seelie mates just a few hours ago, the thought of all those deaths travels with me like a boulder in my stomach.

With every fae who stops and offers any kind of greeting or remark, I push a smile to my lips to show I'm keeping my spirits up and ask them, "Is there anything you could use?" or "Do you need help with anything?"

Most don't seem to want to make any requests of me, although it could be they're simply well-supplied as it is. A couple mention that they'd love it if August sent down more of his duskapple pastries. One asks if I can find anyone skilled with a particular plant's true name around, as she'd like to cultivate some for easy camp meals. To make sure I don't forget, I write it all down on a strip of parchment I grabbed from Whitt's office.

We stop at the far edge of the camp so I can rest my warped foot. The sun beams down over us, warm but not oppressively hot. The weather near the Heart is always pretty much perfect. I sit down on the grass, dragging air full of a lilac-sweet scent into my lungs, and study the camp from this vantage point in case I might notice something else that needs doing.

"They've had several days to get into their routines and figure out any problems that have arisen," Astrid says, staying on her feet next to me. "It'll all be minor matters from here on."

"At least minor matters are still something I can help with." I figure as soon as we're done here, I'll go back to the kitchen and work with August to whip up those pastries extra fast.

Harper hunkers down on the grass beside me and tips her pale face to the sun. Her flaxen hair gleams with the pure natural light. "It's too bad no one needs fancy dresses in a war. I'm getting ready a whole collection for when we can celebrate our win." She pauses. "Not to get ahead of ourselves. I think of it like a good luck charm, encouraging our victory to happen."

"Sounds good to me," I say.

Another familiar figure passes into view briefly before walking on through the camp. Donovan has come down from his castle to check in with his people too. I watch his fiery hair vanish between the buildings and turn to Harper hesitantly. She's looking in the same direction, but I don't see any sign that she's affected by his presence.

"We could go chat him up a little," I suggest. A couple of weeks ago when I was particularly sick, Harper confessed to a crush on the arch-lord.

I expect her to blush, but instead she lets out a light laugh. "No, that's all right. I actually—I've tried to talk to him a couple of times since you and I spoke about it. Because I was thinking about what you said. But… I realized that he doesn't seem to really *see* me. I'm just another random member of Sylas's pack to him, no matter what I say or how I'm dressed. It's better… better to be around someone who notices you for yourself."

Something about her tone makes me raise my eyebrows. "You sound like you're speaking from experience now."

That comment gets me the blush I was anticipating. Harper ducks her head shyly. "There's nothing actually happening. But…

I'm not thinking about Arch-Lord Donovan anymore, so you don't have to worry about that."

Intriguing. I might have pried a little more if Astrid and the other guard weren't standing nearby. Harper deserves her privacy. And if she isn't ready to tell even me about whoever's caught her interest now, that's her right too.

I relax back on my hands for a few minutes longer and then push myself to my feet. "Let's make one more circuit before we head back to Hearth-by-the-Heart. I'd like to find out if there are any—"

My words halt in my throat as my gaze snags on a shape slinking out from between two of the buildings farther down the edge of the camp. It's a wolf, fae-sized and covered in thick white fur with an icy blue sheen. Fur the same color as the hair on the man who took the most glee out of tormenting me in Aerik's cage.

I know Aerik's cadre-chosen Cole when I see him, even in shifted form. My pulse stutters, and I instinctively back up a step. That's all the reaction I would have at the sight of him, except that at the same time, Cole's wolfish head swings in my direction. His lips pull back from his fangs in a silent snarl.

Without any other warning, he charges at me.

It's so much worse than just seeing him with Aerik before. Panic blares through my mind louder than it's ever hit me in the past. In that instant, the sunny summer day around me blackens into a shadowy forest in the dark of evening, with three vicious beasts springing at me and my brother out of the brush. A ghost of the old pain flares in the scars on my shoulder. My skin goes cold, and a scream bursts from my throat.

I come back to myself with the sense of a hand on my back and a firm voice speaking words my mind isn't quite processing. I blink, the world around me coming back into focus. My heart is still racing faster than a runaway train. I've sunk into a crouch, my legs trembling under me, too shaky to fully hold my weight.

It's Harper who's touching my back, rubbing up and down my shoulder blade now, her voice low but frantic. "It's okay, Talia. It's all right. He isn't going to hurt you."

Astrid's voice sinks in next from where she's standing over me, her hands on her hips with one gripping the short sword by its hilt. "I said *back away from her.*"

Cole is poised a few feet away from her, now in the form of a man, the sunlight glinting off his icy hair. He sputters an indignant laugh. "All I was doing was running by. *She* interrupted me in *my* work."

I know that's not true. The image of his bared teeth and the way he charged straight at me flashes through my mind, and another shudder wracks my body.

He provoked me on purpose. But why? My thoughts are too scattered for me to piece together any explanation.

Then Cole offers it up all on his own. He turns away from Astrid and me, and I notice the other Seelie who've stopped in their tracks to see what's going on over here. My scream must have drawn a lot of attention. My throat still stings from it.

"This is the human we've elevated so high," Cole sneers. "She doesn't trust any of *us* at all. She's terrified of our wolves—she thinks we're monsters."

No. He's trying to make me out to be the enemy—as part of Aerik's whole campaign to throw me to the Murk, probably. I suck a breath into my constricted lungs, fighting to get my emotions under control.

He's a monster. And yes, I'm terrified of him. But I don't have to be. I've beaten him and his lord before. I can do it again.

"This is what we're putting up with these days?" Cole goes on with a scoff. "Letting our arch-lords take mates who'll scream at the sight of wolves?"

My pulse hiccups again, but I push myself upright, tensing my legs to hold them straight. It takes me a second to force the words from my throat, but when I do, they're loud enough to carry.

"I'm not afraid of wolves," I say, staring straight at Cole. "I'm afraid of you, because of what you did to me. I've ridden on wolves' backs and fallen asleep with a wolf for a pillow. I have no problem with the Seelie. I only have a problem with *you.*"

Cole jerks around. From the stiffening of his expression, he hadn't expected me to be able to talk back, definitely not that coherently. He upped the ante on purpose—planning to send me into a panic so severe I'd be helpless while he made me look bad. When I managed to stand up to Aerik before, I had my mates all around me and there hadn't been anything to overtly trigger my memories of their abuse. He thought if he pushed me harder, he could get the better of me.

But he's underestimated me again. Hopefully for the last time.

He pulls back his lips just a smidge, just enough to show a glint of the fangs he's let protrude again. Trying to send me spiraling again.

Shivers dart under my skin at the sight, but I ignore them and manage to move toward him rather than away. I'm stronger than he thinks. In the ways that matter most, I'm stronger than *him*.

I propel myself forward to stand where the onlookers can see me just as well as him. None of them were at the meeting of the lords in the Bastion. They might have heard whispers about Aerik's treatment of me, but they've never had to really face it.

Maybe it's time I showed the fae I'm living among everything I can. They've seen me break down, but they haven't seen the full cause. I've tried to cover up my old wounds, to even out my limp, but my scars are a part of me. They tell the story of how I came to be here and what I suffered along the way.

Without letting myself think about the consequences, I jerk the neckline of my dress to the side.

"This is what his lord did to me when I was just a kid," I say, yanking far enough to reveal the angry red ridges that mark my shoulder. No one except my mates has really seen them before now, but I've been wrong to hide them. Wrong to pretend that the Seelie can't be villains, that I support every one of them.

I kick off my braced boot and hold out my misshapen foot. At my gesture, Astrid hefts me up by the waist so those farther off can see the malformed lump of bone where Cole broke it all those years ago. "This is what this man did to me when I was already trapped in a cage. If any of you smash up my body, then I'll be afraid of you too. I hope you won't blame me for that."

Several hostile glances are turning toward Cole now. The cadre-chosen's confidence fades. He shoots me a stealthy glare and marches off without another word.

I wish I could feel triumphant about his departure, but all at once I'm exhausted.

As Astrid sets me down on the grass, a few of the fae who were watching hustle over. "Are you all right, Lady Talia?" one asks in a worried voice.

"I didn't realize it was so bad—how could they get away with hurting you like that?" another says.

I don't know how to answer either of those questions. I tug my boot back on, grappling with my words. "What they did—it technically wasn't a crime. Because I'm human. That's why I've spoken up for the other humans here in the fae world. But I'm all right now. I'm just not going to let him accuse me of ridiculous things."

The murmur of agreement reassures me. No one bought into his awful claims.

Astrid squeezes my shoulder. "Maybe we should get you right home." And then, with a mischievous gleam in her eyes, she bends over into her wolf form. She crouches down so I can clamber onto her back.

I guess there's no better way to prove that it's only certain wolves I take issue with. I swing my leg over her back and curl my fingers into her thick fur. The other guard and Harper shift on either side of us, and we set off through the camp to hushed murmurs and hollered well wishes from all sides.

It really isn't any trial to ride Astrid like this. I've faced my fears of the wolves in general so many times over the past months that it was only the sight of that one specific beast launching himself at me that could still trigger a panic attack. Maybe Cole's strategy will backfire on him, and the rest of the Seelie will appreciate my attempts to help even more.

Most of the good things in my life have come out of facing the things I feared rather than running away from them, haven't they? Memories rise up as if jostled out of the back of my mind by the rhythm of Astrid's wolfish lope.

All the times I stood up to Madoc and spoke my mind even when I wasn't sure how he'd treat me afterward. Crossing the border to the winter realm before I knew much of who Corwin was. Crouching in a cage while Aerik and his men stalked over to me, only to turn the tables on them with my hidden magic. Tossing a blood-smeared rag into my Seelie lovers' mouths while they were in the grips of their savage curse.

I linger on those last two events, something stirring amid my thoughts. I've always been underestimated. *That* fact has led to some of my greatest victories too. And I know how much courage I have in me. I once stood my ground in front of Sylas's wolf while he was raging with the curse, ready to tear me apart.

By the time we reach the border castle, I'm trembling for a totally different reason, one that provokes more excitement than fear. The jitters chase me into the castle, where I find all of my men standing in intense conversation in the living room. They turn at my entrance, but I can't find it in me to hold off this announcement even for greetings.

I halt in the doorway, my heart pounding with determination. "I know how to stop Orion."

CHAPTER TWENTY-ONE

Corwin

Talia's eyes are so wild and defiant they rouse a matching emotion in me. I can't make out any details of the idea that's struck her through our bond, but her resolve radiates into me, as potent as a bonfire.

"Did something happen?" August asks, bristling automatically with his usual protective energy. It's not difficult to see that something must have prompted Talia's sudden furor.

"Yes—it doesn't matter. That's not the point." She marches over to us as briskly as her warped foot allows. "All that matters is it made me think of a way to end the war."

Sylas motions to the nearest armchair. "Why don't you sit down and tell us everything?"

Talia looks a bit reluctant, but she sinks into the chair he indicated, and the rest of us take seats around her. Madoc's stance is tensed, maybe because any attack against the Murk will be more personal to him than to the rest of us. He stays as silent as we do, though, waiting for Talia to gather her words.

"Do you remember," she says, fixing her gaze on the Seelie men, "how we tricked Aerik and his cadre and got them in a position where you could force their yield?"

"Of course," Whitt says for all of them, in a tone that's both dry and wary. "One of your first brilliant brainstorms."

Talia turns to me and Madoc. I've gotten the gist of the story before through her memories, but she explains for both of our benefits. "Technically I was Aerik's 'property,' and Sylas had stolen me. When Aerik's men found out, they demanded that Sylas give me back or they'd reveal the theft to the arch-lords."

Madoc grimaces. "Even more reason to despise those pricks."

"We arranged to meet them with me in a cage and Sylas and the others taking a vow not to make the first attack," Talia goes on. "But Aerik didn't know that I'd been learning true names. We had bronze chains hidden in the grass attached to the base of the cage, and when he and his men came close, I called on bronze to send the chains to restrain them. The effect didn't last for long, but it was enough to count as the first strike so that Sylas, Whitt, and August could jump in without breaking their vow, and the momentary confusion gave them the upper hand. They overpowered Aerik and his men and forced them to yield with a promise that they'd give up all claim on me."

A fresh waft of pride travels through me, thinking of how frightened she must have been facing those men and how she overcame it to conquer them. "It was very clever of you," I say, offering her a fond smile. But beneath my happier feelings, a twisting sensation is forming in my gut. I'm not sure I like my sense of where this might be leading. "How does that relate to Orion? The Murk can't be controlled through yields since they're not bound to the Heart—at least, he and his followers can't."

"I know. It's not the yield part I'm thinking of." Talia glances at Madoc again. "Orion's never shown any sign that he's aware of my other magical powers, right? You never mentioned that I could wield true names, and none of the other Murk figured it out? He definitely wasn't aware of that factor when he asked me about how I'd found the wrench I was using to try to escape."

Madoc cocks his head. "You cast light during the battle the other day, didn't you? Although I couldn't hear you speak the true name, and you talked about the Heart shining through you, so any Murk who noticed that demonstration probably assumed it was some Seelie trick. As far as I know, Orion has no idea that you can work true names. He thinks of you as his own creature—his 'pet'—and I'd imagine it'd be difficult for him to picture the Heart of the Mists granting you any real power when you're so closely tied to him."

He pauses, and a shadow crosses his face before he continues. "He couldn't even believe that you could matter all that much to *me*. He expected me to try to cure your curse, and I don't think it ever occurred to him that it might work."

Talia restrains a wince only I pick up on, with a flash of memory that flickers through our bond: the sight of Madoc's limp body as August and Astrid lifted it off her blood-drenched bed. "All right," she said. "Then we have the same advantage over Orion that we did over Aerik—he doesn't know everything I'm capable of. I can use that against him."

"How?" Sylas asks—not skeptical, just encouraging her onward.

She drags in a breath. "We'd have to work out the exact details. But Orion obviously wants to get his hands on me again—because he's upset that I defied him, because he thinks I'm his possession, whatever. So, what if we give me to him, and I have a chance to surprise him and then—and then kill him before he can recover."

Everything in me recoils at the thought of Talia getting close enough to the Murk king to land a killing blow, putting herself within his grasp, and taking on a horrific task that should be any of ours instead of hers. She isn't a killer. Her uneasiness with the idea wafts off of her.

But her qualms don't diminish her determination. She's resolved to carry through with it—and I know she'll try her best, no matter how she feels about it.

The men around me look similarly discomforted. "It takes a lot to kill a fae," August says. "You'd only get one brief chance, and if anything went wrong…"

Talia meets his gaze. "You're the best warrior our pack has. You can teach me the most effective way to aim a quick strike. And I have another advantage over anyone who's fae, like we've already seen. I can use an iron weapon. If I can stab him in the right spot with an iron blade, that would do the trick, wouldn't it?"

Hearing the specifics only twists me up more inside. I smother my reaction as well as I can and try to focus on the practicalities. "To his heart or perhaps deep enough into his throat should do it—but where are you going to get a weapon like that? Humans don't typically make knives or daggers out of pure iron. None of us can wield magic on iron to create one for you. I don't think even the kind of strategy we used to protect your brother would work for a project that requires such careful attention to detail."

"And even if it could, that assumes you'd be able to get close enough to him and distract him well enough to carry it out," Whitt says, frowning.

Talia shrugs, though I can see the tension running through the casual gesture. "The first part is easy enough. We have humans here who'll help however we ask them to. I spoke to a couple of them when we were preparing for our strategy with the tunnels who do metal work. They could create the blade, and then maybe the Murk who've joined us but aren't yet reconnected with the true Heart could use some magic to make it sharper, or at least to hide it so Orion doesn't realize I have it on me."

From Madoc's expression, I don't think he likes this general plan any more than I do. He didn't give his life to save Talia because he wanted to send her off straight into his king's clutches just weeks later. But he nods. "I think they could probably do both. If I can persuade them to contribute. I'm not going to lie to them about what it's for, and a lot of them still have conflicted feelings about Orion."

"We might need even more of their help," Talia says, her mouth slanting at a pensive angle. "Or maybe some of Delta's followers. The hardest part will probably be making sure I can get face to face with Orion rather than him sending lackeys to deal with me… Maybe if I'm already being escorted, or if they provide an additional distraction… Obviously we still need to figure that part out."

"And what is the distraction you're imagining using when you *are* face to face with him?" Sylas asks.

One corner of her lips curls upward with a hint of a smile. "I thought I'd use light. It seems fitting. A strong blast of it, right into his eyes."

All at once, I can picture it: Talia standing before Orion, light flaring from her hands. But I can also all too easily imagine him springing at her and cutting her down before she can strike any kind of blow. My stomach is outright churning now.

"There have to be other ways," I say, fighting to keep my tone even. "You shouldn't have to put yourself in danger ahead of all of us. It's *our* war."

Talia looks at me, her green eyes so solemn my heart nearly stops beating. "No, it's my war as much as any of yours. Orion used me my whole life. He destroyed my family, left me to be enslaved, tortured me, and almost killed me. He stole the child we should have had from us. Maybe none of that is as big as what he's done to the fae, but it's my entire life. I want to take it back."

I don't know how to argue with that. Perhaps I shouldn't attempt to.

"We've mostly been holding them off," Whitt says. "There's no need to rush into a plan so risky."

Talia's gaze snaps to him. "Do you really think we're going to find a definitive move that's less risky? And we're not really holding them off when Orion can murder children hundreds of miles from the front. We have no idea how much farther he'll go or how soon. The longer we leave it, the more likely he'll hurt the fae more, or figure out a way to get at Jamie, or who knows what else. We have to end this as quickly as we can before even more people suffer."

Slowly, the other men incline their heads in acceptance. I can't quite let go of the protest blaring in my head. "We're your mates," I say. "We should be the ones defending you." A desperate urge rises up in me to fly all the way to the front and charge at Orion myself, to do whatever I can to kill him before Talia even has to try, no matter how small my chances.

Perhaps Sylas can read that impulse in me. He's the one who

caught me on the verge of racing off to the Murk's Refuge when Talia was dying. He clears his throat and stands up. "As Talia's mates, I think we should discuss the matter amongst ourselves for a moment to determine how we can all best lend our skills." He brushes his hand over Talia's hair. "Why don't you find Astrid and have her see about bringing in the humans who have metal-working skills?"

I manage to hold my tongue until Talia has left the room. Then, holding as solid a wall against our bond as I can, I spit out, "You're going through with this? You think we should let her tackle this monster on her own?"

Madoc's mouth tightens. "She's already faced him on her own before. I don't like it, but I think she's right—her plan could work. His biggest weakness is his arrogance. He assumes he has everything under control, that no one could possibly get the better of him—her more than anyone."

"But she—she shouldn't *have* to." My hands clench at my sides with all the frustration and despair I'm reining in. How can I let my soul-twined mate take on the burden of saving my people on my behalf?

How can I face the possibility of losing her to that fiend all over again?

August has started pacing the room as if he needs to let out similar uneasy energy. He doesn't speak, though.

Sylas folds his arms over his chest. "She shouldn't have to, no. You're not going to get any argument on that subject from us. But she *doesn't* have to. You heard her—she *wants* to. I have tried so many times to protect her, but in the end, she knows her own mind. I swore to myself a long time ago that I wasn't going to let my love for her turn into a cage."

I flinch at that framing of the situation. Whitt speaks up before I can argue further. "You weren't there when she took on Aerik and his men. She was spectacular. I have no doubt at all that she can handle this if we give her the chance, whether we like it or not. She's committed to it. That means our job is figuring out how to mitigate the risks and set her up for success in every way we can."

August stops, letting out a huff of breath. I wait, half expecting him to side with me, but he shakes his head. "There's nothing I'd like more than to kill that mangy vermin for her. But I know where my limits are—and so does she. We have to trust in her strength. All of us. We owe her that much." He meets my eyes, a matching anguish dancing behind his—but one he's managed to overcome.

I look down at my hands. My jaw tightens. I want to yell and rage and tear the room apart, but I won't, because that won't help Talia either.

I have faith in Talia. I love her, so much. It could be that's the problem. I'm not afraid only of what fate she could meet at Orion's hands… but also what fate our bond could meet if she succeeds.

When we realized the depth of Orion's meddling in our relationship, I swore to her I'd be hers no matter what happens. That's still true. But I'm not deluded enough to think that nothing will change if the soul-deep connection between us disintegrates. If my soul then clamors for another.

If Talia is willing to face her worst fears, though, shouldn't I? I can't hold her back to protect *myself* from the possibility of a complicated future.

I sigh and swipe my hand across my face. Resignation settles into a hard lump in my chest, but I manage to summon a spark of my own resolve alongside it.

If she's going to do this, she needs every one of us behind her, like Whitt said. She needs *me*.

"All right," I say. "How are we going to get her where she needs to be to kill Orion?"

When I cross my domain to the palace of Heart's Cadence some hours later, meaning to consult with my coterie on the plans we're gradually piecing together, the sky is darkening with evening. The purple tones smudging the sky like a bruise match my uneasy mood.

I'm greeted by one of my staff at the front door. "My lord," she says, "Kara of Hazeleven came to call on you. I told her I wasn't sure of your return, but she insisted on staying… She's in the front parlor."

A starker trepidation winds through my gut. But I can't cast off this young woman without giving her a chance to speak. My thoughts have been so much on my relationship with Talia, but Kara has had no compensation for the soul-twined bond she can sense but not fully experience.

I haven't really discussed the situation with her since our first meeting. There hasn't been time what with the war. But perhaps I owe her more consideration than that despite the turmoil around us. And she needs to understand that nothing is separating me from the mate I already have. I've already caught hints from my awareness of Talia that Kara's resentment has led to minor hostilities.

I find her sitting in a chair near the parlor's hearth. She rises up at my entrance, her welcoming smile a bittersweet mix of pain and hope. I wish I could offer more to the second part.

"Good evening," I say. "I apologize—I should have taken the initiative to attend to you sooner." I pause, grappling with my words. "You already know from the messages I've conveyed that I haven't yet tracked down a solution to your predicament."

Kara blinks. "A solution? You mean make the partial bond go away? That's not what I want." She takes a step toward me and then stops there when I remain rigidly still.

"I believe I've made it clear that I have no intention of attempting to sever the soul-twined bond I've already formed, regardless of its source," I say, gently but firmly.

She looks down at her hands and then back at me. "Yes, that has been clear. I came because I've been thinking… Severing it wouldn't necessarily be required, would it? Many lords take more than one partner. And if we spend more time together, perhaps the real bond that was meant to be will emerge on both sides."

The suggestion is more accepting of Talia than Kara's previous approach, but every particle of my body resists it all the same. I don't *want* another woman dividing my attention—and I have no feelings for the woman in front of me at all, other than sympathy. Perhaps that would change if the Heart decides to impose its original bond more firmly, but I have to speak from where my own heart is right now.

"I've found that I prefer to focus my attentions on one mate," I say.

Kara tilts her head to the side. "*She* has four others, doesn't she?"

"Yes, but…" I grope for the right words to convey the impressions I've gleaned of my mate's experiences and emotions, as well as the certainty that's become ever more solid since the possibility of another mate first presented itself to me.

"Talia didn't seek to bring more than one mate into her life," I say finally. "It happened by chance, and to some extent she resisted the idea." It's easy for me to remember that she hardly leapt at the idea of joining herself to me when our bond first exerted itself. "Her heart is so large and generous that she's found herself bound to all of us as circumstances brought us together. I fear my own capacity for affection is somewhat smaller. And I honestly don't know you at all. I would be forcing myself to attempt the relationship, not pursuing it because of feelings that already exist."

"But we were meant—"

I hold up my hand to cut her off, for her sake so she doesn't cling on to hope even a second longer than she has to. "You know I can't feel the bond that might have been between us at all. As long as that remains true, I can't help imagining that it would be far more torturous for you to remain in my presence, seeking a connection that isn't going to form and watching me with the mate I *am* bound to, than for you to set off on a different path. I'll support whatever endeavors you wish to pursue, contribute anything I can that would help you reach a happier future."

Kara's mouth slants at a tense angle. "You don't understand," she says. "Hazeleven is a desolate domain—I have nothing to offer a mate if I have no bond. I don't even have a home right now."

"We're going to get your home back," I assure her. "And—you shouldn't need finery or prestige to find a mate. You offer yourself."

Her eyebrow twitches. "That's easy for you to say," she murmurs, and then shakes herself. "I just—if there is any chance of us—"

I stop her again before she goes any further. "I'm sorry, but as my feelings stand right now, there isn't a chance. I'll do everything I can to improve your situation and help you gain the happiness you deserve, but it won't be at my side. I also ask that you don't raise any further concerns with my mate. This matter is between you and me, and unless forces beyond our control shift what is, that matter is settled."

Kara gazes at me for a long moment. Something comes over her expression—a chilliness that I don't entirely like.

"Well," she says, "I suppose we'll see. We can't know for sure how the future will play out. Maybe the bond will be fulfilled after all."

Then she sweeps out of the room without another word. She could have simply meant the same consideration I've already had of what may happen when Orion's power is destroyed. But her remark leaves my skin itching with a deeper apprehension than I can fully explain.

CHAPTER TWENTY-TWO

Talia

I peer over the maps spread on Whitt's desk, doing my best to match the lines and words to my memories of the landscape. "How many sightings have there been of Orion himself? Has he been sticking to any specific part of the front or moving around all the time?"

Whitt taps a spot on the map at the edge of the Seelie realm not far from the border with winter. "We believe he was nearby when we acted out your plan with the salt and iron in the tunnels. He certainly reacted quickly. Other than that, he's been fairly elusive. We've had reports claiming to have spotted him along the front in one place or another, but of course with the Murk's fondness for illusion, it's hard to know how much credence to give those sightings."

"I've spoken with the refugees who've joined us from his army," Madoc says from where he's perched on the arm of the sofa for this late-night meeting. "They say he's been traveling through the ranks regularly, encouraging everyone on… and dealing out punishments for poor performance when he feels it's necessary. With the carriages we've learned to conjure, he could easily make it from the farthest end of the front to the other end in less than an hour."

"Then no matter where I put myself forward, someone should be able to get a hold of him and get him to me fairly quickly." I rub my temple as I wrap my head around the many variables. "We wouldn't necessarily need to give the Murk warriors a heads-up very far ahead of time for the plan to work. That's good. Less time for them to make a counter plan. Right?"

Whitt gives me an approving smile. "I'll totally agree with that reasoning."

I stifle a yawn that tries to stretch my jaw. We spent what was left of yesterday and the whole day today brainstorming possible tactics and gathering the information and resources we need. It's nearly midnight, and my brain feels like it's turned into mush.

I can't hide my exhaustion, especially from my soul-twined mate. Corwin gets up from the armchair where he's been sitting and grasps my shoulder. "You're wearing yourself thin. You'll think better in the morning after you've gotten some rest."

His own weariness comes through in his tone and through our connection—along with a lingering trepidation he can't hide from *me*. But he hasn't argued about this plan again since we started working on it. I know he's grappling with his doubts and making every effort to be supportive despite his worries about my safety.

I slip my hand around his. "I think the same would go for all of you too. You've been working on our strategy as hard or even harder than I have." I pause, my hesitance feeling odd when all five of my mates have been collaborating for days—but they haven't come together in exactly *this* way since Madoc joined us. "I think… my bed is big enough for all of us. I'll feel better having you all around me going into tomorrow."

Tomorrow I might be able to move forward with my plan against Orion. We can't afford to wait if the opportunity presents itself. And that means this could be the last night I ever get with the men I love so much.

Sylas and August were already straightening up from their positions around the room. They halt now, August with the most open glance toward the Murk man, although I can feel all four of my other mates' attention focus on him.

Madoc stiffens a bit, probably sensing he's on the spot. He pushes himself off the chair with an air as if he's making a concentrated effort to pretend he hasn't noticed. "I'd be happy to join you… if I'm welcome."

I don't even have to speak up first. Whitt does, with the playful geniality that's smoothed over so many tense or awkward situations in the past. "I'd say you've well and truly infested our home, and there's no coming back from that. Which is a good thing considering how much our mate enjoys your presence."

Madoc looks like he isn't sure whether to be offended or pleased by that statement. Sylas chuckles softly and motions us all out of the room. "I'd say we're all coming to appreciate your contributions, if not in *quite* the same ways Talia does. And we've gotten plenty of practice at sharing already."

Madoc's shoulders drop down a bit as we walk down the hall. He comes up beside me, and I grip his fingers with my free hand, still holding on to Corwin at my other side. So much affection for all of my mates swells inside me that I half expect it to spill out of my skin in a giddy glow.

I can't remember if they've ever all been in my bedroom at the same time. It shouldn't feel so momentous after I've already been so intimately entwined with all of them, but it does. Adrenaline starts to thrum through my body, eating away at my earlier fatigue.

Maybe I don't want to sleep *just* yet.

I suspect my mates must be able to pick up on the shift in my mood, but as so often, they let me take the lead in showing what I want. I stop by the edge of the massive bed, picturing myself snuggled there between my five fae lovers, and a strange ache wakes up in my chest that's more bittersweet than I was prepared for.

What if this *is* the last night we have together? What if I don't survive my gambit against Orion? What if his supporters manage to hurt one of my men before I can end the war?

What if it's all for nothing, and I die only for the war to keep raging on?

I close my eyes against that last, despairing thought. I can't let my mind veer in that direction. There've been so many challenges and enemies before that none of the fae would have believed I could survive, and I've beaten all of them.

I'll keep believing in me for as long as I'm still breathing.

Moving forward, I kick off my boots, climb onto the bed, and sit in the middle of the mattress with my dress pooled across my thighs. My mates circle the bed and sink onto the edges around me. There's something mildly predatory in their approach, but not to the point that it stirs up anything other than desire in me.

Sylas, so often the most confident, eases right next to me first. He kisses the crook of my jaw and teases his fingers along the side of my neck. "What did you have in mind now, my love?"

"I—I don't know," I admit. "I just know I want all of you."

The Seelie arch-lord turns toward Madoc. "Perhaps we should give our newcomer a head start, seeing as he has some catching up to do."

The rat shifter gives the other man a baleful look, but there's no real rancor in it. "I think I'd like to see just how much our mate benefits from having all of us together. But I can definitely make a start of it."

Sliding over, he lifts one of my feet and presses a kiss to the top. His gaze holds mine, the gray irises like molten clouds with the heat of his hunger. He kisses the side of my foot and then my ankle before moving to my other foot, the broken one.

His fingers trace the arch of misaligned bone, an angrier flare sparking in his gaze. He kisses that too, as tenderly as if it were an enhancement rather than a flaw.

As he strokes his hands up my calf, taking his time with this gentle seduction, my other men converge around me. Sylas slides over so he's directly behind me, trailing his fingertips up and down my spine and nipping the back of my neck. August steals a kiss from beside me and caresses my belly. Corwin nuzzles my ear and claims my mouth after August releases it.

Whitt kneels nearby, watching us all with an approving expression. He catches my hand to squeeze it just for a second as if to reassure me that he doesn't feel left out. "I'll take my moment when it comes. There's something to be said for simply taking in your responses. You're radiant when that flush of desire comes over you."

A sharper blush colors my cheeks, and he grins. Then August is kissing me again, Madoc's exploring touch reaches my knee, and there's no room in me for embarrassment.

What's there to be embarrassed about? I'm with my mates as we're intended to be.

Madoc lowers his head to kiss the side of my knee, his hands skimming up my thigh. Sylas helpfully tugs the skirt of my dress higher and then fiddles with the bindings down the back to loosen them. He eases my head around so he can kiss me from behind while August takes advantage of my loosened bodice to cup my breast. Corwin nibbles a path down my shoulder. And all the while I feel Whitt's gaze taking us in, as warm as if he's touching me too.

The flush is spreading through my whole body, from where my breasts tingle with jolts of pleasure to the heady need growing between my legs, dampening my panties. I twist my head around to kiss Corwin more urgently than before. Madoc slicks his tongue from my knee partway up my inner thigh and pauses with a stuttered intake of breath.

He looks up, catching my gaze when I release the Unseelie arch-lord. The emotion in his eyes is so fraught my throat closes up. But then he says, in a voice that's barely more than a whisper, "You're fertile."

Those two words send a stillness over the men gathered around me. Sylas lets out a pleased-sounding rumble and kisses me just behind my ear. Madoc stays braced in front of me, his fingers lightly caressing my inner thigh. They're all waiting for my signal, but he is most of all.

An odd bubbling sensation fills my chest, exhilarating but tinged with grief. I know there isn't much chance I'd get pregnant so quickly after the first time. Even the first time, for it to happen right away, was unexpected. But maybe that's not the point. The point is that I want it to happen again, whenever it does. I want to try as many times as it takes before we have that child our family deserves—and more.

I'm going to believe that we'll have all those chances, no matter what's ahead of us.

In that instant, the decision to simply hold on to faith feels so momentous that I have trouble speaking. "Good," I say. "We have a chance to try again. Maybe the Heart will shine on us now, but if not, there's lots more time for it to come."

Corwin's love courses into me through our bond like a wash of sunlight. Madoc still looks oddly uncertain.

"Are you sure—?" he starts, and seems to grapple with his words. "We aren't officially mated yet…"

I don't know if that's what his hesitation is really about or if it's because of what he is, but he should know that I don't see him as any less than my other men. I told him so before, but after everything he's experienced, it isn't surprising it'd take a while sinking in.

I push myself forward so I can touch his cheek. "We're mated in every way that needs to count as far as I'm concerned. I'm your mate as much as I am anyone else's in this room. Don't hold back on me."

Heat flares in his eyes again, and a small but sly smile curves his lips. "Well, I don't see any reason to rush to the finish line. You still deserve to get every bit of enjoyment out of tonight that we can give you."

He drops his head to my thigh again, tasting my skin in a steady path toward my core. My sex aches with anticipation. Corwin finishes the job Sylas started by tugging my dress off me completely and continues to nibble my shoulder as he fondles one of my breasts. The Seelie arch-lord reclaims my mouth, August teases my other breast with his teeth, and I'm adrift on a whirlwind of bliss.

As Madoc reaches my sex, that storm becomes a tsunami. He presses his mouth to me, his hot breath spilling through the fabric of my panties to delicious effect, and then wrenches them down to lick my sensitive nub directly. I whimper, unable to stop myself from squirming.

Madoc worships me with his lips and tongue, drawing more and more pleasure into my sex with every skillful movement. Quivers race from my core to the tips of my toes and the top of my scalp. I moan again, into Corwin's mouth now, my hips arching up of their own accord. Madoc grips them and urges me to buck into his mouth as he drives me closer and closer to that edge of ecstasy—and then sends me careening right over.

I come, gasping and quivering, and then he's surging over me with a groan of need that can't be denied. As he fumbles with his pants, I throw my arms around his shoulders. He plunges his shaft into me, filling me so perfectly.

I'm so sensitized it only takes a few strokes before I come again, my sex clamping around him. Madoc's chest hitches. "You always feel so fucking good," he mutters, and kisses me hard, thrusting into me almost frantically. I clutch him and rock against him, supported on all sides by my other mates, propelled toward even greater heights by their mouths and hands.

Another groan escapes Madoc as he comes. He kisses me again, long and lingering, and then he withdraws, glancing around him.

August is there in an instant, with no hint of any resentment at the new man in my life or the role he got to take first tonight. He kisses me with a flick of his tongue between my lips and kicks off his trousers. I grasp his rigid length, reveling in the twitch of it against my palm, the strength that emanates from it. "Please," I murmur.

August doesn't make me outright beg. With a joyful sigh, he slides into me, nipping my lip as he sinks all the way in. Another wave of desire swells inside me. I hook my feet around his waist and urge him onward.

"Always so sweet," he murmurs in a rough voice, picking up speed. "My Sweetness."

I whimper and cling on as pleasure blazes through me again. My fingers tangle in the short tufts of his hair. August grunts at the tug on his scalp, his thrusts turning wilder, and then he's spilling himself inside me with a low, drawn-out growl.

My reaching hands find Corwin next. My soul-twined mate pulls me around and onto his lap where he's already stripped off his slacks. I find him with eager fingers and line him up so he can push up into me.

My muscles feel as if they've turned to jelly, but somehow I find the energy to ride him, rewarded by the surges of bliss that race through me with every plunge of his shaft. Corwin dapples kisses across my face and neck, his inner monologue a constant stream of praise and devotion as he careens toward his release. *My mate. My love. My soul. You are all I could ever have asked for.*

His delight spirals into me in that familiar giddying cycle. As he comes with a spurt of heat inside me, I come yet again, shuddering in his arms.

Corwin draws back, but not too far. As he eases me into a kneeling position before him, kissing my neck and stroking my breasts, I realize what he's getting me in position for. Or rather who. Sylas nuzzles the other side of my neck, his rich earthy scent filling my nose, and fills me from behind.

I sway between the two arch-lords, soaring higher with every buck of Sylas's hips and every swipe of Corwin's thumbs over my breasts. Madoc takes the initiative to slip his hand between them and finger my nub, and something in me explodes. My eyes roll back, every nerve quaking with fulfilled desire, my vision fracturing with a burst of stars. Sylas follows me with a roar.

When the Seelie arch-lord releases me with a gentle peck to my shoulder, my sly strategist is waiting. Whitt takes in my sated body and bliss-hazed eyes, and grins. "You are well-loved, aren't you, my mighty one?"

He lays me back down on the bedspread and takes his time kissing me and caressing me between peeling off his clothes. I run my hands over his muscular, tattooed chest, thinking of all the power those true-name marks speak of. All the trust this man has in me that he's supporting *my* strategy, letting me call the ultimate shots.

I am well-loved—so well it takes my breath away.

By the time Whitt's practiced fingers drift over my sex, I'm already quaking with renewed desire. He strokes me carefully, running his hand over my nub and slit and then delving his fingers inside, until I'm writhing and moaning beneath him. Then he sheaths himself in me with one swift movement that brings a gasp to my lips.

I'm tossed up on wave after wave, floating on a heady current that races toward that inevitable peak. Whitt brings out his claws just long enough to tease them down my side, his fangs nicking my shoulder, and I shatter apart beneath him with a cry.

"That's right," he says. "Just like that." The words come out ragged, and a few moments later, he's bowing over me with the impact of his own release.

There's nothing left in me but joy and satisfaction. I drift in that bliss, holding on to it tightly, ignoring all thought of how long it might last—or not. My mates assemble themselves around me, sprawling out across the huge bed with an arm tucked around me here and there, and my eyelids slide shut.

If this is our last night, then I couldn't have asked for a better one.

CHAPTER TWENTY-THREE

Talia

The three humans who've ended up taking over the metal workshop in Heart's Cadence bring the best of their efforts out for me to examine by the light of the mid-morning sun. They lay the weapons on the long table next to the forge building and then step back as I walk right up to it.

Zelpha and Domhnall, today's babysitters from Corwin's coterie, don't come any closer. Based on Zelpha's grimace as we approached the workshop, just the faint whiffs of iron that've caught in the breeze made her uncomfortable. There's no way any of the fae of the seasons could have done this work themselves.

Madoc crosses about half of the distance between them and me before halting there. With his new connection to the Heart of the Mists, I know the noxious substance bothers him too.

Altogether, there are ten weapons lying on the table. The man in the middle, a grizzled figure with a trim beard who took over as leader after we determined he was the most experienced of the bunch, nods to them. "We felt it'd be best to offer a range of sizes and shapes so you can find what you'll be able to handle well. These were our best creations. We haven't worked with iron like this before… If you need us to go back to the drawing board, we can."

I shake my head. "I'm sure one of these will be fine." Madoc has convinced a few of the Murk newcomers to perfect the weapon once I've chosen it. The blades before me already look deadly.

I pick up one and then the next, testing them in my hand. First I simply get a feel for the grip, each of them wrapped with a thin leather binding, and practice drawing them from my pocket. Then I take a few trial jabs with the dagger.

August led me through several training exercises yesterday to hone the moves I'll need. We quickly decided that I'm best off going for Orion's throat. As satisfying as stabbing him in his heart might be, it's guarded by ribs I'd have to pierce at just the right spot and angle to avoid them deflecting my blow. The throat has cartilage to get through, but it isn't as tough as bone, and there's a broad expanse to work with. August showed me exactly where I should strike if I get the chance, a little to the side where the flesh is softer.

I run through those movements with nausea pooling in my stomach. As much as I hate Orion and what he did to me and so many of the fae—what he's still doing to us now—I don't get any joy from imagining his blood splattering all over me like Madoc's did not long ago. Killing has never been a talent I wanted to add to my repertoire.

But if this is the only way to protect myself and all those other people, then I'm not going to let my personal preferences get in the way.

I narrow my options down to my favorite three and experiment with each of them again. I like the ones that are on the longer and thinner side—they move more swiftly in my hand and fly free of my clothes more easily. But the length makes them more difficult to carry and conceal, and I need some heft to the blade if I'm going to be sure of it completely severing Orion's life from his body.

Finally, I settle on the middle one, not the longest or the lightest. As I swing it through the air once more, the sunlight glinting off its surface, a sense of rightness fills my chest.

Yes. This is the one.

"Thank you," I say to the metalworkers. "This is exactly what I needed. I guess you should hold on to the others just in case it turns out this won't quite do the job—I'm not really the best judge of that—but I think I'm ready."

All three of them bob their heads. "Thank you, and God speed," the woman on the left murmurs. They have a vague idea that I'm going to use this weapon to win their freedom, which is true in a roundabout way.

I pull a silk pouch reinforced with shielding magic out of my pocket and slip the dagger into it. Only then do I walk over to Madoc to hand it over. His mouth twitches uneasily as he tucks the pouch into a carry-sack slung over his shoulder.

"They should make the blade as sharp as possible, with a sheath it'll slide free from quickly but won't cut through, and dull whatever impressions the metal gives off so Orion and his people won't realize I have it on me beforehand," I remind him.

My Murk mate touches the side of my face. "I know. They've already researched the spells. And I'll be right there the whole time to make sure they stick to the plan." He pauses. "Then you'll train a little more with August now that you have the specific weapon, while we get the rest of the pieces in place… and that's all there is to it?"

"We can only hope," I say with a halting chuckle. My stomach clenches tighter.

Madoc brushes his thumb over my cheek and hurries off to cross the border so his Murk companions can get started right away. I linger behind for a while, helping the humans tidy up despite their faint protests. August won't need me until the dagger is ready.

"You can go to the palace and get washed up," I say, pointing to the tall diamond building a short distance across the snow-swept plateau. "Then Arch-Lord Corwin's chef will have a hot meal waiting for you."

The metalworkers offer more thank yous and set off for the palace. I turn toward the border castle. As soon as I leave the workshop behind, Zelpha and Domhnall fall into step on either side of me.

"Are you sure it's a good idea to trust the rats with the task of enhancing the blade?" Domhnall asks, frowning. "I don't like so much relying on them staying true to their word."

Zelpha swats him behind my back. "You've been off wrangling the lords in the far-flung domains for too many of the past few months, Dom. Madoc's a good one, and he'll watch over the others more closely than *you* would. There's no way he'd risk Talia getting hurt if he can help it."

Domhnall looks abashed, and I can tell he's heard the story of how Madoc cured my curse. "I'm sorry," he says to me. "I just—I'm so used to thinking of all of the Murk as vermin."

I give him a tight smile. "I know. It's been an adjustment for everyone. But you can definitely trust Madoc. He's more honorable than an awful lot of summer and winter fae I've met."

Zelpha clucks her tongue. "Sad but true. What are you going to do while you're waiting on them enchanting the dagger?"

I blow out a breath. "I guess I'll see what progress Whitt has made on figuring out the final details of how we'll draw Orion out."

When I spoke to him earlier this morning, he was making some kind of calculation about the most ideal spot for me to venture across the front. We're still waiting to see if any of the Murk will agree to go in a little ahead of my arrival and make sure Orion knows to expect me. I'm going to say I'm giving up to save any more deaths among the fae children, but that I want to hear Orion tell me he'll back off on them to my face.

I don't actually expect him to do that. I figure he'll come specifically so he can rub it in my face that he'll attack the fae of the seasons however he wants. But that'll still bring him to me, which is all I need.

If we can't find a rat shifter who's willing to pass on the message, though, we'll have to come up with some other way of getting the king's attention. One he won't suspect is a trick. Too much depends on this gambit for us to get careless with any part.

We're just coming up on the winter side of the joint castle when a shout rings out from farther down the border. My head jerks up to see a slim form, face obscured by a heavy hood, waving to us maybe a quarter mile along the hazy wall. There's a panicked jerkiness to the movement that sets my nerves immediately on the alert.

Zelpha tenses, probably torn between sticking with me and going to investigate. But then the figure calls out, "Lady Talia, please hurry!" and it becomes clear that I'm the one who's most needed there.

We hustle over, my bad foot starting to ache against the frozen ground. As we get closer, I make out the woman's features within the hood. It's Kara. I'd stop in my tracks, the memories of our most recent encounters making me wary, but at the same moment she gestures toward the border.

"A couple just came with their child. We assumed you were on the summer side. The little girl's been taken by the curse—I think she's almost gone."

Her frantic tone and the words themselves send a jolt of chilling adrenaline through my veins. Every second might make a difference in whether I can save this child. I dash in my uneven way into the haze where she's indicating.

If I wasn't in such a hurry, if the past deaths hadn't weighed on my conscience so much, I might have wondered why the couple wouldn't have come to the border castle on the winter side, where the attendants could have told them exactly where I was. Or why Kara happened to be wandering around in Corwin's domain to coincidentally encounter them. But in the moment, horror drives me onward with no thought in my head except reaching the cursed girl.

After just a few steps, a yelp and a grunt sound behind me. I've already dashed across the dwindling ice onto the grass of the summer side of the border. I spin around, squinting into the haze for my companions who've unexpectedly vanished—and rigidly muscled arms slam around me from behind.

One hand yanks a swath of dark fabric over my face, shutting out all light. In the same motion, it clamps over my mouth to muffle my instinctive cry of protest. The other arm locks my arms against my sides, pressing into my ribs so hard my next breath comes with an ache.

"Quickly," someone hisses, and I'm heaved off the ground. I

squirm and kick in every direction, but the arms around me only squeeze tighter. Someone else snatches my flailing legs and wraps a stiff cord around them.

There's a murmur, and a fog starts to sweep over my mind. I fight against it, mumbling the true name for light against the fabric nearly smothering me. It slips out faintly, but it's just enough to drive back the worst of the mental haze. I cling to consciousness by a thread.

Corwin! I call out through our bond with the tenuous focus I have left. *Corwin, help!*

The figures who've grabbed me dump me onto a hard surface and tie another cord around my hands behind my back. They don't seem to have noticed that I'm not totally unconscious, but I can't command my body well enough to take any advantage of that oversight. My limbs refuse to respond. It's all I can do to hold my mind from spiraling into darkness.

What's happened, Talia? Corwin's voice reaches me from inside. *Where are you?*

The surface beneath me lurches into motion. I recognize vaguely that I must be in some kind of vehicle—a carriage from the feel of it. Wind whips over me even sprawled on the floor, tugging at the fabric pulled over my head. My captors are getting out of here as fast as they can, which isn't surprising.

I was— It's a struggle to form my thoughts into anything coherent. *The border… with Zelpha…*

Then the men poised around me start to speak, and I let my inner voice go silent, instead opening myself up so that hopefully Corwin will make out their words through my ears. They might reveal more than I'm able to convey.

"Are you sure that vermin 'king' wants her enough to barter much of anything?" one asks, and a deeper chill sinks into me. I know that voice. It's Cole.

And the one that answers is his lord. "Half of what he's done to us seems to be because of this blasted dung-body. We offer her in trade and win some concession that'll show our arch-lords and the others that they all should have listened to me to begin with."

A hysterical laugh bubbles in my chest. Aerik and his cadre are going to hand me over to Orion just like I was going to hand myself over—except I don't have my weapon, and who knows if they'll even let me be conscious for the transaction. They could have had exactly what they want if they'd just waited until the end of the day.

Except that's not totally true, is it? They didn't just want to bargain with Orion and score a win against the Murk. They also wanted the glory of doing it for themselves. And I have no doubt that Aerik would love to never again have to see me standing alongside one of his arch-lords, stirring the people's sympathies for me.

Did you hear? I think at Corwin. *It's—Aerik—they're—*

Before I can get any further than that, the carriage jostles, and my body flinches instinctively. One of my captors lets out a curse. A hand smacks onto my head alongside a muttered word, and I lose my grasp on the world around me completely.

CHAPTER TWENTY-FOUR

August

"He *what*?" I burst out with an edge of a roar when Corwin finishes his hurried explanation of his last contact with Talia. Rage sears through me, and my vision flares red. "I'll tear that mangy bastard limb from limb, and his cadre too."

The Unseelie arch-lord is looking even paler than usual, adjusting his weight on his feet as if he's seconds away from launching himself after her. I guess I should be glad he took the time to tell us at all.

"I tried to give chase, and I sent the members of my coterie nearby and a few other guards as well," he says in a strained voice. "But Aerik obviously planned this carefully. We couldn't pick up any clear trail or spot him from above. They're concealing themselves too well. And unfortunately, I don't have very many people to call on for the search with so many focused on the war."

"We know they're headed toward the front," Sylas says. He's gotten up from behind the desk in his study, his dark eye glowing fiercely. "We have to catch them there before they have the chance to set up their 'trade'."

"What if they hurt Talia before they get there?" I demand. My claws come out where I'm gripping the top of the nearest chair, piercing the fabric, but I can't draw them back in. "They've done it before—to make her easier to restrain. They might even think Orion will be happier if they show they've tormented her first."

Whitt lets out a low growl. "We won't let it come to that."

"How could they even have taken her at all?" I ask. "They vowed to leave her alone with their yield."

Sylas grimaces. "There must have been some loophole they worked around with the wording. I believe I said they couldn't attempt to put her under their control. It could be that taking her for the purpose of letting Orion control her made enough of a difference that the vow didn't stop them. Or perhaps someone else helped by taking the initial steps to subdue her." He gestures to Corwin. "You said that Unseelie woman, the one who claims she should have been your soul-twined mate, was involved?"

Corwin nods like he's got a heavy weight on his shoulders. "I suspect she believed that if she removed Talia from consideration, her soul-twined bond with me would solidify after all. She set up the trap and prevented my coterie from intervening. Zelpha would have been right there with Talia if Kara hadn't tangled her in a spell. They have her in custody now. No one saw, and she didn't say—we're not sure if anyone else was helping Aerik."

"He could have had a couple of his pack-kin with him if necessary to pull it off." Whitt lets out a rough breath and turns to Corwin. "No offense to your sharp raven eyes, but I think wolfish noses will tackle this task more easily, especially when the trail should be fresh. Exactly how long ago did this happen?"

Corwin winces. "About half an hour ago now. I went after her first—there wasn't any way to quickly tell the rest of you—"

"That's fine," Sylas says. "That still gives us plenty to work with. The trail won't go cold immediately. We'll set out at once—with Astrid and the best trackers we can summon from the packs around the Heart—if we can get a message to our forces on the front to keep watch in case they reach it ahead of us—"

"I doubt Aerik will race right in without any preamble," Whitt says. "He's a prick, but he's not stupid. He'll have to make arrangements with the Murk for a hand-off and figure out a way to do that without tipping the rest of us off. I wouldn't be surprised if he finds a place to camp out until after nightfall when he'll have darkness for additional cover."

It's not even noon yet. If my brother is right, that should give us more than enough time to track the brutes down. I swivel toward the door, every muscle itching to get started on the rescue. "I'll find Astrid and send out the word for trackers. We should get going as soon as—"

I open the study door to find a sentry standing on the other side with her hand raised to knock, her face flushed with exertion and her jaw tensed. I step back, startled. Does she already have news about Talia?

But her hasty report has nothing to do with our mate at all.

"My lord, the Murk have pressed forward in another attack along the front," she says, her gaze seeking out Sylas beyond me. "They're sending some sort of projectiles at our warriors that are weakening their powers. When I left, we'd already lost another two domains. I don't know if the fae already on the front line will be able to hold them off at all."

Sylas growls a curse under his breath. "We'll have to send everyone from the camps—every fae who can contribute any magical power at all. If they press forward all the way to the Heart…"

He doesn't finish that sentence, but he doesn't need to for dread to wind around my gut. If the Murk topple our forces, it won't matter what happens to Talia. We'll all be done for.

The sentry dashes off to alert the other arch-lords. Sylas strides out of the room with Corwin close at his heels. The Unseelie arch-lord looks just as sick as I feel. "If they're advancing on the summer side, they'll be doing the same in my realm as well. I'll have to get back."

But he doesn't want to. None of us wants to be shepherding our people into a desperate battle with the Murk while our mate is in the hands of fae who are just as villainous. My lips pull back from the fangs that've sprung free from my gums. One clear thought blazes through all the rest.

"I'll go after Talia," I say. "I'm the best tracker out of us, and I'll be able to take on all three of those bastards in a fight when I find them, as long as I catch them by surprise. If the Murk have taken up some unexpected new tactic, you won't need one more fighter on the front that much. Our people will need leadership and strategy."

Sylas grits his teeth, but understanding simmers in his eyes. "I don't like you going alone."

"I'll travel faster that way. Chances are they'll be close to the front as it is by the time I catch up with them, and I can call on a little assistance if anyone's able to offer it then." I hold his gaze, my own imploring. "Let me do this. The faster I go after her now—"

Sylas waves his hand, releasing me from any other obligations I had to him. I dash down the hall, already springing into wolf form as I go. "Be careful as well as fast," my brother calls after me. "Aerik has to know someone will come after him."

I charge out of the castle to find the fields outside are already a swarm of activity. Warriors are shouting to each other and passing weapons to pack-kin who look much more uncertain. Every fae on hand is being ushered to the front. Messengers are rushing this way and that through the chaos.

I dodge through the bustle and plunge into the thick underbrush of one of the stretches of forest. Corwin said Aerik stole Talia from a spot just north of here, near where the hill starts to slope downward. I'll sniff him out, whether with my nose or my magic.

He won't get away with this. And when I'm through with him, he's never going to terrorize my mate again.

As I emerge again farther along the border, I mark the spot where the carriage took off easily from the disturbed grass. They raced away too hastily to totally cover their tracks here, probably figuring that there were too many witnesses to the scene of the crime to bother with it. But after they left this spot, they vanished.

To Corwin and his coterie's senses, anyway. I circle the area, expanding my search a little farther with each iteration, taking deep whiffs of scent into my wolfish nose. It takes five circuits, but then I pick up on the clue that will lead me to them.

All of the smells I'm taking in are what you'd expect for this strip of land, no trace of recent fae or human presence. But along one path away from the launch spot, those scents take on a slightly more pungent edge. It's an incredibly subtle difference, and with Corwin and the other Unseelie being unfamiliar with the odors of the summer realm, I'm not surprised they'd have failed to pick up on it.

But I know it for what it is. Aerik used magic to exaggerate the other scents just enough to swallow up his own. The effect will dissipate over time—it's already faded so much I'm lucky I caught it at all. I have to follow it quickly.

I set off at a lope, veering left and right at periodic intervals to make sure I'm still on the right track. As Aerik's course takes clearer shape in my mind, I speed up to a full-out run.

I should have gotten a small carriage of my own before I left Hearth-by-the-Heart. I can't conjure one myself. Is it worth racing back to the castle to see if I can take one now? Will I lose more time doing that or staying on foot?

Before I can finish debating, a shape flits into view at the corner of my vision. I jerk my head around to see a ragtag vehicle made of what looks like scraps of wood and woven leaves, only about twice as big as I am. Madoc is braced by the bow. When he sees me looking his way, he raises his hand.

As he draws up next to me, I straighten up in the form of a man, my pulse thrumming with the need to keep on the move. "What are you doing here?"

The Murk man's expression reminds me of the morning I found him standing over Talia's bed with a knife in his hand, ready to sacrifice himself to save her. "I heard what happened. I have the feeling I'll be more useful helping you than doing battle on the front. Stealth and sneaky escapes are much more my thing than combat."

Some part of me bristles a little, as if it resents his intrusion on my mission, which is ridiculous because it was a risk making the journey alone—and he has gone as far as supplying a vehicle so I don't even need to worry about speed. "I'll accept your offer," I say. "So far the trail leads that way." I motion to the southwest. "Can you handle the steering and change course quickly as need be? I need to focus all my energy on scenting them."

Madoc nods and motions for me to get in. I shift back into wolf form as I leap.

The carriage is narrow enough that I can swing my body from one side to the other and catch the edges of Aerik's concealing spell without needing to divert from our course farther. Madoc sets us off at a pace about twice as fast as I could have run, urging the carriage swifter still at my barks of encouragement. When the trail of exaggerated scent veers farther west, I thump my paw against the hull, and the Murk man adjusts our angle. Sometime later, I smack the other side to get him aiming more south again.

During the straight stretches, Madoc murmurs a few spell words around us, chaining bits of magic together with a tingle that washes through the atmosphere. "I'm disguising us too," he tells me. "Better if they don't see us coming, right?"

I can't argue with that point. I should have thought of it myself.

The extra vividness of the landscape's smells has thickened, still subtle but obvious enough now that I don't need to strain as hard to keep track of it. We must be getting closer, catching up with them. I wonder if Aerik even realizes that the Murk have launched a renewed attack. How will that fit into his plans?

If he's just picking a spot a good distance from the front to hide out until nightfall, he may not have any idea at all what a mess he's set himself up to wade into. Of course, if I have my way, he's never going to get the chance to go anywhere near Orion and his army.

The sun is starting to sink toward the horizon when the carriage slows. I glance at Madoc with a huff of consternation, but he points into the distance where there's a clump of forest with gold-tinged leaves. "I think they've taken shelter there. There's a quality to the light around that spot… Some kind of illusionary magic's been cast there."

I guess as an expert on illusions, he should know.

He draws us up within about fifty feet of the patch of woods, and we both leap out. I stay in wolf form. Madoc casts another spell around the two of us, and we set off toward the trees.

"They won't be able to hear us or see us," he says under his breath. "But if we bump into them, they'll feel us. So don't go barging in there until you're sure you're ready."

I snort to say that should be obvious.

We slink between the trees, which grow sparsely at first and then closer together as we get deeper into the woodlands. I almost miss the glade until Madoc points out the shimmer in the air nearby. Aerik's people have had to get less subtle to expend enough magic to hide their presence entirely. I can't see, hear, or smell the fae themselves yet, but this close, there's an obvious visual clue.

When we reach the edge of the glade where the spell was cast, the figures swim into focus where moments ago it appeared to be empty. My stance goes rigid.

If Aerik had one of his pack-kin helping with the abduction, they left that person behind. Or maybe they sent that one off to try to barter with the Murk. It's just him and his two cadre-chosen sitting on a semi-circle of logs, eating slabs of smoked meat they brought along for the journey. Their narrow carriage, which they must have navigated carefully through the trees, is parked off to one side of the glade.

I straighten up as a man and ease closer, setting my feet softly even though Madoc's spell should stop the other fae from hearing me. With just a few steps, I make out Talia's slender form curled on the floor of the carriage between two of the benches. There's a loose sack over her head, hiding her face and her vivid hair, but she's wearing her usual boots, and I'd know the curves of her body anywhere, just as I know her other features.

My lips pull back in a silent snarl. At least they don't appear to have hurt her—yet—other than binding her wrists and ankles. From the slow rise and fall of her chest, she's unconscious.

My attention slides back to the men who wrenched her away from us and meant to barter with her like she's worthy of no more consideration than the meat they're digging into. My claws spring from my fingertips. But something in me hesitates just for a second.

What will Talia think if we wake her up to a clearing splattered with blood, to that same blood splattered all over me from my rage? How will she look at me?

I close my eyes, gathering myself. Talia has reassured me again and again that she doesn't see a monster in me. That she appreciates the ferocity with which I'm willing to protect her. There's no way I can keep her safe when she goes through with her plan to confront Orion, but right here, right now, I can defend her in the most primal way there is.

She deserves that.

When I open my eyes again, Madoc has come up beside me. My muscles have bunched, ready to spring. I'm not going to bother with my sword for the initial assault. I can't wield it as effectively as I can my fangs and claws anyway.

"I'm not a particularly skilled fighter," Madoc says, "but I can help even the playing field. If you want, I can use an illusion to distract them, scatter them so it'll be easier for you to tear through them all."

He says it without any judgment of the tactics he assumes I'll take or the slightest hint that he'd argue with them. I find myself smiling at him—a real smile, with a sense of companionship I hadn't quite felt toward the newest member of our family before.

"Be my guest."

Madoc smiles back, grimly but determinedly, and steps to the side again. He intones several words under his breath, his gaze trained on a point at the other side of the glade.

There's a rustling in the underbrush. All three of the men's heads jerk up. Twigs crackle and then a stomping sound rushes off as if away from the glade.

"What in the lands?" Cole mutters, leaping up.

Aerik waves at him. "Go see what that's about, but stay hidden unless you need to… deal with it."

The pale-haired man strides off between the trees. The second he's vanished from view, Madoc murmurs again—and an image that looks just like Sylas appears half-cloaked in the shadows at another end of the clearing.

Aerik sees it first and startles, springing up. As he strides forward, his other cadre-chosen stiffens on his log. And I see my perfect opening.

I burst through the trees and launch myself at the man on the log. He barely has time to get out the start of a yelp before it turns into a gurgle as my claws slash through his throat. I slam his skull under my heel for good measure and spin toward Aerik, my pulse thumping, my blood humming with anticipation.

Aerik whirls, but it's Cole I have to deal with next. He bolts into the glade in wolf form, gnashing his teeth. I fling myself forward and shift at the same time. My paws slam into him, digging in as I slam him to the ground.

His claws rake across my side, but I ignore the stinging sensation and snap at his throat. He manages to wriggle just out of reach. I pummel him into the ground with all my weight, hard enough to crack ribs.

A frantic whine creeps from Cole's wolfish mouth that only spurs me onward. He *should* be afraid. I hope he feels every bit as terrified as he's made Talia so many times.

He tries to squirm away, and I shift in an instant, snatching the sword from my belt and driving it into his chest, straight through his heart.

I look up to see Aerik standing over me, his own sword in his hand. He lunges at me, and I dodge to the side, rolling across the blood-damp grass. Then more illusionary images flicker into being around him.

They're all Talia—a Talia at every side of him. They glare at him with the fierceness my mate can bring to bear so well and open their mouths to say in a chorus, "You shouldn't have done this. You're the vermin here."

Aerik can obviously tell they're not real, but they shake him for just long enough for me to recover my balance and hurtle toward him. I ram my elbow into his wrist as I crash into his body, snapping the delicate bones there and sending his sword flying. He slices clawed fingers at my neck, but I twist away and sink my fangs into his shoulder.

Words start to rasp over his lips, but I cut them off with a barked spell of my own that deflects his magic. My feet kick his legs out from under him. As he falls, I rear back to make my final blow.

"Hold!" he sputters, his eyes wide. "I yield. I yield. You can't—"

I snarl at him. "You already broke the terms of our last yield, however you weaseled around them."

"I stuck to the letter of the—"

"I think the Heart will side with me and justice," I roar, and clamp my fangs around his throat to tear it right out.

Blood sprays across me and the glade. Aerik's body sags beneath me. I push away from him, disgusted with the taste of him in my mouth but with a rush sweeping over me that's more relief than triumph. I stare down at his limp form and swipe the back of my hand across my mouth.

It's over. It was a long time coming, and he's finally finished. He'll never lay one more finger on my mate.

CHAPTER TWENTY-FIVE

Talia

My mind swims back into consciousness. I blink, my vision blurring and then steadying to reveal two faces hovering over mine with matching looks of concern.

"Sweetness?" August says, and my pulse hiccups. All at once, I register the hard slats of the carriage floor beneath me, the ache around my forearms and ankles where a rope bound them not long ago, the faint throbbing in the back of my head.

I jerk upright, and Madoc catches my shoulder to steady me. "Aerik," I gasp. "He and Cole and—and I don't know who else."

"We dealt with them," August says with a savage smile, and only then do I notice the flecks of blood at the corners of his lips. There's more splashed across his shirt. My gaze darts over him, but he doesn't appear to be at all injured himself.

I can't stop myself from throwing my arms around him, hugging him tight. August lets out a pleased rumble that sounds a bit choked as well and nuzzles the side of my face. "You're all right now. And he's gone for good." He lifts his head to glance over at Madoc. "Your new mate showed some creative battle skills to help make that happen too."

I pull back and glance between them. There's a new warmth in the grin August aims at Madoc and an ease to the way the Murk man tips his head in return that wasn't there before. It looks like my mates accomplished more than just destroying Aerik and his cadre.

Talia? Corwin speaks through our bond, his voice both eager and oddly harried. He's supressing most impressions of the world around him. *August reached you? You're well?*

As well as I can be when just rescued from a kidnapping, I think back. *Where are you? What's happening there?*

Don't worry about that, my soul. Let August help you recover, and we'll take care of the rest.

The rest of what? I'd ask, but he's muted our connection completely. Trepidation coils around my gut.

August helps me to my feet and lifts me over the side of Aerik's carriage. I stare into the glade we're at the edge of, taking in the three bodies sprawled there. Aerik's neck is nothing but mangled, bloody flesh, the grass around him soaked red. The burly man's throat has been slashed too and his skull cracked open. Cole lies nearby, his eyes staring sightlessly at the sky, a little blood still oozing from a stab wound on his chest.

My stomach turns at the gore and the meaty smell that's rising into the air, but I don't feel any actual horror at the scene. This is exactly how these men would have happily treated me and my mates if they could have gotten away with it. August ensured they'll never get that chance.

I turn my back on them, a heaviness expanding in my chest before my spirits have much time to lift. Corwin's words and the vague sense of disarray I got from him are still niggling at me. I turn back to my men. "Is everyone *else* all right? They only sent the two of you to look for me?" Not that I'm complaining when they obviously got the job done, but it does seem strange, especially when my mates had to suspect they'd be up against at least three opponents.

August opens his mouth and closes it again. Before he can figure out how to answer, Madoc steps in, his voice a little hoarser than usual but still even. "Orion pushed forward another attack. We didn't get many of the details, but it sounded bad. They needed everyone who could be spared on the front to try to stop his advance. I know Sylas, Whitt, and Corwin would have been racing to your rescue too if they hadn't been determined to ensure you have a home to go back to."

Any relief I'd felt before flees my body. I suck in a shaky breath. "I have to do it, then. The plan. I have to—I need the dagger—did the Murk have a chance to finish it? And we need to get to Orion… I can't let him keep going like this!"

"Hey." August strokes his fingers over my hair. "One thing at a time. You only just came out of Aerik's spell. We *don't* have the dagger you need, and—"

Madoc coughs. "Actually…" Gingerly, he pulls the pouch I gave him out of the deep pocket of his trousers. He hands it to me, looking glad to have it farther from his body. "My people have learned to work quickly. They were just finishing up when I heard what'd happened to you. I thought… better to bring it to wherever you are than leave it behind."

August lets out a noise of disbelief. "I couldn't even tell you were carrying it. Are you sure that's iron?"

Madoc smiles thinly. "Very sure. The essence seeps through a little when it's very close to you. But I'm glad to hear the disguising spells did the trick. Talia should be able to walk right up to Orion without him realizing what she's carrying until she's jabbing it into his throat."

I slip my hand into the pouch and pull out the dagger. When I ease it from its thin but hardy sheath, the blade gleams even brighter than before in the late afternoon sunlight. I slash it through the air, and it seems to sing. Even without trying to cut anything, I can tell how sharp it is.

"We didn't get the chance to practice," I say to August. "Not with the actual weapon I'm going to be using."

August glances off through the woods. "We've got a bit of a trek from here to the front, and we'll want to give that a wide berth until we see what the current situation is. Madoc can steer the carriage, and you and I can try out the motions while we're traveling. His vehicle is steady enough." He turns back to me. "But that isn't the important part. We already trained quite a bit. How are we going to get you in a position to take on Orion while his army is in the middle of battering us?"

I frown. "They can't keep going full tilt forever, right? They'll have to slow down to rest at some point. There'll be a lull."

August nods slowly.

Madoc makes a dismissive motion toward the corpses behind me. "As much as I hate to give those fuckheads any credit, we could take a page from Aerik's strategy book. It seemed like he was waiting until nightfall before he'd attempt his 'trade.' You might be better off approaching Orion with the cover of darkness too."

"Yes." I don't know if that will be enough, though. And what if the Murk topple the Seelie and Unseelie forces before they ever need to rest?

"I need to know what's going on," I say. "You said the others all went to the front?"

"As far as I know," August says. "That's what we discussed when I set off to look for you."

"They were just heading out when I left the hill around the Heart," Madoc puts in.

"Let me try to talk to Corwin and then Whitt," I say. "I'm going to find a quiet spot so I can totally concentrate." Distractions shouldn't matter much when it comes to my soul-twined mate, but reaching out to Whitt with his true name has always been harder. At least I'm nowhere near as far away as when I tried to speak to him from the Refuge.

August and Madoc let me pick my way a short distance from them into the trees. I find a mossy stone at the base of a broad oak and sink onto it, leaning my back against the trunk. Closing my eyes, I focus on the energy of the bond inside me.

Corwin? Please, I realize you're dealing with a lot, but I have to know what's happening. August told me the Murk were starting to overwhelm the rest of you. Have you managed to stop them?

Corwin's voice reaches me a moment later, more frayed than

before. *Not quite. We've slowed them down, but we haven't found a strategy that completely offsets their new one.*

What's that? What are they doing?

They've brought out these devices that launch projectiles, and they've been shooting spikes of iron at us. They can't launch very many at once because having the metal around affects them too, but the things can pierce right through any defensive wall we throw up and they weaken us faster than they do the Murk. We've had to keep pulling back as they pollute the territory.

I think back to my own strategy using iron. *That means they're advancing over land that's already got iron scattered across it, and you're pulling back onto clean terrain. It should be wearing down on them the longer they're surrounded by it.*

I agree—and that may be part of the reason their advance has slowed. I don't know if it'll be enough for them to stop for good, though.

I might not need them stopped. I just need there to be enough breaks in the fighting for me to have a chance to get Orion's attention. I bite my lip. *Have you seen Orion? Is he on your side of the border?*

What are you thinking, my soul? You can't go after him in the middle of this.

I'm not asking you for permission. If I see an opening, I'm going to take it. I'll be a lot safer doing that if I have a better idea what I'm up against.

I get the impression of a mental sigh, and distant yells that Corwin's trying to keep from traveling through our bond. *I understand. That determination is part of why I love you, and I won't stifle it. I haven't seen any sign or heard any report of Orion's presence along the front. That doesn't mean he isn't here, but he hasn't shown himself at all if he is.*

Thank you. Stay safe—as safe as you can be. I send him an image of me kissing him and let him refocus on the war waging around him.

I shift my attention to Whitt next, picturing his sparkling ocean-blue eyes and sly grin. "*Wye-con-ell*," I whisper. "Hear me and let me hear you."

Reaching out to the spymaster this time doesn't provoke the same instant headache that came when I tried from the human world. I hear his voice as if through a long tunnel, faintly echoed. *Talia? What's going on? August was coming for you—has he—?*

Yes, I say before he has to go on. *I'm safe now. But from what I'm hearing, the rest of you aren't. Corwin says the Murk are firing iron spikes at the Unseelie. I assume it's the same on the Seelie side?*

Yes, Whitt says. *We've had a little luck deflecting them. A squad of Madoc's Murk followers decided to come with us, and their magic isn't as weak to the iron. But Orion's still gained a lot of ground. We're in a stand-off now.*

Have you seen Orion himself? I ask quickly. Now an ache is starting to creep up the back of my head, and I can tell it'll soon get harder to say or hear anything completely coherent. The true-name connection isn't meant for extended conversations.

I get a sense of Whitt shaking his head. *Not directly. But he hollered out a few taunts with that megaphone spell of his earlier.* He pauses. *What are you thinking, mite?*

Orion's probably on the Seelie side, then. I know where I need to go. *I still have my plan to go through with,* I tell him. *Try to hold your ground until I can make it there. It'll be a lot easier if there's not a battle in full swing.*

I'll see what I can do. There isn't—

My connection to him falters. The ache in my head has only deepened to a dull throbbing, but Aerik's spell has left my mind a little groggy as well.

I know enough, don't I? I get to my feet and head back to August and Madoc. Now I have a destination, and I have my weapon.

I just don't know how I'm going to convince Orion to meet me halfway—the part that we were stuck on all along.

"Did you find out everything you were hoping to?" August asks me when I rejoin them. "Are the others okay?"

"Whitt and Corwin are," I say. "And I'm sure Sylas must be, or I'd have been able to tell something was wrong. I just…"

As I rub my forehead, my gaze drifts across the ruined bodies in the clearing again. My body goes abruptly still. The idea flickers to life like a flame inside my skull.

"What?" Madoc asks, watching me.

"I think I know how I can make it to Orion," I say slowly. "Aerik might have had the right idea in a very wrong sort of way. Let's go, now. I need to try to speak to Whitt again. If they can have everything ready by the time we get there, we might be able to end this war tonight."

CHAPTER TWENTY-SIX

Sylas

I prowl along the crowd of warriors, casting my gaze between those poised to fight at the first sign of another Murk offensive and those scattered behind that line of protection with healers kneeling by their sides. Exhaustion shows on too many of the faces around me. We've been fighting off the Murk onslaught for hours, and we're all wearing thin.

My only comforts are the signs that our rat enemies have also tired and the knowledge that my mate survived her kidnapping uninjured. But even that second fact comes with other worries. Talia is coming back to us, but only to throw herself before the Murk in an even more dangerous scenario than she was facing before.

Whitt finds me as I reach the end of the front near the border haze. He looks weary too, but there's enough optimism in his expression to bring a little hope into my chest.

"I think I might have what we need," he says. "But they want to speak to you first. I think they want some kind of arch-lord guarantee."

I let out a huff, but I'm not going to blame the Murk refugees who've recently come among us for negotiating. Their position here is more precarious than anyone's. "All right. Talia said she needs just two to accompany her?"

Whitt falls into step with me as we head to the area where the rat shifters who volunteered to join us in battle have been sticking together in one small squad. To my pleased surprise, Delta and a contingent of her warriors arrived as well, but they've been keeping their distance from Orion's former followers.

"Yes, just two, as far as I gathered," my strategist says. "The second time she reached out to me, she was struggling more to get her message across. But that number would make sense. Two gives her a decent amount of protection without making Orion feel overly threatened."

"They won't be much protection if he strikes her down too quickly," I can't help muttering.

Whitt sighs. "No. But Talia's been around him; she's seen how he thinks and behaves. And she's got Madoc with her to advise her. I think we have to go by their judgments over our own."

"I know." I restrain a growl of frustration. "If we could kill him ourselves right now…"

"Obviously I'd opt for that plan too if it were available. But he hasn't shown himself to us at all. As much esteem as I have for both the two of us and the rest of our forces, I have to admit we can't offer much that would tempt him."

But the Murk king has had it out for our mate from the moment she fled his colony. The reasoning for her plan is sound. I'll support her in it as much as I can. There's simply nothing that can make me *like* it.

If another opportunity to end Orion's life presented itself right now, I'd take it in an instant.

We have a few dozen Murk who've arrived at the temporary settlement near the Heart, but only eight of them had the courage to accompany us in fighting back directly against their former allies. One of them fell under the first barrage of attacks after we entered the fray. At the moment, the other seven are sitting in a tight cluster, gulping down the rolls other fae have been passing out so the warriors can keep their strength up. From the wary glances they keep shooting over their shoulders, I suspect they haven't gotten the warmest reception from the rest of the fae here.

"Has anyone harassed you?" I ask as I come to a stop before them. If there's been any outright hostility, I need to stamp that out immediately. Not only does it undermine our best chance of finding a peaceful resolution with the Murk even after Orion is gone, but it could threaten Talia's plan to ensure that first part happens at all.

The Murk man who's been the most talkative of the bunch, Flynn, peers at the groups of fae gathered across the plain around us and wrinkles his nose. "Nothing like that. But we'd rather not stick our necks out too far trying to make friends while our lives are already literally on the line, if that's all right with you."

"Of course," I say evenly. "I only asked so that I could set *my* people straight as need be." I motion to Whitt. "I gather that my strategist has informed you of Lady Talia's request? I understand it would be an even more dangerous undertaking than simply standing with us in battle. We wouldn't ask it of any of you if we didn't feel it was our best chance at ending this war."

One of the two women in the bunch narrows her eyes at me. "By killing Orion."

I give her a grim smile. "You must realize that there's no way we can find any kind of peace while he's still determined to take the Mists completely for himself. Can any of you honestly see him agreeing to compromise and live in cooperation with the rest of us?"

The gloom that settles over all their faces is enough of an answer.

"He isn't going to be happy with us," one of the other men says. "Chances are no matter what we say or do, he's going to want to set an example. We'll be walking in there just to be slaughtered if your mate can't put her plan into action the way she's hoping."

I tip my head. "I acknowledge that. As I said, it'll be dangerous. But Lady Talia has accomplished quite a lot of difficult tasks in the past. None of us is safe if we can't defeat Orion—and soon. I honestly believe it's by far the route most likely to see all of us, including the Murk who are willing to work with us, survive."

"Why does it have to be us going with her?" the woman mutters.

"He'll be much more inclined to believe that a couple of *his* people would have regrets and try to make amends than that any of the fae of the seasons would go over to his side," Whitt says. "That'll mean he's less suspicious, more willing to let down his guard, which means more chance for Talia to make her move."

Flynn rubs his mouth. "What does Madoc say about all this? He went after her, didn't he?"

I nod. "Yes, and he's with her now. He'll have consulted with her on this plan. You should have an opportunity to speak to him directly before you actually set off. We'd need you to head west of the front to meet with them and approach the Murk forces from there."

"It won't be easy to back down once we've gone that far," the other woman puts in.

"That's true," I say. "And I gathered you have some conditions you'd like to put on your help. I'm willing to take a vow related to any requests you have—within reason, of course."

One of the men snorts, but Flynn sits up straighter, holding my gaze. "You've got to use plain language, no flowery garbage that's easier to maneuver around. We know the fae of the seasons can be just as tricky as you say the Murk are."

"I have no problem with making the vows as simple as possible."

"All right. We want a guarantee that no matter which of us takes this on, all of us who came out here and have been fighting with you against our own people will be safe in the Mists for the rest of our lives. No banishing us, no attacking us—we'll have a good home and not be hassled about it."

That seems fair. "I can offer you that," I say. "But I'll need to include a caveat that it will only be enforced as long as you don't commit any major crimes. And I can only speak for myself and what I'll insist on. I may be able to get my fellow arch-lords to swear as well, but we can't vow for any future arch-lords, the Unseelie rulers, or anything beyond our scope."

The Murk appear to think this over. Flynn makes a gesture of acceptance. "That's the main thing. I also want—we should have approval to associate with the fae of the seasons however we want, if the other fae want it too. I mean, as friends, or mates, or whatever else comes up."

I restrain myself from raising my eyebrows at that request, wondering if he already has someone in mind. I wouldn't have argued against it even without a vow. "That's not a problem either. Is there anything else?"

The Murk murmur amongst themselves for a few minutes, and then Flynn turns back to me. "That would be enough. We need to approve of the wording before you take the vow. And then we'll decide who goes. We'd like all of the arch-lords to take the vow if possible."

Somehow I suspect he'll be one of those going no matter what. I recognize the determined fire in his eyes.

"I'll speak to them now," I say. "Thank you. We do appreciate the risks you'll be taking."

I expect to have to roam for a while before I can locate both of my colleagues, but I've only just left the Murk when Celia and Donovan stride into view just a short distance away amid the crowded camp. They head straight toward me. Whitt considers them and mutters from the side of his mouth, "This looks like trouble."

I have to agree with him. Both of my fellow arch-lords look solemn and strained.

"What's the matter?" I ask when they reach me. They wouldn't be coming to me together if it wasn't official business.

Donovan glances toward the Murk army on the other side of our latest attempt at a magical wall. "We're seeing new activity among the Murk. We suspect they're gearing up for another large-scale attack, maybe something different than they tried before."

"Maybe something even worse," Celia adds, a stormy expression crossing her dark face. "I say we launch an assault of our own as quickly as possible with all the power we can muster. Catch them before they have the chance to get another edge on us."

My heart sinks. "We've already been fighting them for days without managing to push them very far when we're not implementing a special strategy. What's going to turn the tide this time rather than simply exhausting us even more so we can't even hold our ground after?"

"We have a much larger force assembled today than we've had before," Donovan says, though there's a trace of doubt in his tone. "The Murk have been lingering amid the iron projectiles they fired into that territory—we can hope they've been weakened."

"As we will be if we charge back into that territory," I remind him.

Celia's eyes flash. "We can't simply sit around and wait for them to savage us again."

"We won't," I say with all the confidence I can summon. "Talia is on her way here. The Murk have all but agreed to support her plan. Within the hour, we could see Orion fall, and the majority of his supporters will falter without him leading the charge."

"So you claim. But where is your mate? She may not make it to us at all. And what guarantee do we have that the Murk will follow through? Just days ago, they were on the other side of this war. If we don't act now, we may lose any advantage we could have had."

"If we *do* act now, we'll definitely lose the even greater advantage Talia means to give us." I look at Whitt. "Have we had any other news from her party recently?" I've avoided telling my colleagues exactly how we've communicated with them, letting them make their own assumptions about messenger spells.

Whitt shakes his head, his mouth slanting at a crooked angle. "I don't think it should take very much longer, though."

Celia exhales roughly. "We can't rely on assumptions."

My chest constricts, the responsibilities of my role pressing in on me as never before. I have to make the right choice for my people. Donovan is wavering—I can see I've started to persuade him. But what if I push for this outcome and the Murk tear through our ranks before Talia even arrives?

What if I send so many Seelie to charge at the Murk only to watch most of them fall under the rats' blades and claws?

I think of Talia, standing up to Aerik in the Bastion with all the brilliant strength I've watched growing in her for months. I think of my younger brother, who's fought with unrelenting devotion, and of the rat shifter who was willing to sacrifice his own life for a chance at peace for the rest of his kind.

Resolve winds through me. All three of *them* are my people, and I trust in them. I fully believe that they can see us through this war if we only offer them the chance. If I've learned anything about being a true arch-lord, it's that you need to be able to recognize when those around you are capable of more than you yourself can accomplish—and give them free rein to do so.

"Leave it for half an hour," I say, taking a gamble so I can persuade Celia as well. "If we haven't set Talia's plan in motion by then, we can make our brute force attempt. I swear it. But only if you'll also swear to the conditions of the Murk who'll be risking their lives for that plan. They aren't asking for anything that the rest of us fae don't already have."

Donovan nods slowly. Celia's lips purse, but when she looks toward the opposing army, a flicker of doubt crosses her face. She *wants* to believe we could barge right through their forces, but she must know how precarious her plan is too.

"All right," she says, turning back to me. "I'll hear the Murk out and prepare the pieces of this gambit. But you only have that half an hour."

As we set off toward the Murk squad, Whitt abruptly stiffens. He covers it quickly, but I fall back beside him as his pace slows. After a moment, his gaze clears again. He aims it at me with a crooked smile, lowering his voice.

"She's here. All we have to do is send her rat accomplices to her."

Somehow my spirits lift and plummet at the same time. All we have to do is set the final part of her plan in motion—and hope she comes out of it alive.

CHAPTER TWENTY-SEVEN

Talia

The terrain where the war has currently halted is mostly flat with not much available shelter. Madoc has kept a concealing illusion around us during the whole trip, but we stop the carriage behind a small stand of trees for extra camouflage.

As soon as I've hopped out, I touch the pocket on my dress where the iron dagger is equally well hidden. August adjusted the stitching of the pocket so we can be sure the weapon won't shift too much no matter how my body moves. I've practiced snatching the hilt and brandishing the blade in one swift movement so many times I almost do it automatically the moment I bring my hand near it.

August also carried out more drills on the exact best place to strike for a quick kill. My stomach doesn't outright churn anymore at going through the motions, but it stays knotted as I take in the landscape around us.

What if I falter when I actually have to do it, when Orion's right there in front of me and I need to dig the blade into his literal flesh? It's one thing to imagine it and another altogether to go through with it.

But I have to, because the thought of what will happen if I fail horrifies me even more.

The two men scan the terrain. "Whitt said someone was coming?" August checks.

I nod. "He told me that they were just finishing arrangements. The Murk who agreed to help should be heading this way soon. But I could only give him the general area we're in. We should make some kind of signal so they can find us."

"A signal that Orion's people won't notice," Madoc puts in.

August hums to himself and considers the trees. "They should be coming from the east. I'll make it something that won't show to the south."

Focusing on the branches above us, he speaks the true name I'm planning on using myself in just a little while for an even more crucial task. "*Sole-un-straw.*" Light sparkles into being amid the trees, nestled where it should shine clearly to anyone coming at us from the direction of the Seelie camp but where the foliage will hide it from every other direction.

"Nicely done," Madoc says with genuine approval, and August grins as if the praise matters a lot to him. Even with the danger so close on the horizon now, I have to appreciate their newfound comradery.

While we wait next to the carriage, I practice the fatal strike several more times: standing, crouching, on my knees, even lying down imagining Orion bending over me with his horrible smirk. When my fingers start to ache, I slip the dagger back into its sheath in my pocket. There's a point where more practice will make it harder for me to perform when it counts rather than easier.

August sniffs out some berries on a nearby bush and offers them to me to restore my energy. I'd insist that he and Madoc eat too if I wasn't a little lightheaded. Too much rests on what I do next for me to take any chances with my physical wellbeing.

I'm just gulping down the last of the berries when Madoc lets out a hopeful sound. He straightens up from where he's been leaning against a narrow pine. I squint at the plain ahead of us with its fluffy, pinkish grass. It takes another minute before my human sight picks up on the two small rippling lines weaving through that grass.

The rats reach us within moments. They pause while Madoc extends his concealing spell around them too and then shift into human form. Somehow I'm not surprised to see that one of them is Flynn. His previous bravado obviously wasn't for show.

He stands with his chin high, his eyes bright but his stance a bit rigid with tension. He might have been snarky before, but I can tell he's taking this mission seriously. The woman next to him folds her arms across her chest, but the clenching of her jaw looks determined rather than frightened.

"Thank you for coming," I say to them.

"Yes, you have no idea how much we appreciate you coming through." Madoc tips his head to both of them. "I wish I could join you or take this on completely on my own, but… you already know how Orion feels about *me* right now. Do you understand the basics of what's needed?"

"I think so," Flynn says. "We put a call out for Orion and get him to come, saying we've captured Talia to hand her over to him as a gift with the request that he welcome us back."

"That's the gist of it." Madoc walks around them, checking them over—I guess for anything about them that might tip Orion off to the trick. He finishes his circuit and comes to a stop, apparently satisfied. "We want him away from as many of the other Murk as possible. That'll be safer for you and make Talia's job easier. Walk from here until you're just in view of the front, and a sentry or two should come over to find out what you want. Explain that you're offering up Talia, but that you're not going any farther or handing her over until you can speak to Orion himself. Hold your ground until he comes."

"And if he doesn't come?" the woman asks.

"If you see a larger force heading your way, retreat as quickly as you can," August says. "We don't want this to become a suicide mission."

Flynn's gaze darts over me. "Should we restrain her?" he asks doubtfully. "She's supposed to be our prisoner—but she'll need her hands free to have a go at Orion."

"You'll say that you managed to get her drugged up with cavaral syrup to make her compliant," Madoc says. "Talia can put on a show of supposedly being intoxicated."

"I've had that stuff before," I put in with a wry smile, remembering the time that feels so long ago now when Whitt shared his supply with me at my demand.

"And you should keep a blade on her," August says. "You can borrow my sword if you don't have your own. The implication should be that if the other Murk try to take her from you without Orion coming, you'd rather kill her than give up your bargaining chip. He'll want her alive."

"He will." Flynn exhales sharply and holds out his hand for the sword. "We'd better get going right away. The wolves have spotted some unusual activity on the Murk side. They might be gearing up for a fresh attack, and there's no telling when they'll launch it."

The thought of setting off right now makes my pulse skip even though I've been preparing for this moment for days. Somehow I expected to be able to settle into the mission a little more gradually once it actually started.

I pat my dagger again and drag the warm summer air into my lungs. My heart thumps onward, faster now. I can do this. I *will* do this. I'm not going to let Orion ruin any more of my life than he already has.

"All right," I say. "Let's go."

"Just one second." August tugs me to him and kisses me hard before wrapping me in the tightest of hugs. I lean into his embrace, willing back the nervous tears that want to spring into my eyes. When he lets me go, Madoc grasps my hand and raises his other hand to my cheek.

"You're stronger than he is," he tells me. "By a mile."

I manage an anxious smile in response. Then I turn to our two Murk accomplices and set off toward the front.

Flynn keeps August's sword out but not too close to me. The

woman stays at my other side. After the first few steps, I start to put on my performance of being high on faerie drugs.

My limp makes it easy for me to bring a waver into my gait. I gaze around me as if finding every blade of grass and puff of cloud fascinating. I even swerve off course here and there, letting the Murk guide me back.

The woman snickers and glances at Flynn. "She's good."

"She'll have to be," Flynn says, but he swings the sword with a flourish that's all confidence.

I can't afford to pay too much attention to what's directly ahead of me while I'm supposedly in such a daze, but I do periodically snatch glimpses of the Murk forces in the distance. I see when a few men posted near the edge of the battlefield peel off from the others and trot toward us. Flynn stops me with a hand on my arm and holds the sword ready.

"Hold it there," he snaps when the approaching Murk are several feet away. "We're not here to deal with you. We want to speak to Orion."

One of the sentries sniffs. "I don't think you're anyone to be making demands like that." But his gaze lingers on me. I mumble to myself and cock my head at the sky.

"We've got his human 'pet,'" the woman next to me says. "We stole her from the Seelie while they were distracted with the fighting, and we're bringing her back to her rightful owner. I think that's proof enough that our reasons for leaving were always in support of Orion."

"But we want to hear from his own lips that he recognizes our contribution before we hand her over," Flynn adds. "Why don't you go tell him, and we'll see what he thinks about it? We'll stay right here. For now, she's ours." He motions the sword toward me in a vaguely threatening gesture.

The sentries shift on their feet uneasily. The woman next to me scoffs. "You wouldn't want to make the decision yourself and then find out Orion isn't happy with it, would you?"

She's pushed the right button. The three of them tense, and they scuttle back to the larger mass of Murk warriors. One of them breaks into a sprint, heading for a carriage I can make out past the edge of the crowd.

"And now we wait," Flynn says under his breath with audible trepidation.

I breathe as steadily as I can, willing the rhythm of my lungs to even out the pounding of my pulse. To make the waiting easier, I crouch down and pretend to examine the grass by running my fingers through it, giggling to myself. It's easier to keep up the façade and not give in to the emotional strain when I have something to focus on—and when I don't need to hold myself upright.

The woman's faint cough alerts me that something has changed. The sun has sunk so low by now that our shadows stretch like skinny giants across the plain. I act as if I haven't noticed anything significant, but after a few moments, I let my head swing around in a lazy arc and spot a familiar figure with a head of spiky white hair striding away from his army.

Orion brings a few warriors with him, and he stops a mere ten feet ahead of the rest of his army, where he makes a beckoning gesture. "Let's see her then," he calls. "Let's discover if you've earned your way back into my good graces."

There's an edge to his tone that sets all my nerves on the alert. He doesn't sound happy. He probably assumes that these two fled for real and only recently came to regret that choice.

I can't let him hurt them. I've got to keep them safe too.

But I can't ready myself, can't risk reaching for the dagger or doing anything other than walk with swaying steps as my supposed kidnappers usher me over to where the Murk king is waiting. He sneers as he takes me in, his expression all vicious derision.

"Didn't take much to addle her mind, did it?" he says. "So easy to mold to our will."

Anger swells inside me. I want to raise my fists and shout at him that he doesn't own me, that he never did and he never will, that he's the sorriest excuse for a king I could possibly imagine. To rain judgment down on him like I did with Aerik and Cole.

But that approach isn't going to work here. I'll only get us all killed.

One more time, I'll play the victim—the helpless, frail human. One more time, I'll let the fae around me believe they control my fate. It'll be worth it in the end.

I have to remember that my deception is its own kind of power. I can create this illusion without a single spark of magic, and even Orion buys into it wholeheartedly.

That last thought solidifies the resolve in my chest. I let my glazed eyes continue to drift this way and that as my body weaves from side to side, but within, my attention narrows down to the stance of the man in front of me and the distance from the blade in my pocket to his throat.

My escorts stop again before they've quite reached Orion and his guards. I'd imagine they can pick up on his hostile vibes even better than I can. "You can see what we've brought you," Flynn says. "We've served you the best way we knew how, my king. Will you welcome us back?"

"I think I'd like to examine the merchandise first," Orion says. "Throw away your sword."

Flynn hesitates, but he only needed the weapon for show when he was dealing with the initial sentries. We both know he isn't going to survive a real fight so close to the Murk army, no matter how well-armed he is. He flings the sword off across the grass.

"Back away from her," the king orders next. The two Murk comply, taking one step and another in opposite directions from each other until they're well beyond my reach.

Orion gestures for his guards to walk over to Flynn and the woman. He stalks toward me on his own. Totally assured, never suspecting that I might be more of a threat than they are.

But I am. I can do this. I can sever the life from that smirking face forever. I can silence the voice that's ordered so much pain, still the hands that have dealt so much themselves.

He comes to a halt directly in front of me, close enough that his breath tickles my forehead. I cock my head to the side and peer up at him, still swaying. "Hello?" I say in a dreamy voice, forcing it from my constricted throat.

Orion cackles, a chilling sound that rings across the plain. "You poor, pathetic thing. You should have stayed with me while I was good to you. Now you'll only—"

He starts to move, and adrenaline jolts through my veins. I may not get another chance.

While one hand jerks to my pocket, I whip the other up in front of Orion's face, summoning the joyful memory of drifting off to sleep last night in my mates' combined embrace. The true name tumbles from my lips. "*Sole-un-straw.*"

Light flares from my hand so brightly it glares through my eyelids, which I closed in anticipation. Orion sputters, falling back a step, but I'm already moving with him. My eyes pop open. I lunge at him with a swing of my arm, my fingers clutched around the hilt of the iron dagger.

My strike flies with August's careful training guiding it, with all my fury and horror fueling my strength. The blade plunges into the side of Orion's neck in just the right spot, slamming all the way to the hilt so the point protrudes from the other side.

Blood sprays over my hand and across my arm. Orion gags and gurgles. Even as his legs crumple, he gropes at me, his claws springing from his fingertips. They rake across my forearm before I've quite shoved myself away.

Thin lights of pain sting across my wrist. Every nerve in my body screams at me to get away from him, but I have to make sure I'd done this right. I smack my hand into the hilt of the dagger, driving it even deeper before scrambling backward.

The Murk king crumples further. As blood sputters across his lips, his knees give. He topples over, his head smacking the ground with a dull sound that seems to echo in the sudden silence around us.

The dagger still lodged in his neck gleams in the fading sunlight. His body twitches and then sags.

One of the guards lets out a startled shout. He swivels back toward Flynn, who's backing away with his hands raised.

"It's done now," Flynn says. "It's over."

"It's over!" I repeat, hollering even louder, pitching my voice as far as I can along the front. "Orion is dead. *I* killed him." The words bring a weird mix of exhilaration and dread into my gut. I raise my hands, one of them streaked red with the Murk king's blood. "He died, and so did his war. You can fall like he did, run back to the sewers and subway tunnels, or find a way to make peace with the rest of the fae. They're waiting to welcome you home. The Heart of the Mists is waiting."

Cries ring out along the front. Spells and projectiles hurtle across the gap between the armies, and several Murk warriors charge forward in a last, desperate attempt. A bunch of them at the end of the crowd stalk closer to us, their weapons raised, their lips forming spell words.

My pulse stutters. I retreat as quickly as I can, Flynn and the Murk woman falling in on either side of me—and then a blaze of light sweeps over us all, halting our Murk opponents in their tracks with startled expressions.

It's coming from the Heart of the Mists. The familiar thrum seeps into my skin, recognizable even from so many miles away. The glow like sunlight lights up the ground, and more concentrated beams narrow in on Flynn and his companion on either side of me.

Flynn gasps, his hand smacking into his chest. The woman lets out a choked sound and then a breathless laugh. They glance at each other with matching expressions of awe.

"The Heart," Flynn murmurs. "I can feel it. I never—I never knew it could be like this." He turns to the watching Murk. "You could have this too! Stop the fighting, start negotiating. The Heart of the Mists knows we belong here too."

Our opponents waver on their feet with uncertain expressions. More beams are landing amid the Seelie army where the other Murk who've joined us must be, a few even touching on spots among the Murk forces. I don't know how the Heart is choosing who it welcomes now, but the next cries that ring out are joyful.

A couple of the warriors facing us gnash their teeth and charge forward again. But at the same moment, a Seelie carriage races into view. It plows right into the figures on the attack, knocking them to the ground. My Seelie mates and Madoc lean over the side.

August and Whitt extend their arms to help the three of us in. Sylas directs the carriage to whip around and speed back toward the Seelie side of the front. Then he's with me too, four of my mates around me, passing me from embrace to embrace with soft words of awe and comfort.

"You were amazing," Madoc says. "To face him like that… He had no idea."

My heart still hasn't stopped racing. I meet his gaze. "That was his problem all along."

As the carriage slows behind the Seelie's defensive wall, I glance around to take stock. It looks like maybe a quarter of the Murk force is still hurling attacks at us, although they're so outnumbered now that they hardly feel like a threat. Most of the others have darted off toward the fringes—most likely to the portals that'll lead them to the human world. I'm not sure if they'll hide away for good or if some of them will find the courage to come back to the Mists once they've had time for the new reality to sink in.

There are others crossing the battleground along the edges, their hands raised in surrender. The Murk on our side are hurrying over to beckon them onward.

The Heart's thrum has faded. Orion's body still lies limp where I stabbed him. The sense rises up in me that this isn't totally over after all. The most immediate part of the war is finished, but Orion's legacy doesn't totally die with him.

"The curse," I say. "There's a full moon in a few days. More Unseelie will be hit by the freezing sickness. It isn't going to stop just because Orion died, is it?"

My mates exchange a somber glance. "No," Whitt says. "Most likely it won't. For that, we'd either need to know the counter-curse… or we'd need to destroy the source of the magic that fueled it." He turns to Madoc.

The Murk man grimaces. He might not draw on the power of the Murk Heart anymore, but an awful lot of his people do. He protested before against extinguishing it.

But now he sighs and squares his shoulders. “It has to be done. The Heart of the Mists has shown it’ll accept us. You can’t lord your magic over us.”

“We can’t, and we won’t,” Sylas says firmly. “All of the Murk have a place here if they choose to take it.”

“Then we have one last problem to deal with.” Madoc’s gaze slides toward the fringelands out of view beyond the horizon. “To the Refuge we go. I can lead the way.”

CHAPTER TWENTY-EIGHT

Madoc

If you'd told me a few months ago that I'd end up bringing a bunch of fae of the seasons to the Refuge so they could dismantle the power source Orion so painstakingly grew for our people, I'd have laughed so hard my ribs ached. But here I am, picking apart the spell that guards one of the main entrances in the furnace room of an old mall.

Sylas, Corwin, and a contingent of Seelie and Unseelie fae stand in the dark room around me, waiting for me to finish. I brought a handful of the original Murk refugees too in case their connection to the Murk Heart is needed for whatever we decide to do. Talia insisted on coming as well, even though I can see the tension creeping into her the closer we get to the place where she was essentially held captive for several torturous days.

I understand her wanting to see this through to the end, though. That's why *I'm* here, even though I could have asked any of our other Murk allies to show the way.

If the source of magic that's fueled so many of my people for so long is going to be destroyed, I want to be able to have some say in when and how.

It's clear that Orion brought pretty much all of the Murk who were on his side into the Mists to fight his war. He'd have needed to in order to have any hope of winning. When I intone the last words to release the protective and illusionary spells and the door grinds open, a sole guard peers out at us, the knife in his hand jerking up. I recognize him from doing my rounds here before I left.

"Orion is dead, Hender," I say, in a sympathetic tone I don't have to put on. "But you can still go home to the Mists. We'll even take you there when we're done here if you want. We've just got a little more business to take care of. Will you let us through without a fight? I don't want to see you get hurt."

Hender's jaw works. He'd have trouble taking on me even on my own—I might not be an avid fighter, but when push comes to shove, I give it my all. I wouldn't have made it to my position as Orion's knight otherwise.

And I'm not on my own. The other man's gaze skims over the arch-lords and gathered warriors behind me. I can only imagine the calculations he's making. He has to note the other Murk standing freely in their midst, though.

"Orion's dead?" he repeats, sounding a little hopeless.

I dare to reach into the range of his knife and squeeze his shoulder. "No more unnecessary killings. No more lashing out at anyone who questioned him even a little. No more insisting that every problem be solved through violence and bloodshed. I promise you, it's going to be for the best, if you can let yourself accept it."

He lets out a shaky breath, his eyes searching mine. Then he lowers his knife. "He told me I should stay behind because he didn't think I had enough guts to handle an actual battle. Because I was upset when one of his other knights beat up on my cousin. He didn't even give me a chance."

"It wasn't the kind of chance that'd have brought anything good anyway," I say. "The Heart of the Mists will welcome you back. It's already reached out to me and some of the Murk who came over to us earlier. We're setting up colonies throughout the Mists. The fae of the seasons are *helping* us. It's going to be okay."

His expression still twitches nervously as the other fae draw closer, but he heads on down the tunnel, letting us follow him. At Sylas's motion, the warriors with us keep their weapons sheathed.

"Do you think many of the Murk who fled the battle will come back here?" Talia asks quietly.

I shake my head. "Not right away, at least. This was always Orion's domain first and foremost. They'd have a hard time seeing it as safe after his death. I'm sure they'll be back after they have a chance to realize that his loss isn't the end of the world, though, at least to scrounge up belongings they left behind."

Which makes me think of one particular item I'd like to scrounge up myself. Something that never should have been taken from its owner in the first place.

We tramp along the dark and winding passage for close to half an hour before we finally reach the doorway that leads into the subway tunnels. Hender has fallen into conversation with a couple of the Murk who joined us, and by that time, he's relaxed enough that he opens the entrance for us.

On the other side of the door, the station we come out into is lit with the usual stark yellow glow. Orion didn't cut off the electrical power he got running for this place when he left. But the platforms are eerily vacant, only a couple of my people standing up to gape at us at the far end, the rest of the homes apparently abandoned. The place is unsettlingly quiet with none of the forges or other workshop machinery in operation.

"We're here peacefully," I call out to the women watching us. "You can pass on word to anyone else who stayed behind that the war is over, and we can all move into the Mists now. If you're willing to share our real home with the fae of the seasons, who we've convinced to make plenty of room for us, you're welcome to make your way there with us when we return."

The women murmur to each other and vanish into the nearby tunnel, their tails swishing behind them. I can't tell whether they believe me or not, but I guess we'll find out before too long.

I lead my procession down the tunnel at the other end of the station. The air there is taking on a dank quality it didn't use to have. There haven't been enough Murk around to keep up with Orion's previous cleaning schedule. My pride rankles at what the fae of the seasons must think, imagining we lived like this, but none of them comments on it. I'm sure the warriors have a few thoughts, but the presence of their arch-lords keeps their tongues still.

They can think whatever they want as long as they keep it to themselves. I know what my people were capable of, how much we made of the lot we had. And who was responsible for keeping us in this low situation.

We pass through another station and on into the tunnel Orion's throne room branches off from. At the sight of the quavering orange light spilling across the tracks up ahead and the feel of the erratic thrum of energy that tickles over my skin, I have to restrain a shudder. Now that the magic of the Heart of the Mists courses through my body, I can't tune out how dissonant Orion's Heart is by comparison. No wonder Talia always tensed up in its presence.

She's holding herself steady approaching it now, limping along without a second's hesitation. As much as it might have unnerved her, she never let it get in the way of what she was trying to do.

When we turn the corner into the throne room, several of the fae around me suck in their breaths. "Heart help me," Whitt mutters, staring at the spastically pulsing mass of light at the far end of the dais. "Even after Talia's stories, I didn't imagine it'd be so… so *much*."

Queasiness pools in my stomach, both because of the false Heart before me and because of the thought of what we're going to do with it. First, I walk to a narrow passage in the wall partway down the room. "I'll be right back, and then we'll talk about what to do about it."

I slip down the passage as quickly as I can, Orion's scent thickening around me and raising the hairs on the back of my neck. The tunnel opens up to the room where he usually slept, next to the hoard of his favorite treasures. I paw through them, finding the item I wanted quickly since it was a recent acquisition, and hurry back to rejoin the others.

As I reach them, I hold out the delicate crown in my hands to Talia. "This should never have been taken from you, Lady Talia."

My mate arches her eyebrows slightly at the formal title, but there's no missing the poignant mix of emotions that crosses her face. She takes the crown from me gingerly, her fingers curling around it. No doubt she's remembering the moment it was gifted to her, just as I am—when she took her three Seelie mates with her soul-twined mate's blessing.

That was the night I stole her from her mates and brought her here. How bizarre that committing the crime was the best thing I could have done for my people, but not at all in the way I thought it would be.

Maybe before much longer, she'll bless me with a ceremony like that too, to make our union official. There hasn't exactly been time yet. I can wait. At this point, I trust her and the men she's bound herself to enough to know I'm already part of the family.

"Thank you," she says in a soft voice, and shoots me a smile that could stitch my heart back together even if it'd shattered to pieces.

But it's not my heart we need to worry about now. I turn toward the one Orion created in all its monstrous glory. "What do we do with *this*?"

Sylas lets out a huff, still taking in the mass of energy. "I was hoping you'd have some ideas on that subject."

I speak several words of magic, testing the currents around the Heart. It doesn't feel solid, but in a way that makes the idea of dismantling it more difficult. There's nothing to really get a hold of to tear it apart, nothing to smash or blast to bits.

I motion the other Murk with me who are still connected to its power closer. "Can you get a sense of any weaknesses or a spot where we could even start to prod at it and unravel it, or anything like that?"

They can't hide the reluctance that briefly crosses their faces. "Before long you'll have the other Heart's power to draw on," I add as a reassurance. They nod, girding themselves before launching into some spellwork of their own.

As they prod it, a few other Murk drift through the throne room entrance. They stop just inside, watching us warily. Hender goes over and starts talking to them in hushed tones. I hope he's talking us up and not inciting a rebellion.

"I don't know," one of my comrades says finally, frowning at the Heart. "It doesn't feel like something that can be *killed.* It doesn't feel alive to begin with." He pauses. "Orion fueled it with the suffering of the fae of the seasons—isn't that right?"

"Yes," I say, watching the summer and winter fae around us carefully, but hearing that stated out loud doesn't appear to provoke any of them. Talia will have reported as much when she returned to the Mists—they probably all already knew.

My mate herself eases past the others to step closer to the Heart. Its orange glow ripples over her body. She looks as if she's restrained a wince. She stares into it for a moment that stretches so long I start to itch to wrench her away from it. Then she glances back at us, a sliver of that glow dancing off her eyes.

"Can you move it?" she asks. "Is it attached to this spot?"

One of the other Murk says a few testing magical words and curls her fingers, and the mass shifts a little toward her like a snowball about to hurtle down a hill. She halts abruptly but shoots a smile at Talia. "I think we can manage that. But moving it won't change the spells it's powering."

Talia worries her lower lip under her teeth, her expression pensive. She ponders for a moment longer before going on. "I wonder… It *is* a Heart, even if it's a false one. What if we brought it all the way to the true Heart and let it decide what to do with this one? All this energy came from it to begin with. It knew how to bring Madoc back to life. It knew how to connect to his soul and some of the other Murk's again. All the magic comes back to it in the end."

Her words hit me with a sense of rightness. We'll let the true Heart find the answer. Maybe that will bring many of the Murk still tied to this malformed thing back to where they belong.

"It could go badly," I have to say. "They could clash, or the energy could start dissipating once we reach the Mists and cause some kind of harm there—we don't really know. Are you sure?"

Talia looks at the Murk Heart again and nods firmly. "Yes. Whatever happens, we can handle it. But even the magic in that thing deserves the chance to get back to the home it deserves."

That's such a Talia sentiment that a lump rises in my throat. As the Murk still connected to the false Heart start to murmur and urge the glowing mass across the throne room, Talia steps out of the way. I move to join her, slipping my hand around hers.

"You know," I say, pitching my voice low, "with every passing day I'm more convinced that the real heart of the Mists is you, bright one."

A blush colors Talia's cheeks. She twines her fingers with mine and squeezes. "And you found your way to that heart too."

Yes, I did. And I know that my people will be okay—the ones of them willing to let themselves be okay, at least—as long as this woman is here to shine on all of us.

CHAPTER TWENTY-NINE

Talia

Conveying the Murk Heart back to the Mists and across the fae lands is a slow process. Its energy surges and flares in fits and starts, painting the darkened landscape in fiery shades, and the Murk propelling it along have to pull back and wait until it's settled down again before they can get close enough to maneuver it. We manage to set them up in carriages on either side of it and behind, dragging and pushing at the same time, but we can hardly move the vehicles at full speed.

As the strain of the day's chaotic events creeps up on me, I find I can't keep my eyes open any longer. Sylas shifts into his wolf form and sprawls on the floor of the carriage we're in so I can use his thickly furred side as a pillow. I drift off nestled against him.

My dreams are cast in an eerie orange light, nightmarish images swimming out of the darkness. When I wake up, still groggy, night is just easing back. A thin dawn light is seeping across the sky. And the rhythmic thrum of the true Heart's energy welcomes us back to the domains on the hill.

We draw to a stop on the field beside the Heart. The Murk pull the false Heart within a few feet of the true one and then scoot backward with wary expressions. Five ravens soar out of the sky and land amongst us in human form: Corwin went to gather his fellow Unseelie arch-lords. Celia and Donovan join us a few minutes later.

"Dust and doom," Celia mutters staring up at the Murk Heart. A shudder runs through her. "It's horrifying."

Maybe what's most horrific of all is seeing it next to the true Heart. Orion managed to grow his self-made energy source to nearly a third of the size of the real one in a matter of decades. And it must have been expanding faster as the curse worsened and caused the fae of the seasons to go through even more distress. How much longer would it have taken before he could have fully rivaled their power?

"What now?" Laoni asks, eyeing the thing with equal revulsion.

"I don't know," I admit. "I just thought… it's stolen energy from these lands, from the real Heart. Maybe the Heart of the Mists can take that back."

The idea seems kind of childish now that we're standing here and nothing's happening. More fae are drifting over from the domains around the Heart. There are a couple of clusters of Murk among them. The woman at the front of that group I can recognize as Delta even though I've never met her in person before.

She gazes at the Heart that Orion created and sucks a sharp breath through her teeth. "Those delusions of grandeur weren't all delusion. Too bad he couldn't have put this power to better use."

The true Heart's energy seems to hum a little more emphatically, but I can't see any change in it or the Murk Heart. Maybe it needs guidance. I test the words out in my mind and find that my throat has constricted too much for me to say anything.

If the Murk Heart is destroyed, however that happens, I still don't know what'll happen to my bond with Corwin.

I glance across the clearing to where he's standing with his colleagues. He catches my eyes, and his mouth twists.

It has to be done, he says. *We can't let the curse keep its hold on so many people just to preserve our bond.*

I know. I just… I'm scared.

It's hard to admit that. I've spent so much time being as strong as

I can be, even if only on the inside while I played a victim. But I don't want to pretend I don't care.

I am too, Corwin says, his inner voice going raw. He walks over to me so he can stand next to me and wraps his hand around mine. *But I'm here with you no matter what happens. We'll face it together. And if I don't get another chance to say it to you so intimately, my soul, know how much I love you.*

The connection between us opens completely, and a flood of emotion rushes over me. There's a bittersweet edge of fear and trepidation, but the rest is pure, poignant affection.

I taste how much Corwin cherishes every smile he watches cross my face, even when they're not aimed at him. How proud he is of the way I've stood up for both the fae and humankind while we've fought Orion. How much he longs to pull me into his arms and do nothing but hold me against him, forgetting all these other responsibilities.

I choke up for a totally different reason. *I love you too*, I say. *So much.* I let all the tenderness and devotion I feel for him carry through our bond like liquid sunlight. In that moment, it feels as if we're joined by so much more than our clasped hands and the tenuous magic that first tied us together.

The Hearts still haven't stirred. As I grapple with my thoughts, searching for the right thing to say, another raven swoops through the border and lands by Corwin. It's Verik.

"My lord," he says in a low voice, "your mother—I think she can sense something momentous is happening. She's been battering at her door, crying out that she 'only wants to see it'… None of us have been able to calm her."

Corwin's mouth opens, but at first no sound comes out. He swallows audibly. Then he squares his shoulders. "Let her come. If this works, it'll be the end to the plague that stole my father from her. She deserves to witness that moment if she wants to."

Verik takes off again. I watch his raven fly into the border haze with a prickling sensation winding around my gut.

Corwin's mother was wrecked by her grief when her soul-twined mate died from the curse. She didn't lose just her bond with him but his entire presence in her life. And she's still finding the strength to come and witness the end of that curse despite knowing it won't bring him back.

No matter what happens, Corwin will be here. I can't let any part of me hesitate to believe that destroying the Murk Heart is what must happen.

Gathering my resolve, I wait for the arrival of the former lady of Heart's Cadence. She comes through the border on foot, with Zelpha on one side and Verik on the other holding her steady on her wobbly legs. Her stringy hair is pushed back behind her ears, her face as gaunt as when I first saw her. But when her eyes find Corwin, she shoots him a shaky smile.

Then her gaze veers to the Murk Heart.

As she stares at it, her expression hardens until it contains nothing but pure rage. She remains silent, but her anger practically hums off her, calling for the end to this thing that stole so much of her happiness.

Maybe it'll steal a little of mine too, but that's a small sacrifice to make to see the curse lifted off the entire faerie world.

I let go of Corwin's hand and walk up to the Hearts. August makes a faint noise, but no one moves to stop me. I limp around the Murk Heart to the gap between it and the Heart of the Mists.

Erratic energy hits me from one side, and harmonious power tingles over me from the other. I stare up at the pulsing glow that gave me the magic to win yesterday's war.

"This is all the energy you and your people have lost to Orion," I say. "Take it back. Take it into you and make it something good again. Burn away the curse that's been driving them mad and freezing them to death. Please. It should be yours."

The true Heart's light flares a little brighter, but nothing else changes. Frustration and anxiety tangle together in my chest. What if I was wrong? What if we shouldn't have brought the Murk Heart into the Mists at all?

"There has to be something you can do!" I protest, as if I can argue it into acting. That did sort of work with Madoc. But this doesn't feel like the same situation. There's the faintest hint of confusion in the energy tickling over me.

The Heart of the Mists and the Murk Heart have been totally at odds, opposites to each other, from the beginning. No fae was capable of holding the power from both.

Except for me. In me, they're tied together. In me, both streams of magic meet.

If anyone can bind them back together, it's me.

My mouth goes dry. Without giving myself a chance to chicken out, I thrust one hand into the sun-like glow of the true Heart and the other into the quavering light of the false Heart.

Like the last time I touched the Murk Heart, its energy starts to sear into my skin. I clench my fingers, bracing myself against the pain. Someone lets out a shout from the watching crowd—

And a soothing wave of power gushes into me through my other arm.

The light of the Heart of the Mists surges over me, swallowing me completely in an instant. My vision blazes white; my body seems to crackle with an electric pulse all the way down to my bones. All I'm aware of is that sizzling tsunami and the thudding of my heart, faster with every passing second. The rhythmic thrum roars in my ears. It feels as if the brilliant glow is filling all the tiny vacant spaces inside me, turning me into something more than I was before. It rushes on and on—

And then it pulls back again, like an actual wave drawing back into the sea. I find myself standing there before the Heart gasping as if I've just spent a minute underwater, on the verge of drowning.

Voices are exclaiming all around me. The orange glow has vanished. I'm still gathering my senses when another tendril of light extends from the Heart of the Mists and grazes over my temple, right through my skull and down to my own heart.

As it lets me go, I stumble, but the fae around me are already converging on me. Solid hands catch me by the shoulders. Someone touches my arm, another my cheek. The faces of my mates swim in my vision as I blink to clear the last of the blaze from my eyes.

And a softly eager voice speaks from right inside my head, cutting through the babble I can't quite focus on yet. *My soul?*

A grin springs across my lips so fast I almost crack my cheeks. I spin around and lock eyes with Corwin, his face alight with hope.

And you're my soul, I answer back, joy filling me to the brim. *Even the Heart of the Mists could see that.*

Sylas glances from me to the Unseelie arch-lord and smiles one of his quiet little smiles. "It seems all's ended as it's meant to be, even if not by our conventional patterns of fate."

I grasp Corwin's arm and pull him into a kiss, then plant one on each of my other mates in turn, not caring what anyone looking on thinks of the display. Even Madoc accepts my embrace without hesitation, his arms closing tight around me for a few seconds after. "Our heart," he murmurs, reminding me of what he said to me in the Refuge.

There's a sharp inhalation behind us. I turn to see Corwin's mother approaching the Heart with shaky steps. Its pulsing glow washes over her. She draws in another breath that's part sob, part awed sigh. Then she looks at her son. Her expression is so full of desperate longing it sends an ache all the way through my bones.

Corwin swallows audibly. I can feel his unsettled emotions: old strands of grief that he could never fully put to rest, a wrenching wish that he could help her. But he inclines his head. "Do what you feel you need to."

His mother gives him one last smile, so full of love it shines like the Heart itself. She turns back to the Heart and walks straight into it with open arms as if offering it an embrace.

The light swallows her up. This time, there's no re-emerging. The glow pulses on. A faint melody whispers through the air and fades away.

She's rejoined her soul-twined mate the only way she can. The Heart finally granted her that peace. Maybe something in that fathomless glow has shifted its perspective a little too with everything that's happened in the past several months.

Are you all right? I ask Corwin, who's blinking a bit harder than usual.

Yes, he says, in a tone that tells me he means it. *She waited so long. It was her time.*

The rest of the watching fae gradually disperse. Madoc gives me another gentle squeeze. Then he pauses and touches my skin at the neckline of my dress.

I drop my gaze and tug the fabric a little to the side. My breath catches. There's—there's a true-name mark forming just below my collarbone, darkening into the usual black lines before my eyes. It isn't one I remember having identified for me before, but deep inside, I instinctively know it's the mark for light.

I jerk my gaze up to meet each of my mates. "What does that mean?" Was something in me permanently altered by the Heart's touch? A faint tingling races through my veins, and I can't help wondering if it's somehow made me a little more than human.

Sylas's eyes have widened, but his tone stays mild. "I suppose we'll have to wait and find out."

Those words jerk me out of my startled reverie with the thought of the one person who's still waiting for me, the one I haven't properly saved yet. I glance around at the fae milling close to the Heart of the Mists, all of them exclaiming over the spectacle that just appeared, and a sense of urgency grips me.

"Jamie," I say. "We have to get Jamie. He shouldn't have to stay shut away, missing out on his life, for any longer than he already has. And my aunt and uncle must be worried sick."

Madoc nods. "There has to be someone among all the Murk who've joined us since Orion's death who knows what mine he brought your brother to. I'll find out as quickly as I can." He hurries off.

Whitt tucks a few stray strands of my hair behind my ear. "Do you want us to restore your brother to his home as discreetly as possible? He doesn't need to know the incident has anything to do with you."

I pause to consider, but alongside my urgency, an unexpected conviction has gripped me. "No. Finding out about me and the fae shouldn't put him in danger now—no more than it already has. He'll be so confused… He deserves to know. And I want to be able to be part of his life, however he'll have me once he gets used to the idea."

Sylas grips Whitt's arm. "Corwin and I are still needed here to sort out the aftermath of all the fighting we've been through. Madoc should probably stay nearby as more of the Murk cross over to us. Why don't you and August take her as soon as Madoc reports back on the correct location? And I suppose you'll need to pick out a few of our Murk allies not yet reconnected to the Heart to get the boy free of that iron mine."

Whitt smiles back at his brother. "It would be my pleasure."

When we reach the abandoned iron mine one of Orion's former followers pointed us to, Whitt and August need to stay well back from the boundaries. The stretch of ridged earth drops into a vast pit that I have to venture into with the Murk to retrieve my brother. A couple of Orion's guards have lingered there, but at the sight of us, they shift into rat form and flee. They can't work any magic at all right now with the Murk Heart gone.

Neither can the Murk descending into the mine with me. Their fledgling connection to the Heart of the Mists isn't yet in place, so it's a long trudge down on foot.

We duck into a sort of cave carved into one of the ridges near the bottom of the pit. When the iron case comes into view in the dim light, my heart lurches. My brother is sealed away in there as if in a coffin.

But he's not dead. He's alive *because* I helped build this all-encompassing shield.

When the fae conjured the iron case through me, they had the foresight to key it to my essence. I press my hands to the top, and that part springs open like a lid. The Murk lift Jamie's unconscious form out of the box, cringing at the closeness to so much of the toxic metal, and hurry with him back up the slope.

They lay my brother on the grass where we've parked our

concealed carriage. I kneel next to him, and Whitt comes to stand over me.

"Are you sure about this?" he asks. "Are you ready?"

"Yes," I say to both questions, bracing myself with the water bottle we brought clutched in my hand.

August murmurs the words to bring my brother out of his physical stasis. Jamie's eyelids flutter and then outright blink. He jerks upright with a start before swaying. Slamming his hand into the ground to catch his balance, he stares at me and then the figures around me. "What— Who—?"

His voice comes out in a rasp. I hold the bottle of water out to him. "You should drink something. You've been knocked out for a long time."

His gaze jerks back to me. He studies me for a long time, confusion and a hint of recognition colliding in his face. "You… Who *are* you?"

There's no time like the present. I offer him the gentlest smile I can summon. "It's me, Jamie. It's Talia. I—I know I've got a whole lot of explaining to do. But I promise you that everything's going to be okay now."

"Talia," he repeats in a disbelieving tone, but I can tell he isn't really all that skeptical. He knows my face and my voice, even if it's been years. "This is… very weird. Maybe I'm hallucinating?" He presses his hand to the side of his head.

I give his forearm a tentative squeeze of reassurance. "Nope, this is real. But definitely very weird. It's a long story."

He blinks and focuses on me again. A lopsided smile crosses his lips. "I guess you'd better get started then."

CHAPTER THIRTY

Several months later

Talia

There are few spots as peaceful as the stretch of grass right outside the summer side of the border castle. It's become my favorite spot to relax when I don't have any official business as Lady Talia to attend to—or any of my own responsibilities that I've volunteered for—and Sylas has conjured several permanent wooden loungers with woven grass padding for me and whoever decides to join me.

Today, I'm nestled against those thin but cozy cushions, soaking in the mid-afternoon sun. A yawn stretches my jaw. I thought I slept all right last night—with Sylas and Madoc taking a turn sharing my bed with me—but I haven't felt really rested all day. I'm tempted to close my eyes and drift off for a nap.

But this is one of the rare days when none of my mates have any pressing duties either. Four of them are sprawled on their own seats around me, taking just as much enjoyment out of the sun's warmth. Harper has joined me too, although after we chatted for a while, Flynn stopped by from the nearby Murk colony where he's set up his home. I can't help suspecting he picked that one *because* its nearness lets him drop in quite frequently.

Seeing the way my best friend's face lit up at his arrival and the delighted smile curving her lips now as they sit side by side on one of the other loungers, I definitely don't mind. He's even wearing a shirt Harper designed for him, trim and simple but with multiple pockets in easy reach of his hands. Flynn is apparently quite a collector of whatever happens to catch his interest at any given moment.

I suspect that my mating ceremony with Madoc months ago won't be the only one between a woman of Hearth-by-the-Heart and a Murk man this year.

The sunlight gives Corwin's bronze skin a summery glow, but even when he comes over to the Seelie realm, he's still a practical raven underneath. It's hard for him to totally relax and not talk business at all. He glances from his lounger to the one Sylas is stretched out on. "Were you and your colleagues able to quell that little rebellion without too much trouble?"

Sylas chuckles. "So little I'd almost forgotten about it. Honestly, it works out well. Every pack that decides to take aggressive offense to the rat shifters creates an opening for a new colony when we banish them off to the fringes."

"Only when it's deserved," August puts in, flexing his shoulders against his seat. "There *are* Murk who've purposefully provoked their neighbors."

"And you've shut them down too," I say. "But from what I can tell when I talk to them, most of them are glad just to be alive and not sent into battle by a crazed king, no matter who their neighbors are."

Whitt smirks, pushing himself up on one elbow. "True. We couldn't have expected an instantly smooth transition. I'd say our efforts at placing the colonies and supporting their independence have gone better than anyone would have hoped."

August rolls his eyes playfully. "Of course you'd say that, since you're the one who planned a lot of those efforts."

The strategist holds up his hands. "Hey, credit should be given where it's due."

Flynn glances over at us. "I got the impression that Delta is working up to some big ask the last time I happened to cross paths with her."

"Well, she can make all the 'asks' she wants, and we'll decide whether they're reasonable," Sylas says. "I don't think she's pushed for more than is fair so far. And she and her colony have been very helpful in wrangling the late stragglers who've been drifting in."

"Not to mention the few of Orion's supporters who don't seem to have gotten the memo that his time is over," Whitt mutters. His attention shifts to the border, sliding along it toward the Bastion. "When the new castle is finished being built and the Murk decide on their third arch-lord, I'd imagine we'll be hearing even more from her." He tips his head to Corwin. "Speaking of women with strong opinions, that supposed not-quite-mate of yours has still been following the sanctions placed on her, I assume?"

A sadness laced with a prickle of anger slips into me from Corwin. He hasn't forgiven Kara for her part in my kidnapping, but I know he wishes she hadn't been placed in such an awful situation to begin with. He and the other winter arch-lords took her extenuating circumstances into account when deciding on her punishment, recognizing that a fractured soul-twined bond can affect one's emotions and judgment badly.

"Zelpha and Domhnall have been checking on her regularly," he says. "So far she hasn't left the boundaries of her domain, as we decreed. I expect we'll revisit her sentence within a few years and judge whether she continues to pose any threat."

He sends a wordless sense of questioning my way, and I nod. I don't want Kara to be miserable. I just want to be sure she won't try to hurt me—or anyone I care about—again.

"Does she even still feel any kind of bond?" August asks. "I'd have thought the Heart would take that away when it confirmed the bond between you and Talia."

Corwin shakes his head. "We're not sure what she's feeling now. She was vague when asked about her current impressions."

"She has a long life ahead of her to mend that injury," Sylas says. "Not every wound can be healed in an instant."

Whitt hums to himself. "Very true. But for all the wounds still being mended, I have to say I'm liking the relative peace we're enjoying now a great deal more than all the turmoil that led up to it."

"Here, here," I say, raising my hand as if in a toast.

A familiar carriage glides from the trees at the other end of the clearing. I sit up straighter, bracing my hand against the lounger when the blood rushes from my head faster than I expected.

Madoc pulls the vehicle to a stop and hops out, carrying a sack over his shoulder and wearing a self-satisfied grin. "I have a letter for you," he says, coming to me first as he fishes an envelope out of his pocket.

My heart leaps at the sight of Jamie's narrow handwriting. Since I filled him in on where I've been for the past several years, we've been passing each other letters back and forth.

Madoc's conveyed most of them on his regular trips to the human world, where he's watching over the human servants who chose to return to their old home. It's been a difficult transition for some of them, but I know they were relieved to finally *have* the choice. A surprising number opted to stay here and continue working for their masters on a more equitable basis.

I guess once you get a taste of magic, it's difficult to let go of it, no matter how much it's burned you.

I tear open the flap of the envelope with my thumb and pull out the folded papers inside. The actual letter is typed. I can picture Jamie sitting at his desk in his bedroom, tapping away at his computer keyboard.

Hey Sis,

Thanks for the tart you sent in that last package. If that's how the fae can cook, then I definitely need to come over for dinner sometime. Once I'm eighteen, it'll be easier for me to get away with taking off for a weekend to someplace with no phone service. Just mentioning that so you can get your invitation prepared ahead of time.

Just joking. Mostly. Obviously the first step is you meeting the family, if you're sure you're ready, I can definitely set something up. Do you want to come by the house, or would somewhere public be better? Let me know what the plan is, and I'll get Aunt Becca and Uncle Walter on board.

I'd also really like you to meet Amy, my girlfriend. I know, first things first, but I think she might even be able to wrap her head around the whole fae thing, if you ever feel like it's safe for us to talk about that with anyone else. I get that it's very hush hush. Not pushing.

College acceptances are starting to come in, so keep your fingers crossed for me. I got into one of my second-tier choices but haven't heard from my favorites yet. Sometimes there's so much stressing about it that I want to run away with the faeries too, but I know what you'll say. Best to get my education so I have a backup plan. Aunt Becca totally agrees, so obviously you'll get along fine.

I'm actually pretty excited about the idea of getting to study something I'm really interested in. And obviously crashing a college party or two could be fun. We'll see.

Since you liked my sketches so much, I'm sending another one. It's hard drawing from memory, but it felt better doing that than using a photograph. Let me know what you think.

Talk again soon!

Jamie

The other folded page shows a family standing together, the father's hands on the daughter's shoulders and the mother ruffling the son's hair. It's *our* family—I can recognize us instantly even with the roughness to the lines. Our family before Aerik tore it apart.

I guess in a way that family still lives on in Jamie and me, no matter what.

A twinge of anxiety ripples through me at the thought of making final arrangements to reveal myself to the rest of our surviving family. I've put it off for long enough, and it isn't really fair to Jamie to make him keep so much of a secret for so long. I've just got to perfect my story of where I've been and why it took me so long to reconnect with them, one that won't sound at all insane, but maybe in a week or two…

I'll think on it for a few days and then write him back with a definite plan.

Madoc is handing out the other items he picked up on today's trip. He hands a DVD to Sylas. "A new release. Very good reviews, if you like that sort of thing, which I know you do. Those discs are getting scarce, though. Everyone's switching to streaming now. You're going to need to find a way to get internet access all the way out here."

Sylas guffaws, but he looks pleased as he checks out the latest comedy flick he'll add to his collection before tucking it aside.

Madoc pulls the opening of the sack wide and sets it down in the midst of the loungers with its remaining contents poking out. "I also went looking to restock my snack collection. You all get first dibs on *one* thing. The rest is mine." He gives us a slyly territorial glower.

August leaps up and bounds over with typical eagerness. He counts on Madoc's love of snacks to expand his culinary horizons with human-world flavors. I push myself to my feet, thinking a little treat might be nice, but as I straighten up, my stomach flips. A sudden wave of dizziness washes over me.

My legs stiffen to help me keep my balance. At my abrupt halt, Corwin glances over with a waft of concern through our bond. "Are you all right, Talia?"

"Yeah. I think so. I just—"

My heart skips a beat as the sensations collide in my mind into a pattern I've experienced only once before. I pause, thinking back. It's been two weeks since the last time they said— That's just about the right timing, from what I know about these things… Could it really be—?

I look around at my mates, who are all watching me now. My voice comes out quiet. "I'm just feeling a little off. But it's exactly like —like before when I—" I can't quite get the words out, so I rest my hand on my belly instead.

Understanding flares in all five of the men's eyes. Snacks forgotten, they converge on me like one being, surrounding me and dipping their heads close. As they each breathe in my scent deeply, the heat of their bodies washes over my skin. My pulse keeps skittering giddily on.

Sylas's hand comes to rest on my belly where I touched it a moment ago. August's follows, and then Corwin's, and then Whitt's and Madoc's, until they're overlapping with each other like an echo of our joint relationship.

The Seelie arch-lord speaks first, his voice rough with emotion. "Our family is going to grow again, in a very different way."

A grin stretches across my face. I beam at all of them, lost in the exhilaration of the announcement.

There's no curse on me now, no Murk king out to make me and my mates miserable. The Heart has shone on us all. This baby will be born into a world of joy and compassion, one I'll fight to the death all over again to keep that way.

But surrounded by the men I love right now, I know I'm not going to have to. We're in this together, and like that, we can conquer anything. I will never be caged again.

CELEBRATIONS OF THE HEART

A BOUND TO THE FAE BONUS EPILOGUE

Talia

There's always something so satisfying about the feeling of kneading dough beneath my fingers. The rhythmic sensation and the sweet, bready scent take me back to my first days of relative freedom among the fae, when I started to find my footing by working alongside August in the kitchen of Oakmeet's keep. It speaks of *home* no matter where I happen to be.

Mason squirms on the counter next to me, his bright eyes that match my green ones transfixed on the movements of my hands while his little legs swing over the edge. He informed me this morning that he's a "big boy" now and therefore he should get to help me in the kitchen. I'm not about to give my four-year-old son any major baking duties, but having him here with me and eager to learn brings even more happy warmth into my chest.

"Did you finish stirring the berry mixture?" I ask, shooting him a fond smile.

He nods briskly and waves the goopy spoon. "All mushed up. What do we do with it now?"

"Just watch." I pull off a piece of the dough and flatten it in a rough star shape on the baking tray I've already set out. Then I drop a dollop of the berry jam in the middle. With careful fingers, I fold the arms of the star over to meet in the middle and pinch them.

"It's an old recipe that your Daddy taught me," I tell Mason. "A tradition that got forgotten. The Seelie used to always make these pastries for the end-of-the-year celebrations, but then some arch-lord decided they weren't fancy enough, so a lot of people stopped. But we think what matters most is how tasty they are."

"Of course!" Mason eyes the utensil I took avidly. "Can I lick the spoon?"

I laugh. "Not until the pastries are all filled, but definitely then. Do you want to try some of the folding? I'll help you get it right."

"Oh, yes. And I get to eat the first one when they're done."

I rumple his flaxen hair, even paler than that of the man I know is his father genetically as well as in all the many ways that count even more. "I think your sister might have something to say about that."

"We'll share," Mason says with an air of immense generosity. He hops down onto the stool with a brief swish of his rat tail for balance before it disappears again.

The fae of the seasons are getting more used to seeing the Murk among them, and I never discourage my son from showing what he is, but he's noticed that most fae keep their animalistic features to themselves unless necessary in general. *Also*, he told me a few months ago, *people step on tails a lot more than wings or claws.*

As I lay out more bits of dough and guide Mason in adding the jam, voices carry from beyond the kitchen. It isn't long before Sylas ambles into the room with his cadre close around him.

August makes a beeline for our work area and inspects the assembled pastries. "Looks like you're giving your mother a lot of help," he says to Mason.

Our son beams up at him. "It's fun. I want you to teach me all of your recipes, Daddy." He glances past him to the other men and Astrid. "What were you and Father and Pa doing?"

We weren't sure how our kids would distinguish between their various fathers by name, and in the first couple of years with our eldest, there were a lot of "Dada"s followed by as many as five urgent sets of footsteps as my mates rushed to find out what our daughter wanted. But Ivy quickly came up with her own set of labels to identify them, and Mason has copied it with typical little brother enthusiasm.

It probably isn't surprising that Sylas, with his imposing bearing, has gotten the most formal name as "Father." He walks over with a smile for Mason. "We had to go out and talk with some of the lords about their parts in tomorrow's festivities."

Whitt—a.k.a., "Pa"—grins. "We have to make sure it's as spectacular a party as possible, after all. Let the old year know how much we appreciated it and the new year feel totally welcome."

Mason raises his chin. "I want to stay up for the *whole* thing."

The spymaster chuckles. "You can give it your best shot." He meets my eyes with a twinkle in his, knowing as well as I do that our son is likely to conk out within an hour of his usual evening bedtime.

"Everything went okay?" I venture, not wanting to get too specific in front of Mason.

"If anyone wasn't in a peaceful spirit, they kept it to themselves," Sylas says, which is about as good as we can expect. We've made a lot of strides toward mutual understanding in the last ten years, but some fae have trouble letting go of old grudges, which I guess is understandable. As long as they hold those grudges in rather than aiming any rancor at others, they can keep them.

"Ten years of peace," Mason says. "That's a long time. No wonder we need an extra big party."

The rest of us exchange an amused glance, knowing how little time a decade is in fae years. And possibly in my years too.

Since I stepped into the Heart to help it merge with Orion's false one those ten years ago, my body hasn't felt quite the same as usual. Not even small lines of age have formed on my face yet, though I had my thirtieth birthday more than a year ago. My bad foot is as warped as it's ever been and still aches if I walk on it for very long, but any new scratches or scrapes I've gotten have healed a little faster than is really normal for a human.

It's impossible to know right now, but my mates have speculated that the Heart might have granted me a little extra life as a thank you for bringing that piece of its energy home.

Astrid comes up at my other side and tsks her tongue teasingly at me. "I don't think the lady of the house should be doing all the cooking."

I let out another laugh. "Oh, I'm definitely not doing all of it. It's nice to contribute a little, though." This peace means as much to me as to any of the fae… maybe even more.

With a thunder of paws, a wolf cub charges into the kitchen. She springs onto one of the other countertops, making the pots clang together, and spins around with an eager pant.

I step away from the pastries and set my hands on my hips. "Ivy, what have we told you about running wild in the kitchen?"

Our daughter shifts into the form of an eight-year-old girl, crouched on the counter with a mischievous smile. "Sorry, Mama," she says, not sounding particularly apologetic. "I was playing with Dad. He's got to be in here somewhere." She cranes her neck, scanning the floor from her perch.

I settled on the name Ivy thinking of how that pretty plant could hang on and endure. I've gotten a kid who likes to climb on anything she can reach. But it's hard to feel more than a little consternation and a whole lot of affection watching the vibrant energy that shines from her face and her amber eyes.

We don't know exactly which of my wolfish mates contributed the most to her conception. The dark brown hair that tumbles over her narrow shoulders is a lot like my own, but similar to Sylas's too. Those eyes suggest August. I've never gotten the impression that the men give the question all that much thought, though. She's as much all of theirs as Mason is.

Ivy lets out a squeal and leaps off the counter, shifting into wolf form as she goes. I catch a glimpse of a rat's head peeking around the doorway before Madoc darts away, leading her on another merry chase.

Unlike the summer and winter fae, the Murk don't really have any major traditions to add to the festivities, at least not that any of them seems to recall. They've gone too long without much reason to celebrate. But a twinge passes through my stomach watching Ivy bound off after him. We have to make sure the Murk feel just as welcome during the dual parties as every other fae.

August presses a kiss to my temple as if he's picked up on what I'm thinking and wants to reassure me. "I guess Corwin's busy with the winter-side preparations?" he says.

I nod, vaguely aware of my soul-twined mate in his palace at Heart's Cadence, where he's speaking with the various volunteers who've offered their services to the party that will begin the day after summer's. "He said he'd be back here for dinner." All of my men tend to be busy with their own people's affairs, but we manage to have at least a few meals all together in the border castle every week.

I turn back to the baking tray and my son. "We'd better get on with these pastries. They won't cook themselves!" And I want the festivities to be special in every possible way.

August rolls up his sleeves next to me with a warm, purposeful air. "You're not leaving me out. This is still my kitchen, no matter how much you invade it." He nuzzles the top of Mason's head and flashes a playful smile at me, and for that moment, I'm totally sure we can pull off every part of the upcoming event spectacularly.

Music whirls through the air, and fae spin and sway all across the fields that surround the Heart and the Seelie arch-lords' castles. Harper catches up with me by one of the many refreshment tables scattered across the hilltop, the flush in her face showing that she's recently been dancing too.

She wraps me in a quick hug and turns toward the table. As her gaze roves over the spread, a little gasp escapes her. "There's so much food! I can't believe there are fruits I haven't even tried before."

I smile back at her. "We dug into a lot of old records to see if there was anything interesting that's fallen out of favor. I guess you could say we're celebrating a lot of years past rather than just the most recent one."

"Well, it's amazing." She pivots again, the flared skirt of her blue dress unfurling around her like ocean waves. I can't help noticing that an awful lot of the women in the crowd are wearing similar creations.

"I see you've been busy," I say, nudging her playfully with my elbow.

"Oh, yes." She grins. "Even Delta asked if I could come up with something that would combine her usual style with mine. She seemed pretty happy with it, so I must have succeeded."

"I'm not surprised by that at all." Harper's designs have come into increasingly high demand—my own festival dresses, the one I'm wearing tonight and the one set aside for tomorrow, were her creations. And she seems to have struck a chord with fae of all types. I can spot as nearly as many Unseelie, noticeable because they dance a little more hesitantly amid the wilder Seelie, wearing gowns with her trademark detailing.

Harper lets out a happy sigh. "It's good to see everyone enjoying the holiday together, isn't it? I mean, I know the years before this one we were welcome to cross the border for each other's celebrations, but this is the first time I've seen so many of the Unseelie and Murk taking us up on the offer. And I know so many summer fae who are planning on crossing over tomorrow."

"The more people realize that there's nothing to fear about our alliances, the stronger those alliances will be," I say.

Speaking of alliances of various sorts, Harper's Murk mate bounds out of the mass of dancers at that moment. Flynn shoots me a smile of greeting before beckoning to Harper. "They're going to play one of my favorite songs from the Refuge! I need my favorite partner for that."

Harper beams at him so brightly she could light up a room. "Of course." She gives me a little wave and takes his hand to let him tug her into the crowd.

I've just popped a mirrornut into my mouth, enjoying the caramel-sweet flavor that spreads across my tongue, when gentle arms wrap around me from behind with a presence I can feel inside and out. Corwin tucks his head over mine with a waft of affection.

Will my mate be joining in the dancing tonight? he asks through our bond, easier to be heard over the music than his outward voice.

I slip my arm over his to return his embrace. *I'm sure I can manage to keep up for a couple of songs. Have you seen the kids around?*

He chuckles out loud. *Zelpha found Mason curled up under one of the tables and carried him to his bedroom. Ivy is still going full-tilt. Last time I saw her, she was on August's shoulders.*

Of course she was, I say with amusement, easily able to picture it. A faint pang runs through my chest with the knowledge that I haven't given my Unseelie mate an heir he could fully call his own yet.

It's not as if I could produce a true-blooded child without some special magic from the Heart anyway. But I know what children mean to the fae in general and to Corwin in particular. I suspect he'd take a particular joy in having a little raven to take under his wing both figuratively and literally.

He's never let so much as a whiff of disappointment show, though. And if my men are right and I'll have decades longer in this life than any regular human would, we have lots of time for that joy to still come about.

He dips his head lower to nuzzle my hair, much more at ease with the outward show of affection now than he was when we first met. *May I claim the first of those dances, my soul?*

I twine my fingers with his. *I'd love that.*

The musicians take up a lilting, graceful tune I recognize as Unseelie in origin, which is perfect for a turn across the grass with my winter arch-lord. It's easy to ignore the faint ache in my warped foot when I'm in his arms, surrounded by so much happiness.

We weave through the other dancers and whirl around each other. As the song winds down to begin another, a familiar stormy scent washes over me with a hand on my back.

"Mind if I cut in?" Madoc asks in a tone that's nothing but friendly.

Corwin passes my hand over without hesitation. "She should dance with all her mates tonight."

I grasp the Murk arch-lord's hands, and he beams at me with one of his rare flashes of unbridled emotion. Then he whisks me around with a deftness I probably should have expected given how nimbly he moves in general. But he doesn't often join in the dancing at the various balls and revels, and when he has before, it's been to music that's not quite as lively as this particular tune.

I gaze up at him with a rush of exhilaration. "Have you been enjoying yourself?"

The smile he offers me now is more typically crooked, but it's relaxed rather than stiff. "What's not to enjoy?"

I glance around, catching a glimpse of Delta farther off in the crowd of dancers, the layered dress Harper constructed for her swirling with her movements, and a few other fae I recognize as part of the Murk colonies. "There hasn't been any trouble so far, has there—no one's been less than welcoming to your people?"

"Not in a loud enough way for it to draw attention. Everyone seems to be in a very generous mood tonight."

His last word acknowledges the fact that generosity still isn't always the case when it comes to the rat shifters. But before I can prod at the subject any further, Madoc gives my hands a squeeze and aims a pointed look at me. "You're supposed to be enjoying yourself too, not fretting about politics. Be generous with yourself too for once, bright one?"

I let out a slightly indignant huff, but I can't deny he might have a point. The melody tingles through me, and I welcome it, feeling it sweep through my spirits. "I won't think of anything but dancing and dining for the rest of the night."

Madoc's smile returns. "Perfect. If there's anything else that does need thinking about, your mates can handle that thinking just this once. That's what we're here for."

He tugs me closer. There was a time when he hesitated to even accept a hug from me in front of the other fae for fear of how they'd react, with him being Murk and me seen as some sort of savior to the fae of the seasons. Now, he holds me in his embrace without a hint of reserve. When the music lulls for a moment, he bows his head to claim a quick kiss that I return with a tingle of pleasure.

Corwin said that I should dance with all of my mates, and so I do. After another song, my Murk man passes me on to Whitt. The spymaster whirls us around with his sly smirk. Next I'm swayed by Sylas, and finally I'm scooped up by August, who spins me right off my feet.

"How are you doing, Sweetness?" he asks with his lips brushing my ear.

"Good," I say, although the ache in my foot has deepened, creeping up my ankle now. But the merriment of the festivities really has washed away any lingering nerves about the success of the event. "Wonderful. I think this is going to have to be my last dance of the night, though."

"Then it's a good thing I caught you when I did."

I steal a quick kiss. "I'd have saved the last one for you anyway. Is everything ready for the fire?"

"We'll start when the moon is at its peak."

By the time we've danced one more song away, the Seelie arch-lords are already clearing a large space around the huge heap of firewood collected in the central field. The music dwindles as they raise their hands for attention. All of the fae drift over to form a circle around the pile of wood.

Sylas speaks first. "Long ago, one of the traditions during the end-of-year festivals was a wishing fire. Seeing as we've gotten more peace than most of us could have hoped to wish for in the past ten years, we thought we'd revive that spectacle."

Donovan rubs his hands together beside his older colleague. "There are slips of paper and ink on the tables nearby. Write down whatever you'd like the new year to bring you and toss your wish into the fire for the universe to consume."

Celia inclines her head with typical reserve, but a soft smile has touched her lips. "May the Heart shine on all of us as bright as these flames."

The assembled fae—summer, winter, and Murk alike—hustle to the tables. There's a strange hush over the gathering as everyone contemplates what they'd most want to wish for, as if they expect to receive exactly that as long as they make the request properly. I suppose in this magical world, that isn't an unreasonable thought.

The arch-lords have lit the pile of wood with supernaturally-charged flames that rush up toward the star-speckled sky, flaring with every hue of the rainbow as they perform their own sort of dance. The smoke tickles my nose with a tangy scent. I stare down at the paper I've picked up, finding myself uncertain about the words I'd like to write.

Whitt joins me, his eyebrows arched at their usual sardonic angle but his tone full of fondness. "Already have everything you could wish for, mighty one?"

I look up at him, watching the interplay of wavering colors shift across his handsome face. There's always more I could want, but I've gotten so much that I'm almost afraid to ask for more in case it somehow ruins the amazing life I've already found.

I reach up to touch his cheek. "I have everything I need to be happy, that's for sure."

The spymaster's expression softens. I can remember when he held himself at a distance from everyone around him—even the brothers he was devoted to, even me. But he's opened himself up to me in ways no one else ever has. Even my connection with Corwin isn't quite the same as Whitt offering up his true name, because the soul-twined bond didn't come with any choice. Whitt gave me total access to his soul of his own accord.

He teases his fingers along my jaw and leans in to claim my lips. I kiss him back with a pleased murmur.

"So do I," he murmurs afterward, while a glow of even more joy spreads through my chest. Then a glint of amusement lights in his blue eyes. "But I'm sure I can think of some bit of frivolous fun that won't strain the Heart's powers too much. Our pack deserves many more thrilling revels."

I laugh and consider that—just writing down something small and silly. But it's not really my style. In the end, the best thing I can think to scrawl down is, *I wish for this peace between the fae to continue for many centuries to come.*

We walk together to the flames, their heat surprisingly gentle despite the height of the fire, and toss our slips of paper in together. Ivy comes scampering over to me and grabs my arm, her expression giddy in a way that tells me she's been making quite a few trips to the sweets table.

"I wished for a pony," she announces, and Whitt smothers a guffaw with his hand.

I hug our daughter to me. "Somehow I think that can be arranged. But maybe not until your birthday."

I study the skates Harper's handed me with a mix of awe and amusement. "You managed to fit one of the braces into these?"

"I figured it'd be hard enough for you to keep your balance on the ice even with the extra support," my best friend says, tying up her own skates. "But you shouldn't have to miss out on the fun because of what those jerks did to you."

I smile at the sentiment and slip in my feet before tugging the laces tight. Across the glittering plain around us, thousands of fae are already skidding and gliding this way and that on similar footwear.

For the start of their end-of-the-year festivities, the Unseelie arch-lords—with Corwin's urging—unearthed a pastime that fell out of favor centuries ago because someone decided it had become too human-like. They've transformed most of the plateau around their side of the Heart into a gigantic, glossy ice rink.

And not just any ice. When I push off on slightly unsteady feet, the contact of the metal blades against the surface stirs up a thread of music. More delicate melodies are wavering up all around me as the skaters slide and twirl. It's a dance of its own, one where it's hard to tell whether I'm moving with the music or it's moving with me.

I sway over to where Whitt and August have just gotten Mason and Ivy into their skates. Ivy takes off like a shot, weaving between the other fae as if she's been on ice all her life. Mason wobbles and clutches at Whitt's leg. "This is kind of scary, Pa."

Whitt tugs a strand of our son's pale hair. "If you can't stand up straight, see how much fun you can have tumbling around. The ice won't hurt you. Here, we'll tackle it together, and then we can fall on each other if we lose our balance."

Mason giggles and veers off, clutching Whitt's hand. Verik glides by, with a respectful dip of his head to me. "The whole coterie will be keeping an eye on the young ones as well."

"Thank you!" I call after him.

Corwin is busy getting the next part of the spectacle ready. My impressions of him are muffled because he's partly shutting me out to keep it a surprise. But August catches my hand, and we soar off together across the frozen plane, shivers of song spouting from beneath our blades.

The cool wind flicks through my hair, and for a moment I flash back to cruising around a rink with Jamie and my parents more than twenty years ago, my brother and I laughing as we purposefully collided. An ache forms in my chest that's part lingering grief, part something I can't quite identify. I push it aside, focusing on the celebration around me.

This is my life now. And I helped make it as great as it is. All sorts of fae are sliding across the ice around me, and if there are occasional glowers shot between summer and winter, or between fae of the seasons and Murk, there are far more smiles and laughs of delight.

We pass Ivy, who's in the middle of trying to haul Sylas across the ice while he holds his arms out indulgently, and Mason, who's grabbed Madoc from the crowd and is doing more swinging between his and Whitt's grasp than actual skating. When my foot starts to throb and my face to tingle with the chill despite the warming charms on my clothes, August directs me over to the tables where mugs of a sweetly steaming beverage are waiting.

One gulp sends a fantastic heat bubbling down my throat and leaves an aftertaste like butterscotch in my throat. August hums approvingly. "I'm going to need this recipe. Even if there isn't a whole lot of use for it on the summer side."

"We can pop out the winter entrance just to fully enjoy it," I say with a grin.

The sky is darkening. When the rest of my mates other than Corwin join us, Sylas has Mason cradled in his arms. Our son blinks furiously as he tries to resist sleep for as long as possible.

I extend my awareness to my soul-twined mate. *How's it coming along?*

Just a few more minutes, I promise.

He keeps his word. It can't even be five minutes before an instrument peals out a note for attention across the plain. Everyone hushes, those still skating drawing to a stop.

Laoni's voice, amplified with magic, carries over the crowd. "This has been a fruitful year, finishing off an incredibly productive decade. We offer our gratitude now. Lie back and enjoy the show."

"Productive," Whitt repeats with amusement at the typical Unseelie practicality, but we all hunker down on the ground to witness the spectacle. Ivy comes darting over just in time and squeezes in between me and August, snuggling against us.

A pure white light blazes across the darkened sky like a shooting star. Then another follows, and another. The first few blink out, but as more burst into view, they linger longer, trailing their shimmering tails across the great expanse.

In the hazy glow that seeps from the Heart, I make out figures behind those lights with the flap of feathered wings. I taste a hint of Corwin's exhilaration as he soars over us, coordinating with his fellow arch-lords and dozens of other Unseelie who volunteered to blaze glistening designs across the sky. A different sort of music strikes up, rising and falling in elegant notes in time with the streaks of light.

It's like a meteor shower, the Northern Lights, and a fireworks display all wrapped into one. My breath catches in my throat as my eyes dart this way and that, attempting to take in every glint. But like on the rink, another memory flickers up from the depths of my mind: sitting on a beach with my parents and Jamie while 4th of July fireworks exploded overhead.

I recognize the twist of feeling behind my heart now. It's homesickness. The Mists may have become my new home, but that doesn't mean I should push the one I had first completely aside.

When the spectacle ends, I scramble up and rush across the icy terrain as fast as my limp allows to where I can sense Corwin has landed. He wraps his arms around me and lifts me up to claim a kiss, our breaths mingling hot in contrast with our cooled skin.

"The light show was beautiful," I tell him, and glance around to see that my other mates have followed me. Mason is totally zonked out now, cuddled against Madoc's chest. Ivy is finally starting to droop, but she still finds the energy to run over to Corwin and lift her arms to him.

"Your turn to carry me, Da," she informs him briskly.

Corwin's eyes gleam with so much affection it brings a lump to my throat. "All you have to do is ask," he says, and lifts her up into her favorite position on his shoulders.

She tangles her fingers in his dark curls. "Someday you're going to have to let me fly like this instead of just hugging me."

The winter arch-lord lets out a bemused sound. "We'll see about that."

I feel Sylas's mismatched gaze on me. I'm not sure if he's seen something beyond regular sight with his scarred eye or if my emotions are simply so close to the surface they're obvious when he knows me so well. He wraps one of his brawny arms around me, falling back a little as my other mates stride on ahead toward the border castle.

"Is something on your mind, my love? You look rather pensive after all that reveling."

The warmth of his massive body encircles me like an embrace all its own and melts any worries I might have had about the suggestion I'm going to make. Sylas has always made a point of giving me the freedom to follow my hopes and desires. I don't imagine he'll even find my request all that strange, to be honest.

"It occurred to me that's there's one more thing I'd like to do as we say goodbye to this year," I say. "I think… I think it's time."

He doesn't miss a beat before responding, "Whatever it is, we'll make it happen."

Jamie's living room isn't big enough to easily accommodate eight guests. Especially with five of those guests being fae men larger than the average human. Sylas could almost count as two people.

But we've managed to figure it out. Mason is tucked onto my lap on the sofa where I'm squeezed in between Corwin and Whitt. Sylas sits on the floor near the arm while providing a living chair for Ivy. August and Madoc have perched on chairs pulled over from the dining table, just like my brother. Jamie's wife, Diane, is bouncing their toddler daughter Tori on her lap in the armchair across from the sofa.

August throws back the last of a glass of eggnog spiked with rum and licks his lips. He shoots a playfully accusing glance my way. "I can't believe you never told me about this wonderous stuff. Holding out on us."

I laugh, carefully balancing the plastic cup Mason is clutching in his little hands. "We haven't really celebrated Christmas back home. It didn't occur to me." I've become so immersed in fae traditions that my own from years ago had faded from my mind. But it feels good to be here, with the sticky sweet flavor in my own mouth and the smell of pine drifting from the small tree in the corner. Upbeat Christmas songs are wafting through the room alongside the smells of the cooking dinner that August and I insisted on helping create.

Jamie raises his glass with a warm smile. "You can come back to visit every year for more of it. It's pretty hard to find even around here outside of December."

August considers his empty glass. "That is a shame."

Tori squirms off of Diane's lap and toddles over to gaze at Ivy, who giggles and taps her cousin's little nose. "You're cute. What toys do you have for us to play with? Everything here is so different."

It's the first time I've brought the kids into the human world. The first time we've gotten together as a family like this. Jamie had extended the invite a few weeks ago, suggesting that we could stop by sometime in the week after Christmas once his in-laws had left after their visit, but I hadn't been sure I'd take him up on it.

I've been cautious about how discreet Ivy and Mason will be about their magic, and my brother and his family have never been faced with the reality of just how big *my* family is quite so directly before. When I've visited in the past, it's always been with just one or two of my mates. They've met all of them, but not at the same time.

But the pang of homesickness I felt a couple of days ago told me I shouldn't put the visit off. The eagerness with which Jamie and Diane greeted us makes me wonder if I've actually left it later than I really needed to. Jamie has known about my unusual living situation since we reconnected more than ten years ago, and he eased Diane into the gist of it gradually as they got more serious after they started dating in college.

Tori pulls out a box of jumbled toys, Ivy scampering to join her, and Diane beams at Mason. "Do you want to take a look too? Tori's pretty good at sharing these days."

He curls closer to me for a moment, abruptly shy, and then slips down to go crouch between the girls. In a moment, they're all chattering together as they maneuver plastic figurines around the edge of the box.

"They're so big already," Diane says to me. "How does it work where you live—as far as school and that sort of thing?"

She's an elementary school teacher, so no doubt she's particularly curious about different educational systems. I cock my head. "I mean, it's obviously not the same as here, because the sorts of things they need to learn are pretty different. It's kind of a group effort—we all teach them different skills, and we have a people from our community who specialize in other areas and give them regular lessons. And there's a lot of hands on learning. Ivy's just starting to spend a few hours here and there helping out with the tasks that keep the community running."

"That sounds nice. The whole 'it takes a village' idea." Diane shakes her head with a hint of exasperation. "Sometimes everything feels too regimented here."

"Says the woman who gets annoyed if the grocery store is temporarily out of her favorite brand of tea," Jamie teases with a fond glint in his eyes. "There's something to be said for a certain amount of predictability." Then he perks up. "Oh, Tal, I promised you I'd make the shortbreads from Grandma's recipe. Let me grab those."

I can't help clapping my hands with glee, feeling momentarily transported back to our childhood. "Just wait until you try those," I tell August as Jamie heads to the kitchen. "We had them every Christmas, and the plate was always empty way too fast."

Madoc has been glancing around the room, taking in the vibrant Christmas decorations and the modest furnishings. I've tried to offer my brother some of the fae wealth I've come into, but he's insisted that he wants to build his future completely by his own means. My Murk arch-lord clearly doesn't see anything lacking in the space, though.

"You have a lovely home," he says to Diane. "I can feel the happiness in it."

A pleased smile lights up her face. "We have had a lot of good times here already."

Jamie brings the plate of delicate cookies in and sets it on the coffee table in our midst. As he's straightening up, Ivy glances over at him and blurts out, "Uncle Jamie, what happened to your face?"

In that instant, all us adults freeze. Jamie's hand rises instinctively to the scars that cut across his cheek and one side of his jaw. He hesitates, and I scramble for the right thing to say.

I hadn't thought to coach the kids in preparation for meeting him because I'm so used to how my brother looks, and they've seen scars on enough fae back home, including their fathers, to accept it as normal. But Jamie's are worse than most, and maybe Ivy realizes that she hasn't observed any humans carrying the same markings other than me.

Ivy ends the awkwardness all on her own. "Was it the same mean wolves that hurt Mommy?" she adds, looking over at me. She's seen the similar scars that form ridges on my shoulder, hidden right now under my casual winter dress.

The room seems to let out a collective breath. Jamie nods, his stance relaxing. I don't think he was so uncomfortable about his injury being pointed out as he was about figuring out how to explain it to my kids. "Yeah, the same ones. It was really scary, but we both made it out all right, and that's what matters."

A fierce light gleams in Ivy's eyes. "And my daddies made sure that those criminals wouldn't hurt anyone else ever again."

Sylas chokes on a guffaw with a glance toward Diane, but she appears to take the comment in stride without needing any explanation of how exactly my mates made sure of that. "We're all grateful for that," she says smoothly, and leans forward to grab a cookie. "Only one each for now. You don't want to ruin your appetite for dinner."

"No chance of that for Auggie," Whitt says, smirking as he nudges his younger brother with his foot, and laughter carries around the room at August's look of mock-consternation in response.

I'm savoring the buttery whipped shortbread melting in my mouth when Tori pushes to her feet by the toy box. She points toward the tree. "Presents! Open now?"

"That's not a bad idea, sweetie," Jamie says, and shoots us a grin. "We figured we'd give you the full Christmas treatment. None of it's anything big, but, you know…"

"I'm sure whatever you got is great," I say quickly. "You really didn't have to give us anything at all. But we did bring presents too."

I glance at Corwin, who lifts the large cloth bag he set beside the sofa. "How about you kids bring over the gifts from under the tree?" Diane suggests, and the three of them rush over.

"What are these presents for?" Mason asks, peering at them. "It isn't anyone's birthday."

"That's one of the ways people here celebrate their end-of-the-year holidays," I tell him, with an aside to my brother. "It's not part of the usual fae celebrations."

He chuckles. "That makes it an extra special occasion, then."

The kids—well, mostly Ivy—haul several small packages wrapped in shiny paper into the middle of the room. Ivy squints at the labels on each and hands them out, squealing when she finds her own. "Can I open mine first?"

Corwin motions her over to him as he opens up his bag. "Why don't we give our thank you gifts to our hosts first, and then you can go? You can pass them around."

Our daughter decides this is a suitable compromise, beaming as she brings the first present, tucked into a smaller cloth gift bag, to her little cousin. She patiently shows Tori how to tug open the bow.

Tori reaches inside and pulls out the contents with a babble of excitement. It's a wooden toy in the shape of a wolf, with a mouth that opens and closes and joints that can move—and when she works the mouth, soft little barks emit from within. A little magic, but nothing that a human observer wouldn't assume is somehow mechanically built into the toy.

"It can even wag its tail," Ivy tells her, having provided a lot of consulting on what we should bring for the little girl. Then she grabs the next present to bring to Diane.

My sister-in-law unfurls the bundle of fabric from inside and gasps. "That's beautiful."

It's one of Harper's dresses, specially commissioned. Nothing so fancy that it'd look out of place in the human world, but with patches of fabric designed to look like the panes of a stained-glass window, forming flowers and leaves. When I've visited before, I've noticed that Diane likes unique and playful dresses—she's mentioned that they help keep her students' attention on her in class—so it seemed like a not-too-risky gamble.

"My best friend made it," I say. "The fit should be pretty flexible." Thanks to another whiff of magic we won't mention.

Diane hugs it to her chest. "I love it. I'll wear it for New Year's."

Ivy carries Jamie's present over to him last. Somehow I'm most anxious about how this one will be received, even though it should have been the surest bet.

He pulls out a set of paint brushes and pots of paint. Before he can say anything, I leap to explain. "The brushes are made from the fibers of a plant back home that hold the paint really well and respond to small variations in pressure—they're what all our artists use. They'll work with any kind of paint, but I thought you might like to try out ours. It's kind of halfway between watercolors and oils in texture."

"Amazing." My brother examines the set with awe, gingerly rubbing his thumb over the bristles on one brush. He ended up pursuing a career in digital design, but he's got a studio in one half of the garage where he still works with charcoals, pastels, and all kinds of paint in his spare time. I have one of his city scenes in oils hanging in my bedroom in the border castle.

He looks up at me, his eyes bright with gratitude. "Thank you. I can't wait to see what I can create with these."

A smile stretches across my face. "Me too."

Ivy finally gets to open her own present, which turns out to be a board game that Diane says her 3rd graders love. She and Jamie have gotten Mason a pop-up book full of medieval style castles that he ogles eagerly. There's a set of special mixing bowls for August, a book of classical sheet music that they thought Corwin might find interesting to learn, a couple of recent rom com movies for Sylas, and a bottle of fine whiskey for Whitt.

I unwrap my gift to find a notebook with a handwritten title: *McCarty Family Recipes.* As I flip it open, Jamie seems to watch me with the same nervousness I had about his gift.

"I got as many of the old recipes as I could from Aunt Becca," he says. "And I found some recipe cards that looked like a mix of Grandma's and Mom's in a few boxes of their things that'd been in storage. I wrote everything down in there, even the ones I don't remember us having in case you do or want to see what they're like."

I clasp my hands around the notebook, my heart alight with gratitude. "Thank you. I can't wait to share these with everyone back home."

Madoc has ended up opening his gift last, and it's Diane who looks a little concerned about this one. "It might not seem like much, but I remembered how you're always grabbing more snack foods when you're over here, and I thought these might be some you haven't had a chance to try before. My mom's side of the family is from Peru, and we had a trip down to Trujillo to see some of the relatives in the fall. I grabbed everything that looked interesting and would easily make the trip back."

Madoc paws through the box of crinkly bags and wrappers before grinning at her. "I can't say I've ever been to Peru. I'll have to ration these out so I can enjoy them for as long as possible."

Ivy jumps up with a sweep of her arms. "I *love* Christmas! We should do this every month," she announces to the room at large, and we all break out into laughter again. But as we tuck away our gifts in preparation for dinner, I notice a brief melancholy flickering across Madoc's face as he gazes around the room again.

We've celebrated with the summer fae and winter fae traditions and now my own, but he hasn't gotten to contribute anything. Knowing my Murk mate as well as I do, I suspect that bothers him.

After we're all stuffed from dinner and Jamie has taught the entire family a few Christmas carols that Mason now won't stop singing, we trek through the darkened streets back to the rift we arrived through. I step closer to Madoc and loop my arm around his.

"Did you have any celebrations at this time of year at all in the Refuge?" I ask. "Even if there's something small you could share, I'd love to be a part of that too."

My other mates glance over, Sylas offering an approving nod. Madoc tilts his head to the side, looking abruptly hesitant. Then his eyebrows arch. "You know, we generally skipped anything like Christmas, but we'd never turn down a good New Year's Eve bash…"

I don't think I've ever seen so many people in one space before in my entire life, fae or human. And the revelers shuffling and whooping in the crowd we're standing on the edges of are all very definitely human.

For the occasion, Madoc brought us to a huge street in central Paris, and it's stuffed full of locals and tourists alike. Trees of ruddy lights gleam along the sides of the wide expanse, sheltering booths selling a variety of street foods. We've already stuffed our faces with all kinds of greasy and baked delights, and my stomach is pleasantly full while a trace of custard sweetness lingers in my mouth.

Up ahead, a huge marble arch carved with intricate designs and sculptures looms, a pale giant against the night sky. The crowd has gradually been pressing closer to it, and we've followed them, sticking to the edges where it's easier not to get crushed.

I lift my head toward Madoc at my side and pitch my voice to carry over the noise of the crowd. "Is it always this busy?"

Madoc dips his face by my ear. "Every time I've rung in the new year here. I've heard that tens of thousands of humans come to celebrate at this spot."

Looking around me, I can easily believe that. My pulse thumps faster with both exhilaration and nerves. How has it been so long since I've been surrounded by even a fraction of this many of my fellow human beings?

But it's mostly a thrill. Especially as I've taken in the contentment that relaxed Madoc's expression while he introduced us to the pleasures this event can offer.

Whitt is gazing up at the glistening trees as if taking mental notes for his next revel. August is still nibbling at one last cookie he insisted his stomach could hold. Corwin keeps drifting toward the spots where people have music playing as if trying to absorb as many different tunes of this world as possible.

Sylas has stuck close at my other side, his hand frequently resting on my shoulder, I suspect a little concerned about how I'll fare in the packed street. But he's getting plenty of enjoyment out of the occasion too.

"I've watched New Year's Eve scenes in an awful lot of movies," he admits, "but somehow it never occurred to me to participate myself. I can see why humans consider it such a meaningful occasion."

Since we're out in public, all of my men except August, whose ears are essentially human-shaped, have cast minor spells on themselves to hide their unusual features. As we squeeze closer to the arch, no one gives us a second glance other than the occasional wide eyes at Sylas's impressive bulk. I'm glad Harper agreed to watch over the kids while we took this little trip, though. I can just imagine Ivy bounding off into this crowd and vanishing.

More music starts to play from up ahead. Glowing images light up the arch. Madoc grins and urges us closer. "This is the best part."

Gorgeous imagery, a mix of abstract shapes and scenes from nature and the city, plays out across the stone surface in time with the music. My breath catches at the grandeur of it all. Then all at once, with the striking of midnight, fireworks explode across the sky as if bursting from the arch itself.

The booms seep into my bones and the fiery light sears into my mind. For a few minutes, I'm totally lost in the spectacle.

Madoc grabs me and tugs me into an eager kiss. My men close around me, and I move from one to the next, not caring if anyone around us notices our joint interlude while they exchange their own PDAs to welcome the new year. As the sharper exhilaration of the spectacle fades, a giddy tingle wakes up low in my belly.

Whitt smiles slyly. "I think it's time to get back to the hotel."

We managed to get a room not far from the arch, through some magic my men have kept to themselves. Madoc lets out a chuckle as we step into the ornate but cozy space, taking in the velvet curtains, the Persian rug, and the four-poster bed. "This is definitely fancier than any of the digs I found for myself when I'd come on my own."

"Benefits of being part of the family," August says, nudging the Murk man with his elbow. Then Sylas is sweeping me off my feet so swiftly a gasp slips from my mouth.

As he sets me in the middle of the expansive bed, all five of my men clamber onto the mattress around us. The giddiness I felt earlier expands into a wash of heat running all through my veins. I curl my fingers into Madoc's shirt and offer him the first of many kisses I expect to be granting in this room tonight.

More kisses brand my neck, arms, and calves as my men warm up my body with their mouths and stroking hands. It isn't long before we've all stripped off our clothes.

My Seelie arch-lord guides me onto my back and then lowers his head between my legs. The first swipe of his tongue over my clit makes me moan with the rush of pleasure. I feel nothing less than worshipped by the movements of his lips and the flood of his hot breath while my other men stir up more bliss in the rest of my body.

I buck into Sylas's mouth until he dips his tongue right inside me and I shudder with the wave of my release. As I tangle my fingers in his dark hair, he looks up at me with an impressively regal expression for a man whose mouth is shiny with my arousal.

"We can do even better than that. I say we send our lady up as high as one of those fireworks."

August hums eagerly. "And light her up just as bright."

They turn me in their arms within the ring the five of them have formed. My mouth collides with another and another. Fingers and lips tweak and nip my breasts. Hands delve between my legs to summon even more desire.

They send me soaring higher and higher until I find myself braced over Corwin, letting out a needy keening as he pushes up into me while Madoc crouches behind me, filling my other entrance as well. As they pick up a rhythm, pressing into me together, and Whitt closes his mouth around one nipple while August suckles the other, I really do feel as if I'm spiraling out across the sky.

No one's mentioned anything about my fertility, so I assume it isn't that ideal time of the month for conceiving. Nonetheless, I can't help gazing down at my soul-twined mate with a twinge of sorrow alongside the pleasure he and the men around me are kindling in my body.

I wish I could give you a little raven too.

A flash of concern passes through Corwin's eyes before they roll upward with the sway of my hips. His desire courses into me alongside my own before he answers. *We have so much time still, my soul. I never expected it to happen quickly. And if it doesn't come at all, I have no complaints about the children we've already brought into this world. They own my soul as much as you do.*

The wisp of sadness washes away with the certainty in his inner voice. I can feel just how much he means those words. So I give myself over to the rising bliss, rocking between my two mates, lowering my head to take Sylas and then August into my mouth, coming with the raven and the rat only for Whitt to flip me over and make me cry out in ecstasy all over again.

When we're all well and truly sated, my men sprawl in various positions around me on the bed and we all drift off to the faint strains of music still carrying from the celebrations outside.

I wake up with the ache of thirst in my throat and find only four men still around me. Madoc is standing by the broad window at the far end of the hotel room, gazing out over the street with an odd expression on his face. I scramble off the bed through the opening he's left me and limp over to join him.

Stars are sparkling across the blackness of the sky. I think of the charts tacked to the walls of his office in the border castle. "See anything interesting up there?" I murmur.

He lets out a hum. "Always so many interpretations. Mostly they seem to be saying that I've been away a long time, but unsurprisingly this world has survived in my absence."

His previous expression and something in his voice make me peer into his face. "Is everything all right?"

Madoc wraps his arm around my shoulders. "Everything is wonderful. Sometimes it's still hard to believe that this is where I really belong, after everything. So much of my life was down there on the streets, scrounging for whatever little bit I could get. I believe all fae are equally deserving, but I know I'm not the same as them." He cuts his gaze toward the men still sleeping on the bed.

I reach up toward his hand and intertwine our fingers, a different sort of ache forming behind my collarbone. I guess it isn't totally surprising that the Murk man still has flashes of insecurity, but I wish I could chase them away completely.

"You're not the same," I say, "but that's a good thing. It means you see things they might not see. You know things they might not know. It's because of you we had such a fantastic night."

Madoc raises an eyebrow at me. "A little fun. Not really a grand contribution."

I snort at him. "You offer a lot more than that." I pause, leaning my head against his side. "I don't think I've ever told you why I picked Mason's name."

The rat shifter goes still. "No, you haven't. I assumed you just liked the sound of it."

"Well, I do. But I liked it even more when I heard it because it seemed so perfect for what he represents in our lives. Building something new, setting down a solid foundation. We wouldn't have him if you hadn't trusted us, if you hadn't fought so hard to show that all the fae can live together and respect each other."

Madoc's arm tightens around me. "I trusted *you*," he says, the hoarseness in his voice thickening, and then he's kissing me again, and there isn't a single doubt in *my* mind how much my fifth mate belongs here.

After, I get my drink of water and snuggle up next to Madoc and my other men on the bed. The renewed sense of peace that's settled over me is shaken only by the thought of the first big political decision we need to make in the new year that's just arrived.

Because today's hearing involves both the summer and winter fae, the arch-lords from the two realms as well as the rest of my mates and I have gathered in the audience room in the border castle. After much debate and refinement, we've ended up with a layout with the five silver thrones for the Unseelie arch-lords at the end of the room and the three gold and ebony on either side for the Seelie and Murk.

Out of the Murk arch-lords, only Madoc is present today, and that's more as my mate than as a leader, though he's taken his seat in his throne all the same. I glance over at him from my perch on a cushioned stool between the summer and winter areas. He's poised a little awkwardly on the formal chair, but when I catch his eyes, he flashes me a crooked smile without any hint of reluctance. He's been growing into his new role over the past decade.

I do see concern for me in his stormy gaze, though. He isn't alone in that feeling. Today, Corwin is sitting in the central throne that Laoni usually likes to claim, and I can sense the tension radiating from his rigid posture as well as his inner state. Sylas likewise has taken the center Seelie throne, while Whitt and August flank me on either side.

Whitt teases his fingers down my hair to my shoulder. "She won't get another shot at you while we're still breathing," he says, dry but with a rough undertone that tells me how much he means it—and how much anger he's still harboring toward the woman whose appeal we're about to hear.

Laoni clears her throat from her spot at Corwin's left, looking slightly annoyed, possibly because of her momentarily slightly diminished position. "Before we hear from the petitioner herself, we should go over the objective facts. From the reports I've heard, Kara of Hazeleven has made no attempts to shirk her punishment. She's remained well within her home domain for the entire ten years of her sentence without complaint and has continuously contributed her magic to enhancing supplies for the other fringe domains that suffered most during the curse."

"Yes," Corwin says. "My coterie's reports confirm those accounts."

Sylas inclines his head. "This is also what I've heard from my own channels of information." His spymaster's hand gives my shoulder a reassuring squeeze.

Madoc clears his throat. "Has she made any hostile remarks about Talia or Corwin to the rest of her flock?"

"Not as far as we're aware," Corwin says. "She seems to have kept rather quiet in general."

"It sounds like we can agree that there's nothing in her outward conduct that suggests she shouldn't recover her freedom if her appeal is convincing," Celia puts in. She shifts her attention to me, her gaze a little kinder than it used to be when she'd look at me in the past. "We've all agreed that the final decision will be up to you, Lady Talia. You were the one she wronged by far the most. All we ask is that you judge her today based on how she presents herself now rather than lingering resentments."

I smile tightly at her. "You know I believe in fairness."

And I do, in principle and in practice. But still, when the door swings open and the elegant winter fae woman glides into the room with a guard on either side of her, my stomach twists automatically.

Kara looks just as lovely as she always has from the moment I first encountered her in a temporary refugee camp on the plain beneath the plateau during the war with the Murk. Her auburn hair with its streaks of maroon and burgundy tumbles halfway down her back, and her penetrating dark eyes stand out against her luminously pale skin. She's picked a deep blue dress that's simple by true-blooded fae standards but nonetheless clearly well made.

This woman might have been Corwin's soul-twined mate if the Murk king's magic hadn't interrupted their intended bond with our own. If the Heart hadn't seen fit to maintain my bond with him after it absorbed the energy of Orion's false Heart.

And she was once determined to ensure she got her chance with him regardless of my existence—or rather, by *ending* my existence.

I can't imagine the pain she's gone through, but I also can't imagine holding so much animosity inside me that I'd send another person who'd never done me any purposeful harm off to a torturous death. Maybe it was easier for her because she only needed to trick me into falling into my greater enemies' hands. She didn't need to witness any of the torment. But she knew what they were going to do with me.

If those enemies had seen their plan through, she could have been partly responsible for ruining any chance of reaching the peace we've just been celebrating.

When her gaze passes over me, her eyes twitch, as if she wants to yank them away. Instead, she forces herself to hold my gaze for a moment before continuing her survey of the room. Her expression is coolly implacable like Corwin's so often was when I first met him. She's still a winter fae—there's no doubting that.

The guards lead her to the center of the room on the thick rug with its red and purple pattern, a few paces before the first of the thrones. They take a step back on either side of her but remain within easy reach. And I know that every other fae in this room, which holds the majority of the most powerful in the entire fae world, will leap to my defense if this woman launches any sort of attack. Even Laoni sees me as more valuable alive than dead these days.

Corwin's jaw clenches for just an instant with a jolt of anguished fury through our bond. He's never totally forgiven himself for not realizing what a threat this woman posed to me. But he reins in his emotions and smooths his voice to total calmness.

"Kara of Hazeleven, the first term of your sentence has been completed. We will now consider whether your punishment may be lifted. Please present your case."

Kara bows her head and then looks around at the arch-lords

again. "Thank you for hearing me. I'm grateful for this chance. I know that the crimes I committed against Lady Talia were unforgiveable, so I don't ask for forgiveness, only that I may be allowed to continue to live a productive life with fewer restrictions than I've faced. I freely give my word that I will not make any attempt to harm her, either by my hand or by enabling anyone else's."

I can't hear any loopholes in her statement, but I'm not quite as adept at following fae trickery as the figures around me. Whitt must find it acceptable, though, because he speaks up. "Would you take a vow to that effect?"

"Of course," Kara says without hesitation.

"What will you do if the restrictions on your movements are removed?" Laoni asks.

Kara clasps her hands in front of her. "I was thinking I would ask permission to travel in the summer realm. It might do me some good to get to know more of the fae we're now allied with and possibly discover new ways I could contribute to our world."

Donovan cocks his head. "Is that the *only* reason you'd want to cross the border?"

A hint of a blush colors her cheeks. While fae can lie, they generally avoid it. And Kara seems to be committed to a higher level of honesty than most, because she admits, "No, I suppose it isn't. I also… Many of my fellow Unseelie know me and still carry anger about my actions. I'm not welcome among many flocks here. I was hoping a new realm might allow me more of a fresh start, at least to begin with."

Sylas leans forward in his throne. "We would still enforce a ban around the domains close to the Heart. You'd have no need to venture that close to Talia's home."

"I wouldn't," Kara agrees.

Corwin has been studying her—I can feel the intensity of his focus through our bond. He folds his hands on his lap. "Do you understand now that whatever bond there might have been the potential for between you and me, it is completely gone? That there will never be any connection between us whatsoever?"

A hint of a rasp creeps into Kara's voice. "Yes. I've felt it fading even within me. The Heart has chosen as it wills."

Her elegant posture trembles. Then, to my surprise, she sinks down onto her knees and bows her head down to the floor.

"I don't know how else to show how sorry I am," she says. "The events I set in motion could have been disastrous for you and both realms as well as for Talia. I didn't see—I was so blinded by my sense of the bond—but that's not a real excuse. I should have thought more clearly. I've regretted the cruelty and selfishness of my actions every day since."

Laoni lets out a startled cough. "Get yourself onto your feet, Lady Kara. We don't expect you to act like a dust-destined beggar."

Kara picks herself off the ground almost hesitantly, as if she isn't sure she deserves to obey the command. I watch her, twice as transfixed as I was before, my pulse beating in the base of my throat.

The Heart only knows what Laoni would have made of Corwin's similar display when he begged me for another chance after betraying my trust in the earliest days of our relationship. Winter fae are all about dignity. But he prostrated himself to show that I meant more to him than appearances, and Kara has made almost the same gesture despite her ladylike airs.

They are more alike than I would have thought. Maybe she would have made a good mate for him if the bond that would have been hadn't been interrupted.

I don't mean for that thought to be heard, but it's difficult to pick and choose what my soul-twined mate picks up on. *You are the best possible mate I could have asked for,* he reminds me firmly. *That is all that matters.*

Madoc has been watching the proceedings silently. Now he stirs, sitting up straighter in his throne. "Is there anything *you'd* want to ask, Talia?"

This time, it's August who grips my shoulder encouragingly. I draw in a breath, knowing I could decline to speak if I wanted to. But as Kara turns toward me, her stance tensing, I find there's one important question I do want the answer to before I make my decision.

"You said in your first statement that you're not looking for forgiveness," I say quietly into the stillness of the audience room. "Do *you* forgive *me*?"

Kara's eyes widen. She obviously wasn't expecting a question like that. Her lips part, but at first no sound comes out.

"I— There is nothing to forgive," she says, pulling herself together. "It was never even your choice. The Murk and then the Heart—it came down to them. Your bond is there. You should have it. I didn't really understand what I was asking, when I first suggested that you somehow step aside. I only felt a shadow of a bond, and that was enough to addle my head while I tried to grasp hold of it. I can't imagine, once it's already confirmed and consummated… The Heart gives what we deserve."

There's only the slightest mournful note in those last words, and they're what convince me. She's still grieving the loss. Her declaration isn't some attempt at cold-hearted manipulation. And maybe she believes she was somehow unworthy, and that's why things worked out the way they did.

I don't want to leave her with that thought in her head, unable to pursue anything beyond the boundaries of the domain she admitted to me in the past has little to offer her.

"You don't know what it may give you yet," I say, and look around at the arch-lords. "I don't have any more questions. Does anyone else?"

After a moment of silence, Corwin tips his head toward me. "Do you need some time to come to your decision?"

I push myself to my feet. "No. I'm sure already." I hold Kara's gaze, taking in the mix of hope and fear there, willing her to find a way to follow the hope after today. "I believe the sanctions placed on Kara of Hazeleven should end today, as long as she takes the promised vow and avoids the domains around the Heart."

Kara inhales sharply, as if she didn't really expect this outcome. As the arch-lords get up and gather around the other woman to work out the details of her vow, August slips his arm around my waist. "Always so generous, Sweetness."

One corner of my mouth slants upward. "In some ways, she's been the generous one today."

When the vow is finished, the arch-lords step back, my mates coming to stand around me instead of at their thrones while Kara walks out of the audience room with a more relaxed grace than she entered with. As she steps through the doorway where the guards will escort her out of the castle, I grip Sylas's hand and extend a tendril of silent affection to Corwin.

We spent the last several days saying good-bye to the year that just ended. Now we've achieved another new beginning. And I have faith that the Heart will shine on all of us in peace and happiness, no matter where we started.

ABOUT THE AUTHOR

Eva Chase is an Amazon bestselling author of urban fantasy and paranormal romance. She grew up on a steady diet of magic, mayhem, and romantic angst, and brings plenty of all three to her stories. But no need to fear the dreaded love triangle—Eva's heroines never have to choose. She lives in Ontario, Canada with her family and one velcro-like cat.

Along with the Bound to the Fae series, she is the author of the Royal Spares series, the Rites of Possession series, the Shadowblood Souls series, the Heart of a Monster series, the Gang of Ghouls series, the Flirting with Monsters series, the Cursed Studies trilogy, the Royals of Villain Academy series, the Moriarty's Men series, the Looking Glass Curse trilogy, the Their Dark Valkyrie series, the Witch's Consorts series, the Dragon Shifter's Mates series, the Demons of Fame Romance series, the Legends Reborn trilogy, and the Alpha Project Psychic Romance series.

Connect with Eva online:
www.evachase.com
eva@evachase.com

www.ingramcontent.com/pod-product-compliance
Lightning Source LLC
Chambersburg PA
CBHW020243030826
48979CB00030B/2530/J

* 9 7 8 1 9 9 0 3 3 8 9 4 6 *